GREAT
HORROR
STORIES

GREAT HORROR STORIES

CHANCELLOR
PRESS

Previously published as
The Great Book of Thrillers (1936) by Odhams Press Ltd
Great Tales of Terror (1991) by Chancellor Press

This 2002 edition published by Chancellor Press, an imprint of
Bounty Books, a division of Octopus Publishing Group,
2-4 Heron Quays, London E14 4JP

Reprinted 2002 twice, 2003

ISBN 0 7537 0569 9

Printed in Great Britain by Mackays of Chatham

CONTENTS

A. J. ALAN. *H2, Etc.*   PAGE
How a man went into a neighbour's garden in pursuit
of his cat—and how the grim vision he saw through
his neighbour's window led him into a battle with
Death.   13

MICHAEL ARLEN. *The Smell in the Library.*
Fear of his dead brother haunted Red Antony, and
they found him dead in the room where his brother had
died. The air was acrid with smoke but—there had
been no shot !   18

W. E. AYTOUN. *The Man in the Bell.*
The frightful ordeal of a man at the mercy of an iron-
tongued monster in a belfry.   37

HONORÉ DE BALZAC. *The Mysterious Mansion.*
The wife who lied, the lover and the jealous husband :
a triangle drama with a grim conclusion.   43

MARJORIE BOWEN. *The Folding Doors.*
How, during the French Revolution, a young aristocrat
was late for a rendezvous with his lady—and how her
cunning, bourgeois husband stole the golden hours
from them.   57

WILKIE COLLINS. *The Lady of Glenwith Grange.*
There was a mystery about Rosamond's rich and
charming husband from France. And one terrible day
she learnt what it was.   72

J. S. FLETCHER. *The New Sun.*
A strange and terrible visitant from outer Space rushes
to the destruction of the earth.   92

5

VAL GIELGUD. *Hot Water.*   PAGE

If there had been cold water in the bathroom, the
Secret Service man would not have made his
shattering, almost unbelievable discovery. The
sordidness of espionage had suddenly become tragedy.   110

L. P. HARTLEY. *The Island.*

A house on an island in a storm at night is the appropriate setting for this tale of unexpected terror.   118

NATHANIEL HAWTHORNE. *Edward Randolph's Portrait.*

No one knew what the picture on the wall of the
Province House had once portrayed—it was so
shrouded in the gloom of ages. But when the destiny
of the city was at stake, a strange thing happened.   133

WASHINGTON IRVING. *The Spectre Bridegroom.*

It was a very odd bridegroom who arrived so late for
the feast prepared for him in the castle-home of his
betrothed. It looked as if the goblins had been playing
tricks on the Baron and his lovely daughter.   144

EDGAR ALLAN POE. *The Facts in the Case of M. Valdemar.*

Perhaps the most gruesome story ever conceived by
this famous writer of tales of terror.   158

HUGH WALPOLE. *The Tarn.*

Fenwick hated Foster with a cool, mad hate, and he
saw rising in the deep waters of the tarn the last bubbles
that were the breath of the man he loathed. But even
in death Foster had won.   169

SAMUEL WARREN. *The Resurrectionist.*

How a respectable young medical student became for
one night a body-stealer, and what fears and horrors
assailed him during his gruesome adventure in a moonlit churchyard.   182

PAGE

PROSPER MÉRIMÉE. *The Blue Room.*
Something terrible was happening in the next room—
and the pretty mademoiselle and her handsome
cavalier who had eloped so light-heartedly found
themselves in a horrifying predicament.   194

E. PHILLIPS OPPENHEIM. *The Café of Terror.*
The travellers sensed tragedy in the emptiness of the
little mountain inn. And then the horrible discovery
was made.   206

ANTHONY BERKELEY. *The Avenging Chance.*
The murderer had covered his tracks so thinly—if only
they had known where to look. As it was the Poisoned
Chocolates Case was very nearly added to the list of
unsolved mysteries.   219

G. D. H. AND M. COLE. *A Lesson in Crime.*
One of the popular crime novelist's million readers
obligingly demonstrated to him in the train how a
perfect murder *should* be carried out. The author never
used that plot.   235

FREEMAN WILLS CROFTS. *Mr. Pemberton's Commission.*
Mr. Pemberton was not too staid to be interested in a
pretty Parisienne on the boat-train. He was much
too respectable, however, to dabble in jewel theft.
But one thing leads to another.   247

GILBERT FRANKAU. *Who Killed Castelvetri?*
It seemed a straightforward case to the twelve good
men and true—the *crime passionnelle* and self-defence.
But the lovely little Roumanian with the lazy eyes did
not believe it.   260

R. AUSTIN FREEMAN. *The Aluminium Dagger.*
Hartridge had been stabbed to death in his own room
—yet there was no possible escape for the murderer. 280

HERBERT JENKINS. *The Gylston Slander.*
The village was horrified by a series of anonymous
letters. Then enter Malcolm Sage, detective.   304

MAURICE LEBLANC. *Arsène Lupin in Prison.*
Stone walls do not a prison make nor iron bars a cage
—when the debonair Arsène Lupin decides to commit
another of his brilliant crimes.   323

BARONESS ORCZY. *The Fenchurch Street Mystery.*
With the aid of a piece of string the Old Man in the
Corner unfolded to Miss Polly Burton the amazing
inner history of a most extraordinary crime.   341

EDEN PHILLPOTTS. *Peacock House.*
For the practical Scottish schoolmistress an old crime
was re-enacted but what could it matter after fifty
years? It did matter—very much indeed.   358

JOHN RHODE. *The Vanishing Diamond.*
How sixpence helped a diamond of incalculable value
to disappear—and to be restored.   389

AMBROSE BIERCE. *Staley Fleming's Hallucination.*
The doctor suspected that his patient was suffering
from a malady outside the scope of medical aid. But
even he could not foresee the horrible climax to the
strange symptoms.   405

CATHERINE CROWE. *The Italian's Story.*
A Victorian ghost story whose period atmosphere only
serves to heighten its dramatic effect.   408

DANIEL DEFOE. *The Ghost of Dorothy Dingley.*
The youth who declared that his path to school was
haunted by an apparition had one sympathiser, and
they set out to investigate the mystery.   424

CHARLES DICKENS. *To Be Taken With a Grain of Salt.*
The Old Bailey itself is the unusual setting for this
realistically told story of murder avenged.   432

AMELIA B. EDWARDS. *The Phantom Coach.*
The snowbound traveller hailed the mail-coach with
joy—but once inside what wouldn't he have given
to be out in the snow again !   443

SHERIDAN LE FANU. *Madam Crowl's Ghost.*
A monstrous crime is revealed by the apparition of
wicked Madame Crowl to a little girl.   455

JEFFERY FARNOL. *Black Coffee.*
Professor Jervis had in his study the mummy of an
Egyptian Princess, miraculously preserved. He waited
for her eyes to open and reveal her secret.   471

JOHN GALT. *The Black Ferry.*
The lightning quivered, the thunder roared, the rain
slashed the windows—a cloak for a cruel crime.   484

THÉOPHILE GAUTIER. *The Dreamland Bride.*
The strange story of the monk and Clarimonde—" most
beautiful in all the world."   495

GERALD GRIFFIN. *The Dilemma of Phadrig.*
It was a terrible decision the father had to make, and
the reproachful eyes of his dead wife told him that he had
chosen wrongly.   515

JAMES HOGG. *Mary Burnet.*
A legend from the lowlands of Scotland of magic and
" the Guid Folk " who spirited away a village girl.   523

W. W. JACOBS. *The Three Sisters.*
" Be sure your sins will find you out " might be taken
as the motto for this story of three eccentric ladies.   544

NORMAN MACLEOD.   *The Doctor's Ghost.*
What a horrible night the doctor spent—with his dead
friend restlessly moving all the furniture about?   553

WALTER DE LA MARE.   *Mr. Kempe.*
To prove that Man has a Soul—that was Mr. Kempe's
terrifying problem.   And there was danger for the
stranger on the cliffside where he lived.   559

SIR WALTER SCOTT.   *The Tapestried Chamber.*
The pen of the master transforms a conventional plot
into an eerie tale fraught with the darkest implications. 584

H. RUSSELL WAKEFIELD.   *The Frontier Guards.*
A short story by a modern author calculated to chill the
most sceptical blood.   599

H. G. WELLS.   *The Red Room.*
Something more than a ghost story, this little masterpiece explores the depths of the subconscious mind to
reveal its lurking terror.   605

OSCAR WILDE.   *The Sphinx Without A Secret.*
He loved her madly—that beautiful woman with the
aura of mystery.   She died and took her secret with her. 616

E. F. BENSON.   *The Gardener.*
What happened when the inhabitants of a haunted
house were visited by the ghost of a murderer.   621

ANON.   *A Spanish Ghost Story.*
The foreign governess was puzzled and terrified by
the strange atmosphere of the new household.   At last
she discovered its secret.   634

ILLUSTRATIONS

IT WAS RATHER FUNNY, HE'D GOT HIMSELF UP RATHER LIKE PAGE
A MEMBER OF THE KU KLUX KLAN *by M. Suart* 12

STOPPING IN THE VERY ACT OF STRIKING, SHE LOOKED
ROUND AND SAW HER HUSBAND *by J. S. Goodall* 55

"THE LAND'S ON FIRE!" *by Vernon Smith* 105

"YES; NO; I HAVE BEEN SLEEPING—AND NOW—NOW—
I AM DEAD" *by Ernest Wallcousins* 165

DE BORNEVILLE, AS I HAD IMAGINED HIM, WAS STILL
SWAYING WHERE HE STOOD *by F. G. Moorson* 275

HE SEEMED TO CRUMPLE IN HIS CHAIR AND SHRINK UNDER
HER STARE *by Alfred Sindall* 385

"SHE WAS DRIVIN' ON RIGHT FOR ME, WI' HER ALD
SHRIVELLED HANDS CROOKED AS IF SHE WAS GOIN'
TO CLAW ME" *by Charles De Mornay* 467

AT LENGTH THE PICK OF SÉRAPION SMOTE THE COFFIN LID,
WHICH HE THEN RAISED, AND I SAW CLARIMONDE
by Ernest Wallcousins 513

MARTHA, WITH A HORRIBLE FEAR, FOLLOWED HER GLANCE
TO THE DOOR *by Norman Keene* 551

THE SHEPHERD SPRANG BACK WITH A HALF-SCREAM OF
TERROR *by Fairbairn* 555

I STARTED UP IN BED, AND SAT UPRIGHT, AS I GAZED ON
THIS HORRIBLE SPECTRE *by Reginald Mount* 595

I SNATCHED ANOTHER CANDLE AS I ROSE. ABRUPTLY
THIS WAS BLOWN OUT *by Eric Winter* 613

It was rather funny, he'd got himself up rather like a member of the Ku Klux Klan.

H2, ETC.

WE'VE got a cat. She's a black Persian—a shocking great beast—and she weighs over fifteen pounds on our kitchen scales, but she's awfully delicate. If she stays out too long in the cold she gets bronchitis and has to be sat up with. So, unless it's really hot weather, we reckon to get her indoors by eleven o'clock.

Well, one night not long ago—it was after eleven—in fact ten past twelve, and we were sort of thinking of bed, when my wife said, " I wonder where Tibbins is." Tibbins is, of course, our cat, and at that time in the evening she ought, according to her schedule, to have been lying in a heap with the dogs in front of the fire.

However, the dogs were there but she wasn't. No one remembered having seen her last, so I made a tour of her usual haunts. She wasn't in her basket by the coke stove down in the scullery, where she generally takes her morning nap, neither was she in hell. Hell is a place at the top of the house where the hot-water cistern is. She often retires there in the afternoon. At all events, I drew a complete blank, so we were finally forced to the conclusion that she wasn't in the house at all, and my wife said, " I'm afraid you'll have to go out and meow for her." So I went out and meowed.

I searched our garden, but as she wasn't there I went through the main garden. Perhaps I'd better explain that all the houses in our road have their own gardens at the back, and these have gates into what we call the main garden. This runs right along behind them, and there's one of these main gardens to every eight houses or so, but they are divided off from each other by the side-turnings which run into our road.

I'm afraid it sounds rather complicated. However, our

particular main garden is about a hundred yards long and forty
yards wide, and it's quite big enough for a black cat to hide in,
as I found. I walked round every blooming bush in it and said,
" R-r-r-wow," or words to that effect, in what I considered to
be an ingratiating manner, but without any success, and I was
just going to chuck my hand in when I saw our Tibbins sitting
on the end wall. That is to say, the wall which divides the
garden from the road.

She let me sidle quite close, but just as I was going to grab
her she jumped down on the far side (the road side). Then she
skipped across the road and squeezed through the bars of the
gate into the next main garden. I said a few things and climbed
over the wall and followed her. Of course, I couldn't squeeze
between the bars of the gate so I had to scramble over the top.
She very kindly waited while I did this and then moved off just
ahead. She frolicked about with her tail in the air, as who
should say, " Isn't it fun our going for a walk like this in the
moonlight ? " and I told her what fun I thought it was. I'd
already torn my dinner-jacket getting over the gate, but it's no
good being sarcastic to a cat.

She continued to lead me up the garden, darting from tree to
tree, until we got half-way along, and then she turned off to the
right and went into one of the private gardens. Luckily the
gate was open and I didn't have to climb over it. The house
it belonged to was all in darkness, of course, but when I got to
the middle of the lawn the lights suddenly came on in one of the
ground-floor rooms. It had a French window and the blinds
were up.

Well, this startled the cat and she let me pick her up, so that
was all right, but just as I was turning to come away a little old
man appeared at the window. He was so close that he
couldn't have helped seeing me if I'd moved, so I stood quite
still and held Tibbins up against my shirt front. He was a very
old man indeed, rather inclined to dodder, and he had on a
dark blue dressing-gown. He'd got something white hanging
over his arm, I couldn't quite see what it was, but it looked like
a small towel.

Anyway, he peered out for a bit and then he drew the bolts
and pushed the window open. He came and stood right outside,
and I thought, " He's bound to see me now," but he didn't seem
to. After a minute he wandered back into the room again, and
sat down and began writing a letter.

By the way, this wasn't exactly a sitting-room. It had more

the appearance of a workroom. I mean, there was a large deal table which looked as if it was used for cutting out on, a gas-ring for heating irons, and a sewing-machine, and things like that.

I didn't wait to notice any more. While the old gentleman was busy, me and my cat left.

When I got home my wife had gone to bed. I told her about my adventures and what I'd seen and so on, and she said, " I wonder which house it was." I couldn't tell the number from the back, naturally, but I made a rough guess whereabouts it came and she said, " Oh, then, I think I know the old man. He's usually out in a bath-chair. He doesn't look quite right in his head and he's got asthma or something." And I said, " Well, paddling about the garden won't do his asthma any good. What had we better do ? "

It was no use trying to telephone because we didn't know the name of the people or their number in the road, so there was obviously nothing for it but to go back and see what he was up to and warn his family that he'd got loose.

You mustn't think that we spend our lives doing good deeds, but we both came to the conclusion that it wouldn't be nice to go past the house in a week's time and find a hearse at the door.

At any rate, at perfectly enormous self-sacrifice I went back, over all the walls and gates and what not, and once again fetched up on this precious lawn. The windows had been pulled to but the light was on and I could see in.

The old josser was still sitting at the table, only I couldn't see his face. It was rather funny, he'd got himself up rather like a member of the Ku Klux Klan. You know, you've seen pictures of them. They wear a sort of tall white head-dress going up to a point with two round holes cut out for the eyes. But what he'd got on wasn't a proper head-dress, it was a pillow-case, and there weren't any holes for the eyes.

I wondered for a moment what he was playing at until I noticed that he'd taken the tube off the gas-ring and shoved it up into the pillow-case. He'd buttoned his dressing-gown round it to keep it from falling out.

I said, " Oh, that's it, is it ? " and pulled the windows open (they weren't fastened), and I went in and lugged the pillow-case off his head and turned off the gas.

He wasn't at all dead, but he'd begun to turn grey—well, a silvery colour, and I wouldn't have given much for him in another ten minutes.

The only treatment that occurred to me was fresh air in large quantities, so I rolled him up in the hearthrug and laid him down outside the window. There was a note on the table addressed to the coroner, and I wondered whether I ought to do anything with it, but decided not to.

Next I went through to the bottom of the stairs and set about rousing the house, and you've no idea what a job that was. If I hadn't wanted them to hear me they'd have been yelling blue murder out of the top windows for the last ten minutes. As it was, I called out loudly several times without anyone taking the slightest notice.

I was even looking round for the dinner-gong when a door opened somewhere upstairs and I heard whispering going on. It went on for such a long time that I got annoyed. I said, " Will some one please come down *at once* and not keep me standing here all night." That had an effect. Two middle-aged females appeared. Singularly nasty looking they were, and I loathe boudoir caps at the best of times. They were evidently sisters ; I explained who I was and told them that an old gentleman had just done his very best to make away with himself. They said, " Oh dear, oh dear, that's father. How exasperating of him. He's always doing it." And I said, " What are you talking about, ' always doing it,' it's not a thing people usually make a hobby of." (We were out by the window by this time inspecting the culprit.) And they said, " Well, you see, as a matter of fact, it's like this. Father is very old and he suffers from melancholia. Every now and then, when he gets an especially bad fit, he tries to commit suicide like this. We can't stop him because he simply won't be locked in his room. First of all he creeps down here and writes a letter to the coroner " (they'd apparently got several of them), " and then he goes through this performance with the pillow-case and turns on the gas." I said, " Yes, that's all very well, but why doesn't it work ? I mean it ought to kill him every time." And they said, " Oh, that's all right, we've thought of that. We always turn the gas off at the main before we go to bed." They had the nerve to tell me that once or twice they'd actually watched through the keyhole and seen it all happen. According to them there was just enough gas left in the pipe to send him off to sleep, and at three or four in the morning he'd wake up and crawl back to bed and forget all about it.

Well, it isn't often that I can't think of anything adequate to say, but I couldn't then. I've never in all my life been so angry

with two women at once. It was no use calling them the names
I wanted to call them because they wouldn't have understood.
I did remark on their unsuitability to be in charge of any one, and
I also threatened to run them in, though I don't quite know what
for, but it must be illegal to hazard one's parents like that. Anyway, they got rather haughty. They said there was no need
for any one to interfere because they'd already made arrangements to send their father to a home in Kent. I said, " Mind you
do," and the subject rather dropped. It was a little difficult
to know what to do for the best, because they wouldn't hear of
sending for a doctor, and I couldn't make them—you can't, you
know. Every moment I was expecting them to disapprove my
dictatorial attitude. The patient was recovering, but he still
looked as if he wanted fresh air, so we decided to give him a few
minutes more.

At the same time it wouldn't have done to let him catch his
death of cold, so we covered him up with some more rugs.

After that, by way of something to do, I put the india-
rubber tube back on to the gas-ring with the idea of boiling some
water for hot bottles. When I'd fixed it I just turned the tap
on and off to see if it was working, quite forgetting that there
oughtn't to be any gas. But there was—quite a lot. It came
out with no end of a hiss, and I said, " Oy, you seem to get a
better pressure in this house with the main turned off than we do
with it on," and I turned the tap on again. You could hear it
all over the room. Upon which one of the ugly sisters said to the
other, " Agatha, are you sure you turned it off last thing? "
And Agatha naturally was absolutely certain. She distinctly
remembered doing it. She began to tell us all her reasons for
remembering it so distinctly, but I said, " Why argue when we
can go and look? " So we went and looked, in the pantry, and,
of course, there it was—full on.

THE SMELL IN THE LIBRARY

ONE night we were at a party, George Tarlyon and I, and there were also present some other people. It was not, however, a good party, and we left it before eleven o'clock. I cannot remember now how it was that one had gone there so early, but anyway it is of no significance. As we passed out, a misguided fellow said it would get better later on, but I extracted him from Tarlyon's teeth, and so out into the street. A long string of cars stretched from the door towards Park Lane, and here and there chauffeurs stood in sombre groups, and we wondered if they thought they were missing anything. The heat of the crowded rooms had put us in a fever, the night air penetrated our flimsy evening-coats, and we shivered and murmured. From the open windows of the house we had left there followed us down the length of Green Street that asinine blare which is the punishment of England for having lost America ; and George Tarlyon muttered that there ought to be a law to prevent people from giving fat-headed parties full of crashing bores and plain women, the joints of whose knees cracked in trying any dance which their mothers had not danced before them. I tried to soothe him and myself by saying that parties were not what they were and there it was ; but he would not be soothed, for he had been given a glass of cider-cup in mistake for champagne, and he who touches cider-cup in the watches of the night may neither forget nor forgive.

We walked up Park Lane aimlessly, for we knew not what to do nor whither to go. We were further elated by the fact that we could sum up only one cigarette between us.

I suggested that one might do worse than go to bed, but

Tarlyon said it was too early for that. " It is never too early,"
I said morosely, " to go to bed."

" Pah ! " said Tarlyon, and so we walked down Park
Lane.

Now it is frequently said that Park Lane is full of Jews, but
very few met our eyes, and they might quite well have been
Gentiles. There are many illusions prevalent in the provinces
about life in the great metropolis of London : such as (*a*) that
it is gay : (*b*) that it is wicked : (*c*) that boys will be boys :
(*d*) that there is plenty to do when it rains : (*e*) that you have
only to go for a walk to see many " well-dressed women in costly
furs ; " but the one which has even less foundation in fact
than any of these is that, life in a great city being what it is,
there is never an hour of the twenty-four when the great streets
are not, to a student of life, full of matter for observation. But,
as George Tarlyon said, you might be a student of life until
you burst and still find no matter for observation—though here
we were in Park Lane and the hour not yet eleven !

" The whole thing is a ramp," we said. " Now take this
matter about the Jews. We have been distinctly given to understand that this Lane is full of Jews—but what do we see ? Two
buses and a policeman. But that leads us to an interesting
speculation : can a policeman be a Jew ? Has such a thing
as a Jewish policeman ever been seen or heard of ? And if
not, what is it that prevents a policeman from being a Jew ?
Is the religious feeling among policemen stronger than that
among Privy Councillors ? "

" Let's ask him," I suggested. The policeman was decorating
the corner of Upper Brook Street. Tarlyon asked him, and
the policeman said that Vine Street was not so far off as all
that, while as for Marlborough Street, it was even nearer. He
wasn't there to be accosted, he wasn't, said the policeman
wickedly.

" Ho ! " said Tarlyon. " And have you been arresting any
more respectable old clergymen in Hyde Park for talking to
women without an introduction from a bishop ? Blast me but
I wouldn't dream of entering Hyde Park nowadays, not at night
anyway, without a battalion of chaps fringed with torpedo-
netting."

" Good-night, constable," I said hurriedly.

" Good-night, sir," said he—a discreet man.

" Pah ! " said Tarlyon.

We walked up Park Lane.

And suddenly Tarlyon gripped my arm, and waved his stick and whispered :

" Look at that ! Ralph, just look at that ! "

Ten yards or so ahead of us loomed the back of a giant. He was striding on with huge steps, a black cloak was flung about him, and he wore no hat. Maybe it was the cloak, swaying this way and that, and one end flapping over a shoulder, that made the man seem taller than he really was—but it was a colossal back.

" It's reminiscent," Tarlyon murmured. " I can't help a feeling about that back—it's reminiscent."

" It's reminiscent," I whispered, " of a back I once lent money to. One hundred pounds it was. . . ."

We quickened our pace. The huge figure passed under the light of a lamp, and the light fell on his bare head, and his hair flamed up like fire.

The huge figure, the arrogant walk, the flaming ginger hair. . . .

" Red Antony ! " I murmured.

" And we thought he was dead ! " muttered Tarlyon—as though Red Antony could have died without the noise of his death rattle confounding the thunder of the guns that killed many better men ! Could a man who lived so noisily die as other men ? And yet, because the lean years of peace had passed without sight or sign of him, we had believed the rumour that had had it that Sir Antony Poole had risen to be sergeant in a Canadian storm battalion and had then died ; which had seemed natural in a kind of way, for the worst German shot couldn't, one thought, have consistently missed six-foot-four under a crown of flaming hair.

If there was a man who did not know, or know of, Antony Poole in the careless years before the war, then there must have been something the matter with his eyes or ears. For Red Antony was a famous sight in every crowded place in London, and achieved considerable nonentity as the noisiest and worst-tempered rascal since Fighting Fitzgerald of the Regency. He crashed, did Antony, in furious idiocy from row to row and roguery to roguery, so that the day inevitably came when no decent man or woman would be seen speaking to the man. Oh, a calamitous pair, the brothers Poole ! For one night his brother, the great Sir Roger, brilliant and sardonic Roger, dark and successful Roger, good sportsman and lovable fellow —one night our Roger put a bullet through his head, and at the

inquest the amazed world heard that he had done this unbelievable thing because the police were hammering at the door
with a warrant for his arrest on a charge of fraud. This we, his
friends, did not believe. The police may have been hammering
at the door, we said, but the police are notoriously promiscuous
about the doors they hammer at. " Fraud be damned in connection with Roger Poole ! "—that is what we said. Why, he
was fine, that Roger—*fine* ! Thus we mourned him, once the
wealthiest and wittiest of our company, and we defended his
memory against the few who dared impugn it. But the disappearance of the red giant who was now Sir Antony Poole
we did not mourn, for from the day of the inquest, at which he
broke down and wept like a stricken child, he had not been
seen in London until this night in Park Lane.

II

" Go quietly," Tarlyon restrained me. " We'll learn Red
Antony to walk up Park Lane without a hat."

Gently we approached, one on each side of the colossal back.
" Oi ! " we cried.

A wrench, and he faced us. We are tall, but we were as
children beneath him.

" Oi to you ! " snarled Antony. " Who the blazes are you,
anyway ? " And the great red expanse which was given to
Antony for a face surveyed us intolerantly. Never what you might
call an easy-tempered man, Red Antony.

" We be friends," said Tarlyon sombrely.

" That's uncommonly original of you," drawled Antony.
" I didn't know I had any." And he pretended not to recognise
us—for Antony must always act, always play cussed.

" You haven't," Tarlyon grinned. " But mine was just a
manner of speaking." He knew his man ; and there passed
over Red Antony's face that earthquake and tornado which
was given him for a smile and a laugh.

" Hell ! Always the same Tarlyon ! How are you, George ? "

" Monstrous," says George.

" But there is no sensation in matter," boomed Red Antony,
crushing his hand.

" And this," said Tarlyon, waving his other towards me,
" and this, Sir Antony, is your old friend Ralph Wyndham
Trevor, whom you may quite well have forgotten, since you
owe him a hundred pounds."

Another earthquake across that vast red expanse, so that I feared for the sleep of those mythical Jews. . . .

" Dear old Trevor—fancy having kept you waiting all this time ! Here you are, man, here you are." And from somewhere inside his cloak he jerked a pocket-book into my hand and crushed it against my palm. " You can keep the change, old boy, as you're younger than I am and look as though you need it. Always take vegetables with your meat, Trevor."

" I hate to take money from an impoverished baronet," I got in, just to goad him.

" Impoverished nothing ! " he boomed, and swung on Tarlyon, who backed a step. " D'you remember, George, that Roger always said I had a *flair* for making money——"

" But he added," Tarlyon said, " that you hadn't got the brain of a louse to back that *flair* up with."

Boomed Antony : " I have studied the ways of lice for five years on end and must inform you, George, that my brain, though moth-eaten, is certainly superior. I have made mints of money. I am fat with money. I roll in money. . . ." He was working himself up into that state of chronic excitement in which he might twist the lamp-post. Breakable or twistable things had always a fascination for Red Antony.

" There, there ! " I soothed him. " And we thought the little man was dead ! "

" There, there ! " said George. " Did he make money, now ! And we thought he was lying in some forgotten foreign field with a German bullet in his heart."

Bother the man ! He simply had to make a noise each time he opened his mouth. The policeman who had talked Vine Street to us approached.

" Dead ! Me dead ! " And the sweep of his arm flung wide his cloak, and indeed he looked a mighty man of wrath. " As though a Prooshian bullet could kill me ! "

" You are no doubt reserved for a more terrible end," said Tarlyon.

Blessed if the man didn't wilt ! That roaring red giant—he wilted.

" Don't say that, George," he begged hoarsely. " It's a fool remark to make, that. You didn't mean it, did you ? " And he put the question seriously ! We gaped at him.

" He was only being funny," I explained. " He tries his best. . . ."

" I wish you well, Antony," said Tarlyon, out of his surprise.

" God, I need it ! " Antony growled surprisingly.

And then I laughed—remembering Red Antony's old way of acting cussed, just to surprise and annoy. He'd do anything to make a fool of some one, that man, even if he had to make a fool of himself in doing it. But as I laughed, Antony looked at me with furious, haggard eyes, and I stopped laughing.

I saw Tarlyon looking at him queerly. He knew Antony much better than I did, for many and many a year ago he was a junior subaltern in the mess when Antony threw a bottle at the head of an extremely superior officer. The bottle was full, the aim was true, and Antony was cashiered with all due pomp and dishonour. But, through all his subsequent follies, Tarlyon had liked him. One couldn't, of course, defend Antony ; but the very few who had once liked Red Antony always, somehow, went on liking him. There was something about the man, a sort of tremendous gallantry, an air of shameless bravado, a thunder of individuality, which might have made him a simple and lovable giant—but for a grain of rotten subtlety somewhere in him. Fine timber worm-eaten, Tarlyon said. Not, of course, said Tarlyon, that himself was anything to write home about.

" What's the matter, old Antony ? " Tarlyon asked kindly. " You've changed enormously. . . ."

Now I had noticed no particular change, except, perhaps, that handsome Antony looked his forty years and more ; but Tarlyon knew him better.

" How have I changed ? " snapped Antony. He hated kindness ; he thought he was being pitied.

" You look a bit worn, old boy, that's all," said George lightly.

" If it comes to that, you aren't the man you were, with war, wine, and women ! "

" Talking of wine," I thought to say, " one always understood that you'd die of drink, Antony. That's probably what George meant when he said you looked worn."

I wished I had kept my mouth shut. His eyes blazed over me . . . but he restrained himself ; and Antony's " restraint " was a portentous business—it make a noise like a fast car with the brakes jammed on.

" Drink ! " he said sharply. " I drink nothing to speak of nowadays. There's an end to all things. . . ." Now the lion's bedside manner is a significant thing, and even more significant is it when the lion in the fullness of his strength sways a little, just a little ; and what would make Red Antony sway just a little would be enough to put another man under the table, and no dishonour to the strength of his head, either.

"I do not wish," said Antony reasonably, "that you should think me irresponsible through excess of stimulant. The things that are happening to me are not happening through drink, and you must bear that in mind. I am saner than a sane man, though I can hear and see and smell things that a sane man would die of. . . ."

Tarlyon looked at me meaningly. Antony seemed to have forgotten us. Tarlyon took his arm.

"We can't stay here all night," he said. "Let us now leave Park Lane in a body and go to my house. . . .

Antony woke up ; he threw back his head and howled : "Taxi ! "

"All right, sir, all right," said the policeman gently. "You don't need to shout like that." That was a brave policeman.

"I insist on shouting," boomed Antony. "Taxi ! "

And, thankfully, a taxi appeared from Mount Street, for Red Antony and the police never did mix well. He once arrested two policeman for loitering and took them to Vine Street. . . .

Antony flung open the door. A clock began the lengthy job of striking eleven o'clock.

"We will go to *my* house," said Antony. "I have a charming house, and an appointment to keep in it. Jump in." We jumped in, and we heard him give the driver the address of a house in Regent's Park. How often had we not directed taxis to that house ! Tarlyon whistled.

"So you've got Roger's old house ! " he murmured.

Antony did not answer. The taxi staggered northwards as best it could.

"I don't see," snapped Antony at last, "why you should gape about it. Getting back to England four months ago, I found the house empty, and took it. It seems natural enough."

"I never said it wasn't," Tarlyon murmured. But he thought it wasn't, and so did I. A brother, on coming back to civilisation after many years' absence, does not immediately leap into the house in which his elder brother blew his brains out—anyway, I wouldn't.

The taxi twisted through the gates, round the little drive, and to the great door. An odd feeling it was, to stand again in front of that door after nine years—but now we faced a house black and still where once had been a house of shining windows, gay with music and the laughter of the most brilliant company

in London. Oh, the Georgians, the magnificent young Georgians
—mostly dead !

We told the driver to wait, and followed Antony in. We stood
still in the pitch-black hall until he should switch on the light,
and in the blaze of light in which the cloaked figure faced us I
instantly understood what Tarlyon had meant when he said
that Antony had " changed." I can only describe the change
by saying that the structure of his face seemed to have fallen
into disrepair ; its brick-red complexion of old had dwindled to
a faint pink, so that one had an idea that any ordinary face
would have been a ghastly white ; and he looked worn with
more than the usual wear of passing years. But the wild eyes
were still wild, and uncommonly fine he looked as he faced us
in the sombre hall, the huge dandy in the black cloak with the
head of flaming hair brushed immaculately.

He smiled at us with that sudden charm for which women
had forgiven him much—too much ; he flung out an arm in
the grand manner.

" Welcome to the old house," he said. " And for heaven's
sake try to look as though you didn't miss Roger."

But the magic of Roger Poole was not, I thought, in the
place ; the house was now but a shell for a noisy man.

III

" CHAMPAGNE is indicated," said Antony ; and that indication
led us to the dining-room—a long, oak-panelled room at the
back of the house. The curtains were not drawn across the two
French windows, which gave out to a lawn sloping carelessly
down to the water of Regent's Park ; and in the second in
which Antony fumbled for the electric switch the dark shapes
of the trees looked like the van of an impenetrable forest. But
dark shapes of trees always look more or less like that.

" Didn't you say something about an appointment ? "
Tarlyon asked vaguely, as Antony ravished the wire off a bottle.

" Did I ? " He looked up at us from his business, very
thoughtfully. " Oh, did I ? "

" Pop ! " said the champagne cork.

We drank, and Antony looked at his wrist-watch.

" Damn ! " he said. " It's stopped."

" The time being just 11.25," I helped him.

" Thanks," said Antony, very mild, very thoughtful. " Excuse me a moment, will you ? " And he strode across the room

to the folding doors which led to Roger's old library and card-room. He closed the door behind him, but it did not catch, swung open a few inches. No light filled the dark vertical space.

" Never known him so polite before," I muttered.

" He's absent-minded," said Tarlyon, looking thoughtfully at the dark space.

" What I want to know," he whispered, " is what he's doing in there in the dark ? "

" Keeping his appointment," I suggested facetiously.

Tarlyon looked from the door to me.

" Poor devil ! " he said softly. I thought he was pitying me for my wit, of which I was never very proud.

He put down his empty glass, dug his hands into his pockets, and lounged to the folding-doors. I never knew a man who could walk so casually as Tarlyon ; you never expected him to get anywhere, but he always got there before you expected him to.

He kicked the slightly open door a little wider with the tip of his shoe. I was just behind his shoulder.

" Antony ! " he called softly.

From the light in which we stood the library was a pit of darkness. Nothing moved in the pit. There was no sound.

" He's not there," I whispered ; and I wondered why I whispered.

" Can you smell anything ? " a hoarse voice suddenly asked from the darkness.

Tarlyon lounged into the black room. But, somehow, I did not feel called upon to follow. I leant against the door.

Deeply set in the darkness I could at last make out the faintly white patch which must be Antony's shirt-front ; and I wondered what tomfoolery he was up to now, asking stupid questions in a startling voice out of a poisonously dark room. I could smell nothing at all, and didn't expect to.

" What kind of a smell ? " Tarlyon asked—in a reasonable tone ! He stood just within the door, his back to me.

" Can you smell *nothing* at all ? " the hoarse, subdued voice asked again. " But, of course, it's very faint now."

Tarlyon put up his nose and sniffed. I sniffed. More than faint it was, I thought.

" Been smoking ? " Tarlyon asked, and he sniffed again.

" No," came a whisper.

" Oh," said Tarlyon. This was lunatic talk, and I was just about to say so when Antony asked sharply :

" Why did you ask ? "

"I thought I smelt smoke," said Tarlyon. "Might be cigarette smoke."

"It is," I snapped, for I was smoking a Turkish cigarette just behind his ear.

"You blasted fool!" said Antony—and with such contempt behind it that from being bored I got annoyed. I stretched out my hand on the inside of the library door and switched on the light.

"Turn that out, you fool!" came a frantic roar, and I had a vision of a red giant murdering the distance between us. I've never thanked God for anything so much as for having directed the body of George Tarlyon to be standing between Red Antony and myself. I turned off the light quick enough.

"Steady, Antony, steady!" said Tarlyon.

"Oh, go to hell!" growled Antony.

I thought to myself that we couldn't be very far from it at the moment. But the spell, or smell, it seemed, was broken. I was thankful for that, anyway.

Back in the lighted dining-room Antony emptied his glass; and grinned at me rather shamefacedly.

"Sorry, old boy," he said. I grinned back, as though I had enjoyed it.

Tarlyon asked suddenly:

"Have you got a spare bedroom for me, Antony?"

I stared, Antony stared. Then Antony smiled, and never before had I seen him smile quite like that.

"Thank you, George," he said, almost softly. "Now that's really a friendly action. But I'll be all right—you needn't worry."

Then he addressed me as well; I had never seen Antony so reasonable.

"Come to dinner here to-morrow night," he begged. "Both of you. I can give you quite a good dinner." He seemed very earnest, looking from one to the other of us. I was going to say I was engaged, but Tarlyon answered quickly:

"Right, Antony." And because he looked at me in a certain way, I let it be.

IV

In the taxi, at last, Tarlyon said:

"Ralph, you risked your life by turning on that light, but you did a great service."

" What do you mean ? "

" Didn't you see anything ? "

I then lost my temper.

" No," I shouted. " I neither smelt anything in the dark nor saw anything in the light, except that red lunatic charging at me."

" He was only preserving his illusion," Tarlyon said mildly. " Didn't you see, in that second of light, the open desk just by us, beside the door ? "

" I saw nothing but Antony, but quite enough of him."

" Pity. If you had seen the desk, you would have seen a telephone overturned on it, the receiver hanging down, and a revolver on the floor."

This was getting serious. I struck a match and examined Tarlyon's face. He was not smiling.

" Fact," he assured me. " You would have seen the desk just as it was after Roger Poole had shot himself at it."

" You don't mean——"

" I mean, old boy, that Antony has gone and put everything back exactly as he last saw it in Roger's library. Roger, Roger's wife, Antony and another fellow were in the dining-room. The telephone-bell rang in the library and Roger went to answer it, telling Antony to come with him. He didn't turn on the light in the library. The telephone told Roger that the police were after him. And the two in the dining-room heard Roger telling Antony what he thought of him as a man and brother, then they heard a shot ; and when they got to the door and switched on the light, they saw Roger dead at the desk and Antony standing where he was standing to-night. Antony went out by the window into the garden—and he has reconstructed the scene exactly as he last saw it, even to a dummy telephone and a revolver ! In fact, everything is there except Roger. Silly, isn't it ? "

Silly was not the word. " But why, why ? "

" That's what I want to find out," said Tarlyon. " Antony is playing some sort of a game with himself, and he's frightening himself to death in doing it. He always was a superstitious ass. Giants usually are, somehow—perhaps because, having nothing physical to fear, they fear the psychic. I'll bet he goes into that library every night at the same time—Roger shot himself at about twenty-five past eleven, by the way. Poor old Antony ! "

" But what was all that nonsense about the smell ? " I asked.

Tarlyon did not answer. At last he said :

"Did you ever hear, Ralph, the theory that if Judas Iscariot had not come after Jesus he might have done all that Jesus did? But as he found he could not because he was too late, he was doomed to crime. In a sort of far-fetched way it was the same with Roger and Antony. The tragedy of those two brothers has something absurdly, fantastically reasonable about it. You see, Roger was a year older and did all that Antony wanted to do, the fine and brilliant things, while poor Antony could do nothing but make a fool of himself, which he did only too well. Antony would have been a man of many accomplishments, for he's no fool, but for the fact that Roger was before him—so Antony thought. And Roger loved Antony, while Antony hated and admired and feared Roger. And at last, somehow or another, he managed to betray Roger. No knows what that last moment held for those two—no one knows what lay behind the insults that Roger heaped on Antony at that final moment. For they were overheard, you know, by Roger's wife and the man who was dining there. But something seems to have stuck in Antony's mind and grown very big with years. I'm rather concerned for the poor devil, Ralph. He's still afraid of his elder brother. Or perhaps he feels that Roger left something unsaid which he must hear, and so he wants to recreate him."

It was as the taxi stopped at my door that Tarlyon cried out as though he had made a discovery : "Good God, of course !"

"Of course what?"

"Smoke, you fool ! It *was* smoke !"

V

WHAT was our surprise, on entering the dining-room some minutes after nine o'clock the next evening—for Antony dined late—to see the table laid for four ! And then a lady came in—a tall, dark young lady, a strange and unusual lady with a flash of very white teeth for a smile and a gardenia alight on the wing of her sleek black hair ! I am afraid Tarlyon and I must have seemed very rude, for we were so surprised that we stared. The white teeth flashed at us. We bowed.

"My wife," said Antony. We bowed again. She was the sort of woman one bowed to. Antony's wife !

"Diavalen," said Antony abruptly, "this is Lord Tarlyon and Mr. Trevor."

Diavalen—Lady Poole !—said nothing. With that wonderful

trick of flashing those wonderful teeth she didn't need to say anything.

"She's a Creole," said Antony, as we sat at the table. He said it as he might have said that she was an orange. Those white teeth flashed at me, and I smiled back, feeling an ass. There didn't seem much to say about her being a Creole. . . .

I don't know how Tarlyon felt about it, but it took me some time to get my wind. "My wife," says Antony ! Never a word nor a sign about being married—to that glorious, dark, alien creature with the flashing teeth and sleek black hair ! Diavalen the Creole ! Just like Red Antony to marry a Creole called Diavalen and then spring her on to you with a "my wife." I remembered Antony once saying, years and years ago : "Never give away gratuitous information, old boy." But there are limits. And one of them is to have a wife with flashing teeth, a gardenia in her hair, and a name like Diavalen, and then throw her in with the soup.

Red Antony was never what you might call a good host : not, particularly, at the beginning of dinner. To-night he was morose. But Tarlyon talked—to Lady Poole. It would take more than a lovely Creole to baffle Tarlyon. He seemed to have inside information as to what were the subjects best calculated to excite interest in a Creole married to a morose English baronet with ginger hair. Diavalen did not talk. But one did not realise that she wasn't talking, for she was wonderfully expressive with her smiling, flashing teeth. She seemed to have discovered the art of using teeth for something besides eating.

As Tarlyon talked to her she turned her face towards him, and of this I took advantage to stare at her face bit by bit. The perfection of that face was a challenge to a right-thinking man. "It is too small," I thought. But it was not too small. "It is too white," I thought. But it was not too white. For quite a long time I could not wrench my eyes away from those flashing teeth and scarlet curling lips—they fascinated me. Her face was white, the gardenia in her hair looked almost yellow beside the whiteness of Diavalen's face; and I thought to myself that that white complexion was a considerable achievement, for I was sure her skin underneath was faintly, deliciously brown. It was a small face. It was a decoration, enchanting and unreal. And in the decoration were painted in luminous paint two large black eyes ; the eyelashes swept over them, often she half-closed them—they were very lazy black eyes ; and deep in them there was a sheen, as of a reflection of distant fire. I did not like the lady's eyes very much, I don't know why. But as to that sleek black hair in which lay a gardenia like a light in silken darkness—you felt that you simply must run your hand over that hair to see if it was as beautifully sleek and silky as it looked, and you wouldn't have minded betting that it was. She was the most strangely lovely woman I have ever seen. And she was the most silent.

Even Tarlyon was at last baffled by the silence of Diavalen. A silence fell. The teeth flashed at me, and I was just about to say something to her when Antony's voice hit the drum of my ear and I dropped my fork.

"I shouldn't trouble," said Antony. "She's dumb."

That is why I dropped my fork. The servant picked it up and gave me another. I made a considerable business of it, and then I ate furiously. Red Antony, vile Antony! I didn't look at Tarlyon. He was furious, I knew. He was a man who did not take a very liberal view of jokes like that. But the worst of Antony was that he didn't care what view any one took ; he just said the first thing that came into his great red head.

If the dinner (which was excellent as to food and wine) had been a frost before, it was, naturally, not a howling success after that. The only thing to do was to pretend that Antony had not spoken. It seemed too silly to say to the lovely Creole : " Oh, I'm *so* sorry ! " Poor Diavalen ! But I couldn't pretend, I simply could not find anything to say which didn't need an answer. Just try being suddenly planted with a dumb woman and see if conversation flows naturally from you.

Tarlyon and Antony talked about English heavyweight boxers. Antony was himself a super-heavyweight, and seemed to have a poor opinion of English heavyweights. He wanted to know whether their weight was calculated by the noise they made on being smitten to the ground in the first round. He said that he was tired of opening a newspaper only to read of the domestic history of Famous British Boxers and of seeing photographs of the wives, mothers and children of Famous British Boxers. He said that the whole idea of the press was to impress on the public how gentle, amiable and loving Famous British Boxers were in the home. He pointed out that the whole trouble lay in the fact that Famous British Boxers were too damned gentle, amiable, and loving in the ring. In fact, Antony, having put the lid on his wife, had woken up.

Then, at last, Diavalen rose and we rose. I rushed to the door and held it open. Her teeth flashed at Tarlyon, and he bowed like a courtier. As she passed Antony, he said, "Good-night, Diavalen," but he said it as though he didn't care whether her night was good or bad. As she passed Antony she gave him a look out of her large, black eyes. I was glad I did not know what that look said, but I was sure that Antony deserved it. "Good-night, Lady Poole," I said ; teeth flashed at me, a touch of pleasant scent hovered faintly, and Diavalen was gone.

"Heavens, she's lovely ! " I whispered, as I joined them at the table.

Tarlyon's fingers played with the stem of his port-glass.

"Would you mind explaining, Antony," he asked danger-ously, "why you chose that infamous way of telling us that your wife was—well, not quite like the rest of us ? " There was, I agreed, something blasphemous about the ghastly word "dumb" in relation to that lovely creature.

Red Antony leant back in his chair and dug his hands deep in his pockets, so that his white shirt-front stuck out like the breast-plate of a warrior. He looked bored.

"Favourite trick of hers," he explained morosely. "Always tries to act as though she wasn't dumb. If you had to live with that silly pretence it would get on your nerves, I can tell you. She does it very well, I admit. Takes a pride in it—making a fool of other people, I call it. On board ship from New York she put it over quite a number of people for a day or two. Lord, it would have got on any one's nerves, the way she grinned and grinned and showed her teeth ! Why not be honest and say one's dumb and be done with it ? Or let me say it ! There's no crime in being dumb, especially with a beautiful face like that. But she won't see it, she must smile and flash her teeth—she's got a repertoire of grins that would astonish a movie star ; and she's so proud of them that even if she could speak she wouldn't. And sometimes all that grinning and toothwork gets me so raw that I could put back my head and howl—and she knows it. Sorry I offended you, George. But I'm nervy these days. I'm raw—*raw* ! " He shouted that last word at us with a thump on the table ; and raw he looked, with the eyes blazing out of him, and his once huge, once red, once jolly face shrunk to a mockery of itself, with the skin drawn tight across his jaws and hollow in the cheeks.

Tarlyon picked up a liqueur-glass which the thump had upset. "Sorry about your unhappy marriage, Antony," he said ; "but, you know, it takes a Napoleon to marry a beautiful Creole. How did it happen ? "

" How ? " And Antony laughed ; at least he made a noise which was perhaps intended to sound like laughter. " How ? Because she made it happen—how else ? D'you think because she's dumb that she hasn't got more fascination than a thousand women rolled together ? Those eyes ? Met eyes like that before, George ? If hell has a face its eyes will be like that. I *had* to marry her . . . in Mexico where I went to after the Armistice. I suppose you fellows remember that I went to Mexico three years before the war. I was in love with the girl who became Roger's wife—inevitable, wasn't it, that the only woman I ever loved should fall to Roger ? He didn't do it on purpose, of course—it just happened. So I went to Mexico, to try to do something which Roger could not do before me. Last chance kind of thing, you know——" The rain of words faded out of him. He had moved considerably from the subject of Diavalen, but who could hold a haunted face like that to a subject ? I wished I could, for I didn't want him to run amok about Roger. There was something—well, indecent, in talking about a man dead nine years or more as though he were alive and still wanting to " put it across " Antony at every turn. I wished Tarlyon would saying something, but he was silent, his fingers fiddling with the stem of his port-glass. Antony was drinking next to nothing ; round about his coffee-cup were at least six quarter-smoked cigarettes, and now he began to maul a cigar. I never saw him smoke that cigar.

" In Mexico," Antony said softly, " I found oil. It was very good oil, as Roger said later, but there wasn't much of it. My luck again ! But I made Roger share it this time. You remember how I reappeared in England ? Through that window over there, while Roger was giving a big dinner-party, sitting where I'm sitting now. You were here, George. Roger and I made it up before the lot of you—after a silence of years. Entirely on my side, the quarrel—Roger always loved me. We made it up, you remember, George ? I wanted, you see, to plant Roger with that oil. Cascan Oil—it sounded like a big thing at the time. That was the last big dinner-party Roger ever gave. He was unhappy at home—some love misunderstanding—and he took to me, Roger did. He went head over heels into that bucket-shop. Of course he soon saw through me and my oil—the man wasn't born who could take Roger in—but he let the company go on. He wanted to see how far *I*'d go. Giving me my head, you know. He had packets of money in reserve, and thought he could put the thing right any moment. But he got reckless—

watching me and wondering how far I'd go. Roger had always loved me ever since we were children—he never thought of me but as a naughty baby with a bee in my red head about him. I could see all the time he was wondering how far I *dared* go. And he was unhappy at home, poor Roger ; he and his wife somehow couldn't get their particular ways of loving each other to work well together. So he had nothing to do but get reckless and chuckle over the naughty baby. I went the limit. The bucket-shop crashed on Roger's head. He tried to pull up, chucked his money in, and other people's, but it wouldn't save it. Clear case of dirty work. A greasy bubble, Cascan Oil. Left a nasty mess when it burst. And all the papers signed in Roger's name. Telephone rang in the next room while we were in here. I was sitting where you are, Trevor. Roger looks at me with a kind of crooked smile. 'Come with me,' he says, and I went. Into that room, the library. Roger didn't trouble to switch on the light ; the telephone was on the desk beside the door. The police were after him, said the man on the telephone—the police after Sir Roger Poole, Bart., M.P., and all the rest of it ! 'Listen,' says Roger. And I listened while he told me a few things about myself. 'A poor husk of a man,' he called me. 'A grave-yard of a brother you are,' he said. 'And the epitaph on your grave will be *Dolor Ira*,' he said, for Roger was a great Latin scholar and could lash out bits of Tacitus as easily as a parson might give you the Bible. I thought he was going to shoot me, I was ready for it—but he'd shot himself. Roger loved me, you know——"

"Then why the hell," Tarlyon blazed out, "did you take this cursed house ? "

Antony mauled his cigar.

"Because," he said, with a grin, "it just happened that way. It was fate to find it empty—a fine, large house like this at a low rent while all England was yelling for houses. But I might not have taken it if Diavalen had been against it——"

"Oh," said Tarlyon to that.

Antony looked at his wrist-watch, and jumped up in a mighty hurry. "God, the time's gone ! Excuse me a moment."

"We will not ! " cried Tarlyon, and had his back against the library door almost before you saw him leave the table.

But Antony walked his way to the library door without a word.

"Don't, old Antony, don't ! " Tarlyon begged.

"Out of my way ! " said Antony. He said it as though he

was thinking of something else, which was Antony's most dangerous way of saying anything.

Now Red Antony was a giant, and irresponsible at that. The two of us couldn't have held him from that library door. Tarlyon let him pass with a wicked word, and has regretted it ever since. Antony slammed the door behind him, and we heard the twist of the key.

Without a word to me Tarlyon was at the French window ; opened it, and disappeared. I stayed. I was extremely uncomfortable in that mad-house, you understand. Perhaps two minutes passed, perhaps ten. Where the devil was Tarlyon ? And then I heard through the library door the thud of something falling. And then in there a window smashed, a sharp smash. I measured my distance from that door and crashed my shoulder at it, and fell into the library on top of the panel.

" Light," said Tarlyon's voice. I switched it on. On the floor between us was a heap of a man face downwards, with the back of a red head half-screwed under an outstretched arm. And there was red on the back of Tarlyon's hand where he had put it through the window.

We knelt each side of Red Antony, and turned him over.

" Dead," I said.

" Not he ! " said Tarlyon. " He's fainted—from fright." But he knew as well as I did that Antony was dead—from fright. The huge bulk was as limp as a half-filled sack as we lifted it a little. Antony's eyes were wide open, and they were like the eyes of a child that has just been thrashed.

" He's been shot," I said suddenly.

" There was no noise," said Tarlyon, but he looked at me. There had been no noise, but there was the faint, acrid taste of pistol-smoke in the air. It's unmistakable, that faint, acrid smell of a revolver just spent. But Antony had not been shot.

" It wasn't an illusion, then ! " Tarlyon whispered softly. " That smell . . . of Roger's revolver ! And it's killed Antony in the end ! "

I stared down at the poor haunted face. And then I heard Tarlyon whisper : " My God ! " And again : " My God— look at that ! " But I did not look. I knew he was staring over my shoulder, and I was afraid to look. I was afraid of what I would see. And then I twisted my head over my shoulder, towards the far end of the room, where there was a little door from the hall. And I saw the thing sitting squat in the corner, the black thing with white teeth flashing in a white face and a gardenia in her hair. In the palm of one hand was a little golden bowl, and from this bowl floated up a wisp of smoke, just a wisp of smoke against the blackness of her dress, and this was the faint, acrid smell of a spent bullet. And Diavalen was laughing—the dumb woman was laughing with all the glory of ivory teeth and scarlet lips. . . . We left the thing to its joke. We went out by the window, and did not remember our hats and sticks.

THE MAN IN THE BELL

IN my younger days bell-ringing was much more in fashion
among the young men of —— than it is now. Nobody, I
believe, practises it there at present except the servants of
the church, and the melody has been much injured in consequence. Some fifty years ago about twenty of us who dwelt in
the vicinity of the cathedral formed a club, which used to ring
every peal that was called for ; and from continual practice and
a rivalry which arose between us and a club attached to another
steeple, and which tended considerably to sharpen our zeal,
we became very Mozarts on our favourite instruments. But my
bell-ringing practice was shortened by a singular accident,
which not only stopped my performance, but made even the
sound of a bell terrible to my ears.

One Sunday I went with another into the belfry to ring for
noon prayers, but the second stroke we had pulled showed us
that the clapper of the bell we were at was muffled. Some one
had been buried that morning, and it had been prepared, of
course, to ring a mournful note. We did not know of this, but
the remedy was easy.

" Jack," said my companion, " step up to the loft and cut
off the hat ; " for the way we had of muffling was by tying a
piece of an old hat, or of cloth (the former was preferred), to
one side of the clapper, which deadened every second toll.

I complied, and mounting into the belfry, crept as usual into
the bell, where I began to cut away. The hat had been tied on
in some more complicated manner than usual, and I was perhaps
three or four minutes in getting it off, during which time my
companion below was hastily called away, by a message from his
sweetheart, I believe ; but that is not material to my story.

The person who called him was a brother of the club, who,

knowing that the time had come for ringing for service, and not thinking that any one was above, began to pull. At this moment I was just getting out, when I felt the bell moving ; I guessed the reason at once—it was a moment of terror ; but by a hasty, and almost convulsive effort, I succeeded in jumping down, and throwing myself on the flat of my back under the bell.

The room in which it was was little more than sufficient to contain it, the bottom of the bell coming within a couple of feet of the floor of lath. At that time I certainly was not so bulky as I am now, but as I lay it was within an inch of my face. I had not laid myself down a second when the ringing began. It was a dreadful situation. Over me swung an immense mass of metal, one touch of which would have crushed me to pieces ; the floor under me was principally composed of crazy laths, and if they gave way, I was precipitated to the distance of about fifty feet upon a loft, which would, in all probability, have sunk under the impulse of my fall, and sent me to be dashed to atoms upon the marble floor of the chancel, a hundred feet below.

I remembered—for fear is quick in recollection—how a common clock-wright, about a month before, had fallen, and bursting through the floors of the steeple, driven in the ceilings of the porch, and even broken into the marble tombstone of a bishop who slept beneath. This was my first terror, but the ringing had not continued a minute before a more awful and immediate dread came on me. The deafening sound of the bell smote into my ears with a thunder which made me fear their drums would crack. There was not a fibre of my body it did not thrill through ; it entered my very soul ; thought and reflection were almost utterly banished ; I only retained the sensation of agonising terror.

Every moment I saw the bell sweep within an inch of my face ; and my eyes—I could not close them, though to look at the object was bitter as death—followed it instinctively in its oscillating progress until it came back again. It was in vain I said to myself that it could come no nearer at any future swing than it did at first ; every time it descended I endeavoured to shrink into the very floor to avoid being buried under the down-sweeping mass ; and then reflecting on the danger of pressing too weightily on my frail support, would cower up again as far as I dared.

At first my fears were mere matter of fact. I was afraid the pulleys above would give way and let the bell plunge on me. At another time the possibility of the clapper being shot out in some sweep, and dashing through my body, as I had seen a ramrod glide through a door, flitted across my mind. The dread also, as I have already mentioned, of the crazy floor, tormented me ; but these soon gave way to fears not more unfounded, but more visionary, and of course more tremendous. The roaring of the bell confused my intellect, and my fancy soon began to teem with all sorts of strange and terrifying ideas. The bell pealing above, and opening its jaws with a hideous clamour, seemed to me at one time a ravening monster, raging to devour me ; at another, a whirlpool ready to suck me into its bellowing abyss.

As I gazed on it, it assumed all shapes ; it was a flying eagle, or rather a roc of the Arabian story-tellers, clapping its wings and screaming over me. As I looked upwards into it, it would appear sometimes to lengthen into indefinite extent, or to be twisted at the end into the spiral folds of the tail of a flying-dragon. Nor was the flaming breath, or fiery glance of that fabled animal, wanting to complete the picture. My eyes, inflamed, bloodshot, and glaring, invested the supposed monster with a full proportion of unholy light.

It would be endless were I to merely hint at all the fancies that possessed my mind. Every object that was hideous and roaring presented itself to my imagination. I often thought that I was in a hurricane at sea, and that the vessel in which I was embarked tossed under me with the most furious vehemence. The air, set in motion by the swinging of the bell, blew over me, nearly with the violence, and more than the thunder of a tempest ; and the floor seemed to reel under me, as under a drunken man.

But the most awful of all the ideas that seized on me were drawn from the supernatural. In the vast cavern of the bell hideous faces appeared, and glared down on me with terrifying frowns, or with grinning mockery, still more appalling. At last the devil himself, accoutred, as in the common description of the evil spirit, with hoof, horn and tail, and eyes of infernal lustre, made his appearance, and called on me to curse God and worship him, who was powerful to save me. This dread suggestion he uttered with the full-toned clangour of the bell. I had him within an inch of me and I thought on the fate of the Santon Barsisa. Strenuously and desperately I defied him, and bade him begone.

Reason then, for a moment, resumed her sway, but it was only to fill me with fresh terror, just as the lightning dispels the gloom that surrounds the benighted mariner, but to show him that his vessel is driving on a rock, where she must inevitably be dashed to pieces. I found I was becoming delirious, and trembled lest reason should utterly desert me. This is at all times an agonising thought, but it smote me then with tenfold agony. I feared lest, when utterly deprived of my senses, I should rise, to do which I was every moment tempted by that strange feeling which calls on a man, whose head is dizzy from standing on the battlement of a lofty castle, to precipitate himself from it, and then death would be instant and tremendous.

When I thought of this I became desperate. I caught the floor with a grasp which drove the blood from my nails ; and I yelled with the cry of despair. I called for help, I prayed, I shouted, but all the efforts of my voice were, of course, drowned in the bell. As it passed over my mouth it occasionally echoed my cries, which mixed not with its own sound, but preserved their distinct character. Perhaps this was but fancy. To me, I know, they then sounded as if they were the shouting, howling, or laughing of the fiends with which my imagination had peopled the gloomy cave which swung over me.

You may accuse me of exaggerating my feelings ; but I am not. Many a scene of dread have I since passed through, but they are nothing to the self-inflicted terrors of this half-hour. The ancients have doomed one of the damned in their Tartarus to lie under a rock, which every moment seems to be descending to annihilate him—and an awful punishment it would be. But if to this you add a clamour as loud as if ten thousand furies were howling about you—a deafening uproar banishing reason, and driving you to madness, you must allow that the bitterness of the pang was rendered more terrible. There is no man, firm as his nerves may be, who could retain his courage in this situation.

In twenty minutes the ringing was done. Half of that time passed over me without power of computation—the other half appeared an age. When it ceased, I became gradually more quiet, but a new fear retained me. I knew that five minutes would elapse without ringing, but at the end of that short time the bell would be rung a second time, for five minutes more. I could not calculate time. A minute and an hour were of equal duration. I feared to rise, lest the five minutes should have elapsed, and the ringing be again commenced, in which case I should be crushed, before I could escape, against the walls or framework of the bell. I therefore still continued to lie down, cautiously shifting myself, however, with a careful gliding, so that my eye no longer looked into the hollow.

This was of itself a considerable relief. The cessation of the noise had, in a great measure, the effect of stupefying me, for my attention, being no longer occupied by the chimeras I had conjured up, began to flag. All that now distressed me was the constant expectation of the second ringing, for which, however, I settled myself with a kind of stupid resolution. I closed my eyes, and clenched my teeth as firmly as if they were screwed in a vice. At last the dreaded moment came, and the first swing of the bell extorted a groan from me, as they say the most resolute victim screams at the sight of the rack, to which he is for a second time destined. After this, however, I lay silent and lethargic, without a thought. Wrapped in the defensive armour of stupidity, I defied the bell and its intonations. When it ceased, I was roused a little by the hope of escape. I did not, however, decide on this step hastily, but, putting up my hand with the utmost caution, I touched the rim.

Though the ringing had ceased, it still was tremulous from the sound, and shook under my hand, which instantly recoiled as from an electric jar. A quarter of an hour probably elapsed before I again dared to make the experiment, and then I found it at rest. I determined to lose no time, fearing that I might have delayed already too long, and that the bell for evening service would catch me. This dread stimulated me, and I slipped out with the utmost rapidity and arose. I stood, I suppose, for a minute, looking with silly wonder on the place of my imprisonment, penetrated with joy of escaping, but then rushed down the stony and irregular stair with the velocity of lightning and arrived in the bell-ringer's room. This was the last act I had power to accomplish. I leaned against the wall, motionless and deprived of thought, in which posture my companions found me, when in the course of a couple of hours, they returned to their occupation.

They were shocked, as well they might, at the figure before them. The wind of the bell had excoriated my face, and my dim and stupefied eyes were fixed with a lack-lustre gaze in my raw eyelids. My hands were torn and bleeding, my hair dishevelled, and my clothes tattered. They spoke to me, but I gave no answer. They shook me, but I remained insensible. They then became alarmed, and hastened to remove me. He who had first gone up with me in the forenoon met them as they carried me through the churchyard, and through him, who was shocked at having, in some measure, occasioned the accident, the cause of my misfortune was discovered. I was put to bed at home, and remained for three days delirious, but gradually recovered my senses.

You may be sure the bell formed a prominent topic of my ravings, and if I heard a peal, they were instantly increased to the utmost violence. Even when the delirium abated, my sleep was continually disturbed by imagined ringings, and my dreams were haunted by the fancies which almost maddened me while in the steeple. My friends removed me to a house in the country, which was sufficiently distant from any place of worship to save me from the apprehensions of hearing the church-going bell ; for what Alexander Selkirk, in Cowper's poem, complained of as a misfortune, was then to me as a blessing.

Here I recovered; but, even long after recovery, if a gale wafted the notes of a peal towards me, I started with nervous apprehension. I felt a Mahometan hatred to all the bell tribe, and envied the subjects of the Commander of the Faithful the sonorous voice of their Muezzin. Time cured this, as it does the most of our follies ; but, even at the present day, if, by chance, my nerves be unstrung, some particular tones of the cathedral bell have power to surprise me into a momentary start.

THE MYSTERIOUS MANSION

On the banks of the Loire (said M. Bianchon), there stood an old ruinous-looking mansion in a garden overgrown with weeds. There was no other house near, and its appearance was one of utter desolation, and suggested the idea that it had been the scene of some great crime which had called down the vengeance of Heaven upon it. I frequently stopped to look at it, and imagined a host of crimes which had led to its present forlorn condition. One day I got over the hedge which enclosed the garden in order to examine the house more closely ; and the same evening I had just finished my supper when the landlady came in, and, in a mysterious manner, informed me that M. Regnault wished to speak to me.

"Who is M. Regnault ? " I asked ; but she did not stay to reply, and directly I saw a tall thin man, dressed in black, enter the room. His clothes were very shabby, but he had a diamond pin stuck in his shirt-front, and gold earrings in his ears. "To whom have I the honour of speaking ? " I demanded, as soon as he had taken his seat.

"I am M. Regnault, notary at Vendôme."

"I am delighted, sir, but I am not in a position to make a will, for certain reasons with which I am only too well acquainted."

"Pardon me ; that is not the object of my visit. I understand you are in the habit of visiting La Grande Bretèche."

This was the building to which I have referred, so I answered in the affirmative.

"One moment ! that constitutes a trespass. I am come in the name, and as the executor of the will of the late Countess of Merret, to request that you will discontinue your visits. You appear to be a gentleman of education, and, therefore, must

43

be aware that it is an offence against the law to enter an enclosed property, and a hedge amounts to the same thing as a wall. As far as I am concerned, I should be willing enough to allow you to enter the house, but it is expressly forbidden by Madame de Merret's will, and I have never myself set foot in it since her death. Ah! my dear sir, her will made a great sensation in Vendôme."

"Am I indiscreet, sir, in asking the reason why?" I said.

"I will tell you as far as I may," he answered. "I had not long returned from Paris, where I had been pursuing my studies, and had just established myself in business in this place, when, one night, just as I was going to bed, I was sent for by the Countess de Merret. Her carriage was waiting at the door—but, before I go any further, I may tell you that her husband had died two or three months previously in Paris in a most miserable condition, for he had indulged in all kinds of excesses. The countess had abandoned La Grande Bretèche the very day that her husband left her, and it had been shut up closely from that time just as you see it now; and it was even said that she had caused the whole of the furniture to be burnt before she left. For some months before he left his wife to go to Paris, the count and countess had lived together in a very singular manner; he occupied the first floor, while she lived on the basement story, and neither of them ever received a single person. Even when she had removed to her new house she led the same secluded life, and was never seen even at church. On my way to see her I asked her maid if her mistress was very ill, and she replied that the countess had received the last consolations of religion, and was not expected to live through the night.

"I reached there about eleven o'clock that night. After traversing several large, dismal-looking rooms, I reached the countess's room. From the rumours in circulation respecting her I imagined that I was about to see a coquette. The room was so large, and so dimly-lighted by an old-fashioned argand lamp, which stood on the table, that I had some difficulty in distinguishing the countess in the midst of the enormous bed she occupied. She was propped up in a sitting position, her white hair serving as a kind of frame to a yellow face of such excessive thinness, that you would have supposed it two hands pressed together. Never could I have conceived it possible for a person to have wasted to such a degree and yet retain life. She was frightful to behold, for she had been so devoured by suffering, that she appeared nothing more than a phantom.

The startling effect of her appearance was heightened by two large black eyes, deeply sunk in their orbits. Her lips were of a pale violet colour, and when she spoke to me I could scarcely perceive their movement, so low and feeble was her voice. Although habituated to spectacles of this kind, from the frequency with which I had been called in to draw up the wills of persons in their dying moments during my stay in Paris, I must say that the spectacle of weeping families, and the agonies and other things I saw never affected me to anything like the same degree as the first sight of this mute, solitary woman, who suffered alone in this huge, desolate-looking château. There was not the slightest sound, nor could I perceive the faintest movement of the bed-covering from her respiration. I regarded her with a stupefied air, and remained as if petrified by the spectacle. Presently her large eyes moved slightly ; she made an effort to lift her hand, which immediately fell down on the bed, and she uttered these words in a voice which was no more than the faintest whisper : ' I have been waiting for you impatiently.' I began a reply, but she stopped me by a slight motion of her hand, and the attendant whispered in my my ear, ' Don't speak ; my lady is unable to bear the slightest sound.' I sat down by the head of the bed ; the countess made a great effort, and succeeded in getting her hand under the bolster ; it rested there a moment ; then, by a violent effort, was withdrawn, holding a sealed paper. The exertion requisite to enable her to accomplish this overpowered her, and she had just time to say, as she left it in my hand, which I had stretched out to take it from her, ' I confide to you my testament,' when she suddenly seized a little crucifix lying on the bed and pressed it to her lips, and with an exclamation of 'Ah ! my God !' she ceased to exist. There was even an expression of joy in her eyes when she breathed her last. Certainly she must have suffered greatly in her lifetime.

" When the will was opened it was found that she had left the whole of her property to the hospital at Vendôme, saving a few legacies. I was appointed her executor, and was instructed to leave La Grande Bretèche, the mansion which has excited your curiosity, unopened for fifty years from the day of her death. No repairs were to be made, and I was empowered, if necessary, to pay a man to watch over it. At the expiration of this term, supposing the conditions of her will had been strictly fulfilled, the house was to become the property of my heirs ; for, as you are no doubt aware, sir, the law forbids notaries to accept a legacy. Failing in the due discharge of the conditions imposed, the building was to go to the heir-at-law after the lapse of the said fifty years, subject to the fulfilment of certain conditions specified in a codicil annexed to the will, which was to remain unopened until that epoch arrived. The will has not been disputed, therefore——"

Without finishing the sentence, the notary regarded me with an air of triumph. I made him perfectly happy by paying him a compliment or two, and then I added : " Your narrative has made a profound impression on me. But I presume you must have made some conjectures respecting the contents of the codicil."

" Sir," he replied, with comical reserve, " I should never think of permitting myself to judge the conduct of a person who honoured me with the gift of such a diamond as this," and he carried his hand to his shirt-front.

I soon, however, got him to tell me the opinions regarding it which were current among the gossips of both sexes, but they were so contradictory, that, in spite of the interest I felt in the subject, I could hardly prevent myself from falling asleep. I rose to show him out, and when he was on the staircase he said :

" Ha ! Ha ! many people in Vendôme would like to live forty-eight years longer if it were only to get at this secret. But, one moment ! " Here he laid his finger on the side of his nose, as much as to say, Take particular notice of what I am about to observe. " To get at the secret it is not necessary that one should reach three-score years."

With this parting expression, which he no doubt thought very clever, he made his way downstairs, and I was left to ruminate on the strange tale I had just heard, and to build up a romance upon it, which I did *à la Radcliffe*. I was deep in my dream, when the door of the room opened gently, and my landlady entered the room.

" Well, sir," she began, " M. Regnault has no doubt told you his history of the Grande Bretèche."

" Yes, Mother Lepas."

" What did he tell you ? "

I repeated as briefly as I could the notary's narrative. At each sentence my hostess bent her neck with that expression in her countenance peculiar to the female innkeeper, which is a compound of the instinct of a gendarme, the acuteness of the spy, and the cunning of the trader.

" My dear Madame Lepas," I said, at the termination of
my recital, " you seem to know something more of the matter,
eh ? Else why have you taken the trouble to come up to my
room ? "

" Ah ! faith of an honest woman, and as true as my name
is Lepas——"

" There, don't swear, your eyes are large with a secret. You
knew M. Merret. What sort of a man was he, dame ? "

" M. de Merret, see you, was a handsome man, who was so
long that you could not see the end of him ! A worthy gentleman who came from Picardy. He paid cash for everything, to
avoid the possibility of a dispute with any person. See you, he
was passionate. All the ladies thought him very amiable."

" Because he was passionate ? " I asked my hostess.

" Very likely," said she. " You will readily imagine that
he must have had some special qualities to induce Madame de
Merret to marry him, who, without detracting from others,
was by far the richest and handsomest woman in the province
of Vendôme. The bride was a real jewel of a woman. Ah,
they were a handsome couple in their day ! "

" Were they happy in their wedded life ? "

" Hum ! yes and no. Madame de Merret was a good woman,
pleasant in her manners, who suffered a good deal at times
from the hastiness of her husband ; but though somewhat proud
we liked him. Bah ! it was in his position to be so. When one
is noble, you see——"

" Still, there must have been some catastrophe to cause
their violent separation ? "

" I didn't say that there had been any catastrophe. I don't
know anything about it."

" Good. I am sure now that you know all about it."

" Well, sir, I will tell you everything. When I saw M. Regnault come up to your room, it struck me that he was going to
talk to you about the Grande Bretèche. That has given me the
idea of consulting you on a point which has caused me a great
deal of anxiety. I am sure that you are a gentleman capable
of giving me good advice, and my conscience is greatly troubled
by a matter which I do not feel disposed to confide to a confessor, considering what happened lately at Tours. A widow of
the suburb of St. Pierre-des-Corps accused herself in confession
of having killed her husband. She had, with all deference to
you, salted him like a pig, put him in a cellar and every morning
she threw a small piece of him in the river ; she said he was

travelling, and the fact is, he was journeying in detail under water. At last, there only remained the head. The priest went and told the public prosecutor, and she was put to death in consequence. When the judge asked her why she did not throw the head into the water after the remainder of the body, she answered, that she never could carry it, she found it too heavy. Well, sir, I am not in such a plight as the woman I spoke of, as you will easily believe ; but what I want is the advice of a trustworthy man on a matter which happened to me. Hitherto, I have not dared to open my mind to the people about here, who, when gossiping is concerned, have tongues which move with steel springs. In fact, sir, no traveller has ever stayed so long in my inn as you have to whom I could tell the tale of the fifteen thousand francs——"

" My dear Madame Lepas ! " I said, stopping her flow of words, " if your confidence is one which is of a nature to compromise me, nothing in the world would make me desire to be charged with it."

" Don't be alarmed, sir," she said, interrupting me. " You will see."

This eagerness induced me to imagine that I was not the first to whom my good hostess had communicated the secret of which I was to be the sole depository, and I listened.

" Sir," said she, " when the emperor sent Spanish prisoners here, I had to lodge, at the expense of the government, a young Spaniard, sent here on parole. Notwithstanding he was on parole, he had to go every morning to show himself to the chief of the police. He was a grandee. He had names ending in *os* and *dia*, something like Bagos de Feridia, but I am not quite sure ; however, you can see it in my book. He was a handsome young man for a Spaniard, who, they say, are all ugly. He was only five feet two or three inches high, but he was well made, and had, oh ! such pretty little hands, and such care as he took of them. He had as many brushes for his hands as a woman has for her whole toilette. He was dark-skinned and had a dark bright eye and black hair. He was very grave and silent, regular in his attendance at church, always kneeling in the same place, which happened to be within two or three yards of Madame de Merret's chapel. In the evening, he used to wander about the mountains, and I was rather alarmed at finding, soon after his arrival here, that he did not return until midnight ; but I soon got used to that, and gave him the key so that he might let himself in. One day, a stableman, taking horses to the river, saw the grandee swimming about in the middle of the stream, and he seemed rather annoyed when I cautioned him on his return to be careful of the weeds. At last, sir, one morning we could not find him in his room, and it was clear he had not been there all night. By dint of searching about the room I found a note in a drawer in which there were fifty Spanish gold coins, worth about 200*l.*, also some diamonds in a little box, which were valued at twice that sum. The note stated that in the event of his not returning, we were to appropriate these things on condition of founding masses of thanksgiving for his escape and safety. At that time my husband was alive, and he went in search of the Spaniard ; and here is a strange part of the tale. My husband, in examining the river, found his clothes buried under a large stone on the bank of the river, nearly opposite La Grande Bretèche. My husband was there so early that nobody saw him, and in accordance with the count's desire we burnt the clothes, and gave out that he had made his escape. The authorities sent officers in pursuit, but they were not successful in finding him. My husband thought the count had drowned himself, but I was of a different opinion. I believe that he had something to do in Madam de Merret's affair, seeing that Rosalie told me that the crucifix which madame valued so highly that she had it buried with her, was of ebony and silver, and I had noticed that the count had one like it when he first came here. Now, sir, is it not true that I have the right to enjoy the six hundred pounds without remorse !"

" Certainly ; but have you not questioned Rosalie ? " I asked.

" Oh, yes, indeed, sir ; but that girl is like a wall. She knows something but it's impossible to get her to talk."

After a little more conversation my hostess left me. My curiosity was now excited to the highest pitch. I felt sure that the Grande Bretèche had been the scene of some dreadful crime. Rosalie, who had been Madame de Merret's maid, was now the servant of the inn, and I fancied, from the expression of her face, that she possessed the secret of some fearful occurrence, and I determined I would get that secret from her.

.   .   .   .

At last she consented to tell me the secret, and I will relate it as briefly as I can. The chamber occupied by Madame de Merret was on the ground floor. A little cabinet, about four feet square, which she used as a wardrobe, was at one end of the room. It was made in the thickness of the wall. Three

months before the particular evening of which I am about to
speak, the countess had been so much indisposed that the
count had had a chamber prepared for him on the first floor,
which he occupied from that time. By one of those chances
impossible to foresee, he returned this evening two hours later
than usual from the place where he used to go to read the
papers and talk politics. He had lost forty francs, too, at billiards—an enormous sum in Vendôme, where everybody hoards.
It had been his custom to ask Rosalie, when he came home,
if her mistress had gone to bed, and on receiving an answer
in the affirmative, he invariably went straight up to his room.
This evening, on his return, he took it into his head to go and
see his wife, partly to talk over his loss, and partly, perhaps, to
get some consolation from her ; for he had noticed at dinner
that she was very nicely dressed, and he had observed this, as
husbands do everything, a little late. Instead of calling Rosalie,
who was busy in the kitchen with the cook and coachman, the
count walked towards his wife's room, leaving his candle at
the foot of the stairs. His step was easy to recognise as he moved
along the corridor. At the moment he turned the handle of
the door of his wife's room, he heard the door of the little cabinet
shut, but as his wife was standing beside the fireplace, he took
it for granted that it was Rosalie who had gone in ; still a suspicion forced itself upon his mind ; he looked attentively at his
wife and perceived a confused expression in her eyes. When
she spoke, her voice was slightly altered from its usual tone.
" You have returned late to-night," said she. The count did
not reply, for at that moment Rosalie came into the room.
This was like a thunderbolt to him ; he walked backwards
and forwards from one end of the room to the other, with his
arms folded across his chest.

" Have you had bad news, or are you ill ? " asked his wife
timidly, while Rosalie was assisting her to undress. He remained silent.

" You may go," said the countess to her maid. She divined
some misfortune was about to happen from her husband's
expression, and wished to be alone with him. When Rosalie
had gone, the count stopped in front of his wife, and said to
her calmly :

" Madame, there is somebody in your cabinet."

The countess looked at him quietly, and replied with great
simplicity :

" No, sir."

This negative pierced the count's heart; he did not believe it; yet never had his wife appeared more pure and truthful than at that moment. He rose to open the door of the cabinet, when his wife caught him by the hand, regarded him with melancholy tenderness and said in a touching voice:

"If you do not find anybody there, reflect that all relations between us will be at an end."

The dignified attitude assumed by his wife impressed the count deeply.

"No, Josephine," said he, "I will not go. In either case we should be separated eternally. Listen; I know the purity of your soul, and the holy life you lead; you would not commit a mortal sin to save your life."

At these words the countess regarded her husband with a haggard eye.

"Stay, here is your crucifix," he added. "Swear before God that there is no person there; I will believe you, and will never open that door."

The countess took the crucifix, and said:

"I swear it."

"Speak louder," said the husband, "and repeat: I swear before God that there is no person in that cabinet."

She repeated the phrase without hesitation.

"That is well," said the count coldly.

After a moment's silence he took up the crucifix, which was of ebony, inlaid with silver, and finely chased, and said:

"I did not know you had anything so beautiful of this kind."

"I met with it at Duvivier's, who bought it of one of the Spanish prisoners who passed through Vendôme last year."

"Oh!" ejaculated the count, as he hung the crucifix on the nail, and rang the bell.

Rosalie answered it with remarkable quickness, and as she entered the room, the count hastened to meet her, led her into one of the recesses of the windows and said in a low tone:

"I know Gorenflot wishes to marry you, and that poverty alone prevents you from beginning housekeeping, and that you have told him that you will not marry him until he has found means to establish himself as a master mason. Well! go and find him, and tell him to come here with his tools. Take care you don't wake anybody else besides him in the house where he lives; his fortune shall exceed your desires. Mind, leave the house without gossiping, or else . . ." He frowned.

"Take my key," said he. He then stepped to the door, and shouted in a voice of thunder, "Jean!"

Jean, who was both his coachman and his confidential servant, made his appearance in the passage instantly.

"Go to bed, all of you," said his master, at the same time making a sign for him to approach, and added in a low voice, "When they are all asleep—*asleep*, understand—you will come down quietly and let me know."

The count, who had never lost sight of his wife while he was giving his orders, returned and seated himself gently by her side, near the fire, and related to her his misfortunes in the billiard-room, and the subjects discussed in the reading-room. When Rosalie returned, she found the count and his wife chatting away amicably by the fire. It so happened that some repairs had just been made in the house, and a quantity of mortar had been left which inspired the idea the count was about to put in execution.

"Gorenflot is there, sir."

"Let him come in," said her master, aloud.

The countess paled slightly when she saw the mason.

"Gorenflot," said the count, "go and fetch as many bricks from the coach-house as will be sufficient to brick up the entrance to this cabinet." Then he added, in a low voice, to the mason and Rosalie, "You will sleep here to-night, Gorenflot, but to-morrow morning you will have a passport to a foreign country which I will tell you of. I will give you 240*l.* for your journey. You will remain in that country ten years. You will go to Paris on your way, and there you will wait for me until I arrive. I will then give you a bond for a like sum, which will be paid on your observing the conditions of our agreement, and maintaining the most profound silence on what happens here this night. As for you, Rosalie, I will give you 400*l.* as a marriage portion on the day of your wedding, on condition that you marry Gorenflot, and preserve an absolute silence; otherwise, no marriage portion."

"Rosalie," said the countess, "come and dress my hair."

The husband walked tranquilly to and fro, keeping a close watch on his wife, her maid, and the mason, but without showing any offensive suspicion. Gorenflot was obliged to make a noise about his work, and the countess took advantage of her husband being at the other end of the room to whisper to Rosalie: "An annuity of 40*l.* for you, child, if you will tell Gorenflot to leave an opening at the bottom." Then she said aloud, with great

self-possession, " Go and help him ! " The count and countess
preserved an absolute silence all the time the mason was about
his work. This was intentional on the part of the count, who
did not wish to give his wife the opportunity of uttering words
susceptible of a double construction. When the wall was built
about half-way up, the mason took advantage of a moment
when the count's back was towards him to break one of the
two panes of glass which formed the upper part of the door of
the cabinet. For an instant the mason, the maid, and her
mistress saw a swarthy face with eyes of fire at the opening,
and the countess had just time to make a slight sign of the head,
which seemed to say, " Hope ! " when the face disappeared.

About four o'clock in the morning the wall was finished.
The mason was sent to bed under the guardianship of Jean,
and the count remained with his wife. When they rose in the
morning, he said to his wife :

" I must go to the police office for a passport."

He put on his hat and moved towards the door ; then, as
if thinking of something, he turned back and took down the
crucifix. His wife felt a thrill of joy. He is going to Duvivier's,
thought she. As soon as her husband had gone out, the
countess ran for Rosalie, and said in a terrible voice :

" The pickaxe ! the pickaxe ! I noticed how Gorenflot worked
last night, and we shall have time to make a hole and stop it
up again, so that it will not be seen."

Rosalie fetched a kind of crowbar, and her mistress began
to demolish the wall with incredible strength and fury. She
had already knocked out several bricks, and was in the act of
giving a still more vigorous blow to the remainder, when she
heard a step behind her, and stopping in the very act of striking,
she looked round and saw her husband.

" Put the countess to bed," said he coldly.

Foreseeing what would happen in his absence, he had laid a
snare for his wife ; he had merely written to the magistrate,
and sent for Duvivier. The bricks had been restored to their
places, and the apartment freed from the appearance of disorder when the jeweller arrived.

" Duvivier," said the count, " have you not bought some
crucifixes of the Spaniards who passed this way ! "

" No, sir."

" Good, I thank you," said he, exchanging a tiger-like
glance with his wife. " Jean," added he, turning towards that
confidential person, " you will bring me all the food I require

to this room. The countess is not well, and I shall not leave her until she is quite recovered."

For twenty days did this cruel man remain near his wife. At first, when any noise was made in the cabinet by the dying man, and Josephine was about to plead for mercy on behalf of the unknown, he would stop her before she could utter more than a syllable by saying, " You have sworn on the cross that there is no person there."

Stopping in the very act of striking, she looked round and saw her husband.

THE FOLDING DOORS

A YOUNG man was coming slowly down the wide staircase of a palace in the Rue de Vaugirard. It was, by the new reckoning, the 13th of Brumaire ; evening, and cold, moonlit, and clear ; these things being the same by any reckoning, as the young man thought, pausing by the tall window on the landing-place that looked out on to the blue-shadowed, silent street.

There was a ball overhead in the great state rooms, and he could hear the music, violins, flutes and harpsichord, distinctly, though he had closed the door behind him. He was one of the guests, and had the watchful, furtive air of one who has stolen away unperceived, and fears that he may be discovered. He seemed now to have stopped with an idea of ascertaining if any-one was abroad, for he leant over the smooth gilt banisters and listened. The great staircase was empty, and empty the vast hall below.

Opposite the landing window was a long mirror, with three branched candles before it. The young man turned to this quickly and noiselessly, and pulled from the pocket of his coat a strip of gilt-edged paper, folded tightly. He unrolled this and read the message it contained, written in a light pencil.

" At half-past ten knock four times on the folding doors. *Do not be late ; every moment is one of terror. I am afraid of HIM.*"

The last two sentences were underlined, the last word twice.

The young man looked up and down the stairs, twisted the paper up, and was about to thrust it into the flame of one of the candles, when he caught sight of himself in the tall mirror, and stood staring at the image with the paper held out in his hand.

He saw a figure that to his thinking was that of a mounte-

bank, for it had once been that of the Duc de Jaurès—Citizen
Jaurès now—courtier of his one-time Christian Majesty Louis
XVI., beheaded recently as Louis Capet in the great square
now called by the people the Place de la Revolution.

The People had altered everything, even the person of M.
de Jaurès, who wore the classic mode beloved of liberty—the
fashion of this year one of freedom, hair à la Titus and a
black stock swathing the chin. His face was without colour,
the black, hollow eyes and black hair accentuating this
pallor ; his countenance, though sombre in expression, was
beautiful by reason of the exquisite lines of the mouth and
nostrils, and something elevated and noble in the turn of the
head. As he stared at himself a slow flush of terrible shame
overspread his paleness ; with something like a suppressed
shudder, he gave the paper to the flame, and scattered the
ashes down the stairs.

Then he pulled out the watch hanging from the black
watered-silk fob.

It wanted ten minutes to half-past ten. The dance music
ceased overhead ; in its place came laughter, loud talking, and
presently a woman singing in a rapt and excited fashion.

Monsieur de Jaurès paced to and fro on the landing. He
loathed these people he mixed with, so like him in dress and appearance, but *bourgeois* and *canaille* all of them ; some butchers
of the Terror, some smug deputies, some one-time servants,
some soldiers, some dancers from the opera, some provincials
and their wives—all, by the grace of the People, free and equal.

The Citizen de Jaurès, aristocrat by virtue of birth, tradition,
temper, and qualities, bit his under-lip fiercely to hear these people
rioting in this house. The late owner, his once dear friend, had
been massacred in the prison of La Force a month ago, and the
house now belonged to a deputy from Lyons, married to the
daughter of a nobleman long since sent to the guillotine.

The note that M. de Jaurès had burnt was from
this lady. They had known each other before the rule of chaos,
and when the revolution brought him out of the prison, where
he had been consigned for a political offence by the late King's
ministers, and he had found her, terror-subdued, mistress of a
revolutionary salon, the similarity between their positions, the
common memories of another world, the sense of kinship amidst
a society so alien, so monstrous, so hideous, had grown into
a sad but strong love.

She was spared because she had married one of the tyrants,

and pretended to forget her father's murder ; he, because he had been a prisoner of the King, and affected to subscribe to the new rule of the people. Both had tasted of shame, and together they sought to redeem themselves.

Fired by their mutual sympathy, the horror of what they daily saw round them, the desire to redeem their acquiescence in the overthrow of their order, to redeem, at the risk of death, the lives they should never have consented to save, they had been the instigators of one of the many desperate plots against the Government, the object of which was to rescue the Austrian Queen from the Temple and the ultimate guillotine.

To-night the intrigue, evolved with skill and secrecy, and materially helped by the knowledge Hortense was enabled to obtain through her husband's position, was to be put into execution, and they were either to fly across the frontier with the rescued Queen, or to give up life together, as aristocrats, upon the scaffold.

M. de Jaurès, on the threshold of this hazard, felt that chill suspension of all the faculties which fills that waiting pause before the plunge into great actions. He was conscious of neither exaltation nor despair, but of a strange sense that time had stopped, or had never been, and that all the events which so oppressed his brain were but pictures, that would clear away and reveal at last—reality.

The dance music began again ; the noisy music of the People, with its distinct rise and fall. He and Hortense had been present at the opera the night they had played *Richard Coeur de Lion* and the audience had risen in a frenzy of devotion at the strains of " *O Richard, O mon roi.*"

He recalled the Queen with her children, worshipped and very stately, and Hortense with powdered hair and a hoop festooned with roses ; then he thought of the wretched captive in the Temple, and the haggard woman in a Greek gown with a fillet through her flowing hair, waiting for him downstairs behind the folding doors.

Pacing to and fro, facing now the cold street and bitter night, now his own reflection in the glass, the inner agony of suspense, regret, remorse, broke through the dazed control of his overwrought passions. He gave a little sound, caught into the whirl of the dance music unheard, and stepped back sideways against the gleaming white wall, his hand instinctively to his heart.

The next second he was master of himself, and wondering

wildly what had caused him that sudden utter pang of terror, a terror beyond fear of death or any definition, awful, hideous. He listened, as men will in great dread, and heard what seemed a curious short cry, like the echo of his own, that rose above the dance-beat. He thought it came from the street, and softly opened the window.

Everything was still, but in the distance, where the moon-light fell between two houses, three of the Republican soldiers were dragging a man along, and a girl in a blue gown was following, wringing her hands.

A second, and the little group had passed out of sight. M. de Jaurès closed the window, feeling strangely relieved that his emotion had been caused by such a common thing as the cry of a poor creature following a suspect to the Abbaye. He must, unconsciously, have heard her cry before, and this had given him that sensation of terror.

The dance music fell to a softer measure ; a clock struck the half-hour, and Camille de Jaurès descended to the salon on the next floor.

He entered softly, yet confident of being neither interrupted nor observed.

The room was large, with great windows looking on to the street. It had once been painted with flowers, and shepherds asleep with their flocks, and nymphs seated beside fountains, but had lately been painted white from floor to ceiling by a Republican who detested these remnants of aristocracy. White, with stiff wreaths of classic laurel, candles in plain sconces shaded with dead-hued silk, straight grey curtains before the windows, and very little furniture to cumber the polished floor and that little, simple, bare-legged, and comprising a couch of Grecian shape, covered with striped brocade, such as ladies, dressed in the fashions of the year one of liberty, loved to re-cline on.

A cold, bare room, with a glimmer from the shaded light like the moon-glow, and with no colour, nor gleam, nor bright-ness. The wall that faced the window was almost entirely occu-pied by high, white folding doors with crystal knobs. M. de Jaurès' glance fell at once on these ; they led to the private apartments of Hortense, and through them, by the back way across the garden, they were to escape to-night. He advanced, and was about to knock, when one leaf was opened sharply in his face, and a man stepped out.

It was Citizen Durosoy, husband of Hortense. M. de Jaurès

stepped back ; he saw that the room beyond the folding doors
was dark, but close where the light penetrated he noticed a fold
of soft satin with a pearl border, and an empty white shoe softly
rounded to the shape of a foot, lying sideways, as if it had just
been taken off. Hortense was there, then, he knew, waiting
for him. He straightened himself to meet the unlooked-for
interruption.

He was quite composed as Durosoy closed the doors.

" Your room upstairs is very close," he said, " and I suppose
I am not in a festival mood—it is pleasantly cool here."

" Cool ! " echoed the Deputy of Lyons. " It seems to me
cold," he laughed. " Perhaps it is the singing of La Marguerite,
which is so bad for the nerves, for my wife has a headache, and
must lie down in the dark."

M. de Jaurès smiled. He felt such a contempt for this man
that it put him absolutely at his ease. The Deputy had been a
poor provincial lawyer, to whom the late de Jaurès had been
kind. He affected to remember this now, and was warmly
friendly, even patronising, to his old patron's son. The aristocrat hated him doubly for it, scorned him that no echo of this
hatred seemed ever to awake in his mind ; for the Deputy
was almost familiar in his manner to M. de Jaurès. He was
quiet and modest with everybody.

" I hope my wife is not delicate," he said with an air of
anxiety. " I have thought lately that she was in ill-health."

" I have not noticed it," answered the other.

He seated himself on the striped couch, and looked carelessly at the grate, where a pale fire burnt. The Deputy crossed
to the hearth, and stood looking at his guest with an amiable
smile. He was a slight man, brown-haired and well looking, but
of a common appearance. He wore a grey cloth coat, with a
black sash up under his armpits, and white breeches. This
dress, and the stiff, long straggling locks that fell on to his
bullion-stitched collar, gave him an appearance of anarchy and
wildness not in keeping with his pleasant countenance.

He stood so long smiling at M. de Jaurès, that a feeling of
impatience came over the nobleman. He glanced at the pendule
clock on the mantelpiece, and wondered how long the fool
would stay.

" It is unfortunate that you and the Citizeness should both
be absent at once," he remarked. He had still the tone of an
aristocrat when speaking to Durosoy.

The Deputy held out his right hand

"I cut my finger with a fruit knife," he answered, "and came down to Hortense to tie it up ; but she seemed so to wish to be alone I did not like to press her ; her head hurt so, she said."

A handkerchief was twisted about his hand, and he began to unwind it as he spoke. "Now you are here," he added, "perhaps you could help me tie it up ; it really is bleeding damnably."

M. de Jaurès rose slowly. He let his glance rest for a moment on the folding doors. It was as if he could see Hortense standing at the other side in the dark, listening, waiting for her husband to go.

Durosoy held up his bare hand. There was a deep cut on the forefinger, and the blood was running down the palm and staining the close frill of muslin at his wrist.

"A severe wound for a silver knife," remarked M. de Jaurès, taking him by the wrist.

"A steel knife," said the Deputy—"steel as sharp as La Guillotine—you see, *mon ami*," and he smiled, "what comes of trying to cut a peach with a steel knife."

M. de Jaurès slowly tore his own handkerchief into strips and carefully bound up the wound. He was wondering the while if Hortense had been delayed by the unexpected visit of her husband ; if she was venturing to change her clothes before he finally returned to their guests. By the white shoe he had seen through the folding doors, he thought she had done so.

"Thank you, Camille," said the Deputy. He had a trick of using Christian names, odious to M. de Jaurès. "It is astonishing how faint the loss of a little blood makes one."

"This from our modern Brutus ! " exclaimed M. de Jaurès. That term had been given once, in the Convention, to the Deputy, and the man whose dupe he was dared to quote it ironically, knowing the stupidity of the provincial. As he had expected, the Deputy seemed pleased ; he shrugged modestly.

"Oh, one's own blood, you know, not that of other people. I can endure the loss of *that* with great equanimity." He smiled, as if he had made a joke, and the aristocrat smiled too, for other reasons. "Will you drink with me—down here ? It is, as you say, very close upstairs."

"I fear to detain you, Citizen."

Durosoy rang the bell, then seated himself by the fire.

"No, I am tired of their chatter. I would rather talk with a sensible man like yourself, my dear Camille."

M. de Jaurès did not move from his easy attitude on the brocade couch.

"But we shall disturb the Citizeness," he said. His idea was that if he could make Durosoy leave with him, he could, more or less easily, get rid of him upstairs and return.

The Deputy smiled. "Hortense is not so ill. Besides, the doors are thick enough."

M. de Jaurès wondered—how thick? Could she hear their talk? Would she understand the delay? His straining ears could catch no sound of her movements.

The Deputy continued in a kind of fatuous self-satisfaction.

"I hope she will be well enough to return soon to the ball. When one has a beautiful wife one likes to show her off."

He paused, put his head on one side, and added :

"You do think her beautiful, do you not, Camille ? "

M. de Jaurès looked at him coldly. He felt he could afford to despise this man, since in a few moments he and she would be riding away from his house for ever.

"Naturally, Citizen."

A citizen servant entered, and the Deputy ordered wine.

"I must not stay," said M. de Jaurès. He raised his voice a little that she might hear. "One glass, and I will go back to make my *adieux*."

Durosoy appeared mildly surprised.

"So early ! You cannot have any business this time of night."

The wine was brought in and placed on a thin-legged table by the hearth. M. de Jaurès glanced at the clock. The hand was creeping on towards eleven. His contempt of the Deputy was beginning to change to an impatient hatred of the creature's very presence.

"A matter of mood, not of time," he answered. "I am in no merry-making vein to-night."

The Deputy, pouring out wine, looked at him critically.

"You are too lazy, my friend. You do nothing from one day's end to another—naturally you are wearied. And it is dangerous, too."

M. de Jaurès took the glass offered him. " How dangerous ? "

Durosoy lifted his common brown eyes. "Those who will not serve the Republic are apt to be considered her enemies."

The young noble smiled.

"Oh, as to that, I am a very good friend to France, but I lack the qualities to be of any use."

He sipped his wine, and looked indifferently past the Deputy at the folding doors. His thoughts were : ' The time is getting on. How long will a carriage take from here to the *rue du Temple* ? Half an hour, allowing for the pace we must go and the crowd coming out of the opera.'

" No use ! " exclaimed the Deputy. " Why, you are a soldier, are you not ? "

" Once—that seems a long time ago."

Durosoy laughed and poured out more wine. The tinkling of the glass on the silver stand had the same thin quality as his voice.

" There is always Toulon," he said. " The Royalists there are giving us a good deal of trouble."

" I do not fancy going there to be hewn down by a lot of rascals. I leave that to braver men," smiled de Jaurès lazily ; but his blood leapt with the desire to be with these same Royalists in Toulon, with his sword drawn against such as this Deputy, whose wine seemed to scorch and choke to-night. When would the man go ? The carriage that was waiting at the back might be noticed. The servant in the plot would begin to wonder at the delay ; and she, could she hear ? She must be undergoing torture—as he was.

" Then there is the revolt in Caen," said the Deputy ; " we want good men there."

" I've no fancy to go soldiering."

" You are dull to-night, Citizen. Does the business of the Widow Capet interest you ? It is to come on this month."

" Ah ! The trial ? "

" Yes."

" I heard something of it. No, I am not interested."

When would this babbling cease ? Ten minutes past eleven, and the rendezvous in the *rue du Temple* at twelve.

" Not interested ? " echoed the Deputy. " Now if I might hazard a guess, my friend, I should say that you were rather too interested."

M. de Jaurès looked at him steadily.

" How—too interested ? " he asked in accents painfully calm.

" I do not think you would like the Widow Capet to take the same journey to the Place de la Révolution as her husband did."

" Why should I trouble ? " answered M. de Jaurès, who for one instant had thought himself suspected. He drew his breath a little unevenly ; the delay, the suspense, were beginning to tell on him, were becoming serious, too. He remembered that the hour had been altered at the last moment from one to twelve, and that he had had no opportunity of telling Hortense so. They had to be so careful, there had been so few chances for them to meet at all. Hortense would think they had an hour longer than was the case.

The Deputy was taking his third glass; he seemed to be settled comfortably in his chair. It appeared as if he might maunder on with his idle talk for another hour; and the delay of another hour would be fatal to M. de Jaurès.

" It must seem very strange to you," said the Deputy reflectively, " this year one of liberty."

M. de Jaurès sat forward on the couch. Durosoy had never taken this tone of gravity with him before.

" No stranger to me than to you," he answered. He finished the wine, and set the glass back on the table.

" Well, then, strange to me and to you."

M. de Jaurès laughed; he could not control himself.

"What makes you say that?" he asked. The Deputy shrugged.

" The thought will occur—sitting here in this palace that I used to pass with awe—talking to you whom I used to regard with awe—married to Hortense! Yes, you are right, it is strange to me."

The noble's mouth tightened; a black shame overwhelmed him that he was sitting here listening to this man.

" You," continued the Deputy, " used to know the former owner of this house, did you not? "

M. de Jaurès rose.

" I knew him."

" He was killed at La Force, was he not? "

" I believe so; why do you recall him? " M. de Jaurès leant against the mantelpiece. The cold, white room, the inane Deputy, were fast becoming intolerable. He began to be hideously conscious of two things: the clock whose hands were coming round slowly to the half-hour, and the folding doors behind which Hortense waited. The interruption, of which he had thought nothing at first, was like to prove fatal. Could he do it in less than half an hour? Merciful God! it was not possible! Some of them were already at the rendezvous—the Queen was ready.

" Let us go back upstairs," he said. " It is, after all, rather doleful here."

" On the contrary, I am very comfortable," smiled the Deputy, crossing his legs.

"You will be missed," said M. de Jaurès. His thoughts were racing furiously. How could he convey to Hortense that the time had been altered—that he could not wait?

The Deputy nodded towards the high ceiling. "Missed? You hear the music? I think they are enjoying themselves."

To abandon her, or to miss the appointment in the *rue du Temple*; to break faith with his friends or with her, to lose all chance of redemption, to jeopardise the Queen's escape, or to forsake Hortense (for success meant that he must be across the frontier, and failure meant death; either way he was useless to her)—it was fast narrowing to these terrible decisions.

He looked at his face in the large mirror above the mantel-piece, and was almost startled to see how white it was above the close cravat and blue striped waistcoat. Surely Durosoy must notice!

The Deputy sat looking into the fire. M. de Jaurès, glancing at him out of furtive eyes, observed that he, too, was pale.

A pause of silence was broken by the shrill chimes of the gilt clock striking the half-hour.

M. de Jaurès could not restrain a start. He must go. He could come back for her if alive; his honour (Heaven help him! he still thought of that) was the pledge to them, his affection to her—she would understand. Perhaps by the servant waiting with the carriage at the back entrance he could convey a message, telling her of the changed time.

"You will forgive me," he said with that ease with which breed enabled him to cover his agony, "but I am due at my chambers "—he raised his voice for her to hear—" the truth is I have business—important business to-night. Good-evening, Durosoy."

He went towards the door; it would be quick running to make the *rue du Temple* in time. Heaven enlighten her as to the cause of his desertion.

"Business?" said the Deputy good-humouredly. "There is no business nowadays but politics or plots. I hope you are not engaged in the latter, my dear Camille."

M. de Jaurès had his hand on the door-knob. "This is private business," he answered, "about my property. I am trying to save some of it."

The Deputy turned in his chair.

"Why, I did not know that your estates were confiscated. Why did not you tell me? I might have helped you."

M. de Jaurès opened the door.

" You are such a busy man, Durosoy. I think I shall manage the affair satisfactorily."

" Monseigneur le Duc."

At that title he turned sharply, and saw the Deputy standing before the fire looking at him.

" Why do you say that ? " he asked, and his nostrils widened.

" Forgive me, the expression slipped out. I still think of you as Monseigneur le Duc. It is an astonishing thing, but I believe I am still in awe of you, as I used to be in my little office in Lyons." He smiled fatuously, lowered his eyes to the floor and shook his head.

" Why did you call me ? "

" Well, I wanted to speak to you. Take another glass of wine ; it is still early."

" Indeed, it is impossible for me to stay. I have an appointment."

" Bah ! Make him wait."

" It is a rendezvous that I would rather keep."

" A strange hour for a business appointment. Are you sure it is not a lady that you are so anxious to see ? "

" Say a lady, then," said M. de Jaurès ; " but, believe me that I must go." He was leaving on that, when the Deputy called after him.

" I entreat you to stay. It is also a lady of whom I wish to speak.

M. de Jaurès turned slowly and closed the door.

" Come," smiled the Deputy, " another glass."

" What have you to say to me, Durosoy ? " He felt as if the hand of fate were on his shoulder, dragging him back into the room ; yet every moment—nay, every second—was precious, fast becoming doubly precious.

The Deputy was pouring out the wine. His grey and black figure was illumined by the increasing glow of the fire. He moved bottles and glasses clumsily by reason of the bandaged forefinger of his right hand ; behind him the clock showed twenty minutes to twelve.

M. de Jaurès crossed the long room to the hearth.

" What did you wish to say ? " he asked, " nay "—he put the glass aside—" of what was it that you wished to speak ? "

" My wife."

The noble's first thought was—' This man is not a fool ' ; his second, ' He suspects '—accompanied with a sense of stupor and confusion.

"You," continued Durosoy, "have known her longer than I have ; she was very much admired, was she not, when she was at the Court ? "

"She was admired, naturally. A strange question ! I never knew her well," answered M. de Jaurès. He was sure the fellow suspected, not the plot but the elopement. He desperately readjusted his plans. He could not leave her now ; he must forsake his friends sooner. Had she not said, "I am afraid of *him*."

"Well, that is all," said the Deputy. "Go and keep your appointment, my friend "—his eyes suddenly gleamed—"and I will finish my wine and presently go and fetch Hortense back to the ballroom."

M. de Jaurès answered his look. "No, I will stay," he said with a kind of cold calm.

"Ah ! Now why have you changed your mind ? "

"Because you," was the grim reply, "are so amusing."

He was wondering in his anguish why she did not come out. Surely she might have made some diversion with her presence. Yet she had probably changed her gown. Could she hear—could she understand ?

The man was playing with him ; he might even know of the plot. He must suspect, else why did he remain here, and why did the guests not notice his or her absence, if they had not been prepared ? It was too late to get to the *rue du Temple* now. The governor of the prison was to be abroad for an hour, from twelve to one, and in that time they were to make their attempt. They would make it without him. He could not leave Hortense now. It was certain death ahead of him ; he would be denounced to-morrow, and dishonoured, for he had forsaken his friends.

So raced the thoughts of M. de Jaurès, keeping time to the music of the quadrille coming from the room overhead, while he stood impassive by the head of the brocade sofa, and gazed at the Deputy, who sipped his wine and blinked into the fire.

Two men went by shouting in the street. When their voices had sunk into the distance the Deputy spoke :

"You are rather imprudent, Citizen."

M. de Jaurès was silent ; if he had but some manner of weapon he would kill this man—perhaps with his bare hands even—he came a step nearer.

"I see," continued the Deputy, still looking into the fire,

" that you have a coronet on this handkerchief. Now, do not you think that very imprudent ? "

M. de Jaurès stood arrested. Was this creature, after all, only a fool ? He would, in any case, have killed him ; but the days were gone when noblemen wore swords. Besides, the Deputy sat very near the bell, and was a strong man. Traditions, too, were a clog on the young man's passions. He could not use his hands.

" My dear Camille," exclaimed the Deputy, suddenly glancing up, " you look very pale."

The aristocrat, with the instinct of his breed, was silent under agony. He gazed at the Deputy straightly.

" Are you going to keep this on your linen ? " asked Durosoy, pointing to the coronet on the blood-stained bandage.

" Are you," answered M. de Jaurès, " going to denounce me ? "

The Deputy smiled.

" Because of this ? Why, no, how absurd ! " he laughed. " As if you, of all men, had not given proof of your love for the people by becoming plain Citizen Jaurès. Not so many aristocrats did that."

M. de Jaurès fixed his eyes on the folding doors. It was the one thing that gave him courage to endure, thinking of her waiting there, thinking that he would share the inevitable end with her ; thinking she would know he had waited.

The quadrille music took on another measure. The clock gave a little whirr and struck twelve. The aristocrat shuddered, but held himself erect. Durosoy suddenly grinned up at him.

" What about your appointment ? " he asked.

" I am keeping a more important one," said M. de Jaurès through cold lips.

The Deputy rose.

" Do you not think that I act very well ? " he said in a changed tone.

M. de Jaurès smiled superbly.

" My opinion of you is unchanged, Monsieur."

He had now no longer anything to gain or lose by adopting the manner of the people. The two men took a step towards the middle of the room, still facing each other.

" Your appointment," repeated Durosoy. " Why did you not keep it ? "

M. de Jaurès raised his right hand to his heart and retreated a pace backwards. He hardly heard the words ; the speaker's

presence offended him indescribably ; he lowered his eyes in
instinctive disgust, withdrawn into his own soul. The attempt
in the *rue du Temple* had failed or succeeded without him ;
he had lost the glory of rescuing the Queen, or the glory of being
with the aristocrats in La Force. They would justly despise
him as a coward and a man of broken faith, but the thing
that had induced him to act thus was the thing that rewarded
him—the thought of Hortense. Waiting behind the folding
doors, she must have heard his and her fate. She knew perhaps
before he came that Durosoy suspected and their chance was
over ; she knew now that he had preferred her even to his
word, his pledged honour, for surely that was gone unless it would
be some honour for them to die together—he hoped it would
be the guillotine, not butchery in the prison yard—as befell,
good God—as befell Charles de Maury, with whom he had
once eaten and drunk in this very room——

He steadied his reeling senses with a jerking shudder and
caught the back of the chair near him. That brute Durosoy
was watching him, waiting for him to betray himself, being,
no doubt, very sure of both of them, the man before him and the
woman behind the folding doors.

M. de Jaurès smiled.

" What are you and I looking at each other like this for,
eh ? " he asked.

A soldier went past singing *Ca ira* ; it mingled with the
monotonous repeated music of the quadrille ; the coals fell
together with a little crash ; the Deputy stood in a slack attitude surveying his victim.

M. de Jaurès laughed.

" We will see," said Durosoy slowly, " if Hortense is recovered from her headache."

He turned towards the folding doors. M. de Jaurès longed
for them to open ; at least he would have that moment when
she came forth and walked straight to him, all disguises
over.

The Deputy turned the crystal handle and opened the
door a little way ; he looked over his shoulder and said one
word :

" Aristocrat ! "

" Yes," answered M. de Jaurès. " She and I—both aristocrats."

Durosoy pushed the door a little wider open ; his dull,
foolish manner was changing to a deep breathing ferocity.

" The Widow Capet is still in the Temple, aristocrat," he said, " and your friends are in La Force by now."

M. de Jaurès kept his head high.

" So you knew," he said softly. " You are a cunning rat, Citizen Durosoy."

The Deputy's eyes were suddenly flushed with blood.

" Hortense must thank you, aristocrat, for breaking your appointment for her sake."

M. de Jaurès came nearer. There was darkness beyond the folding doors—the white shoe in the same position and the fold of pearl-braided satin.

The Deputy suddenly flung the other leaf wide.

" I am a cunning rat, am I not ? " he said with a sob of hate. " My wife ! My wife ! " he cried, pointing to her.

She sat just inside the doors, facing them. There was a long red streak down the bosom of her white bodice, her eyes were fixed and her jaw dropped ; across her knee was a knife stained with marks like rust.

The Deputy stood looking at M. de Jaurès.

" You see, I have been cutting peaches with a steel knife. . . ."

THE ANGLER'S STORY OF THE LADY OF GLENWITH GRANGE

I HAVE known Miss Welwyn long enough to be able to bear personal testimony to the truth of many of the particulars which I am now about to relate. I knew her father, and her younger sister Rosamond; and I was acquainted with the Frenchman who became Rosamond's husband. These are the persons of whom it will be principally necessary for me to speak. They are the only prominent characters in my story.

Miss Welwyn's father died some years since. I remember him very well—though he never excited in me, or in any one else that I ever heard of, the slightest feeling of interest. When I have said that he inherited a very large fortune, amassed during his father's time, by speculations of a very daring, very fortunate, but not always very honourable kind, and that he bought this old house with the notion of raising his social position, by making himself a member of our landed aristocracy in these parts, I have told you as much about him, I suspect, as you would care to hear. He was a thoroughly commonplace man, with no great virtues and no great vices in him. He had a little heart, a feeble mind, an amiable temper, a tall figure, and a handsome face. More than this need not, and cannot, be said on the subject of Mr. Welwyn's character.

I must have seen the late Mrs. Welwyn very often as a child; but I cannot say that I remember anything more of her than that she was tall and handsome, and very generous and sweet-tempered towards me when I was in her company. She was her husband's superior in birth, as in everything else; was a great reader of books in all languages; and possessed such admirable talents as a musician, that her wonderful playing on the organ is remembered and talked of to this day among the old people in our country houses about here. All her friends, as I have heard,

THE LADY OF GLENWITH GRANGE 73

were disappointed when she married Mr. Welwyn, rich as he was ; and were afterwards astonished to find her preserving the appearance, at least, of being perfectly happy with a husband who, neither in mind nor heart, was worthy of her.

It was generally supposed (and I have no doubt correctly), that she found her great happiness and her great consolation in her little girl Ida—now the lady from whom we have just parted. The child took after her mother from the first—inheriting her mother's fondness for books, her mother's love of music, her mother's quick sensibilities, and, more than all, her mother's quiet firmness, patience, and loving kindness of disposition. From Ida's earliest years, Mrs. Welwyn undertook the whole superintendence of her education. The two were hardly ever apart, within doors or without. Neighbours and friends said that the little girl was being brought up too fancifully, was not enough among other children, was sadly neglected as to all reasonable and practical teaching, and was perilously encouraged in those dreamy and imaginative tendencies of which she had naturally more than her due share. There was, perhaps, some truth in this ; and there might have been still more, if Ida had possessed an ordinary character, or had been reserved for an ordinary destiny. But she was a strange child from the first, and a strange future was in store for her.

Little Ida reached her eleventh year without either brother or sister to be her playfellow and companion at home. Immediately after that period, however, her sister Rosamond was born. Though Mr. Welwyn's own desire was to have had a son, there were, nevertheless, great rejoicings yonder in the old house on the birth of this second daughter. But they were all turned, only a few months afterwards, to the bitterest grief and despair : the Grange lost its mistress. While Rosamond was still an infant in arms, her mother died.

Mrs. Welwyn had been afflicted with some disorder after the birth of her second child, the name of which I am not learned enough in medical science to be able to remember. I only know that she recovered from it, to all appearance, in an unexpectedly short time ; that she suffered a fatal relapse, and that she died a lingering and a painful death. Mr. Welwyn (who, in after years, had a habit of vain-gloriously describing his marriage as " a love-match on both sides ") was really fond of his wife in his own frivolous feeble way, and suffered as acutely as such a man could suffer, during the latter days of her illness, and at the terrible time when the doctors, one and all, confessed that her life was a thing to be despaired of. He burst into irrepressible passions of tears, and was always obliged to leave the sick-room whenever Mrs. Welwyn spoke of her approaching end. The last solemn words of the dying woman, the tenderest messages that she could give, the dearest parting wishes that she could express, the most earnest commands that she could leave behind her, the gentlest reasons for consolation that she could suggest to the survivors among those who loved her, were not poured into her husband's ear, but into her child's. From the first period of her illness, Ida had persisted in remaining in the sick-room, rarely speaking, never showing outwardly any signs of terror or grief, except when she was removed from it ; and then bursting into hysterical passions of weeping, which no expostulations, no arguments, no commands—nothing, in short, but bringing her back to the bed-side—ever availed to calm. Her mother had been her playfellow, her companion, her dearest and most familiar friend ; and there seemed something in the remembrance of this which, instead of overwhelming the child with despair, strengthened her to watch faithfully and bravely by her dying parent to the very last.

When the parting moment was over, and when Mr. Welwyn, unable to bear the shock of being present in the house of death at the time of his wife's funeral, left home and went to stay with one of his relations in a distant part of England, Ida, whom it had been his wish to take away with him, petitioned earnestly to be left behind. " I promised mamma before she died that I would be as good to my little sister Rosamond as she had been to me," said the child, simply ; " and she told me in return that I might wait here and see her laid in her grave." There happened to be an aunt of Mrs. Welwyn, and an old servant of the family, in the house at this time, who understood Ida much better than her father did, and they persuaded him not to take her away. I have heard my mother say that the effect of the child's appearance at the funeral on her, and on all who went to see it, was something that she could never think of without the tears coming into her eyes, and could never forget to the last day of her life.

It must have been very shortly after this period that I saw Ida for the first time.

I remember accompanying my mother on a visit to the old house we have just left, in the summer, when I was at home for the holidays. It was a lovely, sunshiny morning. There was nobody indoors, and we walked out into the garden. As we approached that lawn yonder, on the other side of the shrubbery, I saw, first, a young woman in mourning (apparently a servant) sitting reading ; then a little girl, dressed all in black, moving towards us slowly over the bright turf, and holding up before her a baby, whom she was trying to teach to walk. She looked, to my ideas, so very young to be engaged in such an occupation as this, and her gloomy black frock appeared to be such an un-naturally grave garment for a mere child of her age, and looked so doubly dismal by contrast with the brilliant sunny lawn on which she stood, that I quite started when I first saw her, and eagerly asked my mother who she was. The answer informed me of the sad family story, which I have been just relating to you. Mrs. Welwyn had then been buried about three months ; and Ida, in her childish way, was trying, as she had promised, to supply her mother's place to her infant sister Rosamond.

I only mention this simple incident, because it is necessary, before I proceed to the eventful part of my narrative, that you should know exactly in what relation the sisters stood towards one another from the first. Of all the last parting words that Mrs. Welwyn had spoken to her child, none had been oftener repeated, none more solemnly urged, than those which had com-mended the little Rosamond to Ida's love and care. To other persons, the full, the all-trusting dependence which the dying mother was known to have placed in a child hardly eleven years old, seemed merely a proof of that helpless desire to cling even to the feeblest consolations, which the approach of death so often brings with it. But the event showed, that the trust so strangely placed had not been ventured vainly when it was committed to young and tender hands. The whole future existence of the child was one noble proof that she had been worthy of her mother's dying confidence, when it was first reposed in her. In that simple incident which I have just mentioned, the new life of the two motherless sisters was all foreshadowed.

Time passed. I left school—went to college—travelled in Germany, and stayed there some time to learn the language. At every interval when I came home, and asked about the Welwyns, the answer was, in substance, almost always the same. Mr. Welwyn was giving his regular dinners, performing his regular duties as a county magistrate, enjoying his regular recreations as an amateur farmer and an eager sportsman. His two daughters were never separate. Ida was the same strange, quiet, retiring girl, that she had always been ; and was still (as the phrase went) " spoiling " Rosamond in every way in which it was possible for an elder sister to spoil a younger by too much kindness.

I myself went to the Grange occasionally, when I was in this neighbourhood, in holiday and vacation time ; and was able to test the correctness of the picture of life there which had been drawn for me. I remember the two sisters, when Rosamond was four or five years old ; and when Ida seemed to me, even then, to be more like the child's mother than her sister. She bore with her little caprices as sisters do not bear with one another. She was so patient at lesson-time, so anxious to conceal any weariness that might overcome her in play-hours, so proud when Rosamond's beauty was noticed, so grateful for Rosamond's kisses when the child thought of bestowing them, so quick to notice all that Rosamond did, and to attend to all that Rosamond said, even when visitors were in the room ; that she seemed, to my boyish observation, altogether different from other elder sisters in other family circles into which I was then received.

I remember then, again, when Rosamond was just growing to womanhood, and was in high spirits at the prospect of spending a season in London, and being presented at Court. She was very beautiful at that time—much handsomer than Ida. Her " accomplishments " were talked of far and near in our country circles. Few, if any, of the people, however, who applauded her playing and singing, who admired her water-colour drawings, who were delighted at her fluency when she spoke French, and amazed at her ready comprehension when she read German, knew how little of all this elegant mental cultivation and nimble manual dexterity she owed to her governesses and masters, and how much to her elder sister. It was Ida who really found out the means of stimulating her when she was idle ; Ida who helped her through all her worst difficulties ; Ida who gently conquered her defects of memory over her books, her inaccuracies of ear at the piano, her errors of taste when she took the brush or pencil in hand. It was Ida alone who worked these marvels, and whose all-sufficient reward for her hardest exertions was a chance word of kindness from her sister's lips. Rosamond was not unaffectionate, and not ungrateful ; but she inherited much of her father's commonness and frivolity of character. She became so accustomed to owe everything to her sister—to resign all her most trifling difficulties to Ida's ever-ready care—to have all her tastes consulted by Ida's ever-watchful kindness—that she never appreciated, as it deserved, the deep devoted love of which she was the object. When Ida refused two good offers of marriage,

Rosamond was as much astonished as the veriest strangers, who wondered why the elder Miss Welwyn seemed bent on remaining single all her life.

When the journey to London, to which I have already alluded, took place, Ida accompanied her father and sister. If she had consulted her own tastes, she would have remained in the country ; but Rosamond declared that she should feel quite lost and helpless twenty times a day, in town, without her sister. It was in the nature of Ida to sacrifice herself to any one whom she loved, on the smallest occasions as well as the greatest. Her affection was as intuitively ready to sanctify Rosamond's slightest caprices as to excuse Rosamond's most thoughtless faults. So she went to London cheerfully, to witness with pride all the little triumphs won by her sister's beauty ; to hear, and never tire of hearing, all that admiring friends could say in her sister's praise.

At the end of the season, Mr. Welwyn and his daughters returned for a short time to the country ; they left home again to spend the latter part of the autumn and the beginning of the winter in Paris.

They took with them excellent letters of introduction, and saw a great deal of the best society in Paris, foreign as well as English. At one of the first of the evening parties which they attended, the general topic of conversation was the conduct of a certain French nobleman, the Baron Franval, who had returned to his native country after a long absence, and who was spoken of in terms of high eulogy by the majority of the guests present. The history of who Franval was, and of what he had done, was readily communicated to Mr. Welwyn and his daughters, and was briefly this :

The Baron inherited little from his ancestors besides his high rank and his ancient pedigree. On the death of his parents, he and his two unmarried sisters (their only surviving children) found the small territorial property of the Franvals, in Normandy, barely productive enough to afford a comfortable subsistence for the three. The Baron, then a young man of three-and-twenty, endeavoured to obtain such military or civil employment as might become his rank ; but, although the Bourbons were at that time restored to the throne of France, his efforts were ineffectual. Either his interest at Court was bad, or secret enemies were at work to oppose his advancement. He failed to obtain even the slightest favour ; and, irritated by undeserved neglect, resolved to leave France, and seek occupation for his energies in foreign countries, where his rank would be no bar to his bettering his fortunes, if he pleased, by engaging in commercial pursuits.

An opportunity of the kind that he wanted unexpectedly offered itself. He left his sisters in care of an old male relative of the family at the château in Normandy, and sailed, in the first instance, to the West Indies ; afterwards extending his wanderings to the continent of South America, and there engaging in mining transactions on a very large scale. After fifteen years of absence (during the latter part of which time false reports of his death had reached Normandy), he had just returned to France ; having realised a handsome independence, with which he proposed to widen the limits of his ancestral property, and to give his sisters (who were still, like himself, unmarried) all the luxuries and advantages that affluence could bestow. The Baron's independent spirit, and generous devotion to the honour of his family and the happiness of his surviving relatives, were themes of general admiration in most of the social circles of Paris. He was expected to arrive in the capital every day ; and it was naturally enough predicted that his reception in society there could not fail to be of the most flattering and most brilliant kind.

The Welwyns listened to this story with some little interest ; Rosamond, who was very romantic, being especially attracted by it, and openly avowing to her father and sister, when they got back to their hotel, that she felt as ardent a curiosity as anybody to see the adventurous and generous Baron. The desire was soon gratified. Franval came to Paris, as had been anticipated—was introduced to the Welwyns—met them constantly in society— made no favourable impression on Ida, but won the good opinion of Rosamond from the first ; and was regarded with such high approval by their father, that when he mentioned his intention of visiting England in the spring of the new year, he was cordially invited to spend the hunting season at Glenwith Grange.

I came back from Germany about the same time that the Welwyns returned from Paris, and at once set myself to improve my neighbourly intimacy with the family. I was very fond of Ida ; more fond, perhaps, than my vanity will now allow me to —but that is of no consequence. It is much more to the purpose to tell you, that I heard the whole of the Baron's story enthusiastically related by Mr. Welwyn and Rosamond ; that he came to the Grange at the appointed time ; that I was introduced to him ; and that he produced as unfavourable an impression upon me as he had already produced upon Ida.

It was whimsical enough ; but I really could not tell why I disliked him, though I could account very easily, according to my own notions, for his winning the favour and approval of Rosamond and her father. He was certainly a handsome man, as far as features went ; he had a winning gentleness and graceful respect in his manner when he spoke to women ; and he sang remarkably well, with one of the sweetest tenor voices I ever heard. These qualities alone were quite sufficient to attract any girl of Rosamond's disposition ; and I certainly never wondered why he was a favourite of hers.

Then, as to her father, the Baron was not only fitted to win his sympathy and regard in the field, by proving himself an ardent sportsman and an excellent rider ; but was also, in virtue of some of his minor personal peculiarities, just the man to gain the friendship of his host. Mr. Welwyn was as ridiculously prejudiced as most weak-headed Englishmen are, on the subject of foreigners in general. In spite of his visit to Paris, the vulgar notion of a Frenchman continued to be *his* notion, both while he was in France and when he returned from it. Now, the Baron was as unlike the traditional " Mounseer " of English songs, plays, and satires, as a man could well be ; and it was on account of this very dissimilarity that Mr. Welwyn first took a violent fancy to him, and then invited him to his house. Franval spoke English remarkably well ; wore neither beard, moustachios nor whiskers ; kept his hair cut almost unbecomingly short ; dressed in the extreme of plainness and modest good taste ; talked little in general society ; uttered his words, when he did speak, with singular calmness and deliberation ; and, to crown all, had the greater part of his acquired property invested in English securities. In Mr. Welwyn's estimation, such a man as this was a perfect miracle of a Frenchman, and he admired and encouraged him accordingly.

I have said that I disliked him, yet could not assign a reason for my dislike ; and I can only repeat it now. He was remarkably polite to me ; we often rode together in hunting, and sat near each other at the Grange table ; but I could never become familiar with him. He always gave me the idea of a man who had some mental reservation in saying the most trifling thing. There was a constant restraint, hardly perceptible to most people, but plainly visible, nevertheless, to me, which seemed to accompany his lightest words, and to hang about his most familiar manner. This, however, was no just reason for my secretly disliking and distrusting him as I did. Ida said as much to me, I remember, when I confessed to her what my feelings towards him were, and tried (but vainly) to induce her to be equally candid with me in return. She seemed to shrink from the tacit condemnation of Rosamond's opinion which such a confidence on her part would have implied. And yet she watched the growth of that opinion—or, in other words, the growth of her sister's liking for the Baron—with an apprehension and sorrow which she tried fruitlessly to conceal. Even her father began to notice that her spirits were not so good as usual, and to suspect the cause of her melancholy. I remember he jested, with all the dense insensibility of a stupid man, about Ida having invariably been jealous, from a child, if Rosamond looked kindly upon anybody except her elder sister.

The spring began to get far advanced towards summer. Franval paid a visit to London ; came back in the middle of the season to Glenwith Grange ; wrote to put off his departure for France ; and, at last (not at all to the surprise of anybody who was intimate with the Welwyns) proposed to Rosamond, and was accepted. He was candour and generosity itself when the preliminaries of the marriage settlement were under discussion. He quite overpowered Mr. Welwyn and the lawyers with references, papers, and statements of the distribution and extent of his property, which were found to be perfectly correct. His sisters were written to, and returned the most cordial answers : saying that the state of their health would not allow them to come to England for the marriage ; but adding a warm invitation to Normandy for the bride and her family. Nothing, in short, could be more straightforward and satisfactory than the Baron's behaviour, and the testimonies to his worth and integrity which the news of the approaching marriage produced from his relatives and his friends.

The only joyless face at the Grange now was Ida's. At any time it would have been a hard trial to her to resign that first and foremost place which she had held since childhood in her sister's heart, as she knew she must resign it when Rosamond married. But, secretly disliking and distrusting Franval as she did, the thought that he was soon to become the husband of her beloved sister filled her with a vague sense of terror which she could not explain to herself ; which it was imperatively necessary that she should conceal ; and which, on those very accounts, became a daily and hourly torment to her that was almost more than she could bear.

One consolation alone supported her : Rosamond and she

were not to be separated. She knew that the Baron secretly disliked her as much as she disliked him ; she knew that she must bid farewell to the brighter and happier part of her life on the day when she went to live under the same roof with her sister's husband ; but, true to the promise made years and years ago, by her dying mother's bed—true to the affection which was the ruling and beautiful feeling of her whole existence—she never hesitated about indulging Rosamond's wish, when the girl, in her bright light-hearted way, said that she could never get on comfortably in the marriage state unless she had Ida to live with her, and help her just the same as ever. The Baron was too polite a man even to *look* dissatisfied when he heard of the proposed arrangement ; and it was therefore settled from the beginning that Ida was always to live with her sister.

The marriage took place in the summer, and the bride and bridegroom went to spend their honeymoon in Cumberland. On their return to Glenwith Grange, a visit to the Baron's sisters, in Normandy, was talked of ; but the execution of this project was suddenly and disastrously suspended by the death of Mr. Welwyn from an attack of pleurisy.

In consequence of this calamity, the projected journey was of course deferred ; and when autumn and the shooting season came, the Baron was unwilling to leave the well-stocked preserves of the Grange. He seemed, indeed, to grow less and less inclined, as time advanced, for the trip to Normandy ; and wrote excuse after excuse to his sisters, when letters arrived from them urging him to pay the promised visit. In the winter-time, he said he would not allow his wife to risk a long journey. In the spring, his health was pronounced to be delicate. In the genial summer-time, the accomplishment of the proposed visit would be impossible, for at that period the Baroness expected to become a mother. Such were the apologies which Franval seemed almost glad to be able to send to his sisters in France.

The marriage was, in the strictest sense of the term, a happy one. The Baron, though he never altogether lost the strange restraint and reserve of his manner, was, in his quiet, peculiar way, the fondest and kindest of husbands. He went to town occasionally on business, but always seemed glad to return to the Baroness ; he never varied in the politeness of his bearing towards his wife's sister ; he behaved with the most courteous hospitality towards all the friends of the Welwyns : in short, he thoroughly justified the good opinion which Rosamond and her father had formed of him when they first met at Paris. And yet no experience of his character thoroughly reassured Ida. Months passed on quietly and pleasantly ; and still that secret sadness, that indefinable, unreasonable apprehension on Rosamond's account, hung heavily on her sister's heart.

At the beginning of the first summer months, a little domestic inconvenience happened, which showed the Baroness, for the first time, that her husband's temper could be seriously ruffled— and that by the veriest trifle. He was in the habit of taking in two French provincial newspapers—one published at Bordeaux, and the other at Havre. He always opened these journals the moment they came, looked at one particular column of each with the deepest attention for a few minutes, then carelessly threw them aside into his waste-paper basket. His wife and her sister were at first rather surprised at the manner in which he read his two papers ; but they thought no more of it when he explained that he only took them in to consult them about French commercial intelligence, which might be, occasionally, of importance to him.

These papers were published weekly. On the occasion to which I have just referred, the Bordeaux paper came on the proper day, as usual ; but the Havre paper never made its appearance. This trifling circumstance seemed to make the Baron seriously uneasy. He wrote off directly to the country post office, and to the newspaper agent in London. His wife, astonished to see his tranquillity so completely overthrown by so slight a cause, tried to retore his good-humour by jesting with him about the missing newspaper. He replied by the first angry and unfeeling words that she had heard issue from his lips. She was then within about six weeks of her confinement, and very unfit to bear harsh answers from anybody—least of all from her husband.

On the second day no answer came. On the afternoon of the third, the Baron rode off to the post town to make inquiries. About an hour after he had gone, a strange gentleman came to the Grange, and asked to see the Baroness. On being informed that she was not well enough to receive visitors, he sent up a message that his business was of great importance, and that he would wait downstairs for a second answer.

On receiving this message, Rosamond turned, as usual, to her elder sister for advice. Ida went downstairs immediately to see the stranger. What I am now about to tell you of the extraordinary interview which took place between them, and of the shocking events that followed it, I have heard from Miss Welwyn's own lips.

She felt unaccountably nervous when she entered the room. The stranger bowed very politely, and asked, in a foreign accent, if she were the Baroness Franval. She set him right on this point, and told him she attended to all matters of business for the Baroness ; adding, that, if his errand at all concerned her sister's husband, the Baron was not then at home.

The stranger answered that he was aware of it when he called, and that the unpleasant business on which he came could not be confided to the Baron—at least in the first instance.

She asked why. He said he was there to explain ; and expressed himself as feeling greatly relieved at having to open his business to her, because she would, doubtless, be best able to prepare her sister for the bad news that he was, unfortunately, obliged to bring. The sudden faintness which overcame her, as he spoke those words, prevented her from addressing him in return. He poured out some water for her from a bottle which happened to be standing on the table, and asked if he might depend on her fortitude. She tried to say " Yes " ; but the violent throbbing of her heart seemed to choke her. He took a foreign newspaper from his pocket, saying that he was a secret agent of the French police—that the paper was the *Havre Journal* for the past week, and that it had been expressly kept from reaching the Baron, as usual, through his (the agent's) interference. He then opened the newspaper, and begged that she would nerve herself sufficiently (for her sister's sake) to read certain lines, which would give her some hint of the business that brought him there. He pointed to the passage as he spoke. It was among the " Shipping Entries," and was thus expressed :

" Arrived, the *Berenice*, from San Francisco, with a valuable cargo of hides. She brings one passenger, the Baron Franval, of Château Franval, in Normandy."

As Miss Welwyn read the entry, her heart, which had been throbbing violently but the moment before, seemed suddenly to cease from all action, and she began to shiver, though it was a warm June evening. The agent held the tumbler to her lips, and made her drink a little of the water, entreating her very earnestly to take courage and listen to him. He then sat down, and referred again to the entry ; every word he uttered seeming to burn itself in for ever (as she expressed it) on her memory and her heart.

He said : " It has been ascertained beyond the possibility of doubt that there is no mistake about the name in the lines you have just read. And it is as certain as that we are here, that there is only *one* Baron Franval now alive. The question, therefore, is, whether the passenger by the *Berenice* is the true Baron, or—I beg you most earnestly to bear with me and to compose yourself—or the husband of your sister. The person who arrived last week at Havre was scouted as an impostor by the ladies at the château, the moment he presented himself there as their brother, returning to them after sixteen years of absence. The authorities were communicated with, and I and my assistants were instantly sent for from Paris.

" We wasted no time in questioning the supposed impostor. He either was, or affected to be, in a perfect frenzy of grief and indignation. We just ascertained, from competent witnesses, that he bore an extraordinary resemblance to the real Baron, and that he was perfectly familiar with places and persons in and about the château : we just ascertained that, and then proceeded to confer with the local authorities, and to examine their private entries of suspected persons in their jurisdiction, ranging back over a past period of twenty years or more. One of the entries thus consulted contained these particulars : ' Hector Auguste Monbrun, son of a respectable proprietor in Normandy. Well educated ; gentlemanlike manners. On bad terms with his family. Character : bold, cunning, unscrupulous, self-possessed. Is a clever mimic. May be easily recognised by his striking like-ness to the Baron Franval. Imprisoned at twenty for theft and assault.' "

Miss Welwyn saw the agent look up at her after he had read this extract from the police-book, to ascertain if she was still able to listen to him. He asked, with some appearance of alarm, as their eyes met, if she would like some more water. She was just able to make a sign in the negative. He took a second extract from his pocket-book, and went on.

He said : " The next entry under the same name was dated four years later, and ran thus : ' H. A. Monbrun, condemned to the galleys for life, for assassination, and other crimes not officially necessary to be here specified. Escaped from custody at Toulon. Is known, since the expiration of his first term of imprisonment, to have allowed his beard to grow, and to have worn his hair long, with the intention of rendering it impossible for those acquainted with him in his native province to recognise him, as heretofore, by his likeness to the Baron Franval.' There were more particulars added, not important enough for extract. We immediately examined the supposed impostor : for, if he was Monbrun, we knew that we should find on his shoulder the two

letters of the convict brand, ' T. F.' standing for (*Traveaux Forcés*).
After the minutest examination with the mechanical and chemical
tests used on such occasions, not the slightest trace of the brand
was to be found. The moment this astounding discovery was
made, I started to lay an embargo on the forthcoming numbers
of the *Havre Journal* for that week, which were about to be sent
to the English agent in London. I arrived at Havre on Saturday
(the morning of publication), in time to execute my design. I
waited there long enough to communicate by telegraph with my
superiors in Paris, then hastened to this place. What my errand
here is, you may——"

He might have gone on speaking for some moments longer ;
but Miss Welwyn heard no more.

Her first sensation of returning consciousness was the feeling
that water was being sprinkled on her face. Then she saw that
all the windows in the room had been set wide open, to give her
air ; and that she and the agent were still alone. At first, she
felt bewildered, and hardly knew who he was ; but he soon
recalled to her mind the horrible realities that had brought him
there, by apologising for not having summoned assistance when
she fainted. He said it was of the last importance, in Franval's
absence, that no one in the house should imagine that anything
unusual was taking place in it. Then, after giving her an interval
of a minute or two to collect what little strength she had left, he
added that he would not increase her sufferings by saying anything more, just then, on the shocking subject of the investigation
which it was his duty to make—that he would leave her to
recover herself, and to consider what was the best course to be
taken with the Baroness in the present terrible emergency—and
that he would privately return to the house between eight and
nine o'clock that evening, ready to act as Miss Welwyn wished,
and to afford her and her sister any aid and protection of which
they might stand in need. With these words he bowed, and
noiselessly quitted the room.

For the first few awful minutes after she was left alone, Miss
Welwyn sat helpless and speechless ; utterly numbed in heart,
and mind, and body—then a sort of instinct (she was incapable
of thinking) seemed to urge her to conceal the fearful news from
her sister as long as possible. She ran upstairs to Rosamond's
sitting-room, and called through the door (for she dared not
trust herself in her sister's presence) that the visitor had come on
some troublesome business from their late father's lawyers, and
that she was going to shut herself up, and write some long letters

in connection with that business. After she had got into her own room, she was never sensible of how time was passing—never conscious of any feeling within her, except a baseless, helpless hope that the French police might yet be proved to have made some terrible mistake—until she heard a violent shower of rain come on a little after sunset. The noise of the rain, and the freshness it brought with it in the air, seemed to awaken her as if from a painful and a fearful sleep. The power of reflection returned to her ; her heart heaved and bounded with an overwhelming terror, as the thought of Rosamond came back vividly to it ; her memory recurred despairingly to the long-past day of her mother's death, and to the farewell promise she had made by her mother's bedside. She burst into an hysterical passion of weeping that seemed to be tearing her to pieces. In the midst of it she heard the clatter of a horse's hoofs in the courtyard, and knew that Rosamond's husband had come back.

Dipping her handkerchief in cold water, and passing it over her eyes as she left the room, she instantly hastened to her sister. Fortunately the daylight was fading in the old-fashioned chamber that Rosamond occupied. Before they could say two words to each other, Franval was in the room. He seemed violently irritated ; said that he had waited for the arrival of the mail—that the missing newspaper had not come by it—that he had got wet through—that he felt a shivering fit coming on—and that he believed he had caught a violent cold. His wife anxiously suggested some simple remedies. He roughly interrupted her, saying there was but one remedy, the remedy of going to bed ; and so left them without another word. She just put her handkerchief to her eyes, and said softly to her sister, " How he is changed ! "—then spoke no more. They sat silent for half an hour or longer. After that, Rosamond went affectionately and forgivingly to see how her husband was. She returned, saying that he was in bed, and in a deep, heavy sleep ; and predicting hopefully that he would wake up quite well the next morning. In a few minutes more the clock struck nine ; and Ida heard the servant's step ascending the stairs. She suspected what his errand was, and went out to meet him. Her presentiment had not deceived her ; the police agent had arrived, and was waiting for her downstairs.

He asked her if she had said anything to her sister, or had thought of any plan of action, the moment she entered the room ; and, on receiving a reply in the negative, inquired further if " the Baron " had come home yet. She answered that he had ; that he was ill and tired, and vexed, and that he had gone to bed. The agent asked in an eager whisper if she knew that he was asleep, and alone in bed ? and, when he received her reply, said that he must go up into the bedroom directly.

She began to feel the faintness coming over her again, and with it sensations of loathing and terror that she could neither express to others nor define to herself. He said that if she hesitated to let him avail himself of this unexpected opportunity, her scruples might lead to fatal results. He reminded her that if " the Baron " were really the convict Monbrun, the claims of society and of justice demanded that he should be discovered by the first available means ; and that if he were not—if some inconceivable mistake had really been committed—then, such a plan for getting immediately at the truth as was now proposed, would ensure the delivery of an innocent man from suspicion, and at the same time spare him the knowledge that he had ever been suspected. This last argument had its effect on Miss Welwyn. The baseless, helpless hope that the French authorities might yet be proved to be in error, which she had already felt in her own room, returned to her now. She suffered the agent to lead her upstairs.

He took the candle from her hand when she pointed to the door ; opened it softly ; and, leaving it ajar, went into the room. She looked through the gap, with a feverish, horror-struck curiosity. Franval was lying on his side in a profound sleep, with his back turned towards the door. The agent softly placed the candle upon a small reading-table between the door and the bedside, softly drew down the bed-clothes a little way from the sleeper's back, then took a pair of scissors from the toilet-table, and very gently and slowly began to cut away, first the loose folds, then the intervening strips of linen from the part of Franval's nightgown, that was over his shoulders. When the upper part of his back had been bared in this way, the agent took the candle and held it near the flesh. Miss Welwyn heard him ejaculate some word under his breath, then saw him looking round to where she was standing, and beckoning to her to come in.

Mechanically she obeyed ; mechanically she looked down where his finger was pointing. It was the convict Monbrun— there, just visible under the bright light of the candle, were the fatal letters " T. F." branded on the villain's shoulder !

Though she could neither move nor speak, the horror of this discovery did not deprive her of her consciousness. She saw the agent softly draw up the bed-clothes again into their proper position, replace the scissors on the toilet-table, and take from it a bottle of smelling-salts. She felt him removing her from the bedroom, and helping her quickly downstairs, giving her the salts to smell by the way. When they were alone again, he said, with the first appearance of agitation that he had yet exhibited, "Now, madam, for God's sake, collect all your courage, and be guided by me. You and your sister had better leave the house immediately. Have you any relatives in the neighbourhood, with whom you could take refuge?" They had none. "What is the name of the nearest town where you could get good accommodation for the night?" Harleybrook (he wrote the name down on his tablets). "How far off is it?" Twelve miles. "You had better have the carriage out at once, to go there with as little delay as possible : leaving me to pass the night here. I will communicate with you to-morrow at the principal hotel. Can you compose yourself sufficiently to be able to tell the head-servant, if I ring for him, that he is to obey my orders till further notice?"

The servant was summoned, and received his instructions, the agent going out with him to see that the carriage was got ready quietly and quickly. Miss Welwyn went upstairs to her sister.

How the fearful news was first broken to Rosamond, I cannot relate to you. Miss Welwyn has never confided to me, has never confided to anybody, what happened at the interview between her sister and herself that night. I can tell you nothing of the shock they both suffered, except that the younger and the weaker died under it ; that the elder and the stronger has never recovered from it, and never will.

They went away the same night, with one attendant, to Harleybrook, as the agent had advised. Before daybreak Rosamond was seized with the pains of premature labour. She died three days after, unconscious of the horror of her situation : wandering in her mind about past times, and singing old tunes that Ida had taught her, as she lay in her sister's arms.

The child was born alive, and lives still. You saw her at the window as we came in at the back way to the Grange. I surprised you, I dare say, by asking you not to speak of her to Miss Welwyn. Perhaps you noticed something vacant in the little girl's expression. I am sorry to say that her mind is more vacant still. If "idiot" did not sound like a mocking word, however tenderly and pityingly one may wish to utter it, I should tell you that the poor thing had been an idiot from her birth.

You will, doubtless, want to hear now what happened at

Glenwith Grange, after Miss Welwyn and her sister had left it. I have seen the letter which the police agent sent the next morning to Harleybrook ; and, speaking from my recollection of that, I shall be able to relate all you can desire to know.

First, as to the past history of the scoundrel Monbrun, I need only tell you that he was identical with an escaped convict, who, for a long term of years, had successfully eluded the vigilance of the authorities all over Europe, and in America as well. In conjunction with two accomplices, he had succeeded in possessing himself of large sums of money by the most criminal means. He also acted secretly as the " banker " of his convict brethren, whose dishonest gains were all confided to his hands for safe keeping. He would have been certainly captured, on venturing back to France, along with his two associates, but for the daring imposture in which he took refuge ; and which, if the true Baron Franval had really died abroad, as was reported, would, in all probability, never have been found out.

Besides his extraordinary likeness to the Baron, he had every other requisite for carrying on his deception successfully. Though his parents were not wealthy, he had received a good education. He was so notorious for his gentlemanlike manners among the villainous associates of his crimes and excesses, that they nicknamed him " the Prince." All his early life had been passed in the neighbourhood of the Château Franval. He knew what were the circumstances which had induced the Baron to leave it. He had been in the country to which the Baron had emigrated. He was able to refer familiarly to persons and localities, at home and abroad, with which the Baron was sure to be acquainted. And, lastly, he had an expatriation of fifteen years to plead for him as his all-sufficient excuse, if he made any slight mistakes before the Baron's sisters, in his assumed character of their long-absent brother. It will be, of course, hardly necessary for me to tell you, in relation to this part of the subject, that the true Franval was immediately and honourably reinstated in the family rights of which the impostor had succeeded for a time in depriving him.

According to Monbrun's own account, he had married poor Rosamond purely for love ; and the probabilities certainly are, that the pretty, innocent English girl had really struck the villain's fancy for the time ; and that the easy, quiet life he was leading at the Grange pleased him, by contrast with his perilous and vagabond existence of former days. What might have happened if he had had time enough to grow wearied of his ill-fated wife and his English home, it is now useless to inquire.

What really did happen on the morning when he awoke after the flight of Ida and her sister can be briefly told.

As soon as his eyes opened they rested on the police agent, sitting quietly by the bedside, with a loaded pistol in his hand. Monbrun knew immediately that he was discovered ; but he never for an instant lost the self-possession for which he was famous. He said he wished to have five minutes allowed him to deliberate quietly in bed, whether he should resist the French authorities on English ground, and so gain time by obliging the one government to apply specially to have him delivered up by the other—or whether he should accept the terms officially offered to him by the agent, if he quietly allowed himself to be captured. He chose the latter course—it was suspected, because he wished to communicate personally with some of his convict associates in France, whose fraudulent gains were in his keeping, and because he felt boastfully confident of being able to escape again, whenever he pleased. Be his secret motives, however, what they might, he allowed the agent to conduct him peaceably from the Grange ; first writing a farewell letter to poor Rosamond, full of heartless French sentiment and glib sophistries about Fate and Society. His own fate was not long in overtaking him. He attempted to escape again, as it had been expected he would, and was shot by the sentinel on duty at the time. I remember hearing that the bullet entered his head and killed him on the spot.

My story is done. It is ten years now since Rosamond was buried in the churchyard yonder ; and it is ten years also since Miss Welwyn returned to be the lonely inhabitant of Glenwith Grange. She now lives but in the remembrances that it calls up before her of her happier existence of former days. There is hardly an object in the old house which does not tenderly and solemnly remind her of the mother, whose last wishes she lived to obey ; of the sister, whose happiness was once her dearest earthly care. Those prints that you noticed on the library walls, Rosamond used to copy in the past time, when her pencil was often guided by Ida's hand. Those music-books that you were looking over, she and her mother have played from together, through many a long and quiet summer's evening. She has no ties now to bind her to the present but the poor child whose affliction it is her constant effort to lighten, and the little peasant population around her, whose humble cares and wants and sorrows she is always ready to relieve. Far and near her modest charities have penetrated among us ; and far and near she is heartily beloved and blessed in many a labourer's household. There is no poor man's hearth, not in this village only, but for miles away from it as well, at which you would not be received with the welcome given to an old friend, if you only told the cottagers that you knew the Lady of Glenwith Grange !

THE NEW SUN

FROM the time that he had taken up the study of astronomy as a pleasant means of spending his newly acquired leisure, and had built himself a small but well-equipped observatory as an adjunct to his house, which stood on one of the highest slopes of Leith Hill, Mequillen had formed the habit of rising from his bed every two or three hours of a cloudy night to see if the sky had cleared. To some men such a habit would have been highly inconvenient, for many obvious reasons. But Mequillen was in a lucky position. He was unmarried ; he possessed much more than ample means ; he had therefore no business or profession to attend to, and accordingly no train to catch of a morning in order to keep office hours. He could sleep at any time of the day he chose ; and if he did jump out of bed at two o'clock in the morning, to find that the sky was still cloudy, he could jump back and go to sleep again on the instant. And he was, moreover, an enthusiast of the first order.

On a certain night in the February of 19—, Mequillen, who had gone to bed at ten o'clock, suddenly awoke, switched on the electric light at the side of his bed, and, seeing that it was then ten minutes past twelve, sprang out, shuffled himself into his thickly padded dressing-gown, and hurried up the winding stair which led to the observatory. One glance into the night showed him a perfectly clear sky. From the vast dome of heaven, wondrously blue, the stars shone out like points of fire. And Mequillen, with a sigh of satisfaction, began his work at the telescope, comparing the sky, field by field, with his star chart, on the chance of finding new variable stars. After his usual fashion, he was immediately absorbed, and the sky remaining clear, he went on working, unconscious of time, until a deep-toned clock in the room beneath struck the hour of three. Then Mequillen started, and realised that he had been so absorbed that he had not noticed the striking of one or two, and he leaned back from the telescope in a suddenly assumed attitude of relaxation, stretching his arms, and casting up his eyes to the still clear vault above him. The next instant he became rigid ; the next he began to tremble with excitement ; the next he could have shouted for joy. For there, in the constellation which astronomers have named Andromeda, Mequillen detected a new star !

He knew as he gazed and gazed, intoxicated with the delight and wonder of his discovery, that the burning and glittering object at which he was looking had never shown its light to man before. There was no need to turn to his star charts. Mequillen, being a rich man, was always equipped with the latest information from all the great observatories of the world. That star, burning with such magnificence, was on no chart. Nay, he himself had taken a photograph of that particular field in the heavens only twenty-four hours previously, wherein were stars to the twelfth magnitude ; but the star at which he gazed was not amongst them. It had suddenly blazed up and as he watched he saw it visibly, plainly, increase in brightness and magnitude.

" A new star ! " he murmured mechanically. " A new star ! I wonder who else has seen it ? "

Mequillen continued to watch until, as the February dawn drew near, the clouds spread great curtains between him and the heavens, and sky and stars were blotted out. Then he went to his bed, and, in spite of his excitement, he slept soundly until ten o'clock in the morning.

When Mequillen woke and looked out across the Surrey hills and vales, the entire landscape was being rapidly blotted out by a curious mist, or fog, which seemed to come from nowhere. A vast, mighty blanket of yellow seemed to be dropped between him and everything as he looked. At one moment he saw the summit of a hill many miles away ; the next he could not even see his own garden beneath his windows. And when he went downstairs, half an hour later, the fog had become of the colour of grey ash, and the house was full of it, and the electric light was turned on everywhere, and to little effect.

Mequillen's sister, Adela, who kept house for him—with the assistance of a housekeeper and several female servants—came to him in his study, looking scared.

" Dan," she said, " isn't there something queer about this fog ? It's—it's getting worse."

Mequillen laid down a bundle of letters which he had just taken up, and walked out to the front door and into the garden. He looked all around him, and he sniffed.

" H'm ! It certainly does seem queer, Addie," he said. " We've certainly never had a fog like this in these parts since we knew them."

The girl sniffed too.

" Dan," she said, " it's like as if it were the very finest dust. And—look there ! "

She had been wiping her hand with a tiny wisp of a handkerchief as she spoke, and now she held the handkerchief out to Mequillen.

" Look ! " she repeated.

Mequillen looked down, and saw a curious stain—a species of smudge or smear of a faint grey colour. Without making any remark he ran the tip of his finger along the nearest object, an espalier. The same smudge or smear appeared on his finger.

" It's on everything," whispered the girl. " See, it's on my cheek ! It is some sort of dust, Dan. What's the matter ? "

But Mequillen made no answer. He asked for breakfast, and they went in together. By that time the interior of the house was as full of the fog as the exterior was hidden by it, and everything that they touched—plate, china, linen—gave off the grey smear. And by noon everything was wrapped in an ashen-grey atmosphere, and the electrical lights had no power beyond a very limited compass.

" This is vexatious," said Mequillen. " I was going to have the motor out and take you across to Greenwich. I wanted to make an inquiry at the Observatory. Do you know, Addie, I found a new star last night ! "

" A new star ! " she said wonderingly. " But you won't go, Dan ? "

" Won't go ? " he said, laughing. " I should like to see anybody go anywhere in this, though it may be only local. By George ! Weren't the Cockerlynes coming out to dine and sleep to-night ? "

Addie nodded.

" Well, I hope they won't run into this," continued Mequillen. " Ah ! I'll ring Dick Cockerlyne up, and ask him what the weather's like in town. And then I'll ring up the Observatory."

He went off to the small room in which the telephone was

placed. His sister followed him, and as they passed close beneath the cluster of lights in the hall Mequillen saw that the girl's face was drawn and pallid. He stopped sharply.

" Why, Addie," he said ; " frightened ? "

She laid her hand on his arm, and he felt it trembling.

" Dan," she whispered. " I'm—I'm horribly frightened ! What—what is this ? You know, there's never been anything like this before—in our time. What's happened ? "

Mequillen laughed, and patted the hand that lay on his arm.

" Come, come, Addie ! " he said soothingly. " This isn't like you. I think this fog is uncommon, and I can't account for it, but I've no doubt it can be accounted for. Now, let me ring up Cockerlyne. I've a notion we shall hear they've got a bright morning there in London."

The girl shook her head, made as if she would follow him to the telephone, and then suddenly turned away. In the silence a woman's shrill scream rang out.

" That's cook—in hysterics," said Addie. " I shall have to be brave for the sake of the servants, Dan. They're all as frightened as—as I am."

Nearly an hour later Mequillen came out of the little room, and called his sister into the study. He closed the door, and beckoned her into the arc of the electric light.

" This is queer ! " he said, in a whisper. " I've been talking to Cockerlyne and to the Observatory. Dick says this fog struck London at ten o'clock. It's just there as it is here, and everything's at a standstill. Dick hasn't the remotest notion how he's going to get away from the city. But—that's nothing. Addie, it's all over Europe."

The girl made a little inarticulate sound of horror in her throat, and her face whitened.

" All over Europe, so they say at Greenwich," continued Mequillen. " From Lisbon to Moscow, and from Inverness to Constantinople ! Land and sea—it's everywhere. It—well, it's something unexplainable. Such a thing has never been known before. But it's no use getting frightened, Addie ; you must be brave. It's no doubt some natural phenomena that will be accounted for. And—phew, how very hot this room is ! "

The girl went close to her brother, and laid her hand on his arm.

" Dan," she said, " it isn't the room. See, the fire's very low, and the ventilating fan's working. It's the same everywhere. Come into the garden."

Mequillen followed her out of the house, knitting his brows, and snapping his fingers, after his wont when he was puzzled. For several days the weather had been unusually cold for the time of year. Released now from the preoccupation of the last few hours, he suddenly realised that the day was as hot as a July day should be under normal conditions. He turned to an outdoor thermometer.

" Why—why," he exclaimed, " it's over seventy now ! Seventy in February ! Addie, something's happened to this old world of ours. That's certain. Look there ! "

As they watched the mercury rose one, two, three figures. The brother and sister stared at each other. And Mequillen suddenly dropped his hand with a gesture of helplessness.

" Well," he said, " there's nothing to be done but to wait. I—I don't understand it."

They went back into the house together, and into Mequillen's study, only to stand and stare at each other in silence. Then Addie made a sudden effort at conversation.

" Tell me about the new star, Dan," she said.

Mequillen started.

" The new star ! " he exclaimed. " The new star ! My God, I wonder if that has anything to do with this ? If——"

The parlourmaid, white and scared, came noiselessly into the circle of electric light within which the brother and sister were standing.

" You are wanted at the telephone, sir," she said.

Mequillen went off. In a few minutes he came back, shaking his head.

" That was the Observatory," he said quietly. " This fog, or whatever it is, is all over the world—over South Africa, North and South America, India, Australia, anyway. And the heat's increasing."

" And—the reason ? " whispered Addie.

Mequillen sat down, and dropped his head in his hands.

" There's no man can tell the reason," he answered. " He can't even make a guess at it. Something's happened, that's all. We must wait—wait."

And he took up the letters which had remained unopened on his desk and began to sort them out and to read them.

" Let us go on with our ordinary routine," he said. " That will be best."

The girl left the room, jangling a bunch of keys. But within half an hour she was back, accompanied by the housekeeper.

" Dan," she said quietly, " the servants want to go. They think the end of the world's come, and they want to get to their own homes."

" How do they propose to reach them ? " asked Mequillen. " They can't see a yard before them."

" I told them that, Mr. Mequillen," said the housekeeper, " but it was of no use. You see, sir, they all live pretty close to here, and they say they can find their way blindfolded. They'd better go, sir, or we shall have more hysterics."

" Give me some money for them, Dan," said Addie.

Mequillen rose, and, unlocking a drawer, handed a cash-box to his sister.

" I don't see what good money can do them if the world's coming to an end," he said, with a laugh. " Well, let them do what they like."

When the two women had left him, Mequillen went outside again, and looked at the thermometer hanging on the wall.

" My God," he said, " eighty already ! What can it mean ? "

And then, standing there in the strange all-wrapping fog in his quiet garden on the slope of the peaceful Surrey hills, Mequillen's thoughts turned to the great city lying only a few miles away. What was happening in London ? He saw, with small exercise of imagination, the congested traffic, the discomfort, the inconvenience, the upsetting of all arrangement and order in an ordinary fog. What, then, must be the effect of this extraordinary one ? For Mequillen was sufficiently versed in science to know that the world had never—never, at any rate, since historical records of it began—known such a day as this. And supposing it lasted, supposing——

And then he interrupted his train of thought to glance once more at the thermometer.

" Yes, yes ! " he muttered to himself. " Yes, but supposing the heat goes on increasing, increasing as it's increased during the last few hours ? My God, it's awful to contemplate ! "

The house was very quiet when the frightened servants had left it. Mequillen and his sister made some attempt to eat the lunch which the housekeeper prepared ; but the attempt was a farce, and presently they found themselves pacing up and down, from room to room, from house to garden, waiting for they knew not what. There was no change in the atmosphere, so far as the fog was concerned, but the thermometer rose steadily, until at six o'clock at night it was at ninety, and they were feeling as if they must soon gasp for breath. And, unknown to Addie,

Mequillen went to the telephone, and eventually got into communication with Dick Cockerlyne, who was still at his city office.

"Dick!" he said as steadily as he could. "Are you still there?"

"I am," came back the answer, in tones that Mequillen could scarcely recognise.

"How is it with you there?"

One word came along. Mequillen felt it to be the only word that could come.

"Hell!"

Mequillen shivered, and again spoke.

"Dick, what is happening? What——"

And then he was sharply rung off. From that moment he had no further communication with the outer world. Once—twice—thrice he tried the telephone again before midnight; no response was given. And all around the house a silence reigned which was like the silence of a deserted ocean. Nothing but the fog was there—not a voice, even of fear or terror, came up from the valley. And the heat went on steadily increasing.

There was no sleep for Mequillen or his sister or the housekeeper that night. They had all changed into the lightest summer garments they could find, by the middle of the night the two women were lying prostrate with exhaustion, and the thermometer was a long way over one hundred degrees. Mequillen did all that knowledge could suggest to him to obtain relief and coolness for them, but there was no air—the atmosphere was still, lifeless, leaden. And when the morning came the all-enveloping fog was still there, and the heat was still increasing.

How they got through that second day Mequillen never knew. He had visions of what might be going on in places where the water supply was bad. He, fortunately, was in command of a splendid and probably inexhaustible supply; he had, too, a well-stocked larder and a well-provided cellar of good wine. Only just able to crawl about, he looked to the two women—the housekeeper, a woman of full habit, was more than once on the verge of collapse; Addie's wiriness and excellent physique kept her going. But as it grew to the second midnight they were all gasping for breath, and Mequillen, making brave efforts to keep the women alive, knew that before many hours were over all would be over with them too. And then, as he lay stretched out in a lounging-chair, anxiously watching his sister who lay on a sofa close by, the door was pushed open, and Dick Cockerlyne, reeling like a drunken man, staggered in, and dropped headlong at Mequillen's side.

II.—*The Refugee*

MEQUILLEN summoned up what strength remained in him, and set himself with clenched teeth and fierce resolution to bring Cockerlyne round. Cockerlyne was a big man, a fellow of brawn and muscle, that in ordinary times would have thought nothing of walking fifty miles on end, if need arose ; now, looking at his great limbs, scarcely hidden by the thin silk shirt and flannel trousers which clothed them, Mequillen saw that he was wasted as if he had undergone starvation. His face had aged by ten years, and there was a look of horror in its lines and in his half-open eyes which told of human fear and terror. And once more Mequillen wondered what was going on in London.

As he poured liquid—a weak mixture of brandy-and-seltzer —down the fallen man's throat, Mequillen glanced at his sister. She had paid no attention whatever to Cockerlyne's entrance ; she lay motionless, her hands clasped across her bosom, slowly and regularly gasping for breath. But Mequillen knew what would rouse her, for she and Cockerlyne had been engaged for the past six months, and were about to be married, and one great source of her anxiety during the past two days had been in her fears for his safety. And as he saw Cockerlyne returning to consciousness, he turned to her.

" Addie ! " he whispered. " Here is Dick ! "

The girl slowly opened her eyes and turned her head, and a faint flush came into her white cheeks. Mequillen reached across, and handed her a glass out of which he had been giving her liquid food at intervals during the past hour.

" Drink that, and then get up and help me with him," he said.

Cockerlyne opened his eyes to the full at last, and saw the brother and sister, and he struggled up from the floor.

" I got through, anyway," he said. " I thought that if we— are all going to—to die, eh ?—I'd see Addie first. I—have I been fainting, Dan ? "

" Lie down again, Addie, this instant ! " commanded Mequillen sharply. " Now then, Dick, drink the rest of that brandy-and-seltzer, and then you shall have some of this concentrated meat extract. No nonsense, now. What we've all got to do is to keep up strength till this—passes. I'm off to our housekeeper. I forbid you two to move or to speak until I come back."

When he returned Mequillen found his sister staring at

Cockerlyne, and Cockerlyne staring at her, as if they were looking their last at each other.

" Come, come ! " he said, with the best imitation of a laugh that he could raise. " We're not at that stage yet. Now, then, obey your doctor."

And he fed them both as if they were children, and presently had the gratification of seeing the colour come back to Cockerlyne's face, and a new light into his eyes. The big man suddenly rose, and shook his limbs, and smiled grimly. There were sandwiches on the table, and he reached over and took one in each hand, and began to eat voraciously.

" Chuck the nursing, Dan," he growled. " I'm all right. I said I'd get it done, and I've done it. I'm here ! "

Mequillen saw with thankfulness that Cockerlyne was going to be something to stand by. He nodded with assumed coolness.

" All right, old chap," he said. " And—how did you get here ? "

Cockerlyne moistened his tongue.

" Fought through it," he said grimly. " I've been thirty hours at it—thirty hours ! "

" Yes ? " said Mequillen.

" You know," continued Cockerlyne, " you know when you telephoned to me at six last night ? After that I think I went mad for a while. Then I got out of the office, and somehow got to the Bank station of the South London—the Tube trains ran now and then. I don't know how I did it, but I travelled that way as far as the train ran—Clapham, or somewhere. And then —well, I just made along this way. Of course, I knew every bit of the road. It was like sleep-walking."

Mequillen nodded, and, picking up a fan, resumed his occupation of trying to agitate the air about his sister's face.

" Well, you're here, Dick," he said. " But—London ? "

Cockerlyne shivered.

" London is—oh, I don't know what London is ! " he answered. " I think half the people are dead, and the other half mad. Once or twice I went out into the streets. One man you met was on his knees, praying aloud ; the next was—oh, I don't know ! It seemed that hell was let loose ; and yet the churches were crammed to the doors. And people were fighting for the liquor in the dram-shops and the public-houses. I—I don't seem to remember much ; perhaps I'm mad myself now. How long will it be, Dan ? "

" How long will what be ? " asked Mequillen.

" The—the end ? I expect this is the end, isn't it ? " said Cockerlyne. " What else can it be ? "

" Don't talk rot ! " said Mequillen sharply. " I thought you'd come round again. Here, pour some of the stuff out of that bottle into that glass, and carry it to the housekeeper in the next room. Pull yourself together, man ! "

" Sorry," said Cockerlyne, and rose to carry out Mequillen's commands. " I—I'm light-headed, perhaps. Don't ask me any more about what I saw. It sends me off."

He went away to the housekeeper, and Mequillen heard him speaking to her in the dry, croaking tones in which they all spoke. And presently Cockerlyne came hurriedly back, and, standing at the open door, beckoned to him with a shaking hand. Mequillen rose, and shambled across to him, looking an interrogation.

" Come out to the garden ! " whispered Cockerlyne, and led the way to the front door. " Listen ! " he said. " I caught the sound in there ! Listen ! "

Mequillen grasped one of the pillars of the porch and strained his ears. And somewhere, so far off that it might have been thousands of miles away, he heard what he knew to be the coming of a mighty wind, and instinctively he tightened his grip on the pillar.

" It's a cyclone coming, Cockerlyne ! " he shouted, though all around them was still and quiet. " It'll sweep all before it— house, everything ! Quick—the two women ! "

But before either man could turn to the open door the great fog was swept away before their eyes as if it had been literally snatched from them by some gigantic hand from heaven, and where it had been was a burning and a dazzling light of such power that in an instant they were grovelling on the ground before it with their eyes pressed instinctively into the crooks of their quivering elbows.

III.—Out of the Illimitable

OF the two men, Mequillen was the first to comprehend what had happened, and with his comprehension came coolness and resource. Never had he thought so quickly in his life.

" Dick," he whispered, " keep your eyes shut tightly, and turn and creep back into the hall. I'm doing the same thing. You know the little room on the left ? Don't open your eyes until you get in there. Now, then," he continued, with a gasp, as the two men reached the room and stood upright, " you can open them here, for the shutters are up. Ah ! And yet, you see, although this room should be quite dark, it's almost as light as a normal winter morning."

Cockerlyne stared stupidly about him.

" For God's sake, Dan, what's happened ? " he exclaimed.

Mequillen was fumbling in a drawer. He brought out two silk mufflers, and passed one to his friend.

" I have a very good idea as to what's happened," he answered gravely. " And I'll tell you in a few minutes. But first muffle your eyes—there, you'll see through two thicknesses of the silk. Now for the women. Fortunately, the curtains are closely drawn in both rooms, or I should have feared for their eyesight in that sudden rush of light—light, Dick, such as this globe has never seen before ! Dick, we've got to blindfold them, and then get them into the darkest place in this house. There's an underground room—not a cellar—which I've sometimes used for experiments. We must get them downstairs."

It was easy to see, in spite of the mufflers, that the light in the hall was blinding, and in the curtained study as bright as on an open sea on a cloudless day in summer. And Addie was lying on her sofa with her arms crossed over her forehead and eyes, obviously surprised and distressed by the sudden glare.

" Don't move your arms ! " exclaimed Mequillen sharply. " Keep your eyes shut as tight as you can."

" What is it ? " she asked. " Has the fog gone, and the sun come ? "

" The fog has gone, and a sun has come," replied Mequillen. " And its light is unbearable—just yet. Now, Addie, I am going to blindfold you and take you and Mrs. Jepson down to the underground room. We shall all have to get used to the light by degrees. do just what I tell you, and Dick and I will make you comfortable."

But when the two women were safely disposed of in a room into which scarcely any light ever penetrated in an ordinary way, but which was then as light as noontide, Mequillen drew Cockerlyne into the study, and, groping his way to the windows, closed the shutters and drew the curtains over them.

" Now you can take off your muffler," he said quietly. " There, you see it's light enough even now, to read print and to see the time. And—you perceive the time ? Half-past twelve, midnight ! "

Cockerlyne's face blanched. He swallowed something, and straightened himself.

"What is this, Mequillen?" he asked quietly. "Do you *know*?"

Mequillen shook his head.

"Not with certainty, he answered. "But I think I know. Forty-eight hours ago I discovered a new star, which increased in magnitude at a surprising rate even while I watched it. Now I think that it is a new sun."

"A—new—sun!" exclaimed Cockerlyne. "Impossible!"

"Call it what you will," said Mequillen. "It is, I am certain, at any rate, a vast heavenly body of fire, which was travelling towards this part of space at an inconceivable rate when I first saw it, and is probably at this moment nearer to us than our sun is. Do you feel that the heat is increasing?"

"Yes," replied Cockerlyne; "but it is different in character."

"It is different in character because the wrapping of infinitely fine dust which has been round us has been drawn away," said Mequillen. "But it will increase in intensity."

Cockerlyne gripped the table.

"And?" he whispered.

"In an hour or two we shall be shrivelled up, consumed, like shreds of wool thrown into a furnace!" answered Mequillen.

Cockerlyne straightened himself.

"All right, Dan," he said quietly. "I'm glad I came here. What's to be done now?"

Mequillen had turned to a nest of drawers in one of the recesses of his study. He brought out some spectacles fitted with lenses of very dark glass, and handed one to Cockerlyne.

"We will make an attempt to see this new sun," he said. "Put these spectacles on, and for the present fold that muffler about your eyes again once. You'll see through both muffler and spectacles. And now come up to the observatory."

In the observatory, Cockerlyne understood little or nothing of the preparations which Mequillen made. Conscious only of the terrible heat, he stood waiting and thinking of the fate which was about to befall them; and suddenly a terrible impatience seized upon him. If there was but an hour or so to live, his place was with the woman he loved.

"Look here, Dan!" he exclaimed. "I'm going down! If the end's coming, then——"

But Mequillen laid a hand on his arm and drew him forward, at the same time removing the muffler from his head.

"We will go down soon, Cockerlyne," he said. "We must, for we shall have to tell them. But first—look! You can look with safety now."

And then Cockerlyne, following his friend's instructions, looked, and saw widespread above him the dome of the heavens. But never had he so seen it in all his life. From north to south, from east to west, it glowed with the effulgence of shining brass; and in the north-east hung a great globe of fiery red, vaster in dimension than the sun which the world had known till then, and, even when seen through the protections which Mequillen had prepared, coruscating and glittering with darting and leaping flame.

"My God!" said Cockerlyne, in a hushed voice. "My God! Dan, is that—It?"

"That is It," answered Mequillen quietly. "It is now nearly twice the magnitude of our sun, and it is coming nearer. This is no time to make calculations, or even speculations; but I believe it is, at any rate, as near to us as our sun is. Come away, Cockerlyne; I want to look out on the world. Hold my hand and follow me."

And he dragged Cockerlyne away through a trap-door and into a dark passage, and then into a darker room.

"Keep your hands over your spectacles for a while, and get accustomed to the light by degrees," he said. "I am going to open an observation shutter here, through which we can see a vast stretch of country to the north. It will be a surprise to me if much of it is not already in flames. Now, if you are ready."

Cockerlyne covered his eyes as he heard the click of the observation shutter. Even then, and through the thick black glasses which he was wearing, he felt the extraordinary glare of the light which entered. Presently Mequillen touched his arm.

"You can look now," he said. "See, it's just as I thought! The land's on fire!"

Cockerlyne looked out upon the great sweep of hill and valley, wood and common which stretches across the fairest part of Surrey from the heights above Shere and Albury to those beyond Reigate. He saw the little villages, with their spires and towers and red roofs and tall grey gables; he saw the isolated farms, the stretches of wood, the hillside coppices, the patches of heath and the expanses of green which indicated land untouched by spade or plough.

It was a scene with which he had been familiar from boyhood. Of late he had explored every nook and corner of it with Addie

" The land's on fire ! "

Mequillen, and at all times of the year it had seemed beautiful to him. But under the glare and brilliance of this extraordinary light everything seemed changed. All over that vast prospect great pillars of smoke and flame were rising to the sky. From the valley beneath them came the shrieks and cries of men and women, and as the two men watched they saw the evergreens in Mequillen's garden suddenly turn to the whiteness of paper, and shrivel and disappear in fine ashes.

" Look there ! " whispered Mequillen, pointing a shaking finger. " There—Dorking's on fire ! And yonder, Reigate, too ! "

Cockerlyne tried to speak, but his tongue rattled in his mouth like a dry pea, in a drier pod. He touched Mequillen's arm and pointed downward, and Mequillen nodded.

" Yes," he said. " We had better go down to them ; they've got to know."

He took Cockerlyne by the hand and led him back to the observatory, which, in spite of the fact that all its shutters were drawn, was full of light. And as they stepped into it a spark of white flame suddenly appeared in the woodwork, and ran like lightning round the rim of the dome.

" On fire ! " said Mequillen quietly. " It's no good, Cockerlyne ; we can't do anything. The end's come ! We—oh, my God, what's this ? What *is* this ? Cockerlyne—Cockerlyne, where *are* you ? "

For just as suddenly as they had seen the greyness of the great fog snatched away from the earth, so now they saw the extraordinary light which had succeeded it snatched away. It was gone in the flash of an eye, with the speed of lightning, and as it went they felt the earth move and shudder, and all around them fell a blackness such as they had never known. And as the two men gripped each other in their terror there suddenly burst upon the dome of the observatory a storm of what seemed to be bullets—fierce, insistent, incessant. The serpent-like trail of fire in the woodwork quivered once and died out. And Mequillen, trembling in every limb, released his hold on Cockerlyne, and staggered against the nearest wall.

" Rain ! " he said. " Rain ! "

In the darkness, Mequillen heard Cockerlyne first stumble about, and then fall heavily. Then he knew that Cockerlyne had fainted, and he made his way to a switch and turned on the electric light, and got water to bring him round. But when he came round, Cockerlyne for some minutes croaked and gabbled incessantly, and it was not until Mequillen had hurried down to the dining-room for brandy for him that he regained his senses and was able to sit up, gasping and staring about him. He pointed a shaking finger to the aperture in the dome, through which the rain was pouring, unheeded by Mequillen, in a ceaseless cascade.

" Where is—It ? " he gasped. " What—what's come of It ? "

Mequillen shook him to his feet, and made him swallow more brandy.

" Pull yourself together, Cockerlyne ! " he said. " This is no time to talk science ; this is a time to act. Come down, man ; we must see to the women ! We've just escaped from fire ; now we're likely to meet our deaths by water. Listen to that rain. Here, help me to close that shutter. Now, downstairs ! It's lucky we're on a hillside, Cockerlyne ! But the people in the valleys ! Come on ! "

And, leaving Cockerlyne to follow him, Mequillen ran down through the house, to find his sister and the housekeeper in the hall. As he saw them, he knew that they had realised what he now had time to realise—that the terrible heat was dying away, and that it was becoming easier and easier to breathe. As he passed it he glanced at a hanging thermometer, and saw the mercury falling in a steady, swift descent.

Mequillen caught his sister in his arms and pressed her to him. She looked anxiously into his face.

" Dick ? " she said.

" He's safe—he's coming," said Mequillen.

Addie suddenly collapsed, and hid her face in her hands. The housekeeper was already in a heap in the nearest chair, sobbing and moaning. And as Cockerlyne came slowly down the stairs, Mequillen saw that, strong man as he was, his nerves had been shaken so much that he was trembling like a leaf. Once more Mequillen had to summon all his energies together in the task of bringing his companions round, and as he moved about from one to the other his quick ear heard the never-ceasing rattle of the rain, which was heavier than any tropical rain that ever fell. And presently he caught the sound of newly forming cascades and waterfalls, cutting new ways from the hill-tops to the level lands of the valleys. Now the normal coolness of middle winter was coming back. The women picked up the wraps they had thrown aside ; the men hurried into greatcoats. And as the February dawn came grey and slow across the hills, Mequillen and Cockerlyne went up to the observatory, and into the little look-out turret from which they had seen the spirals of smoke and flame rising from the land only a few hours before.

The rain was still falling, but with no more violence than that of a tropical rainstorm. But the air was throbbing, pulsating, humming with the noise of falling waters. A hundred yards away from the house a churning and seething mass of yellow foam was tearing a path, wide and deep, through a copse of young pine ; down in the valley immediately beneath them lay a newly formed lake. In the valleys on every side, as far as the eye could reach, lay patches of silvery hue, which they knew to be great sheets of water ; and now the air was cool, and the hitherto tortured lungs could breathe it in comfort.

" Mequillen," said Cockerlyne, after a long silence, " what happened ? "

But Mequillen shook his head.

" I am as a child standing at the edge of a great ocean," he answered. " I cannot say definitely. I think that the great star which we saw, rushing upon us, was suddenly arrested, split into fragments, when that darkness fell, and that we were saved. Once more, Cockerlyne, the old world, a speck in space, will move on. For look there ! "

And Cockerlyne turned as Mequillen pointed, and saw, slowly rising over the Surrey hills, the kindly sun of a grey February morning.

HOT WATER

"THE regrettable truth about all Secret Service work," said Casimir Sipiaghin, " is that it must be devastatingly boring, revoltingly squalid, or unspeakably tragic. Personally I hate boredom, I abominate squalor, and I find tragedy does not suit me."

We were sitting at a small table outside a café in the Avenue du Bois de Boulogne, and it was a delightful spring day—one of those delicious April days when Paris literally sparkles in the sunshine ; and there was nothing pleasanter in the world than to watch the motor-cars flash past and the pretty ladies saunter past ; to watch the fresh green leaves in the foreground and the mass of the Arc du Triomphe in the background against that blue sky which you can see in Paris, but never in London.

" Spying," Casimir went on, " is altogether a dirty business. If you wish me to talk about it, you will have to buy me more *vermouth cassis*."

I beckoned to a waiter without argument, for there was still an hour before lunch, and I do not meet Casimir Sipiaghin every day. Perhaps that is one of the reasons I like him so much : I always want to see more of him. For other reasons, I need only add that he has all the charm and the good manners of a pre-war Russian officer, without any of the bad habits only too frequently to be found among refugees from the Revolution. He does not borrow money ; he does not call himself a count or a prince ; he does not introduce me to beautiful ladies who land me in the devil of a mess ; and he has no connection whatever with any of the *boîtes* in Montmartre or Montparnasse. Finally, he is thirty-eight years old and capital company, making a moderate but honest income by travelling for a firm of mining engineers.

It was a paragraph in one of the Paris papers that had led us to talk about spies. The inevitable Frenchman with his equally inevitable lady friend, energetic and comely, had been arrested by the Fascist militia in a most undesirable part of the Alps, and was to stand his trial for espionage. I had asked Casimir his opinion of the case, for he happens to be the only man I know who has actually been a professional spy. It was some time ago—to be exact, in 1919—when, after his enforced flight from Russia, he took service with the police and was given the job of running the Frontier Intelligence Service against the Bolsheviks, with whom Poland at that time was at war.

" The boredom and the squalor I can believe," I said, as the waiter brought our drinks. " You will forgive me if I put down the tragedy to your Slav instinct for the dramatic ? "

Casimir raised his eyebrows.

" Do you say that, my friend, in Paris ? Do you forget Dreyfus ? Do you forget that tragedy, which was, incidentally, a very complete history of France for the best part of a decade ? But I was not thinking of tragedy on the grand scale. I was thinking of a little one, quite a little one, of my own."

I was careful not to interrupt while he paused to choose and light a cigarette.

" I do not think that you know Lithuania, my friend," he went on. " In those days of 1919 of which you have sometimes heard me speak, my headquarters were in a hotel in Kovno. You should have seen that hotel—you who are so devoted to the Ritz Bar. It was little more than a building in which it was just possible to eat and sleep. Most of its windows were broken but luckily the wooden shutters remained. Modern conveniences had been installed, but water no longer ran, not even in the bathrooms. It had been occupied during the war by every kind of soldier, and you know what that means. And it was kept by a Russian Jew. I had to live in it for four months—the four last months of the year—under an everlastingly grey sky and continual drizzle that changed gradually to continual snow. Streets inches deep in frozen slush and no society but my own agents and the Polish Commandant of Police.

" I do not think that I could have endured it, if it had not been for the fact that nearly all my agents were women——"

I smiled, I hope discreetly. But then he finished his sentence and I stopped smiling.

"—and I was serving for hate."

In the face of Paris, and under that bright sunshine, the last words sounded impossibly melodramatic, but Casimir's eyes had lost their twinkle, and his lean, rather craggy face was very grim. He threw away his cigarette and clasped his hands on the table in front of him.

"Nearly all women," he repeated slowly. "I had collected a dozen or so in Warsaw. Good-looking young girls ; some of noble families ; some merely *bourgeoises* who had lost everything in Russia, and who, to use your English phrase, wanted their own back. I planted them on the other side of the frontier in various capacities, mostly as nurses and typists, and established myself in Kovno as a post office to which they could send their intelligence. It was not a very difficult problem. It is also not very pretty to think of. *À la guerre comme à la guerre.*

"Let me tell you a little more about my hotel. I had three rooms on the first floor, rooms opening out of each other, with one door giving on to the passage. On the other side of the passage a bathroom. It contained an admirable bath, but as I said before, there was no water. Remember that. The innermost of the three rooms was my bedroom. In the middle room slept my chauffeur, and the outer of the three I used as an office— for I was supposed to be an eccentric but enterprising commercial traveller ; though fortunately there were very few inquiries as to what I was supposed to be trying to sell. The Jewish proprietor asked no questions so long as he was monstrously overpaid. Needless to say, these rooms were never left empty : when I had to be away the chauffeur remained on guard, for there was one thing which I could not have carried on my person and which would have given me away for what I was. It was kept in the corner under my bed, and I wore the key on a chain round my neck."

He stopped and groped in an inner pocket.

"Go on," I said.

"I believe a good story should be illustrated," said Casimir. "Just look at this."

He pulled out a pocket-book, and from it took a snapshot which he handed to me. It was a photograph of a girl, and, though the epithet has been worked to death, she was lovely, there was no other word for it. It was the sort of face which the Russian Ballet has made familiar to us : big wide-set eyes ; small, perfectly regular features, slightly oriental ; and smooth dark hair, perfectly parted in the middle. In the photograph she was smiling above a deep fur collar. She looked about nineteen, and tremendously alive.

" She was the best of them all," Casimir continued. " Her name was Tatiana, and she was the daughter of a rich merchant in Moscow, who had been shot by the Reds. She had managed to get herself a job as typist-stenographer to the political commissar attached to the Soviet Fourteenth Army. She had worked with me as my personal secretary in Warsaw for some weeks before she went back into Russia. I was very fond of her.

" Needless to say, it was very seldom that she, or any of my other agents, actually came to me in Kovno. That risk was only run on occasions of the first importance, both for their sakes and for mine. In fact, I think that Tatiana was the only one of them who made that hideously dangerous journey more than two or three times. She did it more often partly because she was getting better and more vital information than any of the others, owing to her position ; and partly, I think, because she liked to see me. Anyhow, I always knew that when she did come it meant that great events were in train and that I had a time of extra hard work ahead of me.

" Now, it happened that I had been away from Kovno on a two days' trip, on some small business which has nothing to do with the story I am telling you. I had gone disguised as a peasant. The weather was vile, and to cut irrelevancies short, I had the devil's own time of it. I got back to the hotel late in the evening, very tired and quite inconceivably dirty and uncomfortable. The oil lamps in the dingy hall were smoking malodorously, and I felt dirty and depressed to the soles of my boots. I shouted for the proprietor, and told him to get some water boiled and carried up to the bathroom opposite my rooms in quick time. Then I lurched painfully up the staircase in semidarkness. At the top of the stairs, I met my chauffeur, who had heard my voice and come to meet me.

" ' Mademoiselle Tatiana is here, monsieur,' he said.

" I blinked at him stupidly.

" ' She is here, monsieur,' he repeated. ' In the inner room.'

" I walked past him into the outer of the three rooms, flopped into a chair, lighted a cigarette, and swore. In the first place, I was in no condition or mood to enjoy feminine society, even Tatiana's, and I was a revolting spectacle. All I desired in the world was a bath and some sleep. In the second place, if Tatiana was there, it meant that a probable crisis was impending which I was in no shape to face, and thirdly, I was bewilderedly irritated that she should be there at all, for she had been in to Kovno only two days before I had gone on my trip, and there had never been less than two or three weeks between her previous visits. However, the thing had to be faced, and I went through into my bedroom feeling thoroughly bad-tempered and at odds with the world.

" Tatiana was sitting on the bed. She had not taken off her heavy fur coat, which was hardly surprising, for the room was abominably cold ; but her round fur cap and big gloves were beside her. Her long boots were caked with slush, and she looked as dead-beat as I felt myself. She was smoking a cigarette and staring straight in front of her. The circles of weariness under her eyes increased their normal magnificence, but her usual vitality was altogether absent. She hardly moved when I came in.

" I dropped on to the bed beside her.

" ' Well ? ' I said. ' What is it ? '

" I expect I sounded pretty irritable. Anyway, she patted my hand soothingly, and I noticed that her fingers were burning hot.

" ' What is it ? ' I repeated. ' Are you ill ? '

" She shook her head.

" ' No, Casimir. I'm not ill. Only a little tired. Change your clothes and have your bath in peace. No, don't pretend you weren't going to change—I heard you shouting for your hot water.'

" ' But are you sure——' I began.

" She got up and went to the bedroom door.

" ' It will give me time to put my thoughts in order,' she said, with a queer little smile, and left me.

" Then I remembered something. I had come back from my trip with a short list of local bad characters whom it was most essential that the Polish Military Police should put under lock and key at the shortest possible notice. Accordingly, I put the list in an envelope, addressed it to the Polish Commandant, and told my chauffeur to take it to his quarters and deliver it in person. Then I threw off my clothes as quickly as possible, slipped on a camel-hair dressing-gown, and left the bedroom.

" ' Mind you don't go out,' I said to Tatiana in the middle room as I passed her, ' at any rate, not until Stefan comes in.'

" And I went into the passage, back along the corridor, and into the bathroom.

" The old Jew had done well by me. The bath was more than half-full, and the room a mass of steam. I flung off the dressing-gown, exulting in the prospect of splashing and soaping and rubbing, and of that extreme of physical content that a bath can give if a man has been deprived of hot water for several days. And then, almost simultaneously, I became aware of two things. The large can of cold water that usually stood beside the bath was not there. And the chain that held the key to the cipher-box was no longer round my neck. For an instant, it seemed as if my heart had missed a beat, and then I remembered how hurriedly I had torn off my clothes, and how I had actually felt the chain catch as I pulled my shirt over my head. Of course it was simply lying in my bedroom amongst my dirty clothes.

" I don't think I should have given the matter another thought if it hadn't been for the absence of that can of cold water. I should simply have had my bath and gone back in due course to collect the chain with my clean clothes. It wasn't as if my rooms had been empty. But however desirous a man may be of plunging into a bath, he cannot plunge into a bath full of boiling water. I cursed the old Jew soundly, put on my dressing-gown again, and very reluctantly quitted the steamy warmth of the bathroom for the draughts and discomforts of my bedroom, where I knew a jug of cold water stood in the cracked basin. And I could retrieve my chain at the same time. . . .

" I had on bedroom slippers with felt soles, and a short course of Secret Service gives one the habit of opening doors quite silently. . . .

" No doubt you have guessed what I found in the bedroom, but for me it was like the end of the world. I have confessed that I was fond of Tatiana, and that she liked me ; but you will hardly appreciate the point of this story, unless I commit what I understand among you English is the unforgivable crime of giving a woman away. For during that time in Warsaw we had been lovers, she and I, though the affair had not lasted. It had ended after the Russian fashion, by her wish, but I still loved her.

" You can imagine, my friend, the sudden tightening of my chest, the hammering of the blood behind my eyes, as I stood quite still there in the doorway of my bedroom, and saw Titiana with her back to me on her knees. The cipher-box was on the bed, and she was opening it with the key from my neck.

" It could only mean one thing. None of my agents, not even she whom I trusted as the most successful of them all, was allowed to touch the cipher-box. It meant treachery, not only treachery to our cause—that I could have forgiven her, for after all, in a way, we were both mercenaries, fighting for our own hands in the service of a foreign power. But she had betrayed me—me who had loved her more than I care ever now to remember. As I stood there and thought of the two rooms we had shared together in Warsaw, and the little table at the Astoria across which I had faced her every day at lunch, and the hundred little things we had had in common, the key twisted harshly in the cipher-box and I thought my brain must burst.

" Instead, the box opened, and at that I suppose I said something. I don't know. For she twisted round and saw me, and the remnants of colour fled out of her face so that it looked like grey paper, and the key tinkled down to the floor. I could not speak. It was beyond words. Mechanically I picked up the key and relocked the accursed box and pushed it back under the bed and hung the chain round my neck. And all the time the girl sat crouched against the bed, her lips twisted and her eyes wide open and staring straight at me.

" At that moment I heard the chauffeur re-enter the outer room, and I realised that here was my opportunity to gain a few moments to think and to make up my mind what to do.

" ' Stefan ! ' I shouted, and I could hardly recognise my own voice. " Stefan, I am going to have a bath. Wait in your room till I come back. Mademoiselle Tatiana will wait in the office. I don't want any one to see that she's here, so I shall lock the outer door.'

" I picked up the jug of cold water and went through into the outer room, Tatiana walking ahead of me. She did not look at me again ; she did not speak ; she simply sat down at the table which I used as a desk, and lighted another cigarette. I locked the office door behind me, and went back into the bedroom.

" I still wonder what I should have done—if I should have handed her over to the Polish Military Police to be shot, if I could have accomplished that hideous climax of duty. I still wonder—for it was only weeks later that I learned that she had been compelled to her treason by the usual Bolshevik practice. They were holding her mother as a hostage and had threatened to shoot that poor old woman of sixty-four if the girl refused to do what was demanded of her.

" All I do know is—and I still thank God for it—is that I had not to put my conscience to the proof. I was still lying in the hot water—water whose heat had been so fantastically significant—when I heard the crash of a single revolver shot and I knew that Tatiana had done the last thing she could for me. I remembered that I had taken off the belt which carried my revolver when I first went in, and slung it across the chair beside the table in the outer office."

Sipiaghin turned away abruptly and signalled to a waiter so that I could not see his face.

" Tragedy or farce, my friend ? " he said. " I do not pretend to make it out. They are too close together. But life is like that."

He snapped his fingers, and blew a long spiral of smoke into the sunlight.

" Just like that."

THE ISLAND

How well I remembered the summer aspect of Mrs. Santander's island, and the gratefully deciduous trees among the pines of that countryside coming down to the water's edge and over it ! How their foliage, sloping to a shallow dome, sucked in the sunlight, giving it back all grey and green ! The sea, tossing and glancing, refracted the light from a million spumy points ; the tawny sand glared, a monochrome unmitigated by shades ; and the cliffs, always bare, seemed to have achieved an unparalleled nudity, every speck on their brown flanks clamouring for recognition.

Now every detail was blurred or lost. In the insufficient, ill-distributed November twilight the island itself was invisible. Forms and outlines survive but indistinctly in the memory ; it was hard to believe that the spit of shingle on which I stood was the last bulwark of that huge discursive land-locked harbour, within whose meagre mouth Mrs. Santander's sea-borne territory seemed to ride at anchor. In the summer I pictured it as some crustacean, swallowed by an ill-turned starfish, but unassimilated. How easy it had been to reach it in Mrs. Santander's gay plunging motor-boat ! And how inaccessible it seemed now, with the motor-boat fallen, as she had written to tell me, into war-time disuse, with a sea running high and so dark that, save for the transparent but scarcely luminous wave-tips, it looked like an agitated solid. The howling of the wind and the oilskins in which he was encased made it hard to attract the ferryman's attention. I shouted to him : " Can you take me over to the island ? "

" No, I can't," said the ferryman, and pointed to the tumultuous waves in the harbour.

" What are you here for ? " I bawled. " I tell you I must get across ; I have to go back to France to-morrow."

In such circumstances it was impossible to argue without heat. The ferryman turned, relenting a little. He asked querulously in the tone of one who must raise a difficulty at any cost : " What if we both get drowned ? "

What a fantastic objection ! " Nonsense," I said, " there's no sea to speak of ; anyhow, I'll make it worth your while."

The ferryman grunted at my unintentional pleasantry. Then as the landing-stage was submerged by the exceptionally high tide, he carried me on his back to the boat, my feet trailing in the water. The man lurched at every step, for I was considerably heavier than he ; but at last, waist-deep in water, he reached the boat and turned sideways for me to embark. How uncomfortable the whole business was. Why couldn't Mrs. Santander spend November in London like other people ? Why was I so infatuated as to follow her here on the last night of my leave when I might have been lolling in the stalls of a theatre ? The craft was behaving oddly, rolling so much that at every other stroke one of the boatman's attenuated seafaring oars would be left high and dry. Once, when we happened to be level with each other, I asked him the reason of Mrs. Santander's seclusion. At the top of his voice he replied : " Why, they do say she be love-sick. Look out ! " he added, for we had reached the end of our short passage and were " standing by " in the surf, a few yards from the shore, waiting for an " easy " in the succession of breakers. But the ferryman misjudged it. Just as the keel touched the steep shingle bank, a wave caught the boat, twisted it round and half-over, and I lost my seat and rolled about in the bottom of the boat, getting very wet.

How dark it was among the trees ! Acute physical discomfort had almost made me forget Mrs. Santander. But as I stumbled up the grassy slope I longed to see her.

She was not in the hall to welcome me. The butler, discreetly noticing my condition, said : " We will see about your things, sir." I was thankful to take them off, and I flung them about the floor of my bedroom—that huge apartment that would have been square but for the bow-window built on to the end. The wind tore at this window, threatening to drive it in : but not a curtain moved. Soundlessness, I remembered, was characteristic of the house. Indeed, I believe you might have screamed yourself hoarse in that room and not have been heard in the adjoining bathroom. Thither I hastened and wallowed long and luxuriously in the marble bath : deliberately I splashed the water over the side, simply to see it collected and marshalled

away down the little grooves that unerringly received it. When
I emerged, swathed in hot towels, I found my clothes already
dried and pressed. Wonderful household. A feeling of unspeakable well-being descended upon me as, five minutes before
dinner-time, I entered the drawing-room. It was empty. What
pains Mrs. Santander must be bestowing on her toilette ! Was
it becoming her chief asset ? I wondered. Perish the thought !
She had a hundred charms of movement, voice and expression,
and yet she defied analysis. She was simply irresistible ! How
Santander, her impossible husband, could have retired to South
America to nurse an injured pride, or as he doubtless called it,
an injured honour, passed my comprehension. She had an art
to make the most commonplace subject engaging. I remembered
having once admired the lighting of the house. I had an odd
fancy that it had a quality not found elsewhere, a kind of whiteness, a power of suggesting silence. It helped to give her house
its peculiar hush. " Yes," she had said, " and it's all so simple :
the sea made it, just by going in and out ! " A silly phrase, but
her intonation made it linger in the memory like a charm.

I sat at the piano and played. There were some songs on
the music-rest—Wolf : full of strange chords and accidentals
so that I couldn't be sure I was right. But they interested me ;
and I felt so happy that I failed to notice how the time was
drawing on—eight o'clock, and dinner should have been at a
quarter to. Growing a little restless, I rose and walked up and
down the room. One corner of it was in shadow, so I turned
on all the lights. I had found it irritating to watch the regular
expansion and shrinkage of my shadow. Now I could see
everything ; but I still felt constrained, sealed up in that admirable room. It was always a shortcoming of mine not to be
able to wait patiently. So I wandered into the dining-room and
almost thought—such is the power of overstrung anticipation—
that I saw Mrs. Santander sitting at the head of the oval table.
But it was only an effect of the candle-light. The two places
were laid, hers and mine ; the glasses with twisty stems were
there, such a number of glasses for the two of us ! Suddenly I
remembered I was smoking and, taking an almond, I left the
room to its four candles. I peeped inside the library ; it was in
darkness, and I realised, as I fumbled for the switch without
being able to find it, that I was growing nervous. How ridiculous !
Of course Mrs. Santander wouldn't be in the library and in the
dark. Abandoning the search for the switch I returned to the
drawing-room.

I vaguely expected to find it altered, and yet I had ceased to expect to see Mrs. Santander appear at any moment. That always happens when one waits for a person who doesn't come. But there *was* an alteration—in me. I couldn't find any satisfaction in struggling with Wolf ; the music had lost its hold. So I drew a chair up to the china-cabinet ; it had always charmed me with its figures of Chinamen, those white figures, conventional and stiff, but so smooth and luminous and significant. I found myself wondering, as often before, whether the ferocious pleasure in their expressions was really the Oriental artist's conception of unqualified good-humour, or whether they were not, after all, rather cruel people. And this disquieting topic aroused others that I had tried successfully to repress : the exact connotation of my staying in the house as Mrs. Santander's guest, an unsporting little mouse playing when the cat was so undeniably, so effectually away. To ease myself of these obstinate questionings, I leant forward to open the door of the cabinet, intending to distract myself by taking one of the figures into my hands. Suddenly I heard a sound and looked up. A man was standing in the middle of the room.

" I'm afraid the cabinet's locked." he said.

In spite of my bewilderment something in his appearance struck me as odd : he was wearing a hat. It was a grey felt hat, and he had an overcoat that was grey too.

" I hope you don't take me for a burglar," I said, trying to laugh.

" Oh, no," he replied, " not that." I thought his eyes were smiling, but his mouth was shadowed by a dark moustache. He was a handsome man. Something in his face struck me as familiar ; but it was not an unusual type and I might easily have been mistaken.

In the hurry of getting up I knocked over a set of fire-irons —the cabinet flanked the fireplace—and there was a tremendous clatter. It alarmed and then revived me. But I had a curious feeling of defencelessness as I stooped down to pick the fire-irons up, and it was difficult to fix them into their absurd sockets. The man in grey watched my operations without moving. I began to resent his presence. Presently he moved and stood with his back to the fire, stretching out his fingers to the warmth.

" We haven't been introduced," I said.

" No," he replied, " we haven't."

Then, while I was growing troubled and exasperated by his behaviour he offered an explanation. " I'm the engineer

Mrs. Santander calls in now and then to superintend her electric plant. That's how I know my way about. She's so inventive, and she doesn't like to take risks." He volunteered this. " And I came in here in case any of the fittings needed adjustment. I see they don't."

" No," I said, secretly reassured by the stranger's account of himself, " but I wish—of course I speak without Mrs. Santander's authority—I wish you'd have a look at the switches in the library. They're damned inconvenient." I was so pleased with myself for having compassed the expletive that I scarcely noticed how the engineer's fingers, still avid of warmth, suddenly became rigid.

" Oh, you've been in the library, have you ? " he said. I replied that I had got no farther than the door. " But if you can wait," I added politely to this superior mechanic who liked to style himself an engineer, " Mrs. Santander will be here in a moment."

" You're expecting her ? " asked the mechanic.

" I'm staying in the house," I replied stiffly. The man was silent for several moments. I noticed the refinement in his face, the good cut of his clothes. I pondered upon the physical disability that made it impossible for him to join the army.

" She makes you comfortable here ? " he asked ; and a physical disturbance, sneezing or coughing, I supposed, seized him, for he took out his handkerchief and turned from me with all the instinct of good breeding. But I felt that the question was one his station scarcely entitled him to make, and ignored it. He recovered himself.

" I'm afraid I can't wait," he said. " I must be going home. The wind is dropping. By the way," he added, " we have a connection in London. I think, I may say it's a good firm. If ever you want electric plant installed—I left a card somewhere." He searched for it vainly. " Never mind," he said, with his hand on the door, " Mrs. Santander will give you all particulars." Indulgently I waved my hand, and he was gone.

A moment later it occurred to me that he wouldn't be able to cross to the mainland without notifying the ferryman. I rang the bell. The butler appeared. " Mrs. Santander is very late, sir," he said.

" Yes," I replied, momentarily dismissing the question. " But there's a man, a mechanic or something—you probably know." The butler looked blank. " Anyhow," I said, " a man has been here attending to the lighting ; he wants to go home ;

would you telephone the boatman to come and fetch him away ? "

When the butler had gone to execute my order, my former discomfort and unease returned. The adventure with the engineer had diverted my thoughts from Mrs. Santander. Why didn't she come ? Perhaps she had fallen asleep, dressing. It happened to women when they were having their hair brushed. Gertrude was imperious and difficult ; her maid might be afraid to wake her. Then I remembered her saying in her letter : " I shall be an awful fright because I've had to give my maid the sack." It was funny how the colloquialisms jarred when you saw them in black and white ; it was different when she was speaking. Ah, just to hear her voice ! Of course, the loss of her maid would hinder her, and account for some delay. Lucky maid, I mused confusedly, to have her hair in your hands ! Her image was all before me as I walked aimlessly about the room. Half-tranced with the delight of that evocation, I stopped in front of a great bowl, ornamented with dragons, that stood on the piano. Half an hour ago I had studied its interior, that depicted terra-cotta fish with magenta fins swimming among conventional weeds. My glance idly sought the pattern again. It was partially covered by a little slip of paper. Ah ! the engineer's card ! His London connection ! Amusedly I turned it over to read the engineer's name :

MR. MAURICE SANTANDER.

I started violently, the more that at the same moment there came a knock at the door. It was only the butler ; but I was so bewildered I scarcely recognised him. Too well-trained perhaps to appear to notice my distress, he delivered himself almost in a speech. " We can't find any trace of the person you spoke of, sir. The ferryman's come across and he says there's no one at the landing-stage."

" The gentleman," I said, " has left this," and I thrust the card into the butler's hand.

" Why, that must be Mr. Santander ! " the servant of Mr. Santander's wife at last brought out.

" Yes," I replied, " and I think perhaps as it's getting late, we ought to try and find Mrs. Santander. The dinner will be quite spoiled."

Telling the butler to wait and not to alarm the servants, I went alone to Gertrude's room. From the end of a long passage

I saw the door standing partly open ; I saw, too, that the room was in darkness. There was nothing strange in that, I told myself ; but it would be methodical, it would save time, to examine the intervening rooms first. Examine ! What a misleading word. I vanished it, and " search " came into my mind. I rejected that too. As I explored the shuttered silences I tried to find a formula that would amuse Gertrude, some facetious understatement of my agitated quest. " A little tour of inspection "—she would like that. I could almost hear her say : " So you expected to find me under a sofa ! " I wouldn't tell her that I had looked under the sofas, unless to make a joke of it ; something about dust left by the housemaid. I rose to my knees, spreading my hands out in the white glow. Not a speck. But wasn't conversation—conversation with Gertrude—made up of little half-truths, small forays into fiction ? With my hand on the door—it was of the last room and led on to the landing— I rehearsed the pleasantry aloud : " During the course of a little tour of inspection, Gertrude, I went from one dust heap to another, from dust unto dust I might almost say . . ." This time I must overcome my unaccountable reluctance to enter her room. Screwing up my courage I stepped into the passage, but for all my resolution I got no farther.

The door still stood as I had first seen it—half-open ; but there was a light in the room—a rather subdued light, possibly from the standard-lamp by the bed. I knocked and called " Gertrude ! " and when there was no reply I pushed open the door. It moved from right to left so as not to expose the bulk of the room, which lay on the left side. It seemed a long time before I was fairly in.

I saw the embers of the fire, the pale troubled lights of the mirror, and, vivid in the pool of light by the bed, a note. It said : " Forgive me, dearest, I have had to go. I can't explain why, but we shall meet sometime. All my love, G." There was no envelope, no direction, but the handwriting was hers and the informality characteristic of her. It was odd that the characters, shaky as they were, did not seem to have been written in haste. I was trying to account for this, trying to stem, by an act of concentration, the tide of disappointment that was sweeping over me, when a sudden metallic whirr sounded in my ear. It was the telephone ; the small subsidiary telephone that communicated with the servants' quarters. " It will save their steps," she had said, when I urged her to have it put in : and I remembered my pleasure in this evidence of consideration, for my own motives had been founded in convenience and even in prudence. Now I loathed the black shiny thing that buzzed so raucously and never moved. And what could the servants have to say to me except that Mr. Santander had—well, gone. What else was there for him to do? The instrument rang again and I took up the receiver.

" Yes ? "

" Please, sir, dinner is served."

" Dinner ! " I echoed. It was nearly ten, but I had forgotten about that much postponed meal.

" Yes, sir, didn't you give orders to have it ready immediately? For two, I think you said, sir." The voice sounded matter of fact enough, but in my bewilderment I nearly lost all sense of what I was doing. At last I managed to murmur in a voice that might have been anybody's : " Yes, of course, for two."

On second thoughts I left the telephone disconnected. I felt just then, that I couldn't bear another summons. And, though my course was clear, I did not know what to do next ; my will had nothing but confusion to work with. In the dark perhaps, I might collect myself. But it didn't occur to me to turn out the light : instead, I parted the heavy curtains that shut off the huge bow-window, and drew them behind me. The rain was driving furiously against the double casements, but not a sound vouched for its energy. A moon shone at intervals, and by the light of one gleam, brighter than the rest, I saw a scrap of paper, crushed up, lying in a corner. I smoothed it out, glad to have employment for my fingers, but darkness descended on the alcove again and I had to return to the room. In spite of its crumpled condition I made out the note ; easily indeed, for it was a copy of the one I had just read. Or perhaps the original ; but why should the same words have been written twice and even three times, not more plainly, for Gertrude never tried to write plainly, but with a deliberate illegibility?

There was only one other person besides Gertrude, I thought, while I stuffed the cartridges into my revolver, who could have written that note ; and he was waiting for me downstairs. How would he look, how would he explain himself? This question occupied me to the exclusion of a more natural curiosity —my appearance, my explanation. They would have to be of the abruptest. Perhaps, indeed, they wouldn't be needed. There were a dozen corners, a dozens points of vantage, all well known to Mr. Santander, between me and the dining-room door. It came to me inconsequently that the crack of a shot in that house would make no more noise than the splintering of a toilet glass on my washing-stand. And Mr. Santander, well versed, no doubt, in South American revolutions, affrays, and shootings-up, would be an adept in the guerrila warfare to which military service hadn't accustomed me. Wouldn't it be wiser, I thought, irresolutely contemplating the absurd bulge in my dinner-jacket, to leave him to his undisputed mastery of the situation, and not put it to the proof? It was not like cutting an ordinary engagement. A knock on the door interrupted my confused consideration of social solecisms.

"Mr. Santander told me to tell you he is quite ready," the butler said. Through his manifest uneasiness I detected a hint of disapproval. He looked at me askance ; he had gone over. But couldn't he be put to some use ? I had an idea.

"Perhaps you would announce me," I said. He couldn't very well refuse, and piloted by him I should have a better chance in the passages and an entry valuably disconcerting. "I'm not personally known to Mr. Santander," I explained. "It would save some little awkwardness."

Close upon the heels of my human shield I threaded the passages. Their bright emptiness reassured me ; it was inconceivable, I felt after several safely negotiated turns, that anything sinister could lurk behind those politely rounded corners—Gertrude had had their angularities smoothed into curves ; it would be so terrible, she said, if going to bed one stumbled (one easily might) and fell against an *edge* ! But innocuous as they were, I preferred to avoid them. The short cut through the library would thus serve a double purpose ; for it would let us in from an unexpected quarter, from that end of the library, in fact, where the large window—so perilous-looking, really so secure on its struts and stays—perched over the roaring sea.

"This is the quickest way," I said to the butler, pointing to the library door. He turned the handle.

"It's locked, sir."

"Oh, well."

We had reached the dining-room at last. The butler paused with his hand on the knob as though by the mere sense of touch he could tell whether he were to be again denied admittance. Or perhaps he was listening or just thinking. The next thing I knew was that he had called out my name and I was standing in the room. Then I heard Mr. Santander's voice. "You can go, Collins." The door shut.

My host didn't turn round at once. All I could make out, in the big dim room lighted only by its four candles and the discreet footlights of dusky pictures, was his back, and his face —the eyes and forehead, reflected in the mirror over the mantelpiece. The same mirror showed my face too, low down on the right-hand side, curiously unrelated. His arms were stretched along the mantelpiece and he was stirring the fire with his foot. Suddenly he turned and face me.

" Oh, you're there," he said. " I'm so sorry."

We moved to the table and sat down. There was nothing to eat.

I fell to studying his appearance. Every line of his dinner-jacket, every fold in his soft shirt, I knew by heart ; I seemed always to have known them.

" What are we waiting for ? " he suddenly demanded rather loudly. " Collins ! " he called. " Collins ! " His voice reverberated through the room, but no one came. " How stupid of me," he muttered, " of course I must ring." Oddly enough he seemed to look to me for confirmation. I nodded ; Collins appeared, and the meal began.

Its regular sequence soothed him, for presently he said : " You must forgive my being so distrait. I've had rather a tiring journey—come from a distance, as they say. South America, in fact," He drank some wine reflectively. " I had one or two things to settle before . . . before joining the army. Now I don't think it will be necessary."

" Necessary to settle them ? " I said.

" No," he replied, " I have settled them."

" You mean that you will claim exemption as an American citizen ? "

Again Mr. Santander shook his head. " It would be a reason, wouldn't it ? But I hadn't thought of that."

Instinct urged me to let so delicate a topic drop ; but my nerves were fearful of a return to silence. There seemed so little, of all that we had in common, to draw upon for conversation.

" You suffer from bad health, perhaps ? " I suggested. But he demurred again.

" Even Gertrude didn't complain of my health," he said, adding quickly, as though to smother the sound of her name, " But you're not drinking."

" I don't think I will," I stammered—I had meant to say I was a teetotaller.

My host seemed surprised. " And yet Gertrude had a long bill at her wine-merchant's," he commented, half to himself.

I echoed it involuntarily : " Had ? "

" Oh," he said, " it's been paid. That's partly," he explained, " why I came home—to pay."

I felt I couldn't let this pass.

" Mr. Santander," I said, " there's a great deal in your behaviour that I don't begin (is that good American ?) to understand."

" No ? " he murmured, looking straight in front of him.

" But," I proceeded, as truculently as I could, " I want you to realise——"

He cut me short. " Don't suppose," he said, " that I attribute all my wife's expenditure to you."

I found myself trying to defend her. " Of course," I said, " she has the house to keep up : it's not run for a mere song, a house like this." And with my arm I tried to indicate to Mr. Santander the costly immensity of his domain. " You wouldn't like her to live in a pig-sty, would you ? And there's the sea to keep out—why, a night like this must do pounds worth of damage ! "

" You are right," he said with a strange look. " You even underestimate the damage it has done."

Of course I couldn't fail to catch his meaning. He meant the havoc wrought in his affections. They had been strong, report said : strong enough for her neglect of them to make him leave the country. They weren't expressed in half-measures, I thought, looking at him with a new sensation. He must have behaved with the high hand, when he arrived. How he must have steeled himself to drive her out of the house, that stormy night, ignoring her piteous protestations, her turns and twists which I had never been able to ignore ! She was never so alluring, never so fertile in emotional appeals, as when she knew she was in for a scolding. I could hear her say : " But, Maurice, however much you hate me, you couldn't really want me to get *wet* ! " and his reply : " Get out of this house, and don't come back till I send for you. As for your lover, leave me to look after him." He was looking after me, and soon, no doubt, he would send for her. And for her sake, since he had really returned to take part in her life, I couldn't desire this estrangement. Couldn't I ever bridge it over, bring it to a close ? *Beati pacifici*. Well, I would be a peacemaker too.

Confident that my noble impulses must have communicated

themselves to my host I looked up from my plate and searched his face for signs of abating rigour. I was disappointed. But should I forgo or even postpone my atonement because he was stiff-necked? Only it was difficult to begin. At last I ventured.

"Gertrude is really very fond of you, you know."

Dessert had been reached and I, in token of amity and goodwill, had helped myself to a glass of port wine.

For answer he fairly glared at me. "Fond of me!" he shouted.

I was determined not to be browbeaten out of my kind offices.

"That's what I said : she has a great heart."

"If you mean," he replied, returning to his former tone, "that it has ample accommodation! But your recommendations come too late : I have delegated her affections."

"To me?" I asked involuntarily.

He shook his head. "And in any case, why do you?"

"Because I——"

"Oh, no," he exclaimed passionately. "Did she deceive you—has she deceived you into believing *that*—that *you* are the alternative to *me*? You aren't unique—you have your re-duplications, scores of them!" My head swam, but he went on, enjoying his triumph. "Why, no one ever told me about you! She herself only mentioned you once. You are the least—the least of all her lovers!" His voice dropped. "Otherwise you wouldn't be here."

"Where should I be?" I fatuously asked. He went on without regarding me. "But I remember this house when its silence, its comfort, its isolation, its uniqueness were for us, Gertrude and me and . . . and for the people we invited. But we didn't ask many—we preferred to be alone. And I thought at first she was alone," he wound up, "when I found her this evening."

"Then why," I asked, "did you send her away and not me?"

"Ah," he replied with an accent of finality, "I wanted you."

While he spoke he was cracking a nut with his fingers, and it must have had sharp edges, for he stopped, wincing, and held the finger to his mouth.

"I've hurt my nail," he said. "See?"

He pushed his hand towards me over the polished table. I watched it, fascinated, thinking it would stop ; but still it came on, his body following, until, if I hadn't drawn back it would have touched me, while his chin dropped to within an inch of the table, and one side of his face was pillowed against his upper arm.

" It's a handicap, isn't it ? " he said, watching me from under his brows.

" Indeed it is," I replied ; for the fine, acorn-shaped nail was terribly torn, a jagged rent revealing the quick, moist and gelatinous. " How did you manage to do that ? " I went on, trying not to look at the mutilation which he still held before my eyes.

" Do you really want to know how I did it ? " he asked. He hadn't moved, and his question, in its awkward, irregular delivery, seemed to reflect the sprawled unnatural position of his body.

" Do tell me," I said, and added, nervously jocular : " But let me guess. Perhaps you met with an accident in the course of your professional activities, when you were mending the lights, I mean, in the library."

At that he jumped to his feet. " You're very warm," he said, " you almost burn. But come into the library with me, and I'll tell you."

I prepared to follow him.

But unaccountably he lingered, walked up and down a little, went to the fireplace and again (it was evidently a favourite relaxation) gently kicked the coals. Then he went to the library door meaning, apparently, to open it ; but he changed his mind and instead turned on the big lights of the dining-room. " Let's see what it's really like," he said. " I hate this half-light." The sudden illumination laid bare that great, rich, still room, so secure, so assured, so content. My host stood looking at it. He was fidgeting with his dinner-jacket and had so little self-control that, at every brush of the material with his damaged finger, he whimpered like a child. His face, now that I saw it fairly again, was twisted and disfigured with misery. There wasn't one imaginable quality that he shared with his sumptuous possessions.

In the library darkness was absolute. My host preceded me and in a moment I had lost all sense of even our relative positions. I backed against the wall, and by luck my groping fingers felt the switch. But its futile click only emphasised the darkness. I began to feel frightened, with an acute immediate alarm very different from my earlier apprehensions and forebodings. To add to my uneasiness my ears began to detect a sound, a small, irregular sound, it might have been water dripping, yet it seemed too definitely consonantal for that ; it

was more like an inhuman whisper. "Speak up," I cried, "if
you're talking to me!" But it had no more effect, my petulant
outcry, than if it had fallen on the ears of the dead. The disquieting noise persisted, but another note had crept into it—
a soft, labial sound, like the licking of lips. It wasn't intelligible,
it wasn't even articulate, yet I felt that if I listened longer it
would become both. I couldn't bear the secret colloquy; and
though it seemed to be taking place all round me I made a rush
into what I took to be the middle of the room. I didn't get very
far, however. A chair sent me sprawling, and when I picked
myself up it was to the accompaniment of a more familiar sound.
The curtains were being drawn apart and the moonlight,
struggling in, showed me shapes of furniture and my own
position, a few feet from the door. It showed me something
else, too.

How could my host be drawing the curtains when I could
see him lounging, relaxed and careless, in an arm-chair that,
from its position by the wall, missed the moon's directer ray?
I strained my eyes. Very relaxed, very careless he must be,
after what had passed between us, to stare at me so composedly
over his shoulder, no, more than that, over his very back!
He faced me, though his shoulder, oddly enough was turned
away. Perhaps he had practised it—a contortionist's trick to
bewilder his friends. Suddenly I heard his voice, not from the
arm-chair at all but from the window."

"Do you know now?"

"What?" I said.

"How I hurt my finger."

"No," I cried, untruthfully, for that very moment all my
fears told me.

"I did it killing my wife!"

I rushed towards the window, only to be driven back by
what seemed a solid body of mingled sleet and wind. I heard
the creak of the great casement before it whirled outwards,
crashing against the mullion and shattering the glass. But
though I fought my way to the opening I wasn't quick enough.
Sixty feet below the eroding sea sucked, spouted and roared.
Out of it jags of rock seemed to rise, float for a moment and then
be dragged under the foam. Time after time great arcs of spray
sprang hissing from the sea, lifted themselves to the window as
though impelled by an insatiable curiosity, condensed and fell
away. Its drops were bitter on my lips. Soaked to the skin and
stiff with cold I turned to the room. The heavy brocade curtains

flapped madly or rose and streamed level with the ceiling, and through the general uproar I could distinguish separate sounds, the clattering fall of small objects and the banging and scraping of pictures against the walls. The whole weather-proof, sound-proof house seemed to be ruining in, to be given up to darkness and furies . . . and to me. But not wholly, not unreservedly, to me. Mrs. Santander was still at her place in the easy-chair.

EDWARD RANDOLPH'S
PORTRAIT

THE old legendary guest of the Province House abode in my remembrance from midsummer till January. One idle evening, last winter, confident that he would be found in the snuggest corner of the bar-room, I resolved to pay him another visit, hoping to deserve well of my country by snatching from oblivion some else unheard-of fact of history. The night was chill and raw, and rendered boisterous by almost a gale of wind, which whistled along Washington Street, causing the gaslights to flare and flicker within the lamps. As I hurried onward, my fancy was busy with a comparison between the aspect of the street, and that which it probably wore when the British governors inhabited the mansion whither I was now going. Brick edifices in those times were few, till a succession of destructive fires had swept, and swept again, the wooden dwellings and warehouses from the most populous quarters of the town. The buildings stood insulated and independent, not, as now, merging their separate existences into connected ranges, with a front of tiresome identity, but each possessing features of its own, as if the owner's individual taste had shaped it, and the whole presenting a picturesque irregularity, the absence of which is hardly compensated by any beauties of our modern architecture. Such a scene, dimly vanishing from the eye by the ray of here and there a tallow candle, glimmering through the small panes of scattered windows, would form a sombre contrast to the street as I beheld it, with the gaslights blazing from corner to corner, flaming within the shops, and throwing a noonday brightness through the huge plates of glass.

But the black, lowering sky, as I turned my eyes upward, wore, doubtless, the same visage as when it frowned upon the ante-Revolutionary New-Englanders. The wintry blast had the same shriek that was familiar to their ears. The Old South Church, too, still pointed its antique spire into the darkness, and was lost between earth and heaven ; and as I passed, its clock, which had warned so many generations how transitory was their lifetime, spoke heavily and slow the same unregarded moral to myself. " Only seven o'clock," thought I. " My old friend's legends will scarcely kill the hours 'twixt this and bedtime."

Passing through the narrow arch, I crossed the courtyard, the confined precincts of which were made visible by a lantern over the portal of the Province House. On entering the bar-room, I found, as I expected, the old tradition-monger seated by a special good fire of anthracite, compelling clouds of smoke from a corpulent cigar. He recognised me with evident pleasure ; for my rare properties as a patient listener invariably make me a favourite with elderly gentlemen and ladies of narrative pro-pensities. Drawing a chair to the fire, I desired mine host to favour us with a glass apiece of whisky punch, which was speedily prepared, steaming hot, with a slice of lemon at the bottom, a dark red stratum of port wine upon the surface, and a sprinkling of nutmeg strewn over all. As we touched our glasses together, my legendary friend made himself known to me as Mr. Bela Tiffany ; and I rejoiced at the oddity of the name, because it gave his image and character a sort of individuality in my con-ception. The old gentleman's draught acted as a solvent upon his memory, so that it overflowed with tales, traditions, anecdotes of famous dead people, and traits of ancient manners, some of which were childish as a nurse's lullaby, while others might have been worth the notice of the grave historian. Nothing impressed me more than a story of a black mysterious picture, which used to hang in one of the chambers of the Province House, directly above the room where we were now sitting. The following is as correct a version of the fact as the reader would be likely to obtain from any other source, although, assuredly, it has a tinge of romance approaching to the marvellous.

In one of the apartments of the Province House there was long preserved an ancient picture, the frame of which was as black as ebony, and the canvas itself so dark with age, damp, and smoke, that not a touch of the painter's art could be discerned. Time had thrown an impenetrable veil over it, and left to tradition and fable and conjecture to say what had once been there portrayed. During the rule of many successive governors it had hung, by prescriptive and undisputed right, over the mantelpiece of the same chamber ; and it still kept its place when Lieutenant-Governor Hutchinson assumed the administration of the province, on the departure of Sir Francis Bernard.

The Lieutenant-Governor sat, one afternoon, resting his head against the carved back of his stately arm-chair, and gazing up thoughtfully at the void blackness of the picture. It was scarcely a time for such inactive musing, when affairs of the deepest moment required the ruler's decision ; for, within that very hour, Hutchinson had received intelligence of the arrival of a British fleet, bringing three regiments from Halifax to overawe the insubordination of the people. These troops awaited his permission to occupy the fortress of Castle William and the town itself. Yet, instead of affixing his signature to an official order, there sat the Lieutenant-Governor, so carefully scrutinising the black waste of canvas, that his demeanour attracted the notice of two young persons who attended him. One, wearing a military dress of buff, was his kinsman, Francis Lincoln, the Provincial Captain of Castle William ; the other, who sat on a low stool beside his chair, was Alice Vane, his favourite niece.

She was clad entirely in white, a pale, ethereal creature, who, though a native of New England, had been educated abroad, and seemed not merely a stranger from another clime, but almost a being from another world. For several years, until left an orphan, she had dwelt with her father in sunny Italy, and there had acquired a taste and enthusiasm for sculpture and painting, which she found few opportunities of gratifying in the undecorated dwellings of the colonial gentry. It was said that the early productions of her own pencil exhibited no inferior genius, though, perhaps, the rude atmosphere of New England had cramped her hand and dimmed the glowing colours of her fancy. But observing her uncle's steadfast gaze, which appeared to search through the mist of years to discover the subject of the picture, her curiosity was excited.

" Is it known, my dear uncle," inquired she, " what this old picture once represented ? Possibly, could it be made visible, it might prove a masterpiece of some great artist ; else, why has it so long held such a conspicuous place ? "

As her uncle, contrary to his usual custom (for he was as attentive to all the humours and caprices of Alice as if she had been his own best-beloved child), did not immediately reply, the young captain of Castle William took that office upon himself.

" This dark old square of canvas, my fair cousin," said he, " has been an heirloom in the Province House from time immemorial. As to the painter, I can tell you nothing ; but if half the stories told of it be true, not one of the great Italian masters has ever produced so marvellous a piece of work as that before you."

Captain Lincoln proceeded to relate some of the strange fables and fantasies, which, as it was impossible to refute them by ocular demonstration, had grown to be articles of popular belief, in reference to this old picture. One of the wildest, and at the same time, the best accredited accounts, stated it to be an original and authentic portrait of the Evil One, taken at a witch meeting near Salem ; and that its strong and terrible resemblance had been confirmed by several of the confessing wizards and witches, at their trial, in open court. It was likewise affirmed that a familiar spirit, or demon, abode behind the blackness of the picture, and had shown himself, at seasons of public calamity, to more than one of the royal governors. Shirley, for instance, had beheld this ominous apparition, on the eve of General Abercrombie's shameful and bloody defeat under the walls of Ticonderoga. Many of the servants of the Province House had caught glimpses of a visage frowning down upon them, at morning or evening twilight, or in the depths of night, while raking up the fire that glimmered on the hearth beneath ; although, if any were bold enough to hold a torch before the picture, it would appear as black and undistinguishable as ever. The oldest inhabitant of Boston recollected that his father, in whose days the portrait had not wholly faded out of sight, had once looked upon it, but would never suffer himself to be questioned as to the face which was there represented. In connection with such stories, it was remarkable that over the top of the frame there were some ragged remnants of black silk, indicating that a veil had formerly hung down before the picture, until the duskiness of time had so effectually concealed it. But, after all, it was the most singular part of the affair, that so many of the pompous governors of Massachusetts had allowed the obliterated picture to remain in the state chamber of the Province House.

" Some of these fables are really awful," observed Alice Vane, who had occasionally shuddered, as well as smiled, while her cousin spoke. " It would be almost worth while to wipe away the black surface of the canvas, since the original picture can hardly be so formidable as those which fancy paints instead of it."

" But would it be possible," inquired her cousin, " to restore this dark picture to its pristine hues ? "

" Such arts are known in Italy," said Alice.

The Lieutenant-Governor had roused himself from his abstracted mood, and listened with a smile to the conversation of his young relatives. Yet his voice had something peculiar in its tones, when he undertook the explanation of the mystery.

"I am sorry, Alice, to destroy your faith in the legends of which you are so fond," remarked he ; "but my antiquarian researches have long since made me acquainted with the subject of this picture—if picture it can be called—which is no more visible, nor ever will be, than the face of the long-buried man whom it once represented. It was the portrait of Edward Randolph, the founder of this house, a person famous in the history of New England."

"Of that Edward Randolph," exclaimed Captain Lincoln, "who obtained the repeal of the first provincial charter, under which our forefathers had enjoyed almost democratic privileges ! He that was styled the arch-enemy of New England, and whose memory is still held in detestation, as the destroyer of our liberties ! "

"It was the same Randolph," answered Hutchinson, moving uneasily in his chair. "It was his lot to taste the bitterness of popular odium."

"Our annals tell us," continued the Captain of Castle William, "that the curse of the people followed this Randolph where he went, and wrought evil in all the subsequent events of his life, and that its effect was seen likewise in the manner of his death. They say, too, that the inward misery of that curse worked itself outward, and was visible on the wretched man's countenance, making it too horrible to be looked upon. If so, and if this picture truly represented his aspect, it was in mercy that the cloud of blackness has gathered over it."

"These traditions are folly, to one who has proved, as I have, how little of historic truth lies at the bottom," said the Lieutenant-Governor. "As regards the life and character of Edward Randolph, too implicit credence has been given to Dr. Cotton Mather, who—I must say it, though some of his blood runs in my veins— has filled our early history with old women's tales, as fanciful and extravagant as those of Greece or Rome."

"And yet," whispered Alice Vane, "may not such fables have a moral ? And, methinks, if the visage of this portrait be so dreadful, it is not without a cause that it has hung so long in a chamber of the Province House. When the rulers feel themselves irresponsible, it were well that they should be reminded of the awful weight of a people's curse."

The Lieutenant-Governor started, and gazed for a moment at his niece, as if her girlish fantasies had struck upon some feeling in his own breast, which all his policy or principles could not entirely subdue. He knew, indeed, that Alice, in spite of her foreign education, retained the native sympathies of a New England girl.

"Peace, silly child," cried he, at last, more harshly than he had ever before addressed the gentle Alice. "The rebuke of a king is more to be dreaded than the clamour of a wild, misguided multitude. Captain Lincoln, it is decided. The fortress of Castle William must be occupied by the Royal troops. The two remaining regiments shall be billeted in the town, or encamped upon the Common, It is time, after years of tumult, and almost rebellion, that his Majesty's government should have a wall of strength about it."

"Trust, sir—trust yet awhile to the loyalty of the people," said Captain Lincoln ; "nor teach them that they can ever be on other terms with British soldiers than those of brotherhood, as when they fought side by side through the French war. Do not convert the streets of your native town into a camp. Think twice before you give up old Castle William, the key of the province, into other keeping than that of true-born New-Englanders."

"Young man, it is decided," repeated Hutchinson, rising from his chair. "A British officer will be in attendance this evening to receive the necessary instructions for the disposal of the troops. Your presence also will be required. Till then, farewell."

With these words the Lieutenant-Governor hastily left the room, while Alice and her cousin more slowly followed, whispering together, and once pausing to glance back at the mysterious picture. The Captain of Castle William fancied that the girl's air and mien were such as might have belonged to one of those spirits of fable—fairies, or creatures of a more antique mythology —who sometimes mingled their agency with mortal affairs, half in caprice, yet with a sensibility to human weal or woe. As he held the door for her to pass, Alice beckoned to the picture and smiled.

"Come forth, dark and evil Shape ! " cried she. " It is thine hour ! "

In the evening, Lieutenant-Governor Hutchinson sat in the same chamber where the foregoing scene had occurred, surrounded by several persons whose various interests had summoned them together. There were the selectmen of Boston, plain, patriarchal fathers of the people, excellent representatives of the old puritanical founders, whose sombre strength had stamped so deep an impress upon the New England character. Contrasting with these were one or two members of Council, richly dressed in the white wigs, the embroidered waistcoats, and other magnificence of the time, and making a somewhat ostentatious display of courtier-like ceremonial. In attendance, likewise, was a major of the British army, awaiting the Lieutenant-Governor's orders for the landing of the troops, which still remained on board the transports. The Captain of Castle William stood beside Hutchinson's chair, with folded arms, glancing rather haughtily at the British officer, by whom he was soon to be superseded in his command. On a table, in the centre of the chamber, stood a branched silver candlestick, throwing down the glow of half a dozen wax-lights upon a paper apparently ready for the Lieutenant-Governor's signature.

Partly shrouded in the voluminous folds of one of the window-curtains, which fell from the ceiling to the floor, was seen the white drapery of a lady's robe. It may appear strange that Alice Vane should have been there, at such a time ; but there was something so childlike, so wayward, in her singular character, so apart from ordinary rules, that her presence did not surprise the few who noticed it. Meantime, the chairman of the selectmen was addressing to the Lieutenant-Governor a long and solemn protest against the reception of the British troops into the town.

"And if your Honour," concluded this excellent but somewhat prosy old gentleman, " shall see fit to persist in bringing these mercenary sworders and musketeers into our quiet streets, not on our heads be the responsibility. Think, sir, while there is yet time, that if one drop of blood be shed, that blood shall be an eternal stain upon your Honour's memory. You, sir, have written, with an able pen, the deeds of our forefathers. The more to be desired is it, therefore, that yourself should deserve honourable mention, as a true patriot and upright ruler, when your own doings shall be written down in history."

" I am not insensible, my good sir, to the natural desire to stand well in the annals of my country," replied Hutchinson, controlling his impatience into courtesy, " nor know I any better method of attaining that end than by withstanding the merely temporary spirit of mischief, which, with your pardon, seems to have infected elder men than myself. Would you have me wait till the mob shall sack the Province House, as they did my private mansion? Trust me, sir, the time may come when you will be glad to flee for protection to the King's banner, the raising of which is now so distasteful to you."

"Yes," said the British major, who was impatiently expecting the Lieutenant-Governor's orders. "The demagogues of this province have raised the devil, and cannot lay him again. We will exorcise him, in God's name and the King's."

"If you meddle with the Devil, take care of his claws!" answered the Captain of Castle William, stirred by the taunt against his countrymen.

"Craving your pardon, young sir," said the venerable select-man, "let not an evil spirit enter into your words. We will strive against the oppressor with prayer and fasting, as our forefathers would have done. Like them, moreover, we will submit to whatever lot a wise Providence may send us—always, after our own best exertions to amend it."

"And there peep forth the Devil's claws!" muttered Hutchinson, who well understood the nature of Puritan submission. "This matter shall be expedited forthwith. When there shall be a sentinel at every corner, and a court of guard before the town-house, a loyal gentleman may venture to walk abroad. What to me is the outcry of a mob, in this remote province of the realm? The King is my master, and England is my country! Upheld by their armed strength, I set my foot upon the rabble, and defy them!"

He snatched a pen, and was about to affix his signature to the paper that lay on the table, when the Captain of Castle William placed his hand upon his shoulder. The freedom of the action, so contrary to the ceremonious respect which was then considered due to rank and dignity, awakened general surprise, and in none more than in the Lieutenant-Governor himself. Looking angrily up, he perceived that his young relative was pointing his finger to the opposite wall. Hutchinson's eye followed the signal; and he saw, what had hitherto been unobserved, that a black silk curtain was suspended before the mysterious picture, so as completely to conceal it. His thoughts immediately recurred to the scene of the preceding afternoon; and, in his surprise, confused by indistinct emotions, yet sensible that his niece must have had an agency in this phenomenon, he called loudly upon her.

"Alice!—come hither, Alice!"

No sooner had he spoken than Alice Vane glided from her station, and pressing one hand across her eyes, with the other snatched away the sable curtain that concealed the portrait. An exclamation of surprise burst from every beholder ; but the Lieutenant-Governor's voice had a tone of horror.

" By Heaven," said he, in a low, inward murmur, speaking rather to himself than to those around him, " if the spirit of Edward Randolph were to appear among us from the place of torment, he could not wear more of the terrors of hell upon his face ! "

" For some wise end," said the aged selectman, solemnly, " hath Providence scattered away the mist of years that had so long hid this dreadful effigy. Until this hour no living man hath seen what we behold ! "

Within the antique frame, which so recently had enclosed a sable waste of canvas, now appeared a visible picture, still dark, indeed, in its hues and shadings, but thrown forward in strong relief. It was a half-length figure of a gentleman in a rich, but very old-fashioned dress of embroidered velvet, with a broad ruff and a beard, and wearing a hat, the brim of which overshadowed his forehead. Beneath this cloud the eyes had a peculiar glare which was almost lifelike. The whole portrait started so distinctly out of the background, that it had the effect of a person looking down from the wall at the astonished and awestricken spectators. The expression of the face, if any words can convey an idea of it, was that of a wretch detected in some hideous guilt, and exposed to the bitter hatred and laughter and withering scorn of a vast surrounding multitude. There was the struggle of defiance, beaten down and overwhelmed by the crushing weight of ignominy. The torture of the soul had come forth upon the countenance. It seemed as if the picture, while hidden behind the cloud of immemorial years, had been all the time acquiring an intenser depth and darkness of expression, till now it gloomed forth again, and threw its evil omen over the present hour. Such, if the wild legend may be credited, was the portrait of Edward Randolph, as he appeared when a people's curse had wrought its influence upon his nature.

" 'Twould drive me mad—that awful face ! " said Hutchinson, who seemed fascinated by the contemplation of it.

" Be warned, then ! " whispered Alice. " He trampled on a people's rights. Behold his punishment—and avoid a crime like his ! "

The Lieutenant-Governor actually trembled for an instant ; but, exerting his energy—which was not, however, his most characteristic feature—he strove to shake off the spell of Randolph's countenance.

"Girl!" cried he, laughing bitterly, as he turned to Alice, "have you brought hither your painter's art—your Italian spirit of intrigue—your tricks of stage effect—and think to influence the councils of rulers and the affairs of nations by such shallow contrivances? See here!"

"Stay yet awhile," said the selectman, as Hutchinson again snatched the pen; "for if ever mortal man received a warning from a tormented soul, your Honour is that man!"

"Away!" answered Hutchinson fiercely. "Though yonder senseless picture cried 'Forbear!' it should not move me!"

Casting a scowl of defiance at the pictured face (which seemed, at that moment, to intensify the horror of its miserable and wicked look), he scrawled on the paper, in characters that betokened it a deed of desperation, the name of Thomas Hutchinson. Then, it is said, he shuddered, as if that signature had granted away his salvation.

"It is done," said he; and placed his hand upon his brow.

"May Heaven forgive the deed," said the soft sad accents of Alice Vane, like the voice of a good spirit flitting away.

When morning came there was a stifled whisper through the household, and spreading thence about the town, that the dark, mysterious picture had started from the wall, and spoken face to face with Lieutenant-Governor Hutchinson. If such a miracle had been wrought, however, no traces of it remained behind; for within the antique frame, nothing could be discerned, save the impenetrable cloud which had covered the canvas since the memory of man. If the figure had, indeed, stepped forth, it had fled back, spirit-like, at the daydawn, and hidden itself behind a century's obscurity. The truth probably was, that Alice Vane's secret for restoring the hues of the picture had merely effected a temporary renovation. But those who, in that brief interval, had beheld the awful visage of Edward Randolph, desired no second glance, and ever afterwards trembled at the recollection of the scene, as if an evil spirit had appeared visibly among them. And as for Hutchinson, when, far over the ocean, his dying hour drew on, he gasped for breath, and complained that he was choking with the blood of the Boston massacre; and Francis Lincoln, the former Captain of Castle William, who was standing at his bedside, perceived a likeness in his frenzied look to that of Edward Randolph. Did his broken spirit feel, at that dread hour, the tremendous burden of a People's curse?

At the conclusion of this miraculous legend, I inquired of

mine host whether the picture still remained in the chamber over our heads ; but Mr. Tiffany informed me that it had long since been removed, and was supposed to be hidden in some out-of-the-way corner of the New England Museum. Perchance some curious antiquary may light upon it there, and, with the assistance of Mr. Howorth, the picture-cleaner, may supply a not unnecessary proof of the authenticity of the facts here set down. During the progress of the story a storm had been gathering abroad, and raging and rattling so loudly in the upper regions of the Province House, that it seemed as if all the old governors and great men were running riot above stairs, while Mr. Bela Tiffany babbled of them below. In the course of generations, when many people have lived and died in an ancient house, the whistling of the wind through its crannies, and the creaking of its beams and rafters, become strangely like the tones of the human voice, or thundering laughter, or heavy footsteps treading the deserted chambers. It is as if the echoes of half a century were revived. Such were the ghostly sounds that roared and murmured in our ears, when I took leave of the circle round the fireside of the Province House, and plunging down the doorsteps, fought my way homeward against a drifting snowstorm.

THE SPECTRE BRIDEGROOM

" He that supper for is dight,
He lyes full cold, I trow, this night !
Yestreen to chamber I him led,
This night Grey-steel has made his bed ! "
SIR EGER, SIR GRAHAME AND SIR GRAY-STEEL.

ON the summit of one of the heights of the Odenwald, a wild and romantic tract of Upper Germany that lies not far from the confluence of the Main and the Rhine, there stood, many, many years since, the Castle of the Baron Von Landshort. It is now fallen to decay, and almost buried among beech trees and dark firs ; above which, however, its old watch-tower may still be seen struggling, like the former possessor I have mentioned, to carry a high head, and look down upon a neighbouring country.

The Baron was a dry branch of the great family of Katzen-ellenbogen, and inherited the relics of the property and all the pride of his ancestors. Though the warlike disposition of his predecessors had much impaired the family possessions, yet the Baron still endeavoured to keep up some show of former state. The times were peaceable, and the German nobles, in general, had abandoned their inconvenient old castles, perched like eagles' nests among the mountains, and had built more con-venient residences in the valleys ; still the Baron remained proudly drawn up in his little fortress, cherishing with hereditary inveteracy all the old family feuds ; so that he was on ill terms with some of his nearest neighbours, on account of disputes that had happened between their great-great-grandfathers.

The Baron had but one child, a daughter ; but Nature, when she grants but one child, always compensates by making it a prodigy ; and so it was with the daughter of the Baron. All the nurses, gossips and country cousins assured her father that she had not her equal for beauty in all Germany ; and who should know better than they ? She had, moreover, been brought up with great care, under the superintendence of two maiden aunts, who had spent some years of their early life at one of the little German courts, and were skilled in all the branches of knowledge necessary to the education of a fine lady. Under their instructions, she became a miracle of accomplishments. By the time she was eighteen she could embroider to admiration, and had worked whole histories of the Saints in tapestry with such stength of expression in their countenances that they looked like so many souls in purgatory. She could read without great difficulty, and had spelled her way through several church legends, and almost all the chivalric wonders of the Heldenbuch. She had even made considerable proficiency in writing, could sign her own name without missing a letter, and so legibly that her aunts could read it without spectacles. She excelled in making little good-for-nothing ladylike knick-knacks of all kinds ; was versed in the most abstruse dancing of the day ; played a number of airs on the harp and guitar ; and knew all the tender ballads of the Minne-lieders by heart.

Her aunts, too, having been great flirts and coquettes in their younger days, were admirably calculated to be vigilant guardians and strict censors of the conduct of their niece ; for there is no duenna so rigidly prudent, and inexorably decorus, as a superannuated coquette. She was rarely suffered out of their sight ; never went beyond the domains of the castle, unless well attended, or, rather, well watched ; had continual lectures read to her about strict decorum and implicit obedience ; and, as to the men—pah ! she was taught to hold them at such distance and distrust that, unless properly authorised, she would not have cast a glance upon the handsomest cavalier in the world—no, not if he were even dying at her feet.

The good effects of this system were wonderfully apparent. The young lady was a pattern of docility and correctness. While others were wasting their sweetness in the glare of the world, and liable to be plucked and thrown aside by every hand, she was coyly blooming into fresh and lovely womanhood under the protection of those immaculate spinsters, like a rosebud blushing forth among guardian thorns. Her aunts looked upon her with pride and exultation, and vaunted that though all the other young ladies in the world might go astray, yet, thank Heaven, nothing of the kind could happen to the heiress of Katzenellenbogen.

But however scantily the Baron Von Landshort might be provided with children, his household was by no means a small one, for Providence had enriched him with abundance of poor relations. They, one and all, possessed the affectionate disposition common to humble relatives ; were wonderfully attached to the Baron, and took every possible occasion to come in swarms and enliven the castle. All family festivals were commemorated by these good people at the Baron's expense ; and when they were filled with good cheer, they would declare that there was nothing on earth so delightful as these family meetings, these jubilees of the heart.

The Baron, though a small man, had a large soul, and it swelled with satisfaction at the consciousness of being the greatest man in the little world about him. He loved to tell long stories about the stark old warriors whose portraits looked grimly down from the walls around, and he found no listeners equal to those who fed at his expense. He was much given to the marvellous, and a firm believer in all those supernatural tales with which every mountain and valley in Germany abounds. The faith of his guests even exceeded his own, they listened to every tale of wonder with open eyes and mouth, and never failed to be astonished, even though repeated for the hundredth time. Thus lived the Baron Von Landshort, the oracle of his table, the absolute monarch of his little territory, and happy, above all things, in the persuasion that he was the wisest man of the age.

At the time of which my story treats there was a great family gathering at the castle, on an affair of the utmost importance : it was to receive the destined bridegroom of the Baron's daughter. A negotiation had been carried on between the father and an old nobleman of Bavaria, to unite the dignity of their houses by the marriage of their children. The preliminaries had been conducted with proper punctilio. The young people were betrothed without seeing each other, and the time was appointed for the marriage ceremony. The young Count Von Altenburg had been recalled from the army for the purpose, and was actually on his way to the Baron's to receive his bride. Missives had even been received from him, from Wurtzburg, where he was accidentally detained, mentioning the day and hour when he might be expected to arrive.

The castle was in a tumult of preparation to give him a suitable welcome. The fair bride had been decked out with uncommon care. The two aunts had superintended her toilet, and quarrelled the whole morning about every article of her dress. The young lady had taken advantage of their contest to follow the bent of her own taste ; and fortunately it was a good one. She looked as lovely as youthful bridegroom could desire ; and the flutter of expectation heightened the lustre of her charms.

The suffusions that mantled her face and neck, the gentle heaving of the bosom, the eye now and then lost in reverie, all betrayed the soft tumult that was going on in her little heart. The aunts were continually hovering around her ; for maiden aunts are apt to take great interest in affairs of this nature : they were giving her a world of staid counsel, how to deport herself, what to say, and in what manner to receive the expected lover.

The Baron was no less busied in preparations. He had, in truth, nothing exactly to do ; but he was naturally a fuming, bustling little man, and could not remain passive when all the world was in a hurry. He worried from top to bottom of the castle, with an air of infinite anxiety ; he continually called the servants from their work to exhort them to be diligent, and buzzed about every hall and chamber, as idle, restless and importunate as a bluebottle fly of a warm summer's day.

In the meantime, the fatted calf had been killed ; the forests had rung with the clamour of the huntsmen ; the kitchen was crowded with good cheer ; the cellars had yielded up whole oceans of *Rhein-wein* and *Ferne-wein*, and even the great Heidelberg Tun had been laid under contribution. Everything was ready to receive the distinguished guest with *Saus und Braus* in the true spirit of German hospitality—but the guest delayed to make his appearance. Hour rolled after hour. The sun that had poured his downward rays upon the rich forests of the Odenwald now just gleamed along the summits of the mountains. The Baron mounted the highest tower, and strained his eyes in hopes of catching a distant sight of the Count and his attendants. Once he thought he beheld them ; the sound of horns came floating from the valley, prolonged by the mountain echoes : a number of horsemen were seen far below, slowly advancing along the road ; but when they had nearly reached the foot of the mountains they suddenly struck off in a different direction. The last ray of sunshine departed—the bats began to flit by in the twilight—the road grew dimmer and dimmer to the view ; and nothing appeared stirring in it but now and then a peasant lagging homeward from his labour.

While the old castle of Landshort was in this state of perplexity, a very interesting scene was transacting in a different part of the Odenwald.

The young Count Von Altenburg was tranquilly pursuing
his route in that sober jog-trot way in which a man travels
toward matrimony when his friends have taken all the trouble
and uncertainty of courtship off his hands, and a bride is waiting
for him, as certainly as a dinner, at the end of his journey. He
had encountered at Wurtzburg a youthful companion in arms,
with whom he had seen some service on the frontiers : Herman
Von Starkenfaust, one of the stoutest hands and worthiest hearts
of German chivalry, who was now returning from the army.
His father's castle was not far distant from the old fortress of
Landshort, although a hereditary feud rendered the families
hostile and strangers to each other.

In the warm-hearted moment of recognition, the young
friends related all their past adventures and fortunes, and the
Count gave the whole history of his intended nuptials with a
young lady whom he had never seen, but of whose charms he
had received the most enrapturing descriptions.

As the route of the friends lay in the same direction, they
agreed to perform the rest of their journey together ; and, that
they might do it more leisurely, set off from Wurtzburg at an
early hour, the Count having given directions for his retinue to
follow and overtake him.

They beguiled their wayfaring with recollections of their
military scenes and adventures ; but the Count was apt to be a
little tedious, now and then, about the reputed charms of his
bride, and the felicity that awaited him.

In this way they had entered among the mountains of the
Odenwald, and were traversing one of its most lonely and thickly
wooded passes. It is well known that the forests of Germany
have always been as much infested with robbers as its castles by
spectres ; and, at this time, the former were particularly
numerous, from the hordes of disbanded soldiers wandering
about the country. It will not appear extraordinary, therefore
that the cavaliers were attacked by a gang of these stragglers in
the midst of the forest. They defended themselves with bravery,
but were nearly overpowered when the Count's retinue arrived
to their assistance. At sight of them the robbers fled, but not
until the Count had received a mortal wound. He was slowly and
carefully conveyed back to the city of Wurtzburg, and a friar
summoned from a neighbouring convent, who was famous for
his skill in administering to both soul and body. But half of his
skill was superfluous ; the moments of the unfortunate Count
were numbered.

With his dying breath he entreated his friend to repair instantly to the castle of Landshort, and explain the fatal cause of his not keeping his appointment with his bride. Though not the most ardent of lovers, he was one of the most punctilious of men, and appeared earnestly solicitous that this mission should be speedily and courteously executed. " Unless this is done," said he, " I shall not sleep quietly in my grave ! " He repeated these last words with peculiar solemnity. A request, at a moment so impressive, admitted no hesitation. Starkenfaust endeavoured to soothe him to calmness ; promised faithfully to execute his wish, and gave him his hand in solemn pledge. The dying man pressed it in acknowledgment, but soon lapsed into delirium— raved about his bride—his engagements—his plighted word ; ordered his horse, that he might ride to the castle of Landshort, and expired in the fancied act of vaulting into the saddle.

Starkenfaust bestowed a sigh and a soldier's tear on the untimely fate of his comrade ; and then pondered on the awkward mission he had undertaken. His heart was heavy, and his head perplexed ; for he was to present himself an unbidden guest among hostile people, and to damp their festivity with tidings fatal to their hopes. Still there were certain whisperings of curiosity in his bosom to see this far-famed beauty of Katzenellenbogen so cautiously shut up from the world ; for he was a passionate admirer of the sex, and there was a dash of eccentricity and enterprise in his character that made him fond of all singular adventure.

Previous to his departure, he made all due arrangements with the holy fraternity of the convent for the funeral solem-nities of his friend, who was to be buried in the cathedral of Wurtzburg, near some of his illustrious relatives ; and the mourning retinue of the Count took charge of his remains.

It is now high time that we should return to the ancient family of Katzenellenbogen, who were impatient for their guest, and still more for their dinner ; and to the worthy little Baron, whom we left airing himself on the watch-tower.

Night closed in, but still no guest arrived. The Baron descended from the tower in despair. The banquet, which had been delayed from hour to hour, could no longer be postponed. The meats were already overdone, the cook in an agony, and the whole household had the look of a garrison that had been reduced by famine. The Baron was obliged reluctantly to give orders for the feast without the presence of the guest. All were seated at table, and just on the point of commencing, when the sound of a horn from without the gate gave notice of the approach of a stranger. Another long blast filled the old courts of the castle with its echoes, and was answered by the warder from the walls. The Baron hastened to receive his future son-in-law.

The drawbridge had been let down, and the stranger was before the gate. He was a tall gallant cavalier, mounted on a black steed. His countenance was pale, but he had a beaming, romantic eye, and an air of stately melancholy. The Baron was a little mortified that he should have come in this simple, solitary style. His dignity for a moment was ruffled, and he felt disposed to consider it a want of proper respect for the important occasion, and the important family with which he was to be connected. He pacified himself, however, with the conclusion that it must have been youthful impatience which had induced him thus to spur on sooner than his attendants.

" I am sorry," said the stranger, " to break in upon you thus unseasonably——"

Here the Baron interrupted him with a world of compliments and greetings ; for, to tell the truth, he prided himself upon his courtesy and his eloquence. The stranger attempted, once or twice, to stem the torrent of words, but in vain ; so he bowed his head and suffered it to flow on. By the time the Baron had come to a pause they had reached the inner court of the castle ; and the stranger was again about to speak, when he was once more interrupted by the appearance of the female part of the family, leading forth the shrinking and blushing bride. He gazed on her for a moment as one entranced ; it seemed as if his whole soul beamed forth in the gaze, and rested upon that lovely form. One of the maiden aunts whispered something in her ear ; she made an effort to speak ; her moist blue eye was timidly raised, gave a shy glance of inquiry on the stranger, and was cast again to the ground. The words died away ; but there was a sweet smile playing about her lips, and a soft dimpling of the cheek, that showed her glance had not been unsatisfactory. It was impossible for a girl of the fond age of eighteen, highly predisposed for love and matrimony, not to be pleased with so gallant a cavalier.

The late hour at which the guest had arrived left no time for parley. The Baron was peremptory, and deferred all particular conversation until the morning, and led the way to the untasted banquet.

It was served up in the great hall of the castle. Around the walls hung the hard-favoured portraits of the heroes of the house of Katzenellenbogen, and the trophies which they had gained in the field and in the chase. Hacked corselets, splintered jousting spears, and tattered banners were mingled with the spoils of sylvan warfare : the jaws of the wolf and the tusks of the boar grinned horribly among crossbows and battle-axes, and a huge pair of antlers branched immediately over the head of the youthful bridegroom.

The cavalier took but little notice of the company or the entertainment. He scarcely tasted the banquet, but seemed absorbed in admiration of his bride. He conversed in a low tone, that could not be overheard—for the language of love is never loud ; but where is the female ear so dull that it cannot catch the softest whisper of the lover ? There was a mingled tenderness and gravity in his manner that appeared to have a powerful effect upon the young lady. Her colour came and went, as she listened with deep attention. Now and then she made some blushing reply, and when his eye was turned away she would steal a sidelong glance at his romantic countenance, and heave a gentle sigh of tender happiness. It was evident that the young couple were completely enamoured. The aunts, who were deeply versed in the mysteries of the heart, declared that they had fallen in love with each other at first sight.

The feast went on merrily, or at least noisily, for the guests were all blessed with those keen appetites that attend upon light purses and mountain air. The Baron told his best and longest stories, and never had he told them so well, or with such great effect. If there was anything marvellous, his auditors were lost in astonishment ; and if anything facetious, they were sure to laugh exactly in the right place. The Baron, it is true, like most great men, was too dignified to utter any joke but a dull one : it was always enforced, however, by a bumper of excellent Hoch-heimer ; and even a dull joke, at one's own table, served up with jolly old wine, is irresistible. Many good things were said by poorer and keener wits that would not bear repeating, except on similar occasions ; many sly speeches whispered in ladies' ears that almost convulsed them with suppressed laughter ; and a song or two roared out by a poor but merry and broad-faced cousin of the Baron, that absolutely made the maiden aunts hold up their fans.

Amid all this revelry, the stranger-guest maintained a most singular and unseasonable gravity. His countenance assumed a deeper cast of dejection as the evening advanced, and, strange as it may appear, even the Baron's jokes seemed only to render him the more melancholy. At times he was lost in thought, and at times there was a perturbed and restless wandering of the eye that bespoke a mind but ill at ease. His conversation with the bride became more and more earnest and mysterious. Lowering clouds began to steal over the fair serenity of her brow, and tremors to run through her tender frame.

All this could not escape the notice of the company. Their gaiety was chilled by the unaccountable gloom of the bridegroom ; their spirits were infected ; whispers and glances were interchanged, accompanied by shrugs and dubious shakes of the head. The song and the laugh grew less and less frequent : there were dreary pauses in the conversation, which were at length succeeded by wild tales and supernatural legends. One dismal story produced another still more dismal, and the Baron nearly frightened some of the ladies into hysterics with the history of the goblin horseman that carried away the fair Leonora—a dreadful, but true story, which has since been put into excellent verse, and is read and believed by all the world.

The bridegroom listened to this tale with profound attention. He kept his eyes steadily fixed on the Baron, and, as the story drew to a close, began gradually to rise from his seat, growing taller and taller, until, in the Baron's entranced eye, he seemed almost to tower into a giant. The moment the tale was finished, he heaved a deep sigh, and took a solemn farewell of the company. They were all amazement. The Baron was perfectly thunderstruck.

What ! going to leave the castle at midnight ? Why, everything was prepared for his reception ; a chamber was ready for him if he wished to retire.

The stranger shook his head mournfully and mysteriously : " I must lay my head in a different chamber to-night ! "

There was something in this reply, and the tone in which it was uttered, that made the Baron's heart misgive him ; but he rallied his forces, and repeated his hospitable entreaties. The stranger shook his head silently, but positively, at every offer ; and, waving his farewell to the company, stalked slowly out of the hall. The maiden aunts were absolutely petrified— the bride hung her head, and a tear stole to her eye.

The Baron followed the stranger to the great court of the

castle, where the black charger stood pawing the earth and snorting with impatience. When they had reached the portal, whose deep archway was dimly lighted by a cresset, the stranger paused, and addressed the Baron in a hollow tone of voice, which the vaulted roof rendered still more sepulchral. " Now that we are alone," said he, " I will impart to you the reason of my going. I have a solemn, an indispensable engagement——"

" Why," said the Baron, " cannot you send some one in your place ? "

" It admits of no substitute—I must attend it in person—I must away to Wurtzburg cathedral——"

" Ay," said the Baron, plucking up spirit, " but not until to-morrow—to-morrow you shall take your bride there."

" No ! no ! " replied the stranger, with tenfold solemnity, " my engagement is with no bride—the worms ! the worms expect me ! I am a dead man—I have been slain by robbers —my body lies at Wurtzburg—at midnight I am to be buried —the grave is waiting for me—I must keep my appointment ! "

He sprang on his black charger, dashed over the drawbridge, and the clattering of his horse's hoofs was lost in the whistling of the night-blast.

The Baron returned to the hall in the utmost consternation, and related what had passed. Two ladies fainted outright ; others sickened at the idea of having banqueted with a spectre. It was the opinion of some that this might be the wild huntsman famous in German legend. Some talked of mountan sprites, of wood-demons, and of other supernatural beings, with which the good people of Germany have been so grievously harassed since time immemorial. One of the poor relations ventured to suggest that it might be some sportive evasion of the young cavalier, and that the very gloominess of the caprice seemed to accord with so melancholy a personage. This, however, drew on him the indignation of the whole company, and especially of the Baron, who looked upon him as little better than an infidel ; so that he was fain to abjure his heresy as speedily as possible, and come into the faith of the true believers.

But, whatever may have been the doubts entertained, they were completely put to an end by the arrival, next day, of regular missives confirming the intelligence of the young Count's murder, and his interment in Wurtzburg cathedral.

The dismay at the castle may well be imagined. The Baron shut himself up in his chamber. The guests who had come to rejoice with him could not think of abandoning him in his distress. They wandered about the courts, or collected in groups in the hall, shaking their heads and shrugging their shoulders at the troubles of so good a man ; and sat longer than ever at table, and ate and drank more stoutly than ever, by way of keeping up their spirits. But the situation of the widowed bride was the most pitiable. To have lost a husband before she had even embraced him—and such a husband ! If the spectre could be so gracious and noble, what must have been the living man ? She filled the house with lamentations.

On the night of the second day of her widowhood, she had retired to her chamber, accompanied by one of her aunts who insisted on sleeping with her. The aunt, who was one of the best tellers of ghost stories in all Germany, had just been recounting one of her longest, and had fallen asleep in the very midst of it. The chamber was remote, and overlooked a small garden. The niece lay pensively gazing at the beams of the rising moon, as they trembled on the leaves of an aspen tree before the lattice. The castle clock had just tolled midnight, when a soft strain of music stole up from the garden. She rose hastily from her bed and stepped lightly to the window. A tall figure stood among the shadows of the trees. As it raised its head, a beam of moonlight fell upon the countenance. Heaven and earth ! She beheld the Spectre Bridegroom ! A loud shriek at that moment burst upon her ear, and her aunt, who had been awakened by the music, and had followed her silently to the window, fell into her arms. When she looked again, the spectre had disappeared.

Of the two females, the aunt now required the most soothing, for she was perfectly beside herself with terror. As to the young lady, there was something, even in the spectre of her lover, that seemed endearing. There was still the semblance of manly beauty ; and though the shadow of a man is but little calculated to satisfy the affections of a lovesick girl, yet, where the substance is not to be had, even that is consoling. The aunt declared that she would never sleep in that chamber again ; the niece, for once, was refractory, and declared as strongly that she would sleep in no other in the castle : the consequence was that she had to sleep in it alone ; but she drew a promise from her aunt not to relate the story of the spectre, lest she should be denied the only melancholy pleasure left her on earth—that of inhabiting the chamber over which the guardian shade of her lover kept its nightly vigils.

How long the good old lady would have observed this promise is uncertain, for she dearly loved to talk of the marvellous, and there is a triumph in being the first to tell a frightful story; it is, however, still quoted in the neighbourhood, as a memorable instance of female secrecy, that she kept it to herself for a whole week; when she was suddenly absolved from all further restraint by intelligence brought to the breakfast-table one morning that the young lady was not to be found. Her room was empty—the bed had not been slept in—the window was open—and the bird had flown!

The astonishment and concern with which the intelligence was received can only be imagined by those who have witnessed the agitation which the mishaps of a great man cause among his friends. Even the poor relations · paused for a moment from the indefatigable labours of the trencher; when the aunt, who had at first been struck speechless, wrung her hands and shrieked out, " The goblin! the goblin! She's carried away by the goblin!"

In a few words she related the fearful scene of the garden, and concluded that the spectre must have carried off his bride. Two of the domestics corroborated the opinion, for they had heard the clattering of a horse's hoofs down the mountain about midnight, and had no doubt that it was the spectre on his black charger, bearing her away to the tomb. All present were struck with the direful probability; for events of the kind are extremely common in Germany, as many well-authenticated histories bear witness.

What a lamentable situation was that of the poor Baron! What a heartrending dilemma for a fond father, and a member of the great family of Katzenellenbogen! His only daughter had either been rapt away to the grave, or he was to have some wood-demon for a son-in-law, and, perchance, a troop of goblin grandchildren. As usual, he was completely bewildered, and all the castle in an uproar. The men were ordered to take horse and scour every road and path and glen of the Odenwald. The Baron himself had just drawn on his jack-boots, girded on his sword, and was about to mount his steed to sally forth on the doubtful quest, when he was brought to a pause by a new apparition. A lady was seen approaching the castle, mounted on a palfrey attended by a cavalier on horseback. She galloped up to the gate, sprang from her horse, and falling at the Baron's feet, embraced his knees. It was his lost daughter, and her companion—the Spectre Bridegroom ! The Baron was astounded. He looked at his daughter, then at the spectre, and almost doubted the evidence of his senses. The latter, too, was wonderfully improved in his appearance, since his visit to the world of spirits. His dress was splendid, and set off a noble figure of manly symmetry. He was no longer pale and melancholy. His fine countenance was flushed with the glow of youth, and joy rioted in his large dark eye.

The mystery was soon cleared up. The cavalier (for, in truth, as you must have known all the while, he was no goblin) announced himself as Sir Herman Von Starkenfaust. He related his adventure with the young Count. He told how he had hastened to the castle to deliver the unwelcome tidings, but that the eloquence of the Baron had interrupted him in every attempt to tell his tale. How the sight of the bride had completely captivated him, and that to pass a few hours near her had tacitly suffered the mistake to continue. How he had been sorely perplexed in what way to make a decent retreat, until the Baron's goblin stories had suggested his eccentric exit. How, fearing the feudal hostility of the family, he had repeated his visits by stealth—had haunted the garden beneath the young lady's window—had wooed—had won— had borne away in triumph—and, in a word, had wedded the fair.

Under any other circumstances the Baron would have been inflexible, for he was tenacious of paternal authority and devoutly obstinate in all family feuds ; but he loved his daughter ; he had lamented her as lost ; he rejoiced to find her still alive ; and, though her husband was of a hostile house, yet, thank Heaven, he was not a goblin. There was something, it must be acknowledged, that did not exactly accord with his notions of strict veracity, in the joke the knight had passed upon him of his being a dead man ; but several old friends present, who had served in the wars, assured him that every stratagem was excusable in love, and that the cavalier was entitled to especial privilege, having lately served as a trooper.

Matters, therefore, were happily arranged. The Baron pardoned the young couple on the spot. The revels at the castle were resumed. The poor relations overwhelmed this new member of the family with loving-kindness ; he was so gallant, so generous—and so rich. The aunts, it is true, were somewhat scandalised that their system of strict seclusion and passive obedience should be so badly exemplified, but attributed all to their negligence in not having the windows grated. One of them was particularly mortified at having her marvellous story marred, and that the only spectre she had ever seen should turn out a counterfeit ; but the niece seemed perfectly happy at having found him substantial flesh and blood—and so the story ends.

THE FACTS IN THE CASE
OF M. VALDEMAR

OF course I shall not pretend to consider it any matter for wonder, that the extraordinary case of M. Valdemar has excited discussion. It would have been a miracle had it not—especially under the circumstances. Through the desire of all parties concerned to keep the affair from the public, at least for the present, or until we had further opportunities for investigation ; through our endeavours to effect this, a garbled or exaggerated account made its way into society, and became the source of many unpleasant misrepresentations, and, very naturally, of a great deal of disbelief.

It is now rendered necessary that I give the *facts*—as far as I comprehend them myself. They are, succinctly, these :

My attention, for the last three years, had been repeatedly drawn to the subject of Mesmerism ; and, about nine months ago, it occurred to me, quite suddenly, that in the series of experiments made hitherto, there had been a very remarkable and most unaccountable omission—no person had as yet been mermerised *in articulo mortis*. It remained to be seen, first, whether in such condition, there existed in the patient any susceptibility to the magnetic influence ; secondly, whether, if any existed, it was impaired or increased by the condition ; thirdly, to what extent, or for how long a period, the encroachments of death might be arrested by the process. There were other points to be ascertained, but these most excited my curiosity—the last in especial, from the immensely important character of its consequences.

In looking around me for some subject by whose means I might test these particulars, I was brought to think of my friend, M. Ernest Valdemar, the well-known compiler of the *Bibliotheca Forensica*, and author (under the *nom de plume* of

Issachar Marx) of the Polish versions of *Wallenstein* and *Gargantua*. M. Valdemar, who has resided principally at Harlem, N.Y., since the year 1839, is (or was) particularly noticeable for the extreme spareness of his person—his lower limbs much resembling those of John Randolph ; and, also for the whiteness of his whiskers, in violent contrast to the blackness of his hair— the latter, in consequence, being very generally mistaken for a wig. His temperament was markedly nervous, and rendered him a good subject for mesmeric experiment. On two or three occasions I had put him to sleep with little difficulty, but was disappointed in other results which his peculiar constitution had naturally led me to anticipate. His will was at no period positively, or thoroughly, under my control, and in regard to *clairvoyance*, I could accomplish with him nothing to be relied upon. I always attributed my failure at these points to the disordered state of his health. For some months previous to my becoming acquainted with him, his physicians had declared him in a confirmed phthisis. It was his custom, indeed, to speak calmly of his approaching dissolution, as of a matter neither to be avoided nor regretted.

When the ideas to which I have alluded first occurred to me, it was of course very natural that I should think of M. Valdemar. I knew the steady philosophy of the man too well to apprehend any scruples from *him* ; and he had no relatives in America who would be likely to interfere. I spoke to him frankly upon the subject, and, to my surprise, his interest seemed vividly excited. I say to my surprise, for, although he had always yielded his person freely to my experiments, he had never before given me any tokens of sympathy with what I did. His disease was of that character which would admit of exact calculation in respect to the epoch of its termination in death ; and it was finally arranged between us that he would send for me about twenty-four hours before the period announced by his physicians as that of his decease.

It is now rather more than seven months since I received, from M. Valdemar himself, the subjoined note :

" *My Dear P——,—You may as well come now. D—— and F—— are agreed that I cannot hold out beyond to-morrow midnight ; and I think they have hit the time very nearly.*"

" Valdemar."

I received this note within half an hour after it was written, and in fifteen minutes more I was in the dying man's chamber.

I had not seen him for ten days, and was appalled by the fearful alteration which the brief interval had wrought in him. His face wore a leaden hue ; the eyes were utterly lustreless ; and the emaciation was so extreme that the skin had been broken through by the cheek-bones. His expectoration was excessive. The pulse was barely perceptible. He retained, nevertheless, in a very remarkable manner, both his mental power and a certain degree of physical strength. He spoke with distinctness, took some palliative medicines without aid, and, when I entered the room, was occupied in pencilling memoranda in a pocket-book. He was propped up in the bed by pillows. Doctors D—— and F—— were in attendance.

After pressing Valdemar's hand, I took these gentlemen aside, and obtained from them a minute account of the patient's condition. The left lung had been for eighteen months in a semi-osseous or cartilaginous state, and was, of course, entirely useless for all purposes of vitality. The right, in its upper portion, was also partially, if not thoroughly, ossified, while the lower region was merely a mass of purulent tubercles, running one into another. Several extensive perforations existed ; and, at one point, permanent adhesion to the ribs had taken place. These appearances in the right lobe were of comparatively recent date. The ossification had proceeded with very unusual rapidity ; no sign of it had been discovered a month before, and the adhesion had only been observed during the three previous days. Independently of the phthisis, the patient was suspected of aneurism of the aorta ; but on this point the osseous symptoms rendered an exact diagnosis impossible. It was the opinion of both physicians that M. Valdemar would die about midnight on the morrow (Sunday). It was then seven o'clock on Saturday evening.

On quitting the invalid's bedside to hold conversation with myself, Doctors D—— and F—— had bidden him a final farewell. It had not been their intention to return ; but, at my request, they agreed to look in upon the patient about ten the next night.

When they had gone, I spoke freely with M. Valdemar on the subject of his approaching dissolution, as well as, more particularly, of the experiment proposed. He still professed himself quite willing and even anxious to have it made, and urged me to commence it at once. A male and a female nurse were in attendance ; but I did not feel myself altogether at liberty to engage in a task of this character with no more reliable witnesses than these people, in case a sudden accident might happen. I therefore postponed operations until about eight the next night, when the arrival of a medical student with whom I had some acquaintance (Mr. Theodore L——l), relieved me from further embarrassment. It had been my design, originally, to wait for the physicians ; but I was induced to proceed, first, by the urgent entreaties of M. Valdemar, and secondly, by my conviction that I had not a moment to lose, as he was evidently sinking fast.

Mr. L——l was so kind as to accede to my desire that he would take notes of all that occurred ; and it is from his memoranda that what I now have to relate is, for the most part, either condensed or copied *verbatim*.

It wanted about five minutes of eight when, taking the patient's hand, I begged him to state, as distinctly as he could, to Mr. L——l, whether he (M. Valdemar) was entirely willing that I should make the experiment of mesmerising him in his then condition.

He replied feebly, yet quite audibly, " Yes, I wish to be mesmerised," adding immediately afterwards, " I fear you have deferred it too long."

While he spoke thus, I commenced the passes which I had already found most effectual in subduing him. He was evidently influenced with the first lateral stroke of my hand across his forehead ; but although I exerted all my powers, no further perceptible effect was induced until some minutes after ten o'clock, when Doctors D—— and F—— called, according to appointment. I explained to them, in a few words, what I designed, and as they opposed no objection, saying that the patient was already in the death agony, I proceeded without hesitation—exchanging, however, the lateral passes for downward ones, and directing my gaze entirely into the right eye of the sufferer.

By this time his pulse was imperceptible and his breathing was stertorous, and at intervals of half a minute.

This condition was nearly unaltered for a quarter of an hour. At the expiration of this period, however, a natural although a very deep sigh escaped the bosom of the dying man, and the stertorous breathing ceased—that is to say, its stertorousness was no longer apparent ; the intervals were undiminished. The patient's extremities were of an icy coldness.

At five minutes before eleven I perceived unequivocal signs of the mesmeric influence. The glassy roll of the eye was changed for that expression of uneasy *inward* examination which is never seen except in cases of sleep-waking, and which it is quite impossible to mistake. With a few rapid lateral passes I made the lids quiver, as in incipient sleep, and with a few more I closed them altogether. I was not satisfied, however, with this, but continued the manipulations vigorously, and with the fullest exertion of the will, until I had completely stiffened the limbs of the slumberer, after placing them in a seemingly easy position. The legs were at full length ; the arms were nearly so, and reposed on the bed at a moderate distance from the loins. The head was very slightly elevated.

When I had accomplished this it was fully midnight, and I requested the gentlemen present to examine M. Valdemar's condition. After a few experiments, they admitted him to an unusually perfect state of mesmeric trance. The curiosity of both the physicians was greatly excited. Dr. D—— resolved at once to remain with the patient all night, while Dr. F—— took leave with a promise to return at daybreak. Mr. L——l and the nurses remained.

We left Mr. Valdemar entirely undisturbed until, about three o'clock in the morning, when I approached him and found him in precisely the same condition as when Dr. F—— went away— that is to say, he lay in the same position ; the pulse was imperceptible ; the breathing was gentle (scarcely noticeable, unless through the application of a mirror to the lips) ; the eyes were closed naturally ; and the limbs were as rigid and as cold as marble. Still, the general appearance was certainly not that of death.

As I approached M. Valdemar I made a kind of half-effort to influence his right arm into pursuit of my own, as I passed the latter gently to and fro above his person. In such experiments with this patient I had never perfectly succeeded before, and assuredly I had little thought of succeeding now ; but to my astonishment his arm very readily, although feebly, followed every direction I assigned it with mine. I determined to hazard a few words of conversation.

" M. Valdemar," I said, "are you asleep ? " He made no answer, but I perceived a tremor about the lips, and was thus induced to repeat the question again and again. At its third repetition, his whole frame was agitated by a very slight shivering; the eyelids unclosed themselves so far as to display a white line of a ball ; the lips moved sluggishly, and from between them, in a barely audible whisper, issued the words :

" Yes ; asleep now. Do not wake me ! Let me die so ! "

I here felt the limbs and found them rigid as ever. The right arm, as before, obeyed the direction of my hand. I questioned the sleep-waker again :

" Do you still feel pain in the breast, M. Valdemar ? "

The answer now was immediate, but even less audible than before.

" No pain—I am dying."

I did not think it advisable to disturb him further just then, and nothing more was said or done until the arrival of Dr. F——, who came a little before sunrise, and expressed unbounded astonishment at finding the patient still alive. After feeling the pulse and applying a mirror to the lips, he requested me to speak to the sleep-waker again. I did so, saying :

" M. Valdemar, do you still sleep ? "

As before, some minutes elapsed ere a reply was made ; and during the interval the dying man seemed to be collecting his energies to speak. At my fourth repetition of the question, he said very faintly, almost inaudibly :

" Yes ; still asleep—dying."

It was not the opinion, or rather the wish, of the physicians, that M. Valdemar should be suffered to remain undisturbed in his present apparently tranquil condition, until death should supervene ; and this it was generally agreed, must now take place within a few minutes. I concluded, however, to speak to him once more, and merely repeated my previous question.

While I spoke, there came a marked change over the countenance of the sleep-waker. The eyes rolled themselves slowly open, the pupils disappearing upwardly ; the skin generally assumed a cadaverous hue, resembling not so much parchment as white paper ; and the circular hectic spots which, hitherto, had been strongly defined to the centre of each cheek, *went out* at once. I use this expression, because the suddenness of their departure put me in mind of nothing so much as the extinguishment of a candle by a puff of the breath. The upper lip, at the same time, writhed itself away from the teeth, which it had previously covered completely ; while the lower jaw fell with an audible jerk, leaving the mouth widely extended, and disclosing in full view the swollen and blackened tongue. I presume that no member of the party then present had been unaccustomed to death-bed horrors ; but so hideous beyond conception was the appearance of M. Valdemar at this moment, that there was a general shrinking back from the region of the bed.

I now feel that I have reached a point of this narrative at which every reader will be startled into positive disbelief. It is my business, however, simply to proceed.

There was no longer the faintest sign of vitality in M. Valdemar ; and, concluding him to be dead, we were consigning him to the charge of the nurses, when a strong vibratory motion was observable in the tongue. This continued for perhaps a minute. At the expiration of this period, there issued from the distended and motionless jaws a voice—such as it would be madness in me to attempt describing. There are, indeed, two or three epithets which might be considered as applicable to it in parts. I might say, for example, that the sound was harsh, and broken, and hollow ; but the hideous whole is indescribable, for the simple reason that no similar sounds have ever jarred upon the ear of humanity. There were two particulars, nevertheless, which I thought then, and still think, might fairly be stated as characteristic of the intonation—as well adapted to convey some idea of its unearthly peculiarity. In the first place, the voice seemed to reach our ears—at least mine—from a vast distance, or from some deep cavern within the earth. In the second place, it impressed me (I fear, indeed, that it will be impossible to make myself comprehended) as gelatinous or glutinous matters impress the sense of touch.

" I have spoken both of " sound " and of " voice." I mean to say that the sound was one of distinct—of even wonderfully, thrillingly distinct—syllabification. M. Valdemar *spoke*—obviously in reply to the question I had propounded to him a few minutes before. I had asked him, it will be remembered, if he still slept. He now said :

" Yes ; no ; I *have been* sleeping—and now—now—*I am dead.*"

No person present even affected to deny, or attempted to repress, the unutterable, shuddering horror which these few words, thus uttered, were so well calculated to convey. Mr. L——l (the student) swooned. The nurses immediately left the chamber, and could not be induced to return. My own impressions I would not pretend to render intelligible to the reader. For nearly an hour, we busied ourselves, silently—without the utterance of a word—in endeavours to revive Mr. L——l. When he came to himself, we addressed ourselves again to an investigation of Mr. Valdemar's condition.

It remained in all respects as I have last described it, with the exception that the mirror no longer afforded evidence of

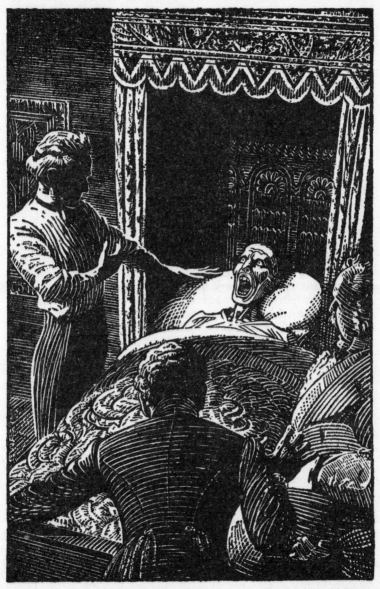

"*Yes ; no ; I have been sleeping—and now—now—I am dead.*"

respiration. An attempt to draw blood from the arm failed. I should mention, too, that this limb was no further subject to my will. I endeavoured in vain to make it follow the direction of my hand. The only real indication, indeed, of the mesmeric influence, was now found in the vibratory movement of the tongue, whenever I addressed M. Valdemar a question. He seemed to be making an effort to reply, but had no longer sufficient volition. To queries put to him by any other person than myself he seemed utterly insensible—although I endeavoured to place each member of the company in mesmeric *rapport* with him. I believe that I have now related all that is necessary to an understanding of the sleep-waker's state at this epoch. Other nurses were procured ; and at ten o'clock I left the house in company with the two physicians and Mr. L——l.

In the afternoon we all called again to see the patient. His condition remained precisely the same. We had now some discussion as to the propriety and feasibility of awakening him ; but we had little difficulty in agreeing that no good purpose would be served by so doing. It was evident that, so far, death (or what is usually termed death) had been arrested by the mesmeric process. It seemed clear to us all that to awaken M. Valdemar would be merely to ensure his instant, or at least his speedy dissolution.

From this period until the close of last week—*an interval of nearly seven months*—we continued to make daily calls at M. Valdemar's house, accompanied, now and then, by medical and other friends. All this time the sleep-waker remained *exactly* as I have last described him. The nurses' attentions were continual.

It was on Friday last that we finally resolved to make the experiment of awakening, or attempting to awaken him ; and it is the (perhaps) unfortunate result of this latter experiment which has given rise to so much discussion in private circles— to so much of what I cannot help thinking unwarranted popular feeling.

For the purpose of relieving M. Valdemar from the mesmeric trace, I made use of the customary passes. These, for a time, were unsuccessful. The first indication of revival was afforded by a partial descent of the iris. It was observed, as especially remarkable, that this lowering of the pupil was accompanied by the profuse outflowing of a yellowish ichor (from beneath the lids) of a pungent and highly offensive odour.

It was now suggested that I should attempt to influence the patient's arm, as heretofore. I made the attempt and failed.

Dr. F—— then intimated a desire to have me put a question. I did so, as follows :

" M. Valdemar, can you explain to us what are your feelings or wishes now ? "

There was an instant return of the hectic circles on the cheeks ; the tongue quivered, or rather rolled violently in the mouth (although the jaws and lips remained rigid as before) ; and at length the same hideous voice which I have already described, broke forth :

" For God's sake !—quick !—quick !—put me to sleep—or, quick !—waken me !—quick !—*I say to you that I am dead !* "

I was thoroughly unnerved, and for an instant remained undecided what to do. At first I made an endeavour to re-compose the patient ; but, failing in this through total abeyance of the will, I retraced my steps and as earnestly struggled to awaken him. In this attempt I soon saw that I should be successful—or at least I soon fancied that my success would be complete—and I am sure that all in the room were prepared to see the patient awaken.

For what really occurred, however, it is quite impossible that any human being could have been prepared.

As I rapidly made the mesmeric passes, amid ejaculations of " dead ! dead ! " absolutely *bursting* from the tongue and not from the lips of the sufferer, his whole frame at once—within the space of a single minute, or even less, shrunk—crumbled—absolutely *rotted* away beneath my hands. Upon the bed, before that whole company, there lay a nearly liquid mass of loathsome —of detestable putridity.

THE TARN

A s Foster moved unconsciously across the room, bent
towards the bookcase, and stood leaning forward a little,
choosing now one book, now another, with his eyes, his
host, seeing the muscles of the back of his thin, scraggy neck
stand out above his low flannel collar, thought of the ease with
which he could squeeze that throat, and the pleasure, the
triumphant, lustful pleasure, that such an action would give
him.

The low, white-walled, white-ceilinged room was flooded
with the mellow, kindly Lakeland sun. October is a wonderful
month in the English Lakes, golden, rich, and perfumed, slow
suns moving through apricot-tinted skies to ruby evening
glories ; the shadows lie then thick about that beautiful country,
in dark purple patches, in long web-like patterns of silver gauze,
in thick splotches of amber and grey. The clouds pass in galleons
across the mountains, now veiling, now revealing, now descending with ghost-like armies to the very breast of the plains,
suddenly rising to the softest of blue skies and lying thin in lazy
languorous colour.

Fenwick's cottage looked across to Low Fells ; on his right,
seen through side windows, sprawled the hills above Ullswater.

Fenwick looked at Foster's back and felt suddenly sick, so
that he sat down, veiling his eyes for a moment with his hand.
Foster had come up there, come all the way from London, to
explain. It was so like Foster to want to explain, to want to
put things right. For how many years had he known Foster ?
Why, for twenty at least, and during all those years Foster
had been for ever determined to put things right with everybody. He could never bear to be disliked ; he hated that

any one should think ill of him ; he wanted every one to be his friends. That was one reason, perhaps, why Foster had got on so well, had prospered so in his career ; one reason, too, why Fenwick had not.

For Fenwick was the opposite of Foster in this. He did not want friends, he certainly did not care that people should like him—that is people for whom, for one reason or another, he had contempt—and he had contempt for quite a number of people.

Fenwick looked at that long, thin, bending back and felt his knees tremble. Soon Foster would turn round and that high, reedy voice would pipe out something about the books. "What jolly books you have, Fenwick!" How many, many times in the long watches of the night, when Fenwick could not sleep, had he heard that pipe sounding close there—yes, in the very shadows of his bed! And how many times had Fenwick replied to it : "I hate you! You are the cause of my failure in life! You have been in my way always. Always, always, always! Patronising and pretending, and in truth showing others what a poor thing you thought me, how great a failure, how conceited a fool! I know. You can hide nothing from me! I can hear you!"

For twenty years now Foster had been persistently in Fenwick's way. There had been that affair, so long ago now, when Robins had wanted a sub-editor for his wonderful review, the *Parthenon*, and Fenwick had gone to see him and they had had a splendid talk. How magnificently Fenwick had talked that day ; with what enthusiasm he had shown Robins (who was blinded by his own conceit, anyway) the kind of paper the *Parthenon* might be ; how Robins had caught his own enthusiasm, how he had pushed his fat body about the room, crying : "Yes, yes, Fenwick—that's fine! That's fine indeed!"—and then how, after all, Foster had got that job.

The paper had only lived for a year or so, it is true, but the connection with it had brought Foster into prominence just as it might have brought Fenwick!

Then, five years later, there was Fenwick's novel, *The Bitter Aloe*—the novel upon which he had spent three years of blood-and-tears endeavour—and then, in the very same week of publication, Foster brings out *The Circus*, the novel that made his name ; although, Heaven knows, the thing was poor enough sentimental trash. You may say that one novel cannot kill another—but can it not? Had not *The Circus* appeared would not that group of London know-alls—that conceited, limited, ignorant, self-satisfied crowd, who nevertheless can do, by their talk, so much to affect a book's good or evil fortunes—have talked about *The Bitter Aloe* and so forced it into prominence? As it was, the book was still-born and *The Circus* went on its prancing, triumphant way.

After that there had been many occasions—some small, some big—and always in one way or another that thin, scraggy body of Foster's was interfering with Fenwick's happiness.

The thing had become, of course, an obsession with Fenwick. Hiding up there in the heart of the Lakes, with no friends, almost no company, and very little money, he was given too much to brooding over his failure. He *was* a failure and it was not his own fault. How could it be his own fault with his talents and his brilliance? It was the fault of modern life and its lack of culture, the fault of the stupid material mess that made up the intelligence of human beings—and the fault of Foster.

Always Fenwick hoped that Foster would keep away from him. He did not know what he would not do did he see the man. And then one day, to his amazement, he received a telegram :

Passing through this way. May I stop with you Monday and Tuesday?—Giles Foster.

Fenwick could scarcely believe his eyes, and then—from curiosity, from cynical contempt, from some deeper, more mysterious motive that he dared not analyse—he had telegraphed —*Come.*

And here the man was. And he had come—would you believe it?—to " put things right." He had heard from Hamlin Eddis that Fenwick was hurt with him, had some kind of grievance.

" I didn't like to feel that, old man, and so I thought I'd just stop by and have it out with you, see what the matter was, and put it right."

Last night after supper Foster had tried to put it right. Eagerly, his eyes like a good dog's who is asking for a bone that he knows he thoroughly deserves, he had held out his hand and asked Fenwick to " say what was up."

Fenwick simply had said that nothing was up ; Hamlin Eddis was a damned fool.

" Oh, I'm glad to hear that ! " Foster had cried, springing up out of his chair and putting his hand on Fenwick's shoulder.

" I'm glad of that, old man. I couldn't bear for us not to
be friends. We've been friends so long."

Lord ! How Fenwick hated him at that moment !

II

" WHAT a jolly lot of books you have ! " Foster turned round
and looked at Fenwick with eager, gratified eyes. " Every book
here is interesting ! I like your arrangement of them, too, and
those open bookshelves—it always seems to me a shame to shut
up books behind glass ! "

Foster came forward and sat down quite close to his host.
He even reached forward and laid his hand on his host's knee.
" Look here ! I'm mentioning it for the last time—positively !
But I do want to make quite certain. There is nothing wrong
between us, is there, old man ? I know you assured me last
night, but I just want . . ."

Fenwick looked at him and, surveying him, felt suddenly
an exquisite pleasure of hatred. He liked the touch of the
man's hand on his knee ; he himself bent forward a little and,
thinking how agreeable it would be to push Foster's eyes in,
deep, deep into his head, crunching them, smashing them to
purple, leaving the empty, staring bloody sockets, said :

" Why, no. Of course not. I told you last night. What
could there be ? "

The hand gripped the knee a little more tightly.

" I am so glad ! That's splendid ! Splendid ! I hope you
won't think me ridiculous, but I've always had an affection for
you ever since I can remember. I've always wanted to know
you better. I've admired your talent so greatly. That novel of
yours—the—the—the one about the aloe——"

" The Bitter Aloe ? "

" Ah, yes, that was it. That was a splendid book. Pessimistic,
of course, but still fine. It ought to have done better. I remember thinking so at the time."

" Yes, it ought to have done better."

" Your time will come, though. What I say is that good
work always tells in the end."

" Yes, my time will come."

The thin, piping voice went on :

" Now, I've had more success than I deserved. Oh, yes, I

have. You can't deny it. I'm not falsely modest. I mean it. I've got some talent, of course, but not so much as people say. And you ! Why, you've got so *much* more than they acknowledge. You have, old man. You have indeed. Only—I do hope you'll forgive my saying this—perhaps you haven't advanced quite as you might have done. Living up here, shut away here, closed in by all these mountains, in this wet climate—always raining— why, you're out of things ! You don't see people, don't talk and discover what's really going on. Why, look at me ! "

Fenwick turned round and looked at him.

" Now, I have half the year in London, where one gets the best of everything, best talk, best music, best plays ; and then I'm three months abroad, Italy or Greece or somewhere, and then three months in the country. Now, that's an ideal arrange- ment. You have everything that way."

Italy or Greece or somewhere !

Something turned in Fenwick's breast, grinding, grinding, grinding. How he had longed, oh, how passionately, for just one week in Greece, two days in Sicily ! Sometimes he had thought that he might run to it, but when it had come to the actual counting of the pennies . . . And how this fool, this fat-head, this self-satisfied, conceited, patronising . . .

He got up, looking out at the golden sun.

" What do you say to a walk ? " he suggested. " The sun will last for a good hour yet."

III

As soon as the words were out of his lips he felt as though some one else had said them for him. He even turned half-round to see whether any one else were there. Ever since Foster's arrival on the evening before he had been conscious of this sensation. A walk ? Why should he take Foster for a walk, show him his beloved country, point out those curves and lines and hollows, the broad silver shield of Ullswater, the cloudy purple hills hunched like blankets about the knees of some recumbent giant ? Why ? It was as though he had turned round to some one behind him, and had said : " You have some further design in this."

They started out. The road sank abruptly to the lake, then the path ran between trees at the water's edge. Across the lake tones of bright yellow light, crocus-hued, rode upon the blue. The hills were dark.

The very way that Foster walked bespoke the man. He was always a little ahead of you, pushing his long, thin body along with little eager jerks, as though, did he not hurry, he would miss something that would be immensely to his advantage. He talked, throwing words over his shoulder to Fenwick as you throw crumbs of bread to a robin.

" Of course I was pleased. Who would not be ? After all, it's a new prize. They've only been awarding it for a year or two, but it's gratifying—really gratifying—to secure it. When I opened the envelope and found the cheque there—well, you could have knocked me down with a feather. You could, indeed. Of course, a hundred pounds isn't much. But it's the honour. . . ."

Whither were they going ? Their destiny was as certain as though they had no free will. Free will ? There is no free will. All is Fate. Fenwick suddenly laughed aloud.

Foster stopped.

" Why, what is it ? "

" What's what ? "

" You laughed."

" Something amused me."

Foster slipped his arm through Fenwick's.

" It *is* jolly to be walking along together like this, arm in arm, friends. I'm a sentimental man. I won't deny it. What I say is that life is short and one must love one's fellow-beings, or where is one ? You live too much alone, old man." He squeezed Fenwick's arm. " That's the truth of it."

It was torture, exquisite, heavenly torture. It was wonderful to feel that thin, bony arm pressing against his. Almost you could hear the beating of that other heart. Wonderful to feel that arm and the temptation to take it in your hands and to bend it and twist it and then to hear the bones crack . . . crack . . . crack. . . . Wonderful to feel that temptation rise through one's body like boiling water and yet not to yield to it. For a moment Fenwick's hand touched Foster's. Then he drew himself apart.

" We're at the village. This is the hotel where they all come in the summer. We turn off at the right here. I'll show you my tarn."

IV

" YOUR tarn ? " asked Foster. " Forgive my ignorance, but
what *is* a tarn exactly ? "

" A tarn is a miniature lake, a pool of water lying in the lap
of the hill. Very quiet, lovely, silent. Some of them are immensely deep."

" I should like to see that."

" It is some little distance—up a rough road. Do you
mind ? "

" Not a bit. I have long legs."

" Some of them are immensely deep—unfathomable—
nobody touched the bottom—but quiet, like glass, with
shadows only——"

" Do you know, Fenwick, I have always been afraid of water
—I've never learnt to swim. I'm afraid to go out of my depth.
Isn't that ridiculous ? But it is all because at my private school,
years ago, when I was a small boy, some big fellows took me
and held me with my head under the water and nearly drowned
me. They did indeed. They went farther than they meant to.
I can see their faces."

Fenwick considered this. The picture leapt to his mind.
He could see the boys—large, strong fellows, probably—and this
skinny thing like a frog, their thick hands about his throat, his
legs like grey sticks kicking out of the water, their laughter,
their sudden sense that something was wrong, the skinny body
all flaccid and still. . . .

He drew a deep breath.

Foster was walking beside him now, not ahead of him, as
though he were a little afraid and needed reassurance. Indeed,
the scene had changed. Before and behind them stretched the
uphill path, loose with shale and stones. On their right, on a
ridge at the foot of the hill, were some quarries, almost deserted,
but the more melancholy in the fading afternoon because a
little work still continued there ; faint sounds came from the
gaunt listening chimneys, a stream of water ran and tumbled
angrily into a pool below, once and again a black silhouette,
like a question-mark, appeared against the darkening hill.

It was a little steep here, and Foster puffed and blew.

Fenwick hated him the more for that. So thin and spare
and still he could not keep in condition ! They stumbled,
keeping below the quarry, on the edge of the running water,

now green, now a dirty white-grey, pushing their way along
the side of the hill.

Their faces were set now towards Helvellyn. It rounded the
cup of hills, closing in the base and then sprawling to the right.

" There's the tarn ! " Fenwick exclaimed ; and then added,
" The sun's not lasting as long as I had expected. It's growing
dark already."

Foster stumbled and caught Fenwick's arm.

" This twilight makes the hills look strange—like living men.
I can scarcely see my way."

" We're alone here," Fenwick answered. " Don't you feel
the stillness ? The men will have left the quarry now and gone
home. There is no one in all this place but ourselves. If you
watch you will see a strange green light steal down over the hills.
It lasts for but a moment and then it is dark.

" Ah, here is my tarn. Do you know how I love this place,
Foster ? It seems to belong especially to me, just as much as
all your work and your glory and fame and success seem to
belong to you. I have this and you have that. Perhaps in the
end we are even, after all. Yes. . . .

" But I feel as though that piece of water belonged to me
and I to it, and as though we should never be separated—yes.
. . . Isn't it black ?

" It is one of the deep ones. No one has ever sounded it.
Only Helvellyn knows, and one day I fancy that it will take
me, too, into its confidence, will whisper its secrets——"

Foster sneezed.

" Very nice. Very beautiful, Fenwick. I like your tarn.
Charming. And now let's turn back. That is a difficult walk
beneath the quarry. It's chilly, too."

" Do you see that little jetty there ? " Fenwick led Foster
by the arm. " Some one built that out into the water. He
had a boat there, I suppose. Come and look down. From
the end of the little jetty it looks so deep and the mountains
seem to close round."

Fenwick took Foster's arm and led him to the end of the
jetty. Indeed, the water looked deep here. Deep and very
black. Foster peered down, then he looked up at the hills.
that did indeed seem to have gathered close around him. He
sneezed again.

" I've caught a cold, I am afraid. Let's turn homewards,
Fenwick, or we shall never find our way."

" Home, then," said Fenwick, and his hands closed about

the thin, scraggy neck. For the instant the head half-turned, and two startled, strangely childish eyes stared ; then, with a push that was ludicrously simple, the body was impelled forward, there was a sharp cry, a splash, a stir of something white against the swiftly gathering dusk, again and then again, then far-spreading ripples, then silence.

V

THE silence extended. Having enwrapped the tarn, it spread as though with finger on lip to the already quiescent hills. Fenwick shared in the silence. He luxuriated in it. He did not move at all. He stood there looking upon the inky water of the tarn, his arms folded, a man lost in intensest thought. But he was not thinking. He was only conscious of a warm, luxurious relief, a sensuous feeling that was not thought at all.

Foster was gone—that tiresome, prating, conceited, self-satisfied fool ! Gone, never to return. The tarn assured him of that. It stared back into Fenwick's face approvingly as though it said : " You have done well—a clean and necessary job. We have done it together, you and I. I am proud of you."

He was proud of himself. At last he had done something definite with his life. Thought, eager, active thought, was beginning now to flood his brain. For all these years he had hung around in this place doing nothing but cherish grievances, weak, backboneless—now at last there was action. He drew himself up and looked at the hills. He was proud—and he was cold. He was shivering. He turned up the collar of his coat. Yes, there was that faint green light that always lingered in the shadows of the hills for a brief moment before darkness came. It was growing late. He had better return.

Shivering now so that his teeth chattered, he started off down the path, and then was aware that he did not wish to leave the tarn. The tarn was friendly—the only friend he had in all the world. As he stumbled along in the dark this sense of loneliness grew. He was going home to an empty house. There had been a guest in it last night. Who was it ? Why, Foster, of course—Foster with his silly laugh and amiable, mediocre eyes. Well, Foster would not be there now. No, he never would be there again.

And suddenly Fenwick started to run. He did not know

why, except that, now that he had left the tarn, he was lonely.
He wished that he could have stayed there all night, but because
it was cold he could not, and so now he was running so that
he might be at home with the lights and the familiar furniture
—and all the things that he knew to reassure him.

As he ran the shale and stones scattered beneath his feet.
They made a tit-tattering noise under him, and some one else
seemed to be running too. He stopped, and the other runner
also stopped. He breathed in the silence. He was hot now.
The perspiration was trickling down his cheeks. He could feel
a dribble of it down his back inside his shirt. His knees were
pounding. His heart was thumping. And all around him the
hills were so amazingly silent, now like india-rubber clouds
that you could push in or pull out as you do those indiarubber
faces, grey against the night sky of a crystal purple, upon whose
surface, like the twinkling eyes of boats at sea, stars were now
appearing.

His knees steadied, his heart beat less fiercely, and he began
to run again. Suddenly he had turned the corner and was out
at the hotel. Its lamps were kindly and reassuring. He walked
then quietly along the lakeside path, and had it not been for
the certainty that some one was treading behind him he would
have been comfortable and at his ease. He stopped once or
twice and looked back, and once he stopped and called out,
" Who's there ? " Only the rustling trees answered.

He had the strangest fancy, but his brain was throbbing
so fiercely that he could not think, that it was the tarn that was
following him, the tarn slipping, sliding along the road, being
with him so that he should not be lonely. He could almost hear
the tarn whisper in his ear : " We did that together, and so I
do not wish you to bear all the responsibility yourself. I will
stay with you, so that you are not lonely."

He climbed down the road towards home, and there were
the lights of his house. He heard the gate click behind him
as though it were shutting him in. He went into the sitting-
room, lighted and ready. There were the books that Foster
had admired.

The old woman who looked after him appeared.

" Will you be having some tea, sir ? "

" No, thank you, Annie."

" Will the other gentleman be wanting any ? "

" No ; the other gentleman is away for the night."

" Then there will be only one for supper ? "

" Yes, only one for supper."

He sat in the corner of the sofa and fell instantly into a deep slumber.

VI

HE woke when the old woman tapped him on the shoulder and told him that supper was served. The room was dark save for the jumping light of two uncertain candles. Those two red candlesticks—how he hated them up there on the mantelpiece ! He had always hated them, and now they seemed to him to have something of the quality of Foster's voice—that thin, reedy, piping tone.

He was expecting at every moment that Foster would enter, and yet he knew that he would not. He continued to turn his head towards the door, but it was so dark there that you could not see. The whole room was dark except just there by the fireplace, where the two candlesticks went whining with their miserable twinkling plaint.

He went into the dining-room and sat down to his meal. But he could not eat anything. It was odd—that place by the table where Foster's chair should be. Odd, naked, and made a man feel lonely.

He got up once from the table and went to the window, opened it and looked out. He listened for something. A trickle as of running water, a stir, through the silence, as though some deep pool were filling to the brim. A rustle in the trees, perhaps. An owl hooted. Sharply, as though some one had spoken to him unexpectedly behind his shoulder, he closed the window and looked back, peering under his dark eyebrows into the room.

Later on he went up to bed.

VII

HAD he been sleeping, or had he been lying lazily, as one does, half-dozing, half-luxuriously not thinking ? He was wide awake now, utterly awake, and his heart was beating with apprehension. It was as though some one had called him by name. He slept always with his window a little open and the blind up. To-night the moonlight shadowed in sickly fashion the objects in his room. It was not a flood of light nor yet a sharp splash, silvering a square, a circle, throwing the rest into ebony darkness. The light was dim, a little green, perhaps, like the shadow that comes over the hills just before dark.

He stared at the window, and it seemed to him that something moved there. Within, or rather against the green-grey light, something silver-tinted glistened. Fenwick stared. It had the look, exactly, of slipping water.

Slipping water ! He listened, his head up, and it seemed to him that from beyond the window he caught the stir of water, not running, but rather welling up and up, gurgling with satisfaction as it filled and filled.

He sat up higher in bed, and then saw that down the wall-paper, beneath the window, water was undoubtedly trickling. He could see it lurch to the projecting wood of the sill, pause, and then slip, slither down the incline. The odd thing was that it fell so silently.

Beyond the window there was that odd gurgle, but in the room itself absolute silence. Whence could it come ? He saw the line of silver rise and fall as the stream on the window-ledge ebbed and flowed.

He must get up and close the window. He drew his legs above the sheets and blankets and looked down.

He shrieked. The floor was covered with a shining film of water. It was rising. As he looked it had covered half the short stumpy legs of the bed. It rose without a wink, a bubble, a break ! Over the sill it poured now in a steady flow, but soundless. Fenwick sat up in the bed, the clothes gathered up to his chin, his eyes blinking, the Adam's apple throbbing like a throttle in his throat.

But he must do something, he must stop this. The water was now level with the seats of the chairs, but still was soundless. Could he but reach the door !

He put down his naked foot, then cried again. The water was icy cold. Suddenly, leaning, staring at its dark, unbroken sheen, something seemed to push him forward. He fell. His head, his face was under the icy liquid ; it seemed adhesive and, in the heart of its ice, hot like melting wax. He struggled to his feet. The water was breast-high. He screamed again and again. He could see the looking-glass, the row of books, the picture of Dürer's " Horse," aloof, impervious. He beat at the water, and flakes of it seemed to cling to him like scales of fish,

clammy to his touch. He struggled, ploughing his way towards
the door.

The water now was at his neck. Then something had caught
him by the ankle. Something held him. He struggled, crying :
" Let me go ! Let me go ! I tell you to let me go ! I hate you !
I hate you ! I will not come down to you ! I will not——"

The water covered his mouth. He felt that some one pushed
in his eyeballs with bare knuckles. A cold hand reached up and
caught his naked thigh.

VIII

In the morning the little maid knocked and, receiving no
answer, came in, as was her wont, with his shaving-water. What
she saw made her scream. She ran for the gardener.

They took the body with its staring, protruding eyes, its
tongue sticking out between the clenched teeth, and laid it on
the bed.

The only sign of disorder was an overturned water-jug. A
small pool of water stained the carpet.

It was a lovely morning. A twig of ivy idly, in the little
breeze, tapped the pane.

THE RESURRECTIONIST

My gentle reader—start not at learning that I have been, in my time, a resurrectionist ! Let not this appalling word, this humiliating confession, conjure up in your fancy a throng of vampire-like images and associations, or earn your " Physician's " dismissal from your hearts and hearths. It is your own groundless fears, my fair trembler !—your own superstitious prejudices—that have driven me, and will drive many others of my brethern, to such dreadful doings as those hereafter detailed. Come, come—let us have one word of reason between us on the abstract question—and then for my tale. You expect us to cure you of disease, and yet deny us the only means of learning *how* ! You would have us bring you the ore of skill and experience, yet forbid us to break the soil or sink a shaft ! Is this fair, *fair* reader ? Is this reasonable ?

What I am now going to describe was my first and last exploit in the way of body-stealing. It was a grotesque if not a ludicrous scene, and occurred during the period of my " walking the hospitals," as it is called, which occupied the two seasons immediately after my leaving Cambridge. A young and rather interesting female was admitted a patient at the hospital I attended ; her case baffled all our skill, and her symptoms even defied diagnosis. *Now*, it seemed an enlargement of the heart—now, an ossification—then this, that, and the other ; and at last it was plain we knew nothing at all about the matter —no, not even whether her disorder was organic or functional, primary or symptomatic—or whether it *was* really the heart that was at fault. She received no benefit at all under the fluctuating schemes of treatment we pursued, and at length fell into dying circumstances. As soon as her friends were apprised of her situation, and had an inkling of our intention to open the body, they insisted on removing her immediately from the hospital, that she might " die at home."

In vain did Sir —— and his dressers expostulate vehemently with them, and represent, in exaggerated terms, the imminent peril attending such a step. Her two brothers avowed their apprehension of our designs, and were inflexible in exercising their right of removing their sister. I used all my rhetoric on the occasion, but in vain ; and at last said to the young men, " Well, if you are afraid only of our *dissecting* her, we can get hold of her, if we are so disposed, as easily if she die with you as with us."

" Well—we'll *troy* that, measter," replied the elder, while his Herculean fist oscillated somewhat significantly before my eyes. The poor girl was removed accordingly to her father's house, which was at a certain village about five miles from London, and survived her arrival scarcely ten minutes ! We soon contrived to receive intelligence of the event ; and as I and Sir ——'s two dressers had taken great interest in the case throughout, and felt intense curiosity about the real nature of the disease, we met together and entered into a solemn compact, that, come what might, we would have her body out of the ground. A trusty spy informed us of the time and exact place of the girl's burial ; and on expressing to Sir —— our determination about the matter, he patted me on the back, saying, " Ah, my fine fellow !—IF you have SPIRIT enough—dangerous," etc., etc.

Was it not skilfully said ? The baronet further told us, he felt himself so curious about the matter that if fifty pounds would be of use to us in furthering our purpose, they were at our service. It needed not this, nor a glance at the *éclat* with which the successful issue of the affair would be attended among our fellow-students, to spur our resolves.

The notable scheme was finally adjusted at my rooms in the Borough. M—— and E——, Sir ——'s dressers, and myself, with an experienced " *grab* "—that is to say, a *professional* resurrectionist—were to set off from the Borough about nine o'clock the next evening—which would be the third day after the burial—in a glass coach provided with all " appliances and means to boot." During the day, however, our friend the grab suffered so severely from an overnight's excess as to disappoint us of his invaluable assistance. This unexpected *contretempts* nearly put an end to our project ; for the few other grabs we knew were absent on *professional tours* ! Luckily, however, I bethought me of a poor Irish porter—a sort of " ne'er-do-weel " hanger-on at the hospital—whom I had several times hired to go on errands. This man I sent for to my room, and, in the presence of my two coadjutors, persuaded, threatened, and bothered into acquiescence, promising him half-a-guinea for his evening's work—and as much whisky as he could drink prudently. As Mr. Tip—that was the name he went by—had some personal acquaintance with the sick grab, he succeeded in borrowing his chief tools ; with which, in a sack large enough to contain our expected prize, he repaired to my rooms about nine o'clock, while the coach was standing at the door. Our Jehu had received a quiet douceur in addition to the hire of himself and coach.

As soon as we had exhibited sundry doses of Irish cordial to our friend Tip—under the effects of which he became quite " bouncible," and *ranted* about the feat he was to take a prominent part in—and equipped ourselves in our worst clothes, and white top-coats, we entered the vehicle—four in number— and drove off. The weather had been exceedingly capricious all the evening—moonlight, rain, thunder, and lightning, fitfully alternating. The only thing we were anxious about was the darkness, to shield us from all possible observation. I must own that, in analysing the feelings that prompted me to undertake and go through with this affair, the mere love of adventure operated quite as powerfully as the wish to benefit the cause of anatomical science. A midnight expedition to the tombs !— It took our fancy amazingly ; and then Sir ——'s cunning hint about the " danger "—and our " spirit ! "

The garrulous Tip supplied us with amusement all the way down—rattle, rattle, rattle, incessantly ; but as soon as we had arrived at that part of the road where we were to stop, and caught sight of —— church, with its hoary steeple— glistening in the fading moonlight, as though it were standing sentinel over the graves around it, one or which we were going so rudely to violate—Tip's spirits began to falter a little. He said little—and that at intervals.

To be very candid with the reader, *none* of us felt over-much at our ease. Our expedition began to wear a somewhat hare-brained aspect, and to be environed with formidable contingencies which we had not taken sufficiently into our calculations. What, for instance, if the two stout fellows, the brothers, should be out watching their sister's grave ? They were not likely to stand on much ceremony with us. And then the manual difficulties ! E—— was the only one of us that had ever assisted

at the exhumation of a body—and the rest of us were likely to
prove but bungling workmen. However, we had gone too far
to think of retreating. We none of us *spoke* our suspicions, but
the silence that reigned within the coach was tolerably significant.
In contemplation, however, of some such contingency we had
put a bottle of brandy in the coach pocket ; and before we
drew up, had all four of us drunk pretty deeply of it. At length
the coach turned down a by-lane to the left, which led directly
to the churchyard wall ; and after moving a few steps down
it, in order to shelter our vehicle from the observation of highway
passengers, the coach stopped, and the driver opened the
door.

" Come, Tip," said I, " out with you."

" Get out, did you say, sir ? To be sure I will—Och ! to be
sure I will." But there was small show of alacrity in his movements as he descended the steps ; for while I was speaking I
was interrupted by the solemn clangour of the church clock
announcing the hour of midnight. The sounds seemed to *warn*
us against what we were going to do.

" 'Tis a cowld night, yer honours," said Tip, in an undertone, as we successively alighted, and stood together, looking
up and down the dark lane, to see if anything was stirring but
ourselves. " 'Tis a cowld night—and—and—and——" he
stammered.

" Why, you cowardly old scoundrel," grumbled M——, " are
you frightened already ? What's the matter, eh ? Hoist up the
bag on your shoulders directly, and lead the way down the lane."

" Och, but yer honours—och ! by the mother that bore
me, but 'tis a murtherous cruel thing, I'm thinking, to wake
the poor cratur from her last sleep."

He said this so querulously, that I began to entertain serious
apprehensions, after all, of his defection ; so I insisted on his
taking a little more brandy, by way of bringing him up to a
par. It was of no use, however. His reluctance increased every
moment—and it even dispirited *us*. I verily believe the turning
of a straw would have decided us all on jumping into the coach
again, and returning home without accomplishing our errand.
Too many of the students, however, were apprised of our
expedition, for us to think of terminating it so ridiculously. As
it were by mutual consent, we stood and paused a few moments,
about half-way down the lane. M—— whistled with infinite
spirit and distinctness ; E—— remarked to me that he always
" thought a churchyard at midnight was the gloomiest object

imaginable ; " and I talked about *business*—" soon be over "—
" shallow grave," etc., etc.

" Confound it—what if those two brothers of hers SHOULD
be there ? " said M—— abruptly, making a dead stop, and
folding his arms on his breast.

" Powerful fellows, both of them ! " muttered E—— We
resumed our march—when Tip, our advanced guard—a title he
earned by anticipating our steps about three inches—suddenly
stood still, let down the bag from his shoulders, elevated both
hands in a listening attitude, and exclaimed, " Whisht !—whisht !
By my soul, *what* was that ? "

We all paused in silence, looking palely at one another—but
could hear nothing except the drowsy flutter of a bat wheeling
away from us a little overhead.

" Fait—an' wasn't it somebody *spaking* on the far side o' the
hedge I heard ? " whispered Tip.

" Pooh—stuff, you idiot ! " I exclaimed, losing my temper.
" Come, M—— and E——, it's high time we had done with all
this cowardly nonsense ; and if we mean really to *do* anything,
we must make haste. 'Tis past twelve—day breaks about four
—and it is coming on wet, you see." Several large drops of
rain, pattering heavily among the leaves and branches, corroborated my words, by announcing a coming shower, and the
air was sultry enough to warrant the expectation of a thunderstorm. We therefore buttoned up our greatcoats to the chin,
and hurried on to the churchyard wall, which ran across the
bottom of the lane. This wall we had to climb over to get
into the churchyard, and it was not a very high one.

Here Tip annoyed us again. I told him to lay down his bag,
mount the wall, and look over into the yard, to see whether
all was clear before us ; and, as far as the light would enable
him, to look about for a new-made grave. Very reluctantly
he complied, and contrived to scramble to the top of the wall.
He had hardly time, however, to peer over into the churchyard, when a fluttering streak of lightning flashed over us,
followed, in a second or two, by a loud burst of thunder ! Tip
fell in an instant to the ground, like a cockchafer shaken from
an elm-tree, and lay crossing himself, and muttering paternosters.
We could scarcely help laughing at the manner in which he
tumbled down, simultaneously with the flash of lightning.
" Now, look ye, gintlemen," said he, still squatting on the
ground, " do you mane to give the poor cratur Christian
burial, when ye've done wid her ? An' will you put her

back again as ye found her? 'Case, if you won't, blood
an' oons——"

"Hark ye now, Tip," said I sternly, taking out one of a
brace of *empty* pistols I had put into my greatcoat pocket, and
presenting it to his head, "we have hired you on this business,
for the want of a better, you wretched fellow! and if you give
us any more of your nonsense, by —— I'll send a bullet through
your brain! Do you hear me, Tip?"

"Och, aisy, aisy wid ye! don't murther me! Bad luck to
me that I ever cam wid ye! Och, and if ivver I live to die,
won't I see and bury my ould body out o' the rache of all the
docthers in the world? if I don't, divel burn me!" We all
laughed aloud at Tip's truly Hibernian expostulation.

"Come, sir, mount! over with you!" said we, helping to
push him upwards. "Now, drop this bag on the other side,"
we continued, giving him the sack that contained our implements. We all three of us then followed, and alighted safely in
the churchyard. It poured with rain; and, to enhance the
dreariness and horrors of the time and place, flashes of lightning
followed in quick succession, shedding a transient awful glare
over the scene, revealing the white tombstones, the ivy-grown
venerable church, and our own figures, a shivering group,
come on an unhallowed errand! I perfectly well recollect the
lively feelings of apprehension—" the compunctious visitings of
remorse "—which the circumstances called forth in my own
breast, and which, I had no doubt, were shared by my companions.

As no time, however, was to be lost, I left the group, for an
instant, under the wall to search out the grave. The accurate
instructions I had received enabled me to pitch on the spot
with little difficulty; and I returned to my companions, who
immediately followed me to the scene of operations. We had
no umbrellas, and our greatcoats were saturated with wet;
but the brandy we had recently taken did us good service, by
exhilarating our spirits and especially those of Tip. He untied
the sack in a twinkling, and shook out the hoes and spades, etc.;
and taking one of the latter himself, he commenced digging
with such energy that we had hardly prepared ourselves for
work before he had cleared away nearly the whole of the mound.
The rain soon abated, and the lightning ceased for a considerable
interval, though thunder was heard occasionally grumbling
sullenly in the distance, as if expressing anger at our unholy
doings—at least I felt it so. The pitchy darkness continued, so

that we could scarcely see one another's figures. We worked on in silence, as fast as our spades could be got into the ground ; taking it in turns, two by two, as the grave would not admit of more. On—on—on we worked till we had hollowed out about three feet of earth. Tip then hastily joined together a long iron screw or borer, which he thrust into the ground, for the purpose of ascertaining the depth at which the coffin yet lay from us.

To our vexation, we found a distance of three feet remained to be got through.

" Sure, and by the soul of St. Patrick, but we'll not be done by the morning ! " said Tip, as he threw down the instrument and resumed his spade.

We were all discouraged. Oh, how earnestly I wished myself at home, in my snug little bed in the Borough ! How I cursed the Quixotism that had led me into such an undertaking ! I had no time, however, for reflection, as it was my turn to relieve one of the diggers ; so into the grave I jumped, and worked away as lustily as before. While I was thus engaged, a sudden noise, close to our ears, so startled me, that I protest I thought I should have dropped down dead in the grave I was robbing.

I and my fellow-digger let fall our spades, and all four stood still for a second or two in an ecstasy of fearful apprehension. We could not see more than a few inches around us, but heard the grass trodden by approaching feet ! They proved to be those of an ass, that was turned at night into the churchyard, and had gone on eating his way towards us ; and, while we were standing in mute expectation of what was to come next, opened on us with an astounding hee-haw ! hee-haw ! hee-haw ! Even after we had discovered the ludicrous nature of the interruption, we were too agitated to laugh. The brute was actually close upon us, and had *given tongue* from under poor Tip's elbow, having approached him from behind as he stood leaning on his spade. Tip started suddenly backward against the animal's head, and fell down.

Away sprang the jackass, as much confounded as Tip, kicking and scampering like a mad creature among the tombstones, and hee-hawing incessantly, as if a hundred devils had got into it for the purpose of discomfiting us. I felt so much fury and fear lest the noise should lead to our discovery I could have killed the brute if it had been within my reach, while Tip stammered, in an affrighted whisper—" Och, the baste ! Och, the baste ! The big black divel of a baste ! The murtherous,

thundering——" and a great many epithets of the same sort.
We gradually recovered from the agitation which this provoking
interruption had occasioned ; and Tip, under the promise of
two bottles of whisky as soon as we arrived safe at home with
our prize, renewed his exertions, and dug with such energy
that we soon cleared away the remainder of the superincumbent
earth, and stood upon the bare lid of the coffin. The grapplers,
with ropes attached to them, were then fixed in the sides and
extremities, and we were in the act of raising the coffin, when
the sound of a human voice, accompanied with footsteps, fell
on our startled ears. We heard both distinctly, and crouched
down close over the brink of the grave, awaiting in breathless
suspense a corroboration of our fears. After a pause of two or
three minutes, however, finding that the sounds were not
renewed, we began to breathe more freely, persuaded that our
ears must have deceived us.

Once more we resumed our work, succeeded in hoisting up
the coffin—not without a slip, however, which nearly precipitated it down again to the bottom, with all four of us upon
it—and depositing it on the graveside. Before proceeding to use
our screws or wrenches, we once more looked and listened, and
listened and looked ; but neither seeing nor hearing anything
we set to work, prized off the lid in a twinkling, and a transient
glimpse of moonlight disclosed to us the shrouded inmate—all
white and damp. I removed the face-cloth, and unpinned the
cap, while M—— loosed the sleeves from the wrists. Thus
were we engaged, when E——, who had hold of the feet, ready
to lift them out, suddenly let them go—gasped, " Oh, my
God ! there they are ! " and placed his hand on my arm. He
shook like an aspen leaf. I looked towards the quarter whither
his eyes were directed, and, sure enough, saw the figure of a
man—if not two—moving stealthily towards us. " Well, we're
discovered, that's clear," I whispered as calmly as I could.

" We shall be murdered ! " groaned E——.

" Lend me one of the pistols you have with you," said
M—— resolutely ; " by ——, I'll have a shot for my life,
however ! "

As for poor Tip, who had heard every syllable of this startling
colloquy, and himself seen the approaching figures, he looked
at me in silence, the image of black horror ! I could have laughed
even then, to see his staring black eyes—his little cocked ruby-
tinted nose—his chattering teeth.

" Hush—hush ! " said I, cocking my pistol, while M—— did

the same ; for none but myself knew that they were unloaded. To add to our consternation, the malignant moon withdrew the small scantling of light she had been doling out to us, and sank beneath a vast cloud, " black as Erebus," but not before we had caught a glimpse of two more figures moving towards us in an opposite direction. " Surrounded ! " two of us muttered in the same breath. We all rose to our feet, and stood together, not knowing what to do—unable in the darkness to see one another distinctly. Presently we heard a voice say, in a subdued tone, " Where are they ? Where ? *Sure* I saw them ! Oh, there they are. Halloa—halloa ! "

That was enough—the signal of our flight. Without an instant's pause, or uttering another syllable, off we sprung, like small-shot from a gun's mouth, all of us in different directions, we knew not whither. I heard the report of a gun—mercy on me ! and pelted away, scarcely knowing what I was about, dodging among the graves—now coming full-butt against a plaguy tombstone, then tumbling on the slippery grass—while some one followed close at my heels, panting and puffing, but whether friend or foe I knew not.

At length I stumbled against a large tombstone ; and, finding it open at the two ends, crept under it, resolved there to abide the issue. At the moment of my ensconcing myself the sound of the person's footsteps who had followed me suddenly ceased. I heard a splashing sound, then a kicking and scrambling, a faint stifled cry of " Ugh—oh, ugh ! " and all was still. Doubtless it must be one of my companions, who had been wounded. What could I do, however ? I did not know in what direction he lay—the night was pitch-dark—and if I crept from my hiding-place, for all I knew, I might be shot myself. I shall never forget that hour—no, never ! There was I, squatting like a toad on the wet grass and weeds, not daring to do more than breathe ! Here was a predicament ! I could not conjecture how the affair would terminate.

Was I to lie where I was till daylight, that then I might step into the arms of my captors ? What was become of my companions ? While turning these thoughts in my mind, and wondering that all was so quiet, my ear caught the sound of the splashing of water, apparently at but a yard or two's distance, mingled with the sounds of a half-smothered human voice— " Ugh ! ugh ! Och, murther ! murther ! murther ! "— another splash—" and isn't it dead, and drowned, and kilt I am——"

Whew ! *Tip* in trouble, thought I, not daring to speak. Yes—it was poor Tip, I afterwards found—who had followed at my heels, scampering after me as fast as fright could drive him, till his career was unexpectedly ended by his tumbling—souse—head over heels, into a newly-opened grave in his path, with more than a foot of water in it. There the poor fellow remained, after recovering from the first shock of his fall, not daring to utter a word for some time, lest he should be discovered—straddling over the water with his toes and elbows stuck into the loose soil on each side, to support him. This was his interesting position, as he subsequently informed me, at the time of uttering the sounds which first attracted my attention. Though not aware of his situation at the time, I was almost choked with laughter as he went on with his soliloquy, somewhat in this strain :

" Och, Tip, ye ould divel ! Don't it sarve ye right, ye fool ? Ye villainous ould coffin-robber ! Won't ye burn for this hereafter, ye sinner ? Ulaloo ! When ye are dead yourself, may ye be trated like that poor cratur—and yourself alive to see it ! Och, hubbaboo ! hubbaboo ! Isn't it sure that I'll be drowned, an' then it's kilt I'll be ! " A loud splash, and a pause for a few moments, as if he were readjusting his footing—" Och ! an' I'm catching my dith of cowld ! Fait, an' it's a divel a drop o' the two bottles o' whisky I'll ever see—Och, och, och ! "—another splash—" och, an' isn't this uncomfortable ! Murther and oons !—if ever I come out of this—sha'n't I be dead before I do ? "

" Tip—Tip—Tip ! " I whispered in a low tone. There was a dead silence. " Tip, Tip, where are you ? What's the matter, eh ? " No answer ; but he muttered in a low tone to himself— " *Where am I ?* by my soul ! Isn't it dead, and kilt, and drowned, and murthered I am—that's all ! "

" Tip—Tip—Tip. ! " I repeated, a little louder.

" Tip, indeed ! Fait, ye may call, bad luck to ye—whoever ye are—but it's divel a word I'll be after spaking to ye."

" Tip, you simpleton ! It's I—Mr. —— "

In an instant there was a sound of jumping and splashing, as if surprise had made him slip from his standing again, and he called out, " Whoo ! whoo ! an' is't you, sweet Mr. —— ! What is the matter wid ye ? Are ye kilt ? Where are they all ? Have they taken ye away, every mother's son of you ? " he asked eagerly, in a breath.

" Why, what are *you* doing, Tip ? Where are *you* ? "

" Fait, an' it's being *washed* I am, in the feet, and in the queerest *tub* your honour ever saw ! " A noise of scuffling not many yards off, silenced us both in an instant.

Presently I distinguished the voice of E——, calling out, " Help, M—— ! " (My name.) " Where are you ? " The noise increased, and seemed nearer than before. I crept from my lurking place, and aided at Tip's resurrection, when both of us hurried towards the spot whence the sound came. By the faint moonlight I could just see the outlines of two figures violently struggling and grappling together. Before I could come up to them both fell down, locked in each other's arms, rolling over each other, grasping one another's collars, gasping and panting as if in mortal struggle. The moon suddenly emerged, and who do you think, reader, was E——'s antagonist ? Why, the person whose appearance had so discomfited and affrighted us all—OUR COACHMAN.

That worthy individual, alarmed at our protracted stay, had, contrary to our injunctions, left his coach to come and search after us. He it was whom we had seen stealing towards us ; his step—his voice had alarmed us, for he could not see us distinctly enough to discover whether we were his fare or not. He was on the point of whispering my name, it seems—when we must all have understood one another—when lo ! we all started off in the manner which has been described ; and he himself, not knowing that he was the reason of it, had taken to his heels, and fled for his life ! He supposed we had fallen into a sort of ambuscade. He happened to hide himself behind the tombstone next but one to that which sheltered E——. Finding all quiet, he and E——, as if by mutual consent, were groping from their hiding-places, when they unexpectedly fell foul of one another—each too affrighted to speak—and hence the scuffle.

After this satisfactory dénouement we all repaired to the grave's mouth, and found the corpse and coffin precisely as we had left them. We were not many moments in taking out the body, stripping it, and thrusting it into the sack we had brought. We then tied the top of the sack, carefully deposited the shroud, etc., in the coffin, re-screwed down the lid—fearful, impious mockery !—and consigned it once more to its resting-place, Tip scattering a handful of earth on the lid, and exclaiming reverently—" An' may the Lord forgive us for what we have done to ye ! " The coachman and I then took the body between us to the coach, leaving M——, and E——, and Tip to fill up the grave.

Our troubles were not yet ended, however. Truly it seemed as though Providence were throwing every obstacle in our way. Nothing went right. On reaching the spot where we had left the coach, behold it lay several yards farther in the lane, tilted into the ditch—for the horses, being hungry, and left to themselves, in their anxiety to graze on the verdant bank of the hedge, had contrived to overturn the vehicle in the ditch—and one of the horses was kicking vigorously when we came up—the whole body off the ground—and resting on that of his companion. We had considerable difficulty in righting the coach, as the horses were inclined to be obstreperous. We succeeded, however —deposited our unholy spoil within, turned the horses' heads towards the high road, and then, after enjoining Jehu to keep his place on the box, I went to see how my companions were getting on. They had nearly completed their task, and told me that " shovelling *in* was surprisingly easier than shovelling *out* ! "

We took great pains to leave everything as neat and as nearly resembling what we found it as possible, in order that our visit might not be suspected. We then carried away each our own tools, and hurried as fast as possible to our coach, for the dim twilight had already stolen a march upon us, devoutly thankful that, after so many interruptions, we had succeeded in effecting our object.

It was broad daylight before we reached town, and a wretched coach company we looked, all wearied and dirty—Tip especially who nevertheless snored in the corner as comfortably as if he had been warm in his bed. I heartily resolved with him, on leaving the coach, that it should be " the devil's own dear self only that should timpt me out again *body-snatching* ! "

THE BLUE ROOM

A YOUNG man was walking with an agitated air about the railway station. He had blue glasses, and although he had not a cold in his head, he kept putting his handkerchief to his nose. In his left hand he held a little black bag, containing, as I learnt later, a silk dressing-gown and some Turkish trousers.

From time to time he went to the entrance and looked up and down the street; then he drew out his watch and studied the timetable. It was an hour before the train went; but there are some folk who are always afraid of being late. The train was not one of those that busy people take—few first-class carriages. And the hour it went was not that which allows business men to leave as soon as their work is done, and arrive in time for dinner at their country-houses. When the passengers began to show themselves, a Parisian would have seen by their air that they were farmers or little traders of the suburbs.

Still, each time any one entered the station, each time a cab stopped at the gate, the heart of the young man in blue glasses swelled out like a balloon; his knees trembled; his bag almost fell from his hand; and his glasses nearly tumbled from his nose, on which, it might be said in passing, they were placed wrong side round.

It was still worse when, after a long wait, there appeared through a side door, coming precisely from the only point that was not subjected to continual observation, a woman clad in black, with a thick veil over her face, holding in her hand a bag of brown morocco, containing, as I afterwards discovered, a wonderful dressing-gown and a pair of blue satin slippers. The woman and the young man came towards each other, looking to the right and the left, but never before them. They came together, touched hands, and stayed for some minutes without saying a word panting, trembling, overcome by one of those poignant emotions, for which I would give a hundred years of philosophic meditations.

" Léon," said the young woman—I have forgotten to say she was young and pretty—" Léon, what happiness ! Never should I have known you in those blue glasses ! "

" What joy ! " said Léon. " I should have never recognised you under that black veil ! "

" What joy ! " she continued. " Let us get our seats quick. If the train started without us ! . . . (And she squeezed his arm.) Nobody guesses what is happening. At this moment I am with Clara and her husband, going to their country-house, where I ought to-morrow to say good-bye ! . . . And," she added laughing and lowering her head, " it is just an hour since I went away with Clara, and to-morrow . . . after having passed the last evening with her . . . (again she squeezed his arm), to-morrow, in the morning, she will leave me at the station, where I shall find Ursule, whom I have sent on ahead at my aunt's. . . . Oh ! I have thought out everything ! Let us get our tickets. . . . It is impossible we should be found out ! Oh ! If they want to know our names at the end ? I have already forgotten. . . ."

" Monsieur and Madame Duru."

" No ! not Duru. There was a shoemaker at the boarding school with that name."

" Then, Dumont ? . . ."

" Daumont ! "

" Very well ! But they will not question us ! "

A bell rang, the door of the waiting-room opened, and the young woman, always carefully veiled, darted into a carriage with her young companion. For the second time the bell rang; a porter shut the door of their compartment.

" We are alone ! " they cried joyfully.

But at that very moment a man of about fifty, dressed all in black, with a broad serious face, entered the carriage and settled down in a corner. The engine whistled and the train set off. The young couple, withdrawing as far as they could from their inconvenient neighbour, began to talk in whispers, and, as an extra precaution, in English.

" Sir," said the other passenger in the same language and with a much purer English accent, " if you want to talk secrets, you had better not use English before me. I am an Englishman. Sorry to trouble you ; but in the other compartment there was only one man, and as a matter of principle I never travel with a single man. He looked to me like a Judas. And this might have tempted him."

He pointed to his travelling-bag that he had thrown on a cushion before him.

" If I can't sleep, I will read."

And he did loyally try to sleep. Opening his bag, he took out a travelling-cap, put it on his head, and kept his eyes shut for some minutes. Then opening them with a movement of impatience, he groped in his bag for spectacles, then for a Greek book. At last he began to read very attentively. In getting the book out of the bag he had overturned many things, all thrown in anyhow. Among other articles he drew out was a pretty thick bundle of Bank of England notes, placed them on the seat in front of him, and before putting them back in the bag he showed them to the young man and asked him if he could change bank-notes at a certain town.

" Probably. It is on the way to England," said Léon.

It was to this town that the young couple were going. There is a little hotel there, fairly clean, where travellers usually stay only on Saturday evening. It is pretended that the rooms are good ; but the landlord and his servants are not far enough removed from Paris to keep a really good inn. Léon had come across the place some time before, when he was not wearing blue glasses, and after the account he gave of it, his sweetheart felt she would like to see it.

Besides, on this day, she was in such a frame of mind that the walls of a prison would have seemed to her full of charm if she had been shut in there with Léon. However, the train went on, the Englishman read his Greek without turning to look at his companions, who chatted in such whispers that only lovers could have understood. Perhaps I shall not surprise my readers by admitting that they were eloping lovers. And what was really deplorable was that they were not married, and there were great difficulties in the way of their marriage.

They reached their stopping-place. The Englishman was the first to alight. While Léon was helping his sweetheart to get out of the carriage without showing her ankles, a man darted from a neighbouring compartment on to the platform. He was pale, even yellow, with sunken, bloodshot eyes and a straggling beard—quite a criminal in appearance. His suit was clean but thread-worn. His frock-coat once black, now grey at the elbows and at the back, was buttoned to the chin, probably to hide a waistcoat still shabbier. He came up to the Englishman, and in a very humble voice :

" Uncle ! " he said to him.

" Leave me alone, you wretch," cried the Englishman, his grey eye lighting up with anger, as he began to walk out of the station.

" Don't drive me to despair," said the other man, in a tone at once sorrowful and threatening.

" Will you be good enough to look after my bag a moment ? " said the old Englishman, throwing his bag at the feet of Léon.

Seizing the arm of the man who had accosted him, he pushed him in a corner, where he hoped he would not be overheard, and there he spoke to him for a moment in a very harsh voice. Then, taking from his pocket some papers, he put them in the hand of the man who had called him uncle. The man took the papers without any thanks, and almost at once went away and disappeared.

There is only one hotel in the town, so you must not be astonished that, at the end of a few minutes, all the characters in this truthful tale met again there. In France every traveller who has the luck to have a well-dressed woman on his arm is sure of obtaining the best room in all the hotel : thus is it established that we are the most polished nation in Europe.

If the room given to Léon was the best, it would be rash to conclude that it was excellent. There was a great wooden bed, with curtains of chintz, on which was printed in violet the magical story of Pyramus and Thisbe. The walls were covered with a painted paper representing a view of Naples, and crowded with figures. Unhappily, idle and indiscreet travellers had added moustaches and pipes to all the figures, male and female ; and many foolish remarks in prose and verse were written in pencil on the sky and on the sea. Against this background hung several engravings : *Louis Philippe swearing to the Charta of* 1830 ; *The First Meeting of Julie and Saint Preux ;* the *Regrets* and the *Hope of Happiness* after Dubuffe. This room was called the Blue Room, because the two arm-chairs to the right and left of the fireplace were in Dutch velvet of this colour. But for many years past they had been hidden under coverings of grey, glazed cloth with amaranth frills.

While the maids of the hotel gathered round the young lady and offered her their services, Léon, who was not wanting in good sense, even when in love, went to the kitchen to order dinner. He had to use all his eloquence and resort to bribery to get the

promise of a private dinner ; but greatly was he disconcerted
when he learnt that in the big dining-room adjoining the Blue
Room the officers of the 3rd Hussars, who were about to relieve
the officers of the 3rd Light Infantry, were joining the latter that
very day in a farewell dinner that would take place with much
cordiality.

The landlord swore by all his gods that, apart from the
gaiety natural to all French soldiers, the Hussars and the Light
Infantry were noted in the town for their gentleness and their
good conduct, and that their presence would not inconvenience
Madame in the least, the custom of the officers being to end
the dinner before midnight.

As Léon went back to the Blue Room, worried over this
affair, he saw that the old Englishman had taken the room next
to his. The door was open. The Englishman, sitting before a
table on which were placed a glass and a bottle, looked at the
ceiling with deep attention, as though he were counting the
flies that were walking there.

" What does it matter who our neighbours are ? " said Léon to
himself. " The Englishman will soon be drunk, and the soldiers
will have gone away before midnight."

In entering the Blue Room his first care was to make sure that
the communicating doors were properly closed and locked. On
the side of the Englishman there was a double door ; the wall
was thick. On the side of the Hussars the partition was thinner ;
but the door had a lock and key. After all, it was a more effectual
barrier against curiosity than the curtains of a cab are ; and how
many people think they are isolated from the world in a cab !

Certainly the richest imagination cannot picture a more
complete happiness than that of two young lovers who, after
long waiting, find themselves alone, far from the eyes of jealous
and curious people, so that they can relate at leisure their
bygone troubles and relish the delights of a perfect meeting. But
the devil always finds some means of pouring his drop of bitterness
into the cup of felicity. While eating a pretty poor dinner in the
Blue Room, composed of some dishes stolen from the banquet
of the officers, Léon and his lady had to suffer a good deal from
the conversation that those gentlemen held in the neighbouring
room. Their talk turned on matters that had nothing to do with
strategy and tactics, and I cannot possibly report it.

It was a long string of coarse stories, accompanied by outbursts
of laughter in which it was sometimes difficult for our lovers not
to take part. Léon's sweetheart was not a prude, but there are

some things a woman does not like to hear, even in company with the man she loves. The situation became more and more embarrassing ; and when the officers were beginning their dessert, Léon went down to the kitchen to beg the landlord to tell the gentlemen there was a sick lady in the next room and to ask them to have the politeness to make a little less noise.

The landlord, as always happens in army dinners, was quite flurried, and did not know what to say. For at the moment when Léon gave him the message for the officers, a waiter asked him for champagne for the Hussars, and a maid for a bottle of port for the Englishman.

" I told him we had no port," she added.

" You are a fool. I keep every kind of wine. I will find him his bottle of port ! Bring me a bottle of ratafia, a bottle of fifteen, and a decanter of brandy."

After having manufactured the port in a turn of the hand, the landlord entered the dining-room and gave the message from Léon. It first excited a furious storm. Then a bass voice, that dominated all the others, demanded what kind of woman they had for a neighbour.

" My faith, messieurs," said the landlord, " she is very pretty and she is very shy. Marie Jeanne says she has a wedding ring. So it may be a bride who has come here for her honeymoon, a they sometimes do."

" A bride ! " shouted forty voices. " She must come and drink with us. We will toast her health, and teach her husband his duties ! "

At these words there was a great clanking of spurs, and our couple trembled, thinking that their room was going to be taken by storm. But suddenly a voice stayed the movement. Evidently it was one of the chiefs that spoke. He reproached the officers with their impoliteness, and told them to sit down, and speak decently without shouting. Then he added some words in too low a voice to be heard in the Blue Room. They were received with deference, but not without exciting a certain restrained hilarity.

From this moment there was a comparative silence in the officers' room, and our loving pair blessed the salutary effects of discipline, and began to talk together with more ease. But after so much upset, it took some time to recover those tender emotions which anxieties, the fatigues of travelling, and above all the coarse merriment of their neighbours, had greatly troubled. At their age, however, the thing is not very difficult, and they soon forgot all the unpleasantness of their adventurous expedition, and began to think only of its pleasures.

They fancied they had made peace with the Hussars. Alas ! it was only a truce. The moment when they were least expecting it, when they were thousands of leagues away from this sublunary world, behold ! twenty-four bugles, sustained by several trombones, poured out the air known to French soldiers, " Ours is the victory ! " How could any one resist such a tempest ? The poor lovers were much to be pitied.

No, not very much. For in the end the officers came out of the dining-room, defiling before the door of the Blue Room with much clank of sabres and spurs, and shouting one after the other, " Good-night, madame, the bride."

Then all sound ceased. No, I am mistaken. The Englishman came out into the corridor and cried :

" Waiter, bring me another bottle of that same port !"

Calmness settled at last on the little inn. The night was sweet, the moon at full. From time immemorial lovers have delighted to look at our satellite. Léon and his lady opened their window, that looked on a little garden, and breathed with joy the cool air, fragrant with the scent of clematis. They did not remain at the window very long. A man was walking in the garden, his head bowed, his arms crossed, a cigar in his mouth. Léon thought he recognised the nephew of the Englishman who loved the good wine of Portugal.

I hate useless details, and besides I am not obliged to tell the reader all that took place, hour by hour, in the inn. So I will only say that the candle, burning on the mantelpiece in the Blue Room, was more than half consumed, when, in the bedroom of the Englishman, hitherto silent, a strange noise was heard, such as a heavy body might produce in its fall. And with this noise there mingled a sort of cracking, not less strange, followed by a stifled cry and several indistinct words, resembling a curse. The young couple in the Blue Room were startled. Perhaps they had been aroused by the fall ; for on both of them the mysterious noise produced an almost sinister impression.

" It is our Englishman dreaming," said Léon, trying to smile. He wished to reassure his companion, but he shivered involuntarily. Two or three minutes afterwards, a door was opened in the corridor, very carefully it seemed, then it was shut very quietly. Some one could be heard walking slowly and uneasily, who, to all appearance, was trying to pass without being heard.

" What a cursed place ! " cried Léon.

" Ah, it is like heaven ! . . ." said the young lady, letting her head fall on Léon's shoulder. " I am so sleepy. . . ."

She sighed and fell asleep again almost at once. But Léon was worried, and his imagination began to dwell on several things that, in another frame of mind, he would have passed over. The sinister figure of the Englishman's nephew was recalled to his memory. There was hatred in the glance he gave his uncle, whilst speaking to him with humility, no doubt because he was asking for money. What could be easier than for a man, still young and vigorous, and desperate besides, to climb from the garden to the window of the next room ? . . . Moreover, he was staying in the inn, since he was walking in the garden at night. Perhaps . . . even probably . . . indubitably, he knew that there was a thick bundle of bank-notes in his uncle's bag. . . . And that heavy blow, like a club falling on a bald head ! . . . that stifled cry ! . . . that frightful oath, and then the creeping steps afterwards ! The nephew had the air of a murderer. . . . But a hotel full of officers is not a good place for a murderer. No doubt this Englishman, like a prudent man, had locked his door, especially knowing what sort of fellow was hanging about. He mistrusted him, since he did not want to go up to him with his bag in his hand. . . . But why think of such hideous things when you are so happy ?

That was what Léon said to himself. In the middle of his thoughts, which I refrain from analysing at length, and which came to him almost as confused as the visions of a dream, he had his eyes fixed mechanically on the communicating door between the Blue Room and the Englishman's room.

In France the doors do not shut well. Between this one and the floor there was an opening of nearly half an inch. Suddenly, through this opening, scarcely lighted by the reflection from the waxed floor, there appeared something blackish, flat, resembling the blade of a knife, for the edge, touched by the light from the candle, showed a thin brilliant line. This moved slowly in the direction of a little slipper of blue satin, thrown indiscreetly a little way from the door. Was it some insect like a centipede ? . . . No ; it was not an insect, it had no fixed shape. . . . Two or three brown trails, each with its line of light at the edge, penetrate into the Blue Room. There movement quickens, owing to the slope of the floor ; they advance rapidly, and begin to touch the little slipper. No more doubt ! It is a liquid, and its colour can now be seen distinctly by the light of the candle—it is blood ! And while Léon, motionless, stared with horror at the frightful thing, the young lady slept on peacefully, and her regular breath warmed the neck and shoulder of the terrified man.

The care that Léon had taken to order dinner as soon as he arrived at the inn is sufficient to prove that he had a good head on his shoulders and was able to look ahead. He did not belie his character on this occasion. He made no movement, and all the force of his mind bent in an effort to come to some decision in the presence of the frightful misfortune that threatened him.

I imagine that most of my readers, and especially my lady readers, full themselves with the spirit of heroism, will blame Léon for his inactivity and his lack of courage. He ought, I shall be told, to have run to the Englishman's room and arrested the murderer. At the very least, he should have pulled his bell and aroused the people of the inn. To this I must answer, first, that in French inns the bell-rope is only an ornament in the bedrooms : there is no apparatus in metal attached to the other end of the cord. I will also add, respectfully but firmly, that, if it is wrong to let an Englishman die in the next room, it is not at all praiseworthy to sacrifice to an old foreigner the young and pretty woman who is sleeping with her head on your shoulder. What would have happened if Léon had shouted out and awakened everybody in the inn ? Gendarmes, a magistrate and his clerk would soon have arrived. Before asking him what he had seen or heard, these gentlemen are so inquisitive by profession that they would have started by asking Léon :

"What is your name ? Where are your papers ? And madame ? Why are you staying together in this Blue Room ? You will both have to appear before the court of assize and give evidence that, on such a date, at such an hour at night, you have been witnesses to such and such things."

Now, it was precisely this idea of the magistrate and the police that first presented itself to the mind of Léon. There are some problems in life that are difficult to solve. Is it better to let an unknown foreigner be murdered, or lose and bring dishonour upon a beloved woman ? Léon did what most men would have done in his place. He did not stir. With his eyes fixed on the blue slipper, and the little red stream that touched it, he remained for some time as though he was fascinated, while a cold sweat came on his forehead, and his heart beat in his breast enough to break it open. A crowd of horrible thoughts and odd images beset him, and an inner voice said to him every minute, " In an hour everything will be known, and it is your fault ! " However, through

continually asking himself, " Whatever shall I do in this affair ? "
a man often ends by finding some rays of hope.

" If we leave this accursed hotel," said Léon to himself,
" before they discover what has happened in the next room,
perhaps we shall be able to cover up our traces. Nobody knows
us here. They have only seen me in blue glasses, and they have
never seen her without her veil. We are only two steps from the
station, and in an hour we shall be far away from this town."

Then, as he had well studied the time-table in arranging his
elopement, he remembered that a train to Paris passed at eight
o'clock. Soon after that, he and his lady would be lost in the
immensity of that city, that hides so many criminals. Who could
there discover two innocent persons ? But if any one entered the
Englishman's room before eight o'clock ? All the problem was
there.

Well convinced there was nothing else he could do, he made a
desperate effort to shake off the drowsiness that had long been
gaining on him. But at his first movement his companion awoke
and kissed him. At the touch of his icy cheek she gave a little
cry.

" What is the matter ? " she said anxiously. " Your forehead
is like marble."

" It is nothing," he replied in a shaky voice. " I heard a
noise in the next room."

Getting out of bed, he took the blue slipper away, and placed
an arm-chair before the communicating door, so as to hide from
his sweetheart the frightful stream which, having now ceased to
spread, formed a large pool on the floor. Then he opened the
door and listened in the corridor. He even dared to try the door
of the Englishman's room. It was locked. There was already
some stir in the inn. The day was dawning. Some stablemen
were grooming the horses in the yard, and, on the second floor,
an officer was coming downstairs with clanking spurs. He was
going to see that the horses were properly looked after.

Léon returned to the Blue Room, and, with circumlocutions
and euphemisms, and all the precautions that love could suggest,
he told his lady in what situation they were.

It was dangerous to remain, and dangerous to go too soon, and
still more dangerous to wait in the inn until the discovery was
made in the next room. It is useless to describe the fright caused
by this information ; the tears that followed it ; the wild
proposals that were made ; how many times the two unhappy
creatures threw themselves in each other's arms, saying, " Pardon

me ! " " Pardon me ! " Each blamed themselves. They promised to die together ; for the young lady was sure they would be found guilty of the murder of the Englishman ; and as they were not certain they would be permitted to kiss on the scaffold, they stifled each other with embraces, and watered each other with their tears.

At last, having said many absurdities and many loving things, they recognised, in the midst of a thousand kisses, that Léon's plan of departing by the eight o'clock train was the only practical one. But there were still two mortal hours to pass. At each step in the corridor they trembled in all their limbs. Each squeak of a boot announced to them the arrival of the police. Their little luggage was packed in the twinkling of an eye. The young lady wished to burn the blue slipper in the fireplace, but Léon took it and after wiping it on the under bedclothes, he kissed it, and put it in his pocket. He was surprised to find it had a vanilla fragrance : his lady liked the same perfume as the Empress Eugénie.

Already everybody was awake in the inn. They could hear the waiters laughing, the maids singing, the soldiers brushing the officers' clothes. Seven o'clock chimed. Léon wished to get his love to take a cup of coffee but she declared her throat was so tight that she would die if she tried to drink anything. Léon, putting on his blue glasses, went down to pay his bill. The landlord begged his pardon for the noise that had been made. He still could not understand it, for the officers were always so quiet. Léon assured him he had heard nothing, and had slept excellently.

" Now your neighbour in the other room," continued the landlord, " cannot have inconvenienced you, for he has not made much noise. I wager he is still sleeping like the dead."

Léon leant heavily against the desk to prevent himself from falling, and his lady, who had resolved to come with him, clutched his arm, pressing her veil over her eyes.

" It is an English lord," went on the landlord pitilessly. " He always wants the best of everything. Ah, he is a gentleman ! But all the English are not like him. There is another here who is a mean rascal. He finds everything too dear—the room and the dinner. He wanted me to give him a hundred and fifty francs for a Bank of England note of five pounds. But is it good ? Here, sir, you ought to know that, for I heard you speaking English with Madame. Is it a good one ? "

He held out a five pound bank-note. On one of the corners was a little red stain that Léon understood.

"I think it is quite good," he said in a strangled voice.

"Oh, you have plenty of time," continued the landlord. "The train is not due till eight o'clock, and it is always late. Won't you sit down, madame? you seem tired."

At this moment a plump maid entered.

"Some warm water, quick," she said, "for the tea of milord! Get a sponge also! He has broken his bottle of port and all his room is flooded."

Léon let himself fall into a chair; his companion did the same. A strong desire to laugh took them both, and they had some trouble not to give way. The young lady shook him joyfully by the hand.

"Decidely," said Léon to the landlord, "we will not go till the afternoon. Prepare a really good lunch for us at twelve."

THE CAFÉ OF TERROR

THE Marquis always talked very bad English when he was angry, and this morning he was very angry indeed. Climbing up narrow and precipitous paths upon a surface of loose stones, pushing his way occasionally through brambles and undergrowth, and looking downwards from heights, which always made him giddy, had been undertakings which had combined to incense him. He was not dressed or built for such mad escapades. The sight of Madelon, bare-headed, and laughing, having the air of one to whom such excursions, instead of being a torture, were a keen pleasure, only irritated him, whereas the final note of exasperation he discovered in the pleasant good temper of Mr. Samuel T. Billingham, their guide and host, who, with a huge cigar in his mouth, was walking with springy steps and unabated cheerfulness up the path which the Marquis had passionately declared to be only fit for goats and idiots.

" I can no further make this absurd promenade," the Marquis announced, sinking on to a heap of stones and dabbing with a scented pocket-handkerchief drops of moisture upon his forehead, which must not be allowed to reach his eyebrows. " It is an absurdity ! I have a pain of the stomach, a pain of the knees, a pain of the back. It is not for this I came. Where is the automobile ? "

" Poor uncle ! " Madelon sympathised. " I had forgotten that you were not used to walking. You should have lived in England as I have done. But the view—you must admit that the view is marvellous ! "

The comments of the Marquis upon the view were delivered in fluent and sacrilegious French. He displayed an acquaintance with the various forms of blasphemy peculiar to his language which moved even Mr. Billingham to wondering admiration.

" When I feel better," he concluded, after a moment's electric pause, " I shall apologise. At present I will only say that the view from the window of my *salon*, which takes in the Casino and all that glorious sea, is better worth having."

" Less than a kilometre to go," Mr. Billingham declared. " I reckon we shall strike the main road just beyond that clump of firs, and that's where I told the car to pick us up. Another quarter of an hour, Marquis, and we shall be in St. Félix."

" If one could only drink something ! " the latter observed pettishly, as he rose to his feet. " I miss my morning apéritif."

" That's coming to you, sure," Mr. Billingham promised. " I've done this tramp before, and unless I'm mistaken there's a little café where this path joins the cart track."

The prospect was sufficiently encouraging to induce the Marquis to struggle to his feet. They clambered another fifty yards or so up the stony path and found themselves in a rough track which had evidently been made by the carting of timber from the other side of the ravine. A little way along there was a small white-plastered building, to which Mr. Billingham pointed.

" The Café du Forêt ! " he exclaimed. " The worst ever, so far as I remember, but a Dubonnet won't poison us."

The Marquis almost smiled.

" A Dubonnet will be acceptable," he admitted. " The place appears poverty-stricken, but if one can secure an unopened bottle——"

" We'll find that," Mr. Billingham interrupted confidently.

A few minutes' further climb brought them to the café. It was small, dilapidated and uninviting. Nevertheless it proclaimed itself in rudely painted black letters to be a restaurant where " *Vins et Consommations* " were to be obtained. There were three iron tables outside with a couple of chairs at each, but no sign of life. The door stood open and his two companions followed Mr. Billingham inside. There was no one behind the little counter, no one in the rude little compartment with its sanded floor and benches in place of chairs. There were bottles upon the shelves, however, and a tumbler half full of brandy upon the couner. Mr. Billingham raised his voice and the glasses around shook.

" Hallo there ! " he shouted.

" Allo, allo ! " the Marquis echoed. " *N'y a-t-il personne ici pour nous servir ?* "

There was a stolid, unsympathetic lack of response. They waited for a moment, then Mr. Billingham opened the door of the room behind the bar and glanced around. It was a rough-looking kitchen, with a stone floor and a few clumsy articles of furniture. A string of onions, a scraggy piece of meat, and a rabbit hung down from iron hooks in the ceiling. There were pots and dishes upon the table, but no fire or any sign of recent occupation. Mr. Billingham raised his voice again without result, opened still another door, and called up a flight of flimsy stairs—also without result. Then he returned to his companions.

"There is no one about at all," he announced.

"You might try outside," Madelon suggested.

Outside there was no garden but a little clearing, a rudely constructed shed built of pine logs from which the bark had not been stripped, and a lean-to shelter, with a corrugated iron roof, against the wall. Mr. Billingham again, in stentorian tones, invited the presence of the missing innkeeper and again without response. He returned to the bar.

"Deserted!" he exclaimed.

"They were preparing for a *fête* at the small village we passed through last," Madelon remarked. "Perhaps the people have gone there, or the man may work in the woods."

The Marquis smiled. He had been studying the labels upon the bottles.

"At least," he pointed out, "they have left a bottle of Dubonnet. Produce that excellent corkscrew of yours, my friend Billingham. We will serve ourselves and leave the money."

They opened the bottle of Dubonnet which the Marquis had dragged down from the shelf, found some thick wine-glasses, and seated themselves before one of the rude tables outside. Madelon gave a little exclamation of relief as they passed out into the pine-scented sunshine.

"That place gave me the shivers," she declared. "It seemed so very empty, so very silent."

"It's a lonely spot," Mr. Billingham agreed, pouring out the Dubonnet. "They seem to have let off felling the timber round here, and I guess that took the trade away."

"So long as they are absent," the Marquis said, "one owes them gratitude that they left the place open. Never have I tasted Dubonnet with a better flavour. Tell me, my friend Billingham, how much further of this abominable promenade before we reach the automobile?"

"Not more than half a kilometre," Mr. Billingham assured

him. "There's a little path which leads straight up to the road from the cart track. There we shall find the automobile. In a few minutes more we shall be in St. Félix. After that—the *déjeuner* ! "

The Marquis breathed a little sigh of content and helped himself once more from the bottle. Madelon, who had set her glass down empty, was fidgeting about as though anxious to start.

"Hungry ? " Mr. Billingham inquired.

She shook her head.

"I have taken a dislike to this place," she confided. "Am I superstitious, I wonder ? I have a terrible feeling about it."

The Marquis was sympathetic but entirely comfortable and not disposed to hurry. He lit a cigarette and leaned back in his chair.

"I understand," he murmured. "A deserted inn on the edge of the forest ! There are all the materials here for drama. There was a story I once read——"

He broke off abruptly and the cigarette fell from his fingers. Mr. Billingham sprang to his feet. Madelon, who had wandered a few yards away from them and turned back towards the house, was standing suddenly rigid, suddenly pale. The cry which had startled them had escaped from her lips. She pointed to the window above the door.

"There was a face there ! " she cried. "Some one up in the room ! "

Mr. Billingham remained composed.

"Well, I guess that isn't so terrible after all," he observed. "I dare say there's some one ill there. Who was it—a man or a woman ? "

"I do not know," Madelon answered faintly. "It was—just a face ! "

"Seems to have given you a shock," Mr. Billingham continued. "Sit down, Miss Madelon, and drink half a glass more of this stuff. Guess I'd better hunt round and see if there's any help wanted."

Madelon—young woman of nerve and courage though she was—staggered into a chair and was utterly unable to raise to her lips the glass which her uncle hastily filled. Mr. Billingham disappeared inside the building. In about five minutes he returned.

"There's only one room upstairs," he announced, "and there ain't a soul in it."

"But I saw some one," Madelon protested.

He strolled a yard or two away and looked back at the
window, pausing a moment to relight his cigar which had gone
out.

"Well, there's no one there now," he assured her. "There's
only one room and not a cupboard for a hiding-place. There
are two beds—both look as though they'd been slept in—but
there isn't a human being in the shanty. You can take my
word for it."

Madelon looked at him steadfastly. She had drunk some
of the Dubonnet and she was becoming herself again.

"Do you believe, then," she asked, "that I saw the face of
some one who does not exist?"

"I shouldn't say you were the sort who saw spooks," Mr.
Billingham admitted. "All I say is, there's no one there now."

"You must surely have realised, my dear Madelon," the
Marquis intervened, "whether the face was the face of a man
or a woman."

"I should have said that it was the face of a young man,"
Madelon replied, "but it might have been the face of a girl.
There was a mass of black hair. The face itself was smooth.
It was the eyes that were horrible."

"You don't say!" Mr. Billingham murmured with tolerant
sympathy. "Kind of scared, were they?"

Madelon rose to her feet.

"Please let us go now," she begged. "I cannot talk about
it any more. I can only assure you of one thing. Something
terrible has happened here. Please, Mr. Billingham!"

"We'll get right along," was the prompt response. "Ten
francs will square us for the bottle of Dubonnet, I guess—ten
francs and what's left of the bottle. I'll put it underneath the
glass—see? Now, we're right! Just a yard or two through the
trees and then we'll leave this place behind us."

"I hope," Madelon murmured as they passed swiftly back
to the cart track, "that I may be able to forget it."

The Marquis smiled.

"Pooh, pooh, my child!" he exclaimed. "You are too
sensitive, too emotional! Material discomforts you scoff at.
A fancy sometimes tortures you. Behold, the good news!"

He pointed upwards. At the end of the path was the curling
main road and by the side of it the automobile Mr. Billingham
had hired for their day's excursion. No vehicle before had ever
appealed so greatly to the Marquis.

"We've struck it right after all," Mr. Billingham declared

with satisfaction. " Gee, how hot the sun is out here ! Lunch on the terrace in twenty minutes, Miss Madelon. Now, let's forget that dirty little shanty and its spook ! "

The spook was not so easy to forget. Madelon, with Mr. Billingham as her escort, was on her way that evening from the Casino to Ciro's when she suddenly gripped her companion's arm.

" Look," she cried, in a tone vibrant with absolute terror. " Look ! The boy at that table ! "

Mr. Billingham's eyes followed her gesture. The young man was certainly an unusual sight in such surroundings. His clothes, although perfectly new, were clumsily fashioned and of the sort worn on fête days by the peasants. His hat was pushed to the back of his head, and, although it was of the sombrero order affected by the mountaineers of the district, it failed to conceal the masses of black hair which gave him almost a grotesque appearance. His complexion was the usual burnt olive of the Provençal labourer. It was again his expression which arrested. His eyes were large and black, without either the vacancy or the humour of the peasant on a holiday. They looked neither at the people who passed, the trees and flowers of the plaza, nor at the bottle of wine which stood half-empty by his side. They seemed to be looking at something which, if it existed at all, existed far away.

" That," Madelon said, " was the face I saw at the upstairs window of that place this morning."

Her hand was clutching nervously at his arm. Mr. Billingham patted it gently.

" Say, this boy has got on your nerves some," he declared. " I'll go across and have a talk to him. Sit down and wait for me."

" I think I will for a moment," Madelon acquiesced.

She seated herself on one of the benches by the side of the pavement. Mr. Billingham crossed the road and addressed the boy in hesitating but comprehensible French.

" Do you belong to the inn up near St. Félix ? " he inquired. " The young lady and I were there this morning."

The boy stared at his questioner for a moment with parted lips and terrified expression. He made absolutely no reply, however.

" We could not find any one there," Mr. Billingham continued, speaking with laborious care. " We hoped there was nothing wrong."

The boy broke out into a stream of rapid, unintelligible speech, to which Mr. Billingham listened in ever-increasing confusion. He turned round to find Madelon by his side.

" Say, this young goat-herd has got hold of a lingo of his own," he complained. " I don't know as any one but a monkey could tell what he's chattering about. Seems kind of annoyed with me, but I can't get a word of it."

" It is the dialect of the Italians here," Madelon explained. " Let me try."

She spoke to him patiently. The boy only shook his head. Presently he poured out another glass of wine and drank it. Then he sat quite still, stolid and inattentive. He took no notice of Madelon's questions. He showed no sign of understanding a word she said. In the end she was seized by a sudden revulsion. She tugged at her companion's arm.

" Come away ! " she begged. " He will not reply. He pretends not to understand me, though I believe that he does. Let us leave him."

" Guess you're right," Mr. Billingham assented. " He's a crazy loon, if ever there was one, or he wouldn't speak such gibberish. Anyway, it's not our business."

They passed on. The young man looked after them sullenly and helped himself to more wine. Ten minutes later, when Mr. Billingham, obeying an unaccountable impulse, chose a moment when Madelon was talking to some acquaintances and hurried back, the chair was empty. The young man was gone.

" Anyway," Mr. Billingham murmured to himself, struggling against a curious feeling of uneasiness, " it ain't our affair."

Notwithstanding the fact that Mr. Billingham had twice declared that whatever trouble there might be or have been at the little inn on the edge of the forest was not his affair, it was barely ten o'clock in the morning when he left the automobile which he had hired in the Square at Monte Carlo, clambered down the steep path, made his way along the cart track, pushed through the clump of trees and found himself before the café. There was no smoke emerging from the chimney, and Mr. Billingham gave a little start of surprise as he saw on the table, in front of the still open door, the half-consumed bottle of Dubonnet and the ten-franc note under one of the glasses.

" I guess passers-by round here are pretty scarce," he ruminated. " Seems queer that whoever quit the place didn't trouble to lock up. Left in a hurry, perhaps."

Mr. Billingham would doubtless have scorned the suggestion that he talked to himself for the fact of any pleasure he might derive from hearing his own voice, and yet it was without a doubt true that the uneasy feeling of the day before had returned to an even larger extent. He pushed open the door. The half-emptied tumbler was still upon the counter. Some little disarrangement of the bottles upon the shelf, effected by their removal of the bottle of Dubonnet, still existed. He threw open the door leading to the kitchen and called out :

" Hallo there ! "

There was no reply. He mounted the stairs with footsteps which he was half-ashamed to admit were reluctant ones. The bedroom was as empty as it had been on the previous day. There was no place to hide anywhere—no other room. As he descended, however, he realised that it was perfectly possible for the owner of the face whom Madelon had seen there to have escaped by the back door and reached the wood in the matter of a very few seconds. He returned to the kitchen. Here he noticed for the first time that by the side of the fireplace was a clumsy framework door, which looked as though it might have led into a pantry or cupboard. He moved towards it and raised the latch. Before he threw the door open, he knew. When he closed it again—in the space of a second or two—there were great beads of perspiration upon his forehead. The colour had left his cheeks and the blood seemed to have been drained from body. He staggered out into the bar, gripped the counter for a moment, saw a bottle of Martell's brandy on the bottom row of the shelf, seized it, made his faltering way outside, knocked off its neck against the top of one of the iron tables, and drank. . . . Mr. Billingham was a strong man and his recovery was prompt. Nevertheless, he was breathing heavily as he hastened up the hill to where his automobile was waiting.

" Drive to the Mairie at St. Félix," he ordered. . . .

Arrived at the Mairie—a small wistaria-covered building on the outskirts of the straggling village of St. Félix—Mr. Billingham was ushered at once by a gendarme into a bare little apartment with whitewashed walls and a row of benches, in which a very formal-looking gentleman with a closely-trimmed black beard, very smoothly brushed hair, and gold-rimmed pince-nez, was seated at a table, signing documents. His work for the morning had consisted of adjudicating upon a highly important case of fowl stealing, and he looked with some surprise at his visitor's precipitate entrance. Mr. Billingham's opening statement was in far from lucid English. The magistrate, with a puzzled expression, waved him to a seat.

"*Comment*, monsieur?" he exclaimed.

Mr. Billingham pulled himself together. His French, though not rapid, was fairly precise, and he had no difficulty in making himself understood.

"A woman has been murdered at a little café at the edge of the forest," he announced.

The magistrate gasped. The gendarme gasped.

"Continue, monsieur," the former begged.

Mr. Billingham told his story. The magistrate gave him his entire attention. It was a great day, this! A murder! Obviously a murder, in his district! He began to make notes of Mr. Billingham's statement. He was friendly but official. It was quite hopeless for him to conceal the fact that the news had filled him with pleasurable interest. It had been the secret desire of his life to have the handling of such a case.

"I will accompany you to the inn myself at once, monsieur," he announced, rising to his feet. "You can accommodate a gendarme, perhaps, on the front of your car. . . . Let the Court remain open till my return," he directed a subordinate. "Tell me again your story as we proceed, monsieur."

Mr. Billingham went through the few facts again. In response to his own inquiries the magistrate gave him certain information.

"The inn," he said, "was kept by a very respectable, good man, of the name of Pierre Anson. He lived there with his wife, the woman who without a doubt is the victim, and his nephew, a young man of whom one hears not too much of good. The wife, it is reported, had savings—savings of some account—and the nephew knew it. Three days ago news came to Anson of the death of a relative in Marseilles. This I know because he came to me for information as to the burying of the relative and as to his journey. He set off last Monday morning. He was expecting to return to-night. He left alone his wife and this nephew. One fears to reflect what may have happened!"

Mr. Billingham sighed, because he was a kind-hearted man, and because a vision of that flashing knife of the guillotine is terrible to such. Nevertheless it was his duty.

"Last night," he confided, "the young man, who apparently was the newphew of Pierre Anson, was drinking wine at the Café de Paris in Monte Carlo. He was pointed out to me by the young lady, who declared that his was the face she saw at the window."

The magistrate nodded gravely.

" It is a crime," he said, " in effect simple, not uncommon amongst this race of people. When heated with wine and drunk with the desire of pleasure, the shedding of blood is nothing. I, who tell you this, know."

They arrived at their destination. The magistrate and the gendarme made their way to the little room. Mr. Billingham sat outside. He had no soul for horrors. It was an hour before they rejoined him. The magistrate was carrying his notebook in his hand.

" All is clear," he announced. " The savings of the poor woman have disappeared. To-night, or to-morrow at the latest, the young man will be in our hands. Your name and address, if you please, monsieur. You will attend the Court? "

" Certainly," Mr. Billingham promised.

" The young man," the magistrate continued, " will have had two nights of that wild pleasure of which he has lain awake, here in this place of tranquillity, and dreamed. Afterwards—well— he may escape with the penitentiary. One knows little of his age."

Mr. Billingham looked up at the blank window. The silence which brooded over the place remained unbroken. A gendarme, having closed the door, seated himself outside.

" Pierre Anson will arrive by the night train," the magistrate remarked. " It will be a sad home-coming for him."

" Better," Mr. Billingham rejoined, with a little shiver, " than if he had found the house empty and opened that door, as I did."

The most pathetic sight in the bare, whitewashed little room of the Mairie on the first morning of the examination was Pierre Anson, the woodman. The tears streamed down his brown, wrinkled face as the magistrate addressed his first few kindly questions. He had, at one time, as was evident, been a man of great stature and strength. Now he seemed shrunken up, stricken with the horror of his home-coming.

" Your wife had savings, Pierre Anson? " the magistrate asked him.

" She was a thrifty woman," was the tremulous reply. " She had always a stocking."

" Do you know how much was in it? "

" She never told me."

" Did your nephew—the young man between the gendarmes

there—the young man whom you trusted alone with your wife —did he know ? "

" I cannot tell," Pierre Anson answered. " He was always wanting money."

" You have been to Marseilles to bury a relative—is it not so ? "

" Yes, monsieur."

" You thought it safe to leave this youth, of whose character we hear little that is good, alone with your wife in such a desolate spot ? "

" She was his aunt," the man announced, with a little sob. " How would I dream of anything so horrible ? "

The magistrate bent over his papers. Mr. Billingham, seated by his side, watched the shaft of sunlight which had found its way through the cobwebbed windows and had fallen upon the boy's face. Madelon, who had also been invited by the magistrate to occupy a chair near him, scribbled something on a piece of paper and passed it to her neighbour. He glanced at it and passed it on to the magistrate, who studied it through his pince-nez with pursed lips. Finally, with a little shrug of the shoulders, he twiddled it between his fingers.

" Where did you stay in Marseilles, Pierre Anson ? " he asked suddenly.

The woodman lifted his head and stared uncomprehendingly at his questioner.

" I asked you where you stayed in Marseilles," the magistrate repeated.

Pierre Anson shook his head.

" I do not remember," he said. " It was a small lodging-house down by the quay."

" You do not remember ? " the magistrate echoed, in a tone of some surprise. " Is that not strange, Pierre Anson ? "

" It was somewhere near where my cousin lay dead," the man answered, a little sullenly. " I could find the place—the name I never knew."

The magistrate's right arm suddenly shot out.

" Or is it that you are lying, Pierre Anson ? " he thundered. " Is it that you yourself, before you left home in the small hours of that Tuesday morning, murdered your wife and stole her savings, forced two of the notes on that half-witted youth, persuaded him to buy clothes and go down to Monte Carlo, and went yourself to Nice—your *rendezvous* at Nice—to your *rendezvous* with Lucie Bérard ? "

The man half-rose to his feet. His eyes seemed suddenly bloodshot. He swayed about as though striving to speak.

" Bring the woman," the magistrate ordered.

Pierre Anson glanced fearfully towards the door. A woman in the care of a gendarme entered. They looked at one another across the room—the man and the woman—and one understood.

" The money of which you robbed your wife, Pierre Anson," the magistrate continued, " was found upon this woman. You have visited her month by month in Nice. You would have thrust the burden of this crime upon your nephew. You yourself are the murderer ! Do you confess ? "

A cry rang through the Court—not from the man, Pierre Anson, who was indeed incapable of speech, whose hands were fighting the air, who fought against unconsciousness, but from the boy who stood between the gendarmes. His eyes were fixed upon the woman who had entered the Court Room. His indifference had vanished. His eyes again were lit with fear.

" Mother ! " he cried.

" It is I ! " she answered.

The boy turned towards the magistrate.

" It was I who killed the woman," he pleaded. " No one else knows anything about it."

" You are a liar and a fool ! " the woman declared angrily. " It was he, the bungler there," she added, pointing to Pierre Anson. " And there is the money."

She dashed a bundle of notes upon the floor and stood with folded arms, defiant, the incarnation of an evil spirit. A gendarme touched Pierre Anson upon the shoulder. The proceedings were over.

Afterwards the magistrate entertained his two distinguished guests with a bottle of sweet wine and biscuits in his retiring-room. He was well pleased with the whole business.

" Amongst the lowest classes of our peasants," he explained, " these family dramas are not uncommon. Pierre Anson, as the story goes now, loved both sisters. He married the older one— a widow with money. The rest of the story unfolds itself. Yet Pierre Anson had cunning which few of these peasants possess. He deceived us all. It is to you, monsieur," he added, turning to Mr. Billingham, " that we owe the clue by means of which we arrived at the truth."

Mr. Billingham shook his head.

" Not to me," he rejoined ; " to the young lady."

The magistrate bowed.

" Then might one inquire," he ventured, " what led the young lady to doubt the lad's guilt ? "

Madelon was once more serious.

" Something in his eyes," she confided, with a little shudder of reminiscence ; " something which was there and something which was not there."

The magistrate raised his glass and bowed first to Madelon, then to Mr. Billingham.

" Something in his eyes," he repeated. " Well, one reads somewhere in a lay commentary upon our laws and the discovery of crime, that the born detective must have an instinct for the truth. Mademoiselle, there is a great vocation open to you."

Madelon smiled. She sipped her wine, but she remained silent.

THE AVENGING CHANCE

ROGER SHERINGHAM was inclined to think afterwards that the Poisoned Chocolates Case, as the papers called it, was perhaps the most perfectly planned murder he had ever encountered. The motive was so obvious, when you knew where to look for it—but you didn't know ; the method was so significant when you had grasped its real essentials—but you didn't grasp them ; the traces were so thinly covered, when you had realised what was covering them—but you didn't realise. But for a piece of the merest bad luck, which the murderer could not possibly have foreseen, the crime must have been added to the classical list of great mysteries.

This is the gist of the case, as Chief-Inspector Moresby told it one evening to Roger in the latter's rooms in the Albany a week or so after it happened :

On Friday morning, the fifteenth of November, at half-past ten in the morning, in accordance with his invariable custom, Sir William Anstruther walked into his club in Piccadilly, the very exclusive Rainbow Club, and asked for his letters. The porter handed him three and a small parcel. Sir William walked over to the fireplace in the big lounge hall to open them.

A few minutes later another member entered the club, a Mr. Graham Beresford. There were a letter and a couple of circulars for him, and he also strolled over to the fireplace, nodding to Sir William, but not speaking to him. The two men only knew each other very slightly, and had probably never exchanged more than a dozen words in all.

Having glanced through his letters, Sir William opened the parcel and, after a moment, snorted with disgust. Beresford looked at him, and with a grunt Sir William thrust out a letter

which had been enclosed in the parcel. Concealing a smile
(Sir William's ways were a matter of some amusement to his
fellow-members), Beresford read the letter. It was from a big
firm of chocolate manufacturers, Mason & Sons, and set forth
that they were putting on the market a new brand of liqueur
chocolates designed especially to appeal to men ; would Sir
William do them the honour of accepting the enclosed two-
pound box and letting the firm have his candid opinion of them ?

" Do they think I'm a blank chorus-girl ? " fumed Sir William.
" Write 'em testimonials about their blank chocolates, indeed !
Blank 'em ! I'll complain to the blank committee. That sort of
blank thing can't blank well be allowed here."

" Well, it's an ill wind so far as I'm concerned," Beresford
soothed him. " It's reminded me of something. My wife and I
had a box at the Imperial last night. I bet her a box of chocolates
to a hundred cigarettes that she wouldn't spot the villain by the
end of the second act. She won. I must remember to get them.
Have you seen it—*The Creaking Skull* ? Not a bad show."

Sir William had not seen it, and said so with force.

" Want a box of chocolates, did you say ? " he added, more
mildly. " Well, take this blank one. I don't want it."

For a moment Beresford demurred politely and then, most
unfortunately for himself, accepted. The money so saved meant
nothing to him for he was a wealthy man ; but trouble was
always worth saving.

By an extraordinarily lucky chance neither the outer wrapper
of the box nor its covering letter were thrown into the fire, and
this was the more fortunate in that both men had tossed the
envelopes of their letters into the flames. Sir William did, indeed,
make a bundle of the wrapper, letter and string, but he handed
it over to Beresford, and the latter simply dropped it inside the
fender. This bundle the porter subsequently extracted and, being
a man of orderly habits, put it tidily away in the waste-paper
basket, whence it was retrieved later by the police.

Of the three unconscious protagonists in the impending
tragedy, Sir William was without doubt the most remarkable.
Still a year of two under fifty, he looked, with his flaming red
face and thick-set figure, a typical country squire of the old
school, and both his manners and his language were in accordance
with tradition. His habits, especially as regards women, were
also in accordance with tradition—the tradition of the bold, bad
baronet which he undoubtedly was.

In comparison with him, Beresford was rather an ordinary

man, a tall, dark, not unhandsome fellow of two-and-thirty,
quiet and reserved. His father had left him a rich man, but
idleness did not appeal to him, and he had a finger in a good
many business pies.

Money attracts money. Graham Beresford had inherited it,
he made it, and, inevitably, he had married it, too. The daughter
of a late shipowner in Liverpool, with not far off half a million
in her own right. But the money was incidental, for he needed
her and would have married her just as inevitably (said his
friends) if she had not had a farthing. A tall, rather serious-
minded, highly cultured girl, and not so young that her character
had not had time to form (she was twenty-five when Beresford
married her, three years ago), she was the ideal wife for him.
A bit of a Puritan perhaps in some ways, but Beresford, whose
wild oats, though duly sown, had been a sparse crop, was ready
enough to be a Puritan himself by that time if she was. To
make no bones about it, the Beresfords succeeded in achieving
that eighth wonder of the modern world, a happy marriage.

And into the middle of it there dropped with irretrievable
tragedy, the box of chocolates.

Beresford gave them to her after lunch as they sat over their
coffee, with some jesting remark about paying his honourable
debts, and she opened the box at once. The top layer, she
noticed, seemed to consist only of kirsch and maraschino.
Beresford, who did not believe in spoiling good coffee, refused
when she offered him the box, and his wife ate the first one
alone. As she did so she exclaimed in surprise that the filling
seemed exceedingly strong and positively burnt her mouth.

Beresford explained that they were samples of a new brand
and then, made curious by what his wife had said, took one
too. A burning taste, not intolerable but much too strong to be
pleasant, followed the release of the liquid, and the almond
flavouring seemed quite excessive.

" By jove," he said, " they are strong. They must be filled
with neat alcohol."

" Oh, they wouldn't do that, surely," said his wife, taking
another. " But they are very strong. I think I rather like them,
though."

Beresford ate another, and disliked it still more. " I don't,"
he said with decision. " They make my tongue feel quite numb.
I shouldn't eat any more of them if I were you. I think there's
something wrong with them."

" Well, they're only an experiment, I suppose," she said.

"But they do burn. I'm not sure whether I like them or not."

A few minutes later Beresford went out to keep a business appointment in the city. He left her still trying to make up her mind whether she liked them, and still eating them to decide. Beresford remembered that scrap of conversation afterwards very vividly, because it was the last time he saw his wife alive.

That was roughly half-past two. At a quarter to four Beresford arrived at his club from the city in a taxi, in a state of collapse. He was helped into the building by the driver and the porter, and both described him subsequently as pale to the point of ghastliness, with staring eyes and livid lips, and his skin damp and clammy. His mind seemed unaffected, however, and when they had got him up the steps he was able to walk, with the porter's help, into the lounge.

The porter, thoroughly alarmed, wanted to send for a doctor at once, but Beresford, who was the last man in the world to make a fuss, refused to let him, saying that it must be indigestion and he would be all right in a few minutes. To Sir William Anstruther, however, who was in the lounge at the time, he added after the porter had gone :

"Yes, and I believe it was those infernal chocolates you gave me, now I come to think of it. I thought there was something funny about them at the time. I'd better go and find out if my wife——" He broke off abruptly. His body, which had been leaning back limply in his chair, suddenly heaved rigidly upright ; his jaws locked together, the livid lips drawn back in a horrible grin, and his hands clenched on the arms of his chair. At the same time Sir William became aware of an unmistakable smell of bitter almonds.

Thoroughly alarmed, believing indeed that the man was dying under his eyes, Sir William raised a shout for the porter and a doctor. The other occupants of the lounge hurried up, and between them they got the convulsed body of the unconscious man into a more comfortable position. Before the doctor could arrive a telephone message was received at the club from an agitated butler asking if Mr. Beresford was there, and if so would he come home at once as Mrs. Beresford had been taken seriously ill. As a matter of fact she was already dead.

Beresford did not die. He had taken less of the poison than his wife, who after his departure must have eaten at least three more of the chocolates, so that its action was less rapid and the doctor had time to save him. As a matter of fact it turned out afterwards that he had not had a fatal dose. By about eight o'clock that night he was conscious ; the next day he was practically convalescent.

As for the unfortunate Mrs. Beresford, the doctor had arrived too late to save her, and she passed away very rapidly in a deep coma.

The police had taken the matter in hand as soon as Mrs. Beresford's death was reported to them and the fact of poison established, and it was only a very short time before things had become narrowed down to the chocolates as the active agent.

Sir William was interrogated, the letter and wrapper were recovered from the waste-paper basket, and, even before the sick man was out of danger, a detective-inspector was asking for an interview with the managing-director of Mason & Sons. Scotland Yard moves quickly.

It was the police theory at this stage, based on what Sir William and the two doctors had been able to tell them, that by an act of criminal carelessness on the part of one of Mason's employees, an excessive amount of oil of bitter almonds had been included in the filling mixture of the chocolates, for that was what the doctors had decided must be the poisoning ingredient. However, the managing-director quashed this idea at once : oil of bitter almonds, he asserted, was never used by Mason's.

He had more interesting news still. Having read with undisguised astonishment the covering letter, he at once declared that it was a forgery. No such letter, no such samples had been sent out by the firm at all ; a new variety of liqueur-chocolates had never even been mooted. The fatal chocolates were their ordinary brand.

Unwrapping and examining one more closely, he called the Inspector's attention to a mark on the underside, which he suggested was the remains of a small hole drilled in the case, through which the liquid could have been extracted and the fatal filling inserted, the hole afterwards being stopped up with softened chocolate, a perfectly simple operation.

He examined it under a magnifying-glass and the Inspector agreed. It was now clear to him that somebody had been trying deliberately to murder Sir William Anstruther.

Scotland Yard doubled its activities. The chocolates were sent for analysis, Sir William was interviewed again, and so was the now conscious Beresford. From the latter the doctor insisted that the news of his wife's death must be kept till the next day, as in his weakened condition the shock might be fatal, so that nothing very helpful was obtained from him.

Nor could Sir William throw any light on the mystery or produce a single person who might have any grounds for trying to kill him. He was living apart from his wife, who was the principal beneficiary in his will, but she was in the South of France, as the French police subsequently confirmed. His estate in Worcestershire, heavily mortgaged, was entailed and went to a nephew ; but as the rent he got for it barely covered the interest on the mortgage, and the nephew was considerably better off than Sir William himself, there was no motive there. The police were at a dead end.

The analysis brought one or two interesting facts to light. Not oil of bitter almonds but nitrobenzine, a kindred substance, chiefly used in the manufacture of aniline dyes, was the somewhat surprising poison employed. Each chocolate in the upper layer contained exactly six minims of it, in a mixture of kirsch and maraschino. The chocolates in the other layers were harmless.

As to the other clues, they seemed equally useless. The sheet of Mason's notepaper was identified by Merton's, the printers, as of their work, but there was nothing to show how it had got into the murderer's possession. All that could be said was that, the edges being distinctly yellowed, it must be an old piece. The machine on which the letter had been typed, of course, could not be traced. From the wrapper, a piece of ordinary brown paper with Sir William's address hand-printed on it in large capitals, there was nothing to be learnt at all beyond that the parcel had been posted at the office in Southampton Street between the hours of 8.30 and 9.30 on the previous evening.

Only one thing was quite clear. Whoever had coveted Sir William's life had no intention of paying for it with his or her own.

" And now you know as much as we do, Mr. Sheringham," concluded Chief-Inspector Moresby ; " and if you can say who sent those chocolates to Sir William, you'll know a good deal more."

Roger nodded thoughtfully.

" It's a brute of a case. I met a man only yesterday who was at school with Beresford. He didn't know him very well because Beresford was on the modern side and my friend was a classical bird, but they were in the same house. He says Beresford's absolutely knocked over by his wife's death. I wish you could find out who sent those chocolates, Moresby."

"So do I, Mr. Sheringham," said Moresby gloomily.

"It might have been any one in the whole world," Roger mused. "What about feminine jealousy, for instance? Sir William's private life doesn't seem to be immaculate. I dare say there's a good deal of off with the old light-o'-love and on with the new."

"Why, that's just what I've been looking into, Mr. Sheringham, sir," retorted Chief-Inspector Moresby reproachfully. "That was the first thing that came to me. Because if anything does stand out about this business it is that it's a woman's crime. Nobody but a woman would send poisoned chocolates to a man. Another man would send a poisoned sample of whisky, or something like that."

"That's a very sound point, Moresby," Roger meditated. "Very sound indeed. And Sir William couldn't help you?"

"Couldn't," said Moresby, not without a trace of resentment, "or wouldn't. I was inclined to believe at first that he might have his suspicions and was shielding some woman. But I don't think so now."

"Humph!" Roger did not seem quite so sure. "It's reminiscent, this case, isn't it? Didn't some lunatic once send poisoned chocolates to the Commissioner of Police himself? A good crime always gets imitated, as you know."

Moresby brightened.

"It's funny you should say that, Mr. Sheringham, because that's the very conclusion I've come to. I've tested every other theory, and so far as I know there's not a soul with an interest in Sir William's death, whether from motives of gain, revenge, or what you like, whom I haven't had to rule quite out of it. In fact, I've pretty well made up my mind that the person who sent those chocolates was some irresponsible lunatic of a woman, a social or religious fanatic who's probably never seen him. And if that's the case," Moresby sighed, "a fat chance I have of ever laying hands on her."

"Unless Chance steps in, as it so often does," said Roger brightly, "and helps you. A tremendous lot of cases get solved by a stroke of sheer luck, don't they? *Chance the Avenger*. It would make an excellent film-title. But there's a lot of truth in it. If I were superstitious, which I'm not, I should say it wasn't chance at all, but Providence avenging the victim."

"Well, Mr. Sheringham," said Moresby, who was not superstitious either, "to tell the truth, I don't mind what it is, so long as it lets me get my hands on the right person."

If Moresby had paid his visit to Roger Sheringham with any hope of tapping that gentleman's brains, he went away disappointed.

To tell the truth, Roger was inclined to agree with the Chief Inspector's conclusion, that the attempt on the life of Sir William Anstruther and the actual murder of the unfortunate Mrs. Beresford must be the work of some unknown criminal lunatic. For this reason, although he thought about it a good deal during the next few days, he made no attempt to take the case in hand. It was the sort of affair, necessitating endless inquiries that a private person would have neither the time nor the authority to carry out, which can be handled only by the official police. Roger's interest in it was purely academic.

It was hazard, a chance encounter nearly a week later, which translated this interest from the academic into the personal.

Roger was in Bond Street, about to go through the distressing ordeal of buying a new hat. Along the pavement he suddenly saw bearing down on him Mrs. Verreker-le-Flemming. Mrs. Verreker-le-Flemming was small, exquisite, rich, and a widow, and she sat at Roger's feet whenever he gave her the opportunity. But she talked. She talked, in fact, and talked, and talked. And Roger, who rather liked talking himself, could not bear it. He tried to dart across the road, but there was no opening in the traffic stream. He was cornered.

Mrs. Verreker-le-Flemming fastened on him gladly.

"Oh, Mr. Sheringham! *Just* the person I wanted to see. Mr. Sheringham, *do* tell me. In confidence. *Are* you taking up this dreadful business of poor Joan Beresford's death?"

Roger, the frozen and imbecile grin of civilised intercourse on his face, tried to get a word in; without result.

"I was horrified when I heard of it—simply horrified. You see, Joan and I were such *very* close friends. Quite intimate. And the awful thing, the truly *terrible* thing is that Joan brought the whole business on herself. Isn't that *appalling*?"

Roger no longer wanted to escape.

"What did you say?" he managed to insert incredulously.

"I suppose it's what they call tragic irony," Mrs. Verreker-le-Flemming chattered on. "Certainly it was tragic enough, and I've never heard anything so terribly ironical. You know about that bet she made with her husband, of course, so that he had to get her a box of chocolates, and if he hadn't Sir William would never have given him the poisoned ones and he'd have eaten them and died himself and good riddance? Well, Mr. Shering-

ham——" Mrs. Verreker-le-Flemming lowered her voice to a
conspirator's whisper and glanced about her in the approved
manner. " I've never told anybody else this, but I'm telling you
because I know you'll appreciate it. *Joan wasn't playing fair!* "
   " How do you mean ? " Roger asked, bewildered.
   Mrs. Verreker-le-Flemming was artlessly pleased with her
sensation.
   " Why, she'd seen the play before. We went together, the
very first week it was on. She *knew* who the villain was all the
time."
   " By jove ! " Roger was as impressed as Mrs. Verreker-le-
Flemming could have wished. " Chance the Avenger ! We're
none of us immune from it."
   " Poetic justice, you mean ? " twittered Mrs. Verreker-le-
Flemming, to whom these remarks had been somewhat obscure.
" Yes, but Joan Beresford of all people ! That's the extraordinary
thing. I should never have thought Joan *would* do a thing like
that. She was such a *nice* girl. A little close with money, of course,
considering how well-off they are, but that isn't anything. Of
course it was only fun, and pulling her husband's leg, but I
always used to think Joan was such a *serious* girl, Mr. Sheringham.
I mean, ordinary people don't talk about honour, and truth, and
playing the game, and all those things one takes for granted.
But Joan did. She was always saying that this wasn't honourable,
or that wouldn't be playing the game. Well, she paid herself
for not playing the game, poor girl, didn't she ? Still, it all goes
to show the truth of the old saying, doesn't it ? "
   " What old saying ? " said Roger, hypnotised by this flow.
   " Why, that still waters run deep. Joan must have been deep,
I'm afraid." Mrs. Verreker-le-Flemming sighed. It was evidently
a social error to be deep. " I mean, she certainly took me in. She
can't have been quite so honourable and truthful as she was
always pretending, can she ? And I can't help wondering whether
a girl who'd deceive her husband in a little thing like that might
not—oh, well, I don't want to say anything against poor Joan
now she's dead, poor darling, but she can't have been *quite* such
a plaster saint after all, can she ? I mean," said Mrs. Verreker-
le-Flemming, in hasty extenuation of these suggestions, " I do
think psychology is so very interesting, don't you, Mr. Sheringham ? "
   " Sometimes, very," Roger agreed gravely. " But you mentioned Sir William Anstruther just now. Do you know him, too ? "
   " I used to," Mrs. Verrêker-le-Flemming replied, without

particular interest. " Horrible man ! Always running after some
woman or other. And when he's tired of her, just drops her—
biff !—like that. At least," added Mrs. Verreker-le-Flemming
somewhat hastily, " so I've heard."

" And what happens if she refuses to be dropped ? "

" Oh, dear, I'm sure I don't know. I suppose you've heard
the latest ? "

Mrs. Verreker-le-Flemming hurried on, perhaps a trifle more
pink than the delicate aids to nature on her cheeks would have
warranted.

" He's taken up with that Bryce woman now. You know,
the wife of the oil man, or petrol, or whatever he made his
money in. It began about three weeks ago. You'd have thought
that dreadful business of being responsible, in a way, for poor
Joan Beresford's death would have sobered him up a little,
wouldn't you ? But not a bit of it ; he——"

Roger was following another line of thought.

" What a pity you weren't at the Imperial with the Beresfords
that evening. She'd never have made that bet if you had been."
Roger looked extremely innocent. " You weren't, I suppose ? "

" I ? " queried Mrs. Verreker-le-Flemming in surprise.
" Good gracious, no. I was at the new revue at the Pavilion.
Lady Gavelstoke had a box and asked me to join her party."

" Oh, yes. Good show, isn't it ? I thought that sketch *The
Sempiternal Triangle* very clever. Didn't you ? "

" *The Sempiternal Triangle* ? " wavered Mrs. Verreker-le-
Flemming.

" Yes, in the first half."

" Oh ! Then I didn't see it. I got there disgracefully late,
I'm afraid. But then," said Mrs. Verreker-le-Flemming with
pathos, " I always do seem to be late for simply everything."

Roger kept the rest of the conversation resolutely upon
theatres. But before he left her he had ascertained that she had
photographs of both Mrs. Beresford and Sir William Anstruther,
and had obtained permission to borrow them some time. As soon
as she was out of view he hailed a taxi and gave Mrs. Verreker-le-
Flemming's address. He thought it better to take advantage of
her permission at a time when he would not have to pay for it a
second time over.

The parlourmaid seemed to think there was nothing odd in
his mission, and took him up to the drawing-room at once. A
corner of the room was devoted to the silver-framed photographs
of Mrs. Verreker-le-Flemming's friends, and there were many

of them. Roger examined them with interest, and finally took away with him not two photographs but six, those of Sir William, Mrs. Beresford, Beresford, two strange males who appeared to belong to the Sir William period, and, lastly, a likeness of Mrs. Verreker-le-Flemming herself. Roger liked confusing his trail.

For the rest of the day he was very busy.

His activities would have no doubt seemed to Mrs. Verreker-le-Flemming not merely baffling but pointless. He paid a visit to a public library, for instance, and consulted a work of reference, after which he took a taxi and drove to the offices of the Anglo-Eastern Perfumery Company, where he inquired for a certain Mr. Joseph Lea Hardwick and seemed much put out on hearing that no such gentleman was known to the firm and was certainly not employed in any of their branches. Many questions had to be put about the firm and its branches before he consented to abandon the quest.

After that he drove to Messrs. Weall and Wilson, the well-known institution which protects the trade interests of individuals and advises its subscribers regarding investments. Here he entered his name as a subscriber, and explaining that he had a large sum of money to invest, filled in one of the special inquiry forms which are headed Strictly Confidential.

Then he went to the Rainbow Club, in Piccadilly.

Introducing himself to the porter without a blush as connected with Scotland Yard, he asked the man a number of questions, more or less trivial, concerning the tragedy.

" Sir William, I understand," he said finally, as if by the way, " did not dine here the evening before ? "

There it appeared that Roger was wrong. Sir William had dined in the club, as he did about three times a week.

" But I quite understood he wasn't here that evening ? " Roger said plaintively.

The porter was emphatic. He remembered quite well. So did a waiter, whom the porter summoned to corroborate him. Sir William had dined, rather late, and had not left the dining-room till about nine o'clock. He spent the evening there, too, the waiter knew, or at least some of it, for he himself had taken him a whisky-and-soda in the lounge not less than half an hour later.

Roger retired.

He retired to Merton's, in a taxi.

It seemed that he wanted some new notepaper printed, of a very special kind, and to the young woman behind the counter he specified at great length and in wearisome detail exactly what he did want. The young woman handed him the books of specimen pieces and asked him to see if there was any style there which would suit him. Roger glanced through them, remarking garrulously to the young woman that he had been recommended to Merton's by a very dear friend, whose photograph he happened to have on him at that moment. Wasn't that a curious coincidence? The young woman agreed that it was.

"About a fortnight ago, I think, my friend was in here last," said Roger, producing the photograph. " Recognise this? "

The young woman took the photograph, without apparent interest.

" Oh, yes. I remember. About some notepaper, too, wasn't it? So that's your friend. Well, it's a small world. Now this is a line we're selling a good deal of just now."

Roger went back to his rooms to dine. Afterwards, feeling restless, he wandered out of the Albany and turned up Piccadilly. He wandered round the Circus, thinking hard, and paused for a moment out of habit to inspect the photographs of the new revue hung outside the Pavilion. The next thing he realised was that he had got as far as Jermyn Street and was standing outside the Imperial Theatre. Glancing at the advertisements of *The Creaking Skull,* he saw that it began at half-past eight. Glancing at his watch, he saw that the time was twenty-nine minutes past that hour. He had an evening to get through somehow. He went inside.

The next morning, very early for Roger, he called on Moresby at Scotland Yard.

" Moresby," he said without preamble, " I want you to do something for me. Can you find me a taximan who took a fare from Piccadilly circus or its neighbourhood at about ten-past nine on the evening before the Beresford crime, to the Strand somewhere near the bottom of Southampton Street, and another who took a fare back between those points. I'm not sure about the first. Or one taxi might have been used for the double journey, but I doubt that. Anyhow, try to find out for me, will you? "

" What are you up to now, Mr. Sheringham? " Moresby asked suspiciously.

" Breaking down an interesting alibi," replied Roger serenely. " By the way, I know who sent those chocolates to Sir William. I'm just building up a nice structure of evidence for you. Ring up my rooms when you've got those taximen."

He strolled out, leaving Moresby positively gaping after him.

The rest of the day he spent apparently trying to buy a second-hand typewriter. He was very particular that it should be a Hamilton No. 4. When the shop-people tried to induce him to consider other makes he refused to look at them, saying that he had had the Hamilton No. 4 so strongly recommended to him by a friend, who had bought one about three weeks ago. Perhaps it was at this very shop? No? They hadn't sold a Hamilton No. 4 for the last three months? How odd.

But at one shop they had sold a Hamilton No. 4 within the last month, and that was odder still.

At half-past four Roger got back to his rooms to await the telephone message from Moresby. At half-past five it came.

" There are fourteen taxi-drivers here, littering up my office," said Moresby offensively. " What do you want me to do with 'em?"

" Keep them till I come, Chief Inspector," returned Roger with dignity.

The interview with the fourteen was brief enough, however. To each man in turn Roger showed a photograph, holding it so that Moresby could not see it, and asked if he could recognise his fare. The ninth man did so, without hesitation.

At a nod from Roger, Moresby dismissed them, then sat at his table and tried to look official. Roger seated himself on the table, looking most unofficial, and swung his legs. As he did so, a photograph fell unnoticed out of his pocket and fluttered, face downwards, under the table. Moresby eyed it but did not pick it up.

" And now, Mr. Sheringham, sir," he said, " perhaps you'll tell me what you've been doing ? "

" Certainly, Moresby," said Roger blandly. " Your work for you. I really have solved the thing, you know. Here's your evidence." He took from his note-case an old letter and handed it to the Chief Inspector. " Was that typed on the same machine as the forged letter from Mason's, or was it not ? "

Moresby studied it for a moment, then drew the forged letter from a drawer of his table and compared the two minutely.

" Mr. Sheringham," he said soberly, " where did you get hold of this ? "

" In a second-hand typewriter shop in St. Martin's Lane. The machine was sold to an unknown customer about a month ago. They identified the customer from that same photograph. As it happened, this machine had been used for a time in the office after it was repaired, to see that it was O.K., and I easily got hold of that specimen of its work."

ANTHONY BERKELEY

"And where is the machine now?"

"Oh, at the bottom of the Thames, I expect," Roger smiled. "I tell you, this criminal takes no unnecessary chances. But that doesn't matter. There's your evidence."

"Humph! It's all right so far as it goes," conceded Moresby. "But what about Mason's paper?"

"That," said Roger calmly, "was extracted from Merton's book of sample notepapers, as I'd guessed from the very yellowed edges might be the case. I can prove contact of the criminal with the book, and there is a gap which will certainly turn out to have been filled by that piece of paper."

"That's fine," Moresby said more heartily.

"As for that taximan, the criminal had an alibi. You've heard it broken down. Between ten-past nine and twenty-five past, in fact, during the time when the parcel must have been posted, the murderer took a hurried journey to that neighbourhood, going probably by bus or Underground, but returning, as I expected, by taxi, because time would be getting short."

"And the murderer, Mr. Sheringham?"

"The person whose photograph is in my pocket," Roger said unkindly. "By the way, do you remember what I was saying the other day about Chance the Avenger, my excellent film-title? Well, it's worked again. By a chance meeting in Bond Street with a silly woman I was put, by the merest accident, in possession of a piece of information which showed me then and there who had sent those chocolates addressed to Sir William. There were other possibilities, of course, and I tested them, but then and there on the pavement I saw the whole thing, from first to last."

"Who was the murderer, then, Mr. Sheringham?" repeated Moresby.

"It was so beautifully planned," Roger went on dreamily. "We never grasped for one moment that we were making the fundamental mistake that the murderer all along intended us to make."

"And what was that?" asked Moresby.

"Why, that the plan had miscarried. That the wrong person had been killed. That was just the beauty of it. The plan had *not* miscarried. It had been brilliantly successful. The wrong person was *not* killed. Very much the right person was."

Moresby gaped.

"Why, how on earth do you make that out, sir?"

"Mrs. Beresford was the objective all the time. That's why

the plot was so ingenious. Everything was anticipated. It was perfectly natural that Sir William should hand the chocolates over to Beresford. It was foreseen that we should look for the criminal among Sir William's associates and not the dead woman's. It was probably even foreseen that the crime would be considered the work of a woman ! "

Moresby, unable to wait any longer, snatched up the photograph.

"Good heavens ! But Mr. Sheringham, you don't mean to tell me that . . . Sir William himself ! "

" He wanted to get rid of Mrs. Beresford," Roger continued. " He had liked her well enough at the beginning, no doubt, though it was her money he was after all the time.

" But the real trouble was that she was too close with her money. He wanted it, or some of it, pretty badly ; and she wouldn't part. There's no doubt about the motive. I made a list of the firms he's interested in and got a report on them. They're all rocky, every one. He'd got through all his own money, and he had to get more.

" As for the nitrobenzine which puzzled us so much, that was simple enough, I looked it up and found that beside the uses you told me, it's used largely in perfumery. And he's got a perfumery business. The Anglo-Eastern Perfumery Company. That's how he'd know about it being poisonous, of course. But I should think he got his supply from there. He'd be cleverer than that. He probably made the stuff himself. Any schoolboy knows how to treat benzol with nitric acid to get nitrobenzine."

" But," stammered Moresby, " but Sir William. . . . He was at Eton."

" Sir William ? " said Roger sharply. " Who's talking about Sir William ? I told you the photograph of the murderer was in my pocket." He whipped out the photograph in question and confronted the astounded Chief Inspector with it. " Beresford, man ! Beresford's the murderer of his own wife.

" Beresford, who still had hankerings after a gay life," he went on more mildly, " didn't want his wife but did want her money. He contrived this plot, providing as he thought against every contingency that could possibly arise. He established a mild alibi, if suspicion ever should arise, by taking his wife to the Imperial, and slipped out of the theatre at the first interval. (I sat through the first act of the dreadful thing myself last night to see when the interval came.) Then he hurried down to the Strand, posted his parcel, and took a taxi back. He had ten minutes, but nobody would notice if he got back to the box a minute late.

" And the rest simply followed. He knew Sir William came to the club every morning at ten-thirty, as regularly as clock-work ; he knew that for a psychological certainty he could get the chocolates handed over to him if he hinted for them ; he knew that the police would go chasing after all sorts of false trails starting from Sir William. And as for the wrapper and the forged letter, he carefully didn't destroy them because they were calculated not only to divert suspicion but actually to point away from him to some anonymous lunatic."

" Well, it's very smart of you, Mr. Sheringham," Moresby said, with a little sigh, but quite ungrudgingly. " Very smart indeed. What was it the lady told you that showed you the whole thing in a flash ? "

" Why, it wasn't so much what she actually told me as what I heard between her words, so to speak. What she told me was that Mrs. Beresford knew the answer to that bet ; what I deduced was that, being the sort of person she was, it was quite incredible that she should have made a bet to which she knew the answer. *Ergo*, she didn't. *Ergo*, there never was such a bet. *Ergo*, Beresford was lying. *Ergo*, Beresford wanted to get hold of those chocolates for some reason other than he stated. After all, we only had Beresford's word for the bet, hadn't we ?

" Of course he wouldn't have left her that afternoon till he'd seen her take, or somehow made her take, at least six of the chocolates, more than a lethal dose. That's why the stuff was in those meticulous six-minim doses. And so that he could take a couple himself, of course. A clever stroke, that."

Moresby rose to his feet.

" Well, Mr. Sheringham, I'm much obliged to you, sir. And now I shall have to get busy myself." He scratched his head. " Chance the Avenger, eh ? Well, I can tell you one pretty big thing Beresford left to Chance the Avenger, Mr. Sheringham. Suppose Sir William hadn't handed over the chocolates after all ? Supposing he'd kept 'em, to give to one of his own ladies ? "

Roger positively snorted. He felt a personal pride in Beresford by this time.

" Really, Moresby ! It wouldn't have had any serious results if Sir William had. Do give my man credit for being what he is. You don't imagine he sent the poisoned ones to Sir William, do you ? Of course not ! He'd send harmless ones, and exchange them for the others on his way home. Dash it all, he wouldn't go right out of his way to present opportunities to Chance.

" If," added Roger, " Chance really is the right word."

A LESSON IN CRIME

JOSEPH NEWTON settled himself comfortably in his corner of
a first-class compartment on the Cornish Riviera express.
So far, he had the compartment to himself; and if, by
strewing rugs, bags, books and papers about he could make
himself look numerous enough to drive fellow-travellers away,
there was hope he might remain undisturbed—for the long
train was far from full. Let us take a look at him, and learn
a little about him before his adventures begin—and end.

Age? Forty-five would not be a bad guess, though, in
fact, he is rather less. As for his physical condition, " well-
nourished " is a polite description ; and we, who desire to have
no illusions, can safely call him paunchy, and, without positive
grossness, flabby with good living. His face is puffy, and whitish
under the eyes ; his mouth is loose, and inclined to leer.

His fair hair, which is rapidly growing thin, is immaculately
brushed, and his clothes are admirably cut and well-tended,
though he has not the art of wearing them well. Altogether
he looks a prosperous, thoroughly self-satisfied, and somewhat
self-indulgent member of the British middle class ; and that
is precisely what he is.

His walk in life? You would put him down as a business
man, possibly a merchant or a middle-sized employer, not a
professional man. There you would be both right and wrong.
He is a professional man, in a sense ; and he is certainly in
business.

In fact, he is Joseph Newton, the best-seller, whose crime
stories and shockers were plastered all over the bookstall he has
just left with his burden of newspapers under his arm. He has
sold—heaven knows how many million copies of his stories, and his
serial rights, first, second, and third, cost fabulous sums to secure.

235

But why describe him further? All the world knows him. And now he is on his way to Cornwall, where he has a pleasant little seaside cottage with twenty-seven bedrooms.

The train starts, and Newton's carriage still remains empty save for himself. He heaves a fat sigh of relief and picks up a magazine, in which he turns instinctively to a story by himself. For the moment he cannot remember who wrote it. Poor stuff, he thinks. He must find out which " ghost " was responsible, and sack him.

Joseph Newton was interrupted in his reflections at this point by the consciousness that some one was looking at him. He glanced up and saw the figure of a man who was standing in the corridor and staring fixedly at him, with a curious air of abstraction. Newton stared back, trying to look as unwelcoming as possible. It would be really bad luck, he felt, if some one were to invade his compartment now.

The newcomer, after a moment more of staring, pushed back the door and came in, flinging down on top of one of Newton's bags a rug and a pillow done up in a strap. He seemed to have no other luggage. Newton unwillingly got up and cleared a corner of his belongings, and the stranger sat down and began to unbuckle his strap. Then he settled himself comfortably with the pillow behind his head, and closed his eyes. " I hope to goodness he doesn't snore," Newton thought.

While our second traveller is thus peacefully settling himself for a doze, we may as well take a good look at him also ; for it may be important to know him later on. He is a scraggy little man, probably of sixty or more, with a completely bald pink head and a straggling grey beard which emerges from an incredibly folded and puckered yellow chin. His height is hardly more than five foot six, and his proportions are puny ; but there is a wiriness about his spare person that contrasts strongly with Newton's fleshy bulk.

He is dressed, not so much ill as with a carelessness amounting to eccentricity. His clothes, certainly cut by a good tailor, hang in bags all over him. His pockets bulge. His waistcoat is buttoned up wrong, and sets awry, and his shirt has come apart at the neck, so that a disconsolate shirt-stud is hanging out on one side, while his red tie is leaning towards the other. Moreover, the sole of one of his boots has come loose, and flaps helplessly as his crossed legs swing slowly to the rhythm of the train.

Yet, despite these appearances, the newcomer is certainly a gentleman, and one is inclined to deem him eccentric rather than poor. He might be an exceptionally absent-minded professor ; though, as a matter of fact, he is not. But who he is Joseph Newton has no idea.

For some time there was silence in the compartment, as the Cornish Riviera sped westward past the long spreading ribbon of London. Newton's fellow-traveller did not snore. His eyes were closed whenever Newton glanced at him ; and yet between whiles the novelist had still a queer feeling of being stared at. He told himself it was nonsense, and tried to bury himself in a Wild West story , but the sensation remained with him. Suddenly, as the train passed Maidenhead Station, his companion spoke, in a quiet positive voice, as of one used to telling idiots what idiots they were. A professorial voice, with a touch of Scots accent.

" Talking of murders," it said, " you have really no right to be so careless."

" Eh ? " said Newton, so startled that his magazine dropped from his hand to the floor. " Eh, what's that ? "

" I said you had no right to be so careless," repeated the other.

Newton retrieved his magazine, and looked his fellow-traveller contemptuously up and down. " I am not aware," he said, " that we were talking of murders, or of anything else, for that matter."

" There, you see," said the other, " you did hear what I said the first time. What I mean to say is that, if you expect intelligent people to read your stories, you might at least trouble to make them plausible."

Newton suppressed the rejoinder that rose instantly to his lips. It was that he had far too large a circulation among fools to bother about what intelligent people thought. He only said, " I doubt, sir, if you are likely to find my conversation any more satisfactory than my books," and resumed his magazine.

" Probably not," said the stranger. " I expect success has spoiled you. But you had some brains to begin with. . . . Those Indian stories of yours——"

Perhaps no other phrase would have induced Joseph Newton to embark upon a conversation with the stranger. But nobody nowadays ever read or bothered about his Indian stories, though he was very well aware that they were the best things he had ever done.

"—— had glimmerings of quality," the other was saying, "and you might have accomplished something had you not taken to writing for money."

" Are you aware, sir," Newton said, " that you are being excessively rude ? "

" Quite," said the other with calm satisfaction. " I always am. It is so good for people. And really, in your last book, you have exceeded the limit."

" Which of my last books are you talking about ? " asked Newton, hovering between annoyance and amusement.

" It is called *The Big Noise,*" said the other, sighing softly.

" Oh, that," said Newton.

" Now, in that book," the stranger went on, " you call the heroine Elinor and Gertrude on different pages. You cannot make up your mind whether her name was Robbins with two *b*'s or with one. You have killed the corpse in one place on Sunday and in another on Monday evening. That corpse was discovered twelve hours after the murder still wallowing in a pool of wet blood. The coroner committed no fewer than seventeen irregularities in conducting the inquest ; and, finally, you have introduced three gangs, a mysterious Chinaman, an unknown poison that leaves no trace, and a secret society of international Jews high up in the political world."

The little old man held up his hands in horror as he ended the grisly recital.

" Well," Newton asked, " any more ? "

" Alas, yes," said the other. " The volume includes, besides many misprints, fifteen glaring inconsistencies, nine cases of gross ignorance, and enough grammatical mistakes to—to stretch from Paddington to Penzance."

This time Newton laughed outright. " You seem to be a very earnest student of my writings," he said.

The stranger picked up the rug from his knees and folded it neatly beside him. He removed the pillow, and laid that down too. He then moved across to the corner seat opposite Newton and, taking a jewelled cigarette case from his pocket, selected a cigarette, returned the case to his pocket, found a match, lighted up, and began to smoke. Then he again drew out the case and offered it to Newton. " Lavery's," he said. " I know your favourite brand."

As a matter of fact, Newton never smoked Lavery's ; but for a handsome sum he allowed his face, and a glowing testimonial to their virtues, to appear on their advertisements.

Well, he might as well find out what the things were like. He took the proffered cigarette, and the stranger obligingly gave him a light. Newton puffed. Yes, they were good stuff—better than might be expected, though rather heavy.

"Now, in my view," the stranger was saying, "the essence of a really good murder is simplicity. All your books—all most people's books—have far too much paraphernalia about them. A really competent murderer would need no special appliances, and practically no preparations. Ergo, he would be in far less danger of leaving any clues behind him. Why, oh, why, Mr. Newton, do you not write a murder story on those lines?"

Again Newton laughed. He was disposed to humour the old gentleman. "It wouldn't make much of a story," he said, "if the murderer really left no clues."

"Oh, but there you are wrong," said the other. "What is needed is a perfectly simple murder, followed by a perfectly simple solution—so simple that only a great mind could think of it, by penetrating to the utter simplicity of the mind of the murderer."

"I can't abide those psychological detectives," Newton said. "You'd better go and read Mr. Van Dine." ("Or some of those fellows who would give their ears for a tenth of my sales," his expression added.)

"Dear me, you quite misunderstand me. That wasn't what I meant at all. There would be no psychology in the story I have in mind. It would be more like William Blake's poetry."

"Mad, you mean," said Newton.

"Crystal sane," replied the other. "Perhaps it will help you if I illustrate my point. Shall I outline the sort of murder I have in mind?"

"If you like," said Newton, who found himself growing suddenly very sleepy.

"Very well," said the stranger. "Then I'll just draw down the blinds."

He jumped up and lowered the blinds on the corridor side of the compartment.

"That's better," he said. "Now we shall be undisturbed. Now supposing—only supposing, of course—that there were two men in a railway carriage just like us, and they were perfect strangers, but one of them did not really care for the other's face—— Are you listening, Mr. Newton?"

"Yes," said Newton, very sleepily. He was now having real difficulty in keeping his eyes open.

"And, further, supposing neither of them had brought any special paraphernalia with him, except what any innocent traveller might be carrying—say, a rug, a pillow, and a rug-strap——"

As he spoke, the stranger picked up the rug-strap from the seat beside him.

"Hey, what's that about a rug-strap?" said Newton, roused for a moment by a connection of ideas he was too sleepy to sort out.

"Except, of course, just one doped cigarette, containing an opiate—strong, but in no wise fatal," the other went on blandly.

"What the——?" murmured Newton, struggling now vainly against an absolutely stupefying drowsiness.

"There would really be nothing to prevent him from committing a nice, neat murder, would there?" the old man continued, rising as he spoke with startling agility and flinging the loop of the rug-strap over Newton's head. "Now, would there?" he repeated, as he drew it tight around his victim's neck and neatly fastened it. Newton's mouth came wide open; his tongue protruded, and he began to gurgle horribly; his eyes stuck out from his head.

"And then," said the stranger, "the pillow would come in so handy to finish him off." He dragged Newton down on the seat, placed the pillow firmly on his upturned face, and sat on it, smiling delightedly. The gurgling slowly ceased.

"The rug," the cheerful voice went on, "has proved to be superfluous. Really, Mr. Newton, murder is even easier than I supposed—though it is not often, I imagine, that a lucky chance enables one to do a service to the literary craft at the same time."

Newton said nothing; for he was dead.

The stranger retained his position a little longer, still smiling gently to himself. Then he rose, removed the pillow from Newton's face, and, after a careful survey of the body, undid the strap. Next, he picked up a half-smoked cigarette and threw it out of the window, folded his rug neatly, did it and the pillow up in the strap, and, opening the door into the corridor, walked quietly away down the train.

"What a pity!" he murmured to himself as he went. "It would make such a good story; and I am afraid the poor fellow will never have the sense to write it."

The body of Joseph Newton was actually discovered by a

restaurant-car attendant who was going round to collect orders for the first lunch. Opening the door of a first-class compartment, which had all its blinds drawn down, he found Newton, no pleasant sight and indubitably dead, stretched out upon the seat where his companion had left him.

Without waiting to do more than make sure the man was dead, he scuttled along to fetch the guard. A brief colloquy of train-officials then took place in the fatal compartment, and it was decided to stop the train short of Newbury Station, and send for the police before any one had a chance of leaving it. It seemed clear, as there had been no stop since they left Paddington, that the murderer must still be on it, unless he had leaped from an express travelling at full speed.

The police duly arrived, inspected the body, hunted the compartment in vain for traces of another passenger—for the murderer had taken the precaution of wearing gloves throughout his demonstration—took the name and address of every person on the train, to the number of some hundreds, had the carriage in which the murder had occurred detached, with much shunting and grunting, from the rest of the train, and finally allowed the delayed express to proceed.

Only those travellers who had been actually in the coach of which Newton's compartment had formed a part were kept back for further inquiries. But Newton's companion was not among them. Having given his correct name and address to the police, he proceeded quietly upon his journey in the empty first-class compartment two coaches farther back to which he had moved after his successful experiment in simplicity.

There were four hundred and ninety-eight passengers on the Cornish Riviera express whose names were taken by the police at Newbury ; or, if you count Newton, four hundred and ninety-nine. Add guards and attendants, restaurant-car staff, and the occupants of a travelling Post Office van—total five hundred and nineteen.

Of these one hundred and twenty-six were women, one hundred and fifty-three children, and the rest men. That allowed for quite enough possible suspects for the police to follow up. They were followed up, exhaustively. But it did not appear that any single person among them had any acquaintance with Joseph Newton, or any connection with him save as readers of his books. Nor did a meticulous examination of Newton's past suggest the shadow of a reason why he should have been murdered.

The police tried their hardest, and the public and the Press did their best to assist, for the murder of a best-seller, by a criminal who left no clue, was enough to excite anybody's imagination. Several individuals, in their enthusiasm, went so far as to confess to the crime, and gave Scotland Yard several days' work in disproving their statements. But nothing helpful was forthcoming, and at long last the excitement died down.

It was more than three months later that the young Marquis of Queensferry called upon Henry Wilson, formerly the chief official of Scotland Yard, and now the foremost private detective in England. His modest request was that Wilson should solve for him the mystery of Joseph Newton's murder.

When Wilson asked him why he wanted it solved, the Marquis explained that it was for a bet. It appeared that his old uncle, the Honourable Roderick Dominic Acres-Noel, had bet him fifty thousand pounds to a penny he could not solve the problem, and he, who had the title but not the money, would be very willing to lay his hands on fifty thousand pounds which his uncle, who had the money but not the title, would never miss. Asked the reason for so unusual a bet, he replied that the reason was Uncle Roderick, who was always betting on something, the sillier the better.

" Our family's like that, you know," the Marquis added. " We're all mad. And my uncle was quite excited about the case, because he was on the train when it happened. He even wrote to the *Times* about it."

Wilson rejected the idea that he could solve a case which had utterly baffled Scotland Yard when the trail was fresh, now that it was stone cold, and all clues, presumably, vanished into limbo. Even the most lavish promises of shares in the fifty thousand pounds did not tempt him, and he sent the young Marquis away with a flea in his ear.

But, after the Marquis had gone, he found that he could not get the case out of his head. In common with everybody else, he had puzzled his brains over it at the time ; but it was weeks since he had given it a thought. But now—here it was again—bothering his mind.

Hang it all, it wasn't reasonable—it was against nature— that a man should be able to murder another man and get away without leaving any clue at all. So, at any rate, the Marquis's crazy old uncle seemed to think, unless, indeed, he was merely crazy. Most likely he was.

Wilson could not say exactly at what moment he decided

to have one more shot at this impossible mystery. Perhaps it was when he recollected that, according to the Marquis, Mr. Acres-Noel had himself travelled on that train to Cornwall. It might be that Mr. Acres-Noel had noticed something that the police had missed ; he was just the sort of old gentleman who would enjoy keeping a tit-bit of information to himself. At any rate, it was one thing one could try.

Wilson rang up his old colleague, Inspector Blaikie, at Scotland Yard, and Blaikie guffawed at him.

" Solve it, by all means," he said. " We'll be delighted. We're sick of the sound of Newton's name. . . . Yes, old Acres-Noel was on the train—I don't know anything more about him. . . . Oh, mad as a hatter. Completely. . . . Yes, he wrote to the *Times*, and they printed it. . . . Three days afterwards, I think. Shall I have it looked up for you ? . . . Right you are. Let us know when you catch the murderer, won't you ? "

Wilson sent for his own file of the *Times*, and looked up the letter of Mr. Acres-Noel. The *Times* had not thought it worth the honour of the middle page, but fortunately had not degraded it into the " Points " column.

" *Sir*," it ran,—

" *The methods of the police in dealing with the so-called Newton Mystery appear to show more than the usual official incompetence. As one of the passengers on the train on which Mr. Newton died, I have been subjected to considerable annoyance—and I may add compensated in part by some amusement—at the fruitless and irrelevant inquiries made by the police.*

" *It is plain the police have no notion of the motives which prompted the murder. Their inquiries show that. If they would devote more attention to thinking what the motive was, and less to the accumulation of useless information, the apparent complexity of the case would disappear. The truth is usually simple—too simple for idiots to see. Why was Newton murdered ? Answer that, and it will appear plainly that only one person could have murdered him. Motive is essentially individual.*

" *I am, yours, etc.,*
" *R. D. Acres-Noel.*"

" Upon my word," said Wilson to himself, " that's a very odd letter."

He read it several times over, staring at it as if the name of the murderer was written between the lines.

Suddenly he leaped to his feet, and with an excitement he seldom showed, dashed down Whitehall to Inspector Blaikie's office. Within ten minutes he was making a proposition to that official which left him starkly incredulous.

"I know," Wilson persisted, "it isn't a certainty, it's a thousand to one chance. But it *is* a chance, and I want to try it. I'm not asking the Department to commit itself in any way, only to let me have a couple of men standing by. Don't you see, the whole point about this extraordinary letter is the way it stresses the question of motive? And, more than that, it suggests that the writer knows what the motive was. Now, how could he do that unless——"

"But, if that's so, the man's mad!" Blaikie protested. "Whoever heard of anyone murdering a complete stranger just to *show* him?"

"Well, he certainly is mad, isn't he? You said so yourself, and his family's notoriously crazy."

"He'll have to be pretty well off his rocker," Blaikie remarked, "if he's to be kind enough to come and shove his neck in a noose for you."

"One can but try," Wilson said. "If you won't help me I'm going to try alone. I must have one shot at getting to the bottom of it." And eventually Blaikie agreed.

The upshot was that Wilson, immediately after his interview, arranged for the posting of the following letter, forged with extreme care so as to imitate the handwriting of the supposed author. It was dispatched from the pillar-box nearest to Joseph Newton's Cornish cottage.

"*Dear Mr. Acres-Noel*," it said,—

"*Ever since our chance meeting a few months ago, I have been thinking over the very interesting demonstration you were kind enough to give me on that occasion. May I confess, however, that I am still not quite satisfied; and I should be even more deeply obliged if I could induce you to repeat it. As it happens, I shall be returning to London this week-end, and travelling down again to Cornwall on the Riviera express next Wednesday. If you too should chance to be travelling that way, perhaps we may meet again.*

"*Yours very truly,*
"*Joseph Newton.*"

Some one remarkably like the late Joseph Newton settled himself comfortably in the corner of a first-class compartment in the Cornish Riviera express. He had the compartment to himself, and, although the train had begun to fill up, no other traveller had entered when the train drew out of the station. Very discreetly, passengers who came near it had been warned away by the station officials.

The train had not yet gathered its full speed when the solitary traveller became conscious that some one was standing outside the compartment, and staring in at him. He raised his eyes from the magazine he was reading, and looked back. Slowly, the newcomer pushed back the sliding door, entered the compartment, and sat down in the far corner.

He was a little old man, with a straggling beard, wearing very shabby clothes. He flung down on the seat beside him a rug and a pillow tied up in a strap. Undoing his bundle, he settled himself with the pillow behind his head, the rug over his knees, and the strap on the seat beside him. Then he closed his eyes.

Wilson did and said nothing. It was nervous work, waiting for his cue. But by this time he knew he was right. The millionth chance had come off.

The train flashed at length—it seemed hours—through Maidenhead Station. Suddenly the old man spoke.

" Talking of murders," he said, " it is my turn to apologise. I am afraid I bungled it last time."

" Not at all," said Wilson, hoping that his voice would not give him away ; " but if you would kindly just show me again how——"

" With pleasure," said the old man.

He moved with alacrity to the corner opposite Wilson, took from his pocket a jewelled cigarette-case, and proffered it. Wilson took a cigarette, and did a second's rapid thinking before the match was produced. A cigarette was something he had not allowed for, and it might even turn out to be poisoned. However, no use to hesitate now. He suffered Mr. Acres-Noel to light it, and the heavy sweetish taste confirmed his fears.

Fortunately, however, it was hardly alight before the other rose and went to the window.

" You won't mind my pulling down the blinds, will you ? " he said ; and Wilson took advantage of his movement to effect a lightning exchange of the suspicious cigarette for one of his own. This was a relief, but clearly he must show some signs of being affected by it. Sleepiness seemed the most likely cue. He yawned.

"You follow me so far, I trust," said the other.

"Perfectly," said Wilson slowly. "Please—go——" Slowly his eyes closed, and his head began to wag.

The old man seized the rug-strap.

"This is the next step," he said, attempting to cast it over Wilson's head. But Wilson sprang to his feet, warded off the strap, and pressed a button beside him which had been fixed to communicate with the adjoining compartment.

Almost as he grappled with his now frenzied antagonist, two stalwart policemen in plain clothes rushed in to his aid. Mr. Acres-Noel, alternately protesting his innocence and shrieking with wild laughter, was soon safely secured. The train slowed down and stopped at the deserted station of Newbury Racecourse, where captors and captive descended almost unnoticed. Then it sped upon its way.

Mr. Acres-Noel, safe in Broadmoor, has only one complaint. The authorities will not supply him with Joseph Newton's new books. He wants to see whether that popular writer has benefited by his lesson in practical criminology.

MR. PEMBERTON'S COMMISSION

MR. COURTNEY PEMBERTON, having placed his bag and rug on his reserved seat in the 8.25 a.m. Boulogne boat express, stepped down once more on the platform of the Gare du Nord in Paris in search of literature wherewith to beguile his journey.

Turning from the news barrow, Mr. Pemberton's eyes met those of a young woman who was standing near. She was looking at him doubtfully, as if meditating speech. Her face was vaguely familiar, and Mr. Pemberton, who was never averse to meeting charming young ladies, decided to claim acquaintance. But before he could take off his hat she withdrew her gaze, turned round and tripped off daintily down the platform.

Mr. Pemberton gazed after her. She was small, dark and piquant and her face was adorable. With a happier expression he felt that in her cheeks there might on occasion be dimples, but now she looked worried and sad. Though quietly, even sombrely dressed, from the top of her small, close-fitting hat to the tips of her tiny, high-heeled shoes, she was a vision to hold the eyes of any man.

"How these Frenchwomen can dress!" he thought, as, after watching her out of sight, he slowly climbed the steps of his carriage.

Mr. Pemberton was a bachelor, stout, small of stature and successful. Formerly a City clerk, he had early found an outlet for his special talents in company promoting, and by means of a number of brilliant experiments with other people's money, had now achieved an assured position and a five-figure income.

Though secure of a good deal more than his necessary bread and cheese, he had not yet gone out of harness. He was in fact even now returning from a bi-monthly meeting of French financial associates. Every first and third Tuesday of the month he spent with his colleagues, and the Wednesday morning following saw his departure from the Gare du Nord on his way back to England.

For a moment after the train started the face of the young Frenchwoman remained in Mr. Pemberton's mind. He wondered where he could have seen her. But soon he turned his attention to his papers, until some time later the incident was recalled to his memory.

Returning along the corridor from lunch, he saw the girl for the second time. Again her face seemed familiar and again she was regarding him with doubt and hesitation. But this time she spoke, in what seemed to him the most entrancing voice to which he had ever listened.

" Pardon, monsieur, that I thus intrude myself on your notice. I am in vair' great trouble, but when I behold M. Pemberton I think to myself : it may be that he will aid me. Will monsieur permit that I beg of him a great favour ? "

" You know me, mademoiselle ? " Mr. Pemberton returned in surprise, delighted at the prospect of an adventure after his own heart.

" But yes, monsieur, though, alas, you do not know me. I am maid to Mme Hill-Brooke. Many times have I seen you at her house."

He recalled her now. Mrs. Hill-Brooke was a wealthy neighbour who lived in one of the finest of the older Hampstead houses, and he remembered having seen this girl on her drive on certain occasions when he had been to call.

" I remember you, of course," he smiled, though his hopes of amatory adventure diminished. " Yes ? I'm sorry to hear you are in trouble. Tell me about it."

" Monsieur is too kind. The last two weeks I stay with Madame in Paris, but last night she leave to visit at Aix. She tell me to go back to London to-day to Mme Bowater. Monsieur without doubt knows Mme Bowater, madame's daughter ? "

Mr. Pemberton recalled Mrs. Hill-Brooke's large and rather overbearing daughter, who lived near Hendon.

" Yes, of course," he answered. " I know her well."

" Before madame leave last night," resumed the young woman, " she give me a parcel to take to London. ' Here, Denise,' she say, ' here is a gift for my grandchild.' That is Mme Bowater's little girl, monsieur understands ? ' It is a

little necklace and I want her to have it for her birthday party.'
That, monsieur, is to-night."

Mr. Pemberton had also seen the child Hermione Bowater.
He thought how characteristic of her grandmother was this
action. Mrs. Hill-Brooke idolised the little girl and Mr. Pemberton felt that the gift of the necklace was a kindness which would
have delighted the old lady even more than her granddaughter.

" Yes ? " he said encouragingly as the girl paused.

" Just before I leave the hotel this morning," she resumed,
" I get a telegram." She took a scrap of paper from her handbag. " It is from the sister of my *fiancé*, and as monsieur see "—
her dark eyes filled with tears—" it tell that my *fiancé* has met
with a vair' serious accident. It is that his life may be in danger."

Mr. Pemberton took the message. It had been handed in
at Boulogne on the previous evening and received early that
morning in Paris. It was in French and read : " Jean seriously
injured in motor accident. Come."

He glanced at the girl. She was certainly very much upset,
though evidently striving hard for composure. As he looked, a
tear escaped from her eye and rolled slowly down her cheek.
She hurriedly wiped it away.

" I am sorry," he said, and his voice took on something
more than a fatherly tone. She certainly was extremely pretty.
" And then ? "

" Monsieur without doubt perceives my difficulty. It is that
I desire to stay at Boulogne, but this package it requires me instead to go to England. If madame were here she would grant
the permission—I know it. But she is not here : I cannot ask
her. And madame would be so greatly distressed if the young
lady was disappointed." She broke off and her shrug was
eloquent of despair.

" And you want me to take it across for you ? " Mr. Pemberton suggested softly.

The girl's face lit up and her eyes sparkled. " Oh, if monsieur would but be so kind ! " She smiled gratefully. " It
would give him but little trouble. I would telephone from
Boulogne to Parker to visit at monsieur's house for it at six
o'clock to-night. It would just be in time. Would six suit
monsieur ? "

Mr. Pemberton knew Parker, Mrs. Hill-Brooke's elderly and
highly respectable chauffeur. He really did not see why he
should not oblige the girl. As she said, it would give him no

trouble. Indeed it would probably please Mrs. Hill-Brooke, who was, he knew, exceedingly considerate to her servants.

"I'll take it with pleasure," he said, gazing admiringly into his companion's dark liquid eyes. "I shall be glad to help you, and I hope you'll find your *fiancé* better than you expect."

Her eyes shone. "Oh, monsieur ! But how kind! Oh, how can I thank monsieur ! "

As she spoke she took from her handbag a small parcel, sealed in an envelope and endorsed in what Mr. Pemberton recognised was Mrs. Hill-Brooke's handwriting : "Miss Hermione Bowater, with love from Grannie." He slipped it into the breast pocket of his inner coat, and after as long and intimate a conversation as he dared, returned to his own compartment, followed by the girl's exuberant thanks.

Mr. Pemberton was what is commonly called a climber. Money had been his first object. He had made it in ways which he now found convenient to forget. But he had placed himself beyond the reach of financial embarrassment. Money had ceased to be his goal and social success had taken its place. From this point of view he valued his acquaintanceship with Mrs. Hill-Brooke and her daughter. This episode of the child's present might even be useful if it gave him an excuse for a more intimate interview than he had yet achieved.

He reached his home in Hampstead as the dark November evening was drawing in. There he took an early opportunity of locking the little parcel in his safe. Shortly before six he was seated in his library, running through the pile of correspondence which awaited him. For several minutes he worked, then suddenly he heard the sound of a car passing the window, followed by that of a distant bell.

"Parker, a trifle before his time," he thought. There was a tramp of footsteps and a knock came to the library door. But when in answer to his invitation it was flung open he received a surprise.

"Detective-Inspector French," the butler announced, and a rather short man with a pleasant expression and blue eyes entered, followed by two companions. One was obviously a police officer in plain clothes, the other a slim man in a blue lounge suit.

"Mr. Courtney Pemberton ? " French said politely. "I'm sorry for this intrusion, but I want a word with you, if you please."

"Certainly, Inspector. Won't you find seats?"

The trio subsided on to three chairs and French continued : "I have been sent from Scotland Yard to make some inquiries about a package which it is alleged you received from Mrs. Hill-Brooke's maid in the Boulogne boat train to-day."

A sudden sense of impending ill came over Mr. Pemberton. "Yes?" he said uneasily. "What about it?"

"May I ask, sir, if you have the package still?"

"I certainly have. But your questions alarm me. I hope nothing is wrong?"

French seemed relieved. "There's not so much wrong if the parcel is safe," he declared. "Have you opened it?"

"Of course not. It's sealed and addressed to Mrs. Hill-Brooke's little granddaughter. The maid said Parker would call for it at six o'clock to-night."

"Parker?"

"Mrs. Hill-Brooke's chauffeur."

A light seemed to dawn on French. "That's the link we want," he replied in satisfied tones, glancing at his subordinate, who nodded obsequiously. "I may admit, sir, we didn't see just where you came in."

"But I don't understand——" Mr. Pemberton was beginning, when the other interrupted him.

"Of course you don't, sir, but I'll explain in a moment. In the meantime I'd be glad if you'd tell me all you know of the affair."

Mr. Pemberton recounted his experiences, to which the trio listened with close attention.

"It's clear enough," French commented when he had finished. "Now I'll tell you something you didn't know. You were not carrying a gift from Mrs. Hill-Brooke to her granddaughter. It was something more valuable even than that. You didn't imagine, sir, that that little package that Denise Marchant gave you was worth not less than twelve thousand pounds?"

Mr. Pemberton stared. "Bless my soul!" he exclaimed. "Twelve thousand pounds! What on earth do you mean?"

"I'll tell you, sir. Mrs. Hill-Brooke had a wonderful jade necklace. You've heard of it?"

At the mention of the necklace Mr. Pemberton's heart fluttered. "Heard of it?" he exclaimed. "Everyone has heard of it. Yes, and I've seen it again and again."

"I dare say. Well, sir, here's something else you didn't know. The necklace has been stolen."

Mr. Pemberton was appalled. " Good heavens ! Stolen ! " he echoed in dismay. " Not surely by that girl ? I can scarcely believe it. She looked so—so innocent."

A twinkle showed in the Inspector's blue eyes. " I can believe it all right," he declared dryly. " She was a thief for all her looks. The necklace was stolen from Mrs. Hill-Brooke's hotel in Paris last night. The girl, Denise Marchant, who has since been recognised as a well-known international thief hailing from Chicago, drugged her mistress and got away with it, at least, so we believe. She was traced to the Gare du Nord and arrested as she stepped from the boat train at Boulogne. A search showed that she had managed to get rid of the necklace, and a passing train official happened to have noticed her handing a package to you in a second-class compartment. Your description was wired to the Yard. We missed you at Victoria, but afterwards found your taxi and so traced you here."

Mr. Pemberton swore. " You horrify me," he exclaimed. " What an unlucky chance that I should have been on the train ! "

"That's the one point I'm not satisfied about," French declared. " All that business of the telegram about her *fiancé* shows premeditation. It looks to me more like as if they knew you would be there and arranged to use you. Did you tell anyone you were going ? "

" No, but I take that journey twice a month—every first and third Wednesday."

" That's it. They knew your movements and thought that you would make a safe messenger. We shall wait here till that chauffeur comes and get hold of him. In the meantime, I should be obliged if you would let us have a look at the necklace to make sure that it's all right."

The financier nodded and crossed the room to his safe. Suddenly he recalled a point he had forgotten.

" Look here," he exclaimed as he took out the package and placed it on the table before French. " It's addressed in Mrs. Hill-Brooke's handwriting. How do you account for that ?"

French took a lens from his pocket and examined the spidery calligraphy.

" I don't know Mrs. Hill-Brooke's hand, myself, sir," he said at last, " but I know enough to tell you that this is not it. Anyone could see this is a forgery. Look for yourself. Those lines have not the smooth curves you get with genuine writing. They are a mass of tiny shakes. They have been drawn slowly from a copy."

Mr. Pemberton was soon convinced, and disgustedly he watched while the Inspector slit open the envelope and brought to light a magnificent necklace of green stones.

"That's it right enough," French said in satisfied tones, beginning laboriously to count the beads. "There should be seventy-two. And there are. That's it all right, I take it, Mr. Hobbs?" He handed it to the slim young man. "Mr. Hobbs, of Devereux' in Bond Street, who supplied the necklace," he explained to Mr. Pemberton.

Hobbs examined the lustrous rope for some minutes without speaking. Indeed, so long did his inspection last that French became impatient.

"Well, what's the matter? It shouldn't be hard to identify."

The young man pored over it for some minutes longer, then replaced it on the table. "It's not so easy to identify," he said slowly, "because I've never seen it before. It's not Mrs. Hill-Brooke's necklace."

French sprang to his feet with an oath, while Mr. Pemberton stiffened suddenly.

"Not the necklace?" the former cried. "Good heavens, man, are you sure?"

The slim young man nodded deliberately. "I'm quite sure. And what's more, it's not a jade necklace at all. It's only glass. Worth about five shillings."

French's jaw dropped. "A fake!" he murmured, sitting down heavily and staring at the gleaming bauble. There was silence for a few moments, then French said bitterly: "They're a smarter crowd than we reckoned on. Well, sir, I must ring up the Yard. I suppose I may use your phone?"

He put through his call, then, returning to the table, he picked up the envelope and absent-mindedly looked at the seals. With a slight frown he took it close to the light and began scrutinising it with his lens. Finally he glanced questioningly at Mr. Pemberton.

"You say, sir, you didn't open this package?" he asked, and his tone was distinctly less suave.

"I certainly did not."

"Then how do you explain the fact that it has been carefully opened and resealed?"

"Good heavens, Inspector! How should I know? I can only tell it wasn't done since I got it."

"Look at these seals, Mr. Pemberton. They have been detached from the lower paper and stuck on again in just not quite the same place."

Once again Mr. Pemberton felt a sense of impending ill.

"This introduces an unpleasant factor," French went on gravely. "The package has been opened, and so far as we know it has been held only by Denise Marchant and yourself. If, as we believe, Marchant made it up and forged the address to deceive you, it's not easy to see why she should have opened it again. If she had wanted to put in a fake necklace she would have done it in the first instance. The suggestion is obvious."

Mr. Pemberton oscillated between anger and dismay. "I have told you everything I know," he retorted. "I suppose you are hardly going to accuse me of stealing the thing?"

"I am not accusing you of anything, but the circumstances are such that you will have to satisfy me. You must see that a good deal of the evidence is against you."

"Really, Inspector, this is perfectly scandalous," Mr. Pemberton declared angrily. "You are making abominable insinuations without an iota of real evidence. I advise you to be careful. I have influential friends——"

French held up his hand. "Now, sir, it won't do you any good to take that line. In your own interest you should be anxious to assist me. What I propose is that you come with me to the Yard and make your statement to the Chief Inspector. I am sure, sir, that it will prove a mere matter of form."

Mr. Pemberton was growing more and more uncomfortable. He recognised now the undistinguished part he had played in the affair. The fair Denise had, so to speak, drawn him, a corpulent and complaisant red herring, across the trail. He swore under his breath as he recalled with rueful admiration the girl's beauty, her appealing, innocent eyes, her real tears. "Ugh!" he thought disgustedly, "they're all the same. There's not one of them you can trust." It was not the first time Mr. Pemberton had intervened to assist a lovely woman in distress, and he had usually come to regret it. He turned back to French.

"How will my going to the Yard affect the matter?" he said indignantly. "I can tell the Chief Inspector nothing more than I've told you. I——"

He was interrupted by the telephone, a long strident ring. He picked up the receiver.

"Mr. Pemberton speaking," he said, then passed the instrument over to French. "It's the Yard."

French listened, spoke, listened again. Then a change came over his manner. He put down the receiver and turned to the financier.

"Mr. Pemberton, sir," he declared in apologetic tones, "it is my duty to tell you that in all good faith I have made a serious mistake. The Yard phones me that news has just come in from Paris. The necklace has been recovered. It was found in Paris in the possession of a man, evidently a confederate. The girl, Marchant, had managed to pass it on before she reached the station and she used you to lay a false trail. There remains therefore nothing but to offer my sincere apologies and, if I may, to say how pleased I am that the matter is closed so far as you are concerned."

Mr. Pemberton was so relieved that he forbore to take a lofty tone.

"My word, Inspector, I'm glad to hear that. I thought you were going to give me no end of trouble."

"I was only doing what I thought was my duty, sir," French returned. "Happily there's no chance now of your being annoyed. All the same, I regret that I have not yet quite finished. I must ask you for a signed statement about your interview with Denise Marchant. You will understand that this is necessary to enable the French police to get a conviction against her."

"Right, Inspector," Mr. Pemberton returned, now once again in an excellent humour. "But you don't expect me to write it all out, do you?"

"I'll do the writing, sir, if you will kindly sign it. It'll only take a minute or two."

As a matter of fact it took twenty, but Mr. Pemberton did not grudge the time. At last it was finished and he signed.

"I suppose, sir, you'd like to keep the faked necklace as a memento?" French went on. "I should have asked you for it if the thieves were not known, but as they are we don't want it. But with your permission I'll take the outside paper. It may help to get a conviction."

Mr. Pemberton thought the necklace might make a good peg whereon to hang his story, and after watching Hobbs roll it up in its soft inside wrapping he took it from him and locked it once more in his safe.

French got up. "Your number, sir, if you please, in case we should want to phone you."

After dinner Mr. Pemberton rang up Mrs. Hill-Brooke's daughter, Mrs. Bowater, to congratulate her on the recovery of the necklace.

"Oh," Mrs. Bowater cried, "how splendid! I hadn't heard. Mother rang me up about the loss, but they hadn't found it at that time. How did you hear?"

"The news has only just come through to Scotland Yard," Mr. Pemberton explained, "so that you would scarcely have had time to hear it yet. As to my connection with the affair, it's a long story. If you'll be there to-morrow I should like to go over in the afternoon and tell you about it."

"Please do," Mrs. Bowater invited, and rang off.

Mr. Pemberton left his office early next day and drove out to Hendon. Mrs. Bowater greeted him pleasantly, but he could see that she had something on her mind.

"That was a curious business last night your telling me the necklace had been found," she began at once. "How did you say you knew?"

"Scotland Yard rang up the police officer who came to interview me on the subject," Mr. Pemberton returned. "He repeated the message to me."

"But it wasn't true," declared Mrs. Bowater.

"It wasn't true?" Mr. Pemberton repeated. "What wasn't true? I don't follow."

"They haven't got the necklace. I expected to hear from mother, and when no message came I rang her up. The Yard must have made some mistake."

Mr. Pemberton was a good deal surprised. "I suppose they must," he repeated slowly. "I haven't a great deal of faith in them, but I must say I shouldn't have expected them to go wrong on a matter of that kind."

"No," she said, "it is strange, isn't it?"

"If you'll let me use your telephone I'll ring them up now and see what they have to say about it."

Presently he got the Yard.

"Is Inspector French in the building?" he asked, and then: "Tell him Mr. Courtney Pemberton wants to speak to him."

After a short silence came a voice: "Inspector French speaking."

"I say, Inspector," went on Mr. Pemberton, "your people were wrong about that necklace. Mrs. Bowater tells me she heard from Paris to-day and it hasn't been recovered."

" What necklace, sir ? " came the unexpected reply. " I don't follow you."

" Why, man, the necklace we discussed last night when you were in with me. What else could it be ? "

" Some mistake, sir. You've got hold of the wrong man. I was here all last evening."

Mr. Pemberton's heart seemed suddenly to lose a beat.

" But, my goodness, Inspector, you gave me your card. ' Inspector Joseph French, C.I.D.' Is there another Inspector French at the Yard ? "

" No, sir, there's been a mistake. Will you tell me the circumstances ? "

Mr. Pemberton did so briefly. From what he could judge of his voice the Inspector seemed impressed.

" I think, sir," the voice went on, " I should like to see you about this. Where are you speaking from ? "

Mr. Pemberton told him.

" Then I shall go out there at once. I'm afraid, sir, you've been hoodwinked."

With a sinking at his heart Mr. Pemberton reported this new development to his hostess, adding a carefully bowdlerised account of his interview with Denise. Presently Inspector French was announced.

Though Mr. Pemberton by this time was prepared for it, the Inspector's appearance gave him something of a shock. This was not the man who had called on him the previous evening !

" Now, sir," said the new arrival gravely, " I should be glad if you'd tell me the whole story."

For the second time in half an hour Mr. Pemberton related his adventure. When he had finished French nodded.

" It's as I thought, sir. You've been hoaxed. Have you got the necklace about you ? "

" It's here. I brought it to show to Mrs. Bowater, but we were so taken up discussing the affair that I forgot to do so."

Mr. Pemberton took the little parcel from his pocket. " It's a perfectly splendid-looking piece of work," he declared as he unwrapped the paper. " No one but an expert would imagine it wasn't genuine. See." He held it out.

Then suddenly he drew it back. He stared fixedly at it while slowly his eyes grew round and an expression of incredulous amazement became stamped on his features. For a time he seemed unable to speak, then he gave a hoarse cry, " Bless my soul ! It's not the same ! "

" Ah," said French with interest, " now we're getting to it. Not the same as what ? "

" As the one I brought across the Channel ! This is quite different ; a poor thing. The other was magnificent ! "

French seemed pleased. " I think that about clears it up, sir," he declared. " Tell me, did you happen to notice if my namesake had a scar on his temple near the hair ? "

Mr. Pemberton looked up in surprise. " Why, yes, Inspector, he had. How on earth did you know that ? "

A slow smile dawned on the other's face. " Because I know who it was, and the others also. They're the Boston gang, and they're wanted by half the police in Europe as well as America. They'll not give us the slip this time. Excuse me while I phone the Yard."

" But *he* phoned the Yard," Mr. Pemberton persisted.

Again French smiled. " An old trick, Mr. Pemberton. Anyone can lift the receiver without letting up the switch. Then you can talk till you're blue in the face and nobody hears you."

The gang, French explained later, consisted of the girl and four men, and made a speciality of theft by ingenious tricks.

" We'll have to find out from Mrs. Hill-Brooke about the details from her end, but apart from that the thing is pretty clear. I may tell you now that the Yard was advised from Paris of the theft. The necklace is well known, and a pretty complete description of it was available. It was believed it would find its way to London as the best place in which to get rid of such stuff. As a matter of fact we're already looking out for it."

As Mr. Pemberton listened to this calm exposition, rage struggled with dismay in his mind. He certainly had been hoaxed—doubly hoaxed ! The very men who were explaining to him how he had been hoaxed were themselves at that moment hoaxing him. " Denise Marchant," " Inspector French," " Mr. Hobbs," the dummy policeman ; Mr. Pemberton choked as he thought of them.

" For goodness' sake explain the thing," he stuttered.

" It's clear enough, as I said," French returned. " Speaking subject to later correction, I imagine a good deal of what my namesake told you was true. The girl, who had probably got her job by means of forged testimonials, stole the necklace during the night. Mrs. Hill-Brooke was in the habit of taking a cup of hot milk just before getting into bed, and Denise drugged this. Mrs. Hill-Brooke slept so soundly that Denise was able to enter her room, take her keys from beneath her pillow, abstract the necklace and return the keys. One of her confederates sent her the telegram from Boulogne and with it she left by the 8.25.

" But she was up against a difficulty. She realised that the loss and her flight would be discovered early in the morning. If so, the services to England would be watched, and she would certainly be taken at one of the ports. Hence she must get rid of her incriminating parcel. The same difficulty obtained in the case of the other members of the gang, so it would not do to pass the necklace to them. You, Mr. Pemberton, became to her a gift from the gods. She knew of your bi-monthly journey and determined to use it. She approached you with her sad tale of an injured fiancé and managed to get you to undertake the carriage of the necklace. At Boulogne she simply disappeared and has not been heard of since.

" But the solution of this first problem raised a second. You had been given the necklace : how was it to be got back from you ? I think you must admit the solution was worthy of the problem. A bogus inspector from Scotland Yard was an old enough idea, but it was effective. The man they called Hobbs is light-fingered ; he began as a sneak thief in New York. He is an expert conjurer ; he learned it as an aid to business. What he did was clear enough. He substituted the mock for the real necklace, probably while you were signing your statement. You say he returned it to you rolled in its inner paper ? "

" Yes," said Mr. Pemberton, " before my eyes. I saw the green stones being rolled up. I would have sworn they were what I brought from France."

" All the same, sir, my double was careful to dull your critical faculties by suggesting the possibility of a criminal charge against you. That was to fill your mind with something else. Quite an astute move ! Then the remaining member rang up as if from the Yard, and that gave them the excuse to decamp. Well, we can but hope for the best."

But unhappily for Mrs. Hill-Brooke, French's hopes were doomed to disappointment. Neither Denise nor her associates were ever heard of again. Some fine jade beads did indeed come on to the market, but no connection between them and the necklace could be proved.

WHO KILLED CASTELVETRI?

HER name is Kyra Sokratesco. She is a Roumanian —*petite*, and rather lovely. And unkind people on the Côte des Maures, which lies west of the more civilised French Riviera, are apt to call her "Gilbert's girl friend." The Chief of the Secret Police of Toulon, however, knows better; and it was at his instigation, with my wife's full cognisance, that Kyra and I spent a day and a night in our Local Assize Town—and disagreed all the time.

"Camille Oustric is innocent," began I, as soon as we reached Draguignan. "He acted in self-defence."

"Camille Oustric is a hired bully and a cold-blooded assassin," began she. "If this were England he, and others with him, would hang."

Our friend of the Secret Police of Toulon said, "I feel with you, mademoiselle. But where is there proof for a court?"

The court at Draguignan is not impressive—bare walls, bare wood, a dais for the Procureur de la République and the three judges, a box with twelve arm-chairs for the jury, a *banc* and a *barreau* for the witnesses, another *banc* for the accused.

When Kyra and I entered the Court-room, the accused was already seated between two gendarmes. He resembled his pictures in the newspapers—a powerfully-built man in his forties, sailorish, with a high dome of bald forehead, big cheek-bones, and an immense brown moustache.

"His eyebrows twitch," observed Kyra, as we took our places in the Press-box. "He is frightened."

"So would you be," I retorted. "Twenty years' penal servitude in French Guiana is worse than death."

We continued sparring—while Counsel for the Defence, little and moustachioed, shook hands with his client; while Counsel

260

WHO KILLED CASTELVETRI? 261

for the Partie Civile (the relatives of the victim, who claim damages for his murder) big and bearded, was arranging his *dossier*; and while the *Greffier* called over the jury-roll. Even the tinny bell and the " *Messieurs, la Cour*," which heralded the entrance of the red-robed " Monsieur le Président," his two brother judges, and the Procureur de la République, bald and clean-shaven, only reduced us to whispers, until the jury had been sworn.

For our disagreement had been of long standing—ever since the first report of the case.

. . . .

The case, as the jury now heard it from the charge-sheet, was rather sordid, but seemed of the simplest. Camille Oustric, owner of a grocer's shop, had shot his brother-in-law, Josef Castelvetri, a *sous-officier* in the French Navy, on the night of the eleventh September at the Villa Fleurie in Toulon. Two witnesses—Oustric's sister, and his sister's fifteen-year-old boy— had witnessed the whole of the shooting. His sister's lover, who owned the villa, had seen the beginning of it. Oustric himself confessed to it—pleading, a plea confirmed by all three witnesses, Self-Defence.

" Tell your story," said the President, after the charge had been read over ; " and please speak up."

" It was like this," said Oustric, rising, and his robust voice carried conviction. " On the night he died my brother-in-law should have come to us before dinner. We waited until nine o'clock for him—his wife, my sister ; his son Jacques ; Monsieur de Borneville, and I. At nine we dined on the veranda. At ten there came a loud knocking on the outside door. I told Jacques to answer the door. He went. A moment later he staggered back, bleeding from a blow on the forehead. ' Papa has killed me,' he cried. My brother-in-law followed. He had a pistol in his hand. ' Woman, I will stand this dishonour no longer,' he shouted. Then he fired twice. My sister fell wounded. Monsieur de Borneville jumped from the veranda. Thinking he would fire again, I rushed at Josef ; I caught his wrists. ' For God's sake ! ' I implored. But he was mad, Monsieur. He fired again—at me ; and the bullet pierced the ceiling. I remembered, then, that my sister had a pistol. It was in a drawer of her writing-table. Before he could fire a fourth shot I was at the writing-table. I wrenched the drawer open. I seized my sister's pistol. I emptied it at him. God forgive me for doing it—but Josef would have killed her. What else could I do ? "

"And do *you* believe that rigmarole," whispered Kyra

"I do," said I. "Or at any rate the essentials of it. The woman was in danger of her life. He defended her."

To which Kyra retorted with the Roumanian equivalent of "Pah!"

The President, however, though he examined at great length, did not succeed in shaking the prisoner's testimony.

"Yes," said Oustric in effect, "I admit that I knew of my sister's relations with Monsieur de Borneville; I admit that Monsieur de Borneville took me to the villa that evening; I admit that I went there to protect my sister should her husband become violent. But I was unarmed. I had no intention of killing. And the thing happened exactly as I have said."

"You say you were unarmed?" was the President's last question. "Yet it has been proved that you possessed a pistol."

"Not a pistol, Monsieur. Only a very old revolver, which Monsieur le Chef de la Sûreté found where I told him he would find it, under the counter of my shop."

When Oustric sat down on his *banc*, while a doctor, pure Dickens from the cut of his old-fashioned coat to the set of his old-fashioned spectacles, came pawkily to the wooden rail of the witnesses, I couldn't help being a little sorry for the Chef de la Sûreté. And the medical evidence made me sorrier still. For after describing Castelvetri's three wounds at length, our Dickensian doctor detailed his examination of Madame Castelvetri, who had been shot, "In the right thigh, gentlemen of the jury; a clean wound at close range; the bullet entering five centimetres higher than its point of exit"—a fact which had hitherto been in dispute.

"*Tu entends, ma chère,*" I whispered, "that blows our friend's theory of her having been hit by a ricochet to atoms."

"I admit it," whispered back Kyra. "But his theory is not mine."

The next evidence, read by the Procureur de la République, was new to both of us—but failed, in my opinion, to throw much light on the case. An architect named Meyrowitz, whose house was eighty yards away from the villa, had heard the shooting—first one shot; then, after a short interval, a second; then a positive fusillade. This witness had also heard de Borneville run past his window, and a woman's voice calling after him, "Marcel! Marcel! Come back."

Kyra, I may say, seemed to think this deposition of some importance. She smiled to herself as she made a note of it;

and nodded to our friend the Chef de la Sûreté just before he took oath at the bar.

"At five-thirty a.m. on the morning of the eleventh September," said our friend, "I was called to the Toulon Hospital. A man had been shot. He wished to make a special deposition. So I went at once. When I got there the man, Josef Castelvetri, was on the point of death. He signed his deposition, however, which is as follows : ' It was my fault. I was mad. I wounded her. Then Camille shot me.' "

"And after that ? " prompted the President.

"After that I rang up the City Police, and told them to make full inquiries at the Villa Fleurie, from which—the ambulance driver told me—the man had been brought in."

"The City Police will tell us the rest, I presume ? "

"*Oui, Monsieur le Président, oui.*"

Our friend, who never appears personally either for or against a prisoner unless, as in this case, circumstances force him to, retired without glancing at us ; and a rather foolish-looking City policeman took his place.

The police, it appeared, had gone to the Villa Fleurie immediately on receipt of our friend's telephone message—but not alone. With them had gone the accused, who had already given himself up and made his confession, and the three principal witnesses, who had reported at the police-station at the same time. At the villa, everything—including a bullet-hole in the ceiling—had confirmed the accused's statement. Both pistols had been left on the dining-table.

"Both of them were seven-shot Brownings," said the City policeman. "Six-point-thirty-five millimetres. Both had been recently fired. One, manufactured at Herbstahl in Belgium, contained three cartridges in the magazine and one in the chamber. This, I was told, had belonged to the victim. The other, marked M.A.B., of French make, belonged, as she admitted, to the woman, and was empty. That is all I know."

But a second policeman, carrying the tale a step further, brought out the one point which—as I had always admitted—was against the accused.

"Acting on instruction," said this second policeman, "I proceeded to the hospital and examined the clothes of the victim. In the pockets I found twenty-nine francs and a few centimes, a watch, a pocket-handkerchief, seventeen six-point-thirty-five millimetre cartridges, and a magazine for a Browning pistol."

" And the mark on that magazine ? " asked the Procureur
de la République, who had hitherto foregone his right to
examine.

" The mark on the magazine, Monsieur, was M.A.B."

.   .   .   .

Since my acquaintance with Kyra and her friend of the
Sûreté, who has particularly requested that I should not describe
him, I have witnessed many " scenes " in French Law Courts.
But rarely such a one as now occurred between Monsieur le
Procureur and Counsel for the Defence.

" I protest," screamed Counsel for the Defence, rising.
" And I shall continue to protest. This evidence is trivial. It
can have no bearing on the issue. The Herbstahl and the
M.A.B. pistol are absolutely identical. The same magazines,
the same cartridges fit either of them."

" Quite so," screamed back the Procureur. " We admit it.
That, we say, is how your client made his mistake."

" Mistake ! But it is you, Monsieur le Procureur, who make
a mistake when you try, as the Juge d'Instruction tried, to
prejudice an innocent man, my unfortunate client——"

" Gentlemen," interrupted the President, " gentlemen——"

But the President's interruption went unheeded—till his bell
rang for the " suspension of debates."

During this suspension Kyra fell into one of those moods
which I can only describe as " Kyraish," her lovely eyes half-
closed, her lips pursed, one thin little hand drawing idle designs
in her notebook—and I, still more or less convinced of Oustric's
innocence, went out to have a cigarette.

Our friend of the Sûreté was outside ; and I condoled with
him a little. He replied, " If Mademoiselle does not aid us, I
fear this villain, and also his accomplices, will go free."

When I came back, the Court seemed much fuller ; Messieurs
les Avocats had apparently made up their differences ; and a
third policeman, a Commissioner, stood at the bar saying :
" Yes, Monsieur. When the accused came to my office on the
morning of the twelfth September, I took all four statements
separately. I noticed nothing peculiar about any of the four
people except that Monsieur de Borneville had a bruise, caused,
as he said, by striking himself against the hood of his motor-car,
on the bridge of his nose."

Two gunsmiths, contradicting one another, as all expert
witnesses in all countries, followed the Commissioner. Both,
however, questioned by the Defence, " If a customer purchases

a six-point-thirty-five millimetre Herbstahl pistol and asks for
a spare magazine with it, is he not as liable to be supplied with
an M.A.B. magazine as a Herbstahl ? " answered, " Yes. That
is so. The magazines are interchangeable."
At which Kyra frowned.

II

KYRA was still frowning while we took our luncheon ; and
with her, too, I condoled a little, for being over-imaginative—
as indeed she is.
"There is no mystery in this case," I told her. " It is all
perfectly straightforward."
She said, quietly, " My friend, no case with a strong sex-
motive behind it is absolutely straightforward. I am a woman—
and I know."
At twenty minutes past two the judges' guard of soldiers came
marching by us ; by half-past we were again in Court. The
Court was fuller than ever. Looking back over my shoulder
at the crowd pressing to the rails behind us, I was reminded of
the French Revolution—as reconstructed by the American
film. But the crowd stood orderly, and only the tiniest shiver
of anticipation ran through it when de Borneville, giving Kyra
a glance as he passed the Press-box, came to the bar.
A highly-strung little man, I judged de Borneville. He had
the long nose of the aristocrat, the " tooth-brush " moustache of
an English officer, and curiously soft, rather imaginative
brown eyes. He gave his age as thirty-nine, unmarried ; his
profession as " landowner " ; took the oath calmly, and turned
to the jury at once.
" Before I make my deposition," he began, " I want to assure
you, gentlemen of the jury, of my deep regret at having been the
unwilling cause of this tragedy. Also of my determination—
once I am assured that Camille Oustric is found innocent—of
compensating the Castelvetri family for the bereavement which
they have suffered—as, indeed, I would have done already had
they not brought suit against the accused."
" Quelle blague," whispered Kyra. But I could see that de
Borneville had impressed the jury ; and the favourable
impression deepened as he went calmly on.
His relations with the woman he admitted frankly, making
no excuse for himself. " What would you ? We are all human.
Despite the difference in our position, I loved her. I still love

her. We should have married had not her husband been an ardent Catholic ; had he not refused to grant her, as most men would have done, a divorce."

" During the two years you and his wife lived together," interrupted the President, " you had often asked Castelvetri to divorce her ? "

" Yes, often. Whenever he came home from a cruise."

" He came home from a cruise on the tenth of September, and the purpose of your meeting on the night of the eleventh was to discuss the same topic ? "

" Precisely."

" And because you were afraid Castelvetri might become violent, you took Oustric with you ? "

" That is so. I am, as you will see, by no means a Hercules." And de Borneville looked towards the foreman of the jury, who smiled.

After that he described the start of the actual shooting, telling the same story as Oustric, quietly, but this time making an excuse for himself. " I ran away after the first shot," he admitted. " It looks cowardly, I know, but I fancied that Castelvetri would follow—that I would draw his fire."

" You ran for help ? " suggested the President. " That hardly bears out what you have just told us."

" I only ran for help after I heard the fusillade, after I guessed that a tragedy must have happened. It seemed to me that the sooner I got some independent witness the better. As soon as I had secured that witness, I jumped into my car ; I drove for the doctor, for the ambulance. At six o'clock I reported myself to the police."

De Borneville, under the President's examination, under that of the Partie Civile and the Procureur, remained imperturbable. The impression he continued to give was that of a man in the most cruel of difficulties, behaving in the correctest way. When asked, " Was Oustric armed when you took him to the villa ? " he retorted instantly : " Had I thought arms necessary, there would have been no need for Oustric. In the war I was not quite unused to firearms. I could have carried a pistol myself."

Only once, or so it seemed to me, did he display any hesitancy, and that at the Procureur's question : " We have been told that Castelvetri, just before he fired, shouted : ' Woman, I will stand this dishonour no longer.' Do you confirm that, or not ? "

" It may have been so," said de Borneville then. " He

certainly said something. But of the actual words I have no recollection. And I do not think he shouted. I would rather describe it that he hissed."

Asked, "Were you not amazed that Castelvetri should have struck his own son?" he answered: "No. The son had always sided with his mother, you see"; and shortly after retired to the *banc.*

"The clever devil!" whispered Kyra, watching him; and in a minute or so the woman stood at the bar.

She was dressed in black, fairly fashionably. A tall creature, dark-haired and slim of figure, with long, expressive hands. Her eyes were big, and held something of fear in them. But her voice, as she gave her age, "Thirty-seven," sounded clear, self-certain, and somehow sweet.

"As the victim's widow," explained the President, "this woman cannot give sworn testimony. But she has volunteered a statement, and she can be interrogated on it. Madame, you may now proceed."

.   .   .   .

The widow's statement tallied, to a nicety, with Oustric's and de Borneville's. Examination revealed no flaws in it. Only at the end were the spectators—Kyra and I, of course, were prepared for it—treated to a surprise.

"In view of what you have just told us," said the President, "how comes it that you told one witness, 'I did it. I killed my husband'? And how comes it that your son told the same witness almost the same thing?"

"I can explain that very easily," the woman answered. "Indeed, I have done so twice already. As the moral culprit, it was my intention to take this crime on my own shoulders. I wanted to save my brother. Therefore, I told my son——"

"To lie, madame?"

"To lie in what I thought a good cause, Monsieur le Président."

"But your son had seen everything?"

"*Oui.*"

"You persist in that? It is claimed, you know, that he told another witness, at his father's funeral, 'I saw nothing. I was not in the veranda. I was outside the door.'"

"Jacques saw everything," asseverated the woman. "The suggestion that he was not in the veranda is mere gossip."

"That," retorted the President, "we shall see."

A little later, after only one admission, secured by the Partie

Civile, " Yes. I called at my brother's shop to buy my usual provisions on the morning of the eleventh," that seemed to me in any way pertinent, the woman joined her lover on the bench of the witnesses, and her son, Castelvetri's orphan, came in.

" He, too," said the President, " cannot give sworn testimony." And I saw Kyra's eyebrows go up as the boy began.

The boy, very strong, dark-haired, stocky of figure, dark-eyed, but not, or so I thought, over-intelligent, made his deposition stoutly. His father had hit him with his pistol-butt. He had seen his father shoot at his mother : seen his uncle struggling with his father ; seen his uncle snatch the pistol from the drawer. When he had finished this deposition the President again " suspended the debates."

" Very unusual before his own examination," I commented to Kyra.

" Very," admitted Kyra. " I suspect our friend's hand in it. However, we shall see."

We saw our friend's hand, and could not help chuckling a little at the subtlety of him, when the bell rang, and the President, full of apologies, turned to the jury saying, " Gentlemen, I am very sorry. I made a mistake. A dead man's son or daughter can give sworn testimony, either for or against his murderer. I am therefore going to ask this witness to repeat what he has just told you. But this time on oath."

And when Jacques Castelvetri repeated his second deposition on oath, it tallied—word for word, as a hidden shorthand writer proved to us that evening—with his first !

" *Tu entends, mon cher*," whispered Kyra triumphantly ; and I, " Supposing he did learn his statement by heart, it proves nothing." Nor did the threefold examination prove very much more.

" I said mother had done it because mother told me to," admitted Jacques Castelvetri.

" Then you lied ? "

" Yes. To save uncle."

" And there is a witness who maintains you told him, ' I saw nothing.' "

" Never, Monsieur le Procureur."

" You are on your oath."

" On my oath, Monsieur."

" You maintain that ? "

" Absolutely."

" Very well."

The boy, his tale told, went to his mother. He took her hand ; held it. The woman was crying a little. He tried to comfort her. De Borneville moved along the bench towards them, thought better of it, moved away.

I called Kyra's attention to the humanity of the picture they made. She whispered, " Yes. They are great actors," as the next, perhaps the all-important, witness came in.

" My name is Henri Piquart, and I am in the Octroi," said that witness, a hefty, clean-shaven youngster, with the manner of the minor French official. " The Octroi (Town Customs) Station is about a quarter of a mile from the Villa Fleurie. At about ten-fifteen on the night of September the eleventh Monsieur de Borneville, who was unknown to me, rushed in. There had been *une bagarre*, he told me. He could find no policeman ; would I come at once ? I went with Monsieur de Borneville, but only after he had proved his identity to me. When we reached his villa, a boy ran out to us, crying, ' He is dead. Mother has killed him.' De Borneville said, ' Not your mother. Surely not your mother.' The boy answered, ' Yes. Yes. Mother.' Then we went in."

The man from the Octroi described the scene—Castelvetri on his back, his wife bleeding, Oustric with a bandage, trying to stanch her wound.

" We saw that the man was not yet dead," he went on. " De Borneville, who seemed very frightened, said, ' I have my car here. I will go for the doctor, for the ambulance.' He took the boy with him. And I remained."

" At de Borneville's suggestion ? " interrupted the President.

" Yes. After he had gone, Castelvetri seemed about to recover consciousness. I sent Camille Oustric to get water for him. While he was away, the woman said to me, ' I will tell you how it happened. I shot him. It was an accident. All the shots in the pistol seemed to go off at once.' Castelvetri was muttering something then ; and Oustric had come back with the water. Oustric said, ' Do not believe her. I did it.' When I gave Castelvetri the water, he opened his eyes and muttered, ' Camille, you have killed me.' Castelvetri seemed in great pain. I did what I could for him. But it was difficult, because of the woman. She seemed quite beside herself. I gathered that there must have been some terrible quarrel. She kept on flinging herself down by her husband, and reproaching him—about some other woman.

This went on all the time till de Borneville returned with the doctor. I was very tired by then. I thought I had done my duty. And after giving my name to de Borneville, I went away."

III

" IF that is the whole case for the prosecution," said I, some hours later, " it fails."

We were sitting, I must admit, in Kyra's bedroom—she on the edge of the bed, legs crossed, a cigarette between her fingers ; I close to her, a brandy-and-soda at my side. Unfortunately for the unkind ones, however, there was a third party present— our friend of the Secret Police.

" We have other evidence for to-morrow," said he. " But only circumstantial. Our main witness, the one who overheard the boy say, ' I saw nothing,' has sent a doctor's certificate to say he is not well enough to attend. All we can actually prove is that Oustric occasionally carried a pistol."

" A pistol," interrupted Kyra, " or a revolver ? "

" Among the lower orders in France, mademoiselle, the terms are unfortunately synonymous."

" I know. It is a pity. And de Borneville's payments to Oustric ? "

" He has always admitted that he financed Oustric's grocery shop."

" He admits everything, that devil."

" Except his complicity in the death of Castelvetri."

" His complicity. And the woman's. She visited her brother that morning. Obviously to arrange the crime."

" But if it was no crime ? " I interrupted. " If it all happened as they say it did ? "

" In that case," Kyra flashed at me, " the wrong magazine would not have been in the dead man's pocket ; there would have been no statement, ' I shot him ; it was an accident,' from the woman ; there would have been no bruise on de Borneville's nose ; the boy's evidence would not have been word-perfect— and de Borneville would have been at the police-station several hours, three at any rate, before six o'clock.

" And besides," she went on, " their story, though plausible, is slightly ridiculous. How could Oustric have wrenched the drawer open to get at the pistol ? The moment he let go of Castelvetri he would have been shot down. And then there is Meyrowitz, who heard the woman cry, ' Marcel, come back ' ;

but never heard the loud knock or the boy's ' Papa has killed me.' or Castelvetri's ' Woman, I will stand this dishonour no longer.'

" And what of Castelvetri's mental state before he went to the villa ? " She turned to our friend. " Have you no evidence on that point ? Somebody must have seen him, spoken with him ? "

" Only his father. And his father is the Partie Civile. He can give no evidence. Castelvetri, it appears, was always very reticent about the whole position."

" Didn't he say anything to his father ? "

" Nothing of importance—except that he had an appointment with de Borneville, who was still bothering him about the divorce."

" Castelvetri did not mean to grant the divorce, then ? "

" No, mademoiselle. He was far too devout. And, as you know, the last man in the world to contemplate violence——"

" Yet he shot his wife in the leg," I interrupted.

" I refuse to believe it," snapped Kyra.

" Then who did shoot her ? De Borneville ? Oustric ? Her own son, perhaps ? Dash it all, her husband himself admitted, on his death-bed, and to our friend here——"

" Castelvetri's deposition," said Kyra, " merely proves him a gentleman—and that he died loving his wife."

In all the detective stories I have ever read—and I have read many, mostly to please her, since my acquaintance with Kyra—the narrator is made out a half-wit. And as such I, of all people, was treated during the next half-hour. Kyra and her pet policeman simply left me out of their discussion—while they pored over plans and photographs of the veranda dining-room, over the two pistols and the ten used cartridge cases, and the whole common-or-garden paraphernalia of their trade.

" You're wasting your time," I said at last—and, I fear, irritably. " Granted all the flaws in the story—and I can see them as well as you can—it will be good enough for the jury. The woman's evidence is unshaken ; the boy's also. And your Juge d'Instruction, when he made his original inquiry, must have been a perfect fool."

" In what way ? " queried our friend, with his usual politeness.

" Eh bien," said I ; " Jacques says, they all say, that his father hit him with his pistol-butt ; that he staggered in bleeding. A blow like that would have left a scar——"

"It did," retorted our friend. "The Juge d'Instruction had it examined by a doctor. It was a superficial head wound, not serious, but such as might easily cause profuse bleeding——"

"And such as might have been inflicted by a pistol-butt?"

"Quite possibly. Since it was under the hair."

A silence followed; and in that silence I looked at Kyra, still smoking, legs crossed, on her bed.

"You're very clever, Gilbert," she said at last. "Almost as clever as de Borneville. But you can't get over the fact that he had eight hours to concoct this story—and that it was supremely in the interest of all of them that Castelvetri should die."

"Not in the boy's," I protested. "Not in Oustric's."

"In theirs too. Financially. De Borneville is a rich man, remember."

"You make the boy out a monster, Kyra."

"The boy still thinks his mother did it. He thinks he is lying to save both her and his uncle. That is why he lies so well."

Another silence followed—with our friend fingering his copy of the *dossier*, and Kyra at her most Kyraish, a picture of applied concentration, cigarette extinguished, eyes closed.

"De Borneville's war record?" she asked, when her eyes opened. "You say it is a good one. About how good? Was he ever wounded?"

"Never." Our friend's eyes were on the *dossier*. "Towards the end he had a touch of shell-shock, and got three months' leave for it. But he returned to duty and was promoted Major for conspicuous coolness and ingenuity during a night raid, almost single-handed, into the enemy's lines."

"H'm!" said Kyra. "That helps."

She closed her eyes again, and sat back for a long time, apparently dreaming. Then she said, "Shell-shock! That explains his bolting. He must have got his nerve back rather quickly. Yet he lost it again, according to Piquart, when the boy said, 'Mother has killed him.' She lost her nerve, too. And so did Oustric. There was no need to empty the whole pistol. Or to plant all those cartridges. I wonder if we dare try it? One could in Roumania. But here! Here!"

IV

BOTH as a law-abiding English citizen and as a friend of France, whose justice in the main is also equitable, I experience a certain diffidence in relating the events of the next hour.

Our friend, when Kyra first broached her plan to him, would have none of it. " It is impossible," he said. " Impossible. Even by the Sureté, it could not be done."

" But he is sleeping in this very hotel," protested Kyra. " I have only to send a note along the corridor."

" He will not come for your note."

" He will—if he is guilty." And in the end, after long argument, Kyra got her way.

She showed us her note before she rang for the waiter ; and though my sense of fair-play revolted, I had to admit the thing a masterpiece. " All is known," it read. " To-morrow, when the Court opens, you and she will be arrested. The Sûreté is watching. Do not try to find me. Be careful.— A FRIEND."

Before she rang for the waiter, too, she made us hide ourselves ; so that it was half-stifled in a slip of a bathroom that I heard her say : " For the gentleman in twenty-eight, garçon. You are to wait until you see him open it. If he asks you from whom it comes, you are to say nothing. When you have delivered the letter, return here."

" Subtle," whispered our friend. " It is a thousand to one he will follow the waiter." And a moment later Kyra turned out her bedroom light.

We waited breathless—and both nervous. We heard the waiter come back ; heard Kyra say, sleepily, " Merci. C'est bon. My petit déjeuner at eight-thirty, please," and about five minutes later, a cautious knock.

Kyra did not answer that knock ; and after an interval it repeated itself. At the third repetition she called out, as one startled : " Who is it ? Who is it ? " and we heard her run to the door.

She gave a tiny cry as she opened the door ; and presently we heard her say, " But this is madness. Madness. They are watching you." Then the door closed, and we knew that de Borneville was inside the darkened room.

" Who are you ? " he asked, and from the tone his teeth must have been chattering.

" A friend. I told you. But it is folly—folly what you have just done."

" Folly or not, I am here. All is known, you wrote. What is known ? Tell me. I insist."

" Enough is known. You are betrayed. The Sûreté has evidence that Oustric habitually carried a pistol, not a revolver. They have evidence, too, that the old revolver under the shop counter was not his, but yours."

I am, as I protest, no half-wit. Nor did it take me more than a few seconds to follow the line Kyra was adopting for her totally illegal experiment in the Third Degree. If the revolver was de Borneville's, and the woman admitted owning one pistol, and Oustric could be proved to have been in the habit of carrying another . . . Yet, even so, I was not prepared for de Borneville's gasp.

He gasped, after Kyra had spoken those two deadly sentences, exactly as I once heard a man gasp when the point of a bayonet took him in the vitals, " Ah ! Ah ! " with a gurgle in the throat. Imaginatively I saw him sway—and in a second Kyra drove at him again.

" They can prove Castelvetri was unarmed," she drove at him.

" Ah ! " Again the gurgle.

" And that the three of you had planned to murder him. They know the truth about Jacques's wound, and about *hers*, and about Castelvetri's dying deposition. They know everything, Monsieur de Borneville." And with her man still gasping, Kyra clicked on the light.

It was our friend's signal to go in ; and he went in, his hand on the weapon in his jacket pocket, very quickly, yet not, as it seemed to me, watching the scene through the bathroom doorway, quite quickly enough.

De Borneville, as I had imagined him, was still swaying where he stood under the chandelier in the centre of the bedroom. His complexion might have been white cheese. Sweat soaked his forehead. The clipped hair on his upper lip twitched like a dog's ear. But his brown eyes were unwinking as they looked on Kyra—and it seemed to me—in fact, I was certain of it—that he must have recognised her, in the second the light went up, for the woman he had glanced at in the Press-box on his way to the bar.

He did not gasp again when our friend came in and past him. But the key, turning in the lock, sent a galvanic shiver

*De Borneville, as I had imagined him, was
still swaying where he stood.*

through his slight body, and I, who have been through shell-shock, knew that he was suffering that peculiar torment which must have been inflicted in other days by the rack.

Our friend, his pistol drawn now, was standing at the locked door. I saw de Borneville's unwinking eyes turn over shoulder at him. Then they switched back to Kyra, who spoke slowly, emphasising every word.

"There is no need to confess," said Kyra. "Unless you feel that a confession may save your mistress by proving that she acted under your instigation. Everything *is* known. When Castelvetri came to the door of your villa, unarmed, you sent Jacques to open it. You had given Jacques his orders—to come back with his father. You knew, when you gave those orders, that the boy's father would not permit him to be present at your discussion. And you calculated that his father would keep the boy out of the veranda long enough for the three of you to do your murder, though possibly not on the struggle that ended in Castelvetri's flinging the boy from him, or the boy's head being struck as he fell.

"Yes. You calculated on being able to kill him before Jacques got back on to the veranda," repeated Kyra ; and I realised, from the pause she made, that she must be expecting an answer. But no answer came from de Borneville, and presently she went on.

"When Castelvetri entered the veranda," went on Kyra, while de Borneville's lips still twitched at her, " he did not see Oustric, or his wife either. He only saw you. You were standing where it had been planned that you should. You had calculated on telling him to approach. As he approached, it was your plan that his wife, who was behind him, should have fired one shot—wide and high. Then Oustric, hidden behind you, could have fired the second shot—to kill. After that, it would have been easy enough to place Oustric's pistol by the dead man's side, to plant the correct magazine in his pocket—and there would have been two of you to swear that a woman, always easy to defend before a French jury, had shot her husband in fear of her own life.

"That was your plan." Again Kyra had paused. Again de Borneville had made no answer. "But you had reckoned without your victim's anger. His struggle with his son had enraged him. He sprang straight at you, his fists clenched. He struck you. The bruise on your nose proves it. And as he struck, your mistress—fearful for your life—fired one shot.

"She fired," repeated Kyra, "and missed. But Oustric

didn't dare to fire. Castelvetri had been too quick for him. Castelvetri had turned. He had caught his wife's wrist. As they struggled the pistol went off, muzzle downwards, wounding her thigh. Castelvetri tore the pistol away. When you saw him with it in his hand, your nerve cracked. You bolted. Oustric's nerve had cracked too. He fired in a panic, seven times. Castelvetri returned that fire—once, with the tenth cartridge, as he was shot down."

Kyra's voice stopped, on a silence such as follows machine-gun fire at night over No Man's Land when a raider is alone. And perhaps de Borneville relived such a moment, for as our friend moved, and the hand of the law rested on his shoulder, his mouth fell open and through thirty dreadful seconds it seemed to me that he must confess.

" It will be better for her if you admit everything," said our friend.

" I——" he began.

But on that, abruptly, another shiver galvanised the slight body ; the feet steadied ; the teeth snapped together ; the lips ceased their twitching, and I—who have been through shell-shock—knew that, for the moment at any rate, de Borneville was past his crisis, keyed up to that tension which makes a man's body more dangerous than magazine-pistols to handle, and his wits sharper than knives.

" *Du* bluff," he said to the Chief. " You know nothing. Release me, Monsieur." And to Kyra : " A pretty trap. A pretty theory."

Our friend, being a man, knew—as he told us later—from the very stiffening of de Borneville's shoulder-muscles that he and Kyra were already beaten. But Kyra, being a woman, for all her cleverness, didn't. Also, or so it seemed to me, she lost her temper a little. For, though our friend's hand released de Bornville, her attack went on.

" Theory ! " she shot at him. " It is the truth. You cannot deny it."

" I do deny it. You cannot get over the evidence."

" Whose evidence ? "

" Castelvetri's dying deposition."

" Begged of him by his wife, under cover of those reproaches heard by the witness Piquart—after his muttering, ' Camille, you have killed me,'—had made even the fool Oustric, who planted the wrong magazine, realise that your story of *crime passionnelle* must be altered—before you, Monsieur de Borneville, had time to consult with your accomplices, to invent a fresh story——"

But de Bornville, still keyed, by his love for the woman perhaps, to that pitch of emotional tension when a man, for good or ill, can accomplish miracles, interrupted, grinning, " *Your* story is certainly the more ingenious, mademoiselle. It might even be the correct version. Yet the law is the law ; and I wager my neck that our twelve honest citizens will find mine the more credible one."

. . . .

And though Kyra still maintains, and our friend with her, that hers is the only possible answer to the question : " Who killed Castelvetri ? " those twelve honest citizens did !

THE ALUMINIUM DAGGER

THE "urgent call"—the instant, peremptory summons to professional duty—is an experience that appertains to the medical rather than the legal practitioner, and I had supposed, when I abandoned the clinical side of my profession in favour of the forensic, that henceforth I should know it no more ; that the interrupted meal, the broken leisure, and the jangle of the night-bell were things of the past ; but in practice it was otherwise. The medical jurist is, so to speak, on the borderland of the two professions, and exposed to the vicissitudes of each calling, and so it happened from time to time that the professional services of my colleague or myself were demanded at a moment's notice. And thus it was in the case that I am about to relate.

The sacred rite of the "tub" had been duly performed, and the freshly-dried person of the present narrator was about to be insinuated into the first instalment of clothing, when a hurried step was heard upon the stair, and the voice of our laboratory assistant, Polton, arose at my colleague's door.

"There's a gentleman downstairs, sir, who says he must see you instantly on most urgent business. He seems to be in a rare twitter, sir——"

Polton was proceeding to descriptive particulars, when a second and more hurried step became audible, and a strange voice addressed Thorndyke.

"I have come to beg your immediate assistance, sir ; a most dreadful thing has happened. A horrible murder has been committed. Can you come with me now ? "

"I will be with you almost immediately," said Thorndyke. "Is the victim quite dead ? "

"Quite. Cold and stiff. The police think——"

"Do the police know that you have come for me?" interrupted Thorndyke.

"Yes. Nothing is to be done until you arrive."

"Very well. I will be ready in a few minutes."

"And if you would wait downstairs, sir," Polton added persuasively, "I could help the doctor to get ready."

With this crafty appeal, he lured the intruder back to the sitting-room, and shortly after stole softly up the stairs with a small breakfast-tray, the contents of which he deposited firmly in our respective rooms, with a few timely words on the folly of "undertaking murders on an empty stomach." Thorndyke and I had meanwhile clothed ourselves with a celerity known only to medical practitioners and quick-change artists, and in a few minutes descended the stairs together, calling in at the laboratory for a few appliances that Thorndyke usually took with him on a visit of investigation.

As we entered the sitting-room, our visitor, who was feverishly pacing up and down, seized his hat with a gasp of relief. "You are ready to come?" he asked. "My carriage is at the door;" and, without waiting for an answer, he hurried out, and rapidly preceded us down the stairs.

The carriage was a roomy brougham which fortunately accommodated the three of us, and as soon as we had entered and shut the door, the coachman whipped up his horse and drove off at a smart trot.

"I had better give you some account of the circumstances, as we go," said our agitated friend. "In the first place, my name is Curtis, Henry Curtis; here is my card. Ah! and here is another card, which I should have given you before. My solicitor, Mr. Marchmont, was with me when I made this dreadful discovery, and he sent me to you. He remained in the rooms to see that nothing is disturbed until you arrive."

"That was wise of him," said Thorndyke. "But now tell us exactly what has occurred."

"I will," said Mr. Curtis. "The murdered man was my brother-in-law, Alfred Hartridge, and I am sorry to say he was —well, he was a bad man. It grieves me to speak of him thus —de mortuis, you know—but, still, we must deal with the facts, even though they be painful."

"Undoubtedly," agreed Thorndyke.

"I have had a great deal of very unpleasant correspondence with him—Marchmont will tell you about that—and yesterday I left a note for him, asking for an interview, to settle the business,

naming eight o'clock this morning as the hour, because I had to
leave town before noon. He replied, in a very singular letter,
that he would see me at that hour, and Mr. Marchmont very
kindly consented to accompany me. Accordingly, we went to
his chambers together this morning, arriving punctually at
eight o'clock. We rang the bell several times and knocked loudly
at the door, but as there was no response, we went down and
spoke tỏ the hall-porter. This man, it seems, had already
noticed, from the courtyard, that the electric lights were full
on in Mr. Hartridge's sitting-room, as they had been all night,
according to the statement of the night-porter ; so now, suspecting that something was wrong, he came up with us, and rang
the bell and battered at the door. Then, as there was still no
sign of life within, he inserted his duplicate key and tried to
open the door—unsuccessfully, however, as it proved to be bolted
on the inside. Thereupon the porter fetched a constable, and,
after a consultation, we decided that we were justified in breaking
open the door ; the porter produced a crowbar, and by our
united efforts the door was eventually burst open. We entered,
and—my God ! Dr. Thorndyke, what a terrible sight it was
that met our eyes ! My brother-in-law was lying dead on the
floor of the sitting-room. He had been stabbed—stabbed to
death ; and the dagger had not even been withdrawn. It was
still sticking out of his back."

He mopped his face with his handkerchief, and was about to
continue his account of the catastrophe when the carriage entered
a quiet side-street between Westminster and Victoria, and drew
up before a block of tall, new, red-brick buildings. A flurried
hall-porter ran out to open the door, and we alighted opposite
the main entrance.

" My brother-in-law's chambers are on the second floor,"
said Mr. Curtis. " We can go up in the lift."

The porter had hurried before us, and already stood with his
hand upon the rope. We entered the lift, and in a few seconds
were discharged on to the second floor, the porter, with furtive
curiosity, following us down the corridor. At the end of the
passage was a half-open door, considerably battered and bruised.
Above the door, painted in white lettering, was the inscription,
" Mr. Hartridge " ; and through the doorway protruded the
rather foxy countenance of Inspector Badger.

" I am glad you have come, sir," said he, as he recognised
my colleague. " Mr. Marchmont is sitting inside like a watch-
dog, and he growls if any of us even walks across the room."

The words formed a complaint, but there was a certain geniality in the speaker's manner which made me suspect that Inspector Badger was already navigating his craft on a lee shore. We entered a small lobby or hall, and from thence passed into the sitting-room, where we found Mr. Marchmont keeping his vigil, in company with a constable and a uniformed inspector. The three rose softly as we entered, and greeted us in a whisper ; and then, with one accord, we all looked towards the other end of the room, and so remained for a time without speaking.

There was, in the entire aspect of the room, something very grim and dreadful. An atmosphere of tragic mystery enveloped the most commonplace objects ; and sinister suggestions lurked in the most familiar appearances. Especially impressive was the air of suspense—of ordinary, everyday life suddenly arrested— cut short in the twinkling of an eye. The electric lamps, still burning dim and red, though the summer sunshine streamed in through the windows ; the half-emptied tumbler and open book by the empty chair, had each its whispered message of swift and sudden disaster, as had the hushed voices and stealthy movements of the waiting men, and, above all, an awesome shape that was but a few hours since a living man, and that now sprawled, prone and motionless, on the floor.

"This is a mysterious affair," observed Inspector Badger, breaking the silence at length, "though it is clear enough up to a certain point. The body tells its own story."

We stepped across and looked down at the corpse. It was that of a somewhat elderly man, and lay, on an open space of floor before the fireplace, face downwards, with the arms extended. The slender hilt of a dagger projected from the back below the left shoulder, and, with the exception of a trace of blood upon the lips, this was the only indication of the mode of death. A little way from the body a clock-key lay on the carpet, and, glancing up at the clock on the mantelpiece, I perceived that the glass front was open.

"You see," pursued the inspector, noting my glance, "he was standing in front of the fireplace, winding the clock. Then the murderer stole up behind him—the noise of the turning key must have covered his movements—and stabbed him. And you see from the position of the dagger on the left side of the back, that the murderer must have been left-handed. That is all clear enough. What is not clear is how he got in, and how he got out again."

"The body has not been moved, I suppose," said Thorndyke.

" No. We sent for Dr. Egerton, the police surgeon, and he certified that the man was dead. He will be back presently to see you and arrange about the post-mortem."

" Then," said Thorndyke, " we will not disturb the body till he comes, except to take the temperature and dust the dagger-hilt."

He took from his bag a long, registering chemical thermo-meter and an insufflator or powder-blower. The former he introduced under the dead man's clothing against the abdomen, and with the latter blew a stream of fine yellow powder on to the black leather handle of the dagger. Inspector Badger stooped eagerly to examine the handle, as Thorndyke blew away the powder that had settled evenly on the surface.

" No finger-prints," said he, in a disappointed tone. " He must have worn gloves. But that inscription gives a pretty broad hint."

He pointed, as he spoke, to the metal guard of the dagger, on which was engraved, in clumsy lettering, the single word, " Traditore."

" That's the Italian for ' traitor,' " continued the inspector, " and I got some information from the porter that fits in with that suggestion. We'll have him in presently, and you shall hear."

" Meanwhile," said Thorndyke, " as the position of the body may be of importance in the inquiry, I will take one or two photographs and make a rough plan to scale. Nothing has been moved, you say ? Who opened the windows ? "

" They were open when we came in," said Mr. Marchmont. " Last night was very hot, you remember. Nothing whatever has been moved."

Thorndyke produced from his bag a small folding camera, a telescopic tripod, a surveyor's measuring-tape, a boxwood scale, and a sketch-block. He set up the camera in a corner, and exposed a plate, taking a general view of the room, and including the corpse. Then he moved to the door and made a second exposure.

" Will you stand in front of the clock, Jervis," he said " and raise your hand as if winding it ? Thanks ; keep like that while I expose a plate."

I remained thus, in the position that the dead man was assumed to have occupied at the moment of the murder, while the plate was exposed, and then, before I moved, Thorndyke marked the position of my feet with a blackboard chalk. He next set up the tripod over the chalk marks, and took two photographs from that position, and finally photographed the body itself.

The photographic operations being concluded, he next proceeded, with remarkable skill and rapidity, to lay out on the sketch-book a ground-plan of the room, showing the exact position of the various objects, on a scale of a quarter of an inch to the foot—a process that the inspector was inclined to view with some impatience.

"You don't spare trouble, doctor," he remarked ; "not time either," he added, with a significant glance at his watch.

"No," answered Thorndyke, as he detached the finished sketch from the block ; "I try to collect all the facts that may bear on a case. They may prove worthless, or they may turn out of vital importance ; one never knows beforehand, so I collect them all. But here, I think, is Dr. Egerton."

The police surgeon greeted Thorndyke with respectful cordiality, and we proceeded at once to the examination of the body. Drawing out the thermometer, my colleague noted the reading, and passed the instrument to Dr. Egerton.

"Dead about ten hours," remarked the latter, after a glance at it. "This was a very determined and mysterious murder."

"Very," said Thorndyke. "Feel that dagger, Jervis."

I touched the hilt, and felt the characteristic grating of bone.

"It is through the edge of a rib !" I exclaimed.

"Yes ; it must have been used with extraordinary force. And you notice that the clothing is screwed up slightly, as if the blade had been rotated as it was driven in. That is a very peculiar feature, especially when taken together with the violence of the blow."

"It is singular, certainly," said Dr. Egerton, "though I don't know that it helps us much. Shall we withdraw the dagger before moving the body ? "

"Certainly," replied Thorndyke, "or the movement may produce fresh inquiries. But wait." He took a piece of string from his pocket, and, having drawn the dagger out a couple of inches, stretched the string in a line parallel to the flat of the blade. Then, giving me the ends to hold, he drew the weapon out completely. As the blade emerged, the twist in the clothing disappeared. "Observe," said he, "that the string gives the direction of the wound, and that the cut in the clothing no longer coincides with it. There is quite a considerable angle, which is the measure of the rotation of the blade."

"Yes, it is odd," said Dr. Egerton, "though, as I said, I doubt that it helps us."

"At present," Thorndyke rejoined dryly, "we are noting the facts."

"Quite so," agreed the other, reddening slightly; "and perhaps we had better move the body to the bedroom, and make a preliminary inspection of the wound."

We carried the corpse into the bedroom, and, having examined the wound without eliciting anything new, covered the remains with a sheet, and returned to the sitting-room.

"Well, gentlemen," said the inspector, "you have examined the body and the wound, and you have measured the floor and the furniture, and taken photographs, and made a plan but we don't seem much more forward. Here's a man murdered in his rooms. There is only one entrance to the flat, and that was bolted on the inside at the time of the murder. The windows are some forty feet from the ground; there is no rain-pipe near any of them; they are set flush in the wall, and there isn't a foothold for a fly on any part of that wall. The grates are modern, and there isn't room for a good-sized cat to crawl up any of the chimneys. Now, the question is—How did the murderer get in, and how did he get out again?"

"Still," said Mr. Marchmont, "the fact is that he did get in, and that he is not here now; and therefore he must have got out; and therefore it must have been possible for him to get out. And, further, it must be possible to discover how he got out."

The inspector smiled sourly, but made no reply.

"The circumstances," said Thorndyke, "appear to have been these: The deceased seems to have been alone; there is no trace of a second occupant of the room, and only one half-emptied tumbler on the table. He was sitting reading when apparently he noticed that the clock had stopped—at ten minutes to twelve; he laid his book, face downwards, on the table, and rose to wind the clock, and as he was winding it he met his death."

"By a stab dealt by a left-handed man, who crept up behind him on tiptoe," added the inspector.

Thorndyke nodded. "That would seem to be so," he said. "But now let us call in the porter, and hear what he has to tell us."

The custodian was not difficult to find, being, in fact, engaged at that moment in a survey of the premises through the slit of the letter-box.

" Do you know what persons visited these rooms last night ? " Thorndyke asked him, when he entered, looking somewhat sheepish.

" A good many were in and out of the building," was the answer, " but I can't say if any of them came to this flat. I saw Miss Curtis pass in about nine."

" My daughter ! " exclaimed Mr. Curtis, with a start. " I didn't know that."

" She left about nine-thirty," the porter added.

" Do you know what she came about ? " asked the inspector.

" I can guess," replied Mr. Curtis.

" Then don't say," interrupted Mr. Marchmont. " Answer no questions."

" You're very close, Mr. Marchmont," said the inspector ; " we are not suspecting the young lady. We don't ask, for instance, if she is left-handed."

He glanced craftily at Mr. Curtis as he made this remark, and I noticed that our client suddenly turned deathly pale, whereupon the inspector looked away again quickly, as though he had not observed the change.

" Tell us about those Italians again," he said, addressing the porter. " When did the first of them come here ? "

" About a week ago," was the reply. " He was a common-looking man—looked like an organ grinder—and he brought a note to my lodge. It was in a dirty envelope, and was addressed ' Mr. Hartridge, Esq., Brackenhurst Mansions,' in a very bad handwriting. The man gave me the note and asked me to give it to Mr. Hartridge ; then he went away, and I took the note up and dropped it into the letter-box."

" What happened next ? "

" Why, the very next day an old hag of an Italian woman— one of them fortune-telling swines with a cage of birds on a stand—came and set up just by the main doorway. I soon sent her packing, but, bless you ! she was back again in ten minutes, birds and all. I sent her off again—I kept on sending her off, and she kept on coming back, until I was reg'lar wore to a thread."

" You seem to have picked up a bit since then," remarked the inspector with a grin and a glance at the sufferer's very pronounced bow-window.

" Perhaps I have," the custodian replied haughtily. " Well,

the next day there was a ice-cream man—a reg'lar waster, *he* was. Stuck outside as if he was froze to the pavement. Kept giving the errand-boys tasters, and when I tried to move him on, he told me not to obstruct his business. Business, indeed ! Well, there them boys stuck, one after the other, wiping their tongues round the bottoms of them glasses, until I was fit to bust with aggravation. And *he* kept me going all day.

" Then, the day after that there was a barrel-organ, with a mangy-looking monkey on it. He was the worst of all. Profane, too, *he* was. Kept mixing up sacred tunes and comic songs : ' Rock of Ages,' ' Bill Bailey,' ' Cujus Animal,' and ' Over the Garden Wall.' And when I tried to move him on, that little blighter of a monkey made a run at my leg ; and then the man grinned and started playing, ' Wait till the Clouds roll by,' I tell you, it was fair sickening."

He wiped his brow at the recollection, and the inspector smiled appreciatively.

" And that was the last of them ? " said the latter ; and as the porter nodded sulkily, he asked : " Should you recognise the note that the Italian gave you ? "

" I should," answered the porter with frosty dignity.

The inspector bustled out of the room, and returned a minute later with a letter-case in his hand.

" This was in his breast-pocket," said he, laying the bulging case on the table, and drawing up a chair. " Now, here are three letters tied together. Ah ! this will be the one." He untied the tape, and held out a dirty envelope addressed in a sprawling, illiterate hand to " Mr. Hartridge, Esq." " Is that the note the Italian gave you ? "

The porter examined it critically. " Yes," said he ; " that is the one."

The inspector drew the letter out of the envelope, and, as he opened it, his eyebrows went up.

" What do you make of that, doctor ? " he said, handing the sheet to Thorndyke.

Thorndyke regarded it for a while in silence, with deep attention. Then he carried it to the window, and, taking his lens from his pocket, examined the paper closely, first with the low power, and then with the hig ly magnifying Coddington attachment.

" I should have thought you could see that with the naked eye," said the inspector, with a sly grin at me. " It's a pretty bold design."

"Yes," replied Thorndyke ; " a very interesting production.
" What do you say, Mr. Marchmont ? "

The solicitor took the note, and I looked over his shoulder.
It was certainly a curious production. Written in red ink, on
the commonest notepaper, and in the same sprawling hand as
the address, was the following message : " You are given six
days to do what is just. By the sign above, know what to expect
if you fail." The sign referred to was a skull and cross-bones,
very neatly, but rather unskilfully, drawn at the top of the
paper.

" This," said Mr. Marchmont, handing the document to Mr.
Curtis, " explains the singular letter that he wrote yesterday.
You have it with you, I think ? "

" Yes," replied Mr. Curtis ; " here it is."

He produced a letter from his pocket and read aloud :

" Yes : come if you like, though it is an ungodly hour.
Your threatening letters have caused me great amusement. They
are worthy of Sadler's Wells in its prime.

" ' ALFRED HARTRIDGE.' "

" Was Mr. Hartridge ever in Italy ? " asked Inspector Badger.

" Oh, yes," replied Mr. Curtis. " He stayed at Capri nearly
the whole of last year."

" Why, then, that gives us our clue. Look here. Here are
these two other letters ; E.C. postmark—Saffron Hill is E.C.
And just look at that ! "

He spread out the last of the mysterious letters, and we
saw that, besides the *memento mori*, it contained only three words :
" Beware ! Remember Capri ! "

" If you have finished, doctor, I'll be off and have a look
round Little Italy. Those four Italians oughtn't to be difficult
to find, and we've got the porter here to identify them."

" Before you go," said Thorndyke, " there are two little
matters that I should like to settle. One is the dagger : it is in
your pocket, I think. May I have a look at it ? "

The inspector rather reluctantly produced the dagger and
handed it to my colleague.

" A very singular weapon, this," said Thorndyke, regarding
the dagger thoughtfully, and turning it about to view its different
parts. " Singular both in shape and material. I have never
seen an aluminium hilt before, and bookbinder's morocco is a
little unusual."

" The aluminium was for lightness," explained the inspector, " and it was made narrow to carry up the sleeve, I expect."

" Perhaps so," said Thorndyke.

He continued his examination, and presently, to the inspector's delight, brought forth his pocket lens.

" I never saw such a man ! " exclaimed the jocose detective. " His motto ought to be, ' We magnify thee.' I suppose he'll measure it next."

The inspector was not mistaken. Having made a rough sketch of the weapon on his block, Thorndyke produced from his bag a folding rule and a delicate calliper-gauge. With these instruments he proceeded, with extraordinary care and precision, to take the dimensions of the various parts of the dagger, entering each measurement in its place on the sketch, with a few brief, descriptive details.

" The other matter," said he at length, handing the dagger back to the inspector, " refers to the houses opposite."

He walked to the window, and looked out at the backs of a row of tall buildings similar to the one we were in. They were about thirty yards distant, and were separated from us by a piece of ground, planted with shrubs and intersected by gravel paths.

" If any of those rooms were occupied last night," continued Thorndyke, " we might obtain an actual eyewitness of the crime. This room was brilliantly lighted, and all the blinds were up, so that an observer at any of those windows could see right into the room, and very distinctly, too. It might be worth inquiring into."

" Yes, that's true," said the inspector ; " though I expect, if any of them have seen anything, they will come forward quick enough when they read the report in the papers. But I must be off now, and I shall have to lock you out of the rooms."

As we went down the stairs, Mr. Marchmont announced his intention of calling on us in the evening, " unless," he added, " you want any information from me now."

" I do," said Thorndyke. " I want to know who is interested in this man's death."

" That," replied Marchmont, " is rather a queer story. Let us take a turn in that garden that we saw from the window. We shall be quite private there."

He beckoned to Mr. Curtis, and, when the inspector had departed with the police surgeon, we induced the porter to let us into the garden.

" The question that you asked," Mr. Marchmont began, looking up curiously at the tall houses opposite, " is very simply answered. The only person immediately interested in the death of Alfred Hartridge is his executor and sole legatee, a man named Leonard Wolfe. He is no relation of the deceased, merely a friend, but he inherits the entire estate—about twenty thousand pounds. The circumstances are these : Alfred Hartridge was the elder of two brothers, of whom the younger, Charles, died before his father, leaving a widow and three children. Fifteen years ago the father died, leaving the whole of his property to Alfred, with the understanding that he should support his brother's family and make the children his heirs."

" Was there no will ? " asked Thorndyke.

" Under great pressure from the friends of his son's widow, the old man made a will shortly before he died ; but he was then very old and rather childish, so the will was contested by Alfred, on the grounds of undue influence, and was ultimately set aside. Since then Alfred Hartridge has not paid a penny towards the support of his brother's family. If it had not been for my client, Mr. Curtis, they might have starved ; the whole burden of the support of the widow and the education of the children has fallen upon him.

" Well, just lately the matter has assumed an acute form, for two reasons. The first is that Charles's eldest son, Edmund, has come of age. Mr. Curtis had him articled to a solicitor, and, as he is now fully qualified, and a most advantageous proposal for a partnership has been made, we have been putting pressure on Alfred to supply the necessary capital in accordance with his father's wishes. This he had refused to do, and it was with reference to this matter that we were calling on him this morning. The second reason involves a curious and disgraceful story. There is a certain Leonard Wolfe, who has been an intimate friend of the deceased. He is, I may say, a man of bad character, and their association has been of a kind creditable to neither. There is also a certain woman named Hester Greene, who had certain claims upon the deceased, which we need not go into at present. Now, Leonard Wolfe and the deceased, Alfred Hartridge, entered into an agreement, the terms of which were these : (1) Wolfe was to marry Hester Greene, and in consideration of this service (2) Alfred Hartridge was to assign to Wolfe the whole of his property, absolutely, the actual transfer to take place on the death of Hartridge."

" And has this transaction been completed ? " asked Thorndyke.

" Yes, it has, unfortunately. But we wished to see if anything could be done for the widow and the children during Hartridge's lifetime. No doubt, my client's daughter, Miss Curtis, called last night on a similar mission—very indiscreetly, since the matter was in our hands ; but, you know, she is engaged to Edmund Hartridge—and I expect the interview was a pretty stormy one."

Thorndyke remained silent for a while, pacing slowly along the gravel path, with his eyes bent on the ground : not abstractedly, however, but with a searching, attentive glance that roved amongst the shrubs and bushes, as though he were looking for something.

" What sort of man," he asked presently, " is this Leonard Wolfe ? Obviously he is a low scoundrel, but what is he like in other respects ? Is he a fool, for instance ? "

" Not at all, I should say," said Mr. Curtis. " He was formerly an engineer, and, I believe, a very capable mechanician. Latterly he has lived on some property that came to him, and has spent both his time and his money in gambling and dissipation. Consequently, I expect he is pretty short of funds at present."

" And in appearance ? "

" I only saw him once," replied Mr. Curtis, " and all I can remember of him is that he is rather short, fair, thin, and clean-shaven, and that he has lost the middle finger of his left hand."

" And he lives at—— ? "

" Eltham, in Kent. Morton Grange, Eltham," said Mr. Marchmont. " And now, if you have all the information that you require, I must really be off, and so must Mr. Curtis."

The two men shook our hands and hurried away, leaving Thorndyke gazing meditatively at the dingy flower-beds.

" A strange and interesting case, this, Jervis," said he, stooping to peer under a laurel-bush. " The inspector is on a hot scent—a most palpable red herring on a most obvious string ; but that is his business. Ah, here comes the porter, intent, no doubt, on pumping us, whereas——" He smiled genially at the approaching custodian, and asked : " Where did you say those houses fronted ? "

" Cotman Street, sir," answered the porter. " They are nearly all offices."

"And the numbers? That open second-floor window, for instance?"

"That is number six; but the house opposite Mr. Hartridge's rooms in number eight."

"Thank you."

Thorndyke was moving away, but suddenly turned again to the porter.

"By the way," said he, "I dropped something out of the window just now—a small flat piece of metal, like this." He made on the back of his visiting card a neat sketch of a circular disc, with a hexagonal hole through it, and handed the card to the porter. "I can't say where it fell," he continued; "these flat things scale about so; but you might ask the gardener to look for it. I will give him a sovereign if he brings it to my chambers, for, although it is of no value to any one else, it is of considerable value to me."

The porter touched his hat briskly, and as we turned out at the gate, I looked back and saw him already wading among the shrubs.

The object of the porter's quest gave me considerable mental occupation. I had not seen Thorndyke drop anything, and it was not his way to finger carelessly any object of value. I was about to question him on the subject, when, turning sharply round into Cotman Street, he drew up at the doorway of number six, and began attentively to read the names of the occupants.

"'Third-floor,'" he read out, "'Mr. Thomas Barlow, Commission Agent.' Hum! I think we will look in on Mr. Barlow."

He stepped quickly up the stone stairs, and I followed, until we arrived, somewhat out of breath, on the third floor. Outside the Commission Agent's door he paused for a moment, and we both listened curiously to an irregular sound of shuffling feet from within. Then he softly opened the door and looked into the room. After remaining thus for nearly a minute, he looked round at me with a broad smile, and noiselessly set the door wide open. Inside, a lanky youth of fourteen was practising, with no mean skill, the manipulation of an appliance known by the appropriate name of diabolo; and so absorbed was he in his occupation that we entered and shut the door without being observed. At length the shuttle missed the string and flew into a large waste-paper basket; the boy turned and confronted us, and was instantly covered with confusion.

"Allow me," said Thorndyke, rooting rather unnecessarily

in the waste-paper basket, and handing the toy to its owner. " I need not ask if Mr. Barlow is in," he added, " nor if he is likely to return shortly."

" He won't be back to-day," said the boy, perspiring with embarrassment ; " he left before I came. I was rather late."

" I see," said Thorndyke. " The early bird catches the worm, but the late bird catches the diabolo. How did you know he would not be back ? "

" He left a note. Here it is."

He exhibited the document, which was neatly written in red ink. Thorndyke examined it attentively, and then asked :

" Did you break the inkstand yesterday ? "

The boy stared at him in amazement. " Yes, I did," he answered. " How did you know ? "

" I didn't, or I should not have asked. But I see that he has used his stylo to write this note."

The boy regarded Thorndyke distrustfully, as he continued :

" I really called to see if your Mr. Barlow was a gentleman whom I used to know ; but I expect you can tell me. My friend was tall and thin, dark, and clean-shaved."

" This ain't him, then," said the boy. " He's thin, but he ain't tall or dark. He's got a sandy beard, and he wears spectacles and a wig. I know a wig when I see one," he added cunningly, " 'cause my father wears one. He puts it on a peg to comb it, and he swears at me when I larf."

" My friend had injured his left hand," pursued Thorndyke.

" I dunno about that," said the youth. " Mr. Barlow nearly always wears gloves ; he always wears one on his left hand, anyhow."

" Ah, well ! I'll just write him a note on the chance, if you will give me a piece of notepaper. Have you any ink ? "

" There's some in the bottle. I'll dip the pen in for you."

He produced, from the cupboard, an opened packet of cheap notepaper and a packet of similar envelopes, and, having dipped the pen to the bottom of the ink-bottle, handed it to Thorndyke, who sat down and hastily scribbled a short note. He had folded the paper, and was about to address the envelope, when he appeared suddenly to alter his mind.

" I don't think I will leave it, after all," he said, slipping the folded paper into his pocket. " No. Tell him I called— Mr. Horace Budge—and say I will look in again in a day or two."

The youth watched our exit with an air of perplexity, and he even came out on to the landing, the better to observe us over the balusters ; until, unexpectedly catching Thorndyke's eye, he withdrew his head with remarkable suddenness, and retired in disorder.

To tell the truth, I was now little less perplexed than the office-boy by Thorndyke's proceedings ; in which I could discover no relevancy to the investigation that I presumed he was engaged upon : and the last straw was laid upon the burden of my curiosity when he stopped at a staircase window, drew the note out of his pocket, examined it with his lens, held it up to the light, and chuckled aloud.

"Luck," he observed, "though no substitute for care and intelligence, is a very pleasant addition. Really, my learned brother, we are doing uncommonly well."

When we reached the hall, Thorndyke stopped at the house-keeper's box, and looked in with a genial nod.

"I have just been up to see Mr. Barlow," said he. "He seems to have left quite early."

"Yes, sir," the man replied. "He went away about half-past eight."

"That was very early ; and presumably he came earlier still ? "

"I suppose so," the man assented, with a grin ; "but I had only just come on when he left."

"Had he any luggage with him ? "

"Yes, sir. There was two cases, a square one and a long, narrow one, about five feet long. I helped him to carry them down to the cab."

"Which was a four-wheeler, I suppose ? "

"Yes, sir."

"Mr. Barlow hasn't been here very long, has he ? " Thorndyke inquired.

"No. He only came in last quarter-day—about six weeks ago."

"Ah, well ! I must call another day. Good-morning." And Thorndyke strode out of the building, and made directly for the cab-rank in the adjoining street. Here he stopped for a minute or two to parley with the driver of a four-wheeled cab, whom he finally commissioned to convey us to a shop in New Oxford Street. Having dismissed the cabman with his blessing and a half-sovereign, he vanished into the shop, leaving me to gaze at the lathes, drills, and bars of metal displayed in the window. Presently he emerged with a small parcel, and explained in answer to my inquiring look : "A strip of tool steel and a block of metal for Polton."

His next purchase was rather more eccentric. We were proceeding along Holborn when his attention was suddenly arrested by the window of a furniture shop, in which was displayed a collection of obsolete French small-arms—relics of the tragedy of 1870—which were being sold for decorative purposes. After a brief inspection, he entered the shop, and shortly reappeared carrying a long sword-bayonet and an old Chassepot rifle.

"What may be the meaning of this martial display?" I asked, as we turned down Fetter Lane.

"House protection," he replied promptly. "You will agree that a discharge of musketry, followed by a bayonet charge, would disconcert the boldest of burglars."

I laughed at the absurd picture thus drawn of the strenuous house-protector, but nevertheless continued to speculate on the meaning of my friend's eccentric proceedings, which I felt sure were in some way related to the murder in Brackenhurst Chambers, though I could not trace the connection.

After a late lunch, I hurried out to transact such of my business as had been interrupted by the stirring events of the morning, leaving Thorndyke busy with a drawing-board, squares, scale, and compasses, making accurate, scaled drawings from his rough sketches ; while Polton, with the brown-paper parcel in his hand, looked on at him with an air of anxious expectation.

As I was returning homeward in the evening by way of Mitre Court, I overtook Mr. Marchmont, who was also bound for our chambers, and we walked on together.

"I had a note from Thorndyke," he explained, "asking for a specimen of handwriting, so I thought I would bring it along myself, and hear if he has any news."

When we entered the chambers, we found Thorndyke in earnest consultation with Polton, and on the table before them I observed, to my great surprise, the dagger with which the murder had been committed.

"I have got you the specimen that you asked for," said Marchmont. "I didn't think I should be able to, but, by a lucky chance, Curtis kept the only letter he ever received from the party in question."

He drew the letter from his wallet, and handed it to Thorndyke, who looked at it attentively and with evident satisfaction.

"By the way," said Marchmont, taking up the dagger. "I thought the inspector took this away with him."

" He took the original," replied Thorndyke. " This is a duplicate, which Polton has made, for experimental purposes, from my drawings."

" Really ! " exclaimed Marchmont, with a glance of respectful admiration at Polton ; " it is a perfect replica—and you have made it so quickly, too."

" It was quite easy to make," said Polton, " to a man accustomed to work in metal."

" Which," added Thorndyke, " is a fact of some evidential value."

At this moment a hansom drew up outside. A moment later flying footsteps were heard on the stairs. There was a furious battering at the door, and, as Polton threw it open, Mr. Curtis burst wildly into the room.

" Here is a frightful thing, Marchmont ! " he gasped. " Edith—my daughter—arrested for the murder. Inspector Badger came to our house and took her. My God ! I shall go mad ! "

Thorndyke laid his hand on the excited man's shoulder. " Don't distress yourself, Mr. Curtis," said he. " There is no occasion, I assure you. I suppose," he added, " your daughter is left-handed ? "

" Yes, she is, by a most disastrous coincidence. But what are we to do ? Good God ! Dr. Thorndyke, they have taken her to prison—to prison—think of it ! My poor Edith ! "

" We'll soon have her out," said Thorndyke. " But listen ; there is some one at the door."

A brisk rat-tat confirmed his statement, and when I rose to open the door, I found myself confronted by Inspector Badger. There was a moment of extreme awkwardness, and then both the detective and Mr. Curtis proposed to retire in favour of the other.

" Don't go, inspector," said Thorndyke ; " I want to have a word with you. Perhaps Mr. Curtis would look in again, say in an hour. Will you ? We shall have news for you by then, I hope."

Mr. Curtis agreed hastily, and dashed out of the room with his characteristic impetuosity. When he had gone, Thorndyke turned to the detective, and remarked dryly :

" You seem to have been busy, inspector ? "

" Yes," replied Badger ; " I haven't let the grass grow under my feet ; and I've got a pretty strong case against Miss Curtis already. You see, she was the last person seen in the company of the deceased ; she had a grievance against him ; she is left-handed, and you remember that the murder was committed by a left-handed person."

" Anything else ? "

" Yes. I have seen those Italians, and the whole thing was a put-up job. A woman, in a widow's dress and veil, paid them to go and play the fool outside the building, and she gave them the letter that was left with the porter. They haven't identified her yet, but she seems to agree in size with Miss Curtis."

" And how did she get out of the chambers, with the door bolted on the inside ? "

" Ah, there you are ! That's a mystery at present—unless you can give us an explanation." The inspector made this qualification with a faint grin, and added : " As there was no one in the place when we broke into it, the murderer must have got out somehow. You can't deny that."

" I do deny it, nevertheless," said Thorndyke. " You look surprised," he continued (which was undoubtedly true), " but yet the whole thing is exceedingly obvious. The explanation struck me directly I looked at the body. There was evidently no practicable exit from the flat, and there was certainly no one in it when you entered. Clearly, then, *the murderer had never been in the place at all.*"

" I don't follow you in the least," said the inspector.

" Well," said Thorndyke, " as I have finished with the case, and am handing it over to you, I will put the evidence before you *seriatim*. Now, I think we are agreed that, at the moment when the blow was struck, the deceased was standing before the fireplace, winding the clock. The dagger entered obliquely from the left, and, if you recall its position, you will remember that its hilt pointed directly towards an open window."

" Which was forty feet from the ground."

" Yes. And now we will consider the very peculiar character of the weapon with which the crime was committed."

He had placed his hand upon the knob of a drawer, when we were interrupted by knock at the door. I sprang up, and, opening it, admitted no less a person than the porter of Bracken-hurst Chambers. The man looked somewhat surprised on recognising our visitors, but advanced to Thorndyke, drawing a folded paper from his pocket.

" I've found the article you were looking for, sir," said he, " and a rare hunt I had for it. It had stuck in the leaves of one of them shrubs."

Thorndyke opened the packet, and, having glanced inside, laid it on the table.

"Thank you," said he, pushing a sovereign across to the gratified official. "The inspector has your name, I think?"

"He have, sir," replied the porter; and, pocketing his fee, he departed, beaming.

"To return to the dagger," said Thorndyke, opening the drawer. "It was a very peculiar one, as I have said, and as you will see from this model, which is an exact duplicate." Here he exhibited Polton's production to the astonished detective. "You see that it is extraordinarily slender, and free from projections, and of unusual materials. You also see that it was obviously not made by an ordinary dagger-maker; that, in spite of the Italian word scrawled on it, there is plainly written all over it 'British mechanic.' The blade is made from a strip of common three-quarter-inch tool steel; the hilt is turned from an aluminium rod; and there is not a line of engraving on it that could not be produced in a lathe by any engineer's apprentice. Even the boss at the top is mechanical, for it is just like an ordinary hexagon nut. Then, notice the dimensions, as shown on my drawing. The parts A and B, which just project beyond the blade, are exactly similar in diameter—and such exactness could hardly be accidental. They are each parts of a circle having a diameter of 10.9 millimetres—a dimension which happens, by a singular coincidence, to be exactly the calibre of the old Chassepot rifle, specimens of which are now on sale at several shops in London. Here is one, for instance."

He fetched the rifle that he had bought, from the corner in which it was standing, and, lifting the dagger by its point, slipped the hilt into the muzzle. When he let go, the dagger slid quietly down the barrel, until its hilt appeared in the open breech.

"Good God!" exclaimed Marchmont. "You don't suggest that the dagger was shot from a gun?"

"I do, indeed; and you now see the reason for the aluminium hilt—to diminish the weight of the already heavy projectile—and also for this hexagonal boss on the end?"

"No, I do not," said the inspector; "but I say that you are suggesting an impossibility."

"Then," replied Thorndyke, "I must explain and demonstrate. To begin with, this projectile had to travel point foremost; therefore it had to be made to spin—and it certainly was spinning when it entered the body, as the clothing and the wound showed us. Now, to make it spin, it had to be fired from a rifle barrel ; but as the hilt would not engage in the rifling, it had to be fitted with something that would. That something was evidently a soft metal washer, which fitted on to this hexagon, and which would be pressed into the grooves of the rifling, and so spin the dagger, but would drop off as soon as the weapon left the barrel. Here is such a washer, which Polton has made for us."

He laid on the table a metal disc, with a hexagonal hole through it.

" This is all very ingenious," said the inspector, " but I say it is impossible and fantastic."

" It certainly sounds rather improbable," Marchmont agreed.

" We will see," said Thorndyke. " Here is a makeshift cartridge of Polton's manufacture, containing an eighth charge of smokeless powder for a 20-bore gun."

He fitted the washer on to the boss of the dagger in the open breech of the rifle, pushed it into the barrel, inserted the cartridge, and closed the breech. Then, opening the office-door, he displayed a target of padded strawboard against the wall.

" The length of the two rooms," said he, " gives us a distance of thirty-two feet. Will you shut the windows, Jervis ? "

I complied, and he then pointed the rifle at the target. There was a dull report—must less loud than I had expected— and when we looked at the target, we saw the dagger driven in up to its hilt at the margin of the bull's-eye.

" You see," said Thorndyke, laying down the rifle, " that the thing is practicable. Now for the evidence as to the actual occurrence. First, on the original dagger there are linear scratches which exactly correspond with the grooves of the rifling. Then there is the fact that the dagger was certainly spinning from left to right—in the direction of the rifling, that is —when it entered the body. And then there is this, which, as you heard, the porter found in the garden."

He opened the paper packet. In it lay a metal disc, per-forated by a hexagonal hole. Stepping into the office, he picked up from the floor the washer that he had put on the dagger, and laid it on the paper beside the other. The two discs were identical in size, and the margin of each was indented with identical markings, corresponding to the rifling of the barrel.

The inspector gazed at the two discs in silence for a while ; then, looking up at Thorndyke, he said :

" I give in, doctor. You're right, beyond all doubt ; but

how you came to think of it beats me into fits. The only question now is, Who fired the gun, and why wasn't the report heard ? "

" As to the latter," said Thorndyke, " it is probable that he used a compressed-air attachment, not only to diminish the noise, but also to prevent any traces of the explosive from being left on the dagger. As to the former, I think I can give you the murderer's name ; but we had better take the evidence in order. You may remember," he continued, " that when Dr. Jervis stood as if winding the clock, I chalked a mark on the floor where he stood. Now, standing on that marked spot, and looking out of the open window, I could see two of the windows of a house nearly opposite. They were the second and third-floor windows of No. 6 Cotman Street. The second floor is occupied by a firm of architects ; the third floor by a commission agent named Thomas Barlow. I called on Mr. Barlow, but before describing my visit, I will refer to another matter. You haven't those threatening letters about you, I suppose ? "

" Yes, I have," said the inspector ; and he drew forth a wallet from his breast-pocket.

" Let us take the first one, then," said Thorndyke. " You see that the paper and envelope are of the very commonest, and the writing illiterate. But the ink does not agree with this. Illiterate people usually buy their ink in penny bottles. Now, this envelope is addressed with Draper's dichroic ink—a superior office ink, sold only in large bottles—and the red ink in which the note is written is an unfixed, scarlet ink, such as is used by draughtsmen, and has been used, as you can see, in a stylographic pen. But the most interesting thing about this letter is the design drawn at the top. In an artistic sense, the man could not draw, and the anatomical details of the skull are ridiculous. Yet the drawing is very neat. It has the clean, wiry line of a machine drawing, and is done with a steady, practised hand. It is also perfectly symmetrical ; the skull, for instance, is exactly in the centre, and, when we examine it through a lens, we see why it is so, for we discover traces of a pencilled centre-line and ruled cross-lines. Moreover, the lens reveals a tiny particle of draughtsman's soft, red rubber, with which the pencil lines were taken out ; and all these facts, taken together, suggest that the drawing was made by some one accustomed to making accurate mechanical drawings. And now we will return to Mr. Barlow. He was out when I called, but I took the liberty of glancing round the office, and this is what I saw. On the mantelshelf was a twelve-inch flat boxwood rule, such as engineers use, a piece of soft, red rubber, and a stone bottle of Draper's dichroic ink. I obtained, by a simple ruse, a specimen of the office notepaper and the ink. We will examine it presently. I found that Mr. Barlow is a new tenant, that he is rather short, wears a wig and spectacles, and always wears a glove on his left hand. He left the office at 8.30 this morning, and no one saw him arrive. He had with him a square case, and a narrow, oblong one about five feet in length ; and he took a cab to Victoria, and apparently caught the 8.51 train to Chatham."

" Ah ! " exclaimed the inspector.

" But," continued Thorndyke, " now examine those three letters, and compare them with this note that I wrote in Mr. Barlow's office. You see that the paper is of the same make, with the same watermark, but that is of no great significance. What is of crucial importance is this : You see, in each of these letters, two tiny indentations near the bottom corner. Somebody has used compasses or drawing-pins over the packet of notepaper, and the points have made little indentations, which have marked several of the sheets. Now, notepaper is cut to its size after it is folded, and if you stick a pin into the top sheet of a section, the indentations on all the underlying sheets will be at exactly similar distances from the edges and corners of the sheet. But you see that these little dents are all at the same distance from the edges and the corner." He demonstrated the fact with a pair of compasses. " And now look at this sheet, which I obtained at Mr. Barlow's office. There are two little indentations—rather faint, but quite visible—near the bottom corner, and when we measure them with the compasses, we find that they are exactly the same distance apart as the others, and the same distance from the edges and the bottom corner. The irresistible conclusion is that these four sheets came from the same packet."

The inspector started up from his chair, and faced Thorndyke. " Who is this Mr. Barlow ? " he asked.

" That," replied Thorndyke, " is for you to determine ; but I can give you a useful hint. There is only one person who benefits by the death of Alfred Hartridge, but he benefits to the extent of twenty thousand pounds. His name is Leonard Wolfe, and I learn from Mr. Marchmont that he is a man of indifferent character—a gambler, and a spendthrift. By profession he is an engineer, and he is a capable mechanician. In appearance he is thin, short, fair, and clean-shaven, and he has lost the middle finger of his left hand. Mr. Barlow is also short, thin, and fair, but wears a wig, a beard, and spectacles, and always wears a glove on his left hand. I have seen the handwriting of both these gentlemen, and should say that it would be difficult to distinguish one from the other."

"That's good enough for me," said the inspector. "Give me his address, and I'll have Miss Curtis released at once."

The same night Leonard Wolfe was arrested at Eltham, in the very act of burying in his garden a large and powerful compressed-air rifle. He was never brought to trial, however, for he had in his pocket a more portable weapon—a large-bore Derringer pistol—with which he managed to terminate an exceedingly ill-spent life.

"And, after all," was Thorndyke's comment, when he heard of the event, "he had his uses. He has relieved society of two very bad men, and he has given us a most instructive case. He has shown us how a clever and ingenious criminal may take endless pains to mislead and delude the police, and yet, by in-attention to trivial details, may scatter clues broadcast. We can only say to the criminal class generally, in both respects, 'Go thou and do likewise.'"

THE GYLSTON SLANDER

IT was through Roger Freynes, the eminent K.C., that Malcolm Sage first became interested in the series of anonymous letters that had created considerable scandal in the little village of Gylston.

Tucked away in the north-west corner of Hampshire, Gylston was a village of some eight hundred inhabitants. The vicar, the Rev. John Crayne, had held the living for some twenty years. Aided by his wife and daughter, Muriel, a pretty and high-spirited girl of nineteen, he devoted himself to the parish, and in return enjoyed great popularity.

Life at the vicarage was an ideal of domestic happiness. Mr. and Mrs. Crayne were devoted to each other and to their daughter, and she to them. Muriel Crayne had grown up among the villagers, devoting herself to parish work as soon as she was old enough to do so. She seemed to find her life sufficient for her needs, and many were the comparisons drawn by other parents in Gylston between the vicar's daughter and their own restless offspring.

A year previously a new curate had arrived in the person of the Rev. Charles Blade. His frank, straightforward personality, coupled with his good looks and masculine bearing, had caused him to be greatly liked, not only by the vicar and his family, but by all the parishioners.

Suddenly and without warning the peace of the vicarage was destroyed. One morning Mr. Crayne received by post an anonymous letter, in which the names of his daughter and the curate were linked together in a way that caused him both pain and anxiety.

A man with a strong sense of humour himself, he cordially

304

despised the anonymous letter-writer, and his first instinct had been to ignore that which he had just received. On second thoughts, however, he reasoned that the writer would be unlikely to rest content with a single letter ; but would, in all probability, make the same calumnious statements to others.

After consulting with his wife, he had reluctantly questioned his daughter. At first she was inclined to treat the matter lightly ; but on the grave nature of the accusations being pointed out to her, she had become greatly embarrassed and assured him that the curate had never been more than ordinarily attentive to her.

The vicar decided to allow the matter to rest there, and accordingly he made no mention of the letter to Blade.

A week later his daughter brought him a letter she had found lying in the vicarage grounds. It contained a passionate declaration of love, and ended with a threat of what might happen if the writer's passion were not reciprocated.

Although the letter was unsigned, the vicar could not disguise from himself the fact that there was a marked similarity between the handwriting of the two anonymous letters and that of his curate. He decided, therefore, to ask Blade if he could throw any light on the matter.

At first the young man had appeared bewildered ; then he had pledged his word of honour, not only that he had not written the letters, but that there was no truth in the statements they contained.

With that the vicar had to rest content ; but worse was to follow.

Two evenings later, one of the churchwardens called at the vicarage and, after behaving in what to the vicar seemed a very strange manner, he produced from his pocket a letter he had received that morning, in which were repeated the scandalous statements contained in the first epistle.

From then on the district was deluged with anonymous letters, all referring to the alleged passion of the curate for the vicar's daughter, and the intrigue they were carrying on together. Some of the letters were frankly indelicate in their expression and, as the whole parish seethed with the scandal, the vicar appealed to the police for aid.

One peculiarity of the letters was that all were written upon the same paper, known as " Olympic Script." This was supplied locally to a number of people in the neighbourhood, among others, the vicar, the curate, and the schoolmaster.

Soon the story began to find its way into the newspapers, and Blade's position became one full of difficulty and embarrassment. He had consulted Robert Freynes, who had been at Oxford with his father, and the K.C., convinced of the young man's innocence, had sought Malcolm Sage's aid.

" You see, Sage," Freynes had remarked, " I'm sure the boy is straight and incapable of such conduct ; but it's impossible to talk to that ass Murdy. He has no more imagination than a tin-linnet."

Freynes's reference was to Chief Inspector Murdy, of Scotland Yard, who had been entrusted with the inquiry, the local police having proved unequal to the problem.

Although Malcolm Sage had promised Robert Freynes that he would undertake the inquiry into the Gylston scandal, it was not until nearly a week later that he found himself at liberty to motor down into Hampshire.

One afternoon the vicar of Gylston, on entering his church, found a stranger on his knees in the chancel. Note-book in hand, he was transcribing the inscription of a monumental brass.

As the vicar approached, he observed that the stranger was vigorously shaking a fountain-pen, from which the ink had evidently been exhausted.

At the sound of Mr. Crayne's footsteps the stranger looked up, turning towards him a pair of gold-rimmed spectacles, above which a bald conical head seemed to contradict the keenness of the eyes and the youthful lines of the face beneath.

" You are interested in monumental brasses ? " inquired the vicar, as he entered the chancel, and the stranger rose to his feet. " I am the vicar," he explained. There was a look of eager interest in the pale grey eyes that looked out from a placid, scholarly face.

" I was taking the liberty of copying the inscription on this," replied Malcolm Sage, indicating the time-worn brass at his feet, " only unfortunately my fountain-pen has given out."

" There is pen and ink in the vestry," said the vicar, impressed by the fact that the stranger had chosen the finest brass in the church, one that had been saved from Cromwell's Puritans by the ingenuity of the then incumbent, who had caused it to be covered with cement. Then as an afterthought the vicar added, " I can get your pen filled at the vicarage. My daughter has some ink ; she always uses a fountain-pen."

Malcolm Sage thanked him, and for the next half-hour the vicar forgot the worries of the past few weeks in listening to a man who seemed to have the whole subject of monumental brasses and Norman architecture at his finger-ends.

Subsequently Malcolm Sage was invited to the vicarage, where another half-hour was occupied in Mr. Crayne showing him his collection of books on brasses.

As Malcolm Sage made a movement to depart, the vicar suddenly remembered the matter of the ink, apologised for his remissness, and left the room, returning a few minutes later with a bottle of fountain-pen ink. Malcolm Sage drew from his pocket his pen, and proceeded to replenish the ink from the bottle. Finally he completed the transcription of the lettering of the brass from a rubbing produced by the vicar.

Reluctant to allow so interesting a visitor to depart, Mr. Crayne pressed him to take tea ; but Malcolm Sage pleaded an engagement.

As they crossed the hall, a fair girl suddenly rushed out from a door on the right. She was crying hysterically. Her hair was disordered, her deep violet eyes rimmed with red, and her moist lips seemed to stand out strangely red against the alabaster paleness of her skin.

" Muriel ! "

Malcolm Sage glanced swiftly at the vicar. The look of scholarly calm had vanished from his features, giving place to a set sternness that reflected the tone in which he had uttered his daughter's name.

At the sight of a stranger the girl had paused, then, as if realising her tear-stained face and disordered hair, she turned and disappeared through the door from which she had rushed.

" My daughter," murmured the vicar, a little sadly, Malcolm Sage thought. " She has always been very highly strung and emotional," he added, as if considering some explanation necessary. " We have to be very stern with her on such occasions. It is the only way to repress it."

" You find it answer ? " remarked Malcolm Sage.

" She has been much better lately, although she has been sorely tried. Perhaps you have heard."

Malcolm Sage nodded absently, as he gazed intently at the thumb-nail of his right hand. A minute later he was walking down the drive, his thoughts occupied with the pretty daughter of the vicar of Gylston.

At the curate's lodgings he was told that Mr. Blade was away, and would not return until late that night.

As he turned from the gate, Malcolm Sage encountered a pale-faced, narrow-shouldered man with a dark moustache and a hard, peevish mouth.

To Malcolm Sage's question as to which was the way to the inn, he nodded in the direction from which he had come and continued on his way.

" A man who has failed in what he set out to accomplish," was Malcolm Sage's mental diagnosis of John Gray, the Gylston schoolmaster.

It was not long before Malcolm Sage realised that the village of Gylston was intensely proud of itself. It had seen in the London papers accounts of the mysterious scandal of which it was the centre. A Scotland Yard officer had been down, and had subjected many of the inhabitants to a careful cross-examination. In consequence Gylston realised that it was a village to be reckoned with.

The Tired Traveller was the centre of all rumour and gossip. Here each night in the public-bar, or in the private-parlour, according to their social status, the inhabitants would forgather and discuss the problem of the mysterious letters. Every sort of theory was advanced, and every sort of explanation offered. Whilst popular opinion tended to the view that the curate was the guilty party, there were some who darkly shook their heads and muttered, " We shall see."

It was remembered and discussed with relish that John Gray, the schoolmaster, had for some time past shown a marked admiration for the vicar's daughter. She, however, had made it clear that the cadaverous, saturnine pedagogue possessed for her no attractions.

During the half-hour that Malcolm Sage spent at the Tired Traveller, eating a hurried meal, he heard all there was to be heard about local opinion.

The landlord, a rubicund old fellow whose baldness extended to his eyelids, was bursting with information. By nature capable of making a mystery out of a sunbeam, he revelled in the scandal that hummed around him.

After a quarter of an hour's conversation, the landlord's conversation, Malcolm Sage found himself possessed of a bewildering amount of new material.

" A young gal don't have them highsterics for nothin'," mine host remarked darkly. " Has fits of 'em every now and then ever since she was a flapper, sobbin' and cryin' fit to break 'er heart, and the vicar that cross with her."

" That is considered the best way to treat hysterical people,"
remarked Malcolm Sage.

" Maybe," was the reply, " but she's only a gal, and a pretty
one too," he added inconsequently.

" Then there's the schoolmaster," he continued, " 'ates the
curate like poison, he does. Shouldn't be surprised if it was him
that done it. 'E's always been a bit sweet in that quarter himself,
has Mr. Gray. Got talked about a good deal one time, 'angin'
about arter Miss Muriel," added the loquacious publican.

By the time Malcolm Sage had finished his meal, the landlord
was well in his stride of scandalous reminiscence. It was with
obvious reluctance that he allowed so admirable a listener to
depart, and it was with manifest regret that he watched Malcolm
Sage's car disappear round the curve in the road.

A little way beyond the vicarage, an admonitory triangle
caused Tims to slow up. Just by the bend Malcolm Sage observed
a youth and a girl standing in the recess of a gate giving access
to a meadow. Although they were in the shadow cast by the
hedge, Malcolm Sage's quick eyes recognised in the girl the
vicar's daughter. The youth looked as if he might be one of
the lads of the village.

In the short space of two or three seconds Malcolm Sage
noticed the change in the girl. Although he could not see her
face very clearly, the vivacity of her bearing and the ready laugh
were suggestive of a gaiety contrasting strangely with the tragic
figure he had seen in the afternoon.

Muriel Crayne was obviously of a very mercurial temperament, he decided, as the car swung round the bend.

The next morning, in response to a telephone message,
Inspector Murdy called on Malcolm Sage.

" Well, Mr. Sage," he cried, as he shook hands, " going to
have another try to teach us our job ? " And his blue eyes
twinkled good-humouredly.

The inspector had already made up his mind. He was a
man with many successes to his record, achieved as a result of
undoubted astuteness in connection with the grosser crimes,
such as train-murders, post-office hold-ups and burglaries. He
was incapable, however, of realising that there existed a subtler
form of law-breaking, arising from something more intimately
associated with the psychic than the material plane.

" Did you see Mr. Blade ? " inquired Malcolm Sage.

" Saw the whole blessed lot," was the cheery reply. " It's
all as clear as milk." And he laughed.

"What did Mr. Blade say?" inquired Malcolm Sage, looking keenly across at the inspector.

"Just that he had nothing to say."

"His exact words. Can you remember them?" queried Malcolm Sage.

"Oh, yes!" replied the inspector. "He said, ' Inspector Murdy, I have nothing to say,' and then he shut up like a real Whitstable."

"He was away yesterday," remarked Malcolm Sage, who then told the inspector of his visit. "How about John Gray, the schoolmaster?" he queried.

"He practically told me to go to the devil," was the genial reply. Inspector Murdy was accustomed to rudeness ; his profession invited it, and to his rough-and-ready form of reasoning, rudeness meant innocence ; politeness, guilt.

He handed to Malcolm Sage a copy of a list of people who purchased "Olympic Script" from Mr. Grainger, the local Whiteley, volunteering the information that the curate was the biggest consumer, as if that settled the question of his guilt.

"And yet the vicar would not hear of the arrest of Blade," murmured Malcolm Sage, turning the copper ash-tray round with his restless fingers.

The inspector shrugged his massive shoulders.

"Sheer good nature and kindliness, Mr. Sage," he said. "He's as gentle as a woman."

"I once knew a man," remarked Malcolm Sage, "who said that in the annals of crime lay the master-key to the world's mysteries, past, present and to come."

"A dreamer, Mr. Sage," smiled the inspector. "We haven't time for dreaming at the Yard," he added good-temperedly, as he rose and shook himself like a Newfoundland dog.

"I suppose it never struck you to look elsewhere than at the curate's lodgings for the writer of the letters?" inquired Malcolm Sage quietly.

"It never strikes me to look about for some one when I'm sitting on his chest," laughed Inspector Murdy.

"True," said Malcolm Sage. "By the way," he continued, without looking up, "in future can you let me see every letter as it is received? You might also keep careful record of how they are delivered."

"Certainly, Mr. Sage. Anything that will make you happy."

"Later I may get you to ask the vicar to seal up any subsequent anonymous letters that reach him without allowing any one to see the contents. Do you think he would do that ? "

" Without doubt if I ask him," said the inspector, surprise in his eyes as he looked down upon the cone of baldness beneath him, realising what a handicap it is to talk to a man who keeps his eyes averted.

" He must then put the letters in a place where no one can possibly obtain access to them. One thing more," continued Malcolm Sage, " will you ask Miss Crayne to write out the full story of the letters as far as she personally is acquainted with it ? "

" Very well, Mr. Sage," said the inspector, with the air of one humouring a child. " Now I'll be going." He walked towards the door, then suddenly stopped and turned.

" I suppose you think I'm wrong about the curate ? "

" I'll tell you later," was the reply.

" When you find the master-key ? " laughed the inspector, as he opened the door.

" Yes, when I find the master-key," said Malcolm Sage quietly and, as the door closed behind Inspector Murdy, he continued to finger the copper ash-tray as if that were the master-key.

II

MALCOLM SAGE was seated at a small green-covered table playing solitaire. A velvet smoking-jacket and a pair of wine-coloured morocco slippers suggested that the day's work was done.

Patience, chess, and the cinema were his unfailing sources, of inspiration when engaged upon a more than usually difficult case. He had once told Sir James Walton that they clarified his brain and co-ordinated his thoughts, the cinema in particular. The fact that in the surrounding darkness were hundreds of other brains, vital and active, appeared to stimulate his own imagination.

Puffing steadily at a gigantic meerschaum, he moved the cards with a deliberation which suggested that his attention rather than his thoughts was absorbed in the game.

Nearly a month had elapsed since he had agreed to take up the inquiry into the authorship of the series of anonymous letters with which Gylston and the neighbourhood had been flooded ; yet still the matter remained a mystery.

A celebrated writer of detective stories had interested himself in the affair, with the result that the Press throughout the country had "stunted" Gylston as if it had been a heavy-weight championship, or a train murder.

For a fortnight Malcolm Sage had been on the Continent in connection with the theft of the Adair Diamonds. Two days previously, after having restored the famous jewels to Lady Adair, he had returned to London, to find that the Gylston affair had developed a new and dramatic phase. The curate had been arrested for an attempted assault upon Miss Crayne and, pleading "not guilty," had been committed for trial.

The incident that led up to this had taken place on the day that Malcolm Sage left London. Late that afternoon Miss Crayne had arrived at the vicarage in a state bordering on collapse. On becoming more collected, she stated that on returning from paying a call, and when half-way through a copse, known locally as "Gipsies Wood," Blade had sprung out upon her and violently protested his passion. He had gripped hold of her wrists, the mark of his fingers was to be seen on the delicate skin, and threatened to kill her and himself. She had been terrified, thinking he meant to kill her. The approach of a farm labourer had saved her, and the curate had disappeared through the copse.

This story was borne out by Joseph Higgins, the farm labourer in question. He had arrived to find Miss Crayne in a state of great alarm and agitation, and he had walked with her as far as the vicarage gate. He did not, however, actually see the curate.

On the strength of this statement the police had applied for a warrant, and had subsequently arrested the curate. Later he appeared before the magistrates, had been remanded, and finally committed for trial, bail being allowed.

Blade protested his innocence alike of the assault and the writing of the letters ; but two handwriting experts had testified to the similarity of the handwriting of the anonymous letters with that of the curate. Furthermore, they were all written upon "Olympic Script," the paper that Blade used for his sermons.

Malcolm Sage had just started a new deal when the door opened and Rogers showed in Robert Freynes. With a nod, Malcolm Sage indicated the chair opposite. His visitor dropped into it and, taking a pipe from his pocket, proceeded to fill and light it.

Placing his meerschaum on the mantelpiece, Malcolm Sage

produced a well-worn briar from his pocket, which, having got into commission, he proceeded once more with the game.

"It's looking pretty ugly for Blade," remarked Freynes, recognising by the substitution of the briar for the meerschaum that Malcolm Sage was ready for conversation.

"Tell me."

"It's those damned handwriting experts," growled Freynes. "They're the greatest anomaly of our legal system. The judge always warns the jury of the danger of accepting their evidence ; yet each side continues to produce them. It's an insult to intelligence and justice."

"To hang a man because his ' s ' resembles that of an implicating document," remarked Malcolm Sage, as he placed a red queen on a black knave, "is about as sensible as to imprison him because he has the same accent as a footpad."

"Then there's Blade's astonishing apathy," continued Freynes. "He seems quite indifferent to the gravity of his position. Refuses to say a word. Any one might think he knew the real culprit and was trying to shield him," and he sucked moodily at his pipe.

"The handwriting expert," continued Malcolm Sage imperturbably, "is too concerned with the crossing of a ' t,' the dotting of an ' i,' or the tail of a ' g,' to give time and thought to the way in which the writer uses, for instance, the compound tenses of verbs. Blade was no more capable of writing those letters than our friend Murdy is of transliterating the Rosetta Stone."

"Yes ; but can we prove it?" asked Freynes gloomily, as with the blade of a penknife he loosened the tobacco in the bowl of his pipe. "Can we prove it?" he repeated and, snapping the knife to, he replaced it in his pocket.

"Blade's sermons," Malcolm Sage continued, "and such letters of his as you have been able to collect, show that he adopted a very definite and precise system of punctuation. He frequently uses the colon and the semicolon, and always in the right place. In a parenthetical clause preceded by the conjunction ' and,' he uses a comma *after* the ' and,' not before it as most people do. Before such words as ' yet ' and ' but,' he without exception uses a semicolon. The word ' only,' he always puts in its correct place. In short, he is so academic as to savour somewhat of the pomposity of the eighteenth century."

"Go on," said Freynes, as Malcolm Sage paused, as if to give the other a chance of questioning his reasoning.

"Turning to the anonymous letters," continued Malcolm Sage, "it must be admitted that the handwriting is very similar ; but there all likeness to Blade's sermons and correspondence ends. Murdy has shown me nearly all the anonymous letters, and in the whole series there is not one instance of the colon or the semicolon being used. The punctuation is of the vaguest, consisting largely of the dash, which after all is a literary evasion.

"In these letters the word ' but ' frequently appears without any punctuation mark before it. At other times it has a comma, a dash, or a full stop."

He paused and for the next two minutes devoted himself to the game before him. Then he continued :

"Such phrases as ' If only you knew,' ' I should have loved to have been,' ' different than,' which appear in these letters, would have been absolutely impossible to a man of Blade's meticulous literary temperament.

As Malcolm Sage spoke, Robert Freynes's brain had been working rapidly. Presently he brought his hand down with a smack upon his knee.

"By heavens, Sage ! " he cried, " this is a new pill for the handwriting expert. I'll put you in the box. We've got a fighting chance after all."

"The most curious factor in the whole case," continued Malcolm Sage, " is the way in which the letters were delivered. One was thrown into a fly on to Miss Crayne's lap, she tells us, when she and her father were driving home after dining at the Hall. Another was discovered in the vicarage garden. A third was thrown through Miss Crayne's bedroom window. A few of the earlier group were posted in the neighbouring town of Whitchurch, some on days that Blade was certainly not there."

"That was going to be one of my strongest points," remarked Freynes.

"The letters always imply that there is some obstacle existing between the writer and the girl he desires. What possible object could Blade have in writing letters to various people suggesting an intrigue between his vicar's daughter and himself ; yet these letters were clearly written by the same hand that addressed those to the girl, her father and her mother."

Freynes nodded his head comprehendingly.

"If Blade were in love with the girl," continued Malcolm Sage, "what was there to prevent him from pressing his suit along legitimate and accepted lines. Murdy frankly acknowledges that there has been nothing in Blade's outward demeanour to suggest that Miss Crayne was to him anything more than the daughter of his vicar."

" What do you make of the story of the assault ? "

" As evidence it is worthless," replied Malcolm Sage, " being without corroboration. The farm-hand did not actually see Blade."

Freynes nodded his agreement.

" Having convinced myself that Blade had nothing to do with the writing of the letters, I next tried to discover if there were anything throwing suspicion on others in the neighbourhood, who were known to use ' Olympic Script ' as notepaper.

" The schoolmaster, John Gray, was one. He is an admirer of Miss Crayne, according to local gossip ; but it was obvious from the first that he had nothing to do with the affair. One by one I eliminated all the others, until I came back once more to Blade.

" It was clear that the letters were written with a fountain-pen, and Blade always uses one. That, however, is not evidence, as millions of people use fountain-pens. By the way, what is your line of defence ? " he inquired.

" Smashing the handwriting experts," was the reply. " I was calling four myself, on the principle that God is on the side of the big battalions ; but now I shall depend entirely on your evidence."

" The assault ? " queried Malcolm Sage.

" There I'm done," said Freynes, " for although Miss Crayne's evidence is not proof, it will be sufficient for a jury. Besides, she's a very pretty and charming girl. I suppose," he added, " Blade must have made some sort of declaration, which she, in the light of the anonymous letters, entirely misunderstood."

" What does he say ? "

" Denies it absolutely, although he admits being in the neighbourhood of the ' Gypsies Wood,' and actually catching sight of Miss Crayne in the distance ; but he says he did not speak to her."

" Is he going into the witness-box ? "

" Certainly," then after a pause he added, " Kelton is prosecuting, and he's as moral as a swan. He'll appeal to the jury as fathers of daughters, and brothers of sisters."

Malcolm Sage made no comment ; but continued smoking mechanically, his attention apparently absorbed in the cards before him.

" If you can smash the handwriting experts," continued the K.C., " I may be able to manage the girl's testimony."

" It will not be necessary," said Malcolm Sage, carefully placing a nine of clubs upon an eight of diamonds.

" Not necessary ? "

" I have asked Murdy to come round," continued Malcolm Sage, still intent upon his game. " I think that was his ring."

A minute later the door opened to admit the burly inspector, more blue-eyed and genial than ever, and obviously in the best of spirits.

" Good-evening, Mr. Sage," he cried cheerfully. " Congratulations on the Adair business. Good-evening, sir," he added, as he shook hands with Freynes.

He dropped heavily into a seat, and taking a cigar from the box on the table, which Malcolm Sage had indicated with a nod, he proceeded to light it. No man enjoyed a good cigar more than Inspector Murdy.

" Well, what do you think of it ? " he inquired, looking from Malcolm Sage to Freynes. " It's a clear case now, I think." He slightly stressed the word " now."

" You mean it's Blade ? " inquired Malcolm Sage, as he proceeded to gather up the cards.

" Who else ? " inquired the inspector, through a cloud of smoke.

" That is the question which involves your being here now, Murdy," said Malcolm Sage dryly.

" We've got three handwriting experts behind us," said the inspector complacently.

" That is precisely where they should be," retorted Malcolm Sage quietly. " In the biblical sense," he added.

Freynes laughed, whilst Inspector Murdy looked from one to the other. He did not quite catch the allusion.

" You have done as I suggested ? " inquired Malcolm Sage, when he had placed the cards in their box and removed the card-table.

" Here are all the letters received up to a fortnight ago," said the inspector, holding out a bulky packet. " Those received since have each been sealed up separately by the vicar, who is keeping half of them, whilst I have the other half ; but really, Mr. Sage, I don't understand——"

" Thank you, Murdy," said Malcolm Sage, as he took the packet. " It is always a pleasure to work with Scotland Yard. It is so thorough."

The inspector beamed ; for he knew the compliment was sincere.

Without a word Malcolm Sage left the room, taking the packet with him.

" A bit quaint at times, ain't he, sir ? " remarked Inspector Murdy to Freynes ; " but one of the best. I'd trust him with anything."

Freynes nodded encouragingly.

" There are some of them down at the Yard that don't like him," he continued. " They call him ' Sage and Onions ; ' but most of us who have worked with him swear by Mr. Sage. He's never out for the limelight himself, and he's always willing to give another fellow a leg up. After all, it's our living," he added, a little inconsequently.

Freynes appreciated the inspector's delicacy in refraining from any mention of the Gylston case during Malcolm Sage's absence. After all, they represented respectively the prosecution and the defence. For nearly half an hour the two talked together upon unprofessional subjects. When Malcolm Sage returned, he found them discussing the prospects of Dempsey against Carpentier.

Handing back the packet of letters to Inspector Murdy, Malcolm Sage resumed his seat, and proceeded to relight his pipe.

" Spotted the culprit, Mr. Sage ? " inquired the inspector, with something that was very much like a wink in the direction of Freynes.

" I think so," was the quiet reply. " You might meet me at Gylston Vicarage to-morrow at three. I'll telegraph to Blade to be there too. You had better bring the schoolmaster also."

" You mean——" began the inspector, rising.

" Exactly," said Malcolm Sage. " It's past eleven, and we all require sleep "

III

THE next afternoon the study of the vicar of Gylston presented a strange appearance.

Seated at Mr. Crayne's writing-table was Malcolm Sage, a small attaché-case at his side, whilst before him were several piles of sealed packets. Grouped about the room were Inspector Murdy, Robert Freynes, Mr. Gray, and the vicar.

All had their eyes fixed upon Malcolm Sage ; but with varying expressions. Those of the schoolmaster were frankly

cynical. The inspector and Freynes looked as if they expected
to see produced from the attaché-case a guinea-pig or a white
rabbit, pink-eyed and kicking ; whilst the vicar had obviously
not yet recovered from his surprise at discovering that the
stranger, who had shown such a remarkable knowledge of
monumental brasses and Norman architecture, was none other
than the famous investigator about whom he had read so much
in the newspapers.

With quiet deliberation Malcolm Sage opened the attaché-
case and produced a spirit lamp, which he lighted. He then
placed a metal plate upon a rest above the flame. On this he
imposed a thicker plate of a similar metal that looked like steel ;
but it had a handle across the middle, rather resembling that
of a tool used by plasterers.

He then glanced up, apparently unconscious of the almost
feverish interest with which his every movement was being
watched.

" I should like Miss Crayne to be present," he said.

As he spoke the door opened and the curate entered, his
dark, handsome face lined and careworn. It was obvious that
he had suffered. He bowed, and then looked about him, without
any suggestion of embarrassment.

Malcolm Sage rose and held out his hand, Freynes followed
suit.

" Ask Miss Muriel to come here," said the vicar to the
maid as she was closing the door.

The curate took the seat that Malcolm Sage indicated beside
him. Silently the six men waited.

A few minutes later Miss Crayne entered, pale but self-
possessed. She closed the door behind her. Suddenly she
caught sight of the curate. Her eyes widened, and her paleness
seemed to become accentuated. A moment later it was followed
by a crimson flush. She hesitated, her hands clenched at her
side, then with a manifest effort she appeared to control herself
and, with a slight smile and inclination of her head, took the
chair the schoolmaster moved towards her. Instinctively she
turned her eyes toward Malcolm Sage.

" Inspector Murdy," he said, without raising his eyes, " will
you please open two of those packets." He indicated the pile
upon his left. " I should explain," he continued, " that each of
these contains one of the most recent of the series of letters with
which we are concerned. Each was sealed up by Mr. Crayne
immediately it reached him, in accordance with Inspector

Murdy's request. Therefore, only the writer, the recipient and the vicar have had access to these letters."

Malcolm Sage turned his eyes interrogatingly upon Mr. Crayne, who bowed.

Meanwhile the inspector had cut open the two top envelopes, unfolded the sheets of paper they contained, and handed them to Malcolm Sage.

All eyes were fixed upon his long, shapely fingers as he smoothed out one of the sheets of paper upon the vicar's blotting-pad. Then, lifting the steel plate by the handle, he placed it upon the upturned sheet of paper.

The tension was almost unendurable. The heavy breathing of Inspector Murdy seemed like the blowing of a grampus. Mr. Gray glanced across at him irritably. The vicar coughed slightly, then looked startled that he had made so much noise.

Every one bent forward, eagerly expecting something ; yet without quite knowing what. Malcolm Sage lifted the metal plate from the letter. There in the centre of the page, in bluish-coloured letters, which had not been there when the paper was smoothed out upon the blotting-pad, appeared the words :

Malcolm Sage,
August 12th, 1919.
No. 138.

For some moments they all gazed at the paper as if the mysterious blue letters exercised upon them some hypnotic influence.

" Secret ink ! "

It was Robert Freynes who spoke. Accustomed as he was to dramatic moments, he was conscious of a strange dryness at the back of his throat, and a consequent huskiness of voice.

His remark seemed to break the spell. Instinctively every one turned to him. The significance of the bluish-coloured characters was slowly dawning upon the inspector ; but the others still seemed puzzled to account for their presence.

Immediately he had lifted the plate from the letter, Malcolm Sage had drawn a sheet of plain sermon paper from the rack before him. This he subjected to the same treatment as the letter. When a few seconds later he exposed it, there in the centre appeared the same words :

Malcolm Sage,
August 12th, 1919.

but on this sheet the number was 203.

Then the true significance of the two sheets of paper seemed to dawn upon the onlookers.

Suddenly there was a scream, and Muriel Crayne fell forward on to the floor.

"Oh ! father, father, forgive me ! " she cried, and the next moment she was beating the floor with her hands in violent hysterics.

IV

"FROM the first I suspected the truth," remarked Malcolm Sage, as he, Robert Freynes and Inspector Murdy sat smoking in the car that Tims was taking back to London at its best pace. "Eighty-five years ago a somewhat similar case occurred in France, that of Marie de Morel, when an innocent man was sentenced to ten years' imprisonment, and actually served eight before the truth was discovered."

The inspector whistled under his breath.

"This suspicion was strengthened by the lengthy account of the affair written by Miss Crayne, which Murdy obtained from her. The punctuation, the phrasing, the inaccurate use of auxiliary verbs, were identical with that of the anonymous letters.

"Another point was that the similarity of the handwriting of the anonymous letters to Blade's became more pronounced as the letters themselves multiplied. The writer was becoming more expert as an imitator."

Freynes nodded his head several times.

"The difficulty, however, was to prove it," continued Malcolm Sage. "There was only one way ; to substitute secretly marked paper for that in use at the vicarage.

"I accordingly went down to Gylston, and the vicar found me keenly interested in monumental brasses, his pet subject, and Norman architecture. He invited me to the vicarage. In his absence from his study I substituted a supply of marked Olympic Script in place of that in his letter-rack, and also in the drawer of his writing-table. As a further precaution, I arranged for my fountain-pen to run out of ink. He kindly supplied me with a bottle, obviously belonging to his daughter. I replenished my pen, which was full of a chemical that would enable me, if necessary, to identify any letter in the writing of which it had been used. When I placed my pen, which is a self-filler, in the ink, I forced this liquid into the bottle."

The inspector merely stared. Words had forsaken him for the moment.

" It was then necessary to wait until the ink in Miss Crayne's pen had become exhausted, and she had to replenish her supply of paper from her father's study. After that discovery was inevitable."

" But suppose she had denied it ? " questioned the inspector.

" There was the ink which she alone used, and which I could identify," was the reply.

" Why did you ask Gray to be present ? " inquired Freynes.

" As his name had been associated with the scandal it seemed only fair," remarked Malcolm Sage, then turning to Inspector Murdy he said, " I shall leave it to you, Murdy, to see that a proper confession is obtained. The case has had such publicity that Mr. Blade's innocence must be made equally public."

" You may trust me, Mr. Sage," said the inspector. " But why did the curate refuse to say anything ? "

" Because he is a high-minded and chivalrous gentleman," was the quiet reply.

" He knew ? " cried Freynes.

" Obviously," said Malcolm Sage. " It is the only explanation of his silence. I taxed him with it after the girl had been taken away, and he acknowledged that his suspicions amounted almost to certainty."

" Yet he stayed behind," murmured the inspector with the air of a man who does not understand. " I wonder why ? "

" To minister to the afflicted, Murdy," said Malcolm Sage. " That is the mission of the Church."

" I suppose you meant that French case when you referred to the ' master-key,' " remarked the inspector, as if to change the subject.

Malcolm Sage nodded.

" But how do you account for Miss Crayne writing such letters about herself," inquired the inspector, with a puzzled expression in his eyes. " Pretty funny letters some of them for a parson's daughter."

" I'm not a pathologist, Murdy," remarked Malcolm Sage dryly, " but when you try to suppress hysteria in a young girl by sternness, it's about as effectual as putting ointment on a plague-spot."

" Sex-repression ? " queried Freynes.

Malcolm Sage shrugged his shoulders ; then after a pause, during which he lighted the pipe he had just refilled, he added :

" When you are next in Great Russell Street, drop in at the British Museum and look at the bust of Faustina. You will see that her chin is similar in modelling to that of Miss Crayne. The girl was apparently very much attracted to Blade, and proceeded to weave what was no doubt to her a romance, later it became an obsession. It all goes to show the necessity for pathological consideration of certain crimes."

" But who was Faustina ? " inquired the inspector, unable to follow the drift of the conversation.

" Faustina," remarked Malcolm Sage, " was the domestic fly in the philosophical ointment of an emperor," and Inspector Murdy laughed ; for, knowing nothing of the marriage or the *Meditations* of Marcus Aurelius, it seemed to him the only thing to do.

ARSÈNE LUPIN IN PRISON

EVERY tripper by the banks of the Seine must have noticed, between the ruins of Jumièges and those of Saint-Wandrille, the curious little feudal castle of the Malaquis, proudly seated on its rock in mid-stream. A bridge connects it with the road. The base of its turrets seems to make one with the granite that supports it, a huge block detached from a mountain-top and flying where it stands by some formidable convulsion of nature. All around, the calm water of the broad river ripples among the reeds, while wagtails perch timidly on the top of the moist pebbles.

The history of the Marquis is as rough as its name, as harsh as its outlines, and consists of endless fights, sieges, assaults, sacks, and massacres. Stories are told in the Caux country, late at night, with a shiver, of the crimes committed there. Mysterious legends are conjured up. There is talk of a famous underground passage that led to the Abbey of Jumièges and to the manor-house of Agnès Sorel, the favourite of Charles VII.

This erstwhile haunt of heroes and robbers is now occupied by Baron Nathan Cahorn, or Baron Satan as he used to be called on the Bourse, where he made his fortune a little too suddenly. The ruined owners of the Malaquis were compelled to sell the abode of their ancestors to him for a song. Here he installed his wonderful collections of pictures and furniture, of pottery and carvings. He lives here alone, with three old servants. No one ever enters the doors. No one has ever beheld, in the setting of those ancient halls, his three Rubens, his two Watteaus, his pulpit carved by Jean Goujon and all the marvels snatched by force of money from before the eyes of the wealthiest frequenters of the public sale-rooms.

Baron Satan leads a life of fear. He is afraid not for himself,

323

but for the treasures which he has accumulated with so tenacious a passion and with the perspicacity of a collector whom not the most cunning of dealers can boast of having ever taken in. He loves his curiosities with all the greed of a miser, with all the jealousy of a lover.

Daily, at sunset, the four iron-barred doors that command both ends of the bridge and the entrance to the principal court are locked and bolted. At the least touch, electric bells would ring through the surrounding silence. There is nothing to be feared on the side of the Seine, where the rock rises sheer from the water.

One Friday in September, the postman appeared as usual at the bridgehead. And, in accordance with his daily rule, the baron himself opened the heavy door.

He examined the man as closely as if he had not for years known that good jolly face and those crafty peasant eyes. And the man said with a laugh :

" It's me all right, monsieur le baron. It's not another chap in my cap and blouse ! "

" One never knows ! " muttered Cahorn.

The postman handed him a bundle of newspapers. Then he added :

" And now, monsieur le baron, I have something special for you."

" Something special ? What do you mean ? "

" A letter . . . and a registered letter at that ! "

Living cut off from everybody, with no friends nor any one that took an interest in him, the baron never received letters ; and this suddenly struck him as an ill-omened event which gave him good cause for nervousness. Who was the mysterious correspondent that came to worry him in his retreat ?

" I shall want your signature, monsieur le baron."

He signed the receipt, cursing as he did so. Then he took the letter, waited until the postman had disappeared round the turn of the road, and after taking a few steps to and fro, leaned against the parapet of the bridge and opened the envelope. It contained a sheet of ruled paper, headed, in writing :

" *Prison de la Santé, Paris.*"

He looked at the signature :

" ARSÈNE LUPIN."

Utterly dumbfounded, he read :

" *Monsieur Le Baron,—In the gallery that connects your two drawing-rooms there is a picture by Philippe de Champaigne, an excellent piece of work, which I admire greatly. I also like your Rubens pictures and the smaller of your two Watteaus. In the drawing-room, on the right, I note the Louis XIII. credence-table, the Beauvais tapestries, the Empire stand, signed by Jacob, and the Renascence chest. In the room on the left, the whole of the case of trinkets and miniatures.*

"*This time, I will be satisfied with these objects, which, I think, can be easily turned into cash. I will therefore ask you to have them properly packed and to send them to my name, carriage paid, to the Gare de Batignolles, on or before this day week, failing which I will myself see to their removal on the night of Wednesday the 27th instant. In the later case, as is only fair, I shall not be content with the above-mentioned objects.*

"*Pray excuse the trouble which I am giving you, and believe me to be,*
"*Yours very truly,*
"*Arsène Lupin.*

"*P.S.—Be sure not to send me the larger of the two Watteaus. Although you paid thirty thousand francs for it at the sale-rooms, it is only a copy, the original having been burnt under the Directory, by Barras, in one of his orgies. See Garat's unpublished Memoirs.*

"*I do not care either to have the Louis XV. chatelaine, the authenticity of which appears to me to be exceedingly doubtful.*"

This letter thoroughly upset Baron Cahorn. It would have alarmed him considerably had it been signed by any other hand. But signed by Arsène Lupin ! . . .

He was a regular reader of the newspapers, knew of everything that went on in the way of theft and crime, and had heard all about the exploits of the infernal housebreaker. He was quite aware that Lupin had been arrested in America, by his enemy, Ganimard ; that he was safely under lock and key ; and that the preliminaries to his trial were now being conducted . . . with great difficulty, no doubt ! But he also knew that one could always expect anything of Arsène Lupin. Besides, this precise knowledge of the castle, of the arrangement of the pictures and furniture, was a very formidable sign. Who had informed Lupin of things which nobody had ever seen ?

The baron raised his eyes and gazed at the frowning outline of the Malaquis, its abrupt pedestal, the deep water that surrounds it. He shrugged his shoulders. No, there was no possible danger. No one in the world could penetrate to the inviolable sanctuary that contained his collections.

No one in the world, perhaps ; but Arsène Lupin ? Did doors, drawbridges, walls so much as exist for Arsène Lupin ? Of what use were the most ingeniously contrived obstacles, the most skilful precautions, once that Arsène Lupin had decided to attain a given object ? . . . .

That same evening he wrote to the public prosecutor at Rouen. He enclosed the threatening letter and demanded police protection.

The reply came without delay : the said Arsène Lupin was at that moment a prisoner at the Santé, where he was kept under strict observation and not allowed to write. The letter, therefore, could only be the work of a hoaxer. Everything went to prove this : logic, common sense, and the actual facts.

However, to make quite sure, the letter had been submitted to a handwriting expert, who declared that, notwithstanding certain points of resemblance, it was not in the prisoner's writing.

"Notwithstanding certain points of resemblance." The baron saw only these five bewildering words, which he regarded as the confession of a doubt which alone should have been enough to justify the intervention of the police. His fears increased. He read the letter over and over again. " I will myself see to their removal." And that fixed date, the night of Wednesday, the 27th of September !

Of a naturally suspicious and silent disposition, he dared not unburden himself to his servants, whose devotion he did not consider proof against all tests. And yet, for the first time for many years, he felt a need to speak, to take advice. Abandoned by the police of his country, he had no hope of protecting himself by his own resources, and thought of going to Paris to beg for the assistance of some retired detective or other.

Two days elapsed. On the third day, as he sat reading his newspapers, he gave a start of delight. The *Réveil de Caudebec* contained the following paragraph :

" *We have had the pleasure of numbering among our visitors, for nearly three weeks, Chief-Inspector Ganimard, one of the veterans of the detective service. M. Ganimard, for whom his last feat, the arrest of Arsène Lupin, has won a European reputation, is enjoying a rest from his arduous labours and spending a short holiday fishing for bleak and gudgeon in the Seine.*"

Ganimard ! The very man that Baron Cahorn wanted ! Who could baffle Lupin's plans better than the cunning and patient Ganimard ?

The baron lost no time. It is a four-mile walk from the castle to the little town of Caudebec. He did the distance with a quick and joyous step, stimulated by the hope of safety.

After many fruitless endeavours to discover the chief-inspector's address, he went to the office of the *Réveil*, which is on the quay. He found the writer of the paragraph, who, going to the window, said :

" Ganimard ! Why, you're sure to meet him, rod in hand, on the quay. That's where I picked up with him and read his name, by accident, on his fishing-rod. Look, there he is, the little old man in the frock-coat and a straw hat, under the trees."

" A frock-coat and a straw hat ? "

" Yes. He's a queer specimen, close-tongued and a trifle testy."

Five minutes later, the baron accosted the famous Ganimard, introduced himself and made an attempt to enter into conversation. Failing in this, he broached the question frankly and laid his case before him.

The other listened, without moving a muscle or taking his eyes from the water. Then he turned his head to the baron, eyed him from head to foot with a look of profound compassion and said :

" Sir, it is not usual for criminals to warn the people whom they mean to rob. Arsène Lupin, in particular, never indulges in that sort of bounce."

" Still . . ."

" Sir, if I had the smallest doubt, believe me, the pleasure of once more locking up that dear Lupin would outweigh every other consideration. Unfortunately, the youth is already in prison."

" Suppose he escapes ? "

" People don't escape from the Santé."

" But Lupin. . . ."

" Lupin no more than another."

" Still . . ."

" Very well, if he does escape, so much the better ; I'll nab him again. Meanwhile, you can sleep soundly and stop frightening my fish."

The conversation was ended. The baron returned home feeling more or less reassured by Ganimard's indifference. He saw to his bolts, kept a watch upon his servants, and another forty-eight hours passed, during which he almost succeeded in persuading himself that, after all, his fears were groundless.

There was no doubt about it : as Ganimard had said, criminals
don't warn the people whom they mean to rob.

The date was drawing near. On the morning of Tuesday,
the twenty-sixth, nothing particular happened. But at three
o'clock in the afternoon a boy rang and handed in this telegram :

" *No goods Batignolles. Get everything ready for to-morrow night.*
                                                    " *Arsène.*"

Once again, Cahorn lost his head, so much so that he asked
himself whether he would not do better to yield to Arsène Lupin's
demands.

He hurried off to Caudebec. Ganimard was seated on a
camp-stool, fishing, in the same spot as before. The baron
handed him the telegram without a word.

" Well ? " said the detective.

" Well what ? It's fixed for to-morrow ! "

" What is ? "

" The burglary ! The theft of my collections ! "

Ganimard turned to him and, folding his arms across his
chest, cried, in a tone of impatience :

" Why, you don't really mean to say that you think I'm
going to trouble myself about this stupid business ? "

" What fee will you take to spend Wednesday night at the
castle ? "

" Not a penny. Don't bother me ! "

" Name your own price. I am a rich man, a very rich man."

The brutality of the offer took Ganimard aback. He replied,
more calmly :

" I am here on leave and I have no right to . . ."

" No one shall ever know. I undertake to be silent, whatever
happens ! "

" Oh, nothing will happen ! "

" Well, look here ; is three thousand francs enough ? "

The inspector took a pinch of snuff, reflected and said :

" Very well. But it's only fair to tell you that you are throwing
your money away."

" I don't mind."

" In that case. . . . And besides, after all, one can never
tell with that devil of a Lupin ! He must have a whole gang at
his orders. . . . Are you sure of your servants ? "

" Well, I . . ."

" Then we must not rely upon them. I'll wire to two of my

own men ; that will make us feel safer. . . . And now leave me ;
we must not be seen together. To-morrow evening, at nine
o'clock."

On the morning of the next day, the date fixed by Arsène
Lupin, Baron Cahorn took down his trophy of arms, polished
up his pistols, and made a thorough inspection of the Malaquis,
without discovering anything suspicious.

At half-past eight in the evening, he dismissed his servants
for the night. They slept in a wing facing the road, but set a
little way back and right at the end of the castle. As soon as he
was alone, he softly opened the four doors. In a little while, he
heard footsteps approaching.

Ganimard introduced his assistants, two powerfully-built
fellows, with bull necks and huge, strong hands, and asked for
certain explanations. After ascertaining the disposition of the
place, he carefully closed and barricaded every issue by which
the threatened rooms could be entered. He examined the walls,
lifted up the tapestries and finally installed his detectives in the
central gallery : " No nonsense, do you understand ? You're
not here to sleep. At the least sound, open the windows on the
court and call me. Keep a look-out also on the water side.
Thirty feet of steep cliff doesn't frighten scoundrels of that
stamp."

He locked them in, took away the keys, and said to the baron :
" And now to our post."

He had selected, as the best place in which to spend the
night, a small room contrived in the thickness of the outer walls
between the two main doors. It had at one time been the
watchman's lodge. A spy-hole opened upon the bridge, another
upon the court. In one corner was what looked like the mouth
of a well.

" You told me, did you not, monsieur le baron, that this
well is the only entrance to the underground passage and that
it had been stopped up since the memory of man ? "

" Yes."

" Therefore, unless there should happen to be another
outlet, unknown to any but Arsène Lupin, which seems pretty
unlikely, we can be easy in our minds."

He placed three chairs in a row, settled himself comfortably
at full length, lit his pipe and sighed :

" Upon my word, monsieur le baron, I must be very eager
to build an additional story to the little house in which I mean

to end my days, to accept so elementary a job as this. I shall tell the story to our friend Lupin ; he'll split his sides with laughter."

The baron did not laugh. With ears pricked up, he questioned the silence with ever-growing restlessness. From time to time, he leaned over the well and plunged an anxious eye into the yawning cavity.

The clock struck eleven ; midnight ; one o'clock.

Suddenly, he seized the arm of Ganimard, who woke with a start :

" Do you hear that ? "

" Yes."

" What is it ? "

" It's myself, snoring ! "

" No, no, listen. . . ."

" Oh, yes, it's a motor-horn."

" Well ? "

" Well, it's as unlikely that Lupin should come by motor-car as that he should use a battering-ram to demolish your castle. So I should go to sleep if I were you, monsieur le baron . . . as I shall have the honour of doing once more. Good-night ! "

This was the only alarm. Ganimard resumed his interrupted slumbers ; and the baron heard nothing save his loud and regular snoring.

At break of day they left their cell. A great calm peace, the peace of the morning by the cool waterside, reigned over the castle. Cahorn, beaming with joy, and Ganimard, placid as ever, climbed the staircase. Not a sound. Nothing suspicious.

" What did I tell you, monsieur le baron ? I really ought not to have accepted . . . I feel ashamed of myself. . . ."

He took the keys and entered the gallery.

On two chairs, with bent bodies and hanging arms, sat the two detectives, fast asleep.

" What in the name of all the . . ." growled the inspector.

At the same moment the baron uttered a cry :

" The pictures ! . . . The credence-table ! "

He stammered and spluttered, with his hand outstretched towards the dismantled walls, with their bare nails and slack cords. The Watteau and the two Rubens had disappeared ! The tapestries had been removed, the glass cases emptied of their trinkets !

"And my Louis XVI. sconces ! . . . And the Regency chandelier ! . . . And my twelfth century Virgin ! . . ."

He ran from place to place, maddened, in despair. Distraught with rage and grief, he quoted the purchase-prices, added up his losses, piled up figures, all promiscuously, in indistinct words and incomplete phrases. He stamped his feet, flung himself about, and, in short, behaved like a ruined man who had nothing before him but suicide.

If anything could have consoled him, it would have been the sight of Ganimard's stupefaction. Contrary to the baron, the inspector did not move. He seemed petrified and, with a dazed eye, examined things. The windows ? They were fastened. The locks of the doors ? Untouched. There was not a crack in the ceiling, not a hole in the floor. Everything was in perfect order. The whole thing must have been carried out methodically, after an inexorable and logical plan.

"Arsène Lupin . . . Arsène Lupin," he muttered, giving way.

Suddenly, he leapt upon the two detectives, as though at last overcome with rage, and shook them and swore at them furiously. They did not wake up !

"The deuce ! " he said. "Can they have been . . . ? "

He bent over them and scrutinised them closely, one after the other : they were both asleep, but their sleep was not natural. He said to the baron :

"They have been drugged."

"But by whom ? "

"By him, of course . . . or by his gang, acting under his instructions. It's a trick in his own manner. I recognise his touch."

"In that case, I am undone : the thing is hopeless."

"Hopeless."

"But this is abominable ; it's monstrous."

"Lodge an information."

"What's the good ? "

"Well, you may as well try . . . the law has its resources. . . ."

"The law ! But you can see for yourself. . . . Why, at this very moment, when you might be looking for a clue, discovering something, you're not even stirring !

"Discover something, with Arsène Lupin ! But, my dear sir, Arsène Lupin never leaves anything behind him ! There's no chance with Arsène Lupin ! I am beginning to wonder whether

he got himself arrested by me of his own free will, in
America ! "

" Then I must give up the hope of recovering my pictures
or anything ! But he has stolen the pearls of my collection. I
would give a fortune to get them back. If there's nothing to
be done against him, let him name his price."

Ganimard looked at him steadily.

" That's a sound notion. Do you stick to it ? "

" Yes, yes, yes ! But why do you ask ? "

" I have an idea."

" What idea ? "

" We'll talk of it if nothing comes of the inquiry. . . .
Only, not a word about me to a soul, if you wish me to
succeed."

And he added, between his teeth :

" Besides, I have nothing to be proud of."

The two men gradually recovered consciousness with the
stupefied look of men awakening from a hypnotic sleep. They
opened astounded eyes, tried to make out what had happened.
Ganimard questioned them. They remembered nothing.

" Still, you must have seen somebody ? "

" No, nobody."

" Try and think ? "

" No, nobody."

" Did you have a drink ? "

They reflected and one of them replied :

" Yes, I had some water."

" Out of that bottle there ? "

" Yes."

" I had some too," said the other.

Ganimard smelt the water, tasted it. It had no particular
scent or flavour.

" Come," he said, " we are wasting our time. Problems
set by Arsène Lupin can't be solved in five minutes. But, by
Jingo, I swear I'll catch him ! He's won the second bout. The
rubber game to me ! "

That day, a charge of aggravated larceny was brought by
Baron Cahorn against Arsène Lupin, a prisoner awaiting trial
at the Santé.

The baron often regretted having laid his information when
he saw the Malaquis made over to the gendarmes, the public
prosecutor, the examining magistrate, the newspaper reporters,

and all the inquisitive people who worm themselves in wherever they have no business to be.

Already the case was filling the public mind. It had taken place under such peculiar conditions, and the name of Arsène Lupin excited men's imaginations to such a pitch that the most fantastic stories crowded the columns of the press and found acceptance with the public.

But the original letter of Arsène Lupin, which was published in the *Écho de France*—and no one ever knew who had supplied the text—the letter in which Baron Cahorn was insolently warned of what threatened him, caused the greatest excitement. Fabulous explanations were offered forthwith. The old legends were revived. The newspapers reminded their readers of the existence of the famous subterranean passages. And the public prosecutor, influenced by these statements, pursued his search in that direction.

The castle was ransacked from top to bottom. Every stone was examined ; the wainscotings and chimneys, the frames of the mirrors and the rafters of the ceilings were carefully inspected. By the light of torches, the searchers investigated the immense cellars in which the lords of the Malaquis had been used to pile up their provisions and munitions of war. They sounded the very bowels of the rock. All to no purpose. They discovered not the slightest trace of a tunnel. No secret passage existed.

Very well, was the answer on every side ; but pictures and furniture don't vanish like ghosts. They go out through doors and windows ; and the people who take them also go in and out through doors and windows. Who are these people ? How did they get in ? And how did they get out ?

The public prosecutor of Rouen, persuaded of his own incompetence, asked for the assistance of the Paris police. M. Dudouis, the chief of the detective-service, sent the most efficient bloodhounds in his employ. He himself paid a forty-eight hours' visit to the Malaquis, but met with no greater success.

It was after his return that he sent for Chief-Inspector Ganimard, whose services he had so often had occasion to value.

Ganimard listened in silence to the instructions of his superior, and then, tossing his head, said :

" I think we shall be on a false scent so long as we continue to search the castle. The solution lies elsewhere."

" With Arsène Lupin ? If you think that, then you believe that he took part in the burglary."

" I do think so. I go further, I consider it certain."

" Come, Ganimard, this is absurd. Arsène Lupin is in prison."

" Arsène Lupin is in prison, I agree. He is being watched, I grant you. But if he had his legs in irons, his hands bound and his mouth gagged, I should still be of the same opinion."

" But why this persistency ? "

" Because no one else is capable of contriving a plan on so large a scale and of contriving it in such a way that it succeeds . . . as this has succeeded."

" Words, Ganimard ! "

" They are true words, for all that. Only, it's no use looking for underground passages, for stones that turn on a pivot, and stuff and nonsense of that kind. Our friend does not employ such antiquated measures. He is a man of to-day, or rather of to-morrow."

" And what do you conclude ? "

" I conclude by asking you straight to let me spend an hour with Lupin."

" In his cell ? "

" Yes. We were on excellent terms during the crossing from America, and I venture to think that he is not without friendly feeling for the man who arrested him. If he can tell me what I want to know, without compromising himself, he will be quite willing to spare me an unnecessary journey."

It was just after midday when Ganimard was shown into Arsène Lupin's cell. Lupin, who was lying on his bed, raised his head and uttered an exclamation of delight.

" Well, this is a surprise ! Dear old Ganimard here ! "

" Himself."

" I have hoped for many things in this retreat of my own choosing, but for none more eagerly than the pleasure of welcoming you here."

" You are too good."

" Not at all, not at all. I have the liveliest regard for you."

" I am proud to hear it."

" I have said it a thousand times : Ganimard is our greatest detective. He's *almost*—see how frank I am—*almost* as clever as Holmlock Shears. But, really, I'm awfully sorry to have nothing better than this stool to offer you. And not a drink of any kind ! Not so much as a glass of beer ! Do forgive me ; I am only just passing through town, you see ! "

Ganimard smiled and sat down on the stool; and the prisoner, glad of the opportunity of speaking, continued :

" By jove, what a treat to see a decent man's face ! I am sick of the looks of all these spies who go through my cell and my pockets ten times a day to make sure that I am not planning an escape. Gad, how fond the Government must be of me ! "

" They show their judgment."

" No, no ! I should be so happy if they would let me lead my own quiet life."

" On other people's money."

" Just so. It would be so simple. But I'm letting my tongue run on, I'm talking nonsense, and I dare say you're in a hurry. Come, Ganimard, tell me to what I owe the honour of this visit."

" The Cahorn case," said Ganimard abruptly.

" Stop ! Wait a bit. . . . You see, I have so many on hand ! First, let me search my brain for the Cahorn pigeon-hole. . . . Ah, I have it ! Cahorn case, Chateau du Malaquis, Seine-Inférieure. . . . Two Rubens, a Watteau, and a few more trifles."

" Trifles ! "

" Oh, yes, all this is of small importance. I have bigger things on hand. However, you're interested in the case and that's enough for me. . . . Go ahead, Ganimard."

" I need not tell you, need I, how far we have got with the investigation ? "

" No, not at all. I have seen the morning papers. And I will even take the liberty of saying that you are not making much progress."

" That's just why I have come to throw myself upon your kindness."

" I am entirely at your service."

" First of all, the thing was done by you, was it not ? "

" From start to finish."

" The registered letter ? The telegram ? "

" Were sent by yours truly. In fact, I ought to have the receipts somewhere."

Arsène opened the drawer of a little deal table which, with the bed and the stool, composed all the furniture of his cell, took out two scraps of paper and handed them to Ganimard.

" Hallo ! " cried the latter. " Why, I thought you were being kept under constant observation and searched on the slightest pretext. And it appears that you read the papers and collect post-office receipts . . ."

" Bah ! Those men are such fools. They rip up the lining of my waistcoat, explore the soles of my boots, listen at the walls of my cell ; but not one of them would believe that Arsène Lupin could be such a fool as to choose so obvious a hiding-place. That's just what I reckoned on."

Ganimard exclaimed, in amusement :

" What a funny chap you are ! You're beyond me. Come, tell me the story."

" Oh, I say ! Not so fast ! Initiate you into all my secrets . . . reveal my little tricks to you ? That's a serious matter."

" Was I wrong in thinking that I could rely on you to oblige me ? "

" No, Ganimard, and as you insist upon it . . ."

Arsène Lupin took two or three strides across his cell. Then, stopping :

" What do you think of my letter to the baron ? " he asked.

" I think you wanted to have some fun, to tickle the gallery a bit."

" Ah, there you go ! Tickle the gallery, indeed ! Upon my word, Ganimard, I gave you credit for more sense ! Do you really imagine that I, Arsène Lupin, waste my time with such childish pranks as that ? Is it likely that I should have written the letter, if I could have rifled the baron without it ? Do try and understand that the letter was the indispensable starting-point, the mainspring that set the whole machine in motion. Look here, let us proceed in order and, if you like, prepare the Malaquis burglary together."

" Very well."

" Now follow me. I have to do with an impregnable and closely-guarded castle. . . . Am I to throw up the game and forgo the treasures which I covet because the castle that contains them happens to be inaccessible ? "

" Clearly not."

" Am I to try to carry it by assault as in the old days, at the head of a band of adventurers ? "

" That would be childish."

" Am I to enter it by stealth ? "

" Impossible."

" There remains only one way, which is to get myself invited by the owner of the aforesaid castle."

" It's an original idea."

" And so easy ! Suppose that, one day, the said owner receives a letter warning him of a plot hatched against him by one Arsène Lupin, a notorious housebreaker. What is he sure to do ? "

" Send the letter to the public prosecutor."

" Who will laugh at him, *because the said Lupin is actually under lock and key*. The natural consequence is the utter bewilderment of the worthy man, who is ready and anxious to ask for the assistance of the first comer. Am I right ? "

" Quite so."

" And if he happens to read in the local rag that a famous detective is staying in the neighbourhood . . . ? "

" He will go and apply to that detective."

" Exactly. But on the other hand, let us assume that, foreseeing this inevitable step, Arsène Lupin has asked one of his ablest friends to take up his quarters at Caudebec, to pick up acquaintance with a contributor to the *Réveil*, a paper, mark you, to which the baron subscribes, and to drop a hint that he is so-and-so, the famous detective. What will happen next ? "

" The contributor will send a paragraph to the *Réveil* stating that the detective is staying at Caudebec."

" Exactly ; and one of two things follows : either the fish—I mean Cahorn—does not rise to the bait, in which case nothing happens ; or else—and this is the more likely presumption—he nibbles, in which case you have our dear Cahorn imploring the assistance of one of my own friends against me ! "

" This is becoming more and more original."

" Of course, the sham detective begins by refusing. Thereupon, a telegram from Arsène Lupin. Dismay of the baron, who renews his entreaties with my friend and offers him so much to watch over his safety. The friend aforesaid accepts and brings with him two chaps of our gang, who, during the night, while Cahorn is kept in sight by his protector, remove a certain number of things through the window and lower them with ropes into a barge freighted for the purpose. It's as simple as . . . Lupin."

" And it's just wonderful," cried Ganimard, " and I have no words in which to praise the boldness of the idea and the ingenuity of the details. But I can hardly imagine a detective so illustrious that his name should have attracted and impressed the baron to that extent."

" There is one and one only."

" Who ? "

" The most illustrious of them all, the arch-enemy of Arsène Lupin, in short, Inspector Ganimard."

" What—myself? "

" Yourself, Ganimard. And that's the delightful part of it : if you go down and persuade the baron to talk, you will end by discovering that it is your duty to arrest yourself, just as you arrested me in America. A humorous revenge, what? I shall have Ganimard arrested by Ganimard ! "

Arsène Lupin laughed loud and long, while the inspector bit his lips with vexation. The joke did not appear to him worthy of so much merriment.

The entrance of a warder gave him time to recover. The man brought the meal which Arsène Lupin, by special favour, was allowed to have sent in from the neighbouring restaurant. After placing the tray on the table, he went away. Arsène sat down, broke his bread, ate a mouthful of two and continued :

" But be easy, my dear Ganimard, you won't have to go. I have something to tell you that will strike you dumb. The Cahorn case is about to be withdrawn."

" What ! "

" About to be withdrawn, I said."

" Nonsense ! I have just left the chief."

" And then ? Does Monsieur Dudouis know more than I do about my concerns ? You must learn that Ganimard—excuse me—that the sham Ganimard remained on very good terms with Baron Cahorn. The baron—and this is his main reason for keeping the thing quiet—charged him with the very delicate mission of negotiating a deal with me ; and the chances are that, by this time, on payment of a certain sum, the baron is once more in possession of his pet knicknacks. In return for which he will withdraw the charge. Wherefore there is no question of theft. Wherefore the public prosecutor will have to abandon . . ."

Ganimard gazed at the prisoner with an air of stupefaction.

" But how do you know all this ? "

" I have just received the telegram I was expecting."

" You have just received a telegram ? "

" This very moment, my friend. I was too polite to read it in your presence. But, if you will allow me. . . ."

" You're poking fun at me, Lupin."

" Have the kindness, my friend, to cut off the top of that egg gently. You will see for yourself that I am not poking fun at you."

Ganimard obeyed mechanically, and broke the egg with the blade of a knife. A cry of surprise escaped him. The shell was empty but for a sheet of blue paper. At Arsène's request, he unfolded it. It was a telegram, or rather a portion of a telegram from which the postal indications had been removed. He read :

" Arrangement settled. Hundred thousand paid over, delivered. All well."

" Hundred thousand paid over ? " he uttered.

" Yes, a hundred thousand francs. It's not much, but these are hard times. . . . And my general expenses are so heavy ! If you knew the amount of my budget . . . it's like the budget of a big town ! "

Ganimard rose to go. His ill-humour had left him. He thought for a few moments and cast a mental glance over the whole business, trying to discover a weak point. Then, in a voice that frankly revealed his admiration as an expert, he said :

" It's a good thing that there are not dozens like you, or there would be nothing for us but to shut up shop."

Arsène Lupin assumed a modest simper and replied :

" Oh, I had to do something to amuse myself, to occupy my spare time . . . especially as the scoop could only succeed while I was in prison."

" What do you mean ? " exclaimed Ganimard. " Your trial, your defence, your examination : isn't that enough for you to amuse yourself with ? "

" No, because I have decided not to attend my trial."

" Oh, I say ! "

Arsène Lupin repeated, deliberately :

" I shall not attend my trial."

" Really ! "

" Why, my dear fellow, you surely don't think that I mean to rot in gaol ? The mere suggestion is an insult. Let me tell you that Arsène Lupin remains in prison as long as he thinks fit and not a moment longer."

" It might have been more prudent to begin by not entering it," said the inspector ironically.

" Ah, so you're chaffing me, sirrah ? Do you remember that you had the honour to effect my arrest ? Well, learn from me, my respectable friend, that no one, neither you nor another, could have laid a hand upon me if a much more important interest had not occupied my attention at that critical moment."

" You surprise me."

" A woman had cast her eyes upon me, Ganimard, and

I loved her Do you realise all that the fact implies when a woman whom one loves casts her eyes upon one ? I cared about little else, I assure you. And that is why I'm here."

" You've been here a long time, allow me to observe."

" I was anxious to forget. Don't laugh : it was a charming adventure and I still have a tender recollection of it. . . . And then I have had a slight nervous breakdown. We lead such a feverish existence nowadays ! It's a good thing to take a rest-cure from time to time. And there's no place for it like this. They carry out the cure in all its strictness at the Santé."

" Arsène Lupin," said Ganimard, " you're pulling my leg."

" Ganimard," replied Lupin, " this is Friday. On Wednesday next, I'll come and smoke a cigar with you, in the Rue Pergolèse, at four o'clock in the afternoon."

" Arsène Lupin, I shall expect you."

They shook hands like two friends who have a proper sense of each other's value and the old detective turned towards the door.

" Ganimard ! "

Ganimard looked round :

" What is it ? "

" Ganimard, you've forgotten your watch."

" My watch ? "

" Yes, I've just found it in my pocket."

He returned it, with apologies :

" Forgive me . . . it's a bad habit. . . . They've taken mine, but that's no reason why I should rob you of yours. Especially as I have a chronometer here which keeps perfect time and satisfies all my requirements."

He took out of the drawer a large, thick, comfortable-looking gold watch, hanging to a heavy chain.

" And out of whose pocket does this come ? " asked Ganimard.

Arsène Lupin carelessly inspected the initials :

" J. B. . . . What on earth does that stand for ? . . . Oh, yes, I remember : Jules Bouvier, my examining magistrate, a charming fellow. . . ."

THE FENCHURCH STREET MYSTERY

THE man in the corner pushed aside his glass, and leant across the table.

"Mysteries!" he commented. "There is no such thing as a mystery in connection with any crime, provided intelligence is brought to bear upon its investigation."

Very much astonished, Polly Burton looked over the top of her newspaper, and fixed a pair of very severe, coldly inquiring eyes upon him.

She had disapproved of the man from the instant when he shuffled across the shop and sat down opposite to her, at the same marble-topped table which already held her large coffee (3d.), her roll and butter (2d.), and plate of tongue (6d.).

Now this particular corner, this very same table, that special view of the magnificent marble hall—known as the Norfolk Street branch of the Aerated Bread Company's depôts—were Polly's own corner, table, and view. Here she had partaken of eleven pennyworth of luncheon and one pennyworth of daily information ever since that glorious never-to-be-forgotten day when she was enrolled on the staff of the *Evening Observer* (we'll call it that, if you please) and became a member of that illustrious and world-famed organisation known as the British Press.

She was a personality, was Miss Burton of the *Evening Observer*. Her cards were printed thus:

MISS MARY J. BURTON

Evening Observer

She had interviewed Miss Ellen Terry and the Bishop of Madagascar, Mr. Seymour Hicks and the Chief Commissioner of Police. She had been present at the last Marlborough House garden party—in the cloak-room, that is to say, where she caught sight of Lady Thingummy's hat, Miss What-you-may-call's sunshade, and of various other things modistical or fashionable, all of which were duly described under the heading "Royalty and Dress," in the early afternoon edition of the *Evening Observer.*

(The article itself is signed M.J.B., and is to be found in the files of that leading halfpennyworth.)

For three reasons—and for various others, too—Polly felt irate with the man in the corner, and told him so with her eyes, as plainly as any pair of brown eyes can speak.

She had been reading an article in the *Daily Telegraph.* The article was palpitatingly interesting. Had Polly been commenting audibly upon it? Certain it is that the man over there had spoken in direct answer to her thoughts.

She looked at him and frowned ; the next moment she smiled. Miss Burton (of the *Evening Observer*) had a keen sense of humour, which two years' association with the British Press had not succeeded in destroying, and the appearance of the man was sufficient to tickle the most ultra-morose fancy.- Polly thought to herself that she had never seen any one so pale, so thin, with such funny light-coloured hair, brushed very smoothly across the top of a very obviously bald crown. He looked so timid and nervous as he fidgeted incessantly with a piece of string ; his long, lean, and trembling fingers tying and untying it into knots of wonderful and complicated proportions.

Having carefully studied every detail of the quaint personality Polly felt more amiable.

"And yet," she remarked kindly but authoritatively, "this article, in an otherwise well-informed journal, will tell you that, even within the last year, no fewer than six crimes have completely baffled the police, and the perpetrators of them are still at large."

"Pardon me," he said gently, "I never for a moment ventured to suggest that there were no mysteries to the *police*; I merely remarked that there were none where intelligence was brought to bear upon the investigation of crime."

"Not even in the Fenchurch Street *mystery*, I suppose," she asked sarcastically.

" Least of all in the so-called Fenchurch Street *mystery*," he replied quietly.

Now the Fenchurch Street mystery, as that extraordinary crime had popularly been called, had puzzled—as Polly well knew—the brains of every thinking man and woman for the last twelve months. It had puzzled her not inconsiderably; she had been interested, fascinated ; she had studied the case, formed her own theories, thought about it all often and often, had even written one or two letters to the Press on the subject —suggesting, arguing, hinting at possibilities and probabilities, adducing proofs which other amateur detectives were equally ready to refute. The attitude of that timid man in the corner, therefore, was peculiarly exasperating, and she retorted with sarcasm destined to completely annihilate her self-complacent interlocutor.

" What a pity it is, in that case, that you do not offer your priceless services to our misguided though well-meaning police."

" Isn't it ! " he replied with perfect good humour. " Well, you know, for one thing I doubt if they would accept them ; and in the second place my inclinations and my duty would —were I to become an active member of the detective force— nearly always be in direct conflict. As often as not my sympathies go to the criminal who is clever and astute enough to lead our entire police force by the nose.

" I don't know how much of the case you remember," he went on quietly. " It certainly, at first, began even to puzzle me. On the 12th of last December a woman, poorly dressed, but with an unmistakable air of having seen better days, gave information at Scotland Yard of the disappearance of her husband, William Kershaw, of no occupation, and apparently of no fixed abode. She was accompanied by a friend—a fat, oily-looking German—and between them they told a tale which set the police immediately on the move.

" It appears that on the 10th of December, at about three o'clock in the afternoon, Karl Müller, the German, called on his friend, William Kershaw, for the purpose of collecting a small debt—some ten pounds or so—which the latter owed him. On arriving at the squalid lodging in Charlotte Street, Fitzroy Square, he found William Kershaw in a wild state of excitement, and his wife in tears. Müller attempted to state the object of his visit, but Kershaw, with wild gestures, waved him aside, and —in his own words—flabbergasted him by asking him point-blank for another loan of two pounds, which sum, he declared, would be the means of a speedy fortune for himself and the friend who would help him in his need.

"After a quarter of an hour spent in obscure hints, Kershaw, finding the cautious German obdurate, decided to let him into the secret plan, which, he averred, would place thousands in their hands."

Instinctively Polly had put down her paper ; the mild stranger, with his nervous air and timid, watery eyes, had a peculiar way of telling his tale, which somehow fascinated her.

"I don't know," he resumed, "if you remember the story which the German told to the police, and which was corroborated in every detail by the wife or widow. Briefly it was this : Some thirty years previously, Kershaw, then twenty years of age, and a medical student at one of the London hospitals, had a chum named Barker, with whom he roomed, together with another.

"The latter, so it appears, brought home one evening a very considerable sum of money, which he had won on the turf, and the following morning he was found murdered in his bed. Kershaw, fortunately for himself, was able to prove a conclusive *alibi* ; he had spent the night on duty at the hospital ; as for Barker, he had disappeared, that is to say, as far as the police were concerned, but not as far as the watchful eyes of his friend Kershaw were able to spy—at least, so the latter said. Barker very cleverly contrived to get away out of the country, and, after sundry vicissitudes, finally settled down at Vladivostok, in Eastern Siberia, where, under the assumed name of Smethurst, he built up an enormous fortune by trading in furs.

"Now, mind you, every one knows Smethurst, the Siberian millionaire. Kershaw's story that he had once been called Barker, and had committed a murder thirty years ago, was never proved, was it ? I am merely telling you what Kershaw said to his friend the German and to his wife on that memorable afternoon of December the 10th.

"According to him Smethurst had made one gigantic mistake in his clever career—he had on four occasions written to his late friend, William Kershaw. Two of these letters had no bearing on the case, since they were written more than twenty-five years ago, and Kershaw, moreover, had lost them, so he said, long ago. According to him, however, the first of these letters was written when Smethurst, alias Barker, had spent all the money he had obtained from the crime and found himself destitute in New York.

"Kershaw, then in fairly prosperous circumstances, sent him a £10 note for the sake of old times. The second, when the tables had turned, and Kershaw had begun to go down-hill, Smethurst, as he then already called himself, sent his whilom friend £50. After that, as Müller gathered, Kershaw had made sundry demands on Smethurst's ever increasing purse, and had accompanied these demands by various threats, which, considering the distant country in which the millionaire lived, were worse than futile.

"But now the climax had come, and Kershaw, after a final moment of hesitation, handed over to his German friend the two last letters purporting to have been written by Smethurst, and which, if you remember, played such an important part in the mysterious story of this extraordinary crime. I have a copy of both these letters here," added the man in the corner, as he took out a piece of paper from a very worn-out pocket-book, and, unfolding it very deliberately, he began to read :

"'SIR,—*Your preposterous demands for money are wholly unwarrantable. I have already helped you quite as much as you deserve. However, for the sake of old times, and because you once helped me when I was in a terrible difficulty, I am willing to let you impose once more upon my good nature. A friend of mine here, a Russian merchant, to whom I have sold my business, starts in a few days for an extended tour to many European and Asiatic ports in his yacht, and has invited me to accompany him as far as England. Being tired of foreign parts, and desirous of seeing the old country once again after thirty years' absence, I have decided to accept his invitation. I don't know when we may actually be in Europe, but I promise you that as soon as we touch a suitable port I will write to you again, making an appointment for you to see me in London. But remember that if your demands are too preposterous I will not for a moment listen to them, and I am the last man in the world to submit to persistent and unwarrantable blackmail.*
"'I am, sir,
"'Yours truly,
"'FRANCIS SMETHURST.'

"The second letter was dated from Southampton," continued the old man in the corner calmly, "and, curiously enough, was the only letter which Kershaw professed to have received from Smethurst of which he had kept the envelope, and which was dated. It was quite brief," he added, referring once more to his piece of paper.

" ' DEAR SIR,—*Referring to my letter of a few weeks ago, I wish to inform you that the " Tsarskoe Selo" will touch at Tilbury on Tuesday next, the 10th. I shall land there, and immediately go up to London by the first train I can get. If you like, you may meet me at Fenchurch Street Station, in the first-class waiting-room, in the late afternoon. Since I surmise that after thirty years' absence my face may not be familiar to you, I may as well tell you that you will recognise me by a heavy Astrakhan fur coat, which I shall wear, together with a cap of the same. You may then introduce yourself to me, and I will personally listen to what you may have to say.*

" ' *Yours faithfully,*
" ' FRANCIS SMETHURST.'

" It was this last letter which caused William Kershaw's excitement and his wife's tears. In the German's own words, he was walking up and down the room like a wild beast, gesticulating wildly, and muttering . sundry exclamations. Mrs. Kershaw, however, was full of apprehension. She mistrusted the man from foreign parts—who, according to her husband's story, had already one crime upon his conscience—who might, she feared, risk another, in order to be rid of a dangerous enemy. Woman-like, she thought the scheme was a dishonourable one, for the law, she knew, is severe on the blackmailer.

" The assignation might be a cunning trap, in any case it was a curious one ; why, she argued, did not Smethurst elect to see Kershaw at his hotel the following day ? A thousand whys and wherefores made her anxious, but the fat German had been won over by Kershaw's visions of untold gold, held tantalisingly before his eyes. He had lent the necessary £2, with which his friend intended to tidy himself up a bit before he went to meet his friend the millionaire. Half an hour afterwards Kershaw had left his lodgings, and that was the last the unfortunate woman saw of her husband, or Müller, the German, of his friend.

" Anxiously his wife waited that night, but he did not return ; the next day she seems to have spent in making purposeless and futile inquiries about the neighbourhood of Fenchurch Street ; and on the 12th she went to Scotland Yard, gave what particulars she knew, and placed in the hands of the police the two letters written by Smethurst."

CHAPTER II

A MILLIONAIRE IN THE DOCK

THE man in the corner had finished his glass of milk. His watery blue eyes looked across at Miss Polly Burton's eager little face, from which all traces of severity had now been chased away by an obvious and intense excitement.

" It was only on the 31st," he resumed after a while, " that a body, decomposed past all recognition, was found by two lightermen in the bottom of a disused barge. She had been moored at one time at the foot of one of those dark flights of steps which lead down between tall warehouses to the river in the East End of London. I have a photograph of the place here," he added, selecting one out of his pocket, and placing it before Polly.

" The actual barge, you see, had already been removed when I took this snapshot, but you will realise what a perfect place this alley is for the purpose of one man cutting another's throat in comfort and without fear of detection. The body, as I said, was decomposed beyond all recognition ; it had probably been there eleven days, but sundry articles, such as a silver ring and a tie pin, were recognisable, and were identified by Mrs. Kershaw as belonging to her husband.

" She, of course, was loud in denouncing Smethurst, and the police had no doubt a very strong case against him, for two days after the discovery of the body in the barge, the Siberian millionaire, as he was already popularly called by enterprising interviewers, was arrested in his luxurious suite of rooms at the Hotel Cecil.

" To confess the truth, at this point I was not a little puzzled. Mrs. Kershaw's story and Smethurst's letters had both found their way into the papers, and following my usual method— mind you, I am only an amateur, I try to reason out a case for the love of the thing—I sought about for a motive for the crime, which the police declared Smethurst had committed. To effectually get rid of a dangerous blackmailer was the generally accepted theory. Well ! did it ever strike you how paltry that motive really was ? "

Miss Polly had to confess, however, that it had never struck her in that light.

" Surely a man who had succeeded in building up an immense fortune by his own individual efforts was not the sort of fool to believe that he had anything to fear from a man like Kershaw. He must have *known* that Kershaw held no damning proofs against him—not enough to hang him, anyway. Have you ever seen Smethurst ? " he added, as he once more fumbled in his pocket-book.

Polly replied that she had seen Smethurst's picture in the illustrated papers at the time. Then he added, placing a small photograph before her :

" What strikes you most about the face ? "

" Well, I think its strange, astonished expression, due to the total absence of eyebrows, and the funny foreign cut of the hair."

" So close that it almost looks as if it had been shaved. Exactly. That is what struck me most when I elbowed my way into the court that morning and first caught sight of the millionaire in the dock. He was a tall, soldierly-looking man, upright in stature, his face very bronzed and tanned. He wore neither moustache nor beard, his hair was cropped quite close to his head, like a Frenchman's ; but, of course, what was so very remarkable about him was that total absence of eyebrows and even eyelashes, which gave the face such a peculiar appearance—as you say, a perpetually astonished look.

" He seemed, however, wonderfully calm ; he had been accommodated with a chair in the dock—being a millionaire —and chatted pleasantly with his lawyer, Sir Arthur Inglewood, in the intervals between the calling of the several witnesses for the prosecution ; whilst during the examination of these witnesses he sat quite placidly, with his head shaded by his hand.

" Müller and Mrs. Kershaw repeated the story which they had already told to the police. I think you said that you were not able, owing to pressure of work, to go to the court that day, and hear the case, so perhaps you have no recollection of Mrs. Kershaw. No ? Ah, well ! Here is a snapshot I managed to get of her once. That is her. Exactly as she stood in the box—over-dressed—in elaborate crape, with a bonnet which once had contained pink roses, and to which a remnant of pink petals still clung obtrusively amidst the deep black.

" She would not look at the prisoner, and turned her head resolutely towards the magistrate. I fancy she had been fond of that vagabond husband of hers ; an enormous wedding-ring encircled her finger, and that, too, was swathed in black. She firmly believed that Kershaw's murderer sat there in the dock, and she literally flaunted her grief before him.

"I was indescribably sorry for her. As for Müller, he was just fat, oily, pompous, conscious of his own importance as a witness ; his fat fingers, covered with brass rings, gripped the two incriminating letters, which he had identified. They were his passports, as it were, to a delightful land of importance and notoriety. Sir Arthur Inglewood, I think, disappointed him by stating that he had no questions to ask of him. Müller had been brimful of answers, ready with the most perfect indictment, the most elaborate accusations against the bloated millionaire who had decoyed his dear friend Kershaw, and murdered him in Heaven knows what an out-of-the-way corner of the East End.

"After this, however, the excitement grew apace. Müller had been dismissed, and had retired from the court altogether, leading away Mrs. Kershaw, who had completely broken down.

"Constable D21 was giving evidence as to the arrest in the meanwhile. The prisoner, he said, had seemed completely taken by surprise, not understanding the cause or history of the accusation against him ; however, when put in full possession of the facts, and realising, no doubt, the absolute futilty of any resistance, he had quietly enough followed the constable into the cab. No one at the fashionable and crowded Hotel Cecil had even suspected that anything unusual had occurred.

"Then a gigantic sigh of expectancy came from every one of the spectators. The ' fun ' was about to begin. James Buckland, a porter at Fenchurch Street railway station, had just sworn to tell all the truth, etc. After all, it did not amount to much. He said that at six o'clock in the afternoon of December the 10th, in the midst of one of the densest fogs he ever remembers, the 5.5 from Tilbury steamed into the station being just about an hour late. He was on the arrival platform, and was hailed by a passenger in a first-class carriage. He could see very little of him beyond an enormous black fur coat and a travelling cap of fur also.

"The passenger had a quantity of luggage, all marked F.S., and he directed James Buckland to place it all upon a four-wheel cab, with the exception of a small handbag, which he carried himself. Having seen that all his luggage was safely bestowed, the stranger in the fur coat paid the porter, and, telling the cabman to wait until he returned, he walked away in the direction of the waiting-room, still carrying his small handbag.

"'I stayed for a bit,' added James Buckland, ' talking to

the driver about the fog and that ; then I went about my business, seein' that the local from Southend 'ad been signalled.'

" The prosecution insisted most strongly upon the hour when the stranger in the fur coat, having seen to his luggage, walked away towards the waiting-rooms. The porter was emphatic. ' It was not a minute later than 6.15,' he averred.

" Sir Arthur Inglewood still had no questions to ask, and the driver of the cab was called.

" He corroborated the evidence of James Buckland as to the hour when the gentleman in the fur coat had engaged him, and having filled his cab in and out with luggage, had told him to wait. And cabby did wait. He waited in the dense fog— until he was tired, until he seriously thought of depositing all the luggage in the lost property office, and of looking out for another fare—waited until at last, at a quarter before nine, whom should he see walking hurriedly towards his cab but the gentleman in the fur coat and cap, who got in quickly and told the driver to take him at once to the Hotel Cecil. This, cabby declared, had occurred at a quarter before nine. Still Sir Arthur Inglewood made no comment, and Mr. Francis Smethurst, in the crowded, stuffy court, had calmly dropped off to sleep.

" The next witness, Constable Thomas Taylor, had noticed a shabbily-dressed individual, with shaggy hair and beard, loafing about the station and waiting-rooms in the afternoon of December the 10th. He seemed to be watching the arrival platform of the Tilbury and Southend trains.

" Two separate and independent witnesses, cleverly unearthed by the police, had seen this same shabbily dressed individual stroll into the first-class waiting room at about 6.15 on Wednesday, December the 10th, and go straight up to a gentleman in a heavy fur coat and cap, who had also just come into the room. The two talked together for a while ; no one heard what they said, but presently they walked off together. No one seemed to know in which direction.

" Francis Smethurst was rousing himself from his apathy ; he whispered to his lawyer, who nodded with a bland smile of encouragement. The employees of the Hotel Cecil gave evidence as to the arrival of Mr. Smethurst at about 9.30 p.m. on Wednesday, December the 10th, in a cab, with a quantity of luggage ; and this closed the case for the prosecution.

" Everybody in that court already *saw* Smethurst mounting

the gallows. It was uninterested curiosity which caused the elegant audience to wait and hear what Sir Arthur Inglewood had to say. He, of course, is the most fashionable man in the law at the present moment. His lolling attitudes, his drawling speech, are quite the rage, and imitated by the gilded youth of society.

" Even at this moment, when the Siberian millionaire's neck literally and metaphorically hung in the balance, an expectant titter went round the fair spectators as Sir Arthur stretched out his long loose limbs and lounged across the table. He waited to make his effect—Sir Arthur is a born actor—and there is no doubt that he made it, when in his slowest, most drawly tones, he said quietly :

" ' With regard to this alleged murder of one William Kershaw, on Wednesday, December the 10th, between 6.15 and 8.45 p.m., your Honour, I now propose to call two witnesses, who saw this same William Kershaw alive on Tuesday afternoon, December the 16th, that is to say, six days after the supposed murder.'

" It was as if a bombshell had exploded in the court. Even his Honour was aghast, and I am sure the lady next to me only recovered from the shock of the surprise in order to wonder whether she need put off her dinner party after all.

" As for me," added the man in the corner, with that strange mixture of nervousness and self-complacency which had set Miss Polly Burton wondering, " well, you see, *I* had made up my mind long ago where the hitch lay in this particular case, and I was not so surprised as some of the others.

" Perhaps you remember the wonderful development of the case which so completely mystified the police—and in fact everybody except myself. Torriani and a waiter at his hotel in the Commercial Road both deposed that at about 3.30 p.m. on December the 10th a shabbily-dressed individual lolled into the coffee-room and ordered some tea. He was pleasant enough and talkative, told the waiter that his name was William Kershaw, that very soon all London would be talking about him, as he was about, through an unexpected stroke of good fortune, to become a very rich man, and so on, and so on, nonsense without end.

" When he had finished his tea he lolled out again, but no sooner had he disappeared down a turning of the road than the waiter discovered an old umbrella, left behind accidentally by the shabby, talkative individual. As is the custom in his highly

respectable restaurant, Signor Torriani put the umbrella care·
fully away in his office, on the chance of his customer calling
to claim it when he had discovered the loss. And sure enough
nearly a week later, on Tuesday, the 16th, at about 1 p.m.,
the same shabbily-dressed individual called and asked for his
umbrella. He had some lunch and chatted once again to the
waiter. Signor Torriani and the waiter gave a description of
William Kershaw, which coincided exactly with that given by
Mrs. Kershaw of her husband.

" Oddly enough he seemed to be a very absent-minded sort
of person, for on this second occasion, no sooner had he left than
the waiter found a pocket-book in the coffee-room, underneath
the table. It contained sundry letters and bills, all addressed
to William Kershaw. This pocket-book was produced, and
Karl Müller, who had returned to the court, easily identified
it as having belonged to his dear and lamented friend,
' Villiam.'

" This was the first blow to the case against the accused. It
was a pretty stiff one, you will admit. Already it had begun to
collapse like a house of cards. Still, there was the assignation,
and the undisputed meeting between Smethurst and Kershaw,
and those two and a half hours of a foggy evening to satisfactorily account for."

The man in the corner made a long pause, keeping the girl
on tenterhooks. He had fidgeted with his bit of string till
there was not an inch of it free from the most complicated and
elaborate knots.

" I assure you," he resumed at last, " that at that very
moment the whole mystery was to me as clear as daylight. I
only marvelled how his Honour could waste his time and
mine by putting what he thought were searching questions to
the accused relating to his past. Francis Smethurst, who had
quite shaken off his somnolence, spoke with a curious nasal
twang, and with an almost imperceptible soupçon of foreign
accent. He calmly denied Kershaw's version of his past ;
declared that he had never been called Barker, and had certainly never been mixed up in any murder case thirty years ago.

" ' But you knew this man Kershaw,' persisted his Honour,
' since you wrote that to him ? '

" ' Pardon me, your Honour,' said the accused quietly, ' I
have never, to my knowledge, seen this man Kershaw, and I
can swear I never wrote to him.'

" ' Never wrote to him ? ' retorted his Honour warningly.

' That is a strange assertion to make when I have two of your letters to him in my hands at the present moment.'

" ' I never wrote those letters, your Honour,' persisted the accused quietly, ' they are not in my handwriting.'

" ' Which we can easily prove,' came in Sir Arthur Inglewood's drawly tones, as he handed up a packet to his Honour ; ' here are a number of letters written by my client since he has landed in this country, and some of which were written under my very eyes.'

" As Sir Arthur Inglewood had said, this could be easily proved, and the prisoner, at his Honour's request, scribbled a few lines, together with his signature, several times upon a sheet of notepaper. It was easy to read upon the magistrate's astounded countenance that there was not the slightest similarity in the two handwritings.

" A fresh mystery had cropped up. Who, then, had made the assignation with William Kershaw at Fenchurch Street railway station ? The prisoner gave a fairly satisfactory account of the employment of his time since his landing in England.

" ' I came over on the *Tsarskoe Selo*,' he said, ' a yacht belonging to a friend of mine. When we arrived at the mouth of the Thames there was such a dense fog that it was twenty-four hours before it was thought safe for me to land. My friend, who is a Russian, would not land at all ; he was regularly frightened at this land of fogs. He was going on to Madeira immediately.

" ' I actually landed on Tuesday, the 10th, and took a train at once for town. I did see to my luggage and a cab, as the porter and the driver told your Honour ; then I tried to find my way to a refreshment-room, where I could get a glass of wine. I drifted into the waiting-room, and there I was accosted by a shabbily-dressed individual who began telling me a piteous tale. Who he was I do not know. He *said* he was an old soldier who had served his country faithfully, and then been left to starve. He begged of me to accompany him to his lodgings, where I could see his wife and starving children, and verify the truth and piteousness of his tale.

" ' Well, your Honour,' added the prisoner with noble frankness, ' it was my first day in the old country. I had come back after thirty years with my pockets full of gold, and this was the first sad tale I had heard ; but I am a business man, and did not want to be exactly " done " in the eye. I followed my man through the fog, out into the streets. He walked silently by my side for a time. I had not a notion where I was.

" ' Suddenly I turned to him with some question, and realised in a moment that my gentleman had given me the slip. Finding, probably, that I would not part with my money till I *had* seen the starving wife and children, he left me to my fate, and went in search of more willing bait.

" ' The place where I found myself was dismal and deserted. I could see no trace of cab or omnibus. I retraced my steps and tried to find my way back to the station, only to find myself in worse and more deserted neighbourhoods. I became hopelessly lost and fogged. I don't wonder that two and a half hours elapsed while I thus wandered on in the dark and deserted streets ; my sole astonishment is that I ever found the station at all that night, or rather close to it a policeman, who showed me the way.'

" ' But how do you account for Kershaw knowing all your movements ? ' still persisted his Honour, ' and his knowing the exact date of your arrival in England ? How do you account for these two letters, in fact ? '

" ' I cannot account for it or them, your Honour,' replied the prisoner quietly. ' I have proved to you, have I not, that I never wrote those letters, and that the man—er—Kershaw is his name ?—was not murdered by me ! '

" ' Can you tell me of any one here or abroad who might have heard of your movements, and of the date of your arrival ? '

" ' My late employees at Vladivostok, of course, knew of my departure, but none of them could have written these letters, since none of them knew a word of English.'

" ' Then you can throw no light upon these mysterious letters ? You cannot help the police in any way towards the clearing up of this strange affair ? '

" ' The affair is as mysterious to me as to your Honour, and to the police of this country.'

" Francis Smethurst was discharged, of course ; there was no semblance of evidence against him sufficient to commit him for trial. The two overwhelming points of his defence which had completely routed the prosecution, were, firstly, the proof that he had never written the letters making the assignation, and secondly, the fact that the man supposed to have been murdered on the 10th was seen to be alive and well on the 16th. But, then, who in the world was the mysterious individual who had apprised Kershaw of the movements of Smethurst, the millionaire ? "

CHAPTER III

HIS DEDUCTION

THE man in the corner cocked his funny thin head on one side and looked at Polly ; then he took up his beloved bit of string and deliberately untied every knot he had made in it. When it was quite smooth he laid it out upon the table.

" I will take you, if you like, point by point along the line of reasoning which I followed myself, and which will inevitably lead you, as it led me, to the only possible solution of the mystery.

" First take this point," he said with nervous restlessness, once more taking up his bit of string and forming with each point raised a series of knots which would have shamed a navigating instructor, " obviously it was *impossible* for Kershaw not to have been acquainted with Smethurst, since he was fully apprised of the latter's arrival in England by two letters. Now it was clear to me from the first that *no one* could have written those two letters except Smethurst. You will argue that those letters were proved not to have been written by the man in the dock. Exactly. Remember, Kershaw was a careless man—he had lost both envelopes. To him they were insignificant. Now it was never *disproved* that those letters were written by Smethurst."

" But——" suggested Polly.

" Wait a minute," he interrupted, while knot number two appeared upon the scene, " it was proved that six days after the murder, William Kershaw was alive, and visited the Torriani Hotel, where already he was known, and where he conveniently left a pocket-book behind, so that there should be no mistake as to his identity ; but it was never questioned where Mr. Francis Smethurst, the millionaire, happened to spend that very same afternoon."

" Surely you don't mean——? " gasped the girl.

" One moment, please," he added triumphantly. " How did it come about that the landlord of the Torriani Hotel was brought into court at all ? How did Sir Arthur Inglewood, or rather his client, know that William Kershaw had on those two memorable occasions visited the hotel, and that its landlord could bring such convincing evidence forward that would for ever exonerate the millionaire from the imputation of murder ? "

" Surely," she argued, " the usual means, the police——"

" The police had kept the whole affair very dark until the arrest at the Hotel Cecil. They did not put into the papers the usual : ' If any one happens to know of the whereabouts, etc., etc.' Had the landlord of that hotel heard of the disappearance of Kershaw through the usual channels, he would have put himself in communication with the police. Sir Arthur Inglewood produced him. How did Sir Arthur Inglewood come on his track ? "

" Surely, you don't mean—— ? "

" Point number four," he resumed imperturbably, " Mrs. Kershaw was never requested to produce a specimen of her husband's handwriting. Why ? Because the police, clever as you say they are, never started on the right tack. They believed William Kershaw to have been murdered ; they looked for William Kershaw.

" On December the 31st, what was presumed to be the body of William Kershaw was found by two lightermen ; I have shown you a photograph of the place where it was found. Dark and deserted it is in all conscience, is it not ? Just the place where a bully and a coward would decoy an unsuspecting stranger, murder him first, then rob him of his valuables, his papers, his very identity, and leave him there to rot. The body was found in a disused barge which had been moored some time against the wall, at the foot of these steps. It was in the last stages of decomposition, and, of course, could not be identified ; but the police would have it that it was the body of William Kershaw.

" It never entered their heads that it was the body of *Francis Smethurst, and that William Kershaw was his murderer.*

" Ah ! it was cleverly, artistically conceived ! Kershaw is a genius. Think of it all ! His disguise ! Kershaw had a shaggy beard, hair, and moustache. He shaved up to his very eyebrows ! No wonder that even his wife did not recognise him across the court ; and remember she never saw much of his face while he stood in the dock. Kershaw was shabby, slouchy, he stooped. Smethurst, the millionaire, might have served in the Prussian army.

" Then that lovely trait about going to revisit the Torriani Hotel. Just a few days' grace, in order to purchase moustache and beard and wig, exactly similar to what he had himself shaved off. Making up to look like himself ! Splendid ! He ! he ! he ! Kershaw was not murdered ! Of course not. He called at the Torriani Hotel six days after the murder, whilst

Mr. Smethurst, the millionaire, hobnobbed in the park with duchesses ! Hang such a man ! Fie ! "

He fumbled for his hat. With nervous, trembling fingers he held it deferentially in his hand whilst he rose from the table. Polly watched him as he strode up to the desk and paid twopence for his glass of milk and his bun. Soon he disappeared through the shop, while she still found herself hopelessly bewildered, with a number of snapshot photographs before her, still staring at a long piece of string, smothered from end to end in a series of knots, as bewildering, as irritating, as puzzling as the man who had lately sat in the corner.

PEACOCK HOUSE

JANE CAMPBELL'S long journey was ended, and in August sunset light, a dogcart, which conveyed her upon the last stage, drove up an avenue of old elms, left the trees, skirted a little lake, and presently brought the visitor before the face of Pole Manor, a minor mansion lying at the foothills of Dartmoor. Two storys high and built of granite, rose this Georgian house, but the porch and its pillars were of red, conglomerate stone. They broke the unbending gravity of the grey front with a touch of colour. Behind rolled blue hills, now melting into the splendour of gold and orange above them ; while southward, beyond a little park, extended meadow lands, wooded ridges, and fields of corn yellowing to harvest.

The dogcart brought up, and a footman descended from the porch. He assisted the traveller, who was a pleasant-looking, red-haired woman of robust build ; then he turned his attention to her luggage, untied a bicycle fastened to the back seat, set it against the steps, and picked up Miss Campbell's plain, leathern trunk and suit-case. These he took into the hall and handed to another man. The cart drove away down a road to the left of the house, and presently a stable boy came up this path and trundled off the bicycle. He waited until beyond observation, then mounted it for his private amusement.

Jane had come to visit her godfather. She was a schoolmistress at Glasgow, and when in doubt as to where the latter part of her summer holiday might be spent, to her amazement received a letter from a friend of her dead father, the old soldier who had been her main gossip. From him she had never heard until now and only once had she seen him, when he came, three-and-thirty years before, to Colonel Campbell's funeral. Then she was but two years old, and had, therefore, no recollection of him. Indeed, if she ever thought of him, it was with impatience, for she had been saddled with his surname and regarded it as rather stupid so to be. Jane Goodenough Campbell she was called, but few knew it save herself. Since her mother's death she was exceedingly alone in the world. She had been an only child, and of her father's people none remained ; of her mother's, but an old aunt and some distant cousins whom she never saw.

She lived a monotonous, independent life, enjoyed the business of teaching, harboured no dreams, and was of a practical and stolid temperament. With men she was cold, and no romance added shadow or lustre to her recollections. She had once liked a man, and even sought to let him know it ; but she understood not how to do so, and the schoolmaster in question soon found out her temperamental lack and turned away.

Now came something of an adventure, and after fearing that such a visit as General George Goodenough proposed was quite out of her province, Jane, greatly daring, determined to accept the invitation, and did so. She had regretted it half a dozen times on the journey, and wished more than once that her destination was one of the whitewashed, thatched cottages that peered from nook and dingle upon her five-mile drive. Some weeks in one of them had better suited her modest ideas of rest and pleasure than a formal visit. But it was too late. She had glimpsed the unpromising front of Pole Manor ; she had passed through the lifeless hall and was waiting in an equally lifeless drawing-room for her host.

A housekeeper welcomed her—a cheerful old woman in black, with a little black cap on her few white hairs. The footman who took her luggage upstairs was also old and grey. A sense of age clung to everything, and the drawing-room seemed naked and archaic to Jane's eye. The furniture was tired-looking, faded, of little worth. Only a magnificent mantelshelf of the Adam period attracted her, and from it she lifted her eyes to the roof and saw that the ceiling was also distinguished.

Then came somebody on a stick. She heard the stick tapping, but no sound of feet. The door opened and a lame, bent figure appeared. Here indeed was eld, and her heart sank. She knew that a contemporary of her father, who had married at forty-five, must be stricken in years, but Time's self stood personified before her, and General Goodenough, by reason of indifference to appearances, looked even more ancient than he was He had been tall, but was now withered and shrunken. He wore a black skull-cap on his bald head, and a great white beard and whiskers still thick and flowing. His face was thin and his cheeks hollow ; his eyes were dim behind their glasses, and a network of wrinkles extended from his high, narrow brow over his temples to his cheek-bones. His expression belied him and belonged, as it seemed, to his soldier days ; for it was still stern. But his voice was not. Though dimmed by the throttle of eighty-five years, it had good, deep notes yet, and it sounded kindly on the ear of all who ever heard it. His clothes seemed ridiculous to Jane. Such a venerable figure, she thought, should have worn Victorian garments at the least ; but the General was clad in a very shabby Norfolk jacket, a waistcoat of fawn-coloured leather, and knickerbockers, from which appeared legs still fairly sturdy, in homespun stockings. On one foot was a red slipper, the other had been tied up in a shawl.

He bowed, shook Jane's hand with gnarled fingers distorted by chalk stones, and sank into a chair.

" Welcome," he said, " I take this visit kindly, young lady. But don't be discouraged. A touch of gout—quite unexpected, probably brought on by the excitement of entertaining you. Deal gently with me ; distract my mind, and it will be gone in twenty-four hours. Have you made a comfortable journey ? "

" Very much so, General Goodenough."

" Do you know Devon ? "

" I do not. I visited Cornwall once and found the air almost too strong."

" Did you ? Here the air is soft, or bracing, at will. The valleys are as good as a Turkish bath this summer ; but Dartmoor, five miles up above us, is always bracing."

" You're not in pain ? " she asked.

" Thank you, no. Mere discomfort. Gout won't kill me. A man is as old as his arteries, Jane Campbell ; and though I'm in my eighty-fifth year, my arteries happen to be only seventy, or thereabouts. So the doctor tells me. Don't think you've come to an invalid. Your good mother—I was so sorry to find she had gone. I hoped to have entertained you both."

" She died ten years ago."

" Well, well. And you don't remember your father, my dear old companion in arms ? "

" Not very well, General. Just a shadow. I was a tiny thing when he died. But I dream about him sometimes—strange to say."

" So do I. It is said, you know, that we never see the faces of the dead in dreams. For that matter, I have no other faces to see now. Your father possessed one or two gifts of the Scots and lacked some of their reputed failings. He had second-sight —couldn't explain it, even disavowed it ; but things happened to him only to be so understood. And he was a Scot in his love of metaphysics. What a man to split straws and prove black was white ! I should have hated it in anybody else ; but nothing was wrong that he did. A great man, and loved a joke, and couldn't keep money in his purse. Dear, dear me ! Really great ; and so he was passed over, and the show puppets, for whom he pulled the strings in such masterly fashion, got the honours. A common thing in India half a century ago. A mad world, Jane, and it always was—it always was. I read little but history nowadays, and I see the only thing that changes not is human nature."

" Psychology is in the air so much," she said. " I suppose there is something in what you speak of as second sight. But it isn't called that now."

" Inherited, they say," answered the old man. " Are you interested in it ? "

" In psychology and second-self, rather than second-sight. I've read Freud. He's a pathologist, but seems to be more useful to the artists than the doctors. So far as I understand it, our unconscious minds seem to be very primitive and earthy and inferior, and impervious to conscience—most disappointing, in fact."

" You never found yourself possessed of any clairvoyant gift ? "

" No, indeed. I'm a schoolmistress, and the most matter-of-fact person in the world. I'm afraid you'll find me very dull, General Goodenough."

" Call me ' Godfather,' " he said. " I expect you think it strange that I should claim such a spiritual relationship after so many years. There's a respectable gap between the silver porringer and spoon I gave you when you were baptized and to-day. Still, bear no grudge. I'm lonely, and I must go soon, and there's no one in the wide world linked to me, even as slightly as you are. The natural fate of all old bachelors, if they refuse to send in their papers at three score and ten. So I thought, if you were willing, that we might have a look at each other. A schoolmistress, eh ? "

" It was very good of you to ask me."

" And rather good of you to come—also rather brave. But

your father's daughter was sure to be brave. I counted on that. It took me some months to hunt you down. I thought you might be married and have a husband and perhaps half a dozen young people."

She shook her head, smiling.

" I shall never marry, Godfather," she said.

" Don't prophesy."

A gong sounded, and the faint rumble reached them.

" You're ready for your dinner, I hope ? Would you like a cup of tea, or anything, now ? "

" No, thank you. I had some tea at Exeter."

They met again at dinner, when Jane, in a new but un-romantic gown, faced the General, who had donned evening dress.

He treated her as though he had known her all his life, and was vivacious, humorous, and cheerful. She admired his tact, for finding that they had nothing of taste or experience in common, he sought to learn what interested her and made her talk about it.

" I catch your father," he said. " It is wonderful to note how young people are often the unconscious echoes of those responsible for them. Not in what they say, or even think, for education has lifted them forward, and their values are changed ; but in the manner of thought and the angle of vision. That is what is handed down—temperament ; here cautious and reserved and self-contained, as you are ; here dashing and reckless ; here cold and calculating ; here big-hearted ; here small. An unconscious inflection of voice, little mannerisms. . . . You have your father's accent, and you lift your chin when you're going to speak, just as he used to do."

" Mother always said I grew up to remind her of him. Have you, by any chance, a picture of my father ? I, to my sorrow, have none. He never would be photographed."

He shook his head.

" I much fear not, save in my old heart ; but we will see. It is barely possible."

A curious emotion made Jane smile to herself that night, though little that happened ever amused her. Her host made her retire early, and, when she had done so, she reflected that he was treating her exactly as she habitually treated her pupils. To them she was old ; to General Goodenough she appeared exceedingly young. She was accustomed to the companionship of immature intellects, as all teachers perforce must be ; but now she perceived that to this venerable man she was immature herself ; and indeed she knew it, for though clever and learned, her knowledge of life outside her scholastic circle was but small.

She asked concerning his health next morning, and he declared his gout to be better. She was touched by his solicitude, and a thousand little attentions that it seemed impossible that a man should have considered.

He took no breakfast himself, but drank a glass of hot water and ate a thin slice of toast only. For her, however, he had planned a generous meal ; porridge, a grouse, scones and marmalade.

" Don't forget the Devonshire cream," he said. " I love to see young people eat."

" But I'm not young, Godfather ; I'm five-and-thirty."

" To be five-and-thirty is to retain all the possibilities of youth, even if the bloom has been rubbed off," he said. " One is generally younger at that age than ten years earlier. To-day you are free of my company, to do as you please ; to-morrow I shall be well enough to drive you to the Moor."

" May I take a long bicycle ride ? It's cool and fresh and 'elicious. I've been in your garden an hour."

" Alas ! We are not gardeners."

" There are splendid possibilities about it."

" Most old Indians make gardens," he said. " I have known old fellows who, if they could not have gardens, amused themselves by growing seeds of date and palm in little pots and watching them spring up. But I am an exception. Horticulture never attracted me."

" You must tell me your hobbies."

" They are easily told : reading and driving. This year I've had an excitement. A regiment, long resident in India, was sent to Dartmoor, to be braced and hardened. With that exquisite foresight so characteristic of our War Office these unfortunate Third Devons were brought straight from the Plains to the side of Cosdon Beacon, and there, under canvas in a harsh April, reminded of the glories of an English spring. The weather, unhappily, could not have been worse ; the ambulance was busy taking poor Tommies to the hospital at Okehampton. A man or two died of pneumonia. The officers welcomed my modest hospitality—good fellows."

" I'll take a long ride ; but I promise not to up go to the Moor. You have to show me that."

" Disregard all hours save that for dinner," he said. " At

eight o'clock I shall expect you to dine. Until then you are free of me."

But this she would not have.

"No, no ; I'm coming back for lunch, please. Perhaps I'll take it with me sometimes—with you on your drives."

"I have no motor-car. You must be resigned to that ; but I love horses and drive myself still very creditably."

They pleased one another, and Jane pleased herself also, to find that she could be so cheerful and at her ease with a strange man. But she understood why. This gracious and kind-hearted old figure was not a man. He had passed beyond manhood into the neuter state of the aged. She liked his physical weakness. It inspired instincts that belonged to her ; for had she not been a schoolmistress, she must have been a nurse.

She thought kindly about him as she rode away, but her imagination was not equal to picturing her future spent at Pole Manor, though her reason told her that such a purpose might lurk in the General's mind. She guessed that he would soon empty her and weary of the content ; while, for her part, she knew that a life plunged into such silence, even with this amiable old spirit for company, must quickly desolate and distract a being devoted to the stir and bustle of a girls' school.

She wondered as to General Goodenough's acquaintance, and suspected he had but few friends. His house did not suggest hospitality, though he himself did.

The cool grey of the morning broke to pearl when Jane had ridden five miles, and she regretted her promise, for the valley lanes were hot and the hills beckoned. Climb indeed she did presently, and won to a little knap crowned with shade of beeches. Then an expanse of country was flung beneath her, and she rejoiced in beholding gentle and distinguished scenery of a sort unfamiliar to her. For she was something of a connoisseur of natural beauty, and protested at those who were learned in art and understood pictures, but cared nothing for the scenes of inspiration where a man had sweated, or frozen, for his achievement. She blamed those who only valued a work itself, but found no pleasure in its sources. She knew the meaning of scenery, distrusted the obvious and rhetorical, but found by experience much that promised least was like a fugue, whose fullness and significance could often only be won after many hours of patient service.

The quiet lands undulating in the diffused light of thin clouds pleased her, and she knew that this manifestation, albeit lumpy and ever-green with the heaviness of English foliage, must be fairer at spring and autumn time. For it was built on a large pattern, finely knit together and broken by great passages of level earth where a river twinkled through the haze.

She thirsted presently, looked for a rooftree, and longed to be on the banks of the distant stream far below. Then, half a mile beneath her, she thought that she saw the gables and twisted chimneys of an old house ; and since inviting meadows sloped towards it, she left her bicycle hidden under a holly and descended for something to drink. Jane remembered at a later date that the hour was just after noon when she took her way.

Descending over a shorn hayfield and passing through a belt of trees, the wanderer entered suddenly upon a different world, and in the glen through which she was now proceeding, the very air seemed charged and charmed with a different quality. It was lustrous, burnished and radiant with light. The sun, that had created but a bright and misty zone behind the clouds all day, here emerged and rained into a woodland whereon no proleptic shadow of autumn had yet appeared. It seemed as though the valley still lay in the lap of early summer ; the very flowers were not the ragworts and hawkweeds of a later time ; but woodbine scented the thickets, the dogrose had not yet dropped her petals, the wayfaring-tree still blossomed.

Jane, emerging from the forest and passing into a meadow, came suddenly to a low bank where the grassland broke, and above which extended a garden to the front of a beautiful dwelling-house. Upon its wall hung a great magnolia with ivory cups glittering in the sunshine, and the lawn of the formal garden was such as the stranger had never seen. To the right and left stood wonders of topiary in the shape of yew trees, clipped to the shape of peacocks with tails outspread, and between them a round pond lay ; while above the water, in the midst of it, stood a marble urchin holding a great fish, from whose mouth leapt up a fountain. It flashed aloft and fell purring upon the water-lilies below.

Two living peacocks strutted on the gravel terrace before the house, and when Jane ascended to the garden by a flight of steps and felt the velvet of the lawn under her feet, one bird lifted the glittering mass of bronze and purple he dragged behind him and opened his tail fanwise, till it arched and quivered like a dark rainbow above his head.

Other sign of life there was none, and seeing no entrance at the front of the house, Jane was about to pass round and follow the path that curved to the right. But the sight of a great magnolia cup low on the tree tempted her to smell the fragrance ; and from that, moved by an impulse that seemed natural at the time, yet made her wonder afterwards, she found herself peeping into the window beyond it.

The room was occupied, but those within did not regard her, and she perceived that their own affairs shut out any thought or sight of another face. The sun beat down, and through two windows of the chamber cast its radiance on the oaken floor. The walls were of dark crimson and upon them hung old portraits in golden frames, while at the centre was a table of polished mahogany spread with a meal. Silver glittered upon the rich wood ; and a bowl of strawberries stood between two tall vases of Bohemian glass, from which sprayed down dark, Tuscan roses and the snowy stars of syringas.

Three people sat at the table, and while the obvious details of the room were unconsciously impressed on the watcher's memory, the living beings she more directly regarded and remembered for ever.

All sense of her own impropriety deserted Jane ; she forgot the glamorous garden and its adornments ; her purpose in being there fled from her ; as still as a statue she stood and stared upon the remarkable trio assembled so near and yet so far removed from her by their own present passions.

A young man and a young woman were seated at each end of the oval table ; while between them sat a man of middle-age, who directly faced the eavesdropper. The girl was fair and seemed to have sprung out of some picture by Reynolds or Gainsborough. Her flaxen hair had been drawn to her crown, yet little curls, amber bright, hid her ears. She was in summer muslin sprigged with blue lavender, with a bunch of lavender ribbon at her throat for sole adornment. Her face was pale and pure—a beautiful, but fragile, Greuze face, with red, small lips, and large, lovely blue eyes. The younger man wore a black tail coat and riding-breeches. He was clean shorn, of good height and well-knit, with a fierce, intent expression on his countenance. Brown, curly hair clustered low on his forehead. The natural expression of neither did Jane see, for the woman was evidently trembling with terror and the youth strained to some great indignation at what he heard. His attitude echoed his emotion, for he leant over the table with a large, white fist clenched upon it, and he had upset and broken a wine-glass at his elbow, from which purple wine trickled over the edge to the floor.

The elder of the men was speaking vehemently and fury contorted his features. He had shaven lips and chin, black, curly whiskers and black hair streaked with grey. He wore a dull russet-coloured coat, very high in the neck, and a black stock with a diamond pin in it. His heavy jowl was as red as a peony, and his round, brown eyes bulged like a fish's from under stormy eyebrows and a wrinkled forehead. Jane had never seen such passion glaze on any human countenance ; she did not know that a face could writhe with such contortions of malice and hate. The stout, middle-aged sufferer shot his lips and spewed moisture, like a gargoyle that she had seen leer down from a mediæval rain-shoot. It seemed that he roared at the others, for the girl shrank back in her chair and put her little white hands over her ears. She wore a wedding ring, Jane noted ; then the watcher, echoing some of this tremendous surge of passion and almost sharing the other woman's terror, turned her eyes again quickly to the raging creature who faced her. She could not hear what he said, but saw the table shiver as he struck, the silver leap, and roses fall from a glass. Then she witnessed death, sudden and terrible, for as the younger man leapt up, with the intention of silencing his tormentor, the elder tore a heavy pistol from his breast, pointed it and fired point-blank at the head of the girl upon his left hand. There was a stab of flame, and the woman, shot through her fair head, fell forward, then slipped out of her chair and dropped to the ground. The murderer had only time to fire once, for as he turned upon the other man, his weapon was torn from his hand and exploded into the air. Then, snatching a great silver knife from the table, the younger drove it with all his strength into the other's breast and left it there. His victim fell and lay without movement, while the man who had slain him hastened to the girl, bent over her, perceived that she was dead, then turned and strode to the window where Jane watched, flung it open and emerged. He almost brushed her elbow, but was apparently unconscious of her presence, for his blazing eyes saw nothing. He passed her and vanished so quickly that she had but a glimpse of the unspeakable agony on his face. It seemed rather an incarnation of all human woe than a living man who swept out of her sight ; and now, looking into the room again, Jane saw the door open and two liveried servants enter.

Then she shrank back, and, alarmed for herself, turned into a shrubbery, where she could not be seen, and so regained the meadows beneath the garden. Still hastening, not without personal fear, she ran, passed the belt of trees and breasted the hayfield as swiftly as she might. Not until she was at the summit of the knoll did she stay her progress, sink down beside her bicycle and slowly regain her breath.

Horror and thankfulness shared Jane's mind. She was appalled at what she had seen, but unspeakably glad that into this tragedy she could not be drawn and need not enter. Neither the murdered man nor woman had seen her, while for the youth, who had so terribly slain the slayer, she could only hope that he might escape. Her sympathies were with him—she knew not why. For an hour she lay retracing every incident of the scene and marvelling that all had happened in so brief a space of time. She looked at her watch and perceived that she had not been half an hour from the hill-top. Then she brooded on the story of these unfortunate people and what must have preceded this grim climax in their lives.

She rose presently, mounted and returned home, conscious that the outer world was changed, that autumn's stealthy signs were now again on field and hedge ; that the sun had retreated behind the clouds. Very poignant emotions filled Jane's heart and head, yet a feeling of gratitude that she had played no part in this awful scene also persisted, and a nature prone to reserve and caution determined her to keep silence before General Goodenough. To tell him was to endanger her own privacy, for it might be that he would demand she should make public what she had accidentally seen, for the benefit of those who must be concerned with the crime. But Jane's conscience did not prompt confession. She was of a practical mind. She knew that she could not bring the dead to life, and had no desire to say one word that might help to bring the living to death. Her instinct indeed forbade it. Therefore she held her peace and waited with profound but secret interest to learn what the morrow would bring and who were the unhappy ones involved.

But the morning came, and neither General Goodenough, the housekeeper, nor any other exclaimed at the contents of the local newspaper. It arrived after breakfast and contained no sensation ; neither, apparently, was any evil thing on the lips of tradesmen, the grooms, or the gardener. Jane marvelled, but still kept silence. Doubtless news travelled slowly upon the countryside, and she guessed it possible that the police, for their own ends, might be keeping the tragedy a secret.

To-day the General found himself well, and drove her in a wagonette to the moor, where she wondered at stone-crowned heights and admired the fabric of autumn furze and heather mingled in a tapestry of purple and gold upon the granite hills.

She called Dartmoor " a little pocket Highlands," and General Goodenough pretended to be greatly annoyed at such patronage.

" A ' pocket Highlands,' indeed ! " he said. " Was ever such a slight put upon our venerable tors ? No, no, Jane, this wilderness echoes no other region on earth, believe me. The mountains are molehills, I grant you : the rivers mere filaments and threads of gold and silver twinkling over their granite aprons and stickles, but for all its smallness, there is a quality here of greatness, too, a spirit of distinction, austerity, and even grandeur that, once received and accepted, soon wins from the heart to the head, and makes you Dartmoor's willing slave. You must confess, before you leave me, that there is nothing like this in Scotland. Better knowledge will show you the weakness of your parallel."

She hoped they might approach the knoll of her adventure, so that an opportunity would offer to ask concerning the house beneath, but they did not go that way, and though the General met a man or two, who saluted him, and one on horseback, who stopped and was introduced to her, nobody brought any startling intelligence ; none appeared aware of the dark events accomplished so near at hand on the previous morning.

For three days Jane Campbell waited in vain expectation of some news, then, to her own amazement, she found the memory already fading under stress of new impressions. Of a stolid temperament, little happened to cause her excitation at any time ; but this event had naturally done so, and she would not let it fade. She shook off the shadow of indifference and grew into an obstinate determination to learn more. It was preposterous that such a thing could occur and make no ripple in a civilised community. Finally, Jane found her mind balanced in uncertain fashion between a choice of actions. First she determined to tell General Goodenough her story in every particular ; then she hesitated before a temptation to visit the house in the vale again. She thought to revisit it upon the old pretext, find the door and ask for a glass of water. Then, surely, something must reach her comprehension concerning, the awful sights of the week before. Dead people must be buried ; such tragedies must wing above the scene of their commission. It was contrary to reason that things so horrible and extravagant could happen and utter no reverberation beyond the spot of their occurrence.

The latter idea more attracted Jane, and, after some few

days, she begged again for a bicycle ride of exploration, took luncheon with her, and set out for a long day alone. Upon certain landmarks she depended to find the former way, and for a time she failed to do so ; then, by chance, she came to a meeting of two roads that crossed at right angles, and she remembered the curious name of the spot lifted up on a sign-post. " Beggar's Bush," it was called, and thence she took the left-hand track, and presently found herself once more upon the knoll. There was no mistake, for the holly bushes reminded her where she had left her bicycle, and she found the spot where she had sat to reflect after her former adventure.

She now prepared to revisit the scene of the tragedy. It was a lonely glen, and none met her on the road, or meadow, as she descended into it. Nor did the sun break forth and shine as on her first visit. Morning, indeed, had opened in clear splendour ; but the day grew oppressively hot before noon, and already a thin web of brown and sulky cloud stole up against the little wind that blew. There was a heavy, sickly feeling in the air, and every sign of electric changes near at hand. Jane looked for the gabled roof and twisted chimneys beneath her, but she could not discern them. Neither were the white pigeons on the wind. The valley seemed to have receded somewhat and the trees towered higher, denser, more numerous than she remembered them. Then she went down over the shorn hayfield as before, passed the belt of wood, and presently, entering the glade beneath, started to cross the meadow, and lifted her eyes to the dwelling as she did so. It had vanished, and the sudden sense of this disappearance terrified Jane as though she had seen a ghost. But the thrill of fear arose from what she did not see, rather than from anything she did. A sensation, strange, and altogether beyond experience, crept into her consciousness, and she believed that she was moving in the spirit rather than the flesh, and standing in some corridor of long, vanished years, before the grey house rose, or the garden spread before it. Time, it seemed, had winged backward to the days when the glen was a wilderness and man had not built a home therein, spread his garden and set his fountain flashing. And into that far, anterior day she, too, had been caught up and whirled back, to behold a scene that existed thus before she was born. She rubbed her eyes and pinched her hand to waken out of this mysterious plunge into the past ; and then she discovered that stark reality awaited her, while what she had before imagined real was the true dream and figment.

The jungles and thickets before her resolved themselves, and beneath them, like a palimpsest of dead writing, that peered ghostly through a later script, she came upon decayed traces and shadows of what she had seen so vividly the week before. Here rose the fragments of steps in the bank up which she had climbed to the garden. They were weed-covered and broken, but again she ascended—to find, amid coarse brakes of thistle, briar and eagle-fern, the shattered circle of the fountain, its marbles green with moss, its statue vanished, and its waters dry. One of the yew trees clipped to the likeness of a peacock had disappeared, while the other still rose above the scrub round it ; and on its now mature and lofty limbs, Jane fancied that she could make out a gesture of the old design. The tree had broken away and taken a natural shape ; yet, to eyes familiar with the earlier form, it still retained some cloudy semblance of a bird grown gigantic. But the house had altogether departed, and in its place hemmed by a cincture of heavy woods with undergrowth of laurel and Pontic rhododendron, lay only an undulating litter of great and small stones—a heap largely concealed under seedling trees that rose above nettle and burdock, darnel and dock. Overhead, where the white pigeons had warped together, a buzzard hung high above the woods ; then it uttered a complaining cry and glided on its way.

No sound or sight of any human being marked the spot ; but a fox, that had been sleeping on the stones, leapt up at Jane's footfall and trotted swiftly into the trees. She marked the white tip of his brush flash through the spinney, and then he was gone. Far distant still, the first murmur of thunder reached her ear, and she saw, amid the weeds, that the yellow goat's-beard had already shut its golden eye for the day.

Here was truth, and despite the loneliness and the melancholy of all human ruins, this seemed a better and purer scene than that her vision had wakened from the past. She feared no longer, but rebuilt the old house, imagined the green lawn, the fountain with its little boy holding a big fish, the magnolia lifting great chalices, that brimmed with scent and sunshine, against the fabric behind it. Only for a few moments she remained ; then followed the way of the fox, climbed the woods and so returned upwards, until once more she reached the hayfield and the summit of the knoll above it.

And there she made no stay, for the thunderstorm was lumbering up with wisps and snakes of fulvous cloud round its head, and diamonds of lightning intermittently flickering in its heart. Her way took her directly from the bad weather, and Jane set off to race this threat of the sky and reach home if possible before it overtook her.

But the thunder was rattling overhead and great splashes of rain spattered the dust before she had ridden half an hour, though she minded little, for she did not dread lightning, nor wince even when it seemed to drop a dazzling ribbon of blue flame a hundred yards ahead of her. Indeed, she rather enjoyed the storm and laughed at General Goodenough, who stood under his porch in anxiety, when she rode up the avenue very bedraggled and wet to the skin.

And while she changed her clothes, Jane considered the significance of all that she had experienced. Her father's reputed gift was hers without a doubt. To him also it had been given, once or twice, to peer through the curtain and survey the past, or future. And yet it was no gift, but rather a peculiarity —part of a psychical diathesis which gave this possessor little pride. She could not control it ; she had never before in her life been subjected to it ; she heartily disliked it. Nothing but a disagreeable impression was left, and Jane perceived no reason in the nature of things why this peculiar and terrible vision had been re-created and re-enacted for her eye and brain alone —why a palingenesis from this decay and ruin had flung off the mantle of years and restored it at the most terrific moment of its past. Presently, indeed, she began to doubt whether any significance whatever attached to the apparition—whether it was, indeed, an echo of things that had really happened, or more probably an hallucination of her own mind, built out of sleeping brain cells, charged, perhaps, with pages from forgotten novels. She even doubted if all were not a dream flashed through her thoughts at some drowsy moment.

Upon this point it was possible to satisfy herself, and after usual cautious deliberation, Jane determined to mention her adventure of that day, while still keeping silence concerning the earlier experience.

She told the General of the incident, and how she had left her bicycle on a little hilltop and then descended into the glen beneath, to find a ruin and frighten a fox. He was interested and able not only to tell her much that belonged to the scene, but narrated more than she knew ; and also less. There was a trace of cynicism in his way of telling the story, which Jane explained to herself as lying in her ears rather than in the tongue of the narrator. For she was so much nearer to these

events than he. To him, the musty record meant nothing but
an old-time tale ; to her it was a living mystery of yesterday.
She had seen what he had only heard from ancient intelligencers ;
and she had seen a great deal more than he had heard.

"Why, Jane, you've found the ruin of Peacock House ! "
said General Goodenough. " What an explorer you are. There's
a story about the ruin, rather famous in these parts, and possibly
truer than some stories."

The General thus played most amiably into her hands.

" It looked as though there ought to be a story," said Jane.

" Yes—I learned it from a farmer, nearly as old as myself,
who had actually known the puppets, or vowed he had. It's
not a particularly novel narrative and the agonists belonged
to another age than this. One victim, however, by all accounts,
was never content to stop in her grave, but visited the scene of
her taking off so frequently that it became uninhabitable for the
living, and was finally pulled down.

" A girl and her elderly spouse dwelt there. But I'll begin
at the beginning. In those days, nearer a hundred than fifty
years ago now, the Poles still reigned here at Pole Manor,
though their stock was already near run out. Sir Walter Pole,
the seventh baronet, his wife and their only child, a son, lived at
Pole Manor, and upon the youth the parents' hopes were set ;
for he was the last of his line. Eustace Pole was a name often
mentioned at that time apparently, but never for any good.
A spoiled boy, hard-hearted, selfish and vicious he appears to
have been ; and while his father and mother made the best
of him and condoned his adventures, yet, when there came a
gleam and possibility of salvation for him, parent-like they
failed to perceive its significance and withstood him at the
turning-point of his career. Not that we can blame them over-
much. Times were different then, and a misalliance—an event
within the experience of most noble families nowadays—was then
held somewhat more appalling. Apparently the only decent
thing Eustace Pole ever did was to fall in love with the daughter
of a small tradesman ; and since she appears to have been a
girl of good education and refinement, had he married her the
story of Peacock House had never been told. Perhaps tragedy
was born with him and must in some shape have crowned his
career. But what happened was this. His parents intrigued
against him, after refusing definitely to sanction the engagement. They found a pretext for sending him to London on
his father's affairs, which appear to have been very involved,

and, while he was away, Sir Walter lied to the girl's father
and explained that Eustace was disillusioned, much to that
worthy man's satisfaction. There were no railroads in those
days that embraced these regions, and the girl certainly heard
nothing to contradict her father's information. Or his letters,
if he wrote any, may have been intercepted. Who can say?
Probably young Pole, busy about saving what he might from
his father's dwindling fortunes, proceeded with his affairs and
felt no suspicion of the things being done behind his back.

   " It happened May Ellis—that was her name—had an
eligible but elderly suitor—a hotel-keeper. He, too, was
superior to her in station, but desired her above all things ;
and to this widower, being convinced that Eustace Pole was,
indeed, a dream of the past, the girl at her father's entreaty
affianced herself. Doubtless she was driven into it after the
fashion of the times ; but she wedded him on the day that
young Pole returned home ; and about the first thing he heard
was that she had done so. Mr. Jonathan Foster had traded
at Plymouth ; but now he was retired, and ignorant of, or
indifferent to, the romance he had shattered, took his treasure
to dwell at his Elizabethan dwelling of Peacock House—a case
he held worthy of such a jewel. Here and there a very old
body can yet remember it, with its fountains and lawns and
fantastic, clipped trees, its little park and the fallow deer that
roamed there.

   " Jonathan Foster—a man of fifty, I imagine—had his own
circle of friends and, of course, did not exist for the county.
He was very well content apparently, and quite ignorant of
the hungry, young, robbed tiger who lived not twenty miles
away.

   " History is silent as to what happened then ; but experience
of life can fill the gap. Young Pole took his defeat ill, no doubt,
and a disposition such as his was certainly concerned to be
level, not only with his supplanter, but the woman also. He
must, however, have hidden his heart for many days, and what
followed can only have resulted, it is supposed, from one cause.
I hesitate to go on with the story in your ears, Jane ; but no
doubt you are a student of human nature and read the newspapers and modern novels. The probability is that Pole must
have met May Foster and learned from her the particulars of
the trick put upon them both. She would tell him that her
father had learned from Sir Walter he was gone, and that
believing it, broken-hearted and indifferent, she had obeyed

her parent. That much is almost certain to have happened; but beyond there lies a measure of guesswork, the truth, or falsehood of which can never be certainly known. The sequel, however, upon which this theory was founded seems to substantiate it solidly enough.

"We are to suppose that for his own reasons Eustace Pole scraped acquaintance with the husband—in the hunting field possibly, for both Foster and his wife rode to hounds. It is then assumed that Pole either attempted to run away with the young wife and failed, or endeavoured to seduce her and was repulsed. Be that as it may, before the end it appears that he hated the woman as much as the man. Clearly they were not aware of it, for Pole came and went from Peacock House and obviously had no recorded quarrel with Jonathan Foster. He was actually lunching there, in a day in June, when he committed his famous crime.

"The meal was over and the servants had withdrawn, when they were suddenly alarmed by two reports of a pistol following each other from the dining-room. They had retired to their own quarters and a full minute probably elapsed when they returned to find their master and mistress murdered and the assassin disappeared. The unhappy girl had been shot through the head; the man was stabbed in the heart with a heavy silver knife from the table. A double-barrelled pistol was found with both barrels discharged; but the murderer had missed with his second shot and the bullet was ultimately discovered in the panelling of the chamber.

"Mounted men rode to this house; but none at Pole Manor knew anything, save that the last hope of his race had ridden from home early that morning and not returned. Nor did he ever return. The countryside was scoured, and Eustace Pole's horse was discovered the day afterwards, dead lame, in a meadow near Exeter. But the villain vanished off the face of the earth from that hour. It is supposed that he committed suicide, and that may well have happened.

"The hiatus in the story is, you see, fairly filled by the theory. If May Foster would neither desert her husband, nor become his mistress in secret, to this lawless young dog might well have come the temptation for such a revenge as he planned; and as he had never fought temptation in his life, it conquered him.

"A grim tale for your young ears, yet that is how it runs. The house was taken again, but May Foster's unhappy spirit was seen so often in the dining-room at the precise hour when her life must have left her, that the tenants could not enjoy their midday meal, or find domestics to stay there. A time therefore came when it was dismantled, and all the material of value removed—some fifty years ago, I believe. Now let us talk of things more cheerful."

"And the Poles vanished, too?" asked his listener. Already inherent caution was fighting with desire ; and though it had seemed the most natural thing in the world, for anybody but Jane Campbell, to confess to her vision, now lifted into a matter of intense interest by its variance from the accepted truth ; none the less she put off her story until she had thought about it, in her canny way, and decided whether to speak or be silent.

"Yes," answered the old man, "the Poles vanished, too. Sir Walter died ten years later and Lady Pole went to live at Torquay, a sanatorium the doctors had just discovered. There are plenty of stories about them, also. The Poles were always rather fond of the knife, apparently—a weakness won, perhaps, from Latin blood, that entered the family with Sir Walter's grandmother. When I came here, a cousin of these dead people was selling the Manor, and I spent a few days with him before deciding whether the place would suit me. I remember a family picture and a story concerning Sir Walter and his wife. I remarked on the beauty of a woman's portrait, and he told me that she was the mother of the murderer. He showed me how the white throat of the woman had been gashed open in the portrait and afterwards restored. He recollected the story, too. At dinner on one occasion—possibly Eustace Pole was of the party—his parents fell out and his mother's tongue loosed his father's temper. He leapt up, doubtless glared at his wife, like the demon he was, and then, taking a knife, turned upon Lady Pole's portrait, hanging behind him, and cut its throat. A new way of committing murder without disturbance to the victim, or danger to the assassin. But consider the woman's emotions ! Surely he murdered her soul when he struck, together with such love as she may still have preserved for him. Let us hope the servants were not in the room. Perhaps the bad-tempered ruffian had a brighter side, made piacular overtures, and was forgiven afterwards. Who can say ? "

But Jane had supped her fill of horrors, and felt not sorry to bid her godfather " good-night " and leave him. Her first impulse was obvious ; yet the cautious lady seldom gratified first impulses. She had thought to tell him her story on the completion of his ; but she changed her mind and went to bed with the two stories—his and her own. She could not dismiss her vision as inferior in probability to the regulation tale. She recognised that the legend made Eustace Pole a fiend ; but in her version it seemed that he was human enough and that, whatever his errors, he had, at least while she watched him, done little more than became a man. She accepted the shadow play and the frenzy of the scene returned to her for a while. Yet, what did it matter, now ? she asked herself impatiently : and why should she, on the strength of a fantastic and futile psychical experience, think twice about the incident ? But she could not thus dismiss the matter. General Goodenough's narrative effectually destroyed her first suspicion, that she had endured a purely subjective and personal illusion ; for her vision, objectively real in every particular, actually served to correct the received opinion of living people. Yet again, what did it matter, since no justice could be served, no name restored to reverence, no wrong righted ? The grave had long since swallowed these figures, and there was none to breathe easier for her story ; while she would certainly breathe less easily if she told her godfather of her experience and he laughed at her. She reduced the situation to one of mild psychologic interest, and no more. General Goodenough had mentioned how her father possessed the gift of second sight, and it was possible that he would be attracted to learn the endowment had been handed down. On second thoughts she felt sure that he would not laugh at her. For herself she took no pleasure in the incident, but rather felt pain, and she trusted that no such adventure would ever again befall her.

She told the General her story on the following evening.

I don't think you've got the tragedy of Peacock House quite right, Godfather," she said after dinner, when she spent an hour with him and he smoked his trichinopoly.

"Don't you, Jane ? That's interesting. Perhaps I have not ; but I'm afraid the facts, if they differ from the chronicle, will be hidden until all things are revealed."

" I saw Peacock House before it was pulled down. I saw it on the very day those poor people died," she said simply, and he stared at her.

" My dear child, what on earth are you talking about ? "

" I have been there twice, and never mentioned the first visit to you. It seemed so mad, because nothing happened

afterwards. And yet it was really like this—unless I dreamed
it."

She told him everything, and his cigar went out as he
listened with closest attention. Not once he interrupted her,
nor did he speak when she had finished. Indeed, his silence
was so lengthy that Jane grew uncomfortable and began to
regret her confession.

" I believe you think I've invented this rigmarole to amuse
you, Godfather," she said presently.

" No, indeed. A great entertainment—a wonderful entertainment, indeed, but not amusing ; much more than that.
There's much to consider here, Jane. You probe the depths.
For what springs from your experience ? A dozen things.
It means, first, that the mysterious property of mind which
your father possessed has been transmitted. That this can
happen is possibly a familiar fact to science, but it is new to
me. And secondly, it means, if these things really fell out
as you saw them, that the old, accepted legend is false, and
you have unearthed a new and very different story from under
the dust of more than half a century."

" I suppose I have. And yet I'm rather annoyed with
myself, Godfather, for it is annoying to find something hidden
inside you that can play such weird tricks. I hope no such
phenomena will ever fall to my lot again ; while, at the same
time, I almost feel that I should like just one more peep into
the past—to round off the adventure. But I know such a last
peep would be painful. The end of that unhappy survivor must
surely have been tragic."

" Only too probable, Jane."

" I've been trying to reconstruct the real truth ever since
I heard your version. Perhaps it lies between the two—a
third story that would more or less reconcile the others."

" No, that could not be," he said. " What you witnessed
is the only basis to argue upon. You must build upon that ;
but do you know enough about human nature to see a plausible
prelude to your vision ? "

" I've tried, only there are difficulties I can't clear up. If
my ears had heard while my eyes were seeing—then perhaps
I should know. The old story comes in my way, I think. Your
tale seems to argue people with rather different characters
from those that I saw."

He nodded.

" Good. The accepted theory probably gave rise to the

assumed qualities of the three actors in the scene. That's where history so often goes wrong. We have only actions to guide us ; and we assume that the actions arose from certain mental properties in those who did, or suffered. The result of action decides us as to character, rather than the motives for action, wherein character really resides. Achievement does not hang on motive. A thousand accidents may determine it. Perhaps these three people were radically different from the old interpretation of them—indeed, they must have been vastly different, and all their values for us are altered now."

" Except the woman's. She was surely deserving of death. And Eustace Pole may, after all, have been as much her murderer as if he had shot her himself. That leaves him a villain still. Everything seems to turn on Jonathan Foster. If he, indeed, destroyed his wife, and meant to destroy her lover too——"

" Wait—wait ! You go too fast, Jane. You have opened the door—not to an alternative, but to a dozen possible variations. We may be as far from the truth as ever, and can only reconstruct on human experience. We lack the touch of poetic vision and inspiration needful to find the truth, I fear. You, for example, are already weaving parts of the apocryphal story into your own. You use the word ' lover ' as a matter of course. But why ? Why should that be taken for granted ? "

" Because it was clearly the opinion of Jonathan Foster. Surely nothing less than that would have made him try to kill them both," argued Jane.

" Is it beyond peradventure that even Jonathan was mistaken ? "

" He is more likely to have been right than wrong, I'm afraid. We have got to argue back from effect to cause, Godfather. We see an elderly man attempt to kill his wife and a young man—her former betrothed. Nothing but jealousy explains that ; and he is a sane, successful business man, who would hardly be led away by a delusion on the subject. After all, he only did what plenty of other jealous men have done."

" True," admitted the General. " But other jealous men have been mistaken, and why not he ? He may have had less ground for his jealousy then we suppose."

" There is Eustace Pole's notorious character."

" Of which, again, we only have oral tradition—largely built on the assumption of a crime that we now know, through your second-sight, he never committed. Perhaps he was not

as evil as we imagine. Then, again, another possibility—
Foster may have been deluded, as Othello was. Perhaps
there existed an Iago, who does not come into our story.
Suppose, for the sake of argument, that Pole, worthless and
probably wicked as he appears to have been, yet entertained
respect for that particular woman, knew that she had been
taken from him through no fault of her own, and still loved
her too well to dishonour her."

But Jane shook her head.

" That is the least likely variation, not the most likely,
Godfather. It's very charitable of you, but I'm afraid too
much like a Sunday School story. At any rate, very improbable.
No, be sure Eustace Pole wasn't that sort of man ; and as to
the woman—possibly she had been found out and didn't know
she had been. That's well inside human nature, isn't it ? "

" It is, Jane ; but many innocent people have been ' found
out ' and paid the price of the guilty. Desdemona was ' found
out.' I don't argue for the man, or the woman. I'm only
trying to show the obvious is not necessarily the true. Once
you dive into problems of character, you drown in a case like
this. Take even the suggested Iago, who comes to poison the
middle-aged husband's ear. Perhaps he was no enemy—no
Iago at all—but a well-meaning friend, who dropped a word
of caution, ignorant that he was setting a match to a train
already laid."

" You want to whitewash them all, I believe ! " said Jane.

" Modern history is largely a matter of whitewashing. We
tend to reconstruct the old giants on the new science of sociology.
We psycho-analyse them. We reduce them to human dimensions
from the fantastic stature of the dead, and find them neither
so black nor white as their contemporaries found them. But
we shall never know enough to reach the truth of this trio. There's
nothing good or evil but thinking makes it so ; and what did
they think ? We can hope for no answer to that. The interesting
thing is how are our own feelings now affected by them ? Do
we find ourselves nearer to forgiving Eustace Pole, or a little
farther from sympathising with Jonathan Foster ? "

" I can't feel they are real people at all, even though I have
seen them," answered Jane. " If you know men and women
have been dead for sixty years, you can't take more interest in
them than you do in characters of fiction—often not so much.
The puppets in a good story are more alive—while you are
reading it."

" I understand that. From your youthful standpoint the
ghosts at Peacock House must be shadows at best, and may
all have been sinners, too ; but I love a forlorn cause ; therefore,
this revelation of yours has made me take the weaker side.
Quixote that I am, I cling to the frail possibility that the young
pair were innocent victims. It is rather a quality of old age
to flout reason and experience, Jane. So I bring to your second-
sight my second childhood."

" It's like you to think well of everybody ; but if you imagine
the young people were innocent, then you make a demon of
the poor, retired hotel-keeper."

" Not if he were *non compos*—driven out of his reason by
fancied disasters to his honour. Suppose that Eustace Pole
were really too convinced of his own integrity to imagine
anybody could doubt it ; while the girl was too innocent to
dream that she had wakened the passion of jealousy in her
husband's hidden heart ? They were both very young and
inexperienced, remember."

" You are on the side of the angels," said Jane, " and I
should be a worldly, cynical wretch to take the other side."

He smiled at that, and lit his cigar again.

" Yes, indeed. The cases ought to be reversed ; yet I, after
eighty-five years in this wicked world, take up the cudgels for
these ghosts, and you—out of a girl's school—snub my senile
charity. And so we win a laugh. And there remains one
certainty—your amazing endowment. Be sure to let me know
if any further revelation overtakes you. I should like to conduct
you to some other of our celebrated houses over which strange
stories brood, and see what happened. Why, you may electrify
the world yet, Jane, and re-write many pages of doubtful
history."

" What a dreadful picture ! It would make me good for
nothing, Godfather, and distrustful of my own shadow, if such
a thing happened again," she assured him.

And then Jane went to bed, while the old man declared
that he was not done with the problem, but intended to work
out new answers, based on a surer interpretation of character
and probability.

" We'll allow ourselves no more fairy stories to-morrow,"
he promised.

But he did not mention the subject on the following day,
nor did she. Other interests filled the remaining week of
Jane's visit, and in her honour General Goodenough gave a

luncheon party. The guests were middle-aged and old. He regretfully confessed that he knew nobody, save Jane herself, to be described as still of the rising generation.

Their friendship grew swiftly during the concluding days of her visit ; and yet, though he lived for five years longer, Jane never saw her godfather again after she bade him " good-night " on her last evening at Pole Manor. For strange things fell out in the final hour of their companionship, and, after dinner, a trivial accident created vast mental changes in their relations from which the veteran found himself unable to recover.

He had promised to give her mementoes, and ordered to his study a large tin cabin box of a vanished type, which he told her was filled with Indian relics.

" I haven't opened it for forty years," he said, " and yours shall be the hand that does. I flung a thousand things into it when I was packing to come home—gifts from native friends, curios, and odds and ends of every description. It will amuse us, Jane, and if there is anything among these treasures that you admire, it shall be yours."

The box indeed offered excellent entertainment and proved to contain trinkets of value among much that was valueless ; but everything had a history for General Goodenough : everything reminded him of some Eastern incident ; he blamed himself heartily that he had never been at the trouble to open the box before, and censured the bygone native servant who had finished his packing.

" I have wondered about that tiger-skin for a generation and never dreamed it was here," he said. " But it's not done for. These metal boxes are vermin-proof, as Indian boxes need to be."

They rummaged together, and he presently presented Jane with a bizarre, but valuable ornament—a golden Buddha with ruby eyes. Then dipping again, he exclaimed in triumph and dragged to the light a roll of faded papers.

" Now, with a shadow of good fortune," he said, " I shall find you something you will value above rubies, Jane."

The roll contained photographs, and he handed to her old, wet-plate pictures of scenery—the Taj, Benares, and familiar wonders. There were groups of natives, too, and elephants and photographs of the chase ; but he same at last upon what he sought and, having looked upon it, handed to Jane a picture of a group of officers in mufti. They wore Early Victorian peg-top trousers and black coats. They were, for the most part, hirsute men, with big beards, long whiskers and moustaches, after the fashion of the time. Some sat, some stood round their colonel—a handsome, grey-whiskered soldier in a white sun-helmet.

" The third from the left is your father, Jane," said General Goodenough, and she thanked him very gratefully.

" That, indeed, will be precious above anything in the world, Godfather ! " she cried. Then she took it ; and, though hungry to see the vanished face, her eyes never reached it. They were arrested by another—one never to be seen again, yet intensely familiar to her. Jane's wish was gratified ; she had the " one more peep " into the past that she desired.

Fortified by her own character and with a tremendous effort, she controlled herself and spoke before her voice had time to waver.

" Who is the second from the left ? " she asked, and the General laughed, as yet not conscious of her profound agitation.

" You mustn't fall in love with him, child ! He doesn't look like that now, though still in the land of the living. That was how your godparent appeared in his green youth—not a bad-looking——"

He broke off at sight of her face.

" My God ! My God ! I forgot," he whispered, stumbling over the words ; and then he seemed to crumple in his chair and shrink under her stare. He fell back and put his hand over his eyes, as though to hide Jane's face, or his own. She, too, was terribly moved ; her countenance grew scarlet, then turned very pale. Her beating heart made her pant.

They were silent for some moments and she breathed hard, grew calmer and wondered what to do or say. She tried to speak and could not ; for it seemed that speech was denied her, or any immediate power of uttering the deep sympathy and compassion that alone filled her mind.

It was her godfather who broke the silence.

" Leave me," he said. " Go to your room now. Retire quickly—quickly, please, Jane."

Something quite unlike her unemotional self hovered over Jane's mind and prompted her to get up and kiss the old man. It seemed that such a caress—a thing she had never offered or imagined until now—might better tell him what was in her heart than words. But her womanly impulse clashed with her inherent quality and character. She felt what any woman might have felt ; but it was something that this woman could not translate into action.

She merely obeyed, went hurriedly, stupidly from the room and, glancing back, saw that his face was still hidden. Her last recollection of him centred about two gout-worn hands and the long, crippled fingers spread over his forehead.

She did not sleep that night, and planned, hour after hour, what she should say next morning ; but when day came and she descended to breakfast, Jane heard that the General was indisposed and much regretted his inability to take a farewell. He would write. And in a week, after she was at home again and a new term beginning, Jane Campbell received a parcel containing a letter, the jewelled Buddha and a flat envelope with the group which embraced her father. The owner had left it just as she set it down in his study, without erasure or defacement.

" *Dear Goddaughter,*" *he wrote,* " *here are your father's picture and your toy. It is no fault of yours that you should have stumbled on agonies that I believed long hidden from any possibility of human knowledge. Even to your father, my best friend on earth, I never imparted the truth. Only an old man's treacherous memory is to be blamed for your shock. But since you know so much, hear all ; and then forget all.*

" *A sort of men are often purer and nobler at one-and-twenty than twenty years afterward. Into adolescence such men take something sweet from childhood, and some it never leaves ; while for the majority it fades and they forget their earlier ideals.*

" *For May Ellis I entertained a worship and reverence that would have scorned anything base or evil ; and, while no paragon, the legend that has grown round my youth owes its colour more to the false story of Peacock House than the true story of my life. If you can remember my arguments in our last conversation you may discount the special pleading ; and further, you may for ever believe that the girl was as pure in soul and flesh as any saint of God. We were a pair of fools, but our actions never exceeded folly.*

" *I knew all manner of people in my harum-scarum country life, and on the hunting field had no difficulty in finding common acquaintance who introduced me to Jonathan Foster. He hoped, through me, to enlarge his own circle, and offered me hospitality, ignorant of the past. He liked me and had no reason not to do so. But he was morbidly jealous of his wife from the first, and when, unknown to her or me, our past*

He seemed to crumple in his chair and shrink under her stare.

relations came to his ears, he allowed himself to read evil into my continued friendship, and quickly created out of a poisoned spirit the conventional disaster for himself. It possessed him, but he concealed it so carefully that his wife did not guess it. She valued him and respected him, for he was a kind and amiable man until the well-springs of his nature were fouled by his imaginary wrongs.

" On the day of his crime and death—all, if expanded, so natural and inevitably springing from our ignorance and his infatuation—I came, at the man's invitation, to dine with him and his wife on a day in June. And I brought news that I had obtained a commission in the Army, and was about to go abroad. We had finished our meal when the storm broke upon us and he denounced us with horrible bitterness, pouring forth a volume of words that led to the final declaration of his purpose. He would not hear me or his wife ; he would not suffer the tissue of imaginary evil he had woven to be broken down. He was a raving maniac for five minutes, and then, drawing a pistol from his breast, he destroyed May.

" And to the Army I went, indeed, enlisting at Exeter, as ' George Good-enough ' on the morning after I had seen the girl murderered and slain her assassin.

" Men did not rise from the ranks in those days, but I was favoured and given the choice between the new Victoria Cross, won in the Mutiny, or a commission. I chose the latter, and when I retired, finding it possible to end my days where I began them, for reasons beyond reason, did so, and spent most of my means in the repurchase of Pole Manor.

" We must not meet again, Jane, because neither of us can be asked to endure any such ordeal now ; but I shall think with affection of you, as you will live to know ; and you, of your charity, must hold me in Christian remembrance if you can.

" Your affectionate Godfather,

" George Goodenough."

Jane pondered long upon this letter and wondered, in her matter-of-fact way, why he had not even asked her to keep silence. He had taken that for granted, and it pleased her he should do so. Henceforward, once a year, she sent him a Christmas card, and devoted much trouble to appropriate words that should go with the picture. And he always wrote and thanked her—in caligraphy that grew more shaky year by year.

When he died, the little he had to leave came to Jane, and she sold Pole Manor for seven thousand pounds. All her life she wondered why the old man had found himself unable to endure the sight of her, or the sound of her voice. Her imagination extended to no solution. And yet imagination seemed to lift a sort of dim question in her head, or heart, sometimes.

"If I had kissed him on that awful night—I wonder——?" she would muse.

THE VANISHING DIAMOND

AT the best of times Dr. Priestley's study, with its heavy furniture and walls lined with dark oak presses, was inclined to be gloomy. At ten o'clock on this particular December morning a dark pall of smoky fog hung over London, and it would have been almost impossible to see across the room, but for the warm glow shed by the carefully shaded lamps.

Dr. Priestley's face was in the shadow. He was leaning back in his chair, dictating, in a deliberate and rather monotonous voice, a series of notes to his secretary, Harold Merefield. The notes dealt with some highly abstruse branch of science, and seemed to Merefield as dismal as the day itself.

In spite of all his efforts, his attention persisted in wandering from the subject in hand. He was aware of the traffic passing the window, of the thousand and one sounds that go to make up the confused murmur of London. As his pencil travelled over the paper mechanically, he caught a glimpse of a large closed car advancing slowly along Westbourne Terrace. It was driven by a chauffeur in a smart livery, who glanced at the houses as he passed, as though seeking a particular number. To Merefield's surprise the car drew up just beyond the window, and a second later he heard the faint sound of the front door bell. A feeling of profound relief swept through him as he realised that this must be a visitor for Dr. Priestley. This meant, at least, a break in the monotony of taking down these interminable notes !

The door opened, and Dr. Priestley's parlourmaid entered the room unobtrusively. But, instead of approaching her master, she came across to Merefield's chair and whispered a few words in his ear. Merefield listened in astonishment, and then glanced apprehensively towards his employer.

Dr. Priestley's expression showed his annoyance at the interruption. " Well, what is it ? " he asked impatiently.

" It's a friend of mine, sir, Wilmot Lillingston," replied Merefield. " He says he wants to see me most urgently. I'll send a message out to him to come some other time——"

But Dr. Priestley interrupted him. " Really, people are most inconsiderate ! " he exclaimed, frowning. " They seem to think that the time of other people is always at their disposal. No, go and and see what he wants, I shall merely be interrupted again if you do not. But see to it that you waste as little time as possible."

Merefield left the room, to return again in less than five minutes. Dr. Priestley motioned him to his chair, and prepared to continue his dictation. But Merefield coughed apologetically. " It seems rather a queer business, sir," he ventured. " Lillingston is very anxious that I should speak to you about it."

" Speak to me ! " exclaimed Dr. Priestley. " What possible concern can I have with your friend's business ? "

" Well, it's like this, sir," replied Merefield, floundering desperately in his confusion. " Wilmot's father has lost a diamond, and Wilmot came here to ask me if I could persuade you to help him find it. He says that he doesn't like to go to the police, under the circumstances. His father's a diamond merchant, and Wilmot's his partner, and they've got offices in Hatton Garden. But the diamond was lost in his house at Weybridge, and Wilmot says he seems nearly frantic."

Dr. Priestley looked over his glasses at his secretary with an expression of marked disfavour. " I gather from that rigmarole that your friend's father has lost a diamond at Weybridge," he said. " But I still fail to see why my assistance should be sought to recover it."

" Well, sir, there's a suspicion that it's been stolen," replied Merefield desperately. " And I thought perhaps that the case might interest you."

Dr. Priestley pushed aside his papers. " Since you have completely interrupted my train of thought, I may as well hear the facts," he said, with an air of resignation. " As you seem incapable of repeating them intelligibly, you had better bring your friend in here."

Merefield dashed out of the room, and returned with Wilmot Lillingston, whom he introduced to Dr. Priestley. He was a bright, well-set up young fellow of about Merefield's own age—

they had, in fact, been at school together, and had kept in touch with one another since.

"It's very good of you to see me, sir," he said, and at the respectful tone of his voice Dr. Priestley's expression relaxed somewhat. "It's awful cheek my coming here at all, but really, I didn't know what else to do. The governor seems to be in a fearful state, and when he talked about a private detective I thought of you at once."

"I am not a private detective," remarked Dr. Priestley severely.

"No, sir, of course not," replied young Lillingston hastily. "I didn't mean that at all. But Harold has told me about some of the problems you've solved, and I thought you might consent to help us with this one."

"Even I cannot be expected to solve a problem without being informed of its nature," said Dr. Priestley tolerantly. "What is it exactly that you wish me to do for you?"

But when it came to it, it soon transpired that Wilmot Lillingston knew very little. He and his father were in partnership as diamond merchants. His father, his sister and himself lived at a house called Fir Grove, near Weybridge. On the previous day Wilmot had been out of London on business, had spent the night with some friends, and had reached the office at half-past nine in the morning. There he had found his father's chauffeur waiting for him, with a note from his master. The handwriting of the note betrayed the writer's agitation. It said that a diamond of inestimable value had been stolen from Fir Grove the previous evening, but that it was impossible to approach the police on the matter. Wilmot was to secure the services of a private detective at once, and bring him down to Fir Grove as soon as possible.

"I thought I'd come to you, first, sir," continued Wilmot Lillingston. "At least you might know of somebody I could go to. What this diamond is, or how it came to be at Fir Grove, I don't know. Nobody at the office seems to know anything about it."

Dr. Priestley nodded, but for a moment or two made no reply. "Your father's note seems to suggest that this is not an ordinary case of theft," he remarked at last. "Do you think that it would help to set his mind at rest if I were to accompany you to Weybridge?"

"The governor and I shall be eternally grateful to you if you will, sir," replied Wilmot fervently.

In just over the hour Dr. Priestley, Harold Merefield and Wilmot arrived at Fir Grove. It was a fair-sized house, standing by itself in an extensive garden, and hidden from the road by a belt of trees. Wilmost hurried the party through the front door and into the hall, where they were met by a smart parlour-maid. In answer to Wilmot's question she informed him that his father was in his study, which he had not left during the whole morning.

Mr. Oscar Lillingston was a middle-aged man, with a nervous manner which, somehow, did not preclude a certain natural dignity. He listened in silence as his son explained how he had persuaded Dr. Priestley to come down, and then turned to the latter.

" It is more than kind of you to put yourself out for a complete stranger, Dr. Priestley," he said. " Perhaps you and Mr. Merefield will sit down and make yourselves comfortable? You, Wilmot, had better get back to the office at once, as there are several matters of importance to attend to. I shall probably not be able to leave here to-day."

Wilmot, thus summarily dismissed, disappeared, leaving his father alone with his visitors. Mr. Lillingston fussed about the room for a few minutes, attending to the comfort of his guests, while Dr. Priestley, as was his habit, took stock of the room in which he found himself.

It was a fairly large room, comfortably furnished, with a number of arm-chairs set round an old-fashioned fireplace. At one side of this fireplace was an alcove, in which stood a table. On the table was a reading-lamp, with a flexible cord leading to a plug in the wall. The only other means of illuminating the room was a three-light pendant hung from the centre of the ceiling. Against the wall on the opposite side of the room to the alcove was a metal stand, upon which stood a small safe which Dr. Priestley recognised as being of the most modern construction. There was only one door, which opened into the passage by which the room was approached. Opposite the door was a bay window, heavily barred.

Mr. Oscar Lillingston seated himself at last, and as the light from the window fell on his face Dr. Priestley saw that it was haggard and lined. " I have asked you to make yourself comfortable here, for this reason, Dr. Priestley," he said. " This is the room from which the diamond disappeared so mysteriously yesterday evening, about half-past nine.

" I must explain that, for the last few months, I and four

friends have been negotiating for the purchase of one of the most valuable stones in existence. We have, in India, a customer for this stone, and we hoped to make a considerable profit by its re-sale. You will understand that it was necessary to conduct such delicate negotiations in the strictest secrecy. Only my four friends, myself, and the former possessor of the stone knew that they were in progress. Even my son was in ignorance of the very existence of the stone.

" The negotiations were finally concluded this week. The seller of the stone arrived from Amsterdam yesterday. I had expected him, and had sent my son into the country on some trumped-up business, with the suggestion that he might care to spend the night with some friends of his. The seller of the stone handed it over to me in my office, and I paid him in notes. He then left at once on his return to Amsterdam. I am perfectly certain, not only that no one was aware of the transaction, but that no living soul but our two selves knew that any transaction had taken place.

" I immediately locked the stone away in the safe in my office, which is exactly similar to the one you see in this room. I then telephoned to my four friends in succession, inviting them here to dinner at half-past seven. This was an arrangement which we had previously made, since we did not care to mention the purchase of the stone on the telephone."

" Then, as soon as your friends received your message, they knew that the purchase had been completed ? " Dr. Priestley asked.

" Yes, and they knew that the stone would be produced for their inspection that evening."

" At what time did you send the messages ? "

" Between three and half-past. The seller left my office just before three. I left myself soon after four, carrying the stone with me. As soon as I arrived here, I placed it in the safe in this room. My friends—their names are Darell, Harvey, Pedder and Tomlinson, duly arrived. The first two drove down in their own cars, the others came by train. We had dinner, and about nine o'clock we left the dining-room and came in here.

" The room was exactly as you see it now, with the lamps in the centre pendant alight. You will see that here by the fireplace are two switches, one controlling the pendant, the other the reading-lamp on the table in the alcove. The reading-lamp was not then switched on. The window was closed, and, in any case, no one could have entered the room by it, owing to the bars. There is a considerable drop from the window into the garden, owing to the ground sloping from the front to the rear of the house, and the window, as you see, is exceptionally low. The bars were presumably put there to prevent any one falling out. The heavy curtain that you see was drawn across the bay.

" I gave a detailed account of the purchase, and my friends and I discussed this matter for some minutes. We were sitting in a circle round the fire, Pedder nearest the door, Darell next to him, myself in the centre, Harvey on my left, and Tomlison next to him. My friends were naturally anxious to see the stone, and I got up to fetch it. I unlocked the safe, took out the small tin box in which the stone was contained, and opened it. The stone was in its place, wrapped up in cotton wool. I then passed the box to Tomlinson, as being the nearest to me.

" Now, Tomlinson's sight is not very good. He peered at the stone for a moment, and then said, as nearly as I can remember his words. ' I can't see the blessed thing properly in this light. Can't you switch on this reading-lamp, Lillingston ? '

" As he spoke, he turned in his chair and put the box down on the table in the alcove. I leant forward to switch on the light—I could reach the switch from where I was sitting. The moment I touched the switch, a very queer thing happened. The lamps in the pendant went out suddenly, and the room was plunged in complete darkness.

" There was instant confusion, as you may suppose. The diamond was the first thought of each of us. I jumped up, and tried the switches every way, but no light came. As I was doing this, I heard Tomlinson call out, ' Here, what's the game ? What's all this foolery ? ' Then Pedder, who was nearest the door, got up and opened it, thinking there would be a light in the passage, but that had failed too. At this, he called out something about fetching candles.

" Meanwhile, every one had been hunting for matches, but it must have been at least twenty seconds before one was struck. Harvey was the first to get a light, and he held it up at arm's length. We were all on our feet by now, crowding towards the table. The tin box was still there, but the diamond had disappeared.

" For a moment or two we stood looking at one another stupidly, and then I heard a noise in the doorway, and saw Vera, the parlourmaid who met you just now, standing there, looking at us with astonishment, as well she might. She had heard Pedder call out and had come to see what was wanted. She said that the lights in the rest of the house were all right, and I told her to bring candles. She did not come inside the room then,. and when, a minute or two later she brought the candles, I took them from her myself at the door.

"When she had gone, we sat down again in a very embarrassed silence. One thing perfectly clear to all of us. The diamond could not have left the room, since nobody had entered or left it. Nor could it have been thrown out of the window or the door. Indeed, it seemed to me that the only person who could have touched it was Tomlinson, since none of the others could have reached it without disturbing his neighbour.

"It was the most uncomfortable experience I have ever known. We all looked suspiciously at one another, and then began to search the room by the light of the candles. The stone was nearly the size of a pullet's egg, and would have sparkled in the first ray of light that fell upon it, so there was no possibility of overlooking it. We searched in every likely and unlikely place, each watching the others, until at last, when we had thoroughly ransacked the room, we gave it up in despair.

"I think it was Darell who was the first to express what we were all feeling. 'This is damned nasty,' he said. 'We all know the stone's in this room somewhere. There's nothing for it but for each of us to submit to a search. You can start with me, if you like.'

"Nobody made any objection, though they knew the ordeal that was before them. A space was cleared in the middle of the room, and each of us in turn stood there and stripped himself to the skin, while the others went over every inch of his clothes and his body. I may say that we all of us had a complete knowledge of the methods used by diamond thieves, and our examination was thorough. When it was over, we were all satisfied that none of us was in possession of the diamond.

"A consultation was held, and it was agreed that since the diamond had been lost in my house, I must be responsible to the rest for its value. I may tell you, Dr. Priestley, that this means that unless the stone is found, I shall be reduced to beggary. Further, it was agreed that since the whole success of the deal depended upon the existence of the stone being kept secret, the police were not to be called in except as a last resource."

Dr. Priestley, who had listened attentively to Mr. Lillingston's story, nodded his head in sign of comprehension. "If the diamond should fall into the hands of one member of the syndicate, would he be able to complete the transaction with your customer by himself ? " he asked.

"Certainly. Our customer is so anxious to obtain the stone that he would purchase it from whoever offered it to him."

" I see. Now, during the search of the room, was anything found that might not be expected ? "

"Nothing whatever. Harvey found a sixpence under his chair, which had probably fallen out of his pocket while he was searching for matches. He put it on the mantelpiece, where it still is."

Without a word Dr. Priestley rose to his feet, walked across to the mantelpiece, and picked up the coin. There was nothing unusual about it, except that on one side it bore a minute black stain.

" Who else, besides the members of the syndicate, were in the house yesterday evening ? " asked Dr. Priestley, absent-mindedly putting the sixpence in his pocket.

" My daughter, who had acted as hostess during dinner, was in the drawing-room. Vera was in the dining-room, clearing away, which accounts for her hearing Pedder's call. The cook and housemaid were in the kitchen."

" How long had the three servants been in your employ ? "

" Only since I bought this house, six weeks ago. Before then, we lived in a service flat. On leaving London, we put an advertisement in *The Times*, and selected these three from the replies we received."

" Had any members of the syndicate visited you here before ? "

" No. They are old acquaintances of mine, and were often at the flat in London. But they had never been here. The dinner last night was in the nature of a house-warming, as well as an opportunity for viewing the diamond."

" When did your daughter know that the dinner was to be held ? She must have had time to make some preparation."

" The evening before last. I knew when I came home that I was to expect the seller of the stone yesterday, and I warned her then that I was asking four friends to dinner. But neither she nor anybody else in the house had an inkling that the diamond would be in the house, or that it ever existed."

" Are you in the habit of bringing home valuable stones for your friends' inspection ? "

" I have never done such a thing before. I only did so

on this occasion because I did not want my office staff to know anything of the stone."

" Who has had access to this room since your friends left yesterday evening ? "

" I have not left this room since the stone disappeared. I spent the night in the very chair you see me in now. Early this morning I sent for my chauffeur, an old and trusted servant, and told him to investigate the cause of the failure of the light. He did so, and said——"

" I should like to question him on that subject myself, if you have no objection, Mr. Lillingston. Has any one else entered the room ? "

" Not until you and Mr. Merefield came in just now."

" Excellent ! Now, one more question, Mr. Lillingston. You are absolutely certain that the light failed at the very instant that you put your hand on the switch of the reading-lamp ? "

" Absolutely. So much so that for the moment I thought I had touched the switch of the pendant and pressed it the wrong way."

" Very well. Now, perhaps, I might be allowed to question the chauffeur ? "

Mr. Lillingston rung the bell and when Vera appeared, gave orders that the chauffeur was to be sent for. He came within a few minutes, and Mr. Lillingston nodded towards a chair. " Sit down, Burdock," he said. " This gentleman would like to ask you a few questions."

Burdock sat down rather gingerly, and Dr. Priestley turned towards him. " When Mr. Lillingston sent for you and told you that the lights in here had failed, what did you do ? " he asked.

" First thing I did, sir, was to look at the lights themselves," replied Burdock briskly. " I took out the lamps, but there was nothing wrong with them or the fittings. So I knew that it was probably a fuse blown. I went to the fuse-box——"

" Where is the fuse-box fitted ? " Dr. Priestley interrupted.

" In the kitchen, sir. I went to the fuse-box, opened it, and found as I expected that the fuse protecting this circuit had blown."

" What lamps are on this circuit ? "

" The ones in this room, the passage, and Mr. Wilmot's bedroom above this, sir."

" Did you find any reason for the fuse having blown ? "

" No, sir, I didn't. Fuses do blow at times, there's no accounting for why."

"The fuse-box had not been interfered with in any way?"

"No, sir, everything was in order. The box hadn't been opened for some time. I could see that. There was a cobweb right across it."

"Did you test the circuit after you had replaced the fuse?"

"Yes, sir. That was all that was wrong. I'll show you, sir." He got up and switched on the lights one after the other. Both the pendant and the reading-lamp came on and lighted perfectly.

"That is a powerful light you have in the reading-lamp," remarked Dr. Priestley.

"Yes, a hundred candle-power," replied Mr. Lillingston. "A powerful light is usually necessary for examining stones."

Burdock was dismissed, and Dr. Priestley requested that the cook might be sent for. She arrived, a large and forbidding-looking woman, and sat down with an air of great dignity.

"Now, Mrs. Lush, would you mind telling me where you were at about half-past nine last night?" Dr. Priestley asked.

"I was in the kitchen, sir, having a cup of tea with Annie, who's the housemaid. There was a cup poured out for Vera, but she hadn't finished clearing up, seeing that there'd been company. I was just saying to Annie that she couldn't be much longer, when there was a pop and a flash from that electric thing up on the wall. I was that startled I upset my teacup. I don't like them things, they're not safe, in my opinion. Never was brought up to them, and that's a fact. Then in runs Vera, saying that the light's gone out in the study, and the gentlemen was in a terrible way about it, and wanted some candles."

"Did Vera say how she knew this?"

"Why, yes, sir. She said she was in the hall, carrying a tray from the dining-room, when she heard the study door open and somebody call out. She started to see what was up, and when she got to the passage she found it all in darkness."

Mrs. Lush was dismissed in her turn, and Dr. Priestley strolled over to the reading-lamp, picked it up, and examined it closely. He remained absorbed in it for so long that Mr. Lillingston could not restrain his impatience. He fussed about the room for some moments, and then burst out. "If you'll forgive me saying so, Dr. Priestley. I don't see that these inquiries can help us much to find the diamond. You see, every minute is of importance——"

"The diamond?" replied Dr. Priestley. "Ah, yes, of course. It is perfectly plain how it disappeared, but the difficulty is to determine what became of it subsequently. But I think I see how we can discover that. Will you lend me Burdock and your car for the rest of the day, Mr. Lillingston? And, if you don't mind, I'll take that reading-lamp with me."

"With the greatest of pleasure. But I confess I don't understand how——"

"I hope to be able to explain that later. Now you said that yesterday afternoon you telephoned to your friends. Will you let me have a list of their names, with the numbers to which you telephoned?"

Mr. Lillingston wrote these out on a piece of paper, and gave it to Dr. Priestley. "Is there anything else before you go?" he asked.

"I think not, thank you; the less time that is wasted now the better. I venture to suggest that it is unnecessary for you to continue your vigil any longer. Wherever the diamond may be now, I am certain that it is not in this room. By the way, when you and your friends came in here after dinner, did you allocate their chairs to them yourself?"

"Oh, no, they sat down where they liked," replied Mr. Lillingston, opening the door. The three passed along the passage into the hall where they met a girl whom Dr. Priestley would have recognised as Miss Lillingston from her likeness to her brother, even without her father's introduction.

"Did you happen to be at home yesterday afternoon, Miss Lillingston?" Dr. Priestley asked her.

"Yes, all the time," she replied. "I didn't go out at all after lunch."

"Did you receive any telephone messages?"

"No, I don't think I did. I answered the telephone once, I remember, but the message was for Vera, from her brother. Her mother has been ill, and he has rung up several times lately. He asked me to tell her that her mother was very much better."

The car was already at the door, and Dr. Priestley and Merefield entered it. They drove first to Scotland Yard, where Dr. Priestley had a brief interview with an old friend of his, Superintendent Hanslet. He requested him to perform a small service for him, and Hanslet made no difficulty about consenting. "I'll find out for you, and ring you up at your house in two or three hours' time," he said.

The next call was at the laboratory of an analytical chemist. Here Dr. Priestley left the reading-lamp, with the request that the contact points of the lamp-holder should be very carefully examined. Then Dr. Priestley ordered Burdock to drive to

Westbourne Terrace, and await further instructions. And, once comfortably installed in his study, Dr. Priestley, to Merefield's supreme disgust, placidly resumed the dictation which had been interrupted that morning.

About three o'clock a messenger came from the analyst, bearing the reading-lamp and a note for Dr. Priestley, which the latter read and put in his pocket. A little later the telephone rang, and Superintendent Hanslet asked to speak to Dr. Priestley. His message was a brief one, and concerned a toll call made from London to Weybridge on the previous afternoon.

Dr. Priestley put down the receiver and smiled. " So that little matter is settled," he remarked complacently. " It only remains to restore the diamond to the custody of Mr. Lillingston. Will you get him on the telephone for me, please, Harold ? "

As soon as the call was through, Dr. Priestley took the instrument and spoke in a tone of command. " Is that you, Mr. Lillingston ? I hope to return to Fir Grove in time for dinner. Meanwhile, will you please request your four friends to call upon you at nine o'clock this evening, without fail ? The matter is of the utmost urgency. I am happy to be able to tell you that the police have discovered the identity of the person who stole the diamond, though they have not laid hands on the stone itself. They will make an arrest in your house at ten o'clock, and for that purpose the presence of all the members of the syndicate will be necessary.

" Will you please telephone to them all at once, giving them this message. Do not breathe a word to anybody else, and do not allow any one but yourself to use your telephone for the rest of the day."

And with this Dr. Priestley replaced the receiver, before the astonished Mr. Lillingston had any chance to reply.

Merefield, who had been listening open-mouthed to this extraordinary message, would have made some remark but Dr. Priestley cut him short. " You can tell Burdock that we shall be ready to drive back to Fir Grove in two hours' time," he said. " That, I think, will give us time to finish the notes we began this morning."

It was seven o'clock when they reached Fir Grove. Mr. Lillingston was waiting for them with ill-concealed impatience, but Dr. Priestley refused point-blank to discuss the affair of the diamond. As soon as he was assured that his message had been given to all the members of the syndicate, and that each one had promised to come, he replaced the reading-lamp in Mr.

Lillingston's room with his own hands, and turned the conversation into an entirely different channel.

Dinner was over at last, and shortly before nine the members of the syndicate began to arrive one by one. They looked suspiciously at one another and at Mr. Lillingston, and were only barely civil when the latter introduced them to Dr. Priestley and Merefield. As soon as they were all assembled, Dr. Priestley took charge of affairs.

" I am anxious to reproduce as nearly as possible the conditions of yesterday evening, before the police arrive," he said. " This room is arranged in exactly the same way as before. Mr. Lillingston, will you place the tin box in which the diamond was contained on the table ? Thank you. Now, gentlemen, will you each kindly take the chairs which you occupied last night."

The company settled themselves down uncomfortably. None of those present seemed to have anything to say. The light from the pendant flooded the room with a soft and subdued glow, leaving the corners in deep shadow. Dr. Priestley glanced round, and then, without being observed, pressed the bell.

The silence was becoming more and more uncomfortable when the door opened suddenly. All turned sharply, expecting the arrival of the police. But it was only Vera. She stood at the door looking expectantly towards her master.

" What is it, Vera ? " asked Mr. Lillingston testily.

" I thought I heard the bell ring, sir," replied Vera.

Mr. Lillingston was about to dismiss her, when Dr. Priestley stepped forward. " One moment," he said, drawing a coin from his pocket. " I have here a sixpence, which belongs to you, I think. It was found on the floor of this room shortly after a valuable object disappeared from that table. I think the police may be interested in that sixpence, Vera."

The girl staggered as though she had been struck. But Dr. Priestley was no longer looking at her. He was watching the members of the syndicate, whose faces expressed the amazement they felt at this extraordinary speech. All but Pedder, seated nearest the door, who sprang to his feet and started to speak incoherently.

But Dr. Priestley waved him imperiously to his seat. " One moment, Mr. Pedder," he said. " There are still a few minutes to go before the police arrive. Please do not leave the room for a minute, Vera. Stay just where you are. Now, in order to reproduce exactly the events of yesterday evening, would you mind switching on the reading-lamp, Mr. Lillingston ? "

Mr. Lillingston leaned forward to touch the switch, and immediately the room was plunged into utter darkness.

So utterly taken by surprise were the whole company that for an instant there was silence. Then arose a confused clamour of imprecation, and as before a search for matches. Merefield would have joined this search, but Dr. Priestley gripped him by the arm. "Stay where you are," he whispered.

At last a match flared up, a feeble glimmer in the wide spaces of the room. But from the table in the alcove came back an answering sparkle, seeming brighter than the flame which it reflected. And suddenly Tomlinson, seated nearest to it, leapt to his feet with a startled exclamation.

"By God ! The diamond ! "

Dr. Priestley's hand was still on Merefield's arm. He impelled him from the room, and out through the passage into the hall. "Put on your coat and hat, quickly ! " he ordered. "We will leave these people to settle their own affairs between them."

It was not until they had once more reached Westbourne Terrace that Dr. Priestley condescended to explain the mysterious vanishing and reappearance of the diamond. "The trick was childishly simple," he said. "I detected it as soon as I heard that a sixpence had been picked up on the floor.

"The whole matter depended, of course, upon the sudden failure of the light. Now fuses do not blow without some cause, which is usually a short circuit somewhere in the system. Such a short circuit can easily be caused by removing a lamp from its holder, and inserting a piece of metal in the holder across the contacts. If this piece of metal is not too thick, the lamp can then be replaced in the holder. A sixpence fulfils this condition admirably.

"The sixpence picked up showed a small stain at one point. The analyst to whom I took the reading-lamp found that one of the contacts of the holder bore minute traces of silver on the point. Both the stain and the silver deposit are exactly what might be expected from the momentary passage of the heavy current which blew the fuse.

"Now, who had inserted the sixpence in the holder? Obviously some one at Fir Grove who had access to Mr. Lillingston's room. But nobody in the house knew that the diamond was to be inspected that evening. On the other hand, all the members of the syndicate knew that the diamond would be so inspected as soon as it was purchased, but they did not know of the purchase until three to half-past that afternoon.

" The obvious deduction was that one of the syndicate was in league with some one in the house, and had evolved a scheme for the abstraction of the stone. It would be necessary for the former to warn the latter that the time had come. Hence my question to Miss Lillingston about the telephone message. I learnt that Vera had received a message that afternoon which was in all probability a code signal to her.

" Here Inspector Hanslet assisted me. I gave him a list of telephone numbers of the members of the syndicate and asked him to find out from the various exchanges concerned if a call to Weybridge had been made from any of those numbers. His message to me was to the effect that such a call had been made from Pedder's number.

" I could then reconstruct exactly the method by which the diamond had been abstracted. I do not know who Vera really is, but I suspect that she is in some way intimately connected with Pedder. No doubt the outlines of the scheme were concerted between them before she answered Miss Lillingston's advertisement for a parlourmaid. Pedder would keep in touch with her, I expect, on her days out and by telephoning to her as her brother on the subject of a supposed illness of her mother.

" Yesterday evening, being warned that the time had come, she left the dining-room shortly before Mr. Lillingston and his guests. She went to his study, inserted the sixpence, and hid behind the curtains drawn across the bay. When the light went out, she slipped out, took the diamond, and removed the sixpence. In the dark this fell on the floor. Then, in the confusion she made her way to the door.

" Pedder, who had purposely sat down next the door, opened it, and called out, thus allowing Vera to slip out into the dark passage. When she appeared in the doorway after the match had been struck, she explained her presence by the fact that she had heard Pedder's call. She still had the diamond about her person. I expect that as she went for the candles she slipped it into the pocket of Peddar's overcoat as it hung in the hall."

Dr. Priestley paused finally as though that concluded the matter. But Merefield was not yet satisfied. " But what about our adventure this evening, sir ? " he asked.

" That surely was obvious," replied Dr. Priestley impatiently. " The problem was to get the stone back with as little unpleasantness as possible. Hence my message to Mr. Lillingston

for transmission to his friends. The only one of them who
would understand it was Pedder, and to him it could only mean
that Vera was to be arrested. He could only avert this by
the return of the stone before ten o'clock.

"I summoned Vera to the room and made it plain to her
that the trick had been discovered. Pedder would have confessed and produced the stone then, had I not stopped him.
But I had thought of an easier course for him. I gave him and
Vera an opportunity of replacing the stone by the same method
as that by which it had been abstracted."

"But how did you contrive that the light should go out
a second time, sir?"

"By the simple process of inserting another sixpence when
I replaced the reading-lamp," replied Dr. Priestley, with a
smile. "It will be interesting to learn whether the discovery
of that coin will enlighten Mr. Lillingston as to the cause of
the mystery."

STALEY FLEMING'S
HALLUCINATION

OF two men who were talking, one was a physician.
"I sent for you, Doctor," said the other, "but I don't
think you can do me any good. Maybe you can recommend a specialist in psychopathy. I fancy I'm a bit loony."

"You look all right," the physician said.

"You shall judge—I have hallucinations. I wake every night
and see in my room, intently watching me, a big black Newfoundland dog with a white forefoot."

"You say you wake ; are you sure about that? 'Hallucinations' are sometimes only dreams."

"Oh, I wake all right. Sometimes I lie still a long time,
looking at the dog as earnestly as the dog looks at me—I always
leave the light going. When I can't endure it any longer I sit
up in bed—and nothing is there !"

"'M, 'm—what is the beast's expression?"

"It seems to me sinister. Of course I know that, except in
art, an animal's face in repose has always the same expression.
But this is not a real animal. Newfoundland dogs are pretty
mild looking, you know ; what's the matter with this one?"

"Really, my diagnosis would have no value : I am not going
to treat the dog."

The physician laughed at his own pleasantry, but narrowly
watched his patient from the corner of his eye. Presently he
said : "Fleming, your description of the beast fits the dog of the
late Atwell Barton."

Fleming half rose from his chair, sat again and made a visible
attempt at indifference. "I remember Barton," he said. "I
believe he was—it was reported that—wasn't there something
suspicious in his death?"

Looking squarely now into the eyes of his patient, the physician said : " Three years ago the body of your old enemy, Atwell Barton, was found in the woods near his house and yours. He had been stabbed to death. There have been no arrests ; there was no clue. Some of us had ' theories.' I had one. Have you ? "

" I ? Why, bless your soul, what could I know about it ? You remember that I left for Europe almost immediately afterward—a considerable time afterward. In the few weeks since my return you could not expect me to construct a ' theory.' In fact, I have not given the matter a thought. What about his dog ? "

" It was first to find the body. It died of starvation on his grave."

We do not know the inexorable law underlying coincidences. Staley Fleming did not, or he would perhaps not have sprung to his feet as the night wind brought in through the open window the long wailing howl of a distant dog. He strode several times across the room in the steadfast gaze of the physician ; then, abruptly confronting him, almost shouted : " What has all this to do with my trouble, Dr. Halderman ? You forget why you were sent for."

Rising, the physician laid his hand upon his patient's arm and said gently : " Pardon me. I cannot diagnose your disorder offhand—to-morrow, perhaps. Please go to bed, leaving your door unlocked ; I will pass the night here with your books. Can you call me without rising ? "

" Yes, there is an electric bell."

" Good. If anything disturbs you, push the button without sitting up. Good-night."

Comfortably installed in an arm-chair, the man of medicine stared into the glowing coals and thought deeply and long, but apparently to little purpose, for he frequently rose and, opening a door leading to the staircase, listened intently, then resumed his seat. Presently, however, he fell asleep, and when he woke it was past midnight. He stirred the failing fire, lifted a book from the table at his side and looked at the title. It was Denneker's *Meditations*. He opened it at random and began to read :

" Forasmuch as it is ordained of God that all flesh hath spirit and thereby taketh on spiritual powers, so, also, the spirit hath powers of the flesh, even when it is gone out of the flesh and liveth as a thing apart, as many a violence performed by wraith and lemure sheweth. And there be who say that man is not single in this, but the beasts have the like evil inducement, and——"

The reading was interrupted by a shaking of the house, as by the fall of a heavy object. The reader flung down the book, rushed from the room and mounted the stairs to Fleming's bed-chamber. He tried the door, but contrary to his instructions it was locked. He set his shoulder against it with such force that it gave way. On the floor near the disordered bed, in his night-clothes, lay Fleming, gasping away his life.

The physician raised the dying man's head from the floor and observed a wound in the throat. "I should have thought of this," he said, believing it suicide.

When the man was dead an examination disclosed the unmis-takable marks of an animal's fangs deeply sunken into the jugular veins.

But there was no animal.

THE ITALIAN'S STORY

"How well your friend speaks English!" I remarked one day to an acquaintance when I was abroad, alluding to a gentleman who had just quitted the room. "What is his name?"

"Count Francesco Ferraldi."

"I suppose he has been in England?"

"Oh, yes; he was exiled and taught Italian there. His history is very curious and would interest you, who like wonderful things."

"Can you tell it me?"

"Not correctly, as I never heard it from himself. But I believe he has no objection to tell it—with the exception of the political transactions in which he was concerned, and which caused his being sent out of the Austrian dominions; that part of it, I believe, he thinks it not prudent to allude to. We'll ask him to dinner, if you'll meet him, and perhaps we may persuade him to tell the story." Accordingly, the meeting took place; we dined *en petit comité*—and the Count very good-naturedly yielded to our request; "but you must excuse me," he said, "beginning a long way back, for my story commences three hundred years ago.

"Our family claims to be of great antiquity, but we were not very wealthy till about the latter half of the tenth century, when Count Jacopo Ferraldi made very considerable additions to the property; not only by getting, but also by saving—he was, in fact, a miser. Before that period the Ferraldis had been warriors, and we could boast of many distinguished deeds of arms recorded in our annals; but Jacopo, although by the death of his brother he ultimately inherited the title and estates, had begun life as a younger son, and being

408

dissatisfied with his portion, had resolved to increase it by commerce.

" Florence then was a very different city to what it is now ; trade flourished, and its merchants had correspondence and large dealings with all the chief cities of Europe. My ancestor invested his little fortune so judiciously, or so fortunately, that he trebled it in his first venture ; and as people grow rapidly rich who gain and don't spend, he soon had wealth to his heart's content. But I am wrong in using that term as applied to him—he was never content with his gains but still worked to add to them, for he grew to love the money for itself, and not for what it might purchase.

" At length, his two elder brothers died, and as they left no issue, he succeeded to their inheritance, and dwelt in the palace of his ancestors ; but instead of circulating his riches, he hoarded them ; and being too miserly to entertain his friends and neighbours, he lived like an anchorite in his splendid halls, exulting in his possessions but never enjoying them. His great pleasure and chief occupation seems to have been counting his money, which he kept hidden in strange out-of-the-way places, or in strong iron chests clamped to the floors and walls. But, notwithstanding these precautions, and that he guarded it like a watch-dog, to his great dismay he one day missed a sum of two thousand pounds which he had concealed in an ingeniously contrived receptacle under the floor of his dining-room, the existence of which was only known to the man who made it ; at least, so he believed. Small as was this sum in proportion to what he possessed, the shock was tremendous ; he rushed out of his house like a madman with the intention of dragging the criminal to justice, but when he arrived at the man's shop he found him in bed and at the point of death. His friends and the doctor swore that he had not quitted it for a fortnight ; in short, according to their showing, he was taken ill on his return from working at the Count's, the very day he finished the job.

" If this were true, he could not be the thief, as the money was not deposited there till some days afterwards, and although the Count had his doubts, it was not easy to disprove what everybody swore, more especially as the man died on the following day, and was buried. Baffled and furious, he next fell foul of his two servants—he kept but two, for he only inhabited a small part of the palace. There was not the smallest reason to suspect them, nor to suppose they knew anything of the hiding-place, for every precaution had been used to conceal it ; moreover, he had found it locked as he himself had locked it after depositing the money, and he was quite sure the key had never been absent from his own person. Nevertheless, he discharged them and took no others. The thief, whoever he was, had evinced so much ingenuity, that he trembled to think what such skill might compass with opportunity. So he resolved to afford none ; and henceforth to have his meals sent in from a neighbouring eating-house, and to have a person once a week to sweep and clean his rooms, whom he could keep an eye on while it was doing. As he had no clue to the perpetrators of the robbery, and the man whom he had most reason to suspect was dead, he took no further steps in the business, but kept it quiet lest he should draw too much attention towards his secret hoards ; nevertheless, though externally calm, the loss preyed on his mind and caused him great anguish.

" Shortly after this occurrence, he received a letter from a sister of his who had several years before married an Englishman, saying that her husband was dead, and it being advisable that her dear and only son should enter into commerce, that she was going to send him to Florence, feeling assured that her brother would advise him for the best, and enable him to employ the funds he brought with him advantageously.

" This was not pleasing intelligence ; he did not want to promote anybody's interest but his own, and he felt that the young man would be a spy on his actions, an intruder in his house, and no doubt an expectant and greedy heir, counting the hours till he died ; for this sister and her family were his nearest of kin, and would inherit if he left no will to the contrary. However, his arrival could not be prevented ; letters travelled slowly in those days, and ere his could reach England his nephew would have quitted it, so he resolved to give him a cold reception and send him back as soon as he could.

" In the meantime, the young man had started on his journey, full of hope and confidence, and immediately on his ·arrival hastened to present himself to this rich uncle who was to show him the path he had himself followed to fortune. It was not for his own sake alone he coveted riches, but his mother and sister were but poorly provided for, and they had collected the whole of their little and risked it upon this venture, hoping, with the aid of their relative, to be amply repaid for the present sacrifice.

" A fine open-countenanced lad was Arthur Allen, just twenty years of age ; such a face and figure had not beamed on those halls for many a day. Well brought up and well instructed too ; he spoke Italian as well as English, his mother having accustomed him to it from infancy.

"Though he had heard his uncle was a miser, he had no conception of the extent to which the mania had arisen ; and his joyous anticipations were somewhat damped when he found himself so coldly received, and when he looked into those hard, grey eyes and contracted features that had never expanded with a genial smile ; so fearing the old man might be apprehensive that he had come as an applicant or for assistance to set him up in trade, he hastened to inform him of the true state of the case, saying that they had got together two thousand pounds.

" ' Of course, my mother,' he said, ' would not have entrusted my inexperience with such a sum ; but she desired me to place it in your hands, and to act entirely under your direction.'

" To use the miser's own expression—for we have learnt all these particulars from a memoir left by himself—' When I heard these words the devil entered into me, and I bade the youth bring the money and dine with me on the following day.'

" I dare say you will think the devil had entered into him long before ; however, now he had recognised his presence, but that did not deter him from following his counsel.

" Pleased that he had so far thawed his uncle's frigidity, Arthur arrived the next day with his money-bags at the appointed hour, and was received in an inner chamber ; their contents were inspected and counted, and then placed in one of the old man's iron chests. Soon afterwards, the tinkle of a bell announced that the waiter from the neighbouring traiteur's had brought the dinner, and the host left the room to see that all was ready. Presently he re-entered, and led his guest to the table. The repast was not sumptuous, but there was a bottle of old Lachryma Christi which he much recommended, and which the youth tasted with great satisfaction. But strange ! He had no sooner swallowed the first glass, than his eyes began to stare —there was a gurgle in his throat—a convulsion passed over his face—and his body stiffened.

" ' I did not look up,' says the old man in his memoir, ' for I did not like to see the face of the boy that had sat down so hearty to his dinner, so I kept on eating mine—but I heard the gurgle, and I knew what had happened ; and presently, lest the servant should come to fetch the dinner things, I pushed the table aside and opened the receptacle from which my two thousand pounds had been stolen—curses on the thief !—and

I laid the body in it, and the wine therewith. I locked it and drove in two strong nails. Then I put back the table—moved away the lad's chair and plate, unlocked the door which was fast, and sat down to finish my dinner. I could not help chuckling as I ate, to think how his had been spoilt.

" ' I closed up that apartment, as I thought there might be a smell that would raise observation, and I selected one on the opposite side of the gallery for my dining-room. All went well until the following day. I counted my two thousand pounds again and again, and I kept gloating over the recovery of it— for I felt as if it was my own money, and I had a right to seize it where I could. I wrote also to my sister, saying that her son had not arrived ; but that when he did I would do my best to forward his views. My heart was light that day—they say that's a bad sign.

" ' Yes, all was so far well ; but the next day we were two of us at dinner ! And yet I had invited no guest ; and the next—and the next—and so on—always ! As I was about to sit down, he entered and took a chair opposite me, an unbidden guest. I ceased dining at home, but it made no difference ; he came, dine where I would. This preyed upon me ; I tried not to mind, but I could not help it. Argument was vain. I lost my appetite, and was reduced nearly to death's door. At last, driven to desperation, I consulted Fra Giuseppe. He had been a fast fellow in his time, and it was said had been too impatient for his father's succession, howbeit, the old man died suddenly ; Giuseppe spent the money and then took to religion. I thought he was a proper person to consult, so I told him my case. He recommended repentance and restitution. I tried, but I could not repent, for I had got the money ; but I thought, perhaps, if I parted with it to another, I might be released ; so I looked about for an advantageous purchase, and hearing that Bartolomeo Malfi was in difficulties, I offered him two thousand pounds, money down for his land—I knew it was worth three times the sum. We signed the agreement, and then I went home and opened the door of the room where it was ; but lo ! he sat there upon the chest where the money was fast locked, and I could not get it. I peeped in two or three times, but he was always there ; so I was obliged to expend other moneys in this purchase, which vexed me, albeit the bargain was a good one. Then I consulted friend Giuseppe again, and he said nothing would do but restitution—but that was bad, so I waited ; and I said to myself. " I'll eat and care not whether he sit there or no." But, woe be to him ! He chilled the marrow of my bones, and I could not away with him ; so I said one day, " What if I go to England with the money ? " And he bowed his head.'

" The old man accordingly took the money-bags from the chest and started for England. His sister and her daughter were still living in the house they had inhabited during the husband's lifetime ; in short, it was their own ; and being attached to the place they hoped, if the young man succeeded in his undertakings, to be able to keep it. It was a small house with a garden full of flowers, which the ladies cultivated themselves. The village church was close at hand, and the church-yard adjoined the garden. The poor ladies had become very uneasy at not hearing of Arthur's arrival ; and when the old man presented himself and declared he had never seen anything of him, great was their affliction and dismay ; for it was clear that some misfortune had happened to the boy, or he had appropriated the money and gone off in some other direction. They scarcely admitted the possibility of the last contingency, although it was the one their little world universally adopted, in spite of his being a very well conducted and affectionate youth ; but people said it was too great a temptation for his years, and blamed his mother for entrusting him with so much money. Whichever it was, the blow fell very heavy on them in all ways, for Arthur was their sole stay and support, and they loved him dearly.

" Since he had set out on this journey, the old man had been relieved from the company of his terrible guest, and was beginning to recover himself a little, but it occasioned him a severe pang when he remembered that this immunity was to be purchased with the sacrifice of two thousand pounds, and he set himself to think how he could jockey the ghost. But while he was deliberating on this subject, an event happened that alarmed him for the immediate safety of the money.

" He had found, on the road, that the great weight of a certain chest he brought with him had excited observation whenever his luggage had to be moved ; on his arrival two labouring men had been called in to carry it into the house, and he had overheard some remarks that induced him to think they had drawn a right conclusion with regard to its contents. Subsequently, he saw these two men hovering about the house in a suspicious manner, and he was afraid to leave it or go to sleep at night, lest he should be robbed.

"So far we learn from Jacopo Ferraldi himself; but here the memoir stops and tradition says that he was found one morning murdered in his bed and his chest rifled. All the family, that is, the mother and daughter and their one servant, were accused of the murder ; and notwithstanding their protestation of innocence were declared guilty and executed.

"The memoir I have quoted was found on his dressing-table, and he appears to have been writing it when he was surprised by the assassins ; for the last words were—' I think I've baulked them, and nobody will understand the——' then comes a large blot and a mark, as if the pen had fallen out of his hand. It seems wonderful that this man, so suspicious and secretive, should thus have entrusted to paper what it was needful he should conceal ; but the case is not singular ; it has been remarked in similar instances, when some mystery is pressing on a human soul, that there exists an irresistible desire to communicate it, notwithstanding the peril of betrayal ; and when no other confidant can be found, the miserable wretch has often had recourse to paper.

"The family of Arthur Allen being now extinct, a cousin of Jacopo's, who was a penniless soldier, succeeded to the title and estate, and the memoir, with a full account of what had happened, being forwarded to Italy, inquiries were made about the missing two thousand pounds ; but it was not forthcoming ; and it was at first supposed that the ladies had some accomplice who had carried it off. Subsequently, however, one of the two men who had borne the money-chest into the house, at the period of the old man's arrival, was detected in endeavouring to dispose of some Italian gold and a diamond ring, which Jacopo was in the habit of wearing. This led to investigation, and he ultimately confessed to the murder committed by himself and his companion, thus exonerating the unfortunate women. He nevertheless declared that they had not rifled the strong box, as they could not open it, and were disturbed by the barking of a dog before they could search for the keys. The box itself they were afraid to carry away, it being a remarkable one and liable to attract notice ; and that therefore their only booty was some loose coin and some jewels that were found on the old man's person. But this was not believed, especially as his accomplice could not be found and appeared, on inquiry, to have left that part of the country immediately after the catastrophe.

"There the matter rested for nearly two centuries and a

half. Nobody sorrowed for Jacopo Ferraldi, and the fate of the Allens was a matter of indifference to the public, who were glad to see the estate fall into the hands of his successor, who appears to have made a much better use of his riches. The family, in the long period that elapsed, had many vicissitudes ; but at the period of my birth my father inhabited the same old palace, and we were in tolerably affluent circumstances. I was born there, and I remember as a child the curiosity I used to feel about the room with the secret receptacle under the floor where Jacopo had buried the body of his guest. It had been found there and had received Christian burial ; but the receptacle still remained and the room was shut up, being said to be haunted. I never *saw* anything extraordinary, but I can bear witness to the frightful groans and moans that issued from it sometimes at night, when, if I could persuade anybody to accompany me, I used to stand in the gallery and listen with wonder and awe. But I never passed the door alone, nor would any of the servants do so after dark. There had been an attempt made to exclude the sounds by walling up the door ; but so far from this succeeding they became twenty times worse, and as the wall was a disfigurement as well as a failure, the unquiet spirit was placated by taking it down again.

"The old man's memoir is always preserved among the family papers, and his picture still hangs in the gallery. Many strangers who have heard something of this extraordinary story, have asked to see it. The palace is now inhabited by an Austrian nobleman. Whether the ghost continues to annoy the inmates by his lamentations, I do not know.

"I now," said Count Francesco, "come to my personal history. Political reasons a few years since obliged me to quit Italy with my family. I had no resources except a little ready money that I had brought with me, and I had resolved to utilise some musical talent which I had cultivated for my amusement. I had not voice enough to sing in public, but I was capable of giving lessons and was considered, when in Italy, a successful amateur. I will not weary you with the sad details of my early residence in England ; you can imagine the difficulties that an unfortunate foreigner must encounter before he can establish a connection. Suffice it to say that my small means were wholly exhausted, and very often I, and what was worse, my wife and child, were in want of bread, and indebted to one of my more prosperous countrymen for the very necessaries of life. I was almost in despair, and I do not

know what rash thing I might have done if I was a single man ;
but I had my family depending on me, and it was my duty not
to sink under my difficulties however great they were.

"One night I had been singing at the house of a nobleman,
in St. James's Square, and had received some flattering compliments from a young man who appeared to be very fond of
Italian music, and to understand it. My getting to this party
was a stroke of good luck in the first instance, for I was quite
unknown to the host, but Signor A., an acquaintance of mine,
who had been engaged for the occasion, was taken ill at the last
moment, and had sent me with a note of introduction to apply
for his place.

"I knew, of course, that I should be well paid for my services,
but I would gladly have accepted half the sum I expected if I
could have had it that night, for our little treasury was wholly
exhausted, and we had not sixpence to purchase a breakfast
for the following day. When the great hall door shut upon
me, and I found myself on the pavement, with all that luxury
and splendour on one side, and I and my desolation on the
other, the contrast struck me cruelly, for I too, had been rich,
and dwelt in illuminated palaces, and had a train of liveried
servants at my command, and sweet music had echoed through
my halls. I felt desperate, and drawing my hat over my eyes I
began pacing the square, forming wild plans for the relief or
escape from my misery. No doubt I looked frantic, for you
know we Italians have such a habit of gesticulating, that I
believe my thoughts were accompanied by movements that
must have excited notice ; but I was too much absorbed to
observe anything, till I was roused by a voice saying, ' Signor
Ferraldi, still here this damp chilly night ! Are you not afraid
for your voice—it is worth taking care of.'

"'To what purpose,' I said savagely, ' It will not give me
bread ! '

"If the interruption had not been so sudden, I should not
have made such an answer, but I was surprised into it before
I knew who had addressed me. When I looked up I saw it was
the young man I had met at Lord L.'s, who had complimented
me on my singing. I took off my hat and begged his
pardon, and was about to move away when he took
my arm.

"'Excuse me,' he said, ' let us walk together,' and then
after a little pause, he added, with an apology, ' I think you are
an exile.'

" ' I am,' I said.

" ' And I think,' he continued, ' I have surprised you out of a secret that you would not voluntarily have told me. I know well the hardships that beset many of your countrymen—as good gentlemen as we are ourselves—when you are obliged to leave your country ; and I beg therefore you will not think me impertinent or intrusive, if I beg you to be frank with me and tell me how you are situated ! '

" This offer of sympathy was evidently so sincere, and it was so welcome, at such a moment, that I did not hesitate to comply with my new friend's request—I told him everything—adding that in time I hoped to get known, and that then I did not fear being able to make my way ; but that meanwhile we were in danger of starving.

" During this conversation we were walking round and round the square, where in fact he lived. Before we parted at his door, he had persuaded me to accept of a gift, I call it, for he had then no reason to suppose I should ever be able to repay him, but he called it an advance of ten guineas upon some lessons I was to give him ; the first instalment of which was to be paid the following day.

" I went home with a comparatively light heart, and the next morning waited upon my friendly pupil, whom I found, as I expected, a very promising scholar. He told me with a charming frankness that he had not much influence in fashionable society, for his family, though rich, was *parvenue*, but he said he had two sisters, as fond of music as himself, who would be shortly in London, and would be delighted to take lessons, as I had just the voice they liked to sing with them.

" This was the first auspicious incident that had occurred to me, nor did the omen fail in its fulfilment. I received great kindness from the family when they came to London. I gave them lessons, sung at their parties, and they took every opportunity of recommending me to their friends.

" When the end of the season approached, however, I felt somewhat about the future—there would be no parties to sing at, and my pupils would all be leaving town ; but my new friends, whose name, by the way, was Greathead, had a plan for me in their heads, which they strongly recommended me to follow. They said they had a house in the country with a large neighbourhood—in fact near a large watering-place ; and if I went there during the summer months, they did not doubt my getting plenty of teaching ; adding, ' We are much greater people there than we are here, you see ; and our recommendation will go a great way.'

" I followed my friends' advice, and soon after they left London I joined them at Salton, which was the name of their place. As I had left my wife and children in town, with very little money, I was anxious that they should join me as soon as possible ; and therefore the morning after my arrival, I proceeded to look for a lodging at S., and to take measures to make my object known to the residents and visitors there. My business done, I sent my family directions for their journey, and then returned to Salton to spend a few days, as I had promised my kind patrons.

" The house was modern ; in fact, it had been built by Mr. Greathead's grandfather, who was the architect of their fortunes ; the grounds were extensive, and the windows looked on a fine lawn, a picturesque ruin, a sparkling rivulet, and a charming flower-garden ; there could not be a prettier view than we enjoyed while sitting at breakfast. It was my first experience of the lovely and graceful English homes, and it fully realised all my expectations, both within doors and without. After breakfast Mr. Greathead and his son asked me to accompany them round the grounds, as they were contemplating some alterations.

" ' Among other things,' said Mr. G., ' we want to turn this rivulet ; but my wife has a peculiar fancy for that old hedge, which is exactly in the way, and she won't let me root it up.'

" The hedge alluded to enclosed two sides of the flower-garden, but seemed out of place, I thought.

" ' Why ! ' said I, ' What is Mrs. Greathead's attachment to the hedge ? '

" ' Why ? it's very old ; it formerly bordered the church-yard, for that old ruin you see there is all that remains of the parish church ; and this flower-garden, I fancy, is all the more brilliant for the rich soil of the burial-ground. But what is remarkable is that the hedge and that side of the garden are full of Italian flowers, and always have been so as long as anybody can remember. Nobody knows how it happens, but they must spring up from some old seeds that have been long in the ground. Look at this cyclamen growing wild in the hedge.'

" The subject of the alterations was renewed at dinner, and Mrs. Greathead, still objecting to the removal of the hedge, her younger son, whose name was Harry, said, ' It is very well for mamma to pretend it is for the sake of the flowers, but I am quite sure that the real reason is that she is afraid of offending the ghost.'

" ' What nonsense, Harry,' she said. ' You must not believe him, Mr. Ferraldi.'

" ' Well, mamma,' said the boy, ' you know you will never be convinced that that was not a ghost you saw.'

" ' Never mind what it was,' she said ; ' I won't have the hedge removed.' Presently, she added, ' I suppose you would laugh at any one believing in a ghost, Mr. Ferraldi.'

" ' Quite the contrary,' I answered ; ' I believe in them myself, and upon very good grounds, for we have a celebrated ghost in our family.'

" ' Well,' she said, ' Mr. Greathead and the boys laugh at me ; but when I came to live here, upon the death of Mr. Greathead's grandfather—for his father never inhabited the place, having died by an accident before the old gentleman— I never heard a word of the place being haunted ; and, perhaps, I should not have believed it if I had. But one evening, when the younger children were gone to bed, and Mr. Greathead and George were sitting with some friends in the dining-room, I and my sister, who was staying with me, strolled into the garden. It was the month of August, and a bright starlight night. We were talking on a very interesting matter, for my sister had that day received an offer from the gentleman she afterwards married. I mention this to show you that we were not thinking of anything supernatural, but, on the contrary, that our minds were quite absorbed with the subject we were discussing. I was looking on the ground, as one often does, when listening intently to what another person is saying ; my sister was speaking, when she suddenly stopped, and laid her hand upon my arm, saying, " Who's that ? " '

" ' I raised my eyes and saw, not many yards from us, an old man, withered and thin, dressed in a curious antique fashion, with a high-peaked hat on his head. I could not conceive who he could be, or what he could be doing there, for it was close to the flower-garden ; so we stood still to observe him. I don't know whether you saw the remains of an old tombstone in a corner of the garden ? It is said to be that of a former rector of the parish ; the date, 1550, is still legible upon it. The old man walked from one side of the hedge to that stone, and seemed to be counting his steps. He walked like a person pacing the ground, to measure it ; then he stopped and appeared to be noting the result of his measurement with a pencil and paper he held in his hand ; then he did the same thing the other side of the hedge, pacing up to the old tombstone and back.

" ' There was a talk, at that time, of removing the hedge, and digging up the old tombstone ; and it occurred to me that my husband might have been speaking to somebody about it, and that this man might be concerned in the business, though, still, his dress and appearance puzzled me. It seemed odd, too, that he took no notice of us ; and I might have remarked that we heard no footsteps, though we were quite close enough to do so ; but these circumstances did not strike me then. However, I was just going to advance, and ask him what he was doing, when I felt my sister's hand release the hold she had of my arm, and she sank to the ground ; at the same instant I lost sight of the mysterious old man, who suddenly disappeared.

" ' My sister had not fainted ; but she said her knees bent under her, and she had slipped down, collapsed by terror. I did not feel very comfortable myself, I assure you ; but I lifted her up, and we hastened back to the house and told what we had seen. The gentlemen went out, and, of course, saw nothing, and laughed at us ; but shortly afterwards, when Harry was born, I had a nurse from the village, and she asked me one day if I had ever happened to see " the old gentleman that walks ! " I had ceased to think of the circumstance, and inquired what old gentlemen she meant. And then she told me that, long ago, a foreign gentleman had been murdered here ; that is, in the old house that Mr. Greathead's grandfather pulled down when he built this ; and that, ever since, the place has been haunted, and that nobody will pass by the hedge and the old tombstone after dark ; for that is the spot to which the ghost confines himself.'

" ' But I should think,' said I, ' that so far from desiring to preserve these objects, you would rather wish them removed, since the ghost would, probably, cease to visit the spot at all.'

" ' Quite the contrary,' answered Mr. G. ' The people of the neighbourhood say that the former possessor of the place entertained the same idea, and had resolved to move them ; but that then the old man became very troublesome, and was even seen in the house ; the nurse positively assured me that her mother had told her old Mr. Greathead had also intended to remove them ; but that he quite suddenly counter-ordered the directions he had given and, though he did not confess to anything of the sort, the people all believed that he had seen the ghost.

Certain it is, that this hedge has always been maintained by the proprietors of the place.'

" The young men laughed and quizzed their mother for indulging in such superstitions ; but the lady was quite firm in her opposition, alleging that, independently of all considerations connected with the ghost, she liked the hedge on account of the Italian flowers ; and she liked the old tombstone on account of its antiquity.

" Consequently some other plan was devised for Mr. Greathead's alterations, which led the course of the rivulet quite clear of the hedge and the tombstone.

" In a few days my family arrived, and I established myself at S. for the summer. The speculation answered very well, and through the recommendations of Mr. and Mrs. Greathead, and their personal kindness to myself and my wife, we passed the time very pleasantly. When the period for our returning to London approached, they invited us to spend a fortnight with them before our departure, and, accordingly, the day we gave up our lodgings, we removed to Salton.

" Preparations for turning the rivulet had then commenced ; and soon after my arrival, I walked out with Mr. Greathead to see the works. There was a boy, about fourteen, amongst the labourers ; and while we were standing close to him, he picked up something and handed it to Mr. G., saying, ' Is this yours, sir ? ' which, on examination, proved to be a gold coin of the sixteenth century—the date on it was 1545. Presently the boy, who was digging, picked up another, and then several more.

" ' This becomes interesting,' said Mr. Greathead, ' I think we are coming upon some buried treasure ; ' and he whispered to me that he had better not leave the spot.

" Accordingly, he did stay till it was time to dress for dinner ; and, feeling interested, I remained also. In the interval, many more coins were found ; and when he went in, he dismissed the workmen, and sent a servant to watch the place—for he saw by their faces that if he had not happened to be present, he would probably never have heard of the circumstance. A few more turned up the following day, and then the store seemed exhausted. When the villagers heard of this money being discovered, they all looked upon it as the explanation of the old gentleman haunting that particular spot. No doubt he had buried the money, and it remained to be seen whether, now that it was found, his spirit would be at rest.

" My two children were with me at Salton on this occasion.

They slept in a room on the third floor, and one morning my wife, having told me that the younger of the two seemed unwell, I went upstairs to look at her. It was a cheerful room, with two little white beds in it, and several old prints and samplers, and bits of work such as you see in nurseries, framed and hung against the wall. After I had spoken to the child, and while my wife was talking to the maid, I stood with my hands in my pockets, idly looking at these things. Among them was one that arrested my attention, because at first I could not understand it, nor see why this discoloured parchment, with a few lines and dots on it, should have been framed and glazed. There were some words here and there which I could not decipher ; so I lifted the frame off the nail and carried it to the window. Then I saw that the words were Italian, written in a crabbed, old-fashioned hand, and the whole seemed to be a plan, or sketch, rudely drawn, of what I thought at first was a camp—but, on closer examination, I saw was part of a churchyard, with tombstones, from one of which various lines were drawn to various dots, and among these lines were numbers, and here and there a word, as *right*, *left*, etc. There were also two lines forming a right angle, which intersected the whole, and after contemplating the thing for some time, it struck me that it was a rude sort of map of the old churchyard and the hedge, which had formed the subject of conversation some days before.

" At breakfast I mentioned what I had observed to Mr. and Mrs. Greathead, and they said they believed it was ; it had been found when the old house was pulled down, and was kept on account of antiquity.

" ' Of what period is it ? ' I asked, ' and how happens it to have been made by an Italian ? '

" ' The last question I can't answer,' said Mr. Greathead, ' but the date is on it, I believe.'

" ' No,' said I,' I examined it particularly—there is no date.'

" ' Oh, there is a date and name, I think—but I never examined it myself.' And to settle the question he desired his son Harry to run up and fetch it, adding, ' You know, Italian architects and designers of various kinds were not rare in this country a few centuries ago.'

" Harry brought the frame, and we were confirmed in our conjectures of what it represented, but we could find no date or name.

" ' And yet I think I've heard there was one,' said Mr. Greathead. ' Let us take it out of the frame.'

" This was easily done, and we found the date and the name."
The Count paused, and then added :
" I dare say you can guess it ? "
" Jacopo Ferraldi ? " I said.

" It was," he answered ; " and it immediately occurred to me that he had buried the money supposed to have been stolen on the night he was murdered, and that this was the plan to guide him to finding it again. So I told Mr. Greathead the story I have now told you, and mentioned my reasons for supposing that if I was correct in my surmise, more gold would be found.

" With the old man's map as our guide, we immediately set to work—the whole family vigorously joining in the search ; and, as I expected, we found that the tombstone in the garden was the point from which all the lines were drawn, and that the dots indicated where the money lay. It was in different heaps, and appeared to have been enclosed in bags, which had rotted away with time. We found the whole sum mentioned in the memoir, and Mr. Greathead, being Lord of the Manor, was generous enough to make it all over to me, as being the lawful heir, which, however, I certainly was not, for it was the spoil of a murderer and thief, and it properly belonged to the Allens. But that family had become extinct ; at least, so we believed, when the two unfortunate ladies were executed, and I accepted the gift with much gratitude and a quiet conscience. It relieved us from our pressing difficulties and enabled me to wait for better times."

" And," said I, " now of the ghost ? Was he pleased or otherwise by the *dénouement* ? "

" I cannot say," replied the Count ; " I have not heard of his being seen since ; I believe, however, that the villagers, who understand these things better than we do, say that they should not be surprised if he allowed the hedge and tombstone to be removed now without opposition ; but Mr. Greathead, on the contrary, wished to retain them as mementoes of these curious circumstances."

THE GHOST OF DOROTHY DINGLEY

In the beginning of this year, a disease happened in this town of Launceston, and some of my scholars died of it. Among others who fell under the malignity then triumphing, was John Elliot, the eldest son of Edward Elliot of Treherse, Esq., a stripling of about sixteen years of age, but of more than common parts and ingenuity. At his own particular request, I preached at the funeral, which happened on the 20th day of June, 1665. In my discourse (*ut mos reique locique postulabat*), I spoke some words in commendation of the young gentleman ; such as might endear his memory to those that knew him, and, withal, tended to preserve his example to the fry which went to school with him, and were to continue there after him. An ancient gentleman, who was then in the church, was much affected with the discourse, and was often heard to repeat, the same evening, an expression I then used out of Vigil :

Et puer ipse fuit cantari dignus.

The reason why this grave gentleman was so concerned at the character, was a reflection he made upon a son of his own, who being about the same age, and, but a few months before, not unworthy of the like character I gave of the young Mr. Elliot, was now, by a strange accident, quite lost as to his parent's hopes and all expectation of any further comfort by him.

The funeral rites being over, I was no sooner come out of the church, but I found myself most courteously accosted by this old gentleman ; and with an unusual importunity almost forced against my humour to see his house that night ; nor could I have rescued myself from his kindness, had not Mr. Elliot interposed and pleaded title to me for the whole of the day, which, as he said, he would resign to no man.

424

Hereupon I got loose for that time, but was constrained to leave a promise behind me to wait upon him at his own house the Monday following. This then seemed to satisfy, but before Monday came I had a new message to request me that, if it were possible, I would be there on the Sunday. The second attempt I resisted, by answering that it was against my convenience, and the duty which mine own people expected from me.

Yet was not the gentleman at rest, for he sent me another letter on the Sunday, by no means to fail on the Monday, and so to order my business as to spend with him two or three days at least. I was indeed startled at so much eagerness, and so many dunnings for a visit, without any business ; and began to suspect that there must needs be some design in the bottom of all this excess of courtesy. For I had no familiarity, scarce common acquaintance with the gentleman or his family ; nor could I imagine whence should arise such a flush of friendship on the sudden.

On the Monday I went, and paid my promised devoir, and met with entertainment as free and plentiful as the invitation was importunate. There also I found a neighbouring minister who pretended to call in accidentally, but by the sequel I suppose it otherwise. After dinner this brother of the coat undertook to show me the gardens, where, as we were walking, he gave me the first discovery of what was mainly intended in all this treat and compliment.

First he began to tell the infortunity of the family in general, and then gave an instance in the youngest son. He related what a hopeful, sprightly lad he lately was, and how melancholic and sottish he was now grown. Then did he with much passion lament, that his ill-humour should so incredibly subdue his reason ; for, says he, the poor boy believes himself to be haunted with ghosts, and is confident that he meets with an evil spirit in a certain field about half a mile from this place, as often as he goes that way to school.

In the midst of our twaddle, the old gentleman and his lady (as observing their cue exactly) came up to us. Upon their approach, and pointing me to the arbour, the parson renews the relation to me ; and they (the parents of the youth) confirmed what he said, and added many minute circumstances, in a long narrative of the whole. In fine, they all three desired my thoughts and advice in the affair.

I was not able to collect thoughts enough on the sudden to frame a judgment upon what they had said, only I answered that the thing which the youth reported to them was strange, yet not incredible, and that I knew not then what to think or say of it ; but if the lad would be free to me in talk, and trust me with his counsels, I had hopes to give them a better account of my opinion the next day.

I had no sooner spoken so much, but I perceived myself in the springe their courtship had laid for me ; for the old lady was not able to hide her impatience, but her son must be called immediately. This I was forced to comply with and consent to, so that drawing off from the company to an orchard near by, she went herself and brought him to me, and left him with me.

It was the main drift of all these three to persuade me that either the boy was lazy, and glad of any excuse to keep from the school, or that he was in love with some wench and ashamed to confess it ; or that he had a fetch upon his father to get money and new clothes, that he might range to London after a brother he had there ; and therefore they begged of me to discover the root of the matter, and accordingly to dissuade, advise, or reprove him, but chiefly, by all means, to undeceive him as to the fancy of ghosts and spirits.

I soon entered into a close conference with the youth, and at first was very cautious not to displease him, but by smooth words to ingratiate myself and get within him, for I doubted he would be too distrustful or too reserved. But we had scarcely passed the first situation, and begun to speak to the business, before I found that there needed no policy to screw myself into his breast ; for he most openly and with all obliging candour did aver, that he loved his book, and desired nothing more than to be bred a scholar ; that he had not the least respect for any of womankind, as his mother gave out ; and that the only request he would make to his parents was, that they would but believe his constant assertions concerning the woman he was disturbed with, in the field called the Higher-Broom Quartils. He told me with all naked freedom, and a flood of tears, that his friends were unkind and unjust to him, neither to believe nor pity him ; and that if any man (making a bow to me) would but go with him to the place, he might be convinced that the thing was real, etc.

By this time he found me apt to compassionate his condition, and to be attentive to his relation of it, and therefore he went on in this way :

"This woman which appears to me," saith he, "lived a neighbour here to my father, and died about eight years since ; her name, Dorothy Dingley, of such a stature, such age, and

THE GHOST OF DOROTHY DINGLEY 427

such complexion. She never speaks to me, but passeth by hastily, and always leaves the footpath to me, and she commonly meets me twice or three times in the breadth of the field.

"It was about two months before I took any notice of it, and though the shape of the face was in my memory, yet I did not recall the name of the person, but without more thoughtfulness, I did suppose it was some woman who lived thereabout, and had frequent occasion that way. Nor did I imagine anything to the contrary before she began to meet me constantly, morning and evening, and always in the same field, and sometimes twice or thrice in the breadth of it.

"The first time I took notice of her was about a year since, and when I first began to suspect and believe it to be a ghost, I had courage enough not to be afraid, but kept it to myself a good while, and only wondered very much about it. I did often speak to it, but never had a word in answer. Then I changed my way and went to school the Under Horse Road, and then she always met me in the narrow lane, between the Quarry Park and the Nursery, which was worse.

"At length I began to be terrified at it, and prayed continually that God would either free me from it or let me know the meaning of it. Night and day, sleeping and waking, the shape was ever running in my mind, and I often did repeat these places of Scripture (with that he takes a small Bible out of his pocket), Job vii, 14 : ' Thou scarest me with dreams, and terrifiest me through visions.' And Deuteronomy xxviii, 67 : ' In the morning, thou shalt say, Would God it were even ; and at even thou shalt say, Would God it were morning ; for the fear of thine heart, wherewith thou shalt fear, and for the sight of thine eyes, which thou shalt see.' "

I was very much pleased with the lad's ingenuity in the application of these pertinent Scriptures to his condition, and desired him to proceed.

"When," says he, "by degrees, I grew very pensive, inasmuch that it was taken notice of by all our family ; whereupon, being urged to it, I told my brother William of it, and he privately acquainted my father and mother, and they kept it to themselves for some time.

"The success of this discovery was only this ; they did sometimes laugh at me, sometimes chide me, but still commanded me to keep to my school, and put such fopperies out of my head. I did accordingly go to school often, but always met the woman in the way."

This, and much more to the same purpose, yea, as much as held a dialogue of near two hours, was our conference in the orchard, which ended with my proffer to him, that, without making any privy to our intents, I would next morning walk with him to the place, about six o'clock. He was even transported with joy at the mention of it, and replied, " But will you, sure, sir ? Will you, sure, sir ? Thank God ! Now I hope I shall be relieved."

From this conclusion we retired into the house.

The gentleman, his wife, and Mr. Sam were impatient to know the event, insomuch that they came out of the parlour into the hall to meet us ; and seeing the lad look cheerfully, the first compliment from the old man was, " Come, Mr. Ruddle, you have talked with him ; I hope now he will have more wit. An idle boy ! an idle boy ! "

At these words, the lad ran up the stairs to his own chamber, without replying, and I soon stopped the curiosity of the three expectants by telling them I had promised silence, and was resolved to be as good as my word ; but when things were riper they might know all. At present, I desired them to rest in my faithful promise, that I would do my utmost in their service, and for the good of their son. With this they were silenced ; I cannot say satisfied.

The next morning before five o'clock, the lad was in my chamber, and very brisk. I arose and went with him. The field he led me to I guessed to be twenty acres, in an open country, and about three furlongs from any house. We went into the field, and had not gone about a third part, before the spectrum, in the shape of a woman, with all the circumstances he had described her to me in the orchard the day before (as much as the suddenness of its appearance and evanition would permit me to discover), met us and passed by. I was a little surprised at it, and though I had taken up a firm resolution to speak to it, yet I had not the power, nor indeed durst I look back ; yet I took care not to show any fear to my pupil and guide, and therefore only telling him that I was satisfied in the truth of his complaint, we walked to the end of the field and returned, nor did the ghost meet us that time above once. I perceived in the young man a kind of boldness, mixed with astonishment : the first caused by my presence, and the proof he had given of his own relation, and the other by the sight of his persecutor.

In short, we went home : I somewhat puzzled, he much animated. At our return, the gentlewoman, whose inquisitiveness had missed us, watched to speak with me. I gave her a convenience, and told her that my opinion was that her son's complaint was not to be slighted, nor altogether discredited ; yet, that my judgment in his case was not settled. I gave her caution, moreover, that the thing might not take wind, lest the whole country should ring with what we had yet no assurance of.

In this juncture of time I had business which would admit no delay ; wherefore I went for Launceston that evening, but promised to see them again next week. Yet I was prevented by an occasion which pleaded a sufficient excuse, for my wife was that week brought home from a neighbour's house very ill. However, my mind was upon the adventure. I studied the case, and about three weeks after went again, resolving, by the help of God, to see the utmost.

The next morning, being the 27th day of July, 1665, I went to the haunted field by myself, and walked the breadth of the field without any encounter. I returned and took the other walk, and then the spectrum appeared to me, much about the same place where I saw it before, when the young gentleman was with me. In my thoughts, it moved swifter than the time before, and about ten feet distance from me on my right hand, insomuch that I had not time to speak, as I had determined with myself beforehand.

The evening of this day, the parents, the son, and myself being in the chamber where I lay, I propounded to them our going all together to the place next morning, and after some asseveration that there was no danger in it, we all resolved upon it. The morning being come, lest we should alarm the family of servants, they went under the pretence of seeing a field of wheat, and I took my horse and fetched a compass another way, and so met at the stile we had appointed.

Thence we all four walked leisurely into the Quartils, and had passed above half the field before the ghost made appearance. It then came over the stile just before us, and moved with that swiftness that by the time we had gone six or seven steps it passed by. I immediately turned head and ran after it, with the young man by my side ; we saw it pass over the stile by which we entered, but no farther. I stepped upon the hedge at one place, he at another, but could discern nothing ; whereas, I dare aver, that the swiftest horse in England could not have conveyed himself out of sight in that short space of time. Two things I observed in this day's appearance. 1. That a spaniel dog, who followed the company unregarded, did bark and run away as the spectrum passed by ; whence it is easy to conclude that it was not our fear or fancy which made the apparition. 2. That the motion of the spectrum was not gradation, or by steps, and moving of the feet, but a kind of gliding, as children upon the ice, or a boat down a swift river, which punctually answers the description the ancients gave of their *Lemures*, which was Κατὰ ῥύμτω ἀέριον καὶ ὁρμὴν ἄπζαποδισον (Heliodorus).

But to proceed. This ocular evidence clearly convinced, but, withal, strangely frightened the old gentleman and his wife, who knew this Dorothy Dingley in her lifetime, were at her burial, and now plainly saw her features in this present apparition. I encouraged them as well as I could, but after this they went no more. However, I was resolved to proceed, and use such lawful means as God hath discovered, and learned men have success-fully practised in these irregular cases.

The next morning being Thursday, I went out very early by myself, and walked for about an hour's space in meditation and prayer in the field next adjoining to the Quartils. Soon after five I stepped over the stile into the disturbed field, and had not gone above thirty or forty paces before the ghost appeared at the farther stile. I spoke to it with a loud voice, in some such sen-tences as the way of these dealings directed me, whereupon it approached, but slowly, and when I came near, it moved not. I spake again, and it answered, in a voice neither very audible nor intelligible. I was not in the least terrified, and therefore persisted until it spake again, and gave me satisfaction. But the work could not be finished at this time ; wherefore the same evening, an hour after sunset, it met me again near the same place, and after a few words on each side, it quietly vanished, and neither doth appear since, nor ever will more to any man's disturbance. The discourse in the morning lasted about a quarter of an hour.

These things are true, and I know them to be so, with as much certainty as eyes and ears can give me ; and until I can be per-suaded that my senses do deceive me about their proper object, and by that persuasion deprive myself of the strongest inducement to believe the Christian religion, I must and will assert that these things in this paper are true.

As for the manner of my proceeding, I find no reason to be ashamed of it, for I can justify it to men of good principles, dis-cretion, and recondite learning, though in this case I choose to content myself in the assurance of the thing, rather than be at the unprofitable trouble to persuade others to believe it ; for I know full well with what difficulty relations of so uncommon a nature and practice obtain relief.* He that tells such a story may expect to be dealt withal as a traveller in Poland by the robbers, viz., first murdered and then searched—first condemned for a liar, or superstitious, and then, when it is too late, have his reasons and proofs examined. This incredulity may be attributed :

1. To the infinite abuses of the people, and impositions upon their faith by the cunning monks and friars, etc., in the days of darkness and popery ; for they made apparitions as often as they pleased, and got both money and credit by quieting the *terriculamenta vulgi*, which their own artifice had raised.

2. To the prevailing of Somatism and the Hobbean principle in these times, which is a revival of the doctrine of the Sadducees ; and as it denies the nature, so it cannot consist with the apparition of spirits ; of which, see *Leviathian*, p. 1, c. 12.

3. To the ignorance of men in our age, in this peculiar and mysterious part of philosophy and of religion, namely, the communication between spirits and men. Not one scholar in ten thousand (though otherwise of excellent learning) knows anything of it or the way how to manage it. This ignorance breeds fear and abhorrence of that which otherwise might be of incomparable benefit to mankind.

But I being a clergyman and young, and a stranger in these parts, do apprehend silence and secrecy to be my best security.

In rebus abstrusissimis abundans cautela non nocet.

TO BE TAKEN WITH A
GRAIN OF SALT

I HAVE always noticed a prevalent want. of courage, even
among persons of superior intelligence and culture, as to
imparting their own psychological experiences when those
have been of a strange sort. Almost all men are afraid that
what they could relate in such wish would find no parallel or
response in a listener's internal life, and might be suspected or
laughed at. A truthful traveller, who should have seen some
extraordinary creature in the likeness of a sea-serpent, would
have no fear of mentioning it ; but the same traveller, having
had some singular presentiment, impulse, vagary of thought,
vision (so called), dream, or other remarkable mental impression,
would hesitate considerably before he would own to it. To this
reticence I attribute much of the obscurity in which such subjects
are involved. We do not habitually communicate our experiences
of these subjective things as we do our experiences of objective
creation. The consequence is, that the general stock of experience
in this regard appears exceptional, and really is so, in respect of
being miserably imperfect.

In what I am going to relate, I have no intention of setting
up, opposing, or supporting any theory whatever. I know the
history of the Bookseller of Berlin, I have studied the case of the
wife of a late Astronomer-Royal as related by Sir David Brewster,
and I have followed the minutest details of a much more remarkable case of Spectral Illusion occurring within my private
circle of friends. It may be necessary to state as to this last,
that the sufferer (a lady) was in no degree, however distant,
related to me. A mistaken assumption on that head might
suggest an explanation of a part of my own case—but only a
part—which would be wholly without foundation. It cannot
be referred to my inheritance of any developed peculiarity, nor

had I ever before any at all similar experience, nor have I ever had any at all similar experience since.

It does not signify how many years ago, or how few, a certain murder was committed in England, which attracted great attention. We hear more than enough of murderers as they rise in succession to their atrocious eminence, and I would bury the memory of this particular brute, if I could, as his body was buried, in Newgate Jail. I purposely abstain from giving any direct clue to the criminal's individuality. When the murder was first discovered, no suspicion fell—or I ought rather to say, for I cannot be too precise in my facts, it was nowhere publicly hinted that any suspicion fell—on the man who was afterwards brought to trial. As no reference was at that time made to him in the newspapers, it is obviously impossible that any description of him can at that time have been given in the newspapers. It is essential that this fact be remembered.

Unfolding at breakfast my morning paper, containing the account of that first discovery, I found it to be deeply interesting, and I read it with close attention. I read it twice, if not three times. The discovery had been made in a bedroom, and, when I laid down the paper, I was aware of a flash—rush—flow—I do not know what to call it—no word I can find is satisfactorily descriptive—in which I seemed to see that bedroom passing through my room, like a picture impossibly painted on a running river. Though almost instantaneous in its passing, it was perfectly clear ; so clear that I distinctly, and with a sense of relief, observed the absence of the dead body from the bed.

It was in no romantic place that I had this curious sensation, but in chambers in Piccadilly, very near to the corner of St. James's Street. It was entirely new to me. I was in my easy-chair at the moment, and the sensation was accompanied with a peculiar shiver which started the chair from its position. (But it is to be noted that the chair ran easily on castors.) I went to one of the windows (there are two in the room, and the room is on the second floor) to refresh my eyes with the moving objects down in Piccadilly. It was a bright autumn morning, and the street was sparkling and cheerful. The wind was high. As I looked out, it brought down from the Park a quantity of fallen leaves, which a gust took, and whirled into a spiral pillar. As the pillar fell and the leaves dispersed, I saw two men on the opposite side of the way, going from west to east. They were one behind the other. The foremost man often looked back over his shoulder. The second man followed him, at a distance of some thirty paces, with his right hand menacingly raised. First, the singularity and steadiness of this threatening gesture in so public a thoroughfare attracted my attention ; and next, the more remarkable circumstance that nobody heeded it. Both men threaded their way among the other passengers with a smoothness hardly consistent even with the action of walking on a pavement ; and no single creature, that I could see, gave them place, touched them, or looked after them. In passing before my windows, they both stared up at me. I saw their two faces very distinctly, and I knew that I could recognise them anywhere. Not that I had consciously noticed anything very remarkable in either face, except that the man who went first had an unusually lowering appearance, and that the face of the man who followed him was of the colour of impure wax.

I am a bachelor, and my valet and his wife constitute my whole establishment. My occupation is in a certain Branch Bank, and I wish that my duties as head of a Department were as light as they are popularly supposed to be. They kept me in town that autumn, when I stood in need of change. I was not ill, but I was not well. My reader is to make the most that can be reasonably made of my feeling jaded, having a depressing sense upon me of a monotonous life, and being "slightly dyspeptic." I am assured by my renowned doctor that my real state of health at that time justified no stronger description, and I quote his own from his written answer to my request for it. As the circumstances of the murder, gradually unravelling, took stronger and stronger possession of the public mind, I kept them away from mine by knowing as little about them as was possible in the midst of the universal excitement. But I knew that a verdict of Wilful Murder had been found against the suspected Murderer, and that he had been committed to Newgate for trial. I also knew that his trial had been postponed over one Sessions of the Central Criminal Court, on the ground of general prejudice and want of time for the preparation of the defence. I may further have known, but I believe I did not, when, or about when, the Sessions to which his trial stood postponed would come on.

My sitting-room, bedroom, and dressing-room are all on one floor. With the last there is no communication but through the bedroom. True, there is a door in it, once communicating with the staircase ; but a part of the fitting of my bath has been —and had been for some years—fixed across it. At the same period, and as a part of the same arrangement, the door had been nailed up and canvased over.

I was standing in my bedroom late one night, giving some directions to my servant before he went to bed. My face was towards the only available door of communication with the dressing-room, and it was closed. My servant's back was towards that door. While I was speaking to him, I saw it open, and a man look in, who very earnestly and mysteriously beckoned to me. That man was the man who had gone second of the two along Piccadilly, and whose face was the colour of impure wax. The figure, having beckoned, drew back, and closed the door. With no longer pause than was made by my crossing the bedroom, I opened the dressing-room door and looked in. I had a lighted candle already in my hand. I felt no inward expectation of seeing the figure in the dressing-room, and I did not see it there.

Conscious that my servant stood amazed, I turned round to him, and said : " Derrick, could you believe that in my cool senses I fancied I saw a——" As I there laid my hand upon his breast, with a sudden start he trembled violently, and said, " O Lord, yes, sir ! A dead man beckoning ! "

Now I do not believe that this John Derrick, my trusty and attached servant for more than twenty years, had any impression whatever of having seen any such figure, until I touched him. The change in him was so startling, when I touched him, that I fully believe he derived his impression in some occult manner from me at that instant.

I bade John Derrick bring some brandy, and I gave him a dram, and was glad to take one myself. Of what had preceded that night's phenomenon I told him not a single word. Reflecting on it, I was absolutely certain that I had never seen that face before, except on the one occasion in Piccadilly. Comparing its expression when beckoning at the door with its expression when it had stared up at me as I stood at my window, I came to the conclusion that on the first occasion it had sought to fasten itself upon my memory, and that on the second occasion it had made sure of being immediately remembered.

I was not very comfortable that night, though I felt a certainty, difficult to explain, that the figure would not return. At daylight I fell into heavy sleep, from which I was awakened by John Derrick's coming to my bedside with a paper in his hand.

This paper, it appeared, had been the subject of an altercation at the door between its bearer and my servant. It was a summons to me to serve upon a Jury at the forthcoming Sessions of the

Central Criminal Court at the Old Bailey. I had never before been summoned on such a Jury, as John Derrick well knew. He believed—I am not certain at this hour whether with reason or otherwise—that that class of Jurors were customarily chosen on a lower qualification than mine, and he had at first refused to accept the summons. The man who served it had taken the matter very coolly. He had said that my attendance or non-attendance was nothing to him ; there the summons was ; and I should deal with it at my own peril, and not at his.

For a day or two I was undecided whether to respond to this call, or take no notice of it. I was not conscious of the slightest mysterious bias, influence, or attraction, one way or other. Of that I am as strictly sure as of every other statement that I make here. Ultimately I decided, as a break in the monotony of my life, that I would go.

The appointed morning was a raw morning in the month of November. There was a dense brown fog in Piccadilly, and it became positively black and in the last degree oppressive east of Temple Bar. I found the passages and staircases of the Court House flaringly lighted with gas, and the Court itself similarly illuminated. I *think* that, until I was conducted by officers into the Old Court and saw its crowded state, I did not know that the Murderer was to be tried that day. I *think* that, until I was so helped into the Old Court with considerable difficulty, I did not know into which of the two Courts sitting my summons would take me. But this must not be received as a positive assertion, for I am not completely satisfied in my mind on either point. I took my seat in the place appropriated to Jurors in waiting, and I looked about the Court as well as I could through the cloud of fog and breath that was heavy in it. I noticed the black vapour hanging like a murky curtain outside the great windows, and I noticed the stifled sound of wheels on the straw or tan that was littered in the street ; also, the hum of the people gathered there, which a shrill whistle, or a louder song or hail than the rest, occasionally pierced. Soon afterwards the Judges, two in number, entered, and took their seats. The buzz in the Court was awfully hushed. The direction was given to put the Murderer to the bar. He appeared there. And in that same instant I recognised in him the first of the two men who had gone down Piccadilly.

If my name had been called then, I doubt if I could have answered to it audibly. But it was called about sixth or eighth in the panel, and I was by that time able to say " Here ! "

Now, observe. As I stepped into the box, the prisoner, who had been looking on attentively, but with no sign of concern, became violently agitated, and beckoned to his attorney. The prisoner's wish to challenge me was so manifest, that it occasioned a pause, during which the attorney, with his hand upon the dock, whispered with his client, and shook his head. I afterwards had it from that gentleman, that the prisoner's first affrighted words to him were, "*At all hazards, challenge that man!*" But that, as he would give no reason for it, and admitted that he had not even known my name until he heard it called and I appeared, it was not done.

Both on the ground already explained, that I wish to avoid reviving the unwholesome memory of that Murderer, and also because a detailed account of his long trial is by no means indispensable to my narrative, I shall confine myself closely to such incidents in the ten days and nights during which we, the Jury, were kept together, as directly bear on my own curious personal experience. It is in that, and not in the Murderer, that I seek to interest my reader. It is to that, and not to a page of the Newgate Calendar, that I beg attention.

I was chosen Foreman of the Jury. On the second morning of the trial, after evidence had been taken for two hours (I heard the church clock strike), happening to cast my eyes over my brother-jurymen, I found an inexplicable difficulty in counting them. I counted them several times, yet always with the same difficulty. In short, I made them one too many.

I touched the brother-juryman whose place was next me, and I whispered to him, "Oblige me by counting us." He looked surprised by the request, but turned his head and counted. "Why," says he, suddenly, "we are Thirt——but no, it's not possible. No. We are twelve." According to my counting that day, we were always right in detail, but in the gross we were always one too many. There was no appearance—no figure— to account for it; but I had now an inward foreshadowing of the figure that was surely coming.

The jury were housed at the London Tavern. We all slept in one large room on separate tables, and we were constantly in the charge and under the eye of the officer sworn to hold us in safe-keeping. I see no reason for suppressing the real name of that officer. He was intelligent, highly polite, and obliging, and (I was glad to hear) much respected in the city. He had an agreeable presence, good eyes, enviable black whiskers, and a fine sonorous voice. His name was Mr. Harker.

When we turned into our twelve beds at night, Mr. Harker's bed was drawn across the door. On the night of the second day, not being disposed to lie down, and seeing Mr. Harker sitting on his bed, I went and sat beside him, and offered him a pinch of snuff. As Mr. Harker's hand touched mine in taking it from my box, a peculiar shiver crossed him, and he said, " Who is this ? "

Following Mr. Harker's eyes, and looking along the room, I saw again the figure I expected—the second of the two men who had gone down Piccadilly. I rose, and advanced a few steps ; then stopped, and looked round at Mr. Harker. He was quite unconcerned, laughed, and said in a pleasant way, " I thought for a moment we had a thirteenth juryman, without a bed. But I see it is the moonlight."

Making no revelation to Mr. Harker, but inviting him to take a walk with me to the end of the room, I watched what the figure did. It stood for a few moments by the bedside of each of my eleven brother jurymen, close to the pillow. It always went to the right-hand side of the bed, and always passed out crossing the foot of the next bed. It seemed, from the action of the head, merely to look down pensively at each recumbent figure. It took no notice of me, or of my bed, which was that nearest to Mr. Harker's. It seemed to go out where the moonlight came in, through a high window, as by an aerial flight of stairs.

Next morning at breakfast, it appeared that everybody present had dreamed of the murdered man last night except myself and Mr. Harker.

I now felt as convinced that the second man who had gone down Piccadilly was the murdered man (so to speak), as if it had been borne into my comprehension by his immediate testimony. But even this took place, and in a manner for which I was not at all prepared.

On the fifth day of the trial, when the case for the prosecution was drawing to a close, a miniature of the murdered man, missing from his bedroom upon the discovery of the deed, and afterwards found in a hiding-place where the murderer had been seen digging, was put in as evidence. Having been identified by the witness under examination, it was handed up to the Bench, and thence handed down to be inspected by the Jury. As an officer in a black gown was making his way with it across to me, the figure of the second man who had gone down Piccadilly impetuously started from the crowd, caught the miniature from the officer, and gave it to me with his own hands, at the same time saying, in a low and hollow tone—before I saw the miniature, which was in a locket—" *I was younger then, and my face was not then drained of blood.*" It also came between me and the brother juryman to whom I would have given the miniature, and between him and the brother juryman to whom he would have given it, and so passed it on through the whole of our number, and back into my possession. Not one of them, however, detected this.

At table, and generally when we were shut up together in Mr. Harker's custody, we had from the first naturally discussed the day's proceedings a good deal. On that fifth day, the case for the prosecution being closed, and we having that side of the question in a completed shape before us, our discussion was more animated and serious. Among our number was a vestry-man—the densest idiot I have ever seen at large—who met the plainest evidence with the most preposterous objections, and who was sided with by two flabby parochial parasites ; all the three impanelled from a district so delivered over to fever that they ought to have been upon their own trial for five hundred murders. When these mischievous blockheads were at their loudest, which was towards midnight, while some of us were already preparing for bed, I again saw the murdered man. He stood grimly behind them, beckoning to me. On my going towards them, and striking into the conversation, he immediately retired. This was the beginning of a separate series of appearances, confined to that long room in which *we* were confined. Whenever a knot of my brother jurymen laid their heads together, I saw the head of the murdered man among theirs. Whenever their comparison of notes was going against him, he would solemnly and irresistibly beckon to me.

It will be borne in mind that down to the production of the miniature, on the fifth day of the trial, I had never seen the Appearance in Court. Three changes occurred now that we entered on the case for the defence. Two of them I will mention together, first. The figure was now in Court continually, and it never there addressed itself to me, but always to the person who was speaking at the time. For instance : the throat of the murdered man had been cut straight across. In the opening speech for the defence it was suggested that the deceased might have cut his own throat. At that very moment, the figure, with its throat in the dreadful condition referred to (this it had concealed before), stood at the speaker's elbow, motioning across and across its windpipe, now with the right hand, now with

the left, vigorously suggesting to the speaker himself the impossibility of such a wound having been self-inflicted by either
hand. For another instance : a witness to character, a woman
deposed to the prisoner's being the most amiable of mankind.
The figure at that instant stood on the floor before her, looking
her full in the face, and pointing out the prisoner's evil countenance with an extended arm and an outstretched finger.

The third change now to be added impressed me strongly
as the most marked and striking of all. I do not theorise upon
it ; I accurately state it, and there leave it. Although the
Appearance was not itself perceived by those whom it addressed,
its coming close to such persons was invariably attended by
some trepidation or disturbance on their part. It seemed to
me as if it were prevented, by laws to which I was not amenable,
from fully revealing itself to others, and yet as if it could invisibly,
dumbly, and darkly overshadow their minds. When the leading
counsel for the defence suggested that hypothesis of suicide, and
the figure stood at the learned gentleman's elbow, frightfully
sawing at its severed throat, it is undeniable that the counsel
faltered in his speech, lost for a few seconds the thread of his
ingenious discourse, wiped his forehead with his handkerchief,
and turned extremely pale. When the witness to character
was confronted by the Appearance, her eyes most certainly
did follow the direction of its pointed finger, and rest in great
hesitation and trouble upon the prisoner's face. Two additional
illustrations will suffice. On the eighth day of the trial, after
the pause which was every day made early in the afternoon for
a few minutes' rest and refreshment, I came back into Court
with the rest of the Jury some little time before the return of
the Judges. Standing up in the box and looking about me, I
thought the figure was not there, until, chancing to raise my
eyes to the gallery, I saw it bending forward, and leaning over
a very decent woman, as if to assure itself whether the Judges
had resumed their seats or not. Immediately afterwards that
woman screamed, fainted and was carried out. So with the
venerable, sagacious, and patient Judge who conducted the
trial. When the case was over, and he settled himself and his
papers to sum up, the murdered man, entering by the Judges'
door, advanced to his Lordship's desk, and looked eagerly over
his shoulder at the pages of his notes which he was turning.
A change came over his Lordship's face ; his hand stopped ;
the peculiar shiver, that I knew so well, passed over him ; he
faltered, " Excuse me, gentlemen, for a few moments. I am some-

what oppressed by the vitiated air ; " and did not recover until he had drunk a glass of water.

Through all the monotony of six of those interminable ten days—the same Judges and others on the bench, the same murderer in the dock, the same lawyers at the table, the same tones of question and answer rising to the roof of the Court, the same scratching of the Judge's pen, the same ushers going in and out, the same lights kindled at the same hour when there had been any natural light of day, the same foggy curtain outside the great windows when it was foggy, the same rain pattering and dripping when it was rainy, the same footmarks of turnkeys and prisoner day after day on the same sawdust, the same keys locking and unlocking the same heavy doors—through all the wearisome monotony which made me feel as if I had been Foreman of the Jury for a vast period of time, and Piccadilly had flourished coevally with Babylon, the murdered man never lost one trace of his distinctness in my eyes, nor was he at any moment less distinct than anybody else. I must not omit, as a matter of fact, that I never once saw the Appearance which I call by the name of the murdered man look at the murderer. Again and again I wondered, " Why does he not ? " But he never did.

Nor did he look at me, after the production of the miniature, until the last closing minutes of the trial arrived. We retired to consider at seven minutes before ten at night. The idiotic vestryman and his two parochial parasites gave us so much trouble that we twice returned into Court to beg to have certain extracts from the Judge's notes re-read. Nine of us had not the smallest doubt about those passages, neither, I believe, had any one in the Court ; the dunder-headed triumvirate, however, having no idea but obstruction, disputed them for that very reason. At length we prevailed, and finally the Jury returned into Court at ten minutes past twelve.

The murdered man at that time stood directly opposite the Jury-box, on the other side of the Court. As I took my place, his eyes rested on me with great attention ; he seemed satisfied, and slowly shook a great grey veil, which he carried on his arm for the first time, over his head and whole form. As I gave in our verdict, " Guilty," the veil collapsed, all was gone, and his place was empty.

The murderer, being asked by the Judge, according to usage whether he had anything to say before sentence of death should be passed upon him, indistinctly muttered something which was described in the leading newspapers of the following day as " a few rambling, incoherent, and half-audible words, in which he was understood to complain that he had not had a fair trial, because the Foreman of the Jury was prepossessed against him." The remarkable declaration that he really made was this : " *My Lord, I knew I was a doomed man, when the Foreman of the Jury came into the box. My Lord, I knew he would never let me off, because before I was taken, he somehow got to my bedside in the night, woke me, and put a rope round my neck.*"

THE PHANTOM COACH

THE circumstances I am about to relate to you have truth to recommend them. They happened to myself, and my recollection of them is as vivid as if they had taken place only yesterday. Twenty years, however, have gone by since that night. During those twenty years I have told the story to but one other person. I tell it now with a reluctance which I find it difficult to overcome. All I entreat, meanwhile, is that you will abstain from forcing your own conclusions upon me. I want nothing explained away. I desire no arguments. My mind on this subject is quite made up, and, having the testimony of my own senses to rely upon, I prefer to abide by it.

Well ! It was just twenty years ago, and within a day or two of the end of the grouse season. I had been out all day with my gun, and had had no sport to speak of. The wind was due east ; the month, December ; the place, a bleak wide moor in the far north of England. And I had lost my way. It was not a pleasant place in which to lose one's way, with the first feathery flakes of a coming snowstorm just fluttering down upon the heather, and the leaden evening closing in all around. I shaded my eyes with my hand, and stared anxiously into the gathering darkness, where the purple moorland melted into a range of low hills, some ten or twelve miles distant. Not the faintest smoke-wreath, not the tiniest cultivated patch, or fence, or sheep-track, met my eyes in any direction. There was nothing for it but to walk on, and take my chance of finding what shelter I could, by the way. So I shouldered my gun again, and pushed wearily forward ; for I had been on foot since an hour after daybreak, and had eaten nothing since breakfast.

Meanwhile, the snow began to come down with ominous steadiness, and the wind fell. After this, the cold became more intense, and the night came rapidly up. As for me, my prospects darkened with the darkening sky, and my heart grew heavy as I thought how my young wife was already watching for me through the window of our little inn parlour, and thought of all the suffering in store for her throughout this weary night. We had been married four months, and, having spent our autumn in the Highlands, were now lodging in a remote little village situated just on the verge of the great English moorlands. We were very much in love, and, of course, very happy. This morning, when we parted, she had implored me to return before dusk, and I had promised her that I would. What would I not have given to have kept my word !

Even now, weary as I was, I felt that with a supper, an hour's rest, and a guide, I might still get back to her before midnight, if only guide and shelter could be found.

And all this time the snow fell and the night thickened. I stopped and shouted every now and then, but my shouts seemed only to make the silence deeper. Then a vague sense of uneasiness came upon me, and I began to remember stories of travellers who had walked on and on in the falling snow until, wearied out, they were fain to lie down and sleep their lives away. Would it be possible, I asked myself, to keep on thus through all the long dark night ? Would there not come a time when my limbs must fail, and my resolution give way ? When I, too, must sleep the sleep of death. Death ! I shuddered. How hard to die just now, when life lay all so bright before me ! How hard for my darling, whose whole loving heart——but that thought was not to be borne ! To banish it, I shouted again, louder and longer, and then listened eagerly. Was my shout answered, or did I only fancy that I heard a far-off cry? I halloed again, and again the echo followed. Then a wavering speck of light came suddenly out of the dark, shifting, disappearing, growing momentarily nearer and brighter. Running towards it at full speed, I found myself, to my great joy, face to face with an old man and a lantern.

" Thank God ! " was the exclamation that burst involuntarily from my lips.

Blinking and frowning, he lifted his lantern and peered into my face.

" What for ? " growled he, sulkily.

" Well—for you. I began to fear I should be lost in the snow."

" Eh, then, folks do get cast away hereabouts fra' time to time, an' what's to hinder you from bein' cast away likewise, if the Lord's so minded ? "

"If the Lord is so minded that you and I shall be lost together, friend, we must submit," I replied ; "but I don't mean to be lost without you. How far am I now from Dwolding?"

"A gude twenty mile, more or less."

"And the nearest village?"

"The nearest village is Wyke, an' that's twelve mile t'other side."

"Where do you live, then?"

"Out yonder," said he, with a vague jerk of the lantern.

"You're going home, I presume?"

"Maybe I am."

"Then I'm going with you."

The old man shook his head, and rubbed his nose reflectively with the handle of the lantern.

"It ain't no use," growled he. "He 'on't let you in—not he."

"We'll see about that," I replied, briskly. "Who is He?"

"The master."

"Who is the master?"

"That's nowt to you," was the unceremonious reply.

"Well, well ; you lead the way, and I'll engage that the master shall give me shelter and a supper to-night."

"Eh, you can try him !" muttered my reluctant guide ; and, still shaking his head, he hobbled, gnome-like, away through the falling snow. A large mass loomed up presently out of the darkness, and a huge dog rushed out, barking furiously.

"Is this the house?" I asked.

"Ay, it's the house. Down, Bey !" And he fumbled in his pocket for the key.

I drew up close behind him, prepared to lose no chance of entrance, and saw in the little circle of light shed by the lantern that the door was heavily studded with iron nails, like the door of a prison. In another minute he had turned the key and I had pushed past him into the house.

Once inside, I looked round with curiosity, and found myself in a great raftered hall, which served, apparently, a variety of uses. One end was piled to the roof with corn, like a barn. The other was stored with flour-sacks, agricultural implements, casks, and all kinds of miscellaneous lumber ; while from the beams overhead hung rows of hams, flitches, and bunches of dried herbs for winter use. In the centre of the floor stood some huge object gauntly dressed in a dingy wrapping-cloth, and reaching half-way to the rafters. Lifting a corner of this cloth, I saw, to my surprise, a telescope of very considerable size, mounted on a rude movable platform, with four small wheels. The tube was made of painted wood, bound round with bands of metal, rudely fashioned ; the speculum, so far as I could estimate its size in the dim light, measured at least fifteen inches in diameter. While I was yet examining the instrument, and asking myself whether it was not the work of some self-taught optician, a bell rang sharply.

"That's for you," said my guide, with a malicious grin. " Yonder's his room."

He pointed to a low black door at the opposite side of the hall. I crossed over, rapped somewhat loudly, and went in, without waiting for an invitation. A huge, white-haired old man rose from a table covered with books and papers, and confronted me sternly.

"Who are you ? " said he. " How came you here ? What do you want ? "

"James Murray, barrister-at-law. On foot across the moor. Meat, drink, and sleep."

He bent his bushy brows into a portentous frown.

"Mine is not a house of entertainment," he said, haughtily. "Jacob, how dared you admit this stranger ? "

"I didn't admit him," grumbled the old man. " He followed me over the moor, and shouldered his way in before me. I'm no match for six foot two."

"And pray, sir, by what right have you forced an entrance into my house ? "

"The same by which I should have clung to your boat, if I were drowning. The right of self-preservation."

"Self-preservation ? "

"There's an inch of snow on the ground already," I replied, briefly ; " and it would be deep enough to cover my body before daybreak."

He strode to the window, pulled aside a heavy black curtain, and looked out.

"It is true," he said. " You can stay, if you choose, till morning. Jacob, serve the supper."

With this he waved me to a seat, resumed his own, and became at once absorbed in the studies from which I had disturbed him.

I placed my gun in a corner, drew a chair to the hearth, and examined my quarters at leisure. Smaller and less incongruous in its arrangements than the hall, this room contained, nevertheless, much to awaken my curiosity. The floor was carpetless. The whitewashed walls were in parts scrawled over with strange diagrams, and in others covered with shelves crowded with philosophical instruments, the uses of many of which were unknown to me. On one side of the fireplace, stood a bookcase filled with dingy folios ; on the other, a small organ, fantastically decorated with painted carvings of mediæval saints and devils. Through the half-opened door of a cupboard at the farther end of the room, I saw a long array of geological specimens, surgical preparations, crucibles, retorts, and jars of chemicals ; while on the mantelshelf beside me, amid a number of small objects, stood a model of the solar system, a small galvanic battery, and a microscope. Every chair had its burden. Every corner was heaped high with books. The very floor was littered over with maps, casts, papers, tracings, and learned lumber of all conceivable kinds.

I stared about me with an amazement increased by every fresh object upon which my eyes chanced to rest. So strange a room I had never seen ; yet seemed it stranger still, to find such a room in a lone farmhouse amid those wild and solitary moors ! Over and over again, I looked from my host to his surroundings, and from his surroundings back to my host, asking myself who and what he could be ? His head was singularly fine ; but it was more the head of a poet than of a philosopher. Broad in the temples, prominent over the eyes, and clothed with a rough profusion of perfectly white hair, it had all the ideality and much of the ruggedness that characterises the head of Louis von Beethoven. There were the same deep lines about the mouth, and the same stern furrows in the brow. There was the same concentration of expression. While I was yet observing him, the door opened, and Jacob brought in the supper. His master then closed his book, rose, and with more courtesy of manner than he had yet shown, invited me to the table.

A dish of ham and eggs, a loaf of brown bread, and a bottle of admirable sherry, were placed before me.

" I have but the homeliest farmhouse fare to offer you, sir," said my entertainer. " Your appetite, I trust, will make up for the deficiencies of our larder."

I had already fallen upon the viands, and now protested, with the enthusiasm of a starving sportsman, that I had never eaten anything so delicious.

He bowed stiffly, and sat down to his own supper, which consisted, primitively, of a jug of milk and a basin of porridge. We ate in silence and, when we had done, Jacob removed the tray. I then drew my chair back to the fireside. My host, somewhat to my surprise, did the same, and turning abruptly towards me, said :

" Sir, I have lived here in strict retirement for three-and-twenty years. During that time, I have not seen as many strange faces, and I have not read a single newspaper. You are the first stranger who has crossed my threshold for more than four years. Will you favour me with a few words of information respecting that outer world from which I have parted company so long ? "

" Pray interrogate me," I replied. " I am heartily at your service."

He bent his head in acknowledgment ; leaned forward, with his elbows resting on his knees and his chin supported in the palms of his hands ; stared fixedly into the fire ; and proceeded to question me.

His inquiries related chiefly to scientific matters, with the later progress of which, as applied to the practical purposes of life, he was almost wholly unacquainted. No student of science myself, I replied as well as my slight information permitted ; but the task was far from easy, and I was much relieved when, passing from interrogation to discussion, he began pouring forth his own conclusions upon the facts which I had been attempting to place before him. He talked, and I listened spellbound. He talked till I believe he almost forgot my presence, and only thought aloud. I had never heard anything like it then ; I have never heard anything like it since. By-and-by—I forget now by what link of conjecture or illustration—he passed on to that field which lies beyond the boundary line of even conjectural philosophy, and reaches no man knows whither. He spoke of the soul and its aspirations ; of the spirit and its powers ; of second sight ; of prophecy ; of those phenomena which, under the names of ghosts, spectres, and supernatural appearances, have been denied by the sceptics and attested by the credulous, of all ages.

" The world," he said, " grows hourly more and more sceptical of all that lies beyond its own narrow radius ; and our men of science foster the fatal tendency. They condemn as fable all that resists experiment. They reject as false all that cannot be brought to the test of the laboratory or the dissecting-room. Against what superstition have they waged so long and obstinate a war as against the belief in apparitions ? And yet what superstition has maintained its hold upon the minds of men so long and so firmly ? Show me any fact in physics, in history, in archæology, which is supported by testimony so wide and so various. Attested by all races of men, in all ages, and in all climates, by the soberest sages of antiquity, by the rudest savage of to-day, by the Christian, the Pagan, the Pantheist, the Materialist, this phenomenon is treated as a nursery tale by the philosophers of our century. Circumstantial evidence weighs with them as a feather in the balance.

The comparison of causes with effects, however valuable in physical science, is put aside as worthless and unreliable. The evidence of competent witnesses, however conclusive in a court of justice, counts for nothing. He who pauses before he pronounces, is condemned as a trifler. He who believes, is a dreamer or a fool."

He spoke with bitterness, and, having said this, relapsed for some minutes into silence. Presently he raised his head from his hands and added, with an altered voice and manner :

" I, sir, paused, investigated, believed, and was not ashamed to state my convictions to the world. I, too, was branded as a visionary, held up to ridicule by my contemporaries, and hooted from that field of science in which I had laboured with honour during all the best years of my life. These things happened just three-and-twenty years ago. Since then I have lived as you see me living now, and the world has forgotten me, as I have forgotten the world. You have my history."

" It is a very sad one," I murmured, scarcely knowing what to answer.

" It is a very common one," he replied. " I have only suffered for the truth, as many a better and wiser man has suffered before me."

He rose, as if desirous of ending the conversation, and went over to the window.

" It has ceased snowing," he observed, as he dropped the curtain and came back to the fireside.

" Ceased ! " I exclaimed, starting eagerly to my feet. " Oh, if it were only possible—but no ! it is hopeless. Even if I could find my way across the moor, I could not walk twenty miles to-night."

" Walk twenty miles to-night ! " repeated my host. " What are you thinking of ? "

" Of my wife," I replied impatiently. " Of my young wife, who does not know that I have lost my way, and who is at this moment breaking her heart with suspense and terror."

" Where is she ? "

" At Dwolding, twenty miles away."

" At Dwolding," he echoed, thoughtfully. " Yes, the distance, it is true, is twenty miles ; but—are you so very anxious to save the next six or eight hours ? "

" So very, very anxious that I would give ten guineas at this moment for a guide and a horse."

" Your wish can be gratified at a less costly rate," said he, smiling. " The night mail from the north, which changes horses at Dwolding, passes within five miles of this spot, and will be due at a certain cross-road in about an hour and a quarter. If Jacob were to go with you across the moor, and put you into the old coach-road, you could find your way, I suppose, to where it joins the new one ? "

" Easily—gladly."

He smiled again, rang the bell, gave the old servant his directions, and, taking a bottle of whisky and a wineglass from the cupboard in which he kept his chemicals, said :

" The snow lies deep, and it will be difficult walking to-night on the moor. A glass of usquebaugh before you start ? "

I would have declined the spirit, but he pressed it on me, and I drank it. It went down my throat like liquid flame, and almost took my breath away.

" It is strong," he said ; " but it will help to keep out the cold. And now you have no moments to spare. Good-night ! "

I thanked him for his hospitality, and would have shaken hands, but that he had turned away before I could finish my sentence. In another minute I had traversed the hall, Jacob had locked the outer door behind me, and we were out on the wide white moor.

Although the wind had fallen, it was still bitterly cold. Not a star glimmered in the black vault overhead. Not a sound, save the rapid crunching of the snow beneath our feet, disturbed the heavy stillness of the night. Jacob, not too well pleased with his mission, shambled on before in sullen silence, his lantern in his hand, and his shadow at his feet. I followed, with my gun over my shoulder, as little inclined for conversation as himself. My thoughts were full of my late host. His voice yet rang in my ears. His eloquence yet held my imagination captive. I remember to this day, with surprise, how my over-excited brain retained whole sentences and parts of sentences, troops of brilliant images, and fragments of splendid reasoning, in the very words in which he had uttered them. Musing thus over what I had heard, and striving to recall a lost link here and there, I strode on at the heels of my guide, absorbed and unobservant. Presently—at the end, as it seemed to me, of only a few minutes—he came to a sudden halt, and said :

" Yon's your road. Keep the stone fence to your right hand, and you can't fail of the way."

" This, then, is the old coach-road ? "

" Ay, 'tis the old coach-road."

" And how far do I go, before I reach the cross-roads ? "

" Nigh upon three mile."

I pulled out my purse, and he became more communicative.

" The road's a fair road enough," said he, " for foot passengers ; but 'twas over steep and narrow for the northern traffic. You'll mind where the parapet's broken away, close again the sign-post. It's never been mended since the accident."

" What accident ? "

" Eh, the night mail pitched right over into the valley below —a gude fifty feet an' more—just at the worst bit o' road in the whole county."

" Horrible ! Were many lives lost ? "

" All. Four were found dead, and t'other two died next morning."

" How long is it since this happened ? "

" Just nine year."

" Near the sign-post, you say ? I will bear it in mind. Good-night."

" Gude-night, sir, and thankee." Jacob pocketed his half-crown, made a faint pretence of touching his hat, and trudged back by the way he had come.

I watched the light of his lantern till it quite disappeared, and then turned to pursue my way alone. This was no longer matter of the slightest difficulty, for, despite the dead darkness overhead, the line of stone fence showed distinctly enough against the pale gleam of the snow. How silent it seemed now with only my foot-steps to listen to ; how silent and how solitary ! A strange dis-agreeable sense of loneliness stole over me. I walked faster. I hummed a fragment of a tune. I cast up enormous sums in my head, and accumulated them at compound interest. I did my best, in short, to forget the startling speculations to which I had but just been listening, and, to some extent, I succeeded.

Meanwhile the night air seemed to become colder and colder, and though I walked fast I found it impossible to keep myself warm. My feet were like ice. I lost sensation in my hands, and grasped my gun mechanically. I even breathed with difficulty, as though, instead of traversing a quiet north country highway, I were scaling the uppermost heights of some gigantic Alp. This last symptom became presently so distressing, that I was forced to stop for a few minutes and lean against the stone fence. As I did so, I chanced to look back up the road, and there, to my infinite relief, I saw a distant point of light, like the gleam of an approaching lantern. I at first concluded that Jacob had retraced his steps and followed me ; but even as the conjecture presented itself, a second light flashed into sight—a light evidently parallel with the first, and approaching at the same rate of motion. It needed no second thought to show me that these must be the carriage-lamps of some private vehicle, though it seemed strange that it should take a road professedly disused and dangerous.

There could be no doubt, however, of the fact, for the lamps grew larger and brighter every moment, and I even fancied I could already see the dark outline of the carriage between them. It was coming up very fast, and quite noiselessly, the snow being nearly a foot deep under the wheels.

And now the body of the vehicle became distinctly visible behind the lamps. It looked strangely lofty. A sudden suspicion flashed upon me. Was it possible that I had passed the cross-roads in the dark without observing the sign-post, and could this be the very coach which I had come to meet?

No need to ask myself that question a second time, for here it came round the bend of the road, guard and driver, one outside passenger, and four steaming greys, all wrapped in a soft haze of light, through which the lamps blazed out, like a pair of fiery meteors.

I jumped forward, waved my hat, and shouted. The mail came down at full speed, and passed me. For a moment I feared that I had not been seen or heard, but it was only for a moment. The coachman pulled up ; the guard, muffled to the eyes in capes and comforters, and apparently sound asleep in the rumble, neither answered my hail nor made the slightest effort to dismount ; the outside passenger did not even turn his head. I opened the door for myself, and looked in. There were but three travellers inside, so I stepped in, shut the door, slipped into the vacant corner, and congratulated myself on my good fortune.

The atmosphere of the coach seemed, if possible, colder than that of the outer air, and was pervaded by a singularly damp and disagreeable smell. I looked round at my fellow-passengers. They were all three men and all silent. They did not seem to be asleep, but each leaned back in his corner of the vehicle, as if absorbed in his own reflections. I attempted to open a conversation.

" How intensely cold it is to-night," I said, addressing my opposite neighbour.

He lifted his head, looked at me, but made no reply.

" The winter," I added, " seems to have begun in earnest."

Although the corner in which he sat was so dim that I could distinguish none of his features very clearly, I saw that his eyes were still turned full upon me. And yet he answered never a word.

At any other time I should have felt, and perhaps expressed, some annoyance, but at the moment I felt too ill to do either. The icy coldness of the night air had struck a chill to my very marrow, and the strange smell inside the coach was affecting me with an intolerable nausea. I shivered from head to foot, and, turning to my left-hand neighbour, asked if he had any objection to an open window?

He neither spoke nor stirred.

I repeated the question somewhat more loudly, but with the same result. Then I lost patience, and let the sash down. As I did so, the leather strap broke in my hand, and I observed that the glass was covered with a thick coat of mildew, the accumulation, apparently, of years. My attention being thus drawn to the condition of the coach, I examined it more narrowly, and saw by the uncertain light of the outer lamps that it was in the last stage of dilapidation. Every part of it was not only out of repair, but in a condition of decay. The sashes splintered at a touch. The leather fittings were crusted over with mould, and literally rotting from the woodwork. The floor was almost breaking away beneath my feet. The whole machine, in short, was foul with damp, and had evidently been dragged from some outhouse in which it had been mouldering away for years, to do another day or two of duty on the road.

I turned to the third passenger, whom I had not yet addressed, and hazarded one more remark.

" This coach," I said, " is in a deplorable condition. The regular mail, I suppose, is under repair ? "

He moved his head slowly, and looked me in the face, without speaking a word. I shall never forget that look while I live. I turned cold at heart under it. I turn cold at heart even now when I recall it. His eyes glowed with a fiery unnatural lustre. His face was livid as the face of a corpse. His bloodless lips were drawn back as if in the agony of death, and showed the gleaming teeth between.

The words that I was about to utter died upon my lips, and a strange horror—a dreadful horror—came upon me. My sight had by this time become used to the gloom of the coach, and I could see with tolerable distinctness. I turned to my opposite neighbour. He, too, was looking at me, with the same startling pallor in his face, and the same stony glitter in his eyes. I passed my hand across my brow. I turned to the passenger on the seat beside my own, and saw—oh Heaven ! how shall I describe what I saw ? I saw that he was no living man—that none of them were living men, like myself ! A pale phosphorescent light—the light of putrefaction—played upon their awful faces ; upon their hair, dank with the dews of the grave ; upon their clothes, earth-stained and dropping to pieces ; upon their hands, which were as the hands of corpses long buried. Only their eyes, their terrible eyes, were living ; and those eyes were all turned menacingly upon me !

A shriek of terror, a wild unintelligible cry for help and mercy, burst from my lips as I flung myself against the door, and strove in vain to open it.

In that single instant, brief and vivid as a landscape beheld in the flash of summer lightning, I saw the moon shining down through a rift of stormy cloud—the ghastly sign-post rearing its warning finger by the wayside—the broken parapet—the plunging horses—the black gulf below. Then, the coach reeled like a ship at sea. There came a mighty crash—a sense of crushing pain—and then darkness. . . .

It seemed as if years had gone by when I awoke one morning from a deep sleep, and found my wife watching by my bedside. I will pass over the scene that ensued, and give you, in half a dozen words, the tale she told me with tears of thanksgiving. I had fallen over a precipice, close against the junction of the old coach-road and the new, and had only been saved from certain death by lighting upon a deep snowdrift that had accumulated at the foot of the rock beneath. In this snowdrift I was discovered at daybreak, by a couple of shepherds, who carried me to the nearest shelter, and brought a surgeon to my aid. The surgeon found me in a state of raving delirium, with a broken arm and a compound fracture of the skull. The letters in my pocket-book showed my name and address ; my wife was summoned to nurse me ; and, thanks to youth and a fine constitution, I came out of danger at last. The place of my fall, I need scarcely say, was precisely that at which the north mail had a frightful accident nine years before.

I never told my wife the fearful events which I have just related to you. I told the surgeon who attended me ; but he treated the whole adventure as a mere dream born of the fever in my brain. We discussed the question over and over again, until we found that we could discuss it with temper no longer, and then we dropped it. Others may form what conclusions they please—I *know* that twenty years ago I was the fourth inside passenger in that Phantom Coach.

MADAM CROWL'S GHOST

I'M an old woman now; and I was but thirteen my last
birthday, the night I came to Applewale House. My aunt
was the housekeeper there, and a sort o' one-horse carriage
was down at Lexhoe to take me and my box up to Applewale.

I was a bit frightened by the time I got to Lexhoe, and
when I saw the carriage and horse, I wished myself back again
with my mother at Hazelden. I was crying when I got into the
" shay "—that's what we used to call it—and old John Mulbery
that drove it, and was a good-natured fellow, bought me a
handful of apples at the Golden Lion, to cheer me up a bit;
and he told me that there was a currant-cake, and tea, and
pork-chops, waiting for me, all hot, in my aunt's room at the
great house. It was a fine moonlight night and I ate the apples,
lookin' out o' the shay winda.

It is a shame for gentlemen to frighten a poor foolish child
like I was. I sometimes think it might be tricks. There was
two on 'em on the tap o' the coach beside me. And they began
to question me after nightfall, when the moon rose, where I
was going to. Well, I told them it was to wait on Dame Arabella
Crowl, of Applewale House, near by Lexhoe.

" Ho, then," says one of them, " you'll not be long
there ! "

And I looked at him as much as to say, " Why not ? " for
I had spoke out when I told them where I was goin', as if 'twas
something clever I had to say.

" Because," says he—" and don't you for your life tell no
one, only watch her and see—she's possessed by the devil, and
more an half a ghost. Have you got a Bible ? "

" Yes, sir," says I. For my mother put my little Bible in
my box, and I knew it was there : and by the same token,

455

though the print's too small for my ald eyes, I have it in my press to this hour.

As I looked up at him, saying " Yes, sir," I thought I saw him winkin' at his friend ; but I could not be sure.

" Well," says he, " be sure you put it under your bolster every night, it will keep the ald girl's claws aff ye."

And I got such a fright when he said that, you wouldn't fancy ! And I'd a liked to ask him a lot about the ald lady, but I was too shy, and he and his friend began talkin' together about their own consarns, and dowly enough I got down, as I told ye, at Lexhoe. My heart sank as I drove into the dark avenue. The trees stands very thick and big, as ald as the ald house, almost, and four people, with their arms out and finger-tips touchin', barely girds round some of them.

Well, my neck was stretched out o' the winda, looking for the first view o' the great house ; and, all at once we pulled up in front of it.

A great white-and-black house it is, wi' great black beams across and right up it, and gables lookin' out, as white as a sheet, to the moon, and the shadows o' the trees, two or three up and down upon the front, you could count the leaves on them, and all the little diamond-shaped winda-panes, glimmering on the great hall winda, and great shutters, in the old fashion, hinged on the wall outside, boulted across all the rest o' the windas in front, for there was but three or four servants, and the old lady in the house, and most o' t'rooms was locked up.

My heart was in my mouth when I sid the journey was over, and this, the great house afore me, and I sa near my aunt that I never sid till noo, and Dame Crowl, that I was come to wait upon, and was afeard on already.

My aunt kissed me in the hall, and brought me to her room. She was tall and thin, wi' a pale face and black eyes, and long thin hands wi black mittins on. She was past fifty, and her word was short ; but her word was law. I hev no complaints to make of her ; but she was a hard woman, and I think she would hev been kinder to me if I had bin her sister's child in place of her brother's. But all that's o' no consequence noo.

The squire—his name was Mr. Chevenix Crowl, he was Dame Crowl's grandson—came down there, by way of seeing that the old lady was well treated, about twice or thrice in the year. I sid him but twice all the time I was at Applewale House.

I can't say but she was well taken care of, notwithstandin', but that was because my aunt and Meg Wyvern, that was her maid, had a conscience, and did their duty by her.

Mrs. Wyvern—Meg Wyvern my aunt called her to herself, and Mrs. Wyvern to me—was a fat, jolly lass of fifty, a good height and a good breadth, always good-humoured, and walked slow. She had fine wages, but she was a bit stingy, and kept all her fine clothes under lock and key, and wore, mostly, a twilled chocolate cotton, wi' red, and yellow, and green sprigs and balls on ħt, and it lasted wonderful.

She never gave me nout, not the vally o' a brass thimble, all the time I was there ; but she was good-humoured, and always laughin', and she talked no end o' proas over her tea ; and, seeing me sa sackless and dowly, she roused me up wi' her laughin' and stories ; and I think I liked her better than my aunt—children is so taken wi' a bit o' fun or a story— though my aunt was very good to me, but a hard woman about some things, and silent always.

My aunt took me into her bed-chamber, that I might rest myself a bit while she was settin' the tea in her room. But first she patted me on the shouther, and said I was a tall lass o' my years, and had spired up well, and asked me if I could do plain work and stitchin' ; and she looked in my face, and said I was like my father, her brother, that was dead and gone, and she hoped I was a better Christian and wad na du a' that lids.

It was a hard sayin' the first time I set my foot in her room, I thought.

When I went into the next room, the housekeeper's room —very comfortable, yak (oak) all round—there was a fine fire blazin' away, wi' coal, and peat, and wood, all in a low together, and tea on the table, and hot cake, and smokin' meat ; and there was Mrs. Wyvern, fat, jolly, and talkin' away, more in an hour than my aunt would in a year.

While I was still at my tea my aunt went upstairs to see Madam Crowl.

" She's a-gone up to see that old Judith Squailes is awake," says Mrs. Wyvern. " Judith sits with Madam Crowl when me and Mrs. Shutters "—that was my aunt's name—" is away. She's a troublesome old lady. Ye'll hev to be sharp wi' her, or she'll be into the fire, or out o' t' winda. She goes on wires, she does, old though she be."

" How old, ma'am ? " says I.

" Ninety-three her last birthday, and that's eight months

gone," says she ; and she laughed. "And don't be askin' questions about her before your aunt—mind, I tell ye ; just take her as you find her, and that's all."

"And what's to be my business about her, please ma'am ? " says I.

"About the old lady ? Well," says she, "your aunt, Mrs. Shutters, will tell you that ; but I suppose you'll hev to sit in the room with your work, and see she's at no mischief, and let her amuse herself with her things on the table, and get her her food or drink as she calls for it, and keep her out o' mischief, and ring the bell hard if she's troublesome."

"Is she deaf, ma'am ? "

"No, nor blind," says she ; "as sharp as a needle, but she's gone quite aupy, and can't remember nout rightly ; and Jack the Giant Killer, or Goody Twoshoes will please her as well as the King's court, or the affairs of the nation."

"And what did the little girl go away for, ma'am, that went on Friday last ? My aunt wrote to my mother she was to go."

"Yes ; she's gone."

"What for ? " says I again.

"She didn't answer Mrs. Shutters, I do suppose," says she. "I don't know. Don't be talkin' ; your aunt can't abide a talkin' child."

"And please, ma'am, is the old lady well in health ? " says I.

"It ain't no harm to ask that," says she. "She's torflin' a bit lately, but better this week past, and I dare say she'll last out her hundred years yet. Hish ! Here's your aunt coming down the passage."

In comes my aunt, and begins talkin' to Mrs. Wyvern, and I, beginnin' to feel more comfortable and at home like, was walkin' about the room lookin' at this thing and at that. There was pretty old china things on the cupboard, and pictures again the wall ; and there was a door open in the wainscot, and I sees a queer old leathern jacket, wi' straps and buckles to it, and sleeves as long as the bed-post, hangin' up inside.

"What's that you're at, child ? " says my aunt, sharp enough, turning about when I thought she least minded. "What's that in your hand ? "

"This, ma'am ? " says I, turning about with the leathern jacket. "I don't know what it is, ma'am."

Pale as she was, the red came up in her cheeks, and her eyes flashed wi' anger, and I think only she had half a dozen steps to take, between her and me, she'd a gov me a sizzup. But she did give me a shake by the shouther, and she plucked the thing out o' my hand, and says she, " While ever you stay here, don't ye meddle wi' nout that don't belong to ye," and she hung it up on the pin that was there, and shut the door wi' a bang and locked it fast.

Mrs. Wyvern was liftin' up her hands and laughin' all this time, quietly in her chair, rolling herself a bit in it, as she used when she was kinkin'.

The tears was in my eyes, and she winked at my aunt, and says she, dryin' her own eyes that was wet wi' the laughin', " Tut, the child meant no harm—come here to me, child. It's only a pair o' crutches for lame ducks, and ask us no questions mind, and we'll tell ye no lies ; and come here and sit down, and drink a mug o' beer before ye go to your bed."

My room, mind ye, was upstairs, next to the old lady's, and Mrs. Wyvern's bed was near hers in her room and I was to be ready at call, if need should be.

The old lady was in one of her. tantrums that night and part of the day before. She used to take fits o' the sulks. Sometimes she would not let them dress her, and other times she would not let them take her clothes off. She was a great beauty, they said, in her day. But there was no one about Applewale that remembered her in her prime. And she was dreadful fond o' dress, and had thick silks, and stiff satins, and velvets, and laces, and all sorts, enough to set up seven shops at the least. All her dresses was old-fashioned and queer, but worth a fortune.

Well, I went to my bed. I lay for a while awake ; for a' things was new to me ; and I think the tea was in my nerves, too, for I wasn't used to it, except now and then on a holiday, or the like. And I heard Mrs. Wyvern talkin', and I listened with my hand to my ear ; but I could not hear Mrs. Crowl, and I don't think she said a word.

There was great care took of her. The people at Applewale knew that when she died they would every one get the sack ; and their situations was well paid and easy.

The doctor come twice a week to see the old lady, and you may be sure they all did as he bid them. One thing was the same every time ; they were never to cross or frump her, any way, but to humour and please her in everything.

So she lay in her clothes all that night, and next day, not
a word she said, and I was at my needlework all that day, in
my own room, except when I went down to my dinner.

I would a liked to see the ald lady, and even to hear her
speak.   But she might as well a'bin in Lunnon a' the time
for me.

When I had my dinner my aunt sent me out for a walk
for an hour.   I was glad when I came back, the trees was so
big, and the place so dark and lonesome, and 'twas a cloudy
day, and I cried a deal, thinkin' of home, while I was walkin'
alone there.   That evening, the candles bein' alight, I was
sittin' in my room, and the door was open into Madam Crowl's
chamber, where my aunt was.   It was, then, for the first time
I heard what I suppose was the ald lady talking.

It was a queer noise like, I couldn't well say which, a bird,
or a beast, only it had a bleatin' sound in it, and was very
small.

I pricked my ears to hear all I could.   But I could not make
out one word she said.   And my aunt answered :

" The evil one can't hurt no one, ma'am, bout the Lord
permits."

Then the same queer voice from the bed says something
more that I couldn't make head nor tail on.

And my aunt med answer again :   " Let them pull faces,
ma'am, and say what they will ; if the Lord be for us, who
can be against us ? "

I kept listenin' with my ear turned to the door, holdin'
my breath, but not another word or sound came in from the
room.   In about twenty minutes, as I was sittin' by the table,
lookin' at the pictures in the old Æsop's Fables, I was aware o'
something moving at the door, and lookin' up I sid my aunt's
face lookin' in at the door, and her hand raised.

" Hish ! " says she, very soft, and comes over to me on
tiptoe, and she says in a whisper :   " Thank God, she's asleep
at last, and don't ye make no noise till I come back, for I'm
goin' down to take my cup o' tea, and I'll be back i' noo—me
and Mrs. Wyvern, and she'll be sleepin' in the room, and you
can run down when we come up, and Judith will gie ye yaur
supper in my room."

And with that away she goes.

I kep' looking at the picture-book, as before, listenin' every
noo and then, but there was no sound, not a breath, that I
could hear ; an' I began whisperin' to the pictures and talkin'

to myself to keep my heart up, for I was growin' feared in that big room.

And at last up I got, and began walkin' about the room, lookin' at this and peepin' at that, to amuse my mind, ye'll understand. And at last what sud I do but peeps into Madame Crowl's bed-chamber.

A grand chamber it was, wi' a great four-poster, wi' flowered silk curtains as tall as the ceilin', and foldin' down on the floor, and drawn close all round. There was a lookin'-glass, the biggest I ever sid before, and the room was a blaze o' light. I counted twenty-two wax-candles, all alight. Such was her fancy, and no one dared say her nay.

I listened at the door, and gaped and wondered all round. When I heard there was not a breath, and did not see so much as a stir in the curtains, I took heart, and I walked into the room on tiptoe, and looked round again. Then I takes a keek at myself in the big glass ; and at last it came in my head, " Why couldn't I ha' a keek at the ald lady herself in the bed ? "

Ye'd think me a fule if ye knew half how I longed to see Dame Crowl, and I thought to myself if I didn't peep now I might wait many a day before I got so gude a chance again.

Well, my dear, I came to the side o' the bed, the curtains bein' close, and my heart a'most failed me. But I took courage, and I slips my finger in between the thick curtains, and then my hand. So I waits a bit, but all was still as death. So, softly, softly I draws the curtain, and there, sure enough, I sid before me, stretched out like the painted lady on the tomb-stean in Lexhoe Church, the famous Dame Crowl, of Applewale House. There she was, dressed out. You never sid the like in they days. Satin and silk, and scarlet and green, and gold and pint lace ; by Jen ! 'twas a sight ! A big powdered wig, half as high as herself, was a-top o' her head, and, wow !— was ever such wrinkles ?—and her old baggy throat all powdered white, and her cheeks rouged, and mouse-skin eyebrows, that Mrs. Wyvern used to stick on, and there she lay grand and stark, wi' a pair o' clocked silk hose on, and heels to her shoon as tall as nine-pins. Lawk ! But her nose was crooked and thin, and half the whites o' her eyes was open. She used to stand, dressed as she was, gigglin' and dribblin' before the lookin'-glass, wi' a fan in her hand, and a big nosegay in her bodice. Her winkled little hands was stretched down by her sides, and such long nails, all cut into points, I never sid in my days.

Could it ever a bin the fashion for grit fowk to wear their finger-nails so?

Well, I think ye'd a bin frightened yourself if ye'd a sid such a sight. I couldn't let go the curtain, nor move an inch, nor take my eyes off her; my very heart stood still. And in an instant she opens her eyes, and up she sits, and spins herself round, and down wi' her, wi' a clack on her two tall heels on the floor, facin' me, ogglin' in my face wi' her two great glassy eyes, and a wicked simper wi' her old wrinkled lips, and lang fause teeth.

Well, a corpse is a natural thing; but this was the dreadfullest sight I ever sid. She had her fingers straight out pointin' at me, and her back was crooked, round again wi' age. Says she:

"Ye little limb! what for did ye say I killed the boy? I'll tickle ye till ye're stiff!"

If I'd a thought an instant, I'd a turned about and run. But I couldn't take my eyes off her, and I backed from her as soon as I could; and she came clatterin' after, like a thing on wires, with her fingers pointing to my throat, and she makin' all the time a sound with her tongue like zizz-zizz-zizz.

I kept backin' and backin' as quick as I could, and her fingers was only a few inches away from my throat, and I felt I'd lose my wits if she touched me.

I went back this way, right into the corner, and I gev a yellock, ye'd think saul and body was partin', and that minute my aunt, from the door, calls out wi' a blare, and the ald lady turns round on her, and I turns about, and ran through my room, and down the back stairs, as hard as my legs could carry me.

I cried hearty, I can tell you, when I got down to the housekeeper's room. Mrs. Wyvern laughed a deal when I told her what happened. But she changed her key when she heard the ald lady's words.

"Say them again," says she.

So I told her.

"Ye little limb! What for did ye say I killed the boy? I'll tickle ye till ye're stiff."

"And did ye say she killed a boy?" says she.

"Not I, ma'am," says I.

Judith was always up with me, after that, when the two elder women was away from her. I would a jumped out at winda, rather than stay alone in the same room wi' her.

It was about a week after, as well as I can remember, Mrs.

Wyvern, one day when me and her was alone, told me a thing about Madam Crowl that I did not know before.

She being young, and a great beauty, full seventy years before, had married Squire Crowl of Applewale. But he was a widower, and had a son about nine year old.

There never was tale or tidings of this boy after one mornin' No one could say where he went to. He was allowed too much liberty, and used to be off in the morning, one day, to the keeper's cottage, and breakfast wi' him, and away to the warren, and not home, mayhap, till evening, and another time down to the lake, and bathe there, and spend the day fishin' there, or paddlin' about in the boat. Well, no one could say what was gone wi' him ; only this, that his hat was found by the lake, under a haathorn that grows thar to this day, and 'twas thought he was drowned bathin'. And the squire's son, by his second marriage, by this Madam Crowl that lived sa dreadful lang, came in for the estates. It was his son, the ald lady's grandson, Squire Chevenix Crowl, that owned the estates at the time I came to Applewale.

There was a deal o' talk lang before my aunt's time about it ; and 'twas said the stepmother knew more than she was like to let out. And she managed her husband, the ald squire, wi' her whiteheft and flatteries. And as the boy was never seen more, in course of time the thing died out of fowks' minds.

I'm goin' to tell you noo about what I sid wi' my own een.

I was not there six months, and it was winter time, when the ald lady took her last sickness.

The doctor was afeard she might a took a fit o' madness, as she did, fifteen years befoore, and was buckled up, many a time, in a strait-waistcoat, which was the very leathern jerkin I sid in the closet, off my aunt's room.

Well, she didn't. She pined, and windered, and went off, torflin', torflin', quiet enough, till a day or two before her flittin', and then she took to rabblin', and sometimes skirlin' in the bed, ye'd think a robber had a knife to her throat, and she used to work out o' the bed, and not being strong enough, then, to walk or stand, she'd fall on the flure, wi' her ald wizened hands stretched before her face, and skirlin' still for mercy.

Ye may guess I didn't go into the room, and I used to be shiverin' in my bed wi' fear, at her skirlin' and scrafflin' on the flure, and blarin' out words that id make your skin turn blue.

My aunt, and Mrs. Wyvern, and Judith Squailes, and a

woman from Lexhoe, was always about her. At last she took fits, and they wore her out.

T' sir (parson) was there, and prayed for her; but she was past prayin' with. I suppose it was right, but none could think there was much good in it, and sa at lang last she made her flittin', and a' was over, and old Dame Crowl was shrouded and coffined and Squire Chevenix was wrote for. But he was away in France, and the delay was sa lang, that t' sir and doctor both agreed it would not du to keep her langer out o' her place, and no one cared but just them two, and my aunt and the rest o' us, from Applewale to go to the buryin'. So the old lady of Applewale was laid in the vault under Lexhoe Church; and we lived up at the great house till such time as the squire should come to tell his will about us, and pay off such as he chose to discharge.

I was put into another room, two doors away from what was Dame Crowl's chamber, after her death, and this thing happened the night before Squire Chevenix came to Applewale.

The room I was in now was a large square chamber, covered wi' yak pannels, but unfurnished except for my bed, which had no curtains to it, and a chair and a table, or so, that looked nothing at all in such a big room. And the big looking-glass, that the old lady used to keek into and admire herself from head to heel, now that there was na mair o' that wark, was put out o' the way, and stood against the wall in my room, for there was shiftin' o' many things in her chambers, ye may suppose, when she came to be coffined.

The news had come that day that the squire was to be down next morning at Applewale; and not sorry was I, for I thought I was sure to be sent home again to my mother. And right glad was I, and I was thinkin' of a' at hame, and my sister, Janet, and the kitten and the pymag, and Trimmer the tike, and all the rest, and I got so fidgety, I couldn't sleep, and the clock struck twelve, and me wide awake, and the room as dark as pick. My back was turned to the door, and my eyes toward the wall opposite.

Well, it could na be a full quarter past twelve, when I sees a lightin' on the wall befoore me, as if something took fire behind, and the shadas o' the bed, and the chair, and my gown, that was hangin' from the wall, was dancin' up and down, on the ceilin' beams and the yak pannels; and I turns my head ower my shouther quick, thinkin' something must a gone a' fire.

And what sud I see, by Jen! but the likeness o' the ald beldame, bedizened out in her satins and velvets, on her dead body, simperin', wi' her eyes as wide as saucers, and her face like the fiend himself. 'Twas a red light that rose about her in a fuffin low, as if her dress round her feet was blazin'. She was drivin' on right for me, wi' her ald shrivelled hands crooked as if she was goin' to claw me. I could not stir, but she passed me straight by, wi' a blast o' cald air, and I sid her, at the wall, in the alcove as my aunt used to call it, which was a recess where the state bed used to stand in ald times, wi' a door open wide, and her hands gropin' in at somethin' was there. I never sid that door befoore. And she turned round to me, like a thing on a pivot, flyrin' (grinning), and all at once the room was dark, and I standin' at the far side o' the bed; I don't know how I got there, and I found my tongue at last, and if I did na blare a yellock, rennin' down the gallery and almost pulled Mrs. Wyvern's door, off t'hooks, and frightened her half out o' her wits.

Ye may guess I did na sleep that night; and wi' the first light, down wi' me to my aunt, as fast as my two legs cud carry me.

Well, my aunt did na frump or flite me, as I thought she would, but she held me by the hand, and looked hard in my face all the time. And she telt me not to be feared; and says she:

" Hed the appearance a key in its hand? "

" Yes," says I, bringin' it to mind, " a big key in a queer brass handle."

" Stop a bit," says she, lettin' go ma hand, and openin' the cupboard-door. " Was it like this? " says she, takin' one out in her fingers and showing it to me, with a dark look in my face.

" That was it," says I, quick enough.

" Are ye sure? " she says, turnin' it round.

" Sart," says I, and I felt like I was gain' to faint when I sid it.

" Well, that will do, child," says she, saftly thinkin', and she locked it up again.

" The squire himself will be here to-day, before twelve o'clock, and ye must tell him all about it," says she, thinkin', " and I suppose I'll be leavin' soon, and so the best thing for the present is, that ye should go home this afternoon, and I'll look out another place for you when I can."

Fain was I, ye may guess, at that word.

My aunt packed up my things for me, and the three pounds
that was due to me, to bring home, and Squire Crowl himself
came down to Applewale that day, a handsome man, about
thirty years ald. It was the second time I sid him. But this
was the first time he spoke to me.

My aunt talked wi' him in the housekeeper's room, and
I don't know what they said. I was a bit feared on the squire,
he bein' a great gentleman down in Lexhoe, and I darn't go
near till I was called. And says he, smilin' :

"What's a' this ye a sen, child ? it mun be a dream, for
ye know there's na sic a thing as a bo or a freet in a' the world.
But whatever it was, ma little maid, sit ye down and tell us
all about it from first to last."

Well, so soon as I med an end, he thought a bit, and says
he to my aunt :

"I mind the place well. In old Sir Oliver's time lame Wyndel
told me there was a door in that recess, to the left, where the
lassie dreamed she saw my grandmother open it. He was
past eighty when he telt me that, and I but a boy. It's twenty
year sen. The plate and jewels used to be kept there, long
ago, before the iron closet was made in the arras chamber,
and he told me the key had a brass handle, and this ye say
was found in the bottom o' the kist where she kept her old
fans. Now, would not it be a queer thing if we found some
spoons or diamonds forgot there ? Ye mun come up wi' us,
lassie, and point to the very spot."

Loth was I, and my heart in my mouth, and fast I held
by my aunt's hand as I stept into that awsome room, and
showed them both how she came and passed me by, and the
spot where she stood, and where the door seemed to open.

There was an ald empty press against the wall then, and
shoving it aside, sure enough there was the tracing of a door
in the wainscot, and a keyhole stopped with wood, and planed
across as smooth as the rest, and the joining of the door all
stopped wi' putty the colour o' yak, and, but for the hinges
that showed a bit when the press was shoved aside, ye would
not consayt there was a door there at all.

"Ha !" says he, wi' a queer smile, "this looks like it."

It took some minutes wi' a small chisel and hammer to
pick the bit o' wood out o' the keyhole. The key fitted, sure
enough, and, wi' a strang twist and a lang skreeak, the boult
went back and he pulled the door open.

There was another door inside, stranger than the first,

She was drivin' on right for me, wi' her ald shrivelled
hands crooked as if she was goin' to claw me.

but the lacks was gone, and it opened easy. Inside was a narrow floor and walls and vault o' brick ; we could not see what was in it, for 'twas dark as pick.

When my aunt had lighted the candle the squire held it up and stept in.

My aunt stood on tiptoe tryin' to look over his shouther, and I did na see nout.

" Ha ! ha ! " says the squire, steppin' backward. " What's that ? Gi'ma the poker—quick ! " says he to my aunt. And as she went to the hearth I peeps beside his arm, and I sid squat down in the far corner a monkey or a flayin' on the chest, or else the maist shrivelled up, wizzened ald wife that ever was sen on yearth.

" By Jen ! " says my aunt, as, puttin' the poker in his hand, she keeked by his shouther, and sid the ill-favoured thing, " hae a care, sir, what ye're doin'. Back wi' ye, and shut to the door ! "

But in place o' that he steps in saftly, wi' the poker pointed like a swoord, and he gies it a poke, and down it a' tumbles together, head and a', in a heap o' bayans and dust, little meyar an' a hatful.

'Twas the bayans o' a child ; a' the rest went to dust at a touch. They said nout for a while, but he turns round the skull as it lay on the floor.

Young as I was I consayted I knew well enough what they was thinkin' on.

" A dead cat ! " says he, pushin' back and blowin' out the can'le, and shuttin' to the door. " We'll come back, you and me, Mrs. Shutters, and look on the shelves by and bye. I've other matters first to speak to ye about ; and this little girl's goin' hame, ye say. She has her wages, and I mun mak' her a present," says he, pattin' my shoulder wi' his hand.

And he did gimma a goud pound, and I went aff to Lexhoe about an hour after, and sa hame by the stagecoach, and fain was I to be at hame again ; and I never saa ald Dame Crowl o' Applewale, God be thanked, either in appearance or in dream, at-efter. But when I was grown to be a woman my aunt spent a day and night wi' me at Littleham, and she telt me there was na doubt it was the poor little boy that was missing sa lang sen that was shut up to die thar in the dark by that wicked beldame, whar his skirls, or his prayers, or his thumpin' cud na be heard, and his hat was left by the water's edge, who-ever did it, to mak' belief he was drowned. The clothes, at the first touch, a' ran into a snuff o' dust in the cell whar the bayans was found. But there was a handful o' jet buttons, and a knife with a green handle, together wi' a couple o' pennies the poor little fella had in his pocket, I suppose, when he was decoyed in thar, and sid his last o' the light. And there was, amang the squire's papers, a copy o' the notice that was prented after he was lost, when the old squire thought he might a' run away or bin took by gipsies, and it said he had a green-hefted knife wi' him, and that his buttons were o' cut jet. Sa that is a' I hev to say consarnin' ald Dame Crowl, o' Applewale House.

BLACK COFFEE

Professor Jarvis sat among piles of reference-books, and stacks of notes and jottings, the silence about him unbroken save for the ceaseless scratching of his pen.

Professor Jarvis hated bustle and noise of all sorts, for they destroyed that continuity of thought, that following out of proved facts to their primary hypotheses, which was to him the chief end and aim of existence ; therefore he inhabited the thirtieth storey.

He had seen none but John, his valet, for nearly a month, sitting night after night, perched high above the great city, busied upon the work of which he had dreamed for years, his treatise upon " The Higher Ethics of Philosophy," and already it neared completion. A spirit of work had come upon him these last few weeks, a spirit that was a devil, cruel, relentless, allowing of no respite from the strain of intricate thought and nerve-racking effort ; hence the Professor sat writing night after night, and had of late done with little sleep and much black coffee.

To-night, however, he felt strangely tired, he laid down his pen, and, resting his throbbing temples between his hands, stared down vacantly at the sheets of manuscript before him.

As he leaned thus, striving against a feeling of nausea that had recurred frequently the last few days, the long, close-written lines became to him " things " endowed with sinuous life, that moved, squirming a thousand legs across the white paper.

Professor Jarvis closed his eyes and sighed wearily. " I really must get some sleep," he said to himself, " I wonder when it was I slept last ? " As he spoke he tried unsuccessfully to yawn and stretch himself. His glance, wandering aimlessly, paused at the lamp upon the desk before him, and as he stared at it, he noticed that the " things " had got from the paper and were writhing and creeping up the green shade. He sighed again, and his fingers fumbled among the papers beside him for the electric bell. Almost immediately, it seemed to him, he heard John's voice rather faint and far-away, responding from the shadow that lay beyond the light of the lamp.

" John, if you are really there, be so good as to switch on the light," said the Professor. " John," he continued, blinking at his valet in the sudden glare, " when did I sleep last ? "

" Why, sir, you haven't rightly slept for a week now, just a doze now and then on the couch, sir, but that's nothing ; if you'll allow me to advise you, sir, the best thing you could do would be to go to bed at once."

" Humph ! " said the Professor. " Thank you, John, but your advice, though excellent, is impracticable. I am engaged upon my last chapter, and sleep is impossible until it is finished."

" Begging your pardon, sir," began John, " but if you were to try undressing and going to bed properly——"

" Don't be a fool, John ! " cried the Professor, with a sudden access of anger that was strangely at variance with his usual placid manner, " do you think I wouldn't sleep if I could ? Can't you see I'm sick for sleep ? I tell you I'd sleep if I could, but I can't—there can be no rest for me I know now, until I've finished my book, and that will be somewhere about dawn," and the Professor glared up at John, his thick brows twitching, and his eyes glowing within the pale oval of his face with an unpleasant light.

" If you would only give up drinking so much black coffee, sir ; they do say it's very bad for the nerves——"

"And I think they are right," put in the Professor, and his voice was as gentle as ever. " Yes, I think they are right. For instance, John, at this precise moment I have a feeling that there is a hand groping behind the curtains yonder. Yet this mental attitude harmonises in a manner with the subject of this last chapter, which deals with the psychic forces of nature. I allude, John, more especially to the following passage :

" ' That mysterious power which some call the soul, if sufficiently educated, may cast off for a time this bodily flesh, and precipitate itself into illimitable spaces, riding upon the winds, walking upon the beds of seas and rivers, and indeed may even re-inhabit the bodies of those that have been long dead, provided they could be kept from corruption.' " The Professor leaned back in his chair, and continued in the voice of one thinking aloud :

"All this was known centuries ago, notably to the priests of Isis and the early Chaldeans, and is practised to-day in some small part by the fakirs of India and the lamas of Tibet, and yet is looked upon by the ignorant world as little more than cheap trickery. By the way," he broke off, becoming suddenly aware of John's presence, " didn't you ask for leave of absence until to-morrow ? "

" Well, yes, sir, I did," admitted John, " but I thought I'd put it off, seeing you are so—so busy, sir."

" Nonsense, John, don't waste the evening, it must be getting late, just brew some more coffee in the samovar, and then you can go." John hesitated, but meeting the Professor's eye, obeyed ; and having set the steaming samovar on a small table at his master's elbow and put the room in order, he turned to the door.

" I shall be back in the morning at eight o'clock, sir."

" Very good, John," said the Professor, sipping his coffee. " Good-night, John."

" Good-night, sir," returned John, and, closing the door behind him, stood for a moment to shake his head. " He isn't fit to be left alone," he muttered, " but I'll get back before eight to-morrow morning, yes, I'll take good care to be back before eight." So saying, he turned, and went softly along the passage.

II

FOR a long time the Professor had sat crouched above his desk, yet in the last half-hour he had not added a single word to the page before him, for somewhere beneath his brain a small hammer seemed tap-tapping, soft and slow and regular, rendering the stillness about him but the more profound. Slowly and gradually a feeling of expectation grew upon him, a foolishly persistent expectation of something that was drawing near and nearer to him with every stroke of the hammer—something that he could neither guess at, nor hope to arrest, only, he knew that it was coming, coming, and he waited with straining ears, listening for the unknown.

Suddenly, from somewhere in the world far below, a clock chimed midnight, and as the last strokes died there was a hurry of footsteps along the corridor without, a knock, and a fumbling at the handle. As the Professor rose, the door opened, and a shortish, stoutish individual, chiefly remarkable for a round, red face, and a bristle of grey hair, trotted in, and was shaking him by the hand—talking meanwhile in that quick jerky style that was characteristic of Magnus McManus, whose researches in Lower Egypt and along the Nile during the last ten years had made his name famous.

" My dear Dick," he began, " good God, how ill you look ! —frightful—overwork as usual, eh ? "

" Why, Magnus ! " exclaimed the Professor, " I thought you were in Egypt ? "

" Exactly—so I was—came back last week with a specimen —been in New York three days—must get back to the Nile at once—booked passage yesterday—sail to-morrow—noon. You see, Dick," continued Magnus, trotting up and down the room, " I received a cable from Tarrant—overseer of the excavations, you know—to say they've come upon a monolith—Coptic inscriptions—curious—may be important—very."

" Yes," nodded the Professor.

" So just looked you up, Dick—to ask you to take charge of this specimen I brought over—thought you wouldn't mind keeping it until I got back."

" Certainly, of course," said the Professor rather absently.

" Undoubtedly the greatest find of the age," pursued Magnus, " stupendous—will throw a new light on Egyptian history—there is not in the whole world, so far as is known, such another mummy."

" A what ? " exclaimed the Professor, " did you say ' mummy ' ? "

" To be sure," nodded Magnus, " though the term is inapt —this is something more than your ordinary dried-up mummy."

" And have you—have you brought it with you, Magnus ? "

" Certainly—it's waiting outside in the corridor."

For no apparent reason the Professor shivered violently, and the nausea came upon him again.

" The deuce of a time getting it here—awkward to handle, you know," and as he spoke Magnus turned and trotted from the room. There came a murmur of voices outside, a shuffle and stagger of approaching footsteps as of men who bore a heavy burden, and above all the excited tones of Magnus.

" Easy there—mind that corner—steady, steady, don't jar it ; now, gently—so." And Magnus reappeared, followed by four men who bent beneath something in shape between a packing-case and a coffin, which by the direction of Magnus they sat carefully down in a convenient corner.

"Now," cried he, as soon as they were alone, drawing a small screwdriver from his pocket, "I'm going to show you something that will make you doubt the evidence of your eyes—as I did myself at first—a wonder, Dick—that will set all the societies gaping—open-mouthed—like fools."

One by one Magnus extracted the screws that held down the lid, while the Professor watched, wide-eyed, waiting— waiting.

"This specimen will be a revelation on the art of embalming," continued Magnus, busy upon the last screw. "Here is no stuffed and withered, dried-up wisp of humanity. Whoever did this was a genius—positively—there has been no disembowelling here—deuce take this screw—body is as perfect as when life first left it—and mark me, Dick—it can't be less than six thousand years old at the very least—probably older. I tell you it's beyond all wonder, but there—judge for yourself!" and with these words, Magnus laid down the screwdriver, lifted off the heavy lid and stood aside.

The Professor drew a deep breath, his fingers clutching convulsively at his chair-arms, as he stared at that which lay, or rather stood, within the glass-fronted shell or coffin.

And what he saw was an oval face framed in black hair, a face full and unshrunken, yet of a hideous ashen-grey, a high, thin, aquiline nose with delicate proud-curving nostrils, and below, a mouth, blue-lipped, yet in whose full, cruel lines lurked a ghastly mockery that carried with it a nameless horror.

"Must have been handsome at one time," said Magnus. "Very much so indeed—regular features and all that—pure Egyptian type, but——"

"It's—the—the face of a devil," muttered the Professor thickly. "I wonder what—what lies behind those eyelids, they seem as if they might lift at any moment, and if they did—— Oh, I tell you it is horrible."

Magnus laughed. "Thought she'd astonish you—will knock science deaf and dumb—not a doubt. The setting of these stones," he continued with a complacent air, "round her neck—uncut emeralds they are—dates quite back to the Fifth Dynasty—yet that scarab on her breast seems even earlier still—the gold embroidery on her gown beats me—quite—and the thumb-ring by its shape would almost seem to belong to the Fifteenth Dynasty. Altogether she's a puzzle. Another peculiar thing was that—mouth and nostrils had been—plugged by a kind of cement—deuce of a time getting it out.

" The inscription upon her sarcophagus," he ran on, "describes her as : ' Ahasuera, Princess of the House of Ra, in the reign of Raman Kau Ra,' possibly another title for Seti The Second. I also came upon a papyrus—very important—and three tablets, have only had time to dip into them hastily—but from what I gather, Ahasuera appears to have been of a very evil reputation—combination of Semiramis, Cleopatra, and Messalína, multiplied by three ! One of her lovers was a certain Ptomes, High Priest of the Temple of Osiris, who is spoken of as ' one greatly versed in the arts and mysteries of Isis and the high Gods.' When I first opened her sarcophagus, from the strange disorder of the wrappings—almost seemed as if she must have moved—also the golden death-mask that had covered her face had fallen off—which was curious—very. Upon examining this mask—found an inscription across the forehead—puzzled me for days—meaning came to me all at once—in bed—might be translated by a line of doggerel verse something like this :

> ' Isis awhile hath stayed my breath,
> Whoso wakes me shall find death.'

which is also curious, eh ? Why, Great heavens, man ! What ails you ? " Magnus broke off, for he had turned and looked at his friend for the first time.

" Nothing," returned the Professor in the same thick voice. " Nothing—only cover it up—cover it up in God's name."

" Certainly—to be sure," said Magnus, staring. " Had no idea it would affect you like that, nerves must be at sixes and sevens, should take more care of yourself, Dick, and stop that confounded black coffee."

As the last screw was driven home, the Professor laughed, a little wildly. " There are eighteen screws, about two and a half inches long, eh, Magnus ? "

" Yes," said Magnus and turned to stare again.

" Good," the Professor rejoined with the same strange laugh. Magnus forced a smile.

" Why, Dick," he began, " you almost talk as though you imagined——"

" Those eyes," the Professor broke in, " they haunt me, they are the eyes of one who waits to take you unawares, they are eyes that watch and follow you behind your back——"

"Pooh! nonsense, Dick," cried Magnus, rather hastily. "This is nothing but imagination—sheer imagination. You ought to take a holiday or you will be suffering from hallucinations next."

"Sit still and listen," said the Professor, and he began to read from the manuscript before him :

"'That mysterious power which some call the soul, if sufficiently educated, may cast off for a time this bodily flesh and precipitate itself into illimitable spaces, riding upon the winds, walking upon the beds of seas and rivers, and indeed may even re-inhabit the bodies of those that have been long dead, provided that body could be kept free from corruption.'"

"Humph!" said Magnus, crossing his legs. "Well?"

"'Provided that body could be kept free from corruption,'" repeated the Professor, then, raising his arm with a sudden gesture, he pointed at the thing in the corner : "That is not death," he said.

Magnus leaped to his feet. "Man, are you mad," he cried, "what do you mean?"

"Suspended animation!" said the Professor.

For a long moment there was silence, during which the two men stared into each other's eyes ; the face of Magnus had lost some of its colour, and the Professor's fingers moved nervously upon his chair-arms. Suddenly Magnus laughed, though perhaps a trifle too boisterously.

"Bosh!" he exclaimed, "what folly are you talking, Dick? What you require is a good stiff glass of brandy and bed afterwards," and with the knowledge and freedom of an old friend, he crossed to a corner cabinet, and took thence a decanter and glasses, pouring out a stiff peg into each.

"So you don't agree with me, Magnus?"

"Agree, no," said Magnus, swallowing his brandy at a gulp, "it's all nerves—damn 'em."

The Professor shook his head. "There are more things in heaven and earth——"

"Yes—yes, I know—I have cursed Shakespeare frequently for that same quotation."

"But you yourself wrote a paper, Magnus, only a few years ago, on the hypnotic trances practised by the Egyptians."

"Now, Dick," expostulated Magnus, "be reasonable, for heaven's sake! Is it possible that any trance could extend into six or seven thousand years? Preposterous, utterly. Come, get to bed, man, like a sensible chap—where's John?"

"I gave him leave of absence until to-morrow."

"The deuce you did?" exclaimed Magnus, glancing round the room with an uneasy feeling. "Well, I'll take his place—see you into bed and all that."

"Thanks, Magnus, but it's no good," returned the Professor, shaking his head. "I couldn't sleep until I've finished this last chapter, and it won't take long."

"One o'clock, by Gad!" exclaimed Magnus, glancing at his watch. "Must hurry off, Dick—hotel—sail to-morrow, you know."

The Professor shivered, and rose to his feet. "Good-bye, Magnus," he said as they shook hands. "I hope your monolith will turn out a good find. Good-bye!"

"Thanks, old fellow," said Magnus, returning the pressure. "Now, no more poisonous coffee, mind." So saying he trotted to the door, nodded, and was gone.

The Professor sat for a moment with puckered brows, then, rising hastily, crossed to the door, turned the handle, and peered out into the dim light of the corridor.

"Magnus," he called in a hoarse whisper. "Magnus."

"Well?" came the answer.

"Then you don't think It will open Its eyes, do you, Magnus?"

"Good God—no!"

"Ah!" said the Professor, and closed the door.

III

"I WISH," said the Professor, as he took up his pen, "I wish that I had not let John go, I feel strangely lonely to-night, and John is so very matter of fact," so saying he bent to his writing again. His brain had grown singularly bright and clear, all his faculties seemed strung to their highest pitch, a feeling of exaltation had taken possession of him. His ideas grew luminous, intricate thoughts became coherent, the words shaping themselves beneath his pen with a subtle power and eloquence.

Yet all at once, and for no apparent reason, in the very middle of a sentence, a desire seized upon him to turn his head and look back over his shoulder at that which stood in the corner. He checked it with an effort, and his pen resumed its scratching; though all the time he was conscious that the desire was growing, and that sooner or later it would master him. Not that he expected to see anything unusual, that was absurd, of course. He began trying to remember how many screws there were holding down the lid upon that Thing, whose lips had mocked at God and man through centuries and whose eyes—ah, whose eyes—— The Professor turned suddenly, and with his pen extended before him, began counting the glinting screw-heads to himself in an undertone.

" One, two three, four, five, six—six along each side, and three along the top and bottom—eighteen in all. And they were steel screws, too, a quarter of an inch thick, and two and a half inches in length ; they ought to be strong enough, and yet eighteen after all was not many ; why hasn't Magnus used more of them, it would have been so much——" The Professor checked himself, and turned back to his work ; but he tried vainly to write, for now the impulse held him without respite, growing more insistent each moment, an impulse that had fear beneath it, fear born of things that move behind one. ' Ah, yes, behind one—why had he let It be placed in the corner that was directly behind his chair ? ' He rose and began pulling and dragging at his desk, but it was heavy, and defied his efforts ; yet the physical exertion, futile though it was, seemed to calm him, but though he bent resolutely above his task—the finishing of his great book—his mind was absent, and the pen between his fingers traced idle patterns and meaningless scribbles upon the sheet before him, so he tossed it aside, and buried his face in his hands.

Could it be possible that in the darkness behind the lid with the eighteen screws the eyes were still shut, or were they—— ? The Professor shivered. Ah, if he could but know, if he could only be certain—he wished John was here—John was so very matter of fact—he might have sat and watched It—yes, he had been foolish to let John go. The Professor sighed, and, opening his eyes, remained motionless—staring down at the sheet of foolscap before him—staring at the two uneven lines scrawled across it in ragged capitals that were none of his :

> " Isis awhile hath stayed my breath,
> Whoso wakes me shall find death."

A sudden piping, high-pitched laugh startled him—" Could it really be issuing from his own lips ? " he asked himself, and indeed he knew it must be so. He sat with every nerve tingling —hoping, praying for something to break the heavy silence— the creak of a footstep—a shout—a scream—anything rather than that horrible laugh ; and as he waited it came again, louder, wilder than before. And now he felt it quivering between his teeth, rattling in his throat, shaking him to and fro in its grip, then, swift as it had come it was gone, and the Professor was looking down at a litter of torn paper at his feet. He reached out a trembling hand to the rack upon his desk and taking down a pipe already filled, lighted it. The tobacco seemed to soothe him, and he inhaled it deeply, watching it rise in blue, curling spirals above his head, watched it roll in thin clouds across the room, until he noticed that it always drifted in the same direction, to hang like a curtain above one point, an ever-moving curtain behind which were shadowy " some-things " that moved and writhed.

The Professor got unsteadily to his legs.

" Magnus was right," he muttered, " I am ill, I must try to sleep—I must—I must." But as he stood there, leaning his shaking hands upon the table-edge, the blind fear, the unreason-ing dread against which he had battled so vainly all night swept over him in an irresistible wave ; his breath choked, a loathing horror shook him from head to foot, yet all the time his gaze never left the great white box, with its narrow screw-heads that stared at him like little searching eyes. Something glittered upon the floor beside it, and almost before he knew he had snatched up the screwdriver. He worked feverishly until but one screw remained, and as he stopped to wipe the sweat from his cheek he was surprised to find himself singing a song he had heard at a music-hall years before, in his college days ; then he held his breath as the last screw gave.

. . . The oval face framed in a mist of black hair, the long voluptuous eyes with their heavy lids, the aquiline nose, the cruel curve of the nostrils, and the full-lipped sensual mouth, with its everlasting mockery ; he had seen it all before, and yet as he gazed he was conscious of a change, subtle and horrible, a change that he could not define, yet which held him as one entranced. With an effort he turned away his eyes, and tried to replace the lid, but could not ; he looked about him wildly, then snatching up a heavily fringed rug, covered the horror from sight.

" Magnus was right," he repeated, " I must sleep," and crossing to the couch, he sank upon it and hid his face among the cushions.

A long time he lay there, but sleep was impossible, for the sound of the hammers was in his ears again, but louder now and seeming to beat upon his very brain. What was that other sound—that came to him beneath the hammer-strokes—could it be a footstep? He sat up listening, and then he noticed that the fringe upon the rug was moving. He rubbed his eyes, disbelieving, until all at once it was shaken by another movement that ran up it with a strange rippling motion. He rose, trembling, and creeping forward, tore away the rug. Then he saw and understood the change that had baffled him before ; and with the knowledge, the might of his learning, the strength of his manhood, deserted him, and covering his face, Professor Jarvis rocked his body to and fro making a strange whimpering noise, like a little child ; for the ashen grey was gone from the face, and the lips which had been black were blood-red. For a while the Professor continued to rock to and fro, whimpering behind his hands, till with a sudden gesture, wild and passionate, he tossed his arms above his head.

"My God !" he cried, "I'm going mad—I am mad, oh, anything but that—not mad, no, not mad—I am not mad—no." Chancing to catch sight of himself in a mirror, he shook his head and chuckled. "Not mad," he whispered to his reflection, "oh, no," then he turned to the case once more, and began patting and stroking the glass.

"Oh, Eyes of Death, lift thy lashes, for I am fain to know the mystery beyond. What though I be the Priest Ptomes, even he that put this magic upon thee, yet am I come back to thee, Beloved, and my soul calleth unto thine even as in Thebes of old. Oh, Eyes of Death, lift thy lashes, for I am fain to know the mystery beyond. While thy soul slept, mine hath hungered for thee through countless ages, and now is the time of waiting accomplished. Oh, Eyes of Death, lift thy lashes, for I am fain to know the mystery beyond. Ah, God," he broke out suddenly, "she will not wake—I cannot wake her." And he writhed his fingers together. All at once his aspect changed, his mouth curved with a smile of cunning, he crept to where a small mirror hung upon the wall, and, with a swift movement, hid it beneath his coat, and, crossing to his desk, propped it up before him.

"They will not open while I look and wait for it," he said, nodding and smiling to himself. "They are the eyes of one who waits to take you unawares, that watch and follow you behind your back, yet I shall see them, yes, I shall see them."

From the world below came the long-drawn tooting of a

steamer on the river, and with the sound, faint and far-away though it was, reason reasserted itself.

"Good heavens!" he exclaimed, trying to laugh. "What a fool I am to let a pitiful bit of dead humanity drive me half-wild with fear, and in New York too, it seems inconceivable." So saying the Professor crossed to the brandy, and, with his back turned resolutely, slowly drained his glass, yet even then he was vaguely conscious of eyes that watched him, followed his every movement, and with difficulty he forbore from swinging round on his heel. With the same iron will crushing down his rebellious nerves, he arranged his papers and took up his pen.

The human body after all has certain attributes of the cur, for let that master, the mind, chastise it, and it will cringe, let him command and it will obey. So the Professor sat, his eye clear, his hand firm, scarcely noticing the mirror beside him, even when he paused to take a fresh sheet.

The sickly grey of dawn was at the windows as he paused to glance at his watch. "Another half-hour," he muttered, "and my work is done, ended, fin——" The word died upon his lips, for his glance by accident had fallen upon the mirror, and the eyes were wide open. For a long moment they looked into his ere their lids fluttered and fell.

"I am suffering from hallucinations," he groaned. "It is one of the results of loss of sleep, but I wish John was back, John is such a matter-of-fact——"

There was a sound behind him, a sound soft and gentle like the whisper of wind in trees, or the brushing of drapery against a wall—and it was moving across the floor behind him. A chill as of death shuddered through him, and he knew the terror that is dumb.

Scarcely daring to look, full of a dread of expectation, he lifted his eyes to the mirror. The case behind him was empty; he turned swiftly, and there, so close that he might almost touch it was, the "Thing" he had called a pitiful bit of dead humanity. Slowly, inch by inch, it moved towards him, with a scrape and rustle of stiff draperies:

> "*Isis awhile hath stayed my breath,*
> *Whoso wakes me, shall find—death!*"

With a cry that was something between a scream and a laugh he leaped to his feet and hurled himself upon It; there was the sound of a dull blow, a gasp, and Professor Jarvis was lying upon the floor, his arms wide-tossed, and his face hidden in the folds of a rug.

. . . .

Next day there was a paragraph in the papers, which read as follows :

"STRANGE DEATH.

"*Yesterday at his chambers in —— Street, Professor Jarvis, the famous Scientist, was found dead, presumably of heart-failure. A curious feature of the case was that a mummy which had stood in a rough travelling-case in a corner on the opposite side of the room was found lying across the Professor's dead body.*"

THE BLACK FERRY

I was then returning from my first session at college. The weather had for some time been uncommonly wet, every brook and stream was swollen far beyond its banks, the meadows were flooded, and the river itself was increased to a raging Hellespont, insomuch that the ferry was only practicable for an hour before and after high tide.

The day was showery and stormy, by which I was detained at the inn until late in the afternoon, so that it was dark before I reached the ferry-house, and the tide did not serve for safe crossing until midnight. I was therefore obliged to sit by the fire and wait the time, a circumstance which gave me some uneasiness, for the ferryman was old and infirm, and Dick his son, who usually attended the boat during the night, happened to be then absent, the day having been such that it was not expected any travellers would seek to pass over that night.

The presence of Dick was not, however, absolutely necessary, for the boat swung from side to side by a rope anchored in the middle of the stream, and, on account of the strong current, another rope had been stretched across by which passengers could draw themselves over without assistance, an easy task to those who had the sleight of it, but it was not so to me, who still wore my arm in a sling.

While sitting at the fireside conversing with the ferryman and his wife, a smart, good-looking country lad, with a recruit's cockade in his hat, came in, accompanied by a young woman who was far advanced in pregnancy. They were told the state of the ferry, and that unless the recruit undertook to conduct the boat himself, they must wait the return of Dick.

They had been only that day married, and were on their way to join a detachment of the regiment in which Ralph Nocton, as

THE BLACK FERRY 485

the recruit was called, had that evening enlisted, the parish officers having obliged him to marry the girl. Whatever might have been their former love and intimacy, they were not many minutes in the house when he became sullen and morose towards her ; nor was she more amiable towards him. He said little, but he often looked at her with an indignant eye, as she reproached him for having so rashly enlisted, to abandon her and his unborn baby, assuring him that she would never part from him while life and power lasted.

Though it could not be denied that she possessed both beauty and an attractive person, there was yet a silly vixen humour about her ill calculated to conciliate. I did not therefore wonder to hear that Nocton had married her with reluctance ; I only regretted that the parish officers were so inaccessible to commiseration, and so void of conscience as to be guilty of rendering the poor fellow miserable for life to avert the hazard of the child becoming a burden on the parish.

The ferryman and his wife endeavoured to reconcile them to their lot ; and the recruit, who appeared to be naturally reckless and generous, seemed willing to be appeased ; but his weak companion was capricious and pettish. On one occasion, when a sudden shower beat hard against the window, she cried out, with little regard to decorum, that she would go no farther that night.

"You may do as you please, Mary Blake," said Nocton, "but go I must, for the detachment marches to-morrow morning. It was only to give you time to prepare to come with me that the Captain consented to let me remain so late in the town."

She, however, only remonstrated bitterly at his cruelty in forcing her to travel, in her condition, and in such weather. Nocton refused to listen to her, but told her somewhat doggedly, more so than was consistent with the habitual cheerful cast of his physiognomy, " that although he had already been ruined by her, he trusted she had not yet the power to make him a deserter."

He then went out, and remained some time alone. When he returned, his appearance was surprisingly changed ; his face was of an ashy paleness ; his eyes bright, febrile and eager, and his lip quivered as he said :

"Come, Mary, I can wait no longer ; the boat is ready, the river is not so wild, and the rain is over."

In vain she protested ; he was firm ; and she had no option but either to go or to be left behind. The old ferryman accompanied them to the boat, saw them embark, and gave the recruit some instruction how to manage the ropes, as it was still rather early in the tide. On returning into the house, he remarked facetiously to his wife :

" I can never see why young men should be always blamed, and all pity reserved for the damsels."

At this moment a rattling shower of rain and hail burst like a platoon of small shot on the window, and a flash of vivid lightning was followed by one of the most tremendous peals of thunder I have ever heard.

" Hark ! " cried the old woman, starting, " was not that a shriek ? " We listened, but the cry was not repeated ; we rushed to the door, but no other sound was heard than the raging of the river, and the roar of the sea-waves breaking on the bar.

Dick soon after came home, and the boat having swung back to her station, I embarked with him, and reached the opposite inn, where I soon went to bed. Scarcely had I laid my head on the pillow when a sudden inexplicable terror fell upon me ; I shook with an unknown horror ; I was, as it were, conscious that some invisible being was hovering beside me, and could hardly muster fortitude enough to refrain from rousing the house. At last I fell asleep ; it was perturbed and unsound ; strange dreams and vague fears scared me awake, and in them were dreadful images of a soldier murdering a female, and open graves, and gibbet-irons swinging in the wind. My remembrance has no parallel to such another night.

In the morning the cloud on my spirit was gone, and I rose at my accustomed hour, and cheerily resumed my journey. It was a bright morning, all things were glittering and fresh in the rising sun, the recruit and his damsel were entirely forgotten, and I thought no more of them.

But when the night returned next year, I was seized with an unaccountable dejection ; it weighed me down ; I tried to shake it off, but was unable ; the mind was diseased, and could no more by resolution shake off its discomfort, than the body by activity can expel a fever. I retired to my bed greatly depressed, but nevertheless I fell asleep. At midnight, however, I was summoned to awake by a hideous and undefinable terror ; it was the same vague consciousness of some invisible visitor being near that I had once before experienced, as I have described, and I again recollected Nocton and Mary Blake in the same instant ; I saw—for I cannot now believe that it was less than apparitional—the unhappy pair reproaching one another.

As I looked, questioning the integrity of my sight, the wretched bride turned round and looked at me. How shall I express my horror, when, for the ruddy beauty which she once possessed, I beheld the charnel visage of a skull ; I started up and cried aloud with such alarming vehemence that the whole inmates of the house, with lights in their hands, were instantly in the room—shame would not let me tell what I had seen, and, endeavouring to laugh, I accused the nightmare of the disturbance.

This happened while I was at a watering-place on the west coast. I was living in a boarding-house with several strangers ; among them was a tall pale German gentleman, of a grave impressive physiognomy. He was the most intelligent and shrewdest observer I have ever met with, and he had to a singular degree the gift of a discerning spirit. In the morning when we rose from the breakfast-table, he took me by the arm, and led me out upon the lawn in front of the house ; and when we were at some distance from the rest of the company, said :

" Excuse me, sir, for I must ask an impertinent question. Was it indeed the dream of the nightmare that alarmed you last night ? "

" I have no objection to answer you freely ; but tell me first why you ask such a question ? "

" It is but reasonable. I had a friend who was a painter ; none ever possessed an imagination which discerned better how nature in her mysteries should appear. One of his pictures was the scene of Brutus when his evil genius summoned him to Philippi, and strange to tell, you bear some resemblance to the painted Brutus. When, with the others, I broke into your room last night, you looked so like the Brutus in his picture that I could have sworn you were amazed with the vision of a ghost."

I related to him what I have done to you.

" It is wonderful," said he, " what inconceivable sympathy hath linked you to the fate of these unhappy persons. There is something more in this renewed visitation than the phantasma of a dream."

The remark smote me with an uncomfortable sensation of dread, and for a short time my flesh cráwled as it were upon my bones. But the impression soon wore off, and was again entirely forgotten.

When the anniversary again returned, I was seized with the same heaviness and objectless horror of mind ; it hung upon me with bodings and auguries until I went to bed, and then after my first sleep I was a third time roused by another fit of the same inscrutable panic. On this occasion, however, the vision was different. I beheld only Nocton, pale and wounded, stretched on a bed, and on the coverlet lay a pair of new epaulettes, as if just unfolded from a paper.

For seven years I was thus annually afflicted. The vision in each was different, but I saw no more of Mary Blake. On the fourth occasion, I beheld Nocton sitting in the uniform of an aide-de-camp at a table, with the customary tokens of conviviality before him ; it was only part of a scene, such as one beholds in a mirror.

On the fifth occasion, he appeared to be ascending, sword in hand, the rampart of a battery ; the sun was setting behind him, and the shadows and forms of a strange land, with the domes and pagodas of an oriental country, lay in wide extent around : it was a picture, but far more vivid than painting can exhibit.

On the sixth time, he appeared again stretched upon a couch ; his complexion was sullen, not from wounds, but disease, and there appeared at his bedside the figure of a general officer, with a star on his breast, with whose conversation he appeared pleased, though languid.

But on the seventh and last occasion on which the horrors of the visions were repeated, I saw him on horseback in a field of battle ; and while I looked at him, he was struck on the face by a sabre, and the blood flowed down upon his regimentals.

Years passed after this, during which I had none of these dismal exhibitions. My mind and memory resumed their healthful tone. I recollected, without these intervening years of oblivion, Nocton and Mary Blake, occasionally, as one thinks of things past, and I told my friends of the curious periodical returns of the visitations to me as remarkable metaphysical phenomena. By an odd coincidence, it so happened that my German friend was always present when I related my dreams. He in the intervals sometimes spoke to me of them, but my answers were vague, for my reminiscences were imperfect. It was not so with him. All I told he distinctly recorded and preserved in a book wherein he wrote down the minutest thing that I had witnessed in my visions. I do not mention his name, because he is a modest and retiring man, in bad health, and who has long sequestered himself from company. His rank, however, is so distinguished that his name could not be stated without the hazard of exposing him to impertinent curiosity. But to proceed.

Exactly fourteen years—twice seven it was—I remember well,

because for the first seven I had been haunted as I have described, and for the other seven I had been placid in my living. At the end of that period of fourteen years, my German friend paid me a visit here. He came in the forenoon, and we spent an agreeable day together, for he was a man of much recondite knowledge. I have seen none so wonderfully possessed of all sorts of occult learning.

He was an astrologer of the true kind, for in him it was not a pretence but a science ; he scorned horoscopes and fortune-tellers with the just derision of a philosopher, but he had a beautiful conception of the reciprocal dependencies of nature. He affected not to penetrate to causes, but he spoke of effects with a luminous and religious eloquence. He described to me how the tides followed the phases of the moon ; but he denied the Newtonian notion that they were caused by the procession of the lunar changes. He explained to me that when the sun entered Aries, and the other signs of the zodiac, how his pro-gression could be traced on this earth by the development of plants and flowers, and the passions, diseases, and affections of animals and man ; but that the stars were more than the celestial signs of these terrestrial phenomena he ridiculed as the conceptions of the insane theory.

His learning in the curious art of alchymy was equally sublime. He laughed at the fancy of an immortal elixir, and his notion of the mythology of the philosopher's stone was the very essence and spirituality of ethics. The elixir of immortality he described to me as an allegory, which, from its component parts, emblems of talents and virtues, only showed that per-severance, industry, goodwill, and a gift from God were the requisite ingredients necessary to attain renown.

His knowledge of the philosopher's stone was still more beautiful. He referred to the writings of the Rosicrucians, whose secrets were couched in artificial symbols, to prove that the sages of that sect were not the fools that the lesser wise of later days would represent them. The self-denial, the patience, the humility, the trusting in God, the treasuring of time by lamp and calcula-tion which the venerable alchymists recommended, he used to say, were only the elements which constitute the conduct of the youth that would attain to riches and honour ; and these different stages which are illuminated in the alchymical volumes as descriptive of stages in the process of making the stone were but hieroglyphical devices to explain the effects of well-applied human virtue and industry.

To me it was amazing to what clear simplicity he reduced all things, and on what a variety of subjects his bright and splendid fancy threw a fair and effecting light. All those demi-sciences—physiognomy—palmistry—scaileology, etc., even magic and witchcraft, obtained from his interpretations a philosophical credibility.

In disquisitions on these subjects we spent the anniversary. He had by them enlarged the periphery of my comprehension ; he had added to my knowledge, and inspired me with a profounder respect for himself.

He was an accomplished musician, in the remotest, if I may use the expression, depths of the art. His performance on the pianoforte was simple, heavy, and seemingly the labour of an unpractised hand, but his expression was beyond all epithet exquisite and solemn ; his airs were grave, devotional, and pathetic, consisting of the simplest harmonic combinations ; but they were wonderful ; every note was a portion of an invocation ; every melody the voice of a passion or a feeling supplied with elocution.

We had spent the day in the fields, where he illustrated his astrological opinions by appeals to plants, and leaves, and flowers, and other attributes of the season, with such delightful perspicuity that no time can efface from the registers of my memory the substance of his discourses. In the evening he delighted me with his miraculous music, and, as the night advanced, I was almost persuaded that he was one of those extraordinary men who are said sometimes to acquire communion with spirits and dominion over demons.

Just as we were about to sit down to our frugal supper, literally or philosophically so, as if it had been served for Zeno himself, Dick, the son of the old ferryman, who by this time was some years dead, came to the door, and requested to speak with me in private. Of course I obeyed, when he informed me that he had brought across the ferry that night a gentleman officer, from a far country, who was in bad health, and whom he could not accommodate properly in the ferry-house.

" The inn," said Dick, " is too far off, for he is lame, and has an open wound in the thigh. I have therefore ventured to bring him here, sure that you will be glad to give him a bed for the night. His servant tells me that he was esteemed the bravest officer in all the service in the Mysore of India."

It was impossible to resist this appeal. I went to the door where the gentleman was waiting, and with true-heartedness expressed how great my satisfaction would be if my house could afford him any comfort.

I took him in with me to the room where my German friend was sitting. I was much pleased with the gentleness and unaffected simplicity of his manners.

He was a handsome middle-aged man—his person was robust and well formed—his features had been originally handsome, but they were disfigured by a scar, which had materially changed their symmetry. His conversation was not distinguished by any remarkable intelligence, but after the high intellectual excitement which I had enjoyed all day with my philosophical companion, it was agreeable and gentlemanly.

Several times during supper, something came across my mind as if I had seen him before, but I could neither recollect when nor where ; and I observed that more than once he looked at me as if under the influence of some research in his memory. At last, I observed that his eyes were dimmed with tears, which assured me that he then recollected me. But I considered it a duty of hospitality not to inquire aught concerning him more than he was pleased to tell himself.

In the meantime, my German friend, I perceived, was watching us both, but suddenly he ceased to be interested, and appeared absorbed in thought, while good manners required me to make some efforts to entertain my guest. This led on to some inquiry concerning the scene of his services, and he told us that he had been many years in India.

" On this day eight years ago," said he, " I was in the battle of Borupknow, where I received the wound which has so disfigured me in the face."

At that moment I accidentally threw my eyes upon my German friend—the look which he gave me in answer caused me to shudder from head to foot, and I began to ruminate of Nocton the recruit, and Mary Blake, while my friend continued the conversation in a light desultory manner, as it would have seemed to any stranger, but to me it was awful and oracular. He spoke to the stranger on all manner of topics, but ever and anon he brought him back, as if without design, to speak of the accidents of fortune which had befallen him on the anniversary of that day, giving it as a reason for his curious remarks that most men observed anniversaries, time and experience having taught them to notice that there were curious coincidences with respect to times, and places, and individuals—things which of themselves form part of the great demonstration of the wisdom and skill

JOHN GALT

displayed in the construction, not only of the mechanical, but the mortal world, showing that each was a portion of one and the same thing.

"I have been," said he to the stranger, "an observer and recorder of such things. I have my book of registration here in this house; I will fetch it from my bed-chamber, and we shall see in what other things, as far as your fortunes have been concerned, how it corresponds with the accidents of your life on this anniversary."

I observed that the stranger paled a little at this proposal, and said, with an affectation of carelessness while he was evidently disturbed, that he would see it in the morning. But the philosopher was too intent upon his purpose to forbear. I know not what came upon me, but I urged him to bring the book. This visibly disconcerted the stranger still more, and his emotion became, as it were, a motive which induced me, in a peremptory manner, to require the production of the book, for I felt that strange horror, so often experienced, returning upon me; and was constrained, by an irresistible impulse, to seek an explanation of the circumstances by which I had for so many years suffered such an eclipse of mind.

The stranger seeing how intent both of us were, desisted from his wish to procrastinate the curious disclosure which my friend said he could make; but it was evident he was not at ease. Indeed he was so much the reverse, that when the German went for his book, he again proposed to retire, and only consented to abide at my jocular entreaty, until he should learn what his future fortunes were to be, by the truth of what would be told him of the past.

My friend soon returned with the book. It was a remarkable volume, covered with vellum, shut with three brazen clasps, secured by a lock of curious construction. Altogether it was a strange, antique, and necromantic-looking volume. The corner was studded with knobs of brass, with a small mirror in the centre, round which were inscribed in Teutonic characters words to the effect, " I WILL SHOW THEE THYSELF." Before unlocking the clasp, my friend gave the book to the stranger, explained some of the emblematic devices which adorned the cover, and particularly the words of the motto that surrounded the little mirror.

Whether it was from design, or that the symbols required it, the explanations of my friend were mystical and abstruse; and I could see that they produced an effect on the stranger, so strong that it was evident he could with difficulty maintain his self-possession. The colour entirely faded from his countenance ; he became wan and cadaverous, and his hand shook violently as he returned the volume to the philosopher, who, on receiving it back, said :

" There are things in this volume which may not be revealed to every eye, yet to those who may not discover to what they relate, they will seem trivial notations."

He then applied the key to the lock, and unclosed the volume. My stranger guest began to breathe hard and audibly. The German turned over the vellum leaves searchingly and carefully. At last he found the record and description of my last vision, which he read aloud. It was not only minute in the main circumstances in which I had seen Nocton, but it contained an account of many things, the still life, as it is called, of the picture, which I had forgotten, and among other particulars a picturesque account of the old General whom I saw standing at the bedside.

" By all that's holy," cried the stranger, " it is old Crippling-ton himself—the queue of his hair was, as you say, always crooked, owing to a habit he had of pulling it when vexed—where could you find the description of all this ? "

I was petrified ; I sat motionless as a statue, but a fearful vibration thrilled through my whole frame.

My friend looked back in his book, and found the description of my sixth vision. It contained the particulars of the crisis of battle in which, as the stranger described, he had received the wound in his face. It affected him less than the other, but still the effect upon him was impressive.

The record of the fifth vision produced a more visible alarm. The description was vivid to an extreme degree—the appearance of Nocton, sword in hand, on the rampart—the animation of the assault, and the gorgeous landscape of domes and pagodas, was limned with words as vividly as a painter could have made the scene. The stranger seemed to forget his anxiety, and was delighted with the reminiscences which the description recalled.

But when the record of the fourth vision was read, wherein Nocton was described as sitting in the regimentals of an aide-de-camp, at a convivial table, he exclaimed, as if unconscious of his words :

" It was on that night I had first the honour of dining with the German general."

The inexorable philosopher proceeded, and read what I had told him of Nocton, stretched pale and wounded on a bed, with new epaulettes spread on the coverlet, as if just unfolded from a paper. The stranger started from his seat, and cried with a hollow and fearful voice :

" This is the book of life."

The German turned over to the second vision, which he read slowly and mournfully, especially the description of my own feelings, when I beheld the charnel visage of Mary Blake. The stranger, who had risen from his seat, and was panting with horror, cried out with a shrill howl, as it were :

" On that night as I was sitting in my tent, methought her spirit came and reproached me."

I could not speak, but my German friend rose from his seat, and holding the volume in his left hand, touched it with his right, and looking sternly at the stranger, said :

" In this volume, and in your own conscience, are the evidences which prove that you are Ralph Nocton, and that on this night, twice seven years ago, you murdered Mary Blake."

The miserable stranger lost all self-command, and cried in consternation :

" It is true, the waters raged ; the rain and the hail came ; she bitterly upbraided me ; I flung her from the boat ; the lightning flashed, and the thunder—Oh ! it was not so dreadful as her drowning execrations."

Before any answer could be given to this confession, he staggered from the spot, and almost in the same instant fell dead upon the floor.

THE DREAMLAND BRIDE

Yᴏᴜ ask me, brother, if I have loved. Yes, I have loved! The story is singular and terrible, and, for all my sixty-six years, I scarce dare stir the ashes of that memory.

To you I can refuse nothing ; to a heart less hardened than yours this tale could never be told by me. For these things were so strange that I can scarce believe they came into my own existence. Three years was I the fool of a delusion of the devil. Three years was I a parish priest by day, while by night, in dreams (God grant they were but dreams !) I led the life of a child of this world, of a lost soul !

For one kind glance at a woman's face was my spirit to be doomed ; but at length, with God to aid, and my patron saint, it was permitted to me to drive away the evil spirit that possessed me.

I lived a double life, by night and by day. All day long was I a pure priest of the Lord, concerned only with prayer and holy things ; but when I closed my eyes in sleep then I was a young knight, a lover of women, of horses and hounds, a drinker, a dicer, a blasphemer, and, when I woke at dawn, meseemed that I was fallen on sleep, and did but dream that I was a priest. From those years of dreaming certain memories yet remain with me ; memories of words and things that will not drown. Aye, though I have never left the walls of my vicarage, he who heard me would rather deem me one that had lived in the world and left it, to die in religion, and end in the breast of God his tumultuous day, than for a priest grown old in a forgotten church, deep in a wood, and far from the things of this earth.

Yes, I have loved as never man loved, with a wild love and a terrible one, so that I marvel my heart did not burst asunder.

Oh, the nights of long ago ! From my earliest childhood had I felt the call to be a priest. This was the end of all my studies, and, till I was twenty-four, my days were one long training. My theological course achieved, I took the lesser orders, and, at length, at the end of Holy Week was to be the hour of my ordination.

I had never entered the world ; my world was the college close. Vaguely I knew that women existed, but of women I never thought. My heart was wholly pure. Even my old and infirm mother I saw but twice a year ; of other worldly relations I had none.

I had no regrets and no hesitations in taking the irrevocable vow ; nay, I was full of an impatient joy. Never did a young bridegroom so eagerly count the hours to his wedding. In my sleep I dreamed of saying the Mass. To be a priest seemed to me the noblest thing in the world, and I would have disdained the estate of poet or of king. To be a priest ! My ambition was nothing higher.

All this I tell you that you may know how little I deserved that which befel me ; that you may know how inexplicable was the fascination by which I was overcome.

The great day came, and I walked to church as if I were winged or walked on air. I felt an angelic beatitude, and marvelled at the gloomy and thoughtful faces of my companions, for we were many.

The night I had passed in prayer. I was all but entranced in ecstasy. The bishop, a venerable old man, was in my eyes like a god, and I seemed to see heaven open beyond the arches of the minster.

You know the ceremony : the Benediction, the Communion in both kinds, the anointing of the palms of the hands with consecrated oil, and finally, the celebration of the holy rite, offered up in company with the bishop.

On these things I will not linger, but oh, how true is the word of Job, that he is foolish who maketh not a covenant with his eyes ! I chanced to raise my head, and saw before me, so near that it seemed I could touch her, though in reality she was at some distance, and on the farther side of a railing, a young dame royally clad, and of incomparable beauty.

It was as if scales had fallen from my eyes ; and I felt like a blind man who suddenly recovers his sight. The bishop, so splendid a moment ago, seemed to fade ; through all the church was darkness, and the candles paled in their sconces of gold, like stars at dawn.

Against the gloom that lovely thing shone out like a heavenly revelation, seeming herself to be the fountain of light, and to give it rather than receive it.

I cast down my eyes, vowing that I would not raise them again ; my attention was failing, and I scarce knew what I did. The moment afterwards I opened my eyes, for through my eyelids I saw her shining in a bright penumbra, as when one has stared at the sun. Ah, how beautiful she was !

The greatest painters, when they have sought in heaven for ideal beauty, and have brought to earth the portrait of Our Lady, came never near unto the glory of this vision ! Pen of poet, palette of painter, can give no vision of her. She was tall, with the bearing we give to a goddess. Her fair hair flowed about her brows in streams of gold. Like a crowned queen she stood there, with her broad, white brow and dark eyebrows ; with her eyes of the brightness and life of the green sea, and at one glance made or marred the destiny of a man. They were astonishingly clear and brilliant, shooting rays like arrows, which I could see winging straight for my heart. I know not if the flame that lighted them came from heaven or hell, but from one or other assuredly it came. Angel or devil, or both ; this woman was no child of Eve, the mother of us all. White teeth shone in her smile, little dimples came and went with each movement of her mouth, among the roses of her cheeks. There was a lustre as of agate on the smooth and shining skin of her half-clad shoulders, and chains of great pearls no whiter than her neck fell over her breast.

From time to time she lifted her head in snake-like motion, and set the silvery ruffles of her raiment quivering. She wore a flame-coloured velvet robe, and from the ermine lining of her sleeves her delicate hands came and went, as transparent as the fingers of the dawn. As I gazed at her, I felt within me, as it were, the opening of gates that had ever been barred ; I saw sudden vistas of an unknown future ; all life seemed altered, new thoughts wakened in my heart. A horrible pain took possession of me ; each minute seemed at once a moment and an age. The ceremony went on and on, and I was being carried far from the world, at whose gates my new desires were beating. I said, " Yes," when I wished to say " No," when my whole soul protested against the words my tongue was uttering. A hidden force seemed to drag them from me. This it is, perhaps, which makes so many young girls walk to the altar with the firm resolve to refuse the husband who is forced on them, and this is why not one of them does what she intends. This is why so many poor novices take the veil, though they are determined to tear it into shreds rather than speak the vows. None dare cause so great a scandal before so many observers, nor thus betray such general expectation. The will of all imposes itself upon you ; the gaze of all presses upon you like a leaden cope. Again, all is so very clearly arranged in advance, so evidently irrevocable, that the intention to refuse is crushed out utterly, for ever.

The expression of the unknown lovely being changed as the ceremony advanced. Tender, caressing at first, it became contemptuous, disdainful. With an effort that might have moved a mountain, I strove to cry out that I would never be a priest ; it was in vain, my tongue would not help in any cry, I could not refuse even by a sign. Though quite awake, I seemed to be in one of the nightmares wherein you cannot utter the word on which your life depends. She appeared to understand the torture which I endured, and cast on me a glance of divine pity and promise.

" Be mine," she seemed to say, " and I shall make thee happier than God, and heaven and His angels will be jealous of thee. Tear the shroud of death wherein thou art swathed, for I am Beauty, and Youth, and Life ; come to me, together we shall be Love. What can Jehovah offer thee in exchange for thy youth ? Our life will flow like a dream in the eternity of a kiss. Cast but the wine from that chalice and thou art free, and I will carry thee to the Unknown Isles, and thou shalt sleep upon my breast in a bed of gold beneath a canopy of silver ; for I love thee, and would fain take thee from thy God, before whom so many noble hearts offer up the incense of their love, which dies before it reaches the heaven where He dwells."

These words I seemed to hear singing in the sweetest of tunes, the words which her eyes sent to me resounded in my heart as if they had been whispered in my soul. I was ready to forswear God, and yet I went through each rite of the ceremony. She cast me a second glance, so full of entreaty and despair that I felt more swords pierce me than ever pierced the heart of Our Lady of Sorrows.

It was over. I was a priest. Then never surely did human force declare so keen a sorrow : the girl who sees her betrothed fall dead at her side, the mother by the empty cradle, Eve at the gate of Eden, the miser who seeks his treasure and finds but a stone, even they look less sorely smitten, less inconsolable. The blood left her sweet face pale ; her lovely arms fell powerless, her feet failed her, and she leaned against a pillar. I staggered to the door with a white face and moist eyes, breathless, and with all the weight of the dome upon my head. As I was crossing the threshold a hand seized one of mine. It was a woman's hand, and though cold, yet it seemed to burn me like a brand.

"Miserable man, what hast thou done?" she whispered, and was then absorbed into the crowd.

The old bishop paused, and gazed severely at me, who was a piteous spectacle, now red, now pale, dazed and faint. One of my colleagues had compassion on me and took me home. I could not have gone alone. At the corner of a street, while the young priest's head was turned, a black page, curiously clad, came up to me and gave me as he passed a little leathern case with corners of wrought gold, signing to me to hide it. I thrust it into my sleeve and kept it till I was alone in my cell. Then I unclasped it. There were but these words written in it—

Clarimonde
at the
Palazzo Concini

So little was I a worldling that I had never heard of Clarimonde despite her fame, nay, nor knew where the Palazzo Concini was. I made many guesses, but so that I did but see her again, I cared little whether Clarimonde were a noble lady or no better than one of the wicked. This love, thus born in an hour, had taken root too deep for me to dream of casting it from me. This woman had made me utterly her own, a glance had been enough to change me, her will swayed mine, I lived not for myself but for her.

Many mad things did I, kissing my hand where hers had touched it, repeating her name for hours—*Clarimonde, Clarimonde*. I had but to close my eyes and she stood before me again as distinctly as if she were present. Then I murmured the words that she had spoken under the porch of the church : "Miserable man, what hast thou done?"

I felt the horror of the strait wherein I was, and the dead and terrible aspect of the life that I had chosen was now revealed. *To be a priest!* Never to love, to know not the call of youth and sex, to turn from beauty, to close the eyes and crawl in the chill shade of cloister or church, to see none but deathly men, to watch by corpses, to wear the cassock in which they would at last bury me !

Then life arose in me like a river in flood, my blood rioted in my veins, my youth burst and flowered forth in a moment. How was I again to have sight of Clarimonde ? I had no excuse for leaving the seminary, for I knew nobody in the town, and indeed was only waiting there till I should be appointed to a parish.

I tried to remove the bars of the window, but to descend without a ladder was almost impossible. Then, again, I could only escape by night, when I should be lost in the labyrinth of streets. Those difficulties which might have been nothing to others were enormous to a poor priest, now first in love without experience, money or knowledge of the world.

Ah ! Had I not been a priest I might have seen her every day, I might have been her lover, her husband, I said to myself in the blindness of my heart. In place of being swathed in a cassock I might have worn silk and velvet, chains of gold, a sword and feather like all the fair young knights. My locks would not be tonsured but would fall in perfumed curls around my throat. But one hour spent before an altar and some garbled words, had cut me off from the company of the living. With my own hands I had sealed the stone upon the tomb of my past life ; I had turned the key in the lock of my prison.

I walked to the window. The sky was heavenly blue, the trees had clothed them in the raiment of spring, all nature smiled with mockery in her smile. The square was full of people coming and going : young exquisites, young beauties, two by two, were walking in the direction of the gardens.

Workmen sang songs as they passed. On all sides there was a life, a movement, a gaiety that did but increase my sorrow and my solitude. A young mother, on the steps of the gate, was playing with her child, kissing its rosy little mouth with a hundred caresses, the childlike and divine caresses that are the secret of mothers.

Near them the father, with folded arms above a happy heart, smiled softly as he watched them. I could not continue to look without pain, but closed the window and flung myself on the bed with a feeling of horrible jealousy and hatred, so that I gnawed my fingers and my coverlet like a starved and untamed beast.

How long I lay thus I know not, but at last, as I turned in a spasm of rage, I saw the Abbé Sérapion curiously regarding me. I bowed my head in shame and hid my face with my hands.

"Romuald, my friend," said he, "some strange thing hath befallen thee. Satan hath desired to have thee, that he may sift thee like wheat ; he goeth about to devour thee as a raging lion. Beware and make thyself a breastplate of prayer, a shield of the mortifying of the flesh. Fight and thou shalt overcome. Be not afraid with any discouragement ; for the firmest hearts and the most surely guarded have known hours like these. Pray, fast, meditate, and the evil spirit will pass away from thee."

Sérapion told me that the priest of C—— was dead, that the bishop had appointed me to this charge, and that I must be ready by the morrow. I nodded assent, and the Abbé departed. I opened my Missal and strove to read in it, but the lines wavered confusedly and the volume slipped unheeded from my hands.

Next day Sérapion came for me ; two mules were waiting for us at the gate with our slender baggage, and we mounted as well as we could. As we traversed the streets I looked around for Clarimonde in each balcony and window. But it was too early, and the city was yet asleep. When we had passed the gates and were climbing the heights, I turned back for a last glance at the place that was the home of Clarimonde. The shadow of a cloud lay on the city, the red roofs and the blue were mingled in a mist, whence rose here and there white puffs of smoke. By some strange optical effect one house stood up golden in a ray of light far above the roofs that were mingled in the mist. A league away though it was, it seemed quite close to us—all was plain to see ; turrets, balconies, parapets, the weathercocks even.

"What is that palace we see yonder in the sunlight ? " said I to Sérapion. He shaded his eyes with his hands, looked and answered—

"That is the old palace which Prince Concini has given to Clarimonde the harlot. Therein dreadful things are done."

Even at that moment, whether it were the actual or the ideal I know not, methought I saw a white and slender shape cross the terrace, glance and disappear. It was Clarimonde ! . . .

Ah ! did she know how in that hour, at the height of the rugged way which led me from her, even at the crest of the ascent I should never tread again, I was watching her, eager and restless, watching the palace where she dwelt ? By a mystery of mirage or light and a shade the palace seemed very near as if inviting me to enter and be lord of all. Doubtless she knew it, so closely bound was her heart to mine ; and this it was which had urged her, in the raiment of the night, to climb the palace terrace in the frosty dews of dawn. The shadow slipped over the palace and, anon, there was but a motionless sea of roofs, marked merely by a billowy undulation of forms. Sérapion pricked on his mule, mine also hastened, and a winding of the road hid from me for ever the city of S——, where I was to return no more. At the end of three days' journey through sad fields we saw the steeple of my parish church high above the trees. Some winding lanes, bordered by cottages and gardens, brought us to the building, which was certainly of no great splendour. A porch with a few mouldings, and two or three pillars rudely carved in sandstone, a tiled roof with counterforts of sandstone—that was all. To the left was the graveyard deep in tall grasses, with an iron cross in the centre. The priests' house was to the right in the shadow of the church. Simplicity could not be further used nor cleanliness made less lovely. There was an old dog and an elderly housekeeper, and when she learned that both were to be retained in my service her joy was great.

When I had been installed Sérapion returned to the college. I was left alone.

Unsupported, uncomforted as I was, the thought of Clarimonde again beset me, nor could I drive her memory away for all my efforts. One evening, as I walked among the box-lined paths of my little garden, I fancied that I saw among the trees the form of a woman, who followed all my movements, and whose green eyes glistened through the leaves. Green as the sea shone her eyes, but it was no more than a vision, for when I crossed to the other side of the alley, nothing did I find but the print of a little foot on the sand—a foot like the foot of a child. Now the garden was girt with high walls, and, for all my search, I could find no living thing within them. I have never been able to explain this incident, which, after all, was nothing to the strange adventures that were to follow.

Thus did I live for a whole year, fulfilling every duty of the priesthood—preaching, praying, fasting, visiting the sick, denying myself necessaries that I might give to the poor. But within me all was dry and barren—the fountains of grace were sealed. I knew not the happiness which goes with the consciousness of a holy mission fulfilled. My heart was otherwhere ; the words of Clarimonde dwelt on my lips like the ballad burden a man repeats against his will. Oh, my brother, consider this ! For the lifting up of mine eyes to behold a woman have I been harried these many years, and my life hath been troubled for ever.

I shall not hold you longer with the story of these defeats and these victories ; let me come to the beginning of the new life.

One night there was a violent knocking at my gate. The old housekeeper went to open it, and the appearance of a man richly clad, tawny of hue, armed with a long dagger, stood before her in the light of her lantern. She was terrified, but he soothed her, saying that he needs must see me instantly concerning a matter of my ministry. Barbara brought him upstairs to the room where I was about going to bed. There the man told me that his mistress, a lady of high degree, was on the point of death, and desired to see a priest. I answered that I was ready to follow him, and, taking with me such matters as are needful for extreme unction, I went down hastily. At the door were two horses, black as night, their breath rising in white clouds of vapour. The man held my stirrup while I mounted ; then he laid one hand on the pommel, and vaulted on the other horse. Gripping his beast with his knees, he gave him his head, and we started with the speed of an arrow, my horse keeping pace with his own. We seemed in running to devour the way, the black trees fled in the darkness like an army in rout. A forest we crossed, so gloomy and so frozen cold that I felt in all my veins a shudder of superstitious dread. The sparks struck from the flints by our coursers' feet followed after us like a trail of fire, and whoever saw us must have deemed us two ghosts riding the nightmare. Will-o'-the-wisps glittered across our path, the night birds clamoured in the forest deeps, and now and again shone out the burning eyes of wild cats. The manes of the horses tossed more wildly on the wind, the sweat ran down their sides, their breath came thick and loud. But whenever they slackened the groom called on them with a cry like nothing that ever came from a human throat, and again they ran their furious course. At last the tempest of their flight reached its goal ; suddenly there stood before us

a great dark mass, with shining points of flame. Our horses'
hoofs clattered louder on a drawbridge, and we thundered
through the dark depths of a vaulted entrance which gaped
between two monstrous towers. Within the castle all was confusion—servants with burning torches ran hither and thither
through the courts ; on the staircases lights rose and fell. I
beheld a medley of vast buildings, columns, arches, parapet
and balcony—a bewildering world of royal or of fancy palaces.
The negro page who had given me the tablets of Clarimonde,
and whom I recognised at a glance, helped me to alight. A
seneschal in black velvet, with a golden chain about his neck,
and an ivory wand in his hand, came forward to meet me,
great tears rolling down his cheeks to his snowy beard.

"Too late," he said, " too late, sir priest ! But if thou hast
not come in time to save the soul, watch, I pray thee, with
the unhappy body of the dead."

He took me by the arm ; he led me to the hall where the
corpse was lying, and I wept as bitterly as he, deeming that
the dead was Clarimonde, the well and wildly loved. There
stood a *prie-dieu* by the bed : a blue flame flickering from a
cup of bronze cast all about the chamber a doubtful light,
and here and there set the shadows fluttering.

In a chiselled vase on the table was one white rose faded,
a single petal clinging to the stem ; the rest had fallen like
fragrant tears, and lay beside the vase. A broken black mask,
a fan, masquerading gear of every kind were huddled on the
chairs, and showed that death had come, unlooked for and
unheralded, to that splendid house. Not daring to cast mine
eyes upon the bed, I knelt, and fervently began to repeat
the Psalms, thanking God that between this woman and me
He had set the tomb, so that now her name might come like
a thing enskied and sainted in my prayers.

By degrees this ardour slackened, and I fell a-dreaming.
This chamber, after all, had none of the air of a chamber of
death. In place of the corpse-laden atmosphere that I was wont
to breathe in these vigils, there floated gently through the
warmth a vapour of orient essences, a perfume of woman and
of love. The pale glimmer of the lamp seemed rather the
twilight of pleasure than the yellow burning of the taper that
watches by the dead. I began to think of the rare hazard that
brought me to Clarimonde in the moment when I had lost
her for ever, and a sigh came from my breast. Then meseemed
that one answered with a sigh behind me, and I turned un-

consciously. 'Twas but an echo ; but, as I turned, mine eyes fell on that which they had shunned—the bed where Clarimonde lay in state. The flowered and crimson curtains, bound up with loops of gold, left the dead woman plain to view, lying at her length, with hands folded on her breast. She was covered with a linen veil, very white and glistering, the more by reason of the dark purple hangings, and so fine was the shroud that her fair body shone through it, with those beautiful, soft, waving lines, as of the swan's neck, that not even death could harden. Fair she was as a statue of alabaster carved by some skilled man for the tomb of a queen ; fair as a young maid asleep beneath new-fallen snow.

I could endure no longer. The air as of a bower of love, the scent of the faded rose intoxicated me, and I strode through the chamber, stopping at each turn to gaze at the beautiful dead beneath the transparent shroud. Strange thoughts haunted my brain. I fancied that she was not really gone, that it was but a device to draw me within her castle gates and to tell me all her love. Nay, one moment methought I saw her foot stir beneath its white swathings, and break the stiff lines of the shroud.

" Is she really Clarimonde ? " I asked myself presently. " What proof have I ? The black page may have entered the household of some other lady. Mad must I be thus to disquiet myself."

But the throbbing of my heart gave me an answer.

" It is she. . . . It is she ! "

I drew near to the bed and looked with fresh attention at that which thus perplexed me. Shall I confess it ? The perfection of her beauty, though shadowed and sanctified by death, harassed my heart, and that long rest of hers was wondrous like a living woman's sleep. I forgot that I had come there to watch by a corpse, and I dreamed that I was a young bridegroom on the threshold of the chamber of the veiled, half-hidden bride !

Broken with sorrow, wild with joy, shuddering with dread and desire, I stooped toward the dreamland bride and raised a corner of the sheet. Gently I raised it, holding my breath as though I feared to waken her. My blood coursed so fearsomely that I heard it surging through the veins of my temples. My brow was moist with sweat, as if I had lifted not filmy linen, but weighty marble.

There lay Clarimonde, even (in the face) as she was upon

the day I was ordained a priest. The pallor of her cheeks, her dead lips fading coral, her long, downcast eyelids with their brown lashes breaking the marble of her cheeks—all gave her an air of sadness and pureness, of pensive patience that had a winsome magic. Her long, loose hair, the small blue flowers yet strewn through it, pillowed her head and veiled the glory of the soft flesh of her shoulders. Her fair hands were crossed. The exquisite roundness and ivory sheen of her arms proved even in death a triumphant lure.

Long did I wait and watch her silently, and still the more I gazed the less I could deem that life had for ever left her beautiful body. I knew not if it were an illusion, or a reflection from the lamp, but it was as if the blood began to flow again beneath that dead white of her flesh, and yet she lay eternally, immovably still. I touched her arm ; it was cold, but no colder han her hand had been on the day when it met mine beneath the church porch.

I fell into my old attitude, stooping my face above her face, while down upon her rained the warm dew of my tears. Oh, the bitterness of impotence and of despair ; oh, wild agony of that death-watch ! The night crept on, and as I felt that the eternal separation drew near, I could not deny myself the sad last delight of one kiss on the dead lips that held all my love.

Oh, miracle ! A light breath mingled with my breath, and the mouth of Clarimonde answered to the touch of mine ! Her eyes opened, and softly shone. She sighed, she uncrossed her arms, and folding them about my neck in a ravished ecstasy,—

" Ah, Romuald, it is thou ! " she said, in a voice as sweet and languishing as the last trembling of a lyre. " Ah, Romuald, what makest thou here ? So long have I waited for thee that I am dead. Yet now we are betrothed, now I may see thee and visit thee. Farewell, Romuald, farewell ! I love thee. It is all that I had to tell thee, and I give thee again that life which thou gavest me with thy kiss. Soon shall we meet again."

Her head sank down, but still her arms clung to me as if they would hold me for ever. A wild gust of wind burst open the window and broke into the room. The last leaf of the white rose fluttered like a bird's wing on the stem, and then fell and flew through the open casement, bearing with it the soul of Clarimonde.

The lamp went out, and I fell fainting on the breast of the beautiful corpse.

When I came to myself I was lying on my own bed in the little chamber of the priest's house ; my hand had slipped from beneath the coverlet, the old dog was licking it. Barbara hobbled and trembled about the room, opening and shutting drawers, and shaking powders into glasses. The old woman gave a cry of delight when she saw me open my eyes. The dog yelped and wagged his tail, but I was too weak to utter a word or make the slightest movement. Later, I learned that for three days I had lain thus, with no sign of life but a scarce-perceptible breathing. These three days do not count in my life ; I know not where my spirit went wandering all that time, whereof I keep not the slightest memory. Barbara told me that the same bronzed man who had come for me at night, brought me back in a closed litter next morning, and instantly went his way. So soon as I could recall my thoughts, I re- viewed each incident of that fatal night. At first I deemed that I had been duped by art magic, but presently actual, palpable circumstances destroyed that belief. I could not suppose that I had been dreaming, for Barbara, no less than myself, had seen the man with the two coal-black steeds, and she described them accurately. Yet no one knew of any castle in the neighbourhood at all like that in which I had found Clarimonde again.

One morning Sérapion entered my room ; he had come with all haste in answer to Barbara's message about my illness.

Though this declared his affection for me, none the more did his visit give me pleasure. There was somewhat inquisitive and piercing, to my mind, in the very glance of Sérapion, and I felt like a criminal in his presence. He it was who first dis-covered my secret disquiet, and I bore him a grudge for being so clear-sighted.

While he was asking about my health in accents of honeyed hypocrisy, his eyes, as yellow as a lion's, were sounding the depths of my soul.

Presently, " The famous harlot Clarimonde is dead," says he in a piercing tone—" dead at the close of an eight-days' revel. It was a feast of Belshazzar or of Cleopatra. Good God, what an age is ours ! The guests were served by dusky slaves, who spoke no tongue known among men, and who seemed like spirits from the pit. The livery of the least of them might have beseemed an emperor on a coronation day. Wild tales are told of this same Clarimonde, and all her lovers have perished miserably or by violence. They say she was a ghost, a female vampire, but I believe she was Satan himself."

He paused and watched me. I could not master a sudden movement at the name of Clarimonde.

"Satan's talons are long," said Sérapion, with a stern look, "and tombs ere now have given up their dead. Three-fold should be the seal upon the grave of Clarimonde, for this is not—it is said—the first time she hath died. God be with thee, Romuald."

So speaking, Sérapion departed with slow steps.

.   .   .   .

Time passed and I was well again. Nay, I deemed that the fears of Sérapion and my own terrors were too great, till one night I dreamed. . . . Scarce had I tasted the first drops of the cup of sleep when I heard the curtains of my bed open, and the rings rang. I raised myself on my arm and saw the one whom straightway I knew for Clarimonde.

She held in her hand a little lamp such as is placed in tombs, and the light touched her dainty fingers to a rosy hue that merged slowly into the milk-white of her arm.

She was clad with naught but the linen shroud in which she had lain in state. The folds were clasped about her breast as it were in pudency by a hand all too small. So white she was that her shroud and her body were blended in the pallid glow of the lamp.

Swathed thus in the fine tissue that betrayed every line of her figure, she seemed a marble image of some lady at the bath rather than a living woman. Dead or living, statue or woman, spirit or flesh, her beauty was ever the same, only the glitter of her sea-green eye was dulled—only the mouth, so red of old, wore but a tender tint of rose, like the white rose of her cheeks. The little blue flowers that I had seen in her hair were sere now, and all but bloomless ; yet so winning was she, so winning that, despite the strangeness of the adventure, and her inexplicable invasion of my chamber, I was not afraid for one moment.

She placed the lamp on the table, and sat down by my bed-foot. Then, in those soft and silver accents which I never heard from any lips but hers,—

"Long have I made thee wait for me," she said, "and thou must have deemed that I had forgotten thee quite. But lo ! I come from far, very far—even from that land whence no traveller has returned. There is no sunlight nor moon in the country whence I wander, only shadow and space. There the foot finds no rest, nor the wandering wing any way ; yet here am I—behold me, for Love can conquer Death. Ah, what sad faces and terrible eyes have I seen in my voyaging, and in what labour hath my soul been to find my body and to make her home therein again ! How hard to lift was the stone that they had laid on me for a covering ! Lo, my hands are sorely wounded in that toil ! Kiss them, my love, and heal them." And she laid her chill palms on my mouth, that I kissed many times, she smiling on me with an inexpressible sweetness of delight.

To my shame be it spoken, I had wholly forgotten the counsels of the Abbé Sérapion, and the sacred character of my ministry. I fell unresisting at the first attack. Nay, I did not even try to bid the tempter avaunt, but succumbed without a struggle before the sweet freshness of Clarimonde's fair body. Poor child ! for all that is come and gone, I can scarce believe that she was indeed a devil ; surely there was naught of the devil in her aspect. Never hath Satan better concealed his claws and his horns ! She was crouching on the side of my bed, her heels drawn up beneath her in an attitude of careless and provoking grace. Once and again she would pass her little hands among my locks, and curl them, as if to try what style best suited my face. It is worth noting that I felt no astonishment at an adventure so marvellous—nay, as in a dream the strangest events fail to surprise us, even so the whole encounter seemed to me perfectly natural.

" I loved thee long before I saw thee, Romuald, my love, and I sought for thee everywhere. Thou wert my dream, and I beheld thee in the church at that fatal hour. ' It is he,' I whispered to myself, and cast on thee a glance fulfilled of all the love wherewith I had loved, and did love, and shall love thee ; a glance that would have ruined the soul of a cardinal, or brought a king with all his court at my feet.

" But thou wert not moved, and before my love thou didst place the love of God.

" Ah, 'tis of God that I am jealous—God whom thou hast loved and lovest more than me.

" Miserable woman that I am ! Never shall I have all thy heart for myself alone—for me, whom thou didst awaken with one kiss ; for me, Clarimonde the dead ; for me, who for thy sake have broken the portals of the grave, and am come to

offer to thee a life that hath been taken up again for this one
end to make thee happy."

So she spoke ; and every word was broken in on by maddening caresses, till my brain swam, and I feared not to console
her by this awful blasphemy ; namely—that my love of her
passed my love of God.

Then the fire of her eyes was rekindled, and they blazed
as it had been the chrysoprase stone.

" Verily thou lovest me with a love like thy love of God,"
she cried, making her arms a girdle for my body. " Then thou
shalt come with me, and whithersoever I go there wilt thou
follow. Thou wilt leave these ugly black robes, thou wilt be of
all knights the proudest and the most envied. The acknowledged
lover of Clarimonde shalt thou be, of her who refused a Pope !
Ah, happy life, ah, golden days, that shall be ours ! When do
we mount and ride, my gentleman ? "

" To-morrow," I cried in my madness.

" To-morrow," she answered. " I shall have time to change
this robe of mine that is somewhat scant, nor fit for voyaging.
Also must I speak with my retainers, that think me dead in
good earnest, and lament me as well as they may. Money,
carriages, change of raiment, all shall be ready for thee ; at
this hour to-morrow will I seek thee. Good-bye, sweetheart."
She touched my brow with her lips, the lamp faded into darkness, the curtains closed, a sleep like lead came down on me,
sleep without a dream. I wakened late, troubled by the memory
of my dream, which at length I made myself believe was but a
vision of the night. Yet it was not without dread that I sought
rest again, praying Heaven to guard the purity of my slumber.

Anon I fell again into a deep sleep, and my dream began
again. The curtains opened, and there stood Clarimonde, not
pale in her pale shroud, nor with the violets of death upon her
cheek ; but gay, bright, splendid, in a travelling robe of green
velvet with strappings of gold, and kilted upon one side to show
a satin undercoat. Her fair, curled locks fell in great masses
from under a large black beaver hat, with strange white plumes ;
in her hand she held a little riding-whip, topped with a golden
whistle. With this she touched me gently, saying—

" Awake, fair sleeper ! Is it thus you prepare for your
voyage ? I had thought to find you alert. Rise, rise quickly ;
we have no time to lose ! "

I leaped out of bed.

" Come, dress, and let us begone," she said, showing me

a little packet she had brought. " Our horses are fretting and champing at the gate. We should be ten leagues from here."

I arrayed myself in haste, while she instructed me, handed me the various articles of a knight's attire, and laughed at my clumsiness. She dressed my hair, and when all was done, gave me a little Venice pocket-mirror in a silver frame, crying—

" What think you of yourself now ? Will you take me for your valet de chambre ? "

I did not know my own face in the glass, and was no more like myself than a statue is like the uncut stone. I was beautiful, and I was vain of the change. The gold embroidered gallant attire made me another man, and I marvelled at the magic of a few ells of cloth, fashioned to a certain device. The character of my clothes became my own, and in ten minutes I was sufficiently conceited. Clarimonde watched me with a kind of maternal fondness as I walked up and down the room, proving my new raiment, as it were ; then—

" Come," she cried, " enough of this child's play ! Up and away, my Romuald ! We have far to go ; we shall never arrive."

She took my hand and led me forth. The gates opened at her touch ; the dog did not waken as we passed.

At the gate we found the groom with three horses like those he had led before, Spanish horses that sped swift as the wind. Presently we came on a plain where a carriage and four horses waited for us. The postilion drove them to a mad gallop. My arm was around the waist of Clarimonde, her head upon my shoulder, her breast pressing against me. From then mine became a double life : within me were two men that knew each other not—the priest who dreamed that by night he was a noble, the noble who dreamed that by night he was a priest.

Certainly I was, or thought I was, in Venice, in a great palace on the Grand Canal. Clarimonde loved life in the great style. Custom could not make her common. To love her was to love a score of mistresses. She returned my love a hundredfold. One day, when she had been unwell for a time, I cut my hand, and she sucked the blood from the wound.

" I shall not die ! I shall not die ! " she exclaimed. " I shall yet love thee long, for my life is in thine. Thy blood has given me back my life ! "

This event and the strange fears it inspired haunted me long.

Sérapion often reproached me. One day he said—

"To drive away the demon that possesses thee, there is but one thing to do. I know where Clarimonde is buried. We must unearth her, and the sight of the worms and the dust of death will make thee thyself again."

So weary was I of my double life that I accepted his plan, and at midnight we found her gravestone. Thereon we read these words—

> Ici gît Clarimonde,
> qui fut de son Vivant
> la Plus Belle du Monde.

. . . .

At length the pick of Sérapion smote the coffin lid, which he then raised, and I saw Clarimonde—on her pale mouth shone one drop of blood.

Sérapion, breaking forth into fury, shouted—

"Ah, there thou art. . . . Devil, Harlot, Vampire ; thou that drainest the blood of men !"

With this he sprinkled holy water over her, and she straightway crumbled into dust.

"There lies thy love, Sir Romuald," he said. "Go now and dally at the Lido with thy beauty."

I bowed my head. Within me all was ruin. Back to my poor priest's house I went. Romuald the lover said farewell to the priest. *But, next night, I saw Clarimonde!*

"Wretched man that thou art," she cried. "What hast thou done ? Why hast thou hearkened to that foolish priest ? Wert thou not happy ? What ill had I done thee that thou must violate my tomb ? Henceforth the link between our souls and bodies is broken. Thou shalt desire me. Farewell !"

Then she fled into space and I saw her never more. . . . Alas ! It was truth she spoke ; I long for her still. Dearly bought hath my salvation been, and the love of my Lord hath not been too much to replace the love of her.

Behold, brother, the story of my youth.

Let not thine eyes gaze upon a woman. Walk with glances that only seek the earth. For, be ye chaste and calm as ye may, one minute may damn thee to all eternity.

*At length the pick of Sérapion smote the coffin lid,
which he then raised, and I saw Clarimonde.*

THE DILEMMA OF PHADRIG

"THERE's no use in talken about it, Phadrig. I know an I feel that all's over wit me. My pains are all gone, to be sure—but in place o' that, there's a weight like a quern stone down upon my heart, an I feel it blackenen within me. All I have to say is—think o' your own Mauria when she's gone, an be kind to poor Patcy."

"Ah, darlen, don't talk that way—there's hopes yet—what'll I do, what'll the child do witout you? "——

"Phadrig, there's noan. I'm goen fast, an if you have any regard for me, you won't say anythin that'll bring the thoughts o' you an him between me an the thoughts o' heaven, for that's what I must think of now. An if you marry again——"

"Oh, Mauria, honey, will you kill me entirely? Is it *I'll* marry again? "

——"If it be a thing you should marry again," Mauria resumed, without taking any notice of her husband's interruption, " you'll bear in mind that the best mother that ever walked the ground will love her own above another's. It stands with raisin an natur. The gander abroad will pull a strange goslen out of his own flock ; and you know yourself, we could never get the bracket hen to sit upon Nelly O'Leary's chickens, do what we could. Everything loves its own. Then, Phadrig, if you see the floury potaties—an the top o' the milk—an the warm seat be the hob—an the biggest bit o' meat on a Sunday goen away from Patcy—you'll think o' your poor Mauria, an do her part by him ; just quietly, and softly, an without blamen the woman —for it is only what's nait'rel, an what many a stepmother does without thinking o' themselves. An above all things, Phadrig, take care to make him mind his books and his religion, to keep out o' bad company, an study his readin-made-aisy, and that's the way he'll be a blessing an a comfort to you in your old days, as I once thought he would be to me in mine."

Here her husband renewed his promises in a tone of deep affliction.

" An now for yourself, Phadrig. Remember the charge that's upon you, and don't be goen out venturen your life in a little canvas canoe, on the bad autumn days, at Ballybunion ; nor wit foolish boys at the Glin and Tarbert fairs ;—an don't be so wake-minded as to be trusten to card-drawers, an fairy doctors, an the like ; for it's the last word the priest said to me was, that you were too superstitious, and that's a great shame an a heavy sin. But tee you ! [1] Phadrig, dear, there's that rogue of a pig at the potaties over——"

Phadrig turned out the grunting intruder, bolted the hurdle-door, and returned to the bedside of his expiring helpmate. That tidy housekeeper, however, exhausted by the exertion which she had made to preserve, from the mastication of the swinish tusk, the fair produce of her husband's conacre of white-eyes, had fallen back on the pillow and breathed her last.

Great was the grief of the widowed Phadrig for her loss—great were the lamentations of her female friends at the evening wake—and great was the jug of whisky-punch which the mourners imbibed at the mouth, in order to supply the loss of fluid which was expended from the eyes. According to the usual cottage etiquette, the mother of the deceased, who acted as mistress of the ceremonies, occupied a capacious hay-bottomed chair near the fireplace—from which she only rose when courtesy called on her to join each of her female acquaintances as they arrived, in the death-wail which (as in politeness bound) they poured forth over the pale piece of earth that lay coffined in the centre of the room. This mark of attention, however, the old lady was observed to omit with regard to one of the fair guests —a round-faced, middle-aged woman, called Milly Rue—or Red Milly, probably because her head might have furnished a solution of the popular conundrum, " Why is a red-haired lady like a sentinel on his post ? "

The fair Milly, however, did not appear to resent this slight, which was occasioned (so the whisper went among the guests) by the fact that she had been an old and neglected love of the new widower. All the fiery ingredients in Milly's constitution appeared to be comprehended in her glowing ringlets—and those, report says, were as ardent in hue as their owner was

[1]To you! Beware!

calm and regulated in her temper. It would be a cold morning, indeed, that a sight of Milly's head would not warm you—and a hot fit of anger which a few tones of her kind and wrath-disarming voice would not cool. She dropped, after she had concluded her " cry," a conciliating curtsey to the sullen old lady, took an unobtrusive seat at the foot of the bed, talked of the " notable " qualities of the deceased, and was particularly attentive to the flaxen-headed little Patcy, whom she held in her lap during the whole night, cross-examining him in his reading and multiplication, and presenting him, at parting, in token of her satisfaction at his proficiency, with a copy of *The Seven Champions of Christendom*, with a fine marble cover and pictures. Milly acted in this instance under the advice of a prudent mother, who exhorted her, " whenever she thought o' maken presents, that way, not to be layen her money out in cakes or gingerbread, or things that would be ett off at wanst, an no more about them or the giver—but to give a strong toy, or a book, or somethen that would last, and bring her to mind now and then, so as that when a person 'ud ask where they got that, or who gev it, they'd say, ' from Milly Rue,' or ' Milly gev it, we're obleest to her,' an talken an thinken of her when she'd be away."

To curb in my tale, which may otherwise become restive and unmanageable—Milly's deep affliction and generous sympathy made a serious impression on the mind of the widower, who more than all was touched by that singularly accidental attachment which she seemed to have conceived for little Patcy. Nothing could be farther from his own wishes than any design of a second time changing his condition ; but he felt that it would be doing a grievous wrong to the memory of his first wife if he neglected this opportunity of providing her favourite Patcy with a protector, so well calculated to supply her place. He demurred a little on the score of true love, and the violence which he was about to do his own constant heart—but like the bluff King Henry, his conscience—" aye—his conscience,"— touched him, and the issue was that a roaring wedding shook the walls which had echoed to the wail of death within the few preceding months.

Milly Rue not only supplied the place of a mother to young Patcy, but presented him in the course of a few years with two merry play-fellows, a brother and a sister. To do her handsome justice, too, poor Mauria's anticipations were completely disproved by her conduct, and it would have been impossible

for a stranger to have detected the stepson of the house from
any shade of undue partiality in the mother. The harmony
in which they dwelt was unbroken by any accident for many
years.

The first shock which burst in with a sudden violence upon
their happiness was one of a direful nature. Disease, that pale
and hungry fiend who haunts alike the abodes of wealth and
of penury ; who brushes away with his baleful wing the bloom
from beauty's cheek, and the balm of slumber from the pillow
of age ; who troubles the hope of the young mother with dreams
of ghastliness and gloom, and fears that come suddenly, she
knows not why nor whence ; who sheds his poisonous dews
alike on the heart that is buoyant and the heart that is broken ;
this stern and conquering demon scorned not to knock, one
summer morning, at the door of Phadrig's cow-house, and to
lay his iron fingers upon a fine milch-cow, a sheeted-stripper
which constituted (to use his own emphatic phrase) the poor
farmer's " substance."

All the " cures " in the pharmacopœia of the village apothe-
cary were expended on the poor animal, without any beneficial
effect ; and Phadrig, after many conscientious qualms about
the dying words of his first wife, resolved to have recourse to that
infallible refuge in such cases—a fairy doctor.

He said nothing to the afflicted Milly about his intention, but
slipped out of the cottage in the afternoon, hurried to the Shannon
side near Money Point, unmoored his light canvas-built canoe,
seated himself in the frail vessel, and fixing his paddles on the
towl-pin, sped away over the calm face of the waters towards
the isle of Scattery, where the renowned Crohoore-na-Oona, or
Connor-of-the-Sheep, the Mohammed of the cottages, at this
time took up his residence. This mysterious personage, whose
prophecies are still commented on among the cottage circles
with looks of deep awe and wonder, was much revered by his
contemporaries as a man " who had seen a dale " ; of what
nature those sights or visions were was intimated by a mysterious
look, and a solemn nod of the head.

In a little time Phadrig ran his little canoe aground on the
sandy beach of Scattery, and, drawing her above high-water
mark, proceeded to the humble dwelling of the gifted Sheep-
shearer with feelings of profound fear and anxiety.

A sudden crash among the stores and dock-weed in an
opposite corner of the ruin made him start and yell. The
noise was occasioned by a little rotund personage, who

had sprung from the mouldering wall, and now stood gazing
fixedly on the terrified Phadrig, who continued returning that
steady glance with a half-frightened, half-crying face—one
hand fast clenched upon his breast, and the other extended,
with an action of avoidance and deprecation. The person of
the stranger was stout and short, rendered still more so by a
stoop, which might almost have been taken for a hump—his
arms hung forward from his shoulders, like those of a long-
armed ape—his hair was grey and bushy, like that of a wanderoo
—and his sullen grey eye seemed to be inflamed with ill-humour
—his feet were bare and as broad as a camel's—and a leathern
girdle buckling round his waist secured a tattered grey frieze
riding-coat, and held an enormous pair of shears, which might
have clipped off a man's head as readily, perhaps, as a lock
of wool.   This last article of costume afforded a sufficient indication to Phadrig that he stood in the presence of the awful object
of his search.

"Well! an who are *you*?" growled the Sheep-shearer, after
surveying Phadrig attentively for some moments.

The first gruff sound of his voice made the latter renew his
start and roar for fright ; after which, composing his terrors as
well as he might, he replied, in the words of Autolycus, "I am
only a poor fellow, sir."

"Well! an what's your business with me?"

"A cure, sir, I wanted for her. A cow o' mine that's very
bad inwardly, an we can do nothen for her ; an I thought may
be you'd know what is it ail'ded her—an prevail on THEM" (this
word was pronounced with an emphasis of deep meaning) " to
leave her to uz."

"Huth!" the Sheep-shearer thundered out, in a tone that
made poor Phadrig jump six feet backwards with a fresh yell,
"do you daare to spake of *them* before me. Go along! you
villyan o' the airth, an wait for me outside the church, an' I'll
tell you all about it there ; but, first—do you think I can get
the *gentlemen* to do anything for me *gratish*—without offeren 'em
a trate or a haip'orth?"

"If their honours wouldn't think two tin-pennies and a
fi'penny bit too little.—It's all I'm worth in the wide world."

"Well! we'll see what they'll say to it. Give it here to me.
Go now—be off with yourself—if you don't want to have 'em
all a-top o' you in a minnit."

This last hint made our hero scamper over the stones like a
startled fawn ; nor did he think himself safe until he reached

the spot where he had left his canoe, and where he expected
the coming of the Sheep-shearer ; conscience-struck by the
breach of his promise to his dying Mauria, and in a state of
agonising anxiety with respect to the lowing patient in the
cow-house.

He was soon after rejoined by Connor-of-the-Sheep.

" There is one way," said he, " of saving your cow—but you
must lose one of your childer if you wish to save it."

" O Heaven presarve uz, sir, how is that, if you plase ? "

" You must go home," said the Sheep-shearer, " and say
nothen to anybody, but fix in your mind which o' your three
childer you'll give for the cow ; an when you do that, look in
his eyes, an he'll sneeze, an don't you bless him, for the world.
Then look in his eyes again, an he'll sneeze again, an still don't
think o' blessen him, be any mains. The third time you'll look
in his eyes he'll sneeze a third time—an if you don't bless him
the third time, he'll die—but your cow will live."

" An this is the only cure you have to gi' me ? " exclaimed
Phadrig, his indignation at the moment overcoming his natural
timidity.

" The only cure.—It was by a dale to do I could prevail on
them to let you make the choice itself."

With a heavy heart Phadrig put forth in his canoe upon the
water and prepared to return. It was already twilight, and as he
glided along the peaceful shores he ruminated mournfully within
his mind on the course which he should pursue. The loss of the
cow would be, he considered, almost equivalent to total ruin
—and the loss of any one of his lovely children was a probability
which he could hardly bear to dwell on for a moment. Still it
behoved him to weigh the matter well. Which of them, now—
supposing it possible that he could think of sacrificing any—
which of them would he select for the purpose ? The choice
was a hard one. There was little Mauria, a fair-haired, blue-eyed
little girl—but he could not, for an instant, think of losing her,
as she happened to be named after his first wife ; her brother,
little Shamus, was the least useful of the three, but he was the
youngest—" the child of his old age—a little one ! " his heart
bled at the idea ; he would lose the cow, and the pig along
with it, before he would harm a hair of the darling infant's head.
He thought of Patcy—and he shuddered and leaned heavier on
his oars, as if to flee away from the horrible doubt which stole
into his heart with that name. It must be one of the three, or
the cow was lost for ever. The two first-mentioned he certainly

would not lose—and Patcy. Again he bade the fiend begone, and trembling in every limb, made the canoe speed rapidly over the tide in the direction of his home.

He drew the little vessel ashore and proceeded towards his cabin. They had been waiting supper for him, and he learned with renewed anxiety that the object of his solicitude, the milch-cow, had rather fallen away than improved in her condition during his absence. He sat down in sorrowful silence with his wife and children to their humble supper of potatoes and thick milk.

He gazed intently on the features of each of the young inno-cents as they took their places on the suggan chairs that flanked the board. Little Mauria and her brother Shamus looked fresh, mirthful, and blooming from their noisy play in the adjoining paddock, while their elder brother, who had spent the day at school, wore—or seemed, to the distempered mind of his father, to wear a look of sullenness and chagrin. He was thinner, too, than most boys of his age—a circumstance which Phadrig had never remarked before. It might be the first indications of his poor mother's disease, consumption, that were beginning to declare themselves in his constitution ; and if so, his doom was already sealed—and whether the cow died or not, Patcy was certain to be lost. Still the father could not bring his mind to resolve on any settled course, and their meal proceeded in silence.

Suddenly the latch of the door was lifted by some person outside, and a neighbour entered to inform Phadrig that the agent to his landlord had arrived in the adjacent village for the purpose of driving matters to extremity against all those tenants who remained in arrear. At the same moment, too, a low moan of anguish from the cow outside announced the access of a fresh paroxysm of her distemper, which it was very evident the poor animal could never come through in safety.

In an agony of distress and horror the distracted father laid his clenched fingers on the table, and looked fixedly in the eyes of the unsuspecting Patcy. The child sneezed, and Phadrig closed his lips hard, for fear a blessing might escape him. The child at the same time, he observed, looked paler than before.

Fearful lest the remorse which began to awake within his heart might oversway his resolution, and prevent the accom-plishment of his unnatural design, he looked hurriedly a second time into the eyes of the little victim. Again the latter sneezed, and again the father, using a violent effort, restrained the blessing which was struggling at his heart. The poor child drooped his head upon his bosom, and letting the untasted food fall from his hand, looked so pale and mournful as to remind his murderer of the look which his mother wore in dying.

It was long—very long—before the heart-struck parent could prevail on himself to complete the sacrifice. The visitor departed ; and the first beams of a full moon began to supplant the faint and lingering twilight which was fast fading in the west. The dead of the night drew on before the family rose from their silent and comfortless meal. The agonies of the devoted animal now drew rapidly to a close, and Phadrig still remained tortured by remorse on the one hand, and by selfish anxiety on the other.

A sudden sound of anguish from the cow-house made him start from his seat. A third time he fixed his eyes on those of his child—a third time the boy sneezed—but here the charm was broken.

Milly Rue, looking with surprise and tenderness on the fainting boy, said, " Why, then, Heaven bless you, child !—it must be a cold you caught, you're sneezen so often."

Immediately the cow sent forth a bellow of deep agony, and expired ; and at the same moment a low and plaintive voice outside the door was heard, exclaiming, " And Heaven bless you, Milly ! and the Almighty bless you, and spare you a long time over your children ! "

Phadrig staggered back against the wall—his blood froze in his veins—his face grew white as death—his teeth chattered—his eyes stared—his hair moved upon his brow, and the chilling damp of terror exuded over all his frame. He recognised the voice of his first wife ; and her pale, cold eye met his at that moment, as her shade flitted by the window in the thin moonlight, and darted on him a glance of mournful reproach. He covered his eyes with his hands, and sunk, senseless, into a chair ; while the affrighted Milly, and Patcy, who at once assumed his glowing health and vigour, hastened to his assistance. They had all heard the voice, but no one saw the shade nor recognised the tone excepting the conscience-smitten Phadrig.

MARY BURNET

THE following incidents are related as having occurred at a shepherd's house, not a hundred miles from St. Mary's Loch ; but, as the descendants of one of the families still reside in the vicinity, I deem it requisite to use names which cannot be recognised, save by those who have heard the story.

John Allanson, the farmer's son of Inverlawn, was a handsome, roving, and incautious young man, enthusiastic, amorous, and fond of adventure, and one who could hardly be said to fear the face of either man, woman, or spirit. Among other love adventures, he fell a-courting Mary Burnet, of Kirkstyle, a most beautiful and innocent maiden, and one who had been bred up in rural simplicity. She loved him, but yet she was afraid of him ; and though she had no objection to meeting with him among others, yet she carefully avoided meeting him alone, though often and earnestly urged to it. One day, the young man, finding an opportunity, at Our Lady's Chapel, after mass, urged his suit for a private meeting so ardently, and with so many vows of love and sacred esteem, that Mary was so far won as to promise, that *perhaps* she would come and meet him.

The trysting place was a little green sequestered spot, on the very verge of the lake, well known to many an angler, and to none better than the writer of this old tale ; and the hour appointed, the time when the King's Elwand (now foolishly termed the Belt of Orion) set his first golden knob above the hill. Allanson came too early ; and he watched the sky with such eagerness and devotion, that he thought every little star that arose in the south-east the top knob of the King's Elwand. At last the Elwand did arise in good earnest, and then the youth, with a heart palpitating with agitation, had nothing for it but to watch the heathery brow by which bonny Mary Burnet was to descend. No Mary Burnet made her appearance, even although the King's Elwand had now measured its own equivocal length five or six times up the lift.

Young Allanson now felt all the most poignant miseries of disappointment ; and, as the story goes, uttered in his heart an unhallowed wish—he wished that some witch or fairy would influence his Mary to come to him in spite of her maidenly scruples. This wish was thrice repeated with all the energy of disappointed love. It was thrice repeated, and no more, when, behold, Mary appeared on the brae, with wild and eccentric motions, speeding to the appointed place. Allanson's excitement seems to have been more than he was able to bear, as he instantly became delirious with joy, and always professed that he could remember nothing of their first meeting, save that Mary remained silent, and spoke not a word, either good or bad. In a short time she fell a-sobbing and weeping, refusing to be comforted, and then, uttering a piercing shriek, sprung up, and ran from him with amazing speed.

At this part of the loch, which, as I said, is well known to many, the shore is overhung by a precipitous cliff, of no great height, but still inaccessible, either from above or below. Save in a great drought, the water comes to within a yard of the bottom of this cliff, and the intermediate space is filled with rough unshapely pieces of rock fallen from above. Along this narrow and rude space, hardly passable by the angler at noon, did Mary bound with the swiftness of a kid, although surrounded with darkness. Her lover, pursuing with all his energy, called out, " Mary ! Mary ! my dear Mary, stop and speak with me. I'll conduct you home, or anywhere you please, but do not run from me. Stop, my dearest Mary—stop ! "

Mary would not stop ; but ran on, till, coming to a little cliff that jutted into the lake, round which there was no passage, and, perceiving that her lover would there overtake her, she uttered another shriek, and plunged into the lake. The loud sound of her fall into the still water rung in the young man's ears like the knell of death ; and if before he was crazed with love, he was now as much so with despair. He saw her floating lightly away from the shore towards the deepest part of the loch ; but, in a short time, she began to sink, and gradually disappeared, without uttering a throb or a cry. A good while previous to this, Allanson had flung off his bonnet, shoes, and coat, and plunged in. He swam to the place where Mary disappeared ; but there was neither boil nor gurgle on the water, nor even a bell of departing breath, to mark the place where his beloved had sunk. Being strangely impressed, at that trying moment, with a determination to live or die with her, he tried to dive, in hopes either to bring her up or to die in her arms ; and he thought of their being so found on the shore of the lake, with a melancholy satisfaction ; but by no effort of his could he reach the bottom, nor knew he what distance he was still from it. With an exhausted frame, and a despairing heart, he was obliged again to seek the shore, and, dripping wet as he was, and half-naked, he ran to her father's house with the woeful tidings. Everything there was quiet. The old shepherd's family, of whom Mary was the youngest, and sole daughter, were all sunk in silent repose ; and oh, how the distracted lover wept at the thoughts of wakening them to hear the doleful tidings ! But waken them he must ; so, going to the little window close by the goodman's bed, he called, in a melancholy tone, " Andrew! Andrew Burnet, are you waking ? "

" Troth, man, I think I be ; or, at least, I'm half-and-half. What hast thou to say to auld Andrew Burnet at this time o' night ? "

" Are you waking, I say ? "

" Gudewife, am I waking ? Because if I be, tell that stravaiger sae. He'll maybe tak your word for it, for mine he winna tak."

" O Andrew, none of your humour to-night ; I bring you tidings the most woeful, the most dismal, the most heart-rending, that ever were brought to an honest man's door."

" To his window, you mean," cried Andrew, bolting out of bed, and proceeding to the door. " Gude sauff us, man, come in, whaever you be, and tell us your tidings face to face ; and then we'll can better judge of the truth of them. If they be in concord wi' your voice, they are melancholy indeed. Have the reavers come, and are our kye driven ? "

" Oh, alas ! waur than that—a thousand times waur than that ! Your daughter—your dear beloved and only daughter, Mary——"

" What of Mary ? " cried the good-man. " What of Mary ? " cried her mother, shuddering and groaning with terror ; and at the same time she kindled a light.

The sight of their neighbour, half-naked, and dripping with wet, and madness and despair in his looks, sent a chillness to their hearts, that held them in silence, and they were unable to utter a word, till he went on thus : " Mary is gone ; your darling and mine is lost, and sleeps this night in a watery grave— and I have been her destroyer ! "

" Thou art mad, John Allanson," said the old man, vehemently, " raving mad ; at least I hope so. Wicked as thou art, thou hadst not the heart to kill my dear child. O yes, you are mad—God be thankful, you are mad. I see it in your looks and demeanour. Heaven be praised, you are mad ! You *are* mad ; but you'll get better again. But what do I say ? " continued he, as recollecting himself—" We can soon convince our own senses. Wife, lead the way to our daughter's bed."

With a heart throbbing with terror and dismay, old Jean Linton led the way to Mary's chamber, followed by the two men, who were eagerly gazing, one over each of her shoulders. Mary's little apartment was in the farther end of the long narrow cottage ; and as soon as they entered it, they perceived a form lying on the bed, with the bedclothes drawn over its head ; and on the lid of Mary's little chest, that stood at the bedside, her clothes were lying neatly folded, as they wont to be. Hope seemed to dawn on the faces of the two old people when they beheld this, but the lover's heart sunk still deeper in despair. The father called her name, but the form on the bed returned no answer ; however, they all heard distinctly sobs, as of one weeping. The old man then ventured to pull down the clothes from her face ; and, strange to say, there indeed lay Mary Burnet, drowned in tears, yet apparently nowise surprised at the ghastly appearance of the three naked figures. Allanson gasped for breath, for he remained still incredulous. He touched her clothes—he lifted her robes one by one—and all of them were dry, neat, and clean, and had no appearance of having sunk in the lake.

There can be no doubt that Allanson was confounded by the strange event that had befallen him, and felt like one struggling with a frightful vision, or some energy beyond the power of man to comprehend. Nevertheless the assurance that Mary was there in life, weeping although she was, put him once more beside himself with joy ; and he kneeled at her bedside, beseeching permission but to kiss her hand. She, however, repulsed him with disdain, saying with great emphasis : " You are a bad man, John Allanson, and I entreat you to go out of my sight. The sufferings that I have undergone this night have been beyond the power of flesh and blood to endure ; and by some cursed agency of yours have these sufferings been brought about. I therefore pray you, in His name, whose law you have transgressed, to depart out of my sight."

Wholly overcome by conflicting passions, by circumstances so contrary to one another, and so discordant with everything either in the works of Nature or Providence, the young man could do nothing but stand like a rigid statue, with his hands lifted up, and his visage like that of a corpse, until led away by the two old people from their daughter's apartment. Then they lighted up a fire to dry him, and began to question him with the most intense curiosity; but they could elicit nothing from him, but the most disjointed exclamations—such as, " Lord in Heaven, what can be the meaning of this ? " And at other times : " It is all the enchantment of the devil ; the evil spirits have got dominion over me ! "

Finding they could make nothing of him, they began to form conjectures of their own. Jean affirmed that it had been the Mermaid of the loch that had come to him in Mary's shape, to allure him to his destruction ; but Andrew Burnet, setting his bonnet to one side, and raising his left hand to a level with it, so that he might have full scope to motion and flourish, suiting his action to his words, thus began, with a face of sapience never to be excelled :

" Gudewife, it doth strike me that thou art very wide of the mark. It must have been a spirit of a great deal higher quality than a meer-maiden, who played this extraordinary prank. The meer-maiden is not a spirit, but a beastly sensitive creature, with a malicious spirit within it. Now, what influence could a cauld clatch of a creature like that, wi' a tail like a great saumont-fish, hae ower our bairn, either to make her happy or unhappy? Or where could it borrow her claes, Jean? Tell me that. Na, na, Jean Linton, depend on it, the spirit that courtit wi' poor sinfu' Jock there, has been a fairy ; but whether a good ane or an ill ane, it is hard to determine."

Andrew's disquisition was interrupted by the young man falling into a fit of trembling that was fearful to look at, and threatened soon to terminate his existence. Jean ran for the family cordial, observing by the way, that " though he was a wicked person, he was still a fellow-creature, and might live to repent ; " and influenced by this spark of genuine humanity, she made him swallow two horn-spoonfuls of strong aquavitæ. Andrew then put a piece of scarlet thread round each wrist, and taking a strong rowan-tree staff in his hand, he conveyed

his trembling and astonished guest home, giving him at parting
this sage advice :

"I'll tell you what it is, Jock Allanson—ye hae run a near
risk o' perdition, and, escaping that for the present, o' losing
your right reason. But take an auld man's advice—never gang
again out by night to beguile ony honest man's daughter, lest a
worse thing befall thee."

Next morning Mary dressed herself more neatly than usual,
but there was manifestly a deep melancholy settled on her
lovely face, and at times the unbidden tear would start into her
eye. She spoke no word, either good or bad, that ever her mother
could recollect, that whole morning ; but she once or twice
observed her daughter gazing at her, as with an intense and
melancholy interest. About nine o'clock in the morning, she
took a hay-raik over her shoulder, and went down to a meadow
at the east end of the loch, to coil a part of her father's hay,
her father and brother engaging to join her about noon, when
they came from the sheepfold. As soon as old Andrew came
home, his wife and he, as was natural, instantly began to con-
verse on the events of the preceding night ; and in the course
of their conversation Andrew said, " Gudeness be about us,
Jean, was not yon an awfu' speech o' our bairn's to young Jock
Allanson last night ? "

" Ay, it was a downsetter, gudeman, and spoken like a good
Christian lass."

" I'm no sae sure o' that, Jean Linton. My good woman,
Jean Linton, I'm no sae sure o' that. Yon speech has gi'en me
a great deal o' trouble o' heart ; for d'ye ken, an' take my life—
ay, an' take your life, Jean—nane o' us can tell whether it was
in the Almighty's name or the devil's that she discharged her
lover."

" O fy, Andrew, how can ye say sae ? How can ye doubt that
it was in the Almighty's name ? "

" Couldna she have said sae then, and that wad hae put it
beyond a' doubt ? And that wad hae been the natural way too ;
but instead of that she says, ' I pray you, in the name of him
whose law you have transgressed, to depart out o' my sight.'
I confess I'm terrified when I think about yon speech, Jean
Linton. Didna she say too that ' her sufferings had been beyond
what flesh and blood could have endured ? ' What was she but
flesh and blood. Didna that remark infer that she was something
mair than a mortal creature ? Jean Linton, Jean Linton ! what
will you say if it should turn out that our daughter *is* drowned,

and that yon was the fairy we had in the house a' the night and this morning ? "

" O haud your tongue, Andrew Burnet, and dinna make my heart cauld within me. We hae aye trusted in the Lord yet, and he has never forsaken us, nor will he yet gie the Wicked One power ower us or ours."

" Ye say very weel, Jean, and we maun e'en hope for the best," quoth old Andrew ; and away he went, accompanied by his son Alexander, to assist their beloved Mary on the meadow.

No sooner had Andrew set his head over the bents, and come in view of the meadow, than he said to his son, " I wish Jock Allanson maunna hae been east-the-loch fishing for geds the day, for I think my Mary has made very little progress in the meadow."

" She's ower muckle ta'en up about other things this while to mind her wark," said Alexander ; " I wadna wonder, father, if that lassie gangs a black gate yet."

Andrew uttered a long and a deep sigh, that seemed to ruffle the very fountains of life, and, without speaking another word, walked on to the hayfield. It was three hours since Mary had left home, and she ought at least to have put up a dozen coils of hay each hour. But, in place of that, she had put up only seven altogether, and the last was unfinished. Her own hay-raik, that had an M and a B neatly cut on the head of it, was leaning on the unfinished coil, and Mary was wanting. Her brother, thinking she had hid herself from them in sport, ran from one coil to another, calling her many bad names, playfully ; but after he had turned them all up, and several deep swathes besides, she was not to be found. This young man, who slept in the byre, knew nothing of the events of the foregoing night, the old people and Allanson having mutually engaged to keep them a profound secret, and he had therefore less reason than his father to be seriously alarmed. When they began to work at the hay Andrew could work none ; he looked this way and that way, but in no way could he see Mary approaching ; so he put on his coat and went away home, to pour his sorrows into the bosom of his wife ; and, in the meantime, he desired his son to run to all the neighbouring farming-houses and cots, every one, and make inquiries if anybody had seen Mary.

When Andrew went home and informed his wife that their darling was missing, the grief and astonishment of the aged couple knew no bounds. They sat down and wept together, and declared over and over that this act of Providence was too strong for them, and too high to be understood. Jean besought her husband to kneel instantly, and pray urgently to God to restore their child to them ; but he declined it, on account of the wrong frame of his mind, for he declared, that his rage against John Allanson was so extreme as to unfit him for approaching the throne of his Maker. " But if the profligate refuses to listen to the entreaties of an injured parent," added he, " he shall feel the weight of an injured father's arm."

Andrew went straight away to Inverlawn, though without the least hope of finding young Allanson at home ; but, on reaching the place, to his amazement, he found the young man lying ill of a burning fever, raving incessantly of witches, spirits, and Mary Burnet. To such a height had his frenzy arrived, that when Andrew went there, it required three men to hold him in the bed. Both his parents testified their opinions openly, that their son was bewitched, or possessed of a demon, and the whole family was thrown into the greatest consternation. The good old shepherd, finding enough of grief there already, was obliged to confine his to his own bosom, and return disconsolate to his little family circle, in which there was a woeful blank that night.

His son returned also from a fruitless search. No one had seen any traces of his sister, but an old crazy woman, at a place called Oxcleuch, said that she had seen her go by in a grand chariot with young Jock Allanson, toward the Birkhill Path, and by that time they were at the Cross of Dumgree. The young man said he asked her what sort of a chariot it was, as there was never such a thing in that country as a chariot, nor yet a road for one. But she replied that he was widely mistaken, for that a great number of chariots sometimes passed that way, though never any of them returned. Those words appearing to be merely the ravings of superannuation, they were not regarded ; but when no other traces of Mary could be found, old Andrew went up to consult this crazy dame once more, but he was not able to bring any such thing to her recollection. She spoke only in parables, which to him were incomprehensible.

Bonny Mary Burnet was lost. She left her father's house at nine o'clock on a Wednesday morning, 17th of September, neatly dressed in a white jerkin and green bonnet, with her hay-raik over her shoulder ; and that was the last sight she was doomed ever to see of her native cottage. She seemed to have had some presentiment of this, as appeared from her demeanour that morning before she left it. Mary Burnet of Kirkstyle was lost, and great was the sensation produced over the whole country by the mysterious event. There was a long ballad extant at one period on the melancholy catastrophe, which was supposed to have been composed by the chaplain of St. Mary's ; but I have only heard tell of it, without ever hearing it sung or recited. Many of the verses concluded thus :

> " But Bonny Mary Burnet
> We will never see again."

The story soon got abroad, with all its horrid circumstances (and there is little doubt that it was grievously exaggerated), and there was no obloquy that was not thrown on the survivor, who certainly in some degree deserved it, for, instead of growing better, he grew ten times more wicked than he was before. In one thing the whole country agreed, that it had been the real Mary Burnet who was drowned in the loch, and that the being which was found in her bed, lying weeping and complaining of suffering, and which vanished the next day, had been a fairy, an evil spirit, or a changeling of some sort, for that it never spoke save once, and that in a mysterious manner ; nor did it partake of any food with the rest of the family. Her father and mother knew not what to say or what to think, but they wandered through this weary world like people wandering in a dream. Everything that belonged to Mary Burnet was kept by her parents as the most sacred relics, and many a tear did her aged mother shed over them. Every article of her dress brought the once comely wearer to mind. Andrew often said, " That to have lost the darling child of their old age in any way would have been a great trial, but to lose her in the way that they had done, was really mair than human frailty could endure."

Many a weary day did he walk by the shores of the loch, looking eagerly for some vestige of her garments, and though he trembled at every appearance, yet did he continue to search on. He had a number of small bones collected, that had belonged to lambs and other minor animals, and, haply, some of them to fishes, from a fond supposition that they might once have formed joints of her toes or fingers. These he kept concealed in a little bag, in order, as he said, " to let the doctors see them." But no relic, besides these, could he ever discover of Mary's body.

Young Allanson recovered from his raging fever scarcely in the manner of other men, for he recovered all at once, after a few days' raving and madness. Mary Burnet, it appeared, was by him no more remembered. He grew ten times more wicked than before, and hesitated at no means of accomplishing his unhallowed purposes. The devout shepherds and cottages around detested him ; and, both in their families and in the wild, when there was no ear to hear but that of Heaven, they prayed protection from his devices, as if he had been the Wicked One ; and they all prophesied that he would make a bad end.

One fine day about the middle of October, when the days begin to get very short, and the nights long and dark, on a Friday morning, the next year but one after Mary Burnet was lost, a memorable day in the fairy annals, John Allanson, younger of Inverlawn, went to a great hiring fair at a village called Moffat in Annandale, in order to hire a housemaid. His character was so notorious, that not one young woman in the district would serve in his father's house ; so away he went to the fair at Moffat, to hire the prettiest and loveliest girl he could there find, with the intention of ruining her as soon as she came home, This is no supposititious accusation, for he acknowledged his plan to Mr. David Welch of Cariferan, who rode down to the market with him, and seemed to boast of it, and dwell on it with delight. But the maidens of Annandale had a guardian angel in the fair that day, of which neither he nor they were aware.

Allanson looked through the hiring-market, and through the hiring-market, and at length fixed on one young woman, which indeed was not difficult to do, for there was no such form there for elegance and beauty. Mr. Welch stood still and eyed him. He took the beauty aside. She was clothed in green, and as lovely as a new-blown rose.

" Are you to hire, pretty maiden ? "

" Yes, sir."

" Will you hire with me ? "

" I care not though I do. But if I hire with you, it must be for a long term."

" Certainly. The longer the better. What are your wages to be ? "

" You know, if I hire, I must be paid in kind. I must have the first living creature that I see about Inverlawn to myself."

" I wish it may be me, then. But what do you know about Inverlawn ? "

" I think I *should* know about it."

" Bless me ! I know the face as well as I know my own, and better. But the name has somehow escaped me. Pray, may I I ask your name ? "

" Hush ! hush ! " said she solemnly, and holding up her hand at the same time. " Hush, hush, you had better say nothing about that here."

" I am in utter amazement ! " he exclaimed. " What is the meaning of this ? I conjure you to tell me your name ! "

" It is Mary Burnet," said she, in a soft whisper ; and at the same time she let down a green veil over her face.

If Allanson's death-warrant had been announced to him at that moment, it could not have deprived him so completely of sense and motion. His visage changed into that of a corpse, his jaws fell down, and his eyes became glazed, so as apparently to throw no reflections inwardly. Mr. Welch, who had kept his eye steadily on them all the while, perceived his comrade's dilemma, and went up to him. " Allanson ? Mr. Allanson ? What is the matter with you, man ? " said he. " Why, the girl has bewitched you, and turned you into a statue ! "

Allanson made some sound in his throat, as if attempting to speak, but his tongue refused its office, and he only jabbered. Mr. Welch, conceiving that he was seized with some fit, or about to faint, supported him into the Johnston Arms ; but he either could not, or would not grant him any explanation. Welch being, however, resolved to see the maiden in green once more, persuaded Allanson, after causing him to drink a good deal, to go out into the hiring-market again, in search of her. They ranged the market through and through, but the maiden in green was gone, and not to be found. She had vanished in the crowd the moment she divulged her name, and even though Welch had his eye fixed on her, he could not discover which way she went. Allanson appeared to be in a kind of stupor as well as terror, but when he found that she had left the market, he began to recover himself, and to look out again for the top of the market.

He soon found one more beautiful than the last. She was like a sylph, clothed in robes of pure snowy white, with green ribands. Again he pointed this new flower out to Mr. David Welch, who declared that such a perfect model of beauty he had never in his life seen. Allanson, being resolved to have this one at any wages, took her aside, and put the usual question : " Do you wish to hire, pretty maiden ? "

" Yes, sir."

" Will you hire with me ? "

" I care not though I do."

" What, then, are your wages to be ? Come—say ? And be

reasonable ; I am determined not to part with you for a trifle."

" My wages must be in a kind ; I work on no other conditions. Pray, how are all the good people about Inverlawn ? "

Allanson's breath began to cut, and a chillness to creep through his whole frame, and he answered, with a faltering tongue : " I thank you—much in their ordinary way."

" And your aged neighbours," rejoined she, " are they still alive and well ? "

" I—I—I think they are," said he, panting for breath. " But I am at a loss to know whom I am indebted to for these kind recollections."

" What," said she, " have you so soon forgot Mary Burnet of Kirkstyle ? "

Allanson started as if a bullet had gone through his heart. The lovely sylph-like form glided into the crowd, and left the astounded libertine once more standing like a rigid statue, until aroused by his friend, Mr. Welch. He tried a third fair one, and got the same answers, and the same name given. Indeed, the first time ever I heard the tale, it bore that he tried *seven*, who all turned out to be Mary Burnets of Kirkstyle ; but I think it unlikely that he would try so many, as he must long ere that time have been sensible that he laboured under some power of enchantment. However, when nothing else would do, he helped himself to a good proportion of strong drink. While he was thus engaged, a phenomenon of beauty and grandeur came into the fair, that caught the sole attention of all present. This was a lovely dame, riding in a gilded chariot, with two livery-men before, and two behind, clothed in green and gold ; and never sure was there so splendid a meteor seen in a Moffat fair. The word instantly circulated in the market, that this was the Lady Elizabeth Douglas, eldest daughter to the Earl of Morton, who then sojourned at Auchincastle, in the vicinity of Moffat, and which lady at that time was celebrated as a great beauty all over Scotland. She was afterwards Lady Keith ; and the mention of this name in the tale, as it were by mere accident, fixes the era of it in the reign of James the Fourth, at the very time that fairies, brownies, and witches, were at the rifest in Scotland.

Every one in the market believed the lady to be the daughter of the Earl of Morton ; and when she came to the Johnston Arms, a gentleman in green came out bareheaded, and received her out of the carriage. All the crowd gazed at such unparalleled beauty and grandeur, but none was half so much overcome as

Allanson. He had never conceived aught half so lovely either
in earth, or heaven, or fairyland ; and while he stood in a
burning fever of admiration, think of his astonishment, and the
astonishment of the countless crowd that looked on, when this
brilliant and matchless beauty beckoned him towards her !
He could not believe his senses, but looked this way and that
way to see how others regarded the affair ; but she beckoned
him a second time, with such a winning courtesy and smile, that
immediately he pulled off his beaver cap and hasted up to her ;
and without more ado she gave him her arm, and the two walked
into the hostel.

Allanson conceived that he was thus distinguished by Lady
Elizabeth Douglas, the flower of the land, and so did all the
people of the market ; and greatly they wondered who the
young farmer could be that was thus particularly favoured ; for
it ought to have been mentioned that he had not one personal
acquaintance in the fair save Mr. David Welch of Cariferan.
The first thing the lady did was to inquire kindly after his health.
Allanson thanked her ladyship with all the courtesy he was
master of ; and being by this time persuaded that she was in
love with him, he became as light as if treading on the air.
She next inquired after his father and mother. Oho ? thought
he to himself, poor creature, she is terribly in for it ! but her
love shall not be thrown away upon a backward or ungrateful
object. He answered her with great politeness, and at length
began to talk of her noble father and young Lord William, but
she cut him short by asking if he did not recognise her.

" Oh, yes ! He knew who her ladyship was, and remembered
that he had seen her comely face often before, although he could
not, at that particular moment, recall to his memory the precise
time or places of their meeting."

She next asked for his old neighbours of Kirkstyle, and if they
were still in life and health !

Allanson felt as if his heart were a piece of ice. A chillness
spread over his whole frame ; he sank back on a seat, and
remained motionless ; but the beautiful and adorable creature
soothed him with kind words, till he again gathered courage
to speak.

" What ! " said he ; " and has it been your own lovely self
who has been playing tricks on me this whole day ? "

" A first love is not easily extinguished, Mr. Allanson," said
she. " You may guess from my appearance, that I have been
fortunate in life ; but, for all that, my first love for you has

continued the same, unaltered and unchanged, and you must forgive the little freedoms I used to-day to try your affections, and the effects my appearance would have on you."

" It argues something for my good taste, however, that I never pitched on any face for beauty to-day but your own," said he. " But now that we have met once more, we shall not so easily part again. I will devote the rest of my life to you, only let me know the place of your abode."

" It is hard by," said she, " only a very little space from this ; and happy, happy, would I be to see you there to-night, were it proper or convenient. But my lord is at present from home and in a distant country."

" I should not conceive that any particular hindrance to my visit," said he.

With great apparent reluctance she at length consented to admit of his visit, and offered to leave one of her gentlemen, whom she could trust, to be his conductor ; but this he positively refused. It was his desire, he said, that no eye of man should see him enter or leave her happy dwelling. She said he was a selfwilled man, but should have his own way ; and after giving him such directions as would infallibly lead him to her mansion, she mounted her chariot and was driven away.

Allanson was uplifted above every sublunary concern. Seeking out his friend, David Welch, he imparted to him his extra-ordinary good fortune, but he did not tell him that she was not the Lady Elizabeth Douglas. Welch insisted on accompanying him on the way, and refused to turn back till he came to the very point of the road next to the lady's splendid mansion ; and in spite of all that Allanson could say, Welch remained there till he saw his comrade enter the court gate, which glowed with lights as innumerable as the stars of the firmament.

Allanson had promised to his father and mother to be home on the morning after the fair to breakfast. He came not either that day or the next ; and the third day the old man mounted his white pony, and rode away towards Moffat in search of his son. He called at Cariferan on his way, and made inquiries at Mr. Welch. The latter manifested some astonishment that the young man had not returned ; nevertheless he assured his father of his safety, and desired him to return home ; and then with reluctance confessed that the young man was engaged in an amour with the Earl of Morton's beautiful daughter ; that he had gone to the castle by appointment, and that he, David Welch, had accompanied him to the gate, and seen him enter, and it was apparent that his reception had been a kind one, since he had tarried so long.

Mr. Welch, seeing the old man greatly distressed, was persuaded to accompany him on his journey, as the last who had seen his son, and seen him enter the castle. On reaching Moffat they found his steed standing at the hostel, whither it had returned on the night of the fair, before the company broke up ; but the owner had not been heard of since seen in company with Lady Elizabeth Douglas. The old man set out for Auchin-castle, taking Mr. David Welch along with him ; but long ere they reached the place, Mr. Welch assured him he would not find his son there, as it was nearly in a different direction that they rode on the evening of the fair. However, to the castle they went, and were admitted to the Earl, who, after hearing the old man's tale, seemed to consider him in a state of derange-ment. He sent for his daughter Elizabeth, and questioned her concerning her meeting with the son of the old respectable countryman—of her appointment with him on the night of the preceding Friday, and concluded by saying he hoped she had him still in safe concealment about the castle.

The lady, hearing her father talk in this manner, and seeing the serious and dejected looks of the old man, knew not what to say, and asked an explanation. But Mr. Welch put a stop to it by declaring to old Allanson that the Lady Elizabeth was not the lady with whom his son made the appointment, for he had seen her, and would engage to know her again among ten thousand ; nor was that the castle towards which he had accompanied his son, nor any thing like it. " But go with me," continued he, " and, though I am a stranger in this district, I think I can take you to the very place."

They set out again ; and Mr. Welch traced the road from Moffat, by which young Allanson and he had gone, until, after travelling several miles, they came to a place where a road struck off to the right at an angle. " Now I know we are right," said Welch ; " for here we stopped, and your son intreated me to return, which I refused, and accompanied him to yon large tree, and a little way beyond it, from whence I saw him received in at the splendid gate. We shall be in sight of the mansion in three minutes."

They passed on to the tree, and a space beyond it ; but then Mr. Welch lost the use of his speech, as he perceived that there was neither palace nor gate there, but a tremendous gulf, fifty fathoms deep, and a dark stream foaming and boiling below.

" How is this ? " said old Allanson. " There is neither mansion nor habitation of man here ! "

Welch's tongue for a long time refused its office, and he stood like a statue, gazing on the altered and awful scene. " He only, who made the spirits of men," said he, at last, " and all the spirits that sojourn in the earth and air, can tell how his is. We are wandering in a world of enchantment, and have been influenced by some agencies above human nature, or without its pale ; for here of a certainty did I take leave of your son— and there, in that direction, and apparently either on the verge of that gulf, or the space above it, did I see him received in at the court gate of a mansion, splendid beyond all conception. How can human comprehension make anything of this ? "

They went forward to the verge, Mr. Welch leading the way to the very spot on which he saw the gate opened, and there they found marks where a horse had been plunging. Its feet had been over the brink, but it seemed to have recovered itself, and deep, deep down, and far within, lay the mangled corpse of John Allanson ; and in this manner, mysterious beyond all example, terminated the career of that wicked and flagitious young man. What a beautiful moral may be extracted from this fairy tale !

But among all these turnings and windings, there is no account given, you will say, of the fate of Mary Burnet ; for this last appearance of hers at Moffat seems to have been altogether a phantom or illusion. Gentle and kind reader, I can give you no account of the fate of that maiden ; for though the ancient fairy tale proceeds, it seems to me to involve her fate in ten times more mystery than what we have hitherto seen of it.

The yearly return of the day on which Mary was lost, was observed as a day of mourning by her aged and disconsolate parents—a day of sorrow, of fasting, and humiliation. Seven years came and passed away, and the seventh returning day of fasting and prayer was at hand. On the evening previous to it, old Andrew was moving along the sands of the loch, still looking for some relic of his beloved Mary, when he was aware of a little shrivelled old man, who came posting towards him. The creature was not above five spans in height, and had a face scarcely like that of a human creature ; but he was, nevertheless, civil in his deportment, and sensible in speech. He bade Andrew a good evening, and asked him what he was looking for. Andrew answered, that he was looking for that which he should never find.

" Pray, what is your name, ancient shepherd ? " said the stranger ; " for methinks I should know something of you, and perhaps have a commission to you."

" Alas ! why should you ask after my name ? " said Andrew. " My name is now nothing to any one."

" Had not you once a beautiful daughter, named Mary ? " said the stranger.

" It is a heartrending question, man," said Andrew ; " but certes, I had once a beloved daughter named Mary."

" What became of her ? " asked the stranger.

Andrew shook his head, turned round, and began to move away ; it was a theme that his heart could not brook. He sauntered along the loch sands, his dim eye scanning every white pebble as he passed along. There was a hopelessness in his stooping form, his gait, his eye, his features—in every step that he took there was a hopeless apathy. The dwarf followed him, and began to expostulate with him. " Old man, I see you are pining under some real or fancied affliction," said he. " But in continuing to do so, you are neither acting according to the dictates of reason nor true religion. What is man that he should fret, or the son of man that he should repine, under the chastening hand of his Maker ? "

" I am far frae justifying myself," returned Andrew, surveying his shrivelled monitor with some degree of astonishment. " But there are some feelings that neither reason nor religion can o'er-master ; and there are some that a parent may cherish without sin."

" I deny the position," said the stranger, " taken either absolutely or relatively. All repining under the Supreme decree is leavened with unrighteousness. But, subtleties aside, I ask you, as I did before, What became of your daughter ? "

" Ask the Father of her spirit, and the framer of her body," said Andrew solemnly ; " ask Him into whose hands I committed her from childhood. He alone knows what became of her, but I do not."

" How long is it since you lost her ? "

" It is seven years to-morrow ! "

" Ay ! you remember the time well. And you have mourned for her all that while ? "

" Yes ; and I will go down to the grave mourning for my only daughter, the child of my age, and of all my affection. Oh, thou unearthly-looking monitor, knowest thou aught of my darling child ? for if thou dost, thou wilt know that she was not like other women. There was a simplicity and a purity about my Mary, that was hardly consistent with our frail nature."

"Wouldst thou like to see her again?" said the dwarf.

Andrew turned round, his whole frame shaking as with a palsy, and gazed on the audacious imp. "See her again, creature!" cried he vehemently. "Would I like to see her again, sayest thou?"

"I said so," said the dwarf, "and I say further, Dost thou know this token? Look, and see if thou dost!"

Andrew took the token, and looked at it, then at the shrivelled stranger, and then at the token again; and at length he burst into tears, and wept aloud; but they were tears of joy, and his weeping seemed to have some breathings of laughter intermingled in it. And still as he kissed the token, he called out in broken and convulsive sentences: "Yes, auld body, I *do* know it!—I *do* know it!—I *do* know it! It is indeed the same golden Edward, with three holes in it, with which I presented my Mary on her birthday, in her eighteenth year, to buy a new suit for the holidays. But when she took it she said—ay, I mind weel what my bonny woman said. 'It is sae bonny and sae kenspeckle,' said she, 'that I think I'll keep it for the sake of the giver.' O dear, dear! Blessed little creature, tell me how she is, and where she is? Is she living, or is she dead?"

"She is living, and in good health," said the dwarf; "and better, and braver, and happier, and lovelier than ever; and if you make haste, you will see her and her family at Moffat to-morrow afternoon. They are to pass there on a journey, but it is an express one, and I am sent to you with that token, to inform you of the circumstance, that you may have it in your power to see and embrace your beloved daughter once before you die."

"And am I to meet my Mary at Moffat? Come away, little, dear, welcome body, thou blessed of heaven, come away, and taste of an auld shepherd's best cheer, and I'll gang foot for foot with you to Moffat, and my auld wife shall gang foot for foot with us too. I tell you, little, blessed, and welcome crile, come alone with me."

"I may not tarry to enter your house, or taste of your cheer, good shepherd," said the being. "May plenty still be within your walls, and a thankful heart to enjoy it! But my directions are neither to taste meat nor drink in this country, but to haste back to her that sent me. Go—haste, and make ready, for you have no time to lose."

" At what time will she be there ? " cried Andrew, flinging
the plaid from him to run home with the tidings.

" Precisely when the shadow of the Holy Cross falls due east,"
cried the dwarf ; and turning round, he hasted on his way.

When old Jean Linton saw her husband coming hobbling
and running home without his plaid, and having his doublet
flying wide open, she had no doubt that he had lost his wits ;
and, full of anxiety, she met him at the side of the kail-yard.
" Gudeness preserve us a' in our right senses, Andrew Burnet,
what's the matter wi' you, Andrew Burnet ? "

" Stand out o' my gate, wife, for, d'ye see, I am rather in a
haste, Jean Linton."

" I see that indeed, gudeman ; but stand still, and tell me
what has putten you *in* sic a haste. Ir ye dementit ? "

" Na, na ; gudewife, Jean Linton, I'm no dementit—I'm
only gaun away till Moffat."

" O, gudeness pity the poor auld body ! How can ye gang
to Moffat, man ? Or what have ye to do at Moffat ? Dinna ye
mind that the morn is the day o' our solemnity ? "

" Haud out o' my gate, auld wife, and dinna speak o'
solemnities to me. I'll keep it at Moffat the morn. Ay, gudewife,
and ye shall keep it at Moffat, too. What d'ye think o' that,
woman ? Too-whoo ! ye dinna ken the metal that's in an auld
body till it be tried."

" Andrew—Andrew Burnet ! "

" Get awa' wi' your frightened looks, woman ; and haste ye,
gang and fling me out my Sabbath-day claes. And, Jean
Linton, my woman, d'ye hear, gang and pit on your bridal
gown, and your silk hood, for ye maun be at Moffat the morn
too ; and it is mair nor time we were awa'. Dinna look sae
surprised, woman, till I tell ye, that our ain Mary is to meet
us at Moffat the morn."

" Oh, Andrew ! dinna sport wi' the feelings of an auld
forsaken heart ! "

" Gude forbid, my auld wife, that I should ever sport wi'
feelings o' yours," cried Andrew, bursting into tears ; " they
are a' as sacred to me as breathings frae the Throne o' Grace.
But it is true that I tell ye ; our dear bairn is to meet us at
Moffat the morn, wi' a son in every hand ; and we maun e'en
gang and see her aince again, and kiss her and bless her afore
we dee."

The tears now rushed from the old woman's eyes like fountains, and dropped from her sorrow-worn cheeks to the earth,

and then, as with a spontaneous movement, she threw her skirt over her head, kneeled down at her husband's feet, and poured out her soul in thanksgiving to her Maker. She then rose up, quite deprived of her senses through joy, and ran crouching away on the road, towards Moffat, as if hasting beyond her power to be at it. But Andrew brought her back ; and they prepared themselves for their journey.

Kirkstyle being twenty miles from Moffat, they set out on the afternoon of Tuesday, the 16th of September ; slept that night at a place called Turnbery Shiel, and were in Moffat next day by noon. Wearisome was the remainder of the day to that aged couple ; they wandered about conjecturing by what road their daughter would come, and how she would come attended. " I have made up my mind on baith these matters," said Andrew ; " at first I thought it was likely that she would come out of the east, because a' our blessings come frae that airt ; but finding now that would be o'er near to the very road we hae come oursells, I now take it for granted she'll come frae the south ; and I just think I see her leading a bonny boy in every hand, and a servant lass carrying a bit bundle ahint her."

The two now walked out on all the southern roads, in hopes to meet their Mary, but always returned to watch the shadow of the Holy Cross ; and, by the time it fell due east, they could do nothing but stand in the middle of the street, and look round them in all directions. At length, about half a mile out on the Dumfries road, they perceived a poor beggar woman approaching with two children following close to her, and another beggar a good way behind. Their eyes were instantly riveted on these objects ; for Andrew thought he perceived his friend the dwarf in the one that was behind ; and now all other earthly objects were to them nothing, save these approaching beggars. At that moment a gilded chariot entered the village from the south, and drove by them at full speed, having two livery-men before, and two behind, clothed in green and gold, " Ach-wow ! the vanity of worldly grandeur ! " ejaculated Andrew, as the splendid vehicle went thundering by ; but neither he nor his wife deigned to look at it farther, their whole attention being fixed on the group of beggars. " Ay, it is just my woman," said Andrew, " it is just hersell ; I ken her gang yet, sair pressed down wi' poortith although she be. But I dinna care how poor she be, for baith her and hers sall be welcome to my fireside as lang as I hae ane."

While their eyes were thus strained, and their hearts melting with tenderness and pity, Andrew felt something embracing his knees, and, on looking down, there was his Mary, blooming in splendour and beauty, kneeling at his feet. Andrew uttered a loud hysterical scream of joy, and clasped her to his bosom ; and old Jean Linton stood trembling, with her arms spread, but durst not close them on so splendid a creature, till her daughter first enfolded her in a fond embrace, and then she hung upon her and wept. It was a wonderful event—a restoration without a parallel. They indeed beheld their Mary, their long-lost darling ; they held her in their embraces, believed in her identity, and were satisfied. Satisfied, did I say ? They were happy beyond the lot of mortals. She had just alighted from her chariot ; and, perceiving her aged parents standing together, she ran and kneeled at their feet. They now retired into the hostel, where Mary presented her two sons to her father and mother. They spent the evening in every social endearment ; and Mary loaded the good old couple with rich presents, watched over them till midnight, when they both fell into a deep and happy sleep, and then she remounted her chariot, and was driven away. If she was any more seen in Scotland, I never heard of it ; but her parents rejoiced in the thoughts of her happiness till the day of their death.

THE THREE SISTERS

THIRTY years ago on a wet autumn evening the household of Mallett's Lodge was gathered round the death-bed of Ursula Mallow, the eldest of the three sisters who inhabited it. The dingy moth-eaten curtains of the old wooden bedstead were drawn apart, the light of a smoking oil-lamp·falling upon the hopeless countenance of the dying woman as she turned her dull eyes upon her sisters. The room was in silence except for an occasional sob from the youngest sister, Eunice. Outside the rain fell steadily over the streaming marshes.

" Nothing is to be changed, Tabitha," gasped Ursula to the other sister, who bore a striking likeness to her, although her expression was harder and colder ; " this room is to be locked up and never opened."

" Very well," said Tabitha brusquely ; " though I don't see how it can matter to you then."

" It does matter," said her sister with startling energy. " How do you know, how do I know that I may not sometimes visit it ? I have lived in this house so long I am certain that I I shall see it again. I *will* come back. Come back to watch over you both and see that no harm befalls you."

" You are talking wildly," said Tabitha, by no means moved at her sister's solicitude for her welfare. " Your mind is wandering ; you know that I have no faith in such things."

Ursula sighed, and beckoning to Eunice, who was weeping silently at the bedside, placed her feeble arms around her neck and kissed her.

" Do not weep, dear," she said feebly. " Perhaps it is best so. A lonely woman's life is scarce worth living. We have no hopes, no aspirations ; other women have had happy husbands and children, but we in this forgotten place have grown old together. I go first, but you must soon follow."

Tabitha, comfortably conscious of only forty years and an iron frame, shrugged her shoulders and smiled grimly.

" I go first," repeated Ursula in a new and strange voice as her heavy eyes slowly closed, " but I will come for each of you in turn, when your lease of life runs out. At that moment I will be with you to lead your steps whither I now go."

As she spoke the flickering lamp went out suddenly as though extinguished by a rapid hand, and the room was left in utter darkness. A strange suffocating noise issued from the bed, and when the trembling women had relighted the lamp, all that was left of Ursula Mallow was ready for the grave.

That night the survivors passed together. The dead woman had been a firm believer in the existence of that shadowy borderland which is said to form an unhallowed link between the living and the dead, and even stolid Tabitha, slightly unnerved by the events of the night, was not free from certain apprehensions that she might have been right.

With the bright morning their fears disappeared. The sun stole in at the window, and seeing the poor earthworn face on the pillow so touched it and glorified it that only its goodness and weakness were seen, and the beholders came to wonder how they could ever have felt any dread of aught so calm and peaceful. A day or two passed, and the body was transferred to a massive coffin long regarded as the finest piece of work of its kind ever turned out of the village carpenter's workshop. Then a slow and melancholy cortège headed by four bearers wound its solemn way across the marches to the family vault in the grey old church, and all that was left of Ursula was placed by the father and mother who had taken that self-same journey some thirty years before.

To Eunice as they toiled slowly home the day seemed strange and Sabbath-like, the flat prospect of marsh wilder and more forlorn than usual, the roar of the sea more depressing. Tabitha had no such fancies. The bulk of the dead woman's property had been left to Eunice, and her avaricious soul was sorely troubled and her proper sisterly feelings of regret for the deceased sadly interfered with in consequence.

" What are you going to do with all that money, Eunice ? " she asked as they sat at their quiet tea.

" I shall leave it as it stands," said Eunice slowly. " We have both got sufficient to live upon, and I shall devote the income from it to supporting some beds in a children's hospital."

"If Ursula had wished it to go to a hospital," said Tabitha in her deep tones, "she would have left the money to it herself. I wonder you do not respect her wishes more."

"What else can I do with it then?" inquired Eunice.

"Save it," said the other with gleaming eyes, "save it."

Eunice shook her head.

"No," said she, "it shall go to the sick children, but the principal I will not touch, and if I die before you it shall become yours and you can do what you like with it."

"Very well," said Tabitha, smothering her anger by a strong effort; "I don't believe that was what Ursula meant you to do with it, and I don't believe she will rest quietly in the grave while you squander the money she stored so carefully."

"What do you mean?" asked Eunice with pale lips. "You are trying to frighten me; I thought that you did not believe in such things."

Tabitha made no answer, and to avoid the anxious inquiring gaze of her sister, drew her chair to the fire, and folding her gaunt arms, composed herself for a nap.

For some time life went on quietly in the old house. The room of the dead woman, in accordance with her last desire, was kept firmly locked, its dirty windows forming a strange contrast to the prim cleanliness of the others. Tabitha, never very talkative, became more taciturn than ever, and stalked about the house and the neglected garden like an unquiet spirit, her brow roughened into the deep wrinkles suggestive of much thought. As the winter came on, bringing with it the long dark evenings, the old house became more lonely than ever, and an air of mystery and dread seemed to hang over it and brood in its empty rooms and dark corridors. The deep silence of night was broken by strange noises for which neither the wind nor the rats could be held accountable. Old Martha, seated in her distant kitchen, heard strange sounds upon the stairs, and once, upon hurrying to them, fancied that she saw a dark figure squatting upon the landing, though a subsequent search with candle and spectacles failed to discover anything. Eunice was disturbed by several vague incidents, and, as she suffered from a complaint of the heart, rendered very ill by them. Even Tabitha admitted a strangeness about the house, but, confident in her piety and virtue, took no heed of it, her mind being fully employed in another direction.

Since the death of her sister all restraint upon her was removed, and she yielded herself up entirely to the stern and hard rules enforced by avarice upon its devotees. Her house-keeping expenses were kept rigidly separate from those of Eunice and her food limited to the coarsest dishes, while in the matter of clothes the old servant was by far the better dressed. Seated alone in her bedroom this uncouth, hard-featured creature revelled in her possessions, grudging even the expense of the candle-end which enabled her to behold them. So completely did this passion change her that both Eunice and Martha became afraid of her, and lay awake in their beds night after night trembling at the chinking of the coins at her unholy vigils.

One day Eunice ventured to remonstrate. " Why don't you bank your money, Tabitha ? " she said ; " it is surely not safe to keep such large sums in such a lonely house."

" Large sums ! " repeated the exasperated Tabitha, " large sums ; what nonsense is this ? You know well that I have barely sufficient to keep me."

" It's a great temptation to housebreakers," said her sister, not pressing the point. " I made sure last night that I heard somebody in the house."

" Did you ? " said Tabitha, grasping her arm, a horrible look on her face. " So did I. I thought they went to Ursula's room, and I got out of bed and went on the stairs to listen."

" Well ? " said Eunice faintly, fascinated by the look on her sister's face.

" There was *something* there," said Tabitha slowly. " I'll swear it, for I stood on the landing by her door and listened ; something scuffling on the floor round and round the room. At first I thought it was the cat, but when I went up there this morning the door was still locked, and the cat was in the kitchen."

" Oh, let us leave this dreadful house," moaned Eunice.

" What ! " said her sister grimly ; " afraid of poor Ursula ? Why should you be ? Your own sister who nursed you when you were a babe, and who perhaps even now comes and watches over your slumbers."

" Oh ! " said Eunice, pressing her hand to her side, " if I saw her I should die. I should think that she had come for me as she said she would. O God ! have mercy on me, I am dying."

She reeled as she spoke, and before Tabitha could save her, sank senseless to the floor.

" Get some water," cried Tabitha, as old Martha came hurrying up the stairs, " Eunice has fainted."

The old woman, with a timid glance at her, retired, reappearing shortly afterwards with the water, with which she proceeded to restore her much-loved mistress to her senses. Tabitha, as soon as this was accomplished, stalked off to her room, leaving her sister and Martha sitting drearily enough in the small parlour, watching the fire and conversing in whispers.

It was clear to the old servant that this state of things could not last much longer, and she repeatedly urged her mistress to leave a house so lonely and so mysterious. To her great delight Eunice at length consented, despite the fierce opposition of her sister, and at the mere idea of leaving gained greatly in health and spirits. A small but comfortable house was hired in Morville, and arrangements made for a speedy change.

It was the last night in the old house, and all the wild spirits of the marshes, the wind and the sea seemed to have joined forces for one supreme effort. When the wind dropped, as it did at brief intervals, the sea was heard moaning on the distant beach, strangely mingled with the desolate warning of the bell-buoy as it rocked to the waves. Then the wind rose again, and the noise of the sea was lost in the fierce gusts which, finding no obstacle on the open marshes, swept with their full fury upon the house by the creek. The strange voices of the air shrieked in its chimneys, windows rattled, doors slammed, and even the very curtains seemed to live and move.

Eunice was in bed, awake. A small night-light in a saucer of oil shed a sickly glare upon the worm-eaten old furniture, distorting the most innocent articles into ghastly shapes. A wilder gust than usual almost deprived her of the protection afforded by that poor light, and she lay listening fearfully to the creakings and other noises on the stairs, bitterly regretting that she had not asked Martha to sleep with her. But it was not too late even now. She slipped hastily to the floor, crossed to the huge wardrobe, and was in the very act of taking her dressing-gown from its peg when an unmistakable footfall was heard on the stairs. The robe dropped from her shaking fingers, and with a quickly beating heart she regained her bed.

The sounds ceased and a deep silence followed, which she herself was unable to break although she strove hard to do so. A wild gust of wind shook the windows and nearly extinguished the light, and when its flame had regained its accustomed steadiness she saw that the door was slowly opening, while the huge shadow of a hand blotted the papered wall. Still her tongue refused its office. The door flew open with a crash, a cloaked figure entered and, throwing aside its coverings, she saw with a horror past all expression the napkin-bound face of the dead

Ursula smiling terribly at her. In her last extremity she raised her faded eyes above for succour, and then as the figure noiselessly advanced and laid its cold hand upon her brow, the soul of Eunice Mallow left its body with a wild shriek and made its way to the Eternal.

Martha, roused by the cry, and shivering with dread, rushed to the door and gazed in terror at the figure which stood leaning over the bedside. As she watched, it slowly removed the cowl and the napkin and exposed the fell face of Tabitha, so strangely contorted between fear and triumph that she hardly recognised it.

" Who's there ? " cried Tabitha in a terrible voice as she saw the old woman's shadow on the wall.

" I thought I heard a cry," said Martha, entering. " Did anybody call ? "

" Yes, Eunice," said the other, regarding her closely. " I, too, heard the cry, and hurried to her. What makes her so strange ? Is she in a trance ? "

" Aye," said the old woman, falling on her knees by the bed and sobbing bitterly, " the trance of death. Ah, my dear, my poor lonely girl, that this should be the end of it ! She has died of fright," said the old woman, pointing to the eyes, which even yet retained their horror. " She has seen something *devilish*."

Tabitha's gaze fell. " She has always suffered with her heart," she muttered ; " the night has frightened her ; it frightened me."

She stood upright by the foot of the bed as Martha drew the sheet over the face of the dead woman.

" First Ursula, then Eunice," said Tabitha, drawing a deep breath. " I can't stay here. I'll dress and wait for the morning."

She left the room as she spoke, and with bent head proceeded to her own. Martha remained by the bedside, and gently closing the staring eyes, fell on her knees and prayed long and earnestly for the departed soul. Overcome with grief and fear, she remained with bowed head until a sudden sharp cry from Tabitha brought her to her feet.

" Well," said the old woman, going to the door.

" Where are you ? " cried Tabitha, somewhat reassured by her voice.

" In Miss Eunice's bedroom. Do you want anything ? "

" Come down at once. Quick ! I am unwell."

Her voice rose suddenly to a scream. " Quick ! For God's sake ! Quick, or I shall go mad. *There is some strange woman in the house.*"

The old woman stumbled hastily down the dark stairs. "What is the matter?" she cried, entering the room. "Who is it? What do you mean?"

"I saw it," said Tabitha, grasping her convulsively by the shoulder. "I was coming to you when I saw the figure of a woman in front of me going up the stairs. Is it—can it be Ursula come for the soul of Eunice, as she said she would?"

"Or for yours?" said Martha, the words coming from her in some odd fashion, despite herself.

Tabitha, with a ghastly look, fell cowering by her side, clutching tremulously at her clothes. "Light the lamps," she cried hysterically. "Light a fire, make a noise; oh, this dreadful darkness! Will it never be day!"

"Soon, soon," said Martha, overcoming her repugnance and trying to pacify her. "When the day comes you will laugh at these fears."

"I murdered her," screamed the miserable woman, "I killed her with fright. Why did she not give me the money? 'Twas no use to her. Ah! *Look there!*"

Martha, with a horrible fear, followed her glance to the door, but saw nothing.

"It's Ursula," said Tabitha, from between her teeth. "Keep her off! Keep her off!"

The old woman, who by some unknown sense seemed to feel the presence of a third person in the room, moved a step forward and stood before her. As she did so Tabitha waved her arms as though to free herself from the touch of a detaining hand, half-rose to her feet, and without a word fell dead before her.

At this the old woman's courage forsook her, and with a great cry she rushed from the room, eager to escape from this house of death and mystery. The bolts of the great door were stiff with age, and strange voices seemed to ring in her ears as she strove wildly to unfasten them. Her brain whirled. She thought that the dead in their distant rooms called to her, and that a devil stood on the step outside laughing and holding the door against her. Then with a supreme effort she flung it open, and heedless of her night-clothes passed into the bitter night. The path across the marshes was lost in the darkness, but she found it; the planks over the ditches slippery and narrow, but she crossed them in safety, until at last, her feet bleeding and her breath coming in great gasps, she entered the village and sank down more dead than alive on a cottage doorstep.

Martha, with a horrible fear, followed her glance to the door.

THE DOCTOR'S GHOST

A FRIEND of mine, a medical man, once went on a fishing expedition with an old college acquaintance, an army surgeon, whom he had not met for many years, from his having been in India with his regiment. McDonald, the army surgeon, was a thorough Highlander, and slightly tinged with what is called the superstition of his countrymen, and at the time I speak of was liable to rather depressed spirits from an unsound liver. His native air was, however, rapidly renewing his youth ; and when he and his old friend paced along the banks of the fishing stream in a lonely part of Argyllshire, and sent their lines like airy gossamers over the pools, and touched the water over a salmon's nose, so temptingly that the best-principled and wisest fish could not resist the bite, McDonald had apparently regained all his buoyancy of spirit.

They had been fishing together for about a week with great success, when McDonald proposed to pay a visit to a family with which he was acquainted, that would separate him from his friend for some days. But whenever he spoke of their intended separation, he sank down into his old gloomy state, at one time declaring that he felt as if they were never to meet again. My friend tried to rally him, but in vain. They parted at the trouting stream, McDonald's route being across a mountain pass, with which, however, he had been well acquainted in his youth, though the road was lonely and wild in the extreme.

The doctor returned early in the evening to his resting-place, which was a shepherd's house lying on the very outskirts of the " settlements," and beside a foaming mountain stream. The shepherd's only attendants at the time were two herd lads and three dogs. Attached to the hut, and communicating with it by a short passage, was rather a comfortable room which " the

Laird " had fitted up to serve as a sort of lodge for himself in the midst of his shooting-ground, and which he had put for a fortnight at the disposal of my friend.

Shortly after sunset on the day I mention the wind began to rise suddenly to a gale, the rain descended in torrents, and the night became extremely dark. The shepherd seemed uneasy, and several times went to the door to inspect the weather. At last he roused the fears of the doctor for McDonald's safety, by expressing the *hope* that by this time he was " owre that awfu' black moss, and across the red burn."

Every traveller in the Highlands knows how rapidly these mountain streams rise, and how confusing the moor becomes in a dark night. The confusion of memory once a doubt is suggested, the utter mystery of places, becomes, as I know from experience, quite indescribable.

" The black moss and red burn " were words that were never after forgot by the doctor, from the strange feelings they produced when first heard that night ; for there came into his mind terrible thoughts and forebodings about poor McDonald, and reproaches for never having considered his possible danger in attempting such a journey alone. In vain' the shepherd assured him that he must have reached a place of safety before the darkness and the storm came on. A presentiment which he could not cast off made him so miserable that he could hardly refrain from tears. But nothing could be done to relieve the anxiety now become so painful.

The doctor at last retired to bed about midnight. For a long time he could not sleep. The raging of the stream below the small window, and the *thuds* of the storm, made him feverish and restless. But at last he fell into a sound and dreamless sleep. Out of this, however, he was suddenly roused by a peculiar noise in his room, not very loud, but utterly indescribable. He heard tap, tap, tap at the window, and he knew, from the relation which the wall of the room bore to the rock, that the glass could not be touched by human hand.

After listening for a moment, and forcing himself to smile at his nervousness, he turned round, and began again to seek repose. But now a noise began too near and loud to make sleep possible. Starting and sitting up in bed, he heard repeated in rapid succession, as if some one was spitting in anger, and close to his bed,—" Fit ! fit ! fit ! " and then a prolonged " whir-r-r " from another part of the room, while every chair began to move, and the table to jerk !

The shepherd sprang back with a half-scream of terror.

The doctor remained in breathless silence, with every faculty intensely acute. He frankly confessed that he heard his heart beating, for the sound was so unearthly, so horrible, and something seemed to come so near him, that he began seriously to consider whether or not he had some attack of fever which affected his brain—for, remember, he had not tasted a drop of the shepherd's small store of whisky! He felt his pulse, composed his spirits, and compelled himself to exercise calm judgment. Straining his eyes to discover anything, he plainly saw at last a white object moving, but without sound, before him. He knew that the door was shut and the window also.

An overpowering conviction then seized him, which he could not resist, that his friend McDonald was dead! By an effort he seized a lucifer-box on a chair beside him, and struck a light. No white object could be seen. The room appeared to be as when he went to bed. The door was shut. He looked at his watch, and particularly marked that the hour was twenty-two minutes past three. But the match was hardly extinguished when, louder than ever, the same unearthly cry of " Fit ! fit ! fit ! " was heard, followed by the same horrible whir-r-r-r, which made his teeth chatter. Then the movement of the table and every chair in the room was resumed with increased violence, while the tapping on the window was heard above the storm. There was no bell in the room, but the doctor, on hearing all this frightful confusion of sounds again repeated, and beholding the white object moving towards him in terrible silence, began to thump the wooden partition and to shout at the top of his voice for the shepherd, and having done so, he dived his head under the blankets !

The shepherd soon made his appearance, in his night-shirt, with a small oil-lamp, or " crusey," over his head, anxiously inquiring as he entered the room :

" What is't, doctor ? What's wrang ? Pity me, are ye ill ? "

" Very ! " cried the doctor. But before he could give any explanation a loud whir-r-r was heard, with the old cry of " Fit ! " close to the shepherd, while two chairs fell at his feet ! The shepherd sprang back, with a half scream of terror the lamp was dashed to the ground, and the door violently shut.

" Come back ! " shouted the doctor. " Come back, Duncan, instantly, I command you ! "

The shepherd opened the door very partially, and said, in terrified accents :

" Gude be aboot us, that was awfu' ! What under heaven is't ? "

"Heaven knows, Duncan," ejaculated the doctor with agitated voice, "but do pick up the lamp, and I shall strike a light."

Duncan did so in no small fear; but as he made his way to the bed in the darkness to get a match from the doctor, something caught his foot; he fell; and then, amidst the same noises and tumults of chairs, which immediately filled the apartment, the "Fit! fit! fit! fit!" was prolonged with more vehemence than ever!

The doctor sprang up, and made his way out of the room, but his feet were several times tripped by some unknown power, so that he had the greatest difficulty in reaching the door without a fall. He was followed by Duncan, and both rushed out of the room, shutting the door after them. A new light having been obtained, they both returned with extreme caution, and, it must be added, real fear, in the hope of finding some cause or other for all those terrifying signs.

Would it surprise our readers to hear that they searched the room in vain?—that, after minutely examining under the table, chairs, bed, everywhere, and with the door shut, not a trace could be found of anything? Would they believe that they heard during the day how poor McDonald had staggered, half dead from fatigue, into his friend's house, and falling into a fit, had died at *twenty-two minutes past three* that morning? We do not ask any one to accept of all this as true. But we pledge our honour to the following facts:

The doctor, after the day's fishing was over, had packed his rod so as to take it into his bedroom; but he had left a minnow attached to the hook. A white cat left in the room swallowed the minnow and was hooked. The unfortunate gourmand had vehemently protested against this intrusion into its upper lip by the violent "Fit! fit! fit!" with which she tried to spit the hook out; the reel added the mysterious whir-r-r-r; and the disengaged line, getting entangled in the legs of the chairs and table, as the hooked cat attempted to flee from her tormentor, set the furniture in motion, and tripped up both shepherd and doctor; while an ivy branch kept tapping at the window! Will any one doubt the existence of ghosts and a spirit-world after this?

I have only to add that the doctor's skill was employed during the night in cutting the hook out of the cat's lip, while his poor patient, yet most impatient, was held by the shepherd in a bag, the head alone of puss, with hook and minnow, being visible. McDonald made his appearance in a day or two, rejoicing once more to see his friend, and greatly enjoying the ghost story.

MR. KEMPE

IT was a mild, clammy evening ; and the swing-door of the
tap-room stood wide open. The brass oil-lamp suspended
from the rafter had not yet been lit ; a small misty drizzle
was drifting between the lime-washed walls and the over
arching trees on the farther side of the lane ; and from my
stool at the counter I could commune, as often as I felt inclined, with the wild white eye of the Blue Boar which fleered
in at the window from the hanging sign.

Autumnal scents, failing day, rain so gentle and persistent
—such phenomena as these have a slightly soporific effect on the
human consciousness. It is as though its busy foreground first
becomes blurred, then blotted out ; and then—the slow steady
sweep of the panorama of dream that never ceases its strange
motioning. The experience is brief, I agree. The footlights,
headlights, skylights brighten again : the panorama retires !

Excluding the landlady, who occasionally waddled in from
her dusky retreat behind the bar, there were only three of us
in the tap-room—three chance customers now met together for
the first time : myself ; a smallish man with an unusually high
crown to his head, and something engagingly monkey-like in
his face ; and a barrel-shaped person who sat humped up
on a stool between us in an old shooting-jacket and leather
leggings, his small eyes set close together on either side a red nose.

I had been the last to put in an appearance, but had not,
it seemed, damped anything in the nature of a conversation.
Such weather does not conduce to it. But three may be some
sort of company where two is none ; and what, at last, set
us more or less at our ease was an " automatic machine " that
stood in the corner of the tap-room under a coloured litho-
graph of Shotover, the winner of the Derby in 1882. It was a

machine of an unusual kind since it gave its patronisers
nothing tangible for their penny—not even their ladylove on
a slip of cardboard, or a clinging jet of perfume.

It reminds me now of the old Miracle plays or Moralities.
Behind its glass it showed a sort of grotto, like a whited sepulchre,
with two compartments, over which descended the tresses of a
weeping willow. You slipped a penny into the slot, and presently
a hump-backed mommet in a rusty-black cowl jerked into
view from the cell on the left. He stood there a moment in the
midst—fixedly looking at you ; then decamped into the gloom
again.

But this was if your luck was out—or so I assumed. If it
was in, then a nymph attired in skirts of pink muslin wheeled
out of the flowery bower on the eastern side ; and danced a
brief but impassioned *pas seul.*

My three pennies had brought me one fandango from the
latter and two prolonged scrutinies from the former—a proportion decided on, no doubt, by the worldly-wise manufacturer
of the machine. But this was not all. In intention at least he
must have been a practical optimist. For if the *nymph* responded
to your penny, you were invited to slip yet another coin into
another slot—but before you could count ten. This galvanised
the young lady into a giddy pursuit of the numbskull in the
black hood—a pursuit, however, which ended merely in the
retirement of them both behind the scenes.

The man in leggings had watched my experiments with
eyes almost as motionless as plums in a pudding. It was my
third penny that had wooed out the nymph. But the " grandfather's clock " in the corner had ticked loudly at least five
times before I managed to insert a fourth. It was a moment
of rapt—of an aching—excitement. What teeming passion
showed itself in that wild horseplay behind the glass ! And
then, alas, the machinery ceased to whirr ; the clock ticked on ;
the faint rustle of the drifting rain sounded once more at the
open door ; I returned to my stool ; and the landlady retired
into her den.

" Bang goes fourpence," I remarked a little sheepishly.
" Still, mine was about the right average, I suppose."

The man in the leather leggings—as if the problem were
not for *his* solution—at once turned his little eyes towards our
companion in the corner, whose face was still wreathed with
the friendliest of grimaces at my efforts.

" Well, now," he took me up, " I'm not so sure. In my view,

that minx there sidles out too often. Most young men and more old ones would be content with once in six. I would myself. It's our credulity. We live on hopes, however long they may be deferred. We *live*, as you might say ; but how many of us learn ? How many of us want to make sure ? " He paused for an answer : his small eyes fixed in his face. " Not one in a million," he decided.

I stole another look into the narrow darkness of the Young Lady's Bower.

" Oh," he interrupted, " I wasn't thinking merely of the ' eternal feminine,' as they call it. That's only one of the problems ; though even an answer to that might be interesting. There's Free Will, for example ; there's Moral Responsibility ; and such little riddles as where we all come from and where we are going to. Why, we don't even know what we are—in ourselves, I mean. And how many of us have tried to find out ? "

The man in leggings withdrew his stare and groped out a hand towards his pint-pot. " Have you ? " he inquired.

The dark-eyed, wizened face lit up once more with its curiously engaging smile. " Well, you see, I was once a schoolmaster, and from an official point of view, I suppose, it is part of the job. To find answers, I mean. But, as you'll agree, we temporise ; we compromise. On the other hand, I once met quite by chance, as we call it, a man who had spent I should guess a good many years on that last problem. All by himself, too. You might almost describe it as a kind of pilgrimage—though I'm not anxious to repeat it. It was my turn for a lesson."

" And what was *his* solution ? " I inquired.

" Have you ever been to Porlock—the Weir ? " the little man inquired.

I shook my head.

" I mention Porlock," he went on, " because if you had ever been there, the place I'm thinking of might perhaps call it to mind. Though mine was on a different scale—a decidedly different scale. I doubt, for example, if it will ever become one of those genial spots frequented by week-end tourists and *chars-a-banc*. In the days I'm speaking of—twenty years or more ago—there wasn't even the rudiments of an inn in the place. Only a beershop about half the size of this tap-room, with a population to match—just a huddle of fishermen's cottages tucked in under the cliff.

" I was walking at the time, covering unfamiliar ground,

and had managed to misread my map. My aim had been to
strike into a cliff-path that runs more or less parallel with the
coast ; but I had taken the wrong turn at the cross-roads. Once
astray, it seemed better manners to keep on. How can you
tell what chance may have secreted in her sleeve, even when
you don't put pennies in slots ?

"I persuaded an old lady to give me tea at one of the cottages, and asked my way. Visitors were rare events, it seemed.
At first she advised me to turn back ; I couldn't do better than
that. But after further questioning, she told me at last of a lower
cliff track or path, some miles apparently this side of the
one I had in view. She marked it out for me with her rheu-
maticky old forefinger on the table-cloth. Follow this path far
enough, I gathered, it would lead me into my right road at
last.

"Not that she suggested my making the attempt. By no
means. It was a matter of seven miles or more. And neither
the natives of the village nor even chance visitors, it seemed,
were tempted to make much use of this particular route."

"Why not ? " inquired the man in leggings, and immediately
coughed, as if he had thought better of it.

"That's what I am coming to," replied the schoolmaster
—as though he had been lying in wait for the question. "You
see my old lady had volunteered her last piece of information
with a queerish look in her eyes—like some shy animal slipping
into cover. She was telling me the truth, but not, I fancied,
the whole truth.

"Naturally I asked what was wrong with the path ; and
was there anything of interest on the way or at the end of it
—worth such a journey ? Once more she took a long slow
look at me, as if my catechism were rather more pressing than
the occasion warranted. There *was* a something marked on
the map, she had been given to understand—' just an old, ancient building, like.'

"Sure enough there was : though unfortunately long
wear of the one I carried had not only left indecipherable more
than an Old English letter or two of any record of it, but had
rubbed off a square half-mile or so of the country round about it.

"It was proving a little irksome to draw Truth out of her
well, and when innocently enough I asked if there was any
one in charge of the place, the old lady was obviously disconcerted. She didn't seem to think it needed being taken charge
of ; though she confessed at last that a house ' not nearly so

old, sir, you will understand,' stood nearby, in which lived a gentleman of the name of Kempe.

" It was easier sailing now that we had come to Mr. Kempe. The land, it appeared, including the foreshore—but apart from the chapel—had been in his family since the beginning of time. Mr. Kempe himself had formerly been in the church— Conformist or otherwise—and had been something of a traveller, but had returned home with an invalid wife many years before.

" Mrs. Kempe was dead now ; and there had been no children, ' none, at least, as you would say grew up to what might be called living.' And Mr. Kempe himself had not only been ailing for some little time, but might, for all my informant knew apparently, be dead himself. Nevertheless, there was still a secretive look in the faded eyes—almost as if she believed Mr. Kempe had discovered little methods of his own against the onsets of mortality ! Anyhow, she couldn't tell ; nobody ever went that way now, so far as she was aware. There was the new road up above. What's more, tidings of Mr. Kempe's end, I gathered, however solitary, would not exactly put the village into mourning.

" It was already latish afternoon ; and in that windless summer weather walking had been à rather arduous form of amusement. I was tired. A snowy low-pitched upper-room overlooking the sea was at my disposal if I wanted it for a night or two. And yet, even while I was following this good soul up her narrow staircase, I had already decided to push on in the direction of Mr. Kempe. If need be, I would come back that evening. Country people are apt to be discreet with strangers—however open in appearance. Those shrewd old eyes—when at least they showed themselves—had hinted that even with an inch to the mile a map-maker cannot exhaust a countryside. The contours, I had noticed, were unusual. Besides, Mr. Kempe was not less likely to be interesting company because he was a recluse.

" I put down five shillings on account for my room, and the kindly old creature laid them aside in an ornament on her mantelpiece. There they lie still, for all I know. I have never reclaimed them."

The man in leggings once more turned his large, shapeless face towards the schoolmaster, but this time he made no audible comment.

" And did you find Mr. Kempe ? " I inquired.

The schoolmaster smiled, looking more like a philanthropic

monkey than ever. " I set out at once : watched by the old lady from her porch, until, with a wave of my hand for adieu, I turned out of the village street, and she was hidden from sight. There was no mistaking the path—even though it led off over a stile into a patch of stinging-nettles, and then past a boggy goose-pond.

" After a few hundred yards it began to dip towards the shore, keeping more or less level with the sea for a mile or so until it entered a narrow and sandy cove—the refuge even in summer of all sorts of flotsam and sea-rubbish ; and a positive maëlstrom, I should imagine, when the winter gales sweep in. Towards the neck of this cove the wheel-marks in the thin turf faded out, and the path meandered on for a while beside a brook and under some fine ash trees, then turned abruptly to the right, and almost due north. The bleached bows of a tarred derelict boat set up on end and full of stones—*The Orion*—was my last touch with civilisation.

" It was a quiet evening ; the leaves and grasses shone green and motionless, the flowers standing erect on their stalks under the blue sky, as if carved out of wax. The air was uncommonly sweet, with its tang of the sea. Taking things easy like this, it was well worth while to be alive. I sat down and rested, chewing a grass-stalk and watching the friendly lapping sea. Then up and on.

" After about an hour's steady walking, the path began once more to ascend. It had by now led shorewards again, though I was softly plodding on out of sight and all but out of sound of the tide. Dense neglected woods rose on either side of me, and though wherever the sun could pierce in there were coverts in plenty, hardly a cry of insect or bird stirred the air. To all intents I might have been exploring virgin country. Now and again indeed the fallen bole of a tree or matted clumps of bramble, briony, and traveller's joy compelled me to make a widish detour. But I was still steadily ascending, and the view tended at length to become more and more open ; with here and there a patch of bright green turf and a few scrub bushes of juniper or sprouting tamarisk.

" Shut in as I had been, until this moment it had been difficult to guess how far above me the actual plateau lay, or precisely how far below, the sea—though I had caught distant glimpses now and again of its spreading silver and the far horizon. Even at this point it would have been flattery to call the track a path. The steeper its incline, the more stony and precarious became one's footing. And then at last I rounded the first of a series of bluffs or headlands, commanding a spectacular view of the coast behind me, though nothing of what lay in front.

"The tiny village had vanished. About a hundred and fifty feet beneath the steep on whose margin I was standing—with a flaming bush of gorse here and there, and an occasional dwarf oak as gray as silk in the evening light—the incoming tide gently mumbled its rocks, rocks of a peculiar patchy green and black.

"I took another look at my map, enjoyed a prolonged 'breather,' and went on. Steadily up and inward now and almost due north-west. And once more untended thickets rose dense on either side, and the air was oppressed with a fragrance sickly as chloroform. Some infernal winter tempest or equinoctial gale must have lately played havoc here. Again and again I had to clamber over the bole or through the head-twigs of monster trees felled by the wind, and still studded with a few sprouting *post-mortem* pale-green buds. It was like edging between this world and the next.

"Apart, too, from the gulls with their saturnine gabbling, and flights of clanging oyster-catchers on the rocks below, what birds I saw were birds of prey : buzzards and kestrels chiefly, suspended as if by a thread from space, their small heads stooping between their quivering wings. And once I overheard what I took to be the cough of a raven to its mate. About twenty minutes afterwards, my second bluff hove into sight. And I paused for a while, staring at it.

"For ordinary purposes I have a fairly good head. And yet I confess that before venturing farther I took a prolonged look at this monster and at the faint patternings of the path that lay before me, curving first in, then out, along and across the face of the cliff, and just faintly etching its precipitous surface as it edged out of sight. It's a foolish thing perhaps to imagine oneself picked out clean against the sky on a precipitous slope—if, that is, you mean to put the fancy into action. You get a sort of double-barrelled view of your mortal body crouching there semi-erect, little better than a framework of bones.

"Not that there was as yet any positive risk or danger. The adventure would have been child's play, no doubt, even for an amateur mountaineer. You had only to pick your way, keeping a sharp eye on the loose stones, and—to avoid megrims—skirting round the final curve without pausing to look up or to look down. A modest man might possibly try all fours. Still, after that, it did not surprise me to remember that visitors to these parts had usually preferred some other method of reaching the road and country up above. Pleasure may be a little *over-spiced* with excitement."

" Steep, eh ? " ejaculated the man in leggings.

" Yes, steep," replied the schoolmaster ; " though taken as mere scenery," he continued, " there was nothing to find fault with. Leagues and leagues of sea stretched out to the vague line of the horizon like an immense plate, mottled green and blue. A deep pinkish glow, too, had begun to spread over the eastern skies, mantling up into heights of space made the more abysmal in appearance by wisps of silver cirrus.

" Now and again I lay back with my heels planted on what was left of the path, and rested a moment, staring up into that infinity. Now and again I all but decided to go back. But sheer curiosity to see the mysterious hermitage of which I had heard, and possibly the shame of proving myself yet another discredited visitor, lured me on. Solitude, too, is like deepening water to a swimmer : that also lures you on. Except for an occasional bloated, fork-tailed, shrimp-like insect that showed itself when a flake of dislodged stone went scuttering down into the abyss below, I was the only living creature abroad. Once more I pushed cautiously forward. But it was an evil-looking prospect, and the intense silence of the evening produced at last a peculiar sense of unreality and isolation. My universe seemed to have become a mere picture—and I out of place in it. It was as if I had been mislaid and forgotten.

" I hung by now, I suppose, about two or three hundred feet above the sea ; and maybe a hundred or so beneath the summit of the wall which brushed my left elbow. Wind-worn boulders, gently whispered over by saplings of ash or birch, jutted shallowly here and there above and below me. Marine plants lifted their windbitten flowers from inch-wide ledges on which their seeds had somehow found a lodging. The colours mirrored in sky and water increased in brilliance and variety as the sunset advanced, though here was only its reflection ; and the flat ocean beneath lapped soundlessly on ; its cream-like surf fringing here and there the very base of the cliff, beneath which, like antediluvian monsters, vast rocks lay drowsing. I refrained from examining them too closely.

" But even if—minute intrusive mote that I was, creeping across that steep of wall—even if I had been so inclined, there was little opportunity. Though for centuries wind, frost and rain had been gnawing and fretting at the face of the cliff, sure foothold and finger-hold became ever more precarious. An occasional ringing reverberation from far below suggested, too, that even the massive bulk of rock itself might be honey-combed to its foundations. What once had been a path was now the negation of one. And the third prodigious bluff towards which I presently found myself slowly, almost mechanically, advancing, projected into space at a knife-like angle ; cut sharp in gigantic silhouette against the skies.

" I made a bewildering attempt to pretend to be casual and cheerful—even to whistle. But my lips were dry, and breath or courage failed me. None the less I had contrived to approach within twenty yards or so of that last appalling preci-pice, when, as if a warning voice had whispered the news in my ear, I suddenly realised the predicament I was in. To turn back now was impossible. Nor had I a notion of what lay on the farther side of the headland. For a few instants my bones and sinews rebelled against me, refusing to commit themselves to the least movement. I could do no more than cling spasmodically with my face to the rock.

" But to hang there on and on and wither like an autumnal fly was out of the question. One single hour of darkness, one spinning puff of wind, would inevitably dislodge me. But dark-ness was some hours distant ; the evening was of a dead calm ; and I thanked my stars there was no sun to roast and confuse me with his blaze and heat. I thanked my stars—but where would my carcass be when those stars began to show them-selves in the coming night ? All this swept through my mind in an instant. Complete self-possession was the one thing needful. I realised that too. And then a frightful cold came over me ; sweat began to pour off my body ; the very soul within me became sick with fear.

" I use the word soul because this renewed nausea was some-thing worse than physical. I was a younger man then, and could still in the long run rely on nerve and muscle, but fear turns one's blood to water—that terror of the spirit, and not merely of the mind or instinct. It bides its moment until the natural edges off into—into the unknown.

" Not that Nature, as we call her, even in the most congenial surroundings, is the sort of old family nurse that makes one's bed every morning, and tucks one up with a ' God bless you ' overnight. Like the ants and the aphides and the elvers and the tadpoles, she produces us humans in millions ; leaving us

otherwise to our own devices. We can't even guess what little
stratagems for the future she may be hiding up her sleeve. We
can't even guess. But that's a mere commonplace. After all,
so far as we can prove, she deserves only a small ' n ' to her
name.

" What I'm suggesting is merely that though she appeared
to have decoyed me into this rat-trap with all her usual artless-
ness, she remained a *passive* enemy, and what now swathed me
in like a breath of poison—as, with face, palms, knees and
belly pressed close against the rock, I began once more working
softly on from inch-wide ledge and inch-deep weed, my tongue
like tinder, my eyes seeming to magnify every glittering atom
they tried to focus—was the consciousness of some power or
influence beyond Nature's. It was not so much of death—and I
actually with my own eyes *saw* my body inertly hurtling to its
doom beneath—that I was afraid. What terrified me beyond
words to express was some positive presence here in a more
desperate condition even than I. I was being waylaid.

" When you come to such a pass as this, you lose count of
time. I had become an automaton—little better than a beetle
obeying the secret dictates of what I believe they call the Life-
Urge ; and how precisely I contrived to face and to circum-
navigate that last bit of precipice, I cannot recall. But this
once done, in a few minutes I was in comparative safety. I
found myself sluggishly creeping again along a path which had
presently widened enough to allow me to turn my face outwards from the rock, and even to rest. And even though the
precipice beneath me was hardly less abrupt and enormous,
and the cliff-face above actually overhung my niche, for the
time being I was out of physical danger. I was, as they say,
my own man again ; had come back.

" It was high time. My skull seemed to have turned to
ice ; I was wet through ; my finger-nails were split ; my hands
covered with blood ; and my clothes would have disgraced a
tramp.

" But all traces of fear had left me, and what now swept
my very wits away in this almost unendurable reaction was
the sheer beauty of the scene that hung before my eyes. Half
reclining, not daring yet to stir, my outstretched hands clasping
two knobs of rocks, my eyeballs gently moving to and fro, I
sat there and feasted on the amazing panorama spread out
before me ; realising none the less that I was in the presence
of something—how can I express it ?—of something a little

different from, stranger and less human than—well, our old friend Nature.

"The whole face of this precipice was alight with colour —dazzling green and orange, drifts of snow and purple— campion, sea-pink, may-weed, samphire, camomile, lichen, stonecrop, with fleshy and aromatic plants that I knew not even the names of, sweeping down drift beyond drift into a narrow rock-bound tranquil bay of the darkest emerald and azure, and then sweeping up once more drift beyond drift into the vault of the sky, its blue fretted over as if by some master architect with silvery interlacings, a scattered feather-like fleece of vapour.

"The steady cry, too, possibly amplified by echo, of the incoming tide reached me here once more ; a whisper and yet not toneless. And on and on into the distance swept the gigantic coast line, crowned summit to base with its emerald springtide woods.

"Still slightly intoxicated as I was by the terror and danger in which I had been, and which were now for the moment past and gone, I gave myself ample opportunity to rest and to drink in this prodigious spectacle. And yet, as I lay there, still at a dizzy altitude, midway between sea and sky but in perfect safety, the odd conviction persisted, that though safe, I was not yet secure. It was as if I were still facing some peril of the mind, and absurd and irrational though it may sound there was a vague disquieting hint within me of disappointment—as if I had lost without realising it a unique opportunity. And yet, all this medley of hints and intuitions was wholly subsidiary to the conviction that from some one point in all this vacancy around me a steady devouring gaze was fixed on me—that I was being watched."

Once more our hard-headed friend fidgeted uneasily on his stool.

"It sounds absurd, I agree," the schoolmaster caught him up. "Simply because, apart from the seabirds and the clouds, I had been and was still the only moving object within view. The sudden apparition of me crawling around that huge nose of rock must have been as conspicuous as it was absurd. Besides, myriads of concealed eyes in the dense forest towering conically up on the other side of the narrow bay beneath me, and looming ever more mistily from headland to headland towards the north and west, could have watched my every movement. A thousand arrows from unseen archers concealed on the opposing heights might at any instant have transfixed me where I lay. One becomes conscious, too, of the sort of empty settled stare which fixes an intruder into such solitudes. It is at the same time vacant, enormous and hostile.

" But I don't mean that. I still mean something far more definite—and more dangerous, too, than that ; and I keep to it even if this precise memory may have been affected by what came after. For I was soon to learn that in actual fact I *was* being watched ; and by as acute and unhuman a pair of eyes as I have ever seen in mortal head.

" With infinite caution I rose to my feet again at last, and continued my journey. The path grew steadily easier ; soil succeeded to bare rock, and this must not very long before, I discovered, have been trodden by other human feet than mine. There were marks of hobnails between its tussocks of grass and moss and thrift.

" It presently descended a little, and then in a while, from out of the glare of the evening, I found myself entering a broader and heavily-shaded track leading straight onwards and tunnelling inland into the woods. It was, to my amazement, close on eight o'clock, and too late to dream of turning back, even if I could have persuaded myself to face again the experience of the last half-hour. Yet whatever curiosity might say for itself, I felt a peculiar disinclination to forge ahead. The bait had ceased to be enticing.

" I paused once more under the dismal funnel of greenery in which I found myself staring at the face of my watch, and then had another look at the map. A minute or two's scrutiny assured me that straight ahead was my only possible course. And why not ? There was company ahead. In this damp soil the impressions of the hobnailed shoes showed more clearly. Quite recently those shoes must have come and gone along this path on three separate occasions at least. Mine had been a rather acutely solitary excursion, and yet for the life of me I had not the smallest desire to meet the maker of those footprints.

" In less than half an hour, however, I came to a standstill beneath ' the old, ancient building, like ' that had once been marked on my map. And an uncompanionable sight it was. Its walls lay a little back from the green track in what appeared to be a natural clearing, or amphitheatre, though at a few yards distance huge pines, in shallow rising semi-circles, hemmed it in. In shape it was all but circular ; and must once no doubt have been a wayside hermitage or cell. It was of stone and was

surmounted by a conical roof of thick and heavy slabs, at the
south side of which rose a minute bell-cote, and towards the
east a stunted stone cross, with one of its arms broken away.

" The round arched door—its chevron edging all but
defaced—refused to open. Nothing was to be seen in the gloom
beyond its gaping keyhole. There was but one narrow slit of
window, and this was beyond my reach. I could not even guess
the age of this forbidding yet beautiful thing, and the gentleman
—as I found afterwards—who had compiled the local guide-
book had omitted to mention it altogether. Here and there in
its fabric decay had begun to show itself, but clumsy efforts had
been made at repair.

" In that deep dark verdurous silence, unbroken even by
drone or twitter, the effect of those walls in their cold minute
simplicity was peculiarly impressive. They seemed to strike a
solemn chill into the air around them—those rain-stained
senseless stones. And what looked like a kind of derelict burial-
ground to the south side of it only intensified its sinister aspect.
No place surely for when the slow dark hours begin.

" The graves were very few in number, and only one name
was decipherable on any of the uncouth and half-buried headstones. Two were mere mounds in the nibbled turf. I had
drawn back to survey once more from this new aspect the walls
beyond, when—from one instant to the next, so to speak—I
became aware of the presence of Mr. Kempe. He was standing
a few paces distant, his gaze in my direction—as unexpected an
apparition as that of Banquo in *Macbeth*. Not even a robin
could have appeared with less disturbance of its surroundings.
Not a twig had snapped, not a leaf had rustled.

" He looked to be a man of about sixty or more, in his old
greenish-black half-clerical garb, his trousers lapping concertina-
like over immense ungainly boots. An antiquated black straw
hat was on his head. From beneath it grey hair flowed out
a little on either side the long colourless face with its straggling
beard. His eyes were clear as water—the lids unusually wide
apart—and they had the peculiarity, perceptible even at this
distance, of not appearing to focus what their attention was
fixed upon. That attention was fixed upon me as a matter of
fact, and, standing as I was, with head turned in his direction, we
so remained, closely regarding one another for what seemed
to be a matter of hours rather than of moments.

" It was I who broke the silence with some affectedly-casual
remark about the weather and the interestingness of the relic

that stood, something like a huge mushroom of stone, nearby.
The voice that sounded in answer was even more astonishing
than Mr. Kempe himself. It seemed to proceed from a throat
rusty from want of use, and carried a kind of vibrant glassy note
in it, like the clash of fine glass slightly cracked. At first I
could not understand what he said. The sound of it reminds me
now of Alexander Selkirk when his rescuers found him in Juan
Fernandez. They said he spoke his words by halves, you'll
remember. So did Mr. Kempe. They sounded like relics of a
tongue as ancient as the unknown hermit's chapel beside which
we had met.

" Still, I was myself as nervous as a cat. With all his oddities
—those wide, colourless eyes, those gestures, that over-loud
voice, there was nothing hostile, nothing even discourteous in his
manner, and he did not appear to be warning me off as a
trespasser. Indeed the finger wagging at me in the air was clearly
beckoning me on. Not that I had any keen inclination to follow.
I preferred to go on watching him, and attempted to mark time
by once more referring to the age and architecture of the chapel
—asked him at last point-blank if it were now too late to beg the
courtesy of a glance inside.

" The evening light momentarily brightened above the
dark spreading tops of the pines and struck down full on this
queer shape with its engrossed yet vacant face. His eyes never
faltered, their pin-prick pupils fixed in their almost hueless
irises. Reflected thus, I seemed to be an object of an extremely
limited significance—a mere speck floating in their intense inane.
The eyes of the larger cats and the hawk-tribe have a similar
effect ; and yet one could hardly assert that their prey has no
significance for *them* !

" He made no attempt to answer my questions, but appeared
to be inquiring, in turn, how I had contrived to invade his
solitude ; what I wanted, in short. I was convinced none the
less that he was deceiving me. He knew well how I had come :
for, of course, meeting as we had, only one way had been possible
—that from the sea.

" It might be impolitic to press the matter. I merely
suggested that my journey had not been ' roses all the way,'
that I must get back to the world above before nightfall ; and
once more gave him to understand my innocent purpose—
the desire to examine this curious relic. His gaze wandered off
to the stone hermitage, returned, and then as if in stealth, rested
an instant intently on my hands. Otherwise he remained

perfectly motionless : his long knotted fingers hanging down out of the sleeves of a jacket too short for his gaunt body—and those ineffable clumsy rusty boots.

" The air in this green niche of the bay was stagnant with the scent of foliage and flowers ; and so magically dark and clear it was as though you were in the presence of a dream. Or of a dreamer indeed—responsible not only for its beauty, but also for its meancing influence on the mind. All this, however, only convinced me the more of the necessity to keep my attention steadily fixed on the figure beside me. There was a something, an aura, about him difficult to describe. It was as if he himself were a long way off from his body—though that's pure nonsense, of course. As the phrase goes—he was not *all there.* Once more his eyes met mine, and the next thing that occurred to me was that I had never seen a human countenance that betrayed so desperate a hunger. But for what ? It was impossible to tell.

" He was pressing me to follow him. I caught the word ' key ' ; and he at once led the way. With a prolonged reluctant look behind me—that antiquated cell of stone ; those gigantic pines ; the few sinking mounds clad in their fresh green turf— I turned in my tracks ; and the glance he cast at me over his shoulder was intended, I gathered, as a smile of encouragement.

" The straggling gabled house to which he conducted me, with its low tower and smokeless chimneys now touched with the last cold red of sunset, was almost more windows than wall. The dark glass of their casements showed like water in its discoloured sides. Beyond it the ravine ascended ever more narrowly, and the house rested here in this green gap like a mummy long since deserted by its ghost.

" We crossed a cobbled courtyard, and Mr. Kempe preceded me up a wooden flight of stairs into a low-ceiled room with one all but ivy-blinded window, and, oddly enough, a stone floor. Except for the space where hung the faded portrait of what appeared to be a youngish woman, her hair dressed in ringlets, bookshelves covered the walls. Books lay hugger-mugger everywhere, indeed : on the table, on the chairs, on the floor, and even piled into the chimney of the rusty grate. The place was fusty with their leather bindings, and with damp.

" They had evidently been both well-used and neglected. There was little opportunity to get the general range of their titles—though a complete row of them I noticed were in Latin— because some vague intuition compelled me to keep my attention fixed upon my host. He had motioned me to a chair, and had

seated himself on another that was already topped with two
or three folios. It must have been even at midday a gloomy
room ; and owing to its situation it was a dark house. The
door having admitted us, stood open ; beyond it yawned the
silent staircase."

At this the schoolmaster paused ; the landlady of the Blue
Boar had once more emerged, and, like one man, we shamefacedly pushed our three glasses across the counter.

" And what happened then ? " I inquired.

At this the man in leggings slightly turned his tortoise-like
head in my direction, as if its usual resort was beneath a shell.

The schoolmaster watched the shape of the landlady till it
had vanished into the dusk beyond. " Mr. Kempe began talking
to me," he said. " Rapidly and almost incoherently at first, but
gradually slowing down till I could understand more or less
what he was saying. He was explaining, a little unnecessarily
as I fancied, that he was a recluse ; that the chapel was not
intended for public worship ; that he had few visitors ; that
he was a scholar and therefore was in need of little company
but his books. He swept his long arm towards these companions
of his leisure. The little light that silted through the window
struck down across his tousled head, just touching his brow and
cheekbones as he talked. And then in the midst of this harangue
he suddenly came to an end, and asked me if I had been sent
there. I assured him that I had come of my own free will, and
would he oblige me before we returned to the chapel, with a
glass of water. He hesitated.

" ' Water ? ' he repeated. ' Oh, water ? ' And then with a
peculiar gesture he crossed the room and shut the door after him.
His boots beat as hollowly on the stairs as sticks on a tom-tom.
I heard the creaking of a pump-handle, and in a moment he
reappeared carrying a blue-lined cup without a handle. With
a glance at the portrait over my head, I drank its ice-cold
contents at a gulp, and pushed the cup in between two dogs-
eared books.

" ' I want to get back to the road up above,' I explained.

" This seemed to reassure him. He shut his mouth and sat
gazing at me. ' Ah ! The road up above ! '

" Then, ' Why ? ' he suddenly almost bawled at me, as if
I were sitting a long way off. His great hands were clasped on
his angled knees, his body bolt upright.

" ' Why what ? '

" ' Why have you come here ? What is there to spy out ?

This is private property. What do you do—for a living? What's the use of it all?'

"It was an unusual catechism—from stranger to stranger. But I had just escaped an unpleasant death, and could afford to be indulgent. Besides, he was years and years older than I. I told him that I was a schoolmaster, on vacation, not thinking it necessary to add that owing to a small legacy I was out of a job at the time. I said I was merely enjoying myself.

"'Enjoying yourself! And you teach!' he cried with a snap of his jaw. 'And what do you teach? Silly, suffocating lies, I suppose; or facts, as you prefer to call them.' He drew his hand down his long colourless face, and I stole a glance towards the door. 'If human beings *are* mere machines, well and good,' he went on. 'But supposing, my young friend, they are not mere machines? Supposing they have souls in their bodies: what then? Supposing *you* have a soul in your body: what then? Ay, and the proof; the proof!'"

The schoolmaster's face puckered up once more into a genial smile.

"I won't attempt," he went on, "to repeat word for word the talk I had that evening. I can give only the gist of it. But I had stumbled pretty abruptly, you'll notice, on Mr. Kempe's King Charles's head. And he presented me with it on a charger. He was possessed, I gathered, by one single aim, thought and desire. All these years of his ' retirement ' had apparently been spent in this one quest—to *prove* Man's possession of a ' Soul.' Certain doubts in my mind sprang up a little later in the evening but it was clear from the beginning that in pursuit of this he had spared neither himself nor the wife that was gone. It was no less clear that he was entirely incapable of what better brains, no doubt, would have considered a scientific treatment of his theme.

"He thrust into my hand a few chapters of a foolscap manuscript that lay on the table—a fly-blown mirky pile of paper at least eighteen inches high. Never have I seen anything to which the term ' reading-*matter* ' seemed more appropriate. The ink was faded on the top page; it was stained as if with tea. This work was entitled briefly, ' The Soul '—though the sub-title that followed it would not have disgraced the author of the ' Anatomy.'

"I could follow no more than a line or two at a time of the crazy handwriting. The pages were heavily interscored, annotated and revised, not only in pencil but in violet and in red ink. A good part of it appeared to be in Latin and Hebrew, and other inactive tongues. But turning them over at haphazard I caught such page-headings as ' Contemplation ' ; ' Dreams ' ; ' Flagellation ' ; ' Cadaver ' ; ' Infancy.' I replaced the sheets a little gingerly on the table ; though one mustn't, of course, judge of the merits of a work by the appearance of it in ms.

" The desolation of its author's looks and his abruptness of manner thinned away awhile as he warmed to his subject. But it was not so much his own sufferings in the cause as the thought of what Mrs. Kempe's last few years on earth must have been to her, that made me an attentive listener. Hers must indeed have proved a lingering death. He had never left her side, I gathered, for weeks at a time, except to tend his patch of garden, and to prepare their niggardly meals. And as her body had wasted, poor soul, his daily inquisition, his daily probings had become ever more urgent and desperate.

" There was no doubt in the world that this afflicted old man had loved his wife. The softening of the vacant inhuman eyes as he told me of that last deathbed colloquy was enough to prove that. Maybe it was in part because of this affection that mere speculation had sharpened into what they call an *idée fixe*. Still, I hardly think so. More probably the insidious germ had shared his cradle. And after all, some degree of conviction on the subject is not out of place in men of his cloth. He had abandoned his calling indeed, he was assuring me, solely as a proof of his zeal !

" He showed me also one or two late photographs of Mrs. Kempe—taken with his own antiquated camera, and ' developed ' maybe in this very room. Soul indeed ! There was little else. The face mirkily represented in them wore a peculiar remote smile. The eyes had been hollowly directed towards the round leather cap of the machine. And so fallen were the features, now fading away on the discoloured paper, they might as well have been the presentment of a ghost.

" What precise proofs he had actually demanded of this companion of his hermitage I cannot even guess. And what proofs might he still be pleading for, pursuing ? Evidently none as yet had satisfied his craving. But it was at least to his credit that his own personal experiments—experiments on himself, I mean—had been as drastic. In one of them I had unwittingly shared. For the cliff path, I discovered, had long been his constant penance. A catlike foot was concealed beneath those Brobdingnagian boots. His had been the hand that had not only helped Nature protect her fastnesses, but had kept off all but one or two occasional stragglers as fatuous as myself.

"It had been his haunt, this path—day and night. He questioned the idle heavens there. In the face of a peril so extreme the spirit wins almost to a point of severance from its earthly clay. Night and a half-moon and the northern constellations— I could at least in fancy share his vigils there. Only an occasional ship ventures into sight of that coast, but almost any day, it seemed, during these last few years a good spy-glass might have discerned from its decks a human shape facing the Infinite from that appalling eyrie.

"Both delusions and illusions, too, are rapid breeders. Which of the two, I wondered—still wonder—was *this* old man's conviction—the conviction, I mean, that one is likely to be more acutely conscious of the spirit within when the body is suspended, as it were, from the lintel of death's door. What dreams may come in such circumstances every practical psychologist no doubt would merely pooh-pooh. Still, after all, Mr. Kempe had been something of a pioneer in this inquest. He had not spared himself. He could not live by faith, it seemed. He must indeed again and again have come uncommonly near dying in the pursuit of it.

"He had fasted moreover, and was now little more than a mere frame of bones within his outlandish clothes. Those boots of his—they kept forcing themselves on my attention—a worse fit than any worn by some homesick desperate soldier clambering ' over the top ' in the Great War. They stuck in my mind.

" ' You don't seem to realise—you folk out there don't seem to realise,' he suddenly began shouting at me, ' that nothing in this world is of the slightest importance compared with a Yes or No to what I ask. If we are nothing more than the brutes that perish—and no sign ever comes from them, I may tell you—then let us perish, I say. Let fire descend from Heaven and shrivel us up. I care not in what cataclysm of horror. I have passed them all. I am suggesting no blasphemy. I make no challenge ; no denial—merely a humble plodder, my dear sir. But no ! Nothing. Nothing. Nothing. Not a word.' He lifted himself out of his chair, opened the door, looked out and came back again.

" ' I disapprove '—he brandished his outspread fingers at me—' I disapprove absolutely of peering and prying. Your vile pernicious interferences with the natural mysteries which we as humanity inherited from the old Adam—away with them !

I declare I am a visitor here. I declare that this '—he swept his hand down his meagre carcass,—' this is my mere tenancy. All that I seek is the simplest proof. A proof that would not so much as stay a pulse-beat in the vile sceptics that give their wretched lives to what they call Science.

" ' I am not even a philosopher,' he ejaculated. ' I am here alone, a wayfaring man and a fool. Alone—in the face of this one supreme mystery. And I need aid ! ' His voice ceased ; he threw out his hands and sat there emptily gazing at me.

" And so he continued. Now he would lift himself out of his chair and prowling from shelf to shelf, scanning at but an inch or two distant the titles of their contents, would thrust volume after volume into my hands for evidence, accompanying his clumsy motions with peevish and broken comments impossible to follow. I was presently surrounded with these things as with a surf.

" Then he would once more seat himself, and embark on a protracted harangue with that cracked disused voice rising steadily until it broke in a discordant screech of argument.

" ' Almighty God,' he yelled at me, ' you sit there, living, breathing, a human being ; and the one justification of this hideous masquerade left uncertain.' He flung his hand into the air. ' What right has he even to share the earth with me ! ' he shouted into the quiet.

" Then once more there followed as swift a return to silence, to self-possession—that intent devouring stare. One at least knows oneself to be something objective in any chance-encountered pair of human eyes. In his, as I have said already, I appeared to have no material existence whatsoever. Mr. Kempe might have been surveying, talking to, his own shadow. It was peculiarly disconcerting.

" After yet another such outburst he had for a moment lain back in his chair as if exhausted. And I was so intent in my scrutiny of him that a second or two went by before I sprang forward to pick up the few dingy photographs that had fallen out of his hand on to the grimy patch of carpet beneath. But he himself had stooped even more abruptly, and our skulls collided together with a crack that for the moment all but dazed me.

" But the eye moves almost as swiftly as the mind, and the collision had not been hasty enough to prevent my snatching a glimpse of one or two of them, photographs of which neither this widower not his wife had been the original. I drew back appalled—their details fixed in my mind as if etched there by a flash of lightning. And, leaving him to gather up his further evidences as best he could, I instantly found myself edging towards the door. Those squalid oblongs of cardboard were easily concealed in his immense palm. He pawed them together as clumsily as a bear might combs of honey ; then slowly raised his grey dishevelled head, and met my eyes.

" I paused. ' You have had other visitors at times ? ' I queried as mildly as my tongue would allow.

" ' What visitors, young man, do you mean, may I ask ? ' An extraordinary change had come into his voice—a flatness, an obsequiousness. The ingratiating tones were muffled, as if he could hardly trust himself to speak. For a while I could only gape in reply.

" ' Like myself,' I blurted out at last. ' Visitors who come to—well, out of sheer curiosity. There's the other route, I suppose ? '

" My one desire just then was to keep my thoughts about Mr. Kempe rational and within bounds. To make a monster of him would be merely to lose my head once more as I had already lost it on that afternoon's journey. None the less I was now looking at him through the after-image of those chance-seen photographs. They were a disturbing medium. The body of a human being who has fallen from a great height is not pleasing and pacifying to look at even though for a while its owner may have survived the fatality. There were others, too ; and yet, it was less his photographs than the amateur photographer that had set my teeth on edge. He looked so old and so helpless— like an animal, as I say, enslaved by—and yet incapable of obeying—some heaven-sent instinct. That terrifying, doglike despair !

" But then, open your newspaper any fine morning of your life, and which is the more likely to greet you on the news-page : the innocent young lady in the pink gauze petticoats over there, or that old figure of fun in the monk's cowl ? "

The tortoiselike shape of the man in leggings once more stirred on its stool. But this time his little eyes were turned in my direction.

" How did you manage to get out at last ? " I inquired of the schoolmaster.

" Well," he said, " all this time Mr. Kempe had been watching me as circumspectly as I had been watching him, but as if, too, he were uncertain how many paces distant from him I stood. Then once more voice and manner changed. He feigned to be reassured. 'It has been a wonderful day,' he remarked, with the dignity of an old retired scholar whose dubious fortune it has been to entertain a foreign prince ; 'a wonderful day. And my only regret is that I was unprepared for the occasion ; that I have so poor a hospitality to offer. You may have had an exceedingly painful experience this afternoon. Why, my dear sir, in the absence of mind that comes over me once I embark on this hobby of mine, I haven't even asked you to wash your hands.'

"Almost involuntarily I glanced down at them. Like Macbeth's they needed the invitation. But I must confess I preferred this old minister when he was not talking to me as if I were an imbecile child in a Sunday School. Besides, I knew pefectly well that—whether from that tumbling watch-tower of his, or from some hiding-place in the woods—there had been one intent witness of that experience. I thrust my hands into my pockets out of his sight.

"'If you will await me here a moment," he went on— and his utterance began to thicken again, 'I will get the key to the chapel—a remarkable, even unique example of its order. There was a well, too, in former times, and even archæologists have failed to agree about its date. They used to come ; they used to come : and would argue, too. Why I can *prove* it is in parts at least not later than the ninth century. And the interior . . . but, dear me, it will soon be dark ; and—no—you mustn't think of leaving the house to-night. I need company ; I *need* it.' He poked forward at me again, while yet furtively and rapidly edging towards the door.

"With a peculiar disinclination to come into the very slightest contact with his person, I had to dodge out of his way to allow him to pass, and attempted to do so without appearing to show like a visitor who has strayed by mischance into the cage of a dangerous animal in some zoological garden. The old grey tousled head turned not an inch upon its heavy angular shoulders as he passed me ; but in the dimming light of the window I caught a glimpse of the wide sea-like eyes intently fixed on me—like lifeless planets in the waste of space.

"Even a young man may have intimations of the fool he is about to prove himself. Intimations, I mean, that come too late. Before the cumbrous door had closed behind him, I was listening for the sound of the key being turned in the lock I didn't even wait to try the handle, but tiptoed as rapidly as possible over the heaped-up books on the floor towards the window. It was one of dingy oblong panes, and the hasp was broken. The drop beneath its sill—to any one at least who had reached the house by the less easy way of the two roads—was almost as easy as getting into bed. It would land me some ten feet below on a heap of vegetable rubbish. But the hinges of the window had been allowed to rust, and the wood to shrink and swell with the changing seasons.

" Not a sound had followed the locking of the door, and unless Mr. Kempe had disencumbered his feet of their boots, he was at that moment collecting his wits immediately outside of it. I tiptoed across once more. ' Please don't let me be any trouble,' I bawled. ' I could come again another time.'

" The next instant I was back at the window, listening. The answer boomed down at me at last from some room above. But I could distinguish no words—merely a senseless babble. It would be indiscreet, it seemed, to hesitate any longer. I seized a frowsy cushion and with all my force thrust it against the rotten frame of the window. It flew open with but one explosive crack. I was prepared for it. Once more I paused. Then after a last hasty glance round that dismal laboratory, its scattered books, fusty papers, blackened ceiling, broken lamp—and that one half-obliterated portrait of the gentle apologetic faded young woman on the wall, I clambered soundlessly on to the sill, and dropped. The refuse below was thoroughly rotten ; not a twig snapped.

" The moment I touched ground I regretted this ignominious exit. There was I, a young man—thirty to forty years at least the junior of Mr. Kempe—a young man who, whether or not possessed of a soul, was at least fairly capable in body. Surely I might have ventured !—life has more riddles than one. But I did not pursue these thoughts far. The very look and appearance of the house as I glanced up at the window out of which I had descended so abruptly, its overhanging gable, its piebald darkened walls rising towards the first stars under the last of twilight—it was hardly less unhappy and unpleasing company than its tenant.

" I groped my way beyond its purlieus as quickly and silently as I could, mounted a low wall and was already in the woods. By luck I had caught a glimpse of the Plough straddling above the chimneys, so I knew my North, and edged off upwards and westwards for some little distance under the motionless trees before I came to a halt.

" The house was now out of sight, its owner once more

abandoned to his own resources, and researches. And I was conscious of no particular desire to return to examine the interior of the small stone chapel nor the inscriptions on the few headstones which memoralised those who had been longest slumbering in the ground nearby.

"Possibly I was not the only visitor who had bidden the recluse in this valley so unmannerly a farewell. I cannot at any rate imagine any one simpleton enough to venture back even in response to the sound of hysterical weeping that came edging across the silence of the woods."

"D'ye mean that old man was *crying*?" queried our friend in leggings.

The drizzle in the lane outside the Inn had plucked up courage as daylight ebbed, and had increased to a steady downpour. He had to repeat his question.

"I mean," said the schoolmaster a little acidly, "exactly what I say. I am nothing much of a traveller, or perhaps I could tell you what resemblance the noise of it had to the cajolings of a crocodile."

"My God!" coughed the other derisively. With this he seemed to have finally made up his mind, and lurched heavily off his stool. And without even so much as a " good-night " to our landlady, he betook himself out of the bar.

Except for the noise of the rain a complete silence followed his departure.

"And you never went back? " I ventured presently. " Or— or spoke about the matter? "

"I mean, do you see," said the schoolmaster, " I acted like a fool. I should have taken Mr. Kempe simply on his face value. There was nothing to complain about. He hadn't *invited* me to come and see him. And it was hardly his fault, I suppose, if an occasional visitor failed to complete so precarious a journey. I wouldn't go so far as that. He was merely one of those would-be benefactors to the human race who go astray ; get lost, ramble on down the wrong turning. *Qua* pioneer, I ask," he rapped his fingers on the pewter of the counter, "was he exceptional? " He was arguing with himself, not with me.

I nodded. " But what was your impression—was *he* sure— Mr. Kempe? Either way? "

" The Soul? "

" Yes," I echoed, " the Soul."

But I repeated the word under my breath, for something

in the sound of our voices seemed to have attracted the attention of the landlady. And, alas, she had decided to light up.

The solemnity of Man's remotest ancestors lay over the schoolmaster's features. " I can't say," he replied. " I am not certain even if he was aware how densely populated his valley appeared to be—to a chance visitor, I mean. What's more, to judge from the tones of his voice, he had scarcely the effect of a single personality. There were at least three Mr. Kempes present that evening. And I haven't the faintest wish in the world to meet any one of them again."

" And afterwards ? Was it comparatively easy finding your way—on to the new cliff road ? "

" Comparatively," said the schoolmaster. " Though it took time. But nights are fairly short in May, even in country as thickly wooded as that."

I continued to look at him without speaking ; yet another unuttered question on my lips.

To judge from the remote friendly smile he just blinked at me, he appeared to have divined it, though it produced no direct answer. He got down from his stool, looked at his empty glass— and for the first time I noticed he was wearing mittens over his small bluish hands. " It's getting late," he said, with an eye fixed vacantly once more on the automatic machine in the corner of the tap-room. There was no denying it ; nor that even the musty interior of the Blue Boar looked more hospitable than the torrential darkness of the night outside.

How strange is man. The spectacle depressed me beyond words—as if it had any more significance than that for its passing hour a dense yet not unbeneficent cloud was spread betwixt this earth of ours and the faithful shining of the stars.

But I did not mention this to the schoolmaster. He seemed to be lost in a dark melancholy, his face a maze of wrinkles. And beyond him—in a cracked looking-glass—I could see his double, sitting there upon its stool. I was conscious that in some way I had bitterly disappointed him. I looked at him—my hand on the door-handle—waiting to go out. . . .

THE TAPESTRIED CHAMBER

ABOUT the end of the American war, when the officers of Lord Cornwallis's army, which surrendered at Yorktown, and others, who had been made prisoners during the impolitic and ill-fated controversy, were returning to their own country to relate their adventures and repose themselves after their fatigues, there was amongst them a general officer, of the name of Browne—an officer of merit, as well as a gentleman of high consideration for family and attainments.

Some business had carried General Browne upon a tour through the western counties, when, in the conclusion of a morning stage, he found himself in the vicinity of a small country town, which presented a scene of uncommon beauty, and of a character peculiarly English.

The little town, with its stately old church, whose tower bore testimony to the devotion of ages long past, lay amidst pastures and cornfields of small extent, but bounded and divided with hedgerow timber of great age and size. There were few marks of modern improvement. The environs of the place intimated neither the solitude of decay nor the bustle of novelty; the houses were old, but in good repair; and the beautiful little river murmured freely on its way to the left of the town, neither restrained by a dam nor bordered by a towing-path.

Upon a gentle eminence, nearly a mile to the southward of the town, were seen, amongst many venerable oaks and tangled thickets, the turrets of a castle as old as the wars of York and Lancaster, but which seemed to have received important alterations during the age of Elizabeth and her successor. It had not been a place of great size ; but whatever accommodation it formerly afforded was, it must be supposed, still to be obtained within its walls ; at least, such was the inference which General Browne drew from observing the smoke arise merrily from several of the ancient wreathed and carved chimney-stalks. The wall of the park ran alongside of the highway for two or three hundred yards ; and through the different points by which the eye found glimpses into the woodland scenery it seemed to be well stocked. Other points of view opened in succession—now a full one of the front of the old castle, and now a side glimpse at its particular towers, the former rich in all the bizarrerie of the Elizabethan school, while the simple and solid strength of other parts of the building seemed to show that they had been raised more for defence than ostentation.

Delighted with the partial glimpses which he obtained of the castle through the woods and glades by which this ancient feudal fortress was surrounded, our military traveller was determined to inquire whether it might not deserve a nearer view, and whether it contained family pictures or other objects of curiosity worthy of a stranger's visit, when, leaving the vicinity of the park, he rolled through a clean and well-paved street and stopped at the door of a well-frequented inn.

Before ordering horses to proceed on his journey, General Browne made inquiries concerning the proprietor of the chateau which had so attracted his admiration, and was equally surprised and pleased at hearing in reply a nobleman named whom we shall call Lord Woodville. How fortunate ! Much of Browne's early recollections, both at school and at college, had been connected with young Woodville, whom, by a few questions, he now ascertained to be the same with the owner of this fair domain. He had been raised to the peerage by the decease of his father a few months before, and, as the General learned from the landlord, the term of mourning being ended, was now taking possession of his paternal estate, in the jovial season of merry autumn, accompanied by a select party of friends, to enjoy the sports of a country famous for game.

This was delightful news to our traveller. Frank Woodville had been Richard Browne's fag at Eton, and his chosen intimate at Christ Church ; their pleasures and their tasks had been the same ; and the honest soldier's heart warmed to find his early friend in possession of so delightful a residence, and of an estate, as the landlord assured him with a nod and a wink, fully adequate to maintain and add to his dignity. Nothing was more natural than that the traveller should suspend a journey which there was nothing to render hurried to pay a visit to an old friend under such agreeable circumstances.

The fresh horses, therefore, had only the brief task of conveying the General's travelling-carriage to Woodville Castle. A porter admitted them at a modern Gothic lodge, built in that style, to correspond with the castle itself, and at the same time rang a bell to give warning of the approach of visitors. Apparently the sound of the bell had suspended the separation of the company, bent on the various amusements of the morning, for, on entering the court of the chateau, several young men were lounging about in their sporting-dresses, looking at and criticising the dogs, which the keepers held in readiness to attend their pastime. As General Browne alighted, the young lord came to the gate of the hall, and for an instant gazed as at a stranger upon the countenance of his friend, on which war, with its fatigues and its wounds, had made a great alteration. But the uncertainty lasted no longer than till the visitor had spoken, and the hearty greeting which followed was such as can only be exchanged betwixt those who have passed together the merry days of careless boyhood or early youth.

" If I could have formed a wish, my dear Browne," said Lord Woodville, " it would have been to have you here, of all men, upon this occasion, which my friends are good enough to hold as a sort of holiday. Do not think you have been unwatched during the years you have been absent from us. I have traced you through your dangers, your triumphs, your misfortunes, and was delighted to see that, whether in victory or defeat, the name of my old friend was always distinguished with applause."

The General made a suitable reply, and congratulated his friend on his new dignities, and the possession of a place and domain so beautiful.

" Nay, you have seen nothing of it as yet," said Lord Woodville, " and I trust you do not mean to leave us till you are better acquainted with it. It is true, I confess, that my present party is pretty large, and the old house, like other places of the kind, does not possess so much accommodation as the extent of the outward walls appears to promise. But we can give you a comfortable old-fashioned room, and I venture to suppose that your campaigns have taught you to be glad of worse quarters."

The General shrugged his shoulders and laughed. " I presume," he said, " the worse apartment in your chateau is considerably superior to the old tobacco-cask in which I was fain to take up my night's lodging when I was in the bush, as the Virginians call it, with the light corps. There I lay, like Diogenes himself, so delighted with my covering from the elements that I made a vain attempt to have it rolled on to my next quarters ; but my commander for the time would give way to no such luxurious provision, and I took farewell of my beloved cask with tears in my eyes."

" Well, then, since you do not fear your quarters," said Lord Woodville, " you will stay with me a week at least. Of guns, dogs, fishing-rods, flies, and means of sport by sea and land, we have enough and to spare ; you cannot pitch on an amusement, but we will find the means of pursuing it. But if you prefer the gun and pointers, I will go with you myself, and see whether you have mended your shooting since you have been amongst the Indians of the back settlements."

The General gladly accepted his friendly host's proposal in all its points. After a morning of manly exercise, the company met at dinner, where it was the delight of Lord Woodville to conduce to the display of the high properties of his recovered friend, so as to recommend him to his guests, most of whom were persons of distinction. He led General Browne to speak of the scenes he had witnessed ; and as every word marked alike the brave officer and the sensible man, who retained possession of his cool judgment under the most imminent dangers, the company looked upon the soldier with general respect, as on one who had proved himself possessed of an uncommon portion of personal courage—that attribute, of all others, of which everybody desires to be thought possessed.

The day at Woodville Castle ended as usual in such mansions. The hospitality stopped within the limits of good order ; music, in which the young lord was a proficient, succeeded to the circulation of the bottle ; cards and billiards, for those who preferred such amusements, were in readiness ; but the exercise of the morning required early hours, and not long after eleven o'clock the guests began to retire to their several apartments.

The young lord himself conducted his friend, General Browne, to the chamber destined for him, which answered the description he had given of it, being comfortable, but old-fashioned. The bed was of the massive form used in the end of the 17th century, and the curtains of faded silk, heavily trimmed with tarnished gold. But then the sheets, pillows and blankets looked delightful to the campaigner, when he thought of his " mansion, the cask." There was an air of gloom in the tapestry hangings which, with their worn-out graces, curtained the walls of the little chamber, and gently undulated as the autumnal breeze found its way through the ancient lattice-window, which pattered and whistled as the air gained

588   SIR WALTER SCOTT

entrance. The toilet, too, with its mirror, turbaned, after the
manner of the beginning of the century, with a coiffure of
murrey-coloured silk, and its hundred strange-shaped boxes,
providing for arrangements which had been obsolete for more
than fifty years, had an antique, and in so far a melancholy
aspect. But nothing could blaze more brightly and cheerfully
than the two large wax candles ; or if aught could rival them,
it was the flaming, bickering fagots in the chimney, that sent
at once their gleam and their warmth through the snug apartment, which, notwithstanding the general antiquity of its
appearance, was not wanting in the least convenience that
modern habits rendered either necessary or desirable.

"This is an old-fashioned sleeping-apartment, General,"
said the young lord, "but I hope you find nothing that makes
you envy your old tobacco-cask."

"I am not particular respecting my lodgings," replied the
General ; "yet were I to make any choice, I would prefer this
chamber by many degrees to the gayer and more modern
rooms of your family mansion. Believe me, that when I unite
its modern air of comfort with its venerable antiquity, and
recollect that it is your lordship's property, I shall feel in better
quarters here than if I were in the best hotel London could
afford."

"I trust—I have no doubt—that you will find yourself as
comfortable as I wish you, my dear General," said the young
nobleman ; and once more bidding his guest good-night, he
shook him by the hand and withdrew.

The General once more looked round him, and internally
congratulating himself on his return to peaceful life, the com-
forts of which were endeared by the recollection of the hardships and dangers he had lately sustained, undressed himself,
and prepared for a luxurious night's rest.

Here, contrary to the custom of this species of tale, we leave
the General in possession of his apartment until the next morning.

The company assembled for breakfast at an early hour, but
without the appearance of General Browne, who seemed the
guest that Lord Woodville was desirous of honouring above all
whom his hospitality had assembled around him. He more
than once expressed surprise at the General's absence, and at
length sent a servant to make inquiry after him. The man
brought back information that General Browne had been
walking abroad since an early hour of the morning, in defiance
of the weather, which was misty and ungenial.

"The custom of a soldier," said the young nobleman to his friends ; "many of them acquire habitual vigilance, and cannot sleep after the early hour at which their duty usually commands them to be alert."

Yet the explanation which Lord Woodville thus offered to the company seemed hardly satisfactory to his own mind, and it was in a fit of silence and abstraction that he awaited the return of the General. It took place near an hour after the breakfast bell had rung. He looked fatigued and feverish. His hair, the powdering and arrangement of which was at this time one of the most important occupations of a man's whole day, and marked his fashion as much as, in the present time, the tying of a cravat, or the want of one, was dishevelled, uncurled, void of powder, and dank with dew. His clothes were huddled on with a careless negligence remarkable in a military man, whose real or supposed duties are usually held to include some attention to the toilet ; and his looks were haggard and ghastly in a peculiar degree.

"So you have stolen a march upon us this morning, my dear General," said Lord Woodville ; " or you have not found your bed so much to your mind as I had hoped and you seemed to expect. How did you rest last night ? "

" Oh, excellently well—remarkably well—never better in my life ! " said General Browne rapidly, and yet with an air of embarrassment which was obvious to his friend. He then hastily swallowed a cup of tea, and, neglecting or refusing whatever else he was offered, seemed to fall into a fit of abstraction.

" You will take the gun to-day, General ? " said his friend and host, but had to repeat the question twice ere he received the abrupt answer, " No, my lord ; I am sorry I cannot have the honour of spending another day with your lordship ; my post-horses are ordered, and will be here directly."

All who were present showed surprise, and Lord Woodville immediately replied, " Post-horses, my good friend ! What can you possibly want with them, when you promised to stay with me quietly for at least a week ? "

" I believe," said the General, obviously much embarrassed, " that I might, in the pleasure of my first meeting with your lordship, have said something about stopping here a few days ; but I have since found it altogether impossible."

" That is very extraordinary," answered the young nobleman. " You seemed quite disengaged yesterday, and you cannot have had a summons to-day, for our post has not come up from the town, and therefore you cannot have received any letters."

General Browne, without giving any further explanation, muttered something of indispensable business, and insisted on the absolute necessity of his departure in a manner which silenced all opposition on the part of his host, who saw that his resolution was taken, and forbore all further importunity.

" At least, however," he said, " permit me, my dear Browne, since go you will or must, to show you the view from the terrace, which the mist, that is now rising, will soon display."

He threw open a sash-window and stepped down upon the terrace as he spoke. The General followed him mechanically, but seemed little to attend to what his host was saying, as, looking across an extended and rich prospect, he pointed out the different objects worthy of observation. Thus they moved on till Lord Woodville had attained his purpose of drawing his guest entirely apart from the rest of the company, when, turning round upon him with an air of great solemnity, he addressed him thus :

" Richard Browne, my old and very dear friend, we are now alone. Let me conjure you to answer me upon the word of a friend and the honour of a soldier. How did you in reality rest during last night ? "

" Most wretchedly indeed, my lord," answered the General, in the same tone of solemnity ; " so miserably, that I would not run the risk of such a second night, not only for all the lands belonging to this castle, but for all the country which I see from this elevated point of view."

" This is most extraordinary," said the young lord, as if speaking to himself ; " then there must be something in the reports concerning that apartment." Again turning to the General, he said, " For God's sake, my dear friend, be candid with me and let me know the disagreeable particulars which have befallen you under a roof where, with consent of the owner, you should have met nothing save comfort."

The General seemed distressed by this appeal, and paused a moment before he replied. " My dear lord," he at length said, " what happened to me last night is of a nature so peculiar and so unpleasant, that I could hardly bring myself to detail it even to your lordship, were it not that, independent of my wish to gratify any request of yours, I think that sincerity on my part may lead to some explanation about a circumstance equally painful and mysterious. To others, the communication I am about to make might place me in the light of a weak-minded, superstitious fool, who suffered his own imagination to delude and bewilder him ; but you have known me in childhood and youth, and will not suspect me of having adopted in manhood the feelings and frailties from which my early years were free." Here he paused, and his friend replied :

" Do not doubt my perfect confidence in the truth of your communication, however strange it may be," replied Lord Woodville ; " I know your firmness of disposition too well to suspect you could be made the object of imposition, and am aware that your honour and your friendship will equally deter you from exaggerating whatever you may have witnessed."

" Well, then," said the General, " I will proceed with my story as well as I can, relying upon your candour, and yet distinctly feeling that I would rather face a battery than recall to my mind the odious recollections of last night."

He paused a second time, and then perceiving that Lord Woodville remained silent and in an attitude of attention, he commenced, though not without obvious reluctance, the history of his night adventures in the Tapestried Chamber.

" I undressed and went to bed, so soon as your lordship left me yesterday evening ; but the wood in the chimney, which nearly fronted my bed, blazed brightly and cheerfully, and, aided by a hundred exciting recollections of my childhood and youth, which had been recalled by the unexpected pleasure of meeting your lordship, prevented me from falling immediately asleep. I ought, however, to say that these reflections were all of a pleasant and agreeable kind, grounded on a sense of having for a time exchanged the labour, fatigues and dangers of my profession for the enjoyments of a peaceful life, and the reunion of those friendly and affectionate ties which I had torn asunder at the rude summons of war.

" While such pleasing reflections were stealing over my mind, and gradually lulling me to slumber, I was suddenly aroused by a sound like that of the rustling of a silken gown and the tapping of a pair of high-heeled shoes, as if a woman were walking in the apartment. Ere I could draw the curtain to see what the matter was, the figure of a little woman passed between the bed and the fire. The back of this form was turned to me, and I could observe, from the shoulders and neck, it was that of an old woman, whose dress was an old-fashioned gown, which,

I think, ladies call a sacque—that is, a sort of robe completely
loose in the body, but gathered into broad plaits upon the
neck and shoulders, which fall down to the ground, and terminate in a species of train.

" I thought the intrusion singular enough, but never harboured for a moment the idea that what I saw was anything
more than the mortal form of some old woman about the establishment, who had a fancy to dress like her grandmother, and
who, having perhaps, as your lordship mentioned that you
were rather straitened for room, been dislodged from her chamber for my accommodation, had forgotten the circumstance
and returned by twelve to her old haunt. Under this persuasion
I moved myself in bed and coughed a little, to make the intruder sensible of my being in possession of the premises. She
turned slowly round, but, gracious Heaven ! my lord, what a
countenance did she display to me ! There was no longer
any question what she was, or any thought of her being a living
being. Upon a face which wore the fixed features of a corpse
were imprinted the traces of the vilest and most hideous passions
which had animated her while she lived. The body of some
atrocious criminal seemed to have been given up from the
grave, and the soul restored from the penal fire, in order to form,
for a space, an union with the ancient accomplice of its guilt.
I started up in bed, and sat upright, supporting myself on my
palms, as I gazed on this horrible spectre. The hag made, as
it seemed, a single and swift stride to the bed where I lay, and
squatted herself down upon it, in precisely the same attitude
which I had assumed in the extremity of horror, advancing her
diabolical countenance within half a yard of mine, with a grin
which seemed to intimate the malice and the derision of an
incarnate fiend."

Here General Browne stopped, and wiped from his brow the
cold perspiration with which the recollection of his horrible
vision had covered it.

" My lord," he said, " I am no coward. I have been in all
the mortal dangers incidental to my profession, and I may truly
boast that no man ever knew Richard Browne dishonour the
sword he wears ; but in these horrible circumstances, under the
eyes, and, as it seemed, almost in the grasp, of an incarnation
of an evil spirit, all firmness forsook me, all manhood melted
from me like wax in the furnace, and I felt my hair individually
bristle. The current of my life-blood ceased to flow, and I sank
back in a swoon, as very a victim to panic terror as ever was a

village girl or a child of ten years old. How long I lay in this condition I cannot pretend to guess.

" But I was roused by the castle clock striking one, so loud that it seemed as if it were in the very room. It was some time before I dared open my eyes, lest they should again encounter the horrible spectacle. When, however, I summoned courage to look up, she was no longer visible. My first idea was to pull my bell, wake the servants, and remove to a garret or a hay-loft, to be ensured against a second visitation. Nay, I will confess the truth, that my resolution was altered, not by the shame of exposing myself, but by the fear that, as the bell-cord hung by the chimney, I might, in making my way to it, be again crossed by the fiendish hag, who, I figured to myself, might be still lurking about some corner of the apartment.

" I will not pretend to describe what hot and cold fever-fits tormented me for the rest of the night, through broken sleep, weary vigils, and that dubious state which forms the neutral ground between them. An hundred terrible objects appeared to haunt me ; but there was the great difference betwixt the vision which I have described and those which followed, that I knew the last to be deceptions of my own fancy and over-excited nerves.

" Day at last appeared, and I rose from my bed ill in health and humiliated in mind. I was ashamed of myself as a man and a soldier, and still more so at feeling my own extreme desire to escape from the haunted apartment, which, however, conquered all other considerations ; so that, huddling on my clothes with the most careless haste, I made my escape from your lordship's mansion, to seek in the open air some relief to my nervous system, shaken as it was by this horrible encounter with a visitant, for such I must believe her, from the other world. Your lordship has now heard the cause of my discomposure, and of my sudden desire to leave your hospitable castle. In other places I trust we may often meet ; but God protect me from ever spending a second night under that roof ! "

Strange as the General's tale was, he spoke with such a deep air of conviction, that it cut short all the usual commentaries which are made on such stories. Lord Woodville never once asked him if he was sure he did not dream of the apparition, or suggested any of the possibilities by which it is fashionable to explain supernatural appearances, as wild vagaries of the fancy or deceptions of the optic nerves. On the contrary, he seemed deeply impressed with the truth and reality of what he had heard ; and, after a considerable pause, regretted, with much appearance of sincerity, that his early friend should in his house have suffered so severely.

" I am the more sorry for your pain, my dear Browne," he continued, " that it is the unhappy, though most unexpected, result of an experiment of my own. You must know that, for my father and grandfather's time, at least, the apartment which was assigned to you last night had been shut on account of reports that it was disturbed by supernatural sights and noises. When I came, a few weeks since, into possession of the estate, I thought the accommodation which the castle afforded for my friends was not extensive enough to permit the inhabitants of the invisible world to retain possession of a comfortable sleeping-apartment. I therefore caused the Tapestried Chamber, as we call it, to be opened, and, without destroying its air of antiquity, I had such new articles of furniture placed in it as became the modern times. Yet, as the opinion that the room was haunted very strongly prevailed among the domestics, and was also known in the neighbourhood and to many of my friends, I feared some prejudice might be entertained by the first occu-pant of the Tapestried Chamber, which might tend to revive the evil report which it had laboured under, and so disappoint my purpose of rendering it a useful part of the house.   I must confess, my dear Browne, that your arrival yesterday, agreeable to me for a thousand reasons besides, seemed the most favourable opportunity of removing the unpleasant rumours which attached to the room, since your courage was indubitable, and your mind free of any preoccupation on the subject. I could not, therefore, have chosen a more fitting subject for my experiment."

" Upon my life," said General Browne, somewhat hastily, " I am infinitely obliged to your lordship—very particularly indebted indeed. I am likely to remember for some time the consequences of the experiment, as your lordship is pleased to call it."

" Nay, now you are unjust, my dear friend," said Lord Woodville. " You have only to reflect for a single moment, in order to be convinced that I could not augur the possibility of the pain to which you have been so unhappily exposed. I was yesterday morning a complete sceptic on the subject of super-natural appearances. Nay, I am sure that, had I told you what was said about that room, those very reports would have in-duced you, by your own choice, to select it for your accommo-dation. It was my misfortune, perhaps my error, but really

I started up in bed, and sat upright, supporting myself
on my palms, as I gazed on this horrible spectre.

cannot be termed my fault, that you have been afflicted so strangely:"

"Strangely indeed!" said the General, resuming his good temper ; "and I acknowledge that I have no right to be offended with your lordship for treating me like what I used to think myself, a man of some firmness and courage. But I see my post-horses are arrived, and I must not detain your lordship from your amusement."

"Nay, my old friend," said Lord Woodville, "since you cannot stay with us another day, which, indeed, I can no longer urge, give me at least half an hour more. You used to love pictures, and I have a gallery of portraits, some of them by Vandyke, representing ancestry to whom this property and castle formerly belonged. I think that several of them will strike you as possessing merit."

General Browne accepted the invitation, though somewhat unwillingly. It was evident he was not to breathe freely or at ease till he left Woodville Castle far behind him. He could not refuse his friend's invitation, however ; and the less so, that he was a little ashamed of the peevishness which he had displayed towards his well-meaning entertainer.

The General, therefore, followed Lord Woodville through several rooms, into a long gallery hung with pictures, which the latter pointed out to his guest, telling the names, and giving some account of the personages whose portraits presented themselves in progression. General Browne was but little interested in the details which these accounts conveyed to him. They were, indeed, of the kind which are usually found in an old family gallery. Here was a cavalier who had ruined the estate in the royal cause ; there a fine lady who had reinstated it by contracting a match with a wealthy Roundhead. There hung a gallant who had been in danger for corresponding with the exiled court at St. Germain's ; here one who had taken arms for William at the Revolution ; and there a third that had thrown his weight alternately into the scale of Whig and Tory.

While Lord Woodville was cramming these words into his guest's ear, "against the stomach of his sense," they gained the middle of the gallery, when he beheld General Browne suddenly start, and assume an attitude of the utmost surprise, not unmixed with fear, as his eyes were caught and suddenly riveted by a portrait of an old lady in a sacque, the fashionable dress of the end of the 17th century.

"There she is!" he exclaimed—"there she is, in form and

features, though inferior in demoniac expression to the accursed hag who visited me last night."

"If that be the case," said the young nobleman, "there can remain no longer any doubt of the horrible reality of your apparition.   That is the picture of a wretched ancestress of mine, of whose crimes a black and fearful catalogue is recorded in a family history in my charter-chest.   The recital of them would be too horrible ; it is enough to say, that in yon fatal apartment incest and unnatural murder were committed.   I will restore it to the solitude to which the better judgment of those who preceded me had consigned it ; and never shall any one, so long as I can prevent it, be exposed to a repetition of the supernatural horrors which could shake such courage as yours."

Thus the friends, who had met with such glee, parted in a very different mood—Lord Woodville to command the Tapestried Chamber to be unmantled and the door built up ; and General Browne to seek in some less beautiful country, and with some less dignified friend, forgetfulness of the painful night which he had passed in Woodville Castle.

THE FRONTIER GUARDS

"WHAT a charming little house ! " said Brinton, as he was walking in from a round of golf at Ellesborough with Lander.

" Yes, from the outside," replied Lander.

" What's the matter with the inside—Eozoic plumbing ? "

" No ; the ' usual offices ' are neat, if not gaudy. Spengler would probably describe them as ' contemporary with the death of Lincoln,' but it's not that—it's haunted."

" Is it, by jove ! " said Brinton, gazing up at it. " Fancy such a dear little Queen Anne piece having such a nasty reputation. I see it's unoccupied."

" It usually is," replied Lander.

" Tell me about it."

" During dinner I will. But you seem to find something of interest about those windows on the second floor." Brinton gazed up for a moment or two longer, and then started to walk back in silence beside his host.

In a few minutes they reached Lander's cottage—it was rather more pretentious than that—an engaging two-storeyed structure added to and modernised from time to time, formerly known as " The Old Vicarage," and rechristened " Laymer's." Black and white and creeper-lined, with a trim little garden of rose-trees and mellow turf, two fine limes, and a great yew, impenetrable and secret. This little garden melted into an arable expanse, and there was a lovely view over to some high Chiltern spurs. The whole place just suited Lander, who was—or it might be more accurate to say, wanted to be—a novelist ; a commonplace and ill-advised ambition, but he had money of his own and could afford to wait.

James Brinton, his guest for a week and a very old friend,

occupied himself with a picture gallery in Mayfair. A very small gallery—one rather small room, to be exact—but he had admirable taste and made it pay.

Two hours later they sat down to dinner. " Now then," said Brinton, as Mrs. Dunkley brought in the soup, " tell me about that house."

" Well," replied Lander, " I have had, as you know, much more experience of such places than most people, and I consider Pailton the worst or the best specimen I have heard or read of or experienced. For one thing, it is a ' killer.' The majority of haunted houses are harmless, the peculiar energy they have absorbed and radiate forth is not hostile to life. But in others the radiation is malignant and fatal. Pailton has been rented five times in the last twelve years ; in each case the tenancy has been marked by a violent death within its walls. For my part, I have no two opinions concerning the morality of letting it at all. It should be razed to the ground."

" How long do its occupants stick it out as a rule ? "

" Six weeks is the record, and that was made by some people called Pendexter. That was three years ago. I knew Pendexter *père*, and he was a courageous and determined person. His daughter was hurled down the stairs one night and killed, and I shall never forget the mingled fury and grief with which he told me about it. Previous to that he had detected eighteen different examples of psychic action—appearances and sounds —several definitely malignant. The family had not enjoyed one single day of freedom from abnormal phenomena."

" How long since it was last occupied ? " asked Brinton.

" It has been empty for a year, and I am inclined to think it will remain so. Any one who comes down to look at it is given a pretty straight tip by one or other of us to keep away."

" Does it affect you violently ? "

" I have never set foot in it."

" What ? You, of all people ! "

" My dear Jim, just for that very reason. When I first discovered I was psychic I felt flattered and anxious to experience all I could. I soon changed my mind. I found I experienced quite enough without any need for *making* opportunities. I do to this day. Several times I have had a visitor in the study here after dinner, an uninvited guest. And it has always been so. I have many times heard and seen things which could not be explained in places with perfectly clean bills of psychic health. And one never gets quite used to it. Terror may pass, but some distress of mind is invariable. Any person gifted or afflicted like myself will tell you the same. It seems to me sometimes as if I actually assist in evoking and materialising these appearances, that I help to establish a connection between them and the place I inhabit, that I am a most unpleasant kind of lightning conductor."

"Is there any possible explanation for that?"

"Well, I have formed one, but it would take rather a long time to explain, and may be quite fallacious. Anyhow, there has never been any need for me to visit such places as Pailton, and I keep away from them if I can."

"Would you very much object to going in for a minute or two?"

"Why?"

"Well, I have been bothered all my life about this business of ghosts. I have never seen one ; in a sense I ' don't believe in them,' yet I am convinced you have known many. It is a maddening dualism of mind. I feel if I could just once come in contact with something of the kind I should feel a sense of enormous relief."

"And you'd like me to conduct you over Pailton?"

"Not if it would really upset you."

"It would be at your own risk," said Lander, smiling.

"I'll risk it !"

"You mustn't imagine that you can go into a disturbed ·spot such as this and expect to see about ten ghosts in as many minutes. Even in the case of such a busy hive as Pailton there are many quiet periods, and some people simply cannot ' see ghosts.' The odds are very much against your desire being granted, though, if you *are* psychic, the atmosphere of the place would affect you at once."

"How?"

"Well, you've often heard of people who know by some obscure but infallible instinct that there's a cat in the room. Just so. However, I'll certainly give you the chance. It won't seriously disturb me. I can get the key in the morning from the woman who looks after it, though I need hardly say she doesn't sleep there. There is no need for a caretaker. It was broken into once, but the burglar was found dead in the dining-room, and since then the crooks have given it a wide berth."

"It really is dangerous, then?"

"Beginning to feel a bit prudent?"

"No, I shall feel safe with you."

" Very well then. After coming back from golf we'll pay it a visit. It will be dark by five, and we'll make the excursion about six. The chances of gratifying your curiosity will be better after dark. I'd better tell you something else. I never quite know how these places are going to affect me. Before now, I have gone off into a kind of trance and been decidedly weird, my dear Jim. My sense of time and space becomes distorted, though for your assurance I may say," he added smiling, " I am never dangerous when in this condition. Furthermore, you must be prepared to make acquaintance with a mode of existence in which the ordinary laws of existence which you have always known abdicate themselves. Bierce called his famous book of ghost stories, *Can These Things Be?* Assuredly they can. Now I'm sounding pompous and pontifical, but some such warning is necessary. When I touch that front door to-morrow I may become in a sense a stranger to you ; once inside we shall cross a frontier into a region with its own laws of time and space, and where the seemingly impossible can happen. . . . Do you understand what I mean and still want to go ? "

" Yes," replied Brinton, " to all your questions."

" Very well then," said Lander, " I will now get out the chess-men and discover a complete answer to Reti's opening which you sprang on me last night ; so you shall have the white pieces."

November 21st was a lazy, drowsy, cloudless day, starting with a sharp ground frost which, thawing unresistingly as the sun climbed, made the tees at Ellesborough like tiny slides. In consequence, neither Brinton nor Lander played very good golf. This upset Brinton not at all, for he was thinking much more of that which was beginning to impress him as a possible ordeal, the crossing of the threshold of Pailton a few hours later. As they finished their second round a mist, spreading like a gigantic spider's web, was beginning to raise the level of the Buckingham-shire fields. As they walked homewards it climbed with them, keeping pace with them like a dog ; sometimes hurrying ahead, then dropping back, but always with them.

It was exactly five o'clock as they reached Laymer's. Tea was ready. " Do you still want to go, Jim ? " asked Lander abruptly.

" Sure, Bo ! " replied Brinton lightly.

" Here's the key," said Lander, smiling, " the Open Sesame to the Chamber of Horrors. The electric light is turned off, so all the light we shall have will be produced by my torch. One last word of advice—if you want to get the best chance of a thrill, try to keep your mind quite empty—don't talk as I personally conduct this tour. Concentrate on *not* concentrating."

"I understand what you mean," said Brinton.

"Well, then, let's get a move on," said Lander.

An idea suddenly occurred to Brinton. "How will you be able to show me over it if you've never been inside it?"

"You needn't worry about that," replied Lander.

The fog was thick by now, and they wavered slightly as they groped their way down the lane, compressed by high hedges, which led to Pailton. When they reached it, Brinton's eyes turned up to observe the windows on the second floor. And then Lander stepped forward and placed the key in the lock.

As the door swung open the fog, which seemed to have been crouching at his heels, leapt forward and entered with him and inundated the passage down which he moved. The moment he was inside, something advanced to meet him. He opened a door on the left of the passage and flashed his torch round it. The fog was in there too. Jim, he could feel, was at this elbow.

"This is where they found the burglar—it's the dining-room."

His voice was not quite under control. "Quite a pleasant room, smells a bit frowsty." The little beam wandered from chair to desk, settling for a moment here and there. Then he shut the door and stepped along the passage till the little beam revealed a flight of stairs which he began to climb. He still heard Brinton's steps coming up behind him. Up on the first floor he opened another door. "This is the drawing-room," he said. "The Proctors' cook was found dead here in 1921." Round swung the tiny beam, fastening on chairs, tables, desks, curtains. He shut the door and began to climb another flight of stairs. He could hear Jim's feet pattering up behind him. On the second floor he opened still another door. "This, my dear Jim, is the nasty one; it was from here Amy Pendexter fell and broke her neck."

His voice had risen slightly, and he was speaking quickly. Once again he flashed his torch over chairs, tables, curtains, and ahead.

"Well, Jim, do you get any reaction? Do you? You can speak now." As there was no answer, he turned, and swung the beam of his torch on to the person just behind him. But it wasn't Brinton who was standing at his elbow. . . .

" What's the matter, Willie ? " asked Brinton, "can't you find the keyhole ? " The figure in front of him remained motionless.

" Can't you find the keyhole ? " asked Brinton more urgently.

As the figure still remained motionless, Jim Brinton lit a match and peered forward. . . . And then he reeled back.

" Who, in God's name, are you ? " he cried.

THE RED ROOM

"I CAN assure you," said I, " that it will take a very tangible ghost to frighten me." And I stood up before the fire with my glass in my hand.

" It is your own choosing," said the man with the withered arm, and glanced at me askance.

" Eight-and-twenty years," said I, " I have lived, and never a ghost have I seen as yet."

The old woman sat staring hard into the fire, her pale eyes wide open. " Ay," she broke in ; " and eight-and-twenty years you have lived and never seen the likes of this house, I reckon. There's a many things to see, when one's still but eight-and-twenty." She swayed her head slowly from side to side. " A many things to see and sorrow for."

I half-suspected the old people were trying to enhance the spiritual terrors of their house by their droning insistence. I put down my empty glass on the table and looked about the room, and caught a glimpse of myself, abbreviated and broadened to an impossible sturdiness, in the queer old mirror at the end of the room. " Well," I said, " if I see anything to-night, I shall be so much the wiser. For I come to the business with an open mind."

" It's your own choosing," said the man with the withered arm once more.

I heard the sound of a stick and a shambling step on the flags in the passage outside, and the door creaked on its hinges as a second old man entered, more bent, more wrinkled, more aged even than the first. He supported himself by a single crutch, his eyes were covered by a shade, and his lower lip, half-averted, hung pale and pink from his decaying yellow teeth. He made straight for an arm-chair on the opposite side of the table, sat down clumsily, and began to cough. The man with the withered arm gave this newcomer a short glance of positive dislike ; the old woman took no notice of his arrival, but remained with her eyes fixed steadily on the fire.

" I said—it's your own choosing," said the man with the withered arm, when the coughing had ceased for a while.

" It's my own choosing," I answered.

The man with the shade became aware of my presence for the first time, and threw his head back for a moment and sideways, to see me. I caught a momentary glimpse of his eyes, small and bright and inflamed. Then he began to cough and splutter again.

" Why don't you drink ? " said the man with the withered arm, pushing the beer towards him. The man with the shade poured out a glassful with a shaky arm that splashed half as much again on the deal table. A monstrous shadow of him crouched upon the wall and mocked his action as he poured and drank. I must confess I had scarce expected these grotesque custodians. There is to my mind something inhuman in senility, something crouching and atavistic ; the human qualities seem to drop from old people insensibly day by day. The three of them made me feel uncomfortable, with their gaunt silences, their bent carriage, their evident unfriendliness to me and to one another.

" If," said I, " you will show me to this haunted room of yours, I will make myself comfortable there."

The old man with the cough jerked his head back so suddenly that it startled me, and shot another glance of his red eyes at me from under the shade ; but no one answered me. I waited a minute, glancing from one to the other.

" If," I said a little louder, " if you will show me to this haunted room of yours, I will relieve you from the task of entertaining me."

" There's a candle on the slab outside the door," said the man with the withered arm, looking at my feet as he addressed me. " But if you go to the red room to-night——"

(" This night of all nights ! " said the old woman.)

" You go alone."

" Very well," I answered. " And which way do I go ? "

" You go along the passage for a bit," said he, " until you come to a door, and through that is a spiral staircase, and half way up that is a landing and another door covered with baize.

Go through that and down the long corridor to the end, and the red room is on your left up the steps."

" Have I got that right ? " I said, and repeated his directions. He corrected me in one particular.

" And are you really going ? " said the man with the shade, looking at me again for the third time, with that queer, unnatural tilting of the face.

(" This night of all nights ! " said the old woman.)

" It is what I came for," I said, and moved towards the door. As I did so, the old man with the shade rose and staggered round the table, so as to be closer to the others and to the fire. At the door I turned and looked at them, and saw they were all close together, dark against the firelight, staring at me over their shoulders, with an intent expression on their ancient faces.

" Good-night," I said, setting the door open.

" It's your own choosing," said the man with the withered arm.

I left the door wide open until the candle was well alight, and then I shut them in and walked down the chilly, echoing passage.

I must confess that the oddness of these three old pensioners in whose charge her ladyship had left the castle, and the deep-toned, old-fashioned furniture of the housekeeper's room in which they foregathered, affected me in spite of my efforts to keep myself at a matter-of-fact phase. They seemed to belong to another age, an older age, an age when things spiritual were different from this of ours, less certain ; an age when omens and witches were credible, and ghosts beyond denying. Their very existence was spectral ; the cut of their clothing, fashions born in dead brains. The ornaments and conveniences of the room about them were ghostly—the thoughts of vanished men, which still haunted rather than participated in the world of to-day. But with an effort I sent such thoughts to the right-about. The long, draughty subterranean passage was chilly and dusty, and my candle flared and made the shadows cower and quiver. The echoes rang up and down the spiral staircase, and a shadow came sweeping up after me, and one fled before me into the darkness overhead. I came to the landing and stopped there for a moment, listening to a rustling that I fancied I heard ; then, satisfied of the absolute silence, I pushed open the baize-covered door and stood in the corridor.

The effect was scarcely what I expected, for the moonlight, coming in by the great window on the grand staircase, picked out everything in vivid black shadow or silvery illumination. Everything was in its place ; the house might have been deserted on the yesterday instead of eighteen months ago. There were candles in the sockets of the sconces, and whatever dust had gathered on the carpets or upon the polished flooring was distributed so evenly as to be invisible in the moonlight. I was about to advance, and stopped abruptly. A bronze group stood upon the landing, hidden from me by the corner of the wall, but its shadow fell with marvellous distinctness upon the white panelling and gave me the impression of some one crouching to waylay me. I stood rigid for half a minute perhaps. Then, with my hand in the pocket that held my revolver, I advanced, only to discover a Ganymede and Eagle glistening in the moonlight. That incident for a time restored my nerve, and a porcelain Chinaman on a buhl table, whose head rocked silently as I passed him, scarcely startled me.

The door of the red room and the steps up to it were in a shadowy corner. I moved my candle from side to side, in order to see clearly the nature of the recess in which I stood before opening the door. Here it was, thought I, that my predecessor was found, and the memory of that story gave me a sudden twinge of apprehension, I glanced over my shoulder at the Ganymede in the moonlight, and opened the door of the red room rather hastily, with my face half-turned to the pallid silence of the landing.

I entered, closed the door behind me at once, turned the key I found in the lock within, and stood with the candle held aloft, surveying the scene of my vigil, the great red room of Lorraine Castle, in which the young duke had died. Or, rather, in which he had begun his dying, for he had opened the door and fallen headlong down the steps I had just ascended. That had been the end of his vigil, of his gallant attempt to conquer the ghostly tradition of the place, and never, I thought, had apoplexy better served the ends of superstition. And there were other and older stories that clung to the room, back to the half-credible beginning of it all, the tale of a timid wife and the tragic end that came to her husband's jest of frightening her. And looking around that large sombre room, with its shadowy window bays, its recesses and alcoves, one could well understand the legends that had sprouted in its black corners, its germinating darkness. My candle was a little tongue of light in its vastness, that failed to pierce the opposite end of the room, and left an ocean of mystery and suggestion beyond its island of light.

I resolved to make a systematic examination of the place at once, and dispel the fanciful suggestions of its obscurity before they obtained a hold upon me. After satisfying myself of the fastening of the door, I began to walk about the room, peering round each article of furniture, tucking up the valances of the bed, and opening its curtains wide. I pulled up the blinds and examined the fastenings of the several windows before closing the shutters, leant forward and looked up the blackness of the wide chimney, and tapped the dark oak panelling for any secret opening. There were two big mirrors in the room, each with a pair of sconces bearing candles, and on the mantelshelf, too, were more candles in china candlesticks. All these I lit one after the other. The fire was laid, an unexpected consideration from the old housekeeper—and I lit it, to keep down any disposition to shiver, and when it was burning well, I stood round with my back to it and regarded the room again. I had pulled up a chintz-covered arm-chair and a table, to form a kind of barricade before me, and this lay my revolver ready to hand. My precise examination had done me good, but I still found the remoter darkness of the place, and its perfect stillness, too stimulating for the imagination. The echoing of the stir and crackling of the fire was no sort of comfort to me. The shadow in the alcove at the end in particular, had that undefinable quality of a presence, that odd suggestion of a lurking, living thing, that comes so easily in silence and solitude. At last, to reassure myself, I walked with a candle into it, and satisfied myself that there was nothing tangible there. I stood that candle upon the floor of the alcove, and left it in that position.

By this time I was in a state of considerable nervous tension, although to my reason there was no adequate cause for the condition. My mind, however, was perfectly clear. I postulated quite unreservedly that nothing supernatural could happen, and to pass the time I began to string some rhymes together, Ingoldsby fashion, of the original legend of the place. A few I spoke aloud, but the echoes were not pleasant. For the same reason I also abandoned, after a time, a conversation with myself upon the impossibility of ghosts and haunting. My mind reverted to the three old and distorted people downstairs, and I tried to keep it upon that topic. The sombre reds and blacks of the room troubled me ; even with seven candles the place was merely dim. The one in the alcove flared in a draught, and the fire-flickering kept the shadows and penumbra perpetually shifting and stirring. Casting about for a remedy, I recalled the candles I had seen in the passage, and, with a slight effort, walked out into the moonlight, carrying a candle and leaving the door open, and presently returned with as many as ten. These I put in various knick-knacks of china with which the room was sparsely adorned, lit and placed where the shadows had lain deepest, some on the floor, some in the window recesses, until at last my seventeen candles were so arranged that not an inch of the room but had the direct light of at least one of them. It occurred to me that when the ghost came, I could warn him not to trip over them. The room was now quite brightly illuminated. There was something very cheery and reassuring in these little streaming flames, and snuffing them gave me an occupation, and afforded a helpful sense of the passage of time.

Even with that, however, the brooding expectation of the vigil weighed heavily upon me. It was after midnight that the candle in the alcove suddenly went out, and the black shadow sprang back to its place there. I did not see the candle go out; I simply turned and saw that the darkness was there, as one might start and see the unexpected presence of a stranger. " By jove ! " said I aloud ; " that draught's a strong one ! " and, taking the matches from the table, I walked across the room in a leisurely manner, to re-light the corner again. My first match would not strike, and as I succeeded with the second, something seemed to blink on the wall before me. I turned my head involuntarily, and saw that the two candles on the little table by the fireplace were extinguished. I rose at once to my feet.

" Odd ! " I said. " Did I do that myself in a flash of absent-mindedness ? "

I walked back, re-lit one, and as I did so, I saw the candle in the right sconce of one of the mirrors wink and go right out, and almost immediately its companion followed it. There was no mistake about it. The flame vanished, as if the wicks had been suddenly nipped between a finger and a thumb, leaving the wick neither glowing nor smoking, but black. While I stood gaping, the candle at the foot of the bed went out, and the shadows seemed to take another step towards me.

" This won't do ! " said I, and first one and then another candle on the mantelshelf followed.

" What's up ? " I cried, with a queer high note getting into my voice somehow. At that the candle on the wardrobe went out, and the one I had re-lit in the alcove followed.

" Steady on ! " I said. " These candles are wanted," speaking

with a half-hysterical facetiousness, and scratching away at a
match the while for the mantel candlesticks. My hands trembled
so much that twice I missed the rough paper of the matchbox.
As the mantel emerged from darkness again, two candles in the
remoter end of the window were eclipsed. But with the same
match I also re-lit the larger mirror candles, and those on the
floor near the doorway, so that for the moment I seemed to gain
on the extinctions. But then in a volley there vanished four
lights at once in different corners of the room, and I struck
another match in quivering haste, and stood hesitating whither
to take it.

As I stood undecided, an invisible hand seemed to sweep out
the candles on the table. With a cry of terror, I dashed at the
alcove, then into the corner, and then into the window, relighting
three, as two more vanished by the fireplace ; then, perceiving
a better way, I dropped the matches on the iron-bound deed-
box in the corner, and caught up the bedroom candlestick.
With this I avoided the delay of striking matches ; but for all
that the steady process of extinction went on, and the shadows
I feared and fought against returned, and crept in upon me,
first a step gained on this side of me and then on that. It was
like a ragged storm-cloud sweeping out the stars. Now and then
one returned for a minute, and was lost again. I was now almost
frantic with the horror of the coming darkness, and my self-
possession deserted me. I leaped panting and dishevelled from
candle to candle, in a vain struggle against that remorseless
advance.

I bruised myself on the thigh against the table, I sent a
chair headlong, I stumbled and fell and whisked the cloth from
the table in my fall. My candle rolled away from me, and I
snatched another as I rose. Abruptly this was blown out, as I
swung it off the table by the wind of my sudden movement, and
immediately the two remaining candles followed. But there was
light still in the room, a red light that staved off the shadows from
me. The fire ! Of course, I could still thrust my candle between
the bars and re-light it !

I turned to where the flames were still dancing between the
glowing coals, and splashing red reflections upon the furniture,
made two steps towards the grate, and incontinently the flames
dwindled and vanished, the glow vanished, the reflections
rushed together and vanished, and as I thrust the candle
between the bars darkness closed upon me like the shutting
of an eye, wrapped about me in a stifling embrace, sealed my

vision, and crushed the last vestiges of reason from my brain. The candle fell from my hand. I flung out my arms in a vain effort to thrust that ponderous blackness away from me, and, lifting up my voice, screamed with all my might—once, twice, thrice. Then I think I must have staggered to my feet. I know I thought suddenly of the moonlit corridor, and, with my head bowed and my arms over my face, made a run for the door.

But I had forgotten the exact position of the door, and struck myself heavily against the corner of the bed. I staggered back, turned, and was either struck or struck myself against some other bulky furniture. I have a vague memory of battering myself thus, to and fro in the darkness, of a cramped struggle, and of my own wild crying as I darted to and fro, of a heavy blow at last upon my forehead, a horrible sensation of falling that lasted an age, of my last frantic effort to keep my footing, and then I remember no more.

I opened my eyes in daylight. My head was roughly bandaged and the man with the withered arm was watching my face. I looked about me, trying to remember what had happened, and for a space I could not recollect. I rolled my eyes into the corner, and saw the old woman, no longer abstracted, pouring out some drops of medicine from a little blue phial into a glass. " Where am I ? " I asked ; " I seem to remember you, and yet I cannot remember who you are."

They told me then, and I heard of the haunted Red Room as one who hears a tale. " We found you at dawn," said he, " and there was blood on your forehead and lips."

It was very slowly I recovered my memory of my experience. " You believe now," said the old man, " that the room is haunted ? " He spoke no longer as one who greets an intruder, but as one who grieves for a broken friend.

" Yes," said I ; " the room is haunted."

" And you have seen it. And we, who have lived here all our lives, have never set eyes upon it. Because we have never dared. . . . Tell us, is it truly the old earl who——"

" No," said I ; " it is not."

" I told you so," said the old lady, with the glass in her hand. " It is his poor young countess who was frightened——"

" It is not," I said. " There is neither ghost of earl nor ghost of countess in that room, there is no ghost there at all ; but worse, far worse——"

" Well ? " they said.

I snatched another candle as I rose.   Abruptly this was blown out.

" The worst of all the things that haunt poor mortal man,"
said I ; " and that is, in all its nakedness—*Fear* ! Fear that will
not have light nor sound, that will not bear with reason, that
deafens and darkens and overwhelms. It followed me through
the corridor, it fought against me in the room——"

I stopped abruptly. There was an interval of silence. My
hand went up to my bandages.

Then the man with the shade sighed and spoke. " That is
it," said he. " I knew that was it. A power of darkness. To put
such a curse upon a woman ! It lurks there always. You can
feel it even in the daytime, even of a bright summer's day,
in the hangings, in the curtains keeping behind you however
you face about. In the dusk it creeps along the corridor and
follows you, so that you dare not turn. There is Fear in that
room of hers—black Fear, and there will be—so long as this
house of sin endures."

THE SPHINX WITHOUT
A SECRET

ONE afternoon I was sitting outside the Café de la Paix, watching the splendour and shabbiness of Parisian life, and wondering over my vermouth at the strange panorama of pride and poverty that was passing before me, when I heard some one call my name. I turned round and saw Lord Murchison. We had not met since we had been at college together, nearly ten years before, so I was delighted to come across him again, and we shook hands warmly. At Oxford we had been great friends. I had liked him immensely, he was so handsome, so high-spirited, and so honourable. We used to say of him that he would be the best of fellows, if he did not always speak the truth, but I think we really admired him all the more for his frankness. I found him a good deal changed. He looked anxious and puzzled, and seemed to be in doubt about something. I felt it could not be modern scepticism, for Murchison was the stoutest of Tories, and believed in the Pentateuch as firmly as he believed in the House of Peers ; so I concluded that it was a woman, and asked him if he was married yet.

" I don't understand women well enough," he answered.

" My dear Gerald," I said, " women are meant to be loved, not to be understood."

" I cannot love where I cannot trust," he replied.

" I believe you have a mystery in your life, Gerald," I exclaimed ; " tell me about it."

" Let us go for a drive," he answered, " it is too crowded here. No, not a yellow carriage, any other colour—there, that dark green one will do " ; and in a few moments we were trotting down the boulevard in the direction of the Madeleine.

" Where shall we go to ? " I said.

" Oh. anywhere you like ! " he answered—" to the restaurant

in the Bois ; we will dine there, and you shall tell me all about
yourself."

" I want to hear about you first," I said. " Tell me your
mystery."

He took from his pocket a little silver-clasped morocco case,
and handed it to me. I opened it. Inside there was the photograph of a woman. She was tall and slight, and strangely
picturesque with her large vague eyes and loosened hair. She
looked like a *clairvoyante*, and was wrapped in rich furs.

" What do you think of that face ? " he said ; " is it truthful ? "

I examined it carefully. It seemed to me the face of some
one who had a secret, but whether that secret was good or evil
I could not say. Its beauty was a beauty moulded out of many
mysteries—the beauty, in fact, which is psychological, not
plastic—and the faint smile that just played across the lips was
far too subtle to be really sweet.

" Well," he cried impatiently, " what do you say ? "

" She is the Gioconda in sables," I answered. " Let me
know all about her."

" Not now," he said ; " after dinner," and began to talk of
other things.

When the waiter brought us our coffee and cigarettes I reminded Gerald of his promise. He rose from his seat, walked
two or three times up and down the room, and, sinking into
an arm-chair, told me the following story :

" One evening," he said, " I was walking down Bond Street
about five o'clock. There was a terrific crush of carriages,
and the traffic was almost stopped. Close to the pavement
was standing a little yellow brougham, which, for some reason
or other, attracted my attention. As I passed by there looked
out from it the face I showed you this afternoon. It fascinated
me immediately. All that night I kept thinking of it, and all
the next day. I wandered up and down that wretched Row,
peering into every carriage, and waiting for the yellow brougham ; but I could not find *ma belle inconnue*, and at last I began
to think she was merely a dream. About a week afterwards I
was dining with Madame de Rastail. Dinner was for eight
o'clock ; but at half-past eight we were still waiting in the
drawing-room. Finally the servant threw open the door, and
announced Lady Alroy. It was the woman I had been looking
for. She came in very slowly, looking like a moonbeam in grey
lace, and, to my intense delight, I was asked to take her in to

dinner. After we had sat down, I remarked quite innocently,
'I think I caught sight of you in Bond Street some time ago,
Lady Alroy.' She grew very pale, and said to me in a low
voice, 'Pray do not talk so loud ; you may be overheard.' I felt
miserable at having made such a bad beginning, and plunged
recklessly into the subject of the French plays. She spoke
very little, always in the same low musical voice, and seemed
as if she was afraid of some one listening. I fell passionately,
stupidly in love, and the indefinable atmosphere of mystery
that surrounded her excited my most ardent curiosity. When
she was going away, which she did very soon after dinner, I
asked her if I might call and see her. She hesitated for a moment,
glanced round to see if any one was near us, and then said,
'Yes ; to-morrow at a quarter to five.' I begged Madame
de Rastail to tell me about her ; but all that I could learn
was that she was a widow with a beautiful house in Park Lane,
and as some scientific bore began a dissertation on widows,
as exemplifying the survival of the matrimonially fittest, I left
and went home.

"The next day I arrived at Park Lane punctual to the
moment, but was told by the butler that Lady Alroy had just
gone out. I went down to the club quite unhappy and very
much puzzled, and after long consideration wrote her a letter,
asking if I might be allowed to try my chance some other afternoon. I had no answer for several days, but at last I got a
little note saying she would be at home on Sunday at four and
with this extraordinary postscript : 'Please do not write to me
here again ; I will explain when I see you.' On Sunday she
received me, and was perfectly charming ; but when I was
going away she begged of me, if I ever had occasion to write
to her again, to address my letter to 'Mrs. Knox, care of Whit-
taker's Library, Green Street.' 'There are reasons,' she said,
'why I cannot receive letters in my own house.'

"All through the season I saw a great deal of her, and the
atmosphere of mystery never left her. Sometimes I thought
she was in the power of some man, but she looked so unap-
proachable that I could not believe it. It was really very difficult
for me to come to any conclusion, for she was like one of those
strange crystals that one sees in museums, which are at one
moment clear, and at another clouded. At last I determined
to ask her to be my wife ; I was sick and tired of the incessant
secrecy that she imposed on all my visits, and on the few letters
I sent her. I wrote to her at the library to ask her if she could

see me the following Monday at six. She answered yes, and I
was in the seventh heaven of delight. I was infatuated with her :
in spite of the mystery, I thought then—in consequence of it,
I see now. No ; it was the woman herself I loved. The mystery
troubled me, maddened me. Why did chance put me in its
track ? ''

" You discovered it, then ? " I cried.

" I fear so," he answered. " You can judge for yourself."

" When Monday came round I went to lunch with my
uncle, and about four o'clock found myself in the Marylebone
Road. My uncle, you know, lives in Regent's Park. I wanted
to get to Piccadilly, and took a short cut through a lot of shabby
little streets. Suddenly I saw in front of me Lady Alroy, deeply
veiled and walking very fast. On coming to the last house in
the street, she went up the steps, took out a latch-key, and let
herself in. ' Here is the mystery,' I said to myself ; and I hurried
on and examined the house. It seemed a sort of place for letting
lodgings. On the doorstep lay her handkerchief which she
had dropped. I picked it up and put it in my pocket. Then I
began to consider what I should do. I came to the conclusion
that I had no right to spy on her, and I drove down to the
club. At six I called to see her. She was lying on a sofa, in a
tea-gown of silver tissue looped up by some strange moonstones
that she always wore. She was looking quite lovely. ' I am so
glad to see you,' she said ; ' I have not been out all day.' I
stared at her in amazement, and pulling the handkerchief out
of my pocket, handed it to her. ' You dropped this in Cumnor
Street this afternoon, Lady Alroy,' I said very calmly. She
looked at me in terror, but made no attempt to take the handkerchief. ' What were you doing there ? ' I asked. ' What right
have you to question me ? ' she answered. ' The right of a
man who loves you,' I replied ; ' I came here to ask you to
be my wife.' She hid her face in her hands, and burst into
floods of tears. ' You must tell me,' I continued. She stood
up, and, looking me straight in the face, said, ' Lord Murchison,
there is nothing to tell you.'—' You went to meet some one,' I
cried ; ' this is your mystery.' She grew dreadfully white,
and said, ' I went to meet no one.'—' Can't you tell the truth ? '
I exclaimed. ' I have told it,' she replied. I was mad, frantic ;
I don't know what I said, but I said terrible things to her. Finally
I rushed out of the house. She wrote me a letter the next day ;
I sent it back unopened, and started for Norway with Alan
Colville. After a month I came back, and the first thing I saw

in the *Morning Post* was the death of Lady Alroy. She had caught a chill at the Opera, and had died in five days of congestion of the lungs. I shut myself up and saw no one. I had loved her so much, I had loved her so madly. Good God! how I had loved that woman ! "

" You went to the street, to the house in it ? " I said.

" Yes," he answered.

" One day I went to Cumnor Street. I could not help it ; I was tortured with doubt. I knocked at the door, and a respectable-looking woman opened it to me. I asked her if she had any rooms to let. ' Well, sir,' she replied, ' the drawing-rooms are supposed to be let ; but I have not seen the lady for three months, and as rent is owing on them, you can have them.'—' Is this the lady ? ' I said, showing the photograph. ' That's her, sure enough,' she exclaimed ; ' and when is she coming back, sir ? '—' The lady is dead,' I replied. ' Oh, sir, I hope not ! ' said the woman ; ' she was my best lodger. She paid me three guineas a week merely to sit in my drawing-rooms now and then.'—' She met some one here ? ' I said ; but the woman assured me that it was not so, that she always came alone, and saw no one. ' What on earth did she do here ? ' I cried. ' She simply sat in the drawing-room, sir, reading books, and sometimes had tea,' the woman answered. I did not know what to say, so I gave her a sovereign and went away. Now, what do you think it all meant ? You don't believe the woman was telling the truth ? "

" I do."

" Then why did Lady Alroy go there ? "

" My dear Gerald," I answered, " Lady Alroy was simply a woman with a mania for mystery. She took these rooms for the pleasure of going there with her veil down, and imagining she was a heroine. She had a passion for secrecy, but she herself was merely a Sphinx without a secret."

" Do you really think so ? "

" I am sure of it," I replied.

He took out the morocco case, opened it, and looked at the photograph. " I wonder ? " he said at last.

THE GARDENER

Two friends of mine, Hugh Grainger and his wife, had taken for a month of Christmas holiday the house in which we were to witness such strange manifestations, and when I received an invitation from them to spend a fortnight there I returned them an enthusiastic affirmative. Well already did I know that pleasant heathery countryside, and most intimate was my acquaintance with the subtle hazards of its most charming golf-links. Golf, I was given to understand, was to occupy the solid day for Hugh and me, so that Margaret should never be obliged to set her hand to the implements with which the game, so detestable to her, was conducted. . . .

I arrived there while yet the daylight lingered, and as my hosts were out, I took a ramble round the place. The house and garden stood on a plateau facing south ; below it were a couple of acres of pasture that sloped down to a vagrant stream crossed by a foot-bridge, by the side of which stood a thatched cottage with a vegetable patch surrounding it. A path ran close past this across the pasture from a wicket-gate in the garden, conducted you over the foot-bridge, and, so my remembered sense of geography told me, must constitute a short cut to the links that lay not half a mile beyond. The cottage itself was clearly on the land of the little estate, and I at once supposed it to be the gardener's house. What went against so obvious and simple a theory was that it appeared to be untenanted. No wreath of smoke, though the evening was chilly, curled from its chimneys, and, coming closer, I fancied it had that air of " waiting " about it which we so often conjure into unused habitations. There it stood, with no sign of life whatever about it, though ready, as its apparently perfect state of repair seemed to warrant, for fresh tenants to put the breath of life into it again.

Its little garden, too, though the palings were neat and newly painted, told the same tale ; the beds were untended and unweeded, and in the flower-border by the front door was a row of chrysanthemums which had withered on their stems. But all this was but the impression of a moment, and I did not pause as I passed it, but crossed the foot-bridge and went on up the heathery slope that lay beyond. My geography was not at fault, for presently I saw the club-house just in front of me. Hugh no doubt would be just about coming in from his afternoon round, and so we would walk back together. On reaching the club-house, however, the steward told me that not five minutes before Mrs. Grainger had called in her car for her husband, and I therefore retraced my steps by the path along which I had already come. But I made a detour, as a golfer will, to walk up the fairway of the seventeenth and eighteenth holes just for the pleasure of recognition, and looked respectfully at the yawning sandpit which so inexorably guards the eighteenth green, wondering in what circumstances I should visit it next, whether with a step complacent and superior, knowing that my ball reposed safely on the green beyond, or with the heavy footfall of one who knows that laborious delving lies before him.

The light of the winter evening had faded fast, and when I crossed the foot-bridge on my return the dusk had gathered. To my right, just beside the path, lay the cottage, the white-washed walls of which gleamed whitely in the gloaming ; and as I turned my glance back from it to the rather narrow plank which bridged the stream I thought I caught out of the tail of my eye some light from one of its windows, which thus disproved my theory that it was untenanted. But when I looked directly at it again I saw that I was mistaken : some reflection in the glass of the red lines of sunset in the west must have deceived me, for in the inclement twilight it looked more desolate than ever. Yet I lingered by the wicket gate in its low palings, for though all exterior evidence bore witness to its emptiness, some inexplicable feeling assured me, quite irrationally, that this was not so, and that there was somebody there. Certainly there was nobody visible, but, so this absurd idea informed me, he might be at the back of the cottage concealed from me by the intervening structure, and, still oddly, still unreasonably, it became a matter of importance to my mind to ascertain whether this was so or not, so clearly had my perceptions told me that the place was empty, and so firmly had some conviction assured me that it was tenanted. To cover my inquisitiveness, in case there was some one there, I could inquire whether this path was a short cut to the house at which I was staying, and, rather rebelling at what I was doing, I went through the small garden, and rapped at the door. There was no answer, and, after waiting for a response to a second summons, and having tried the door and found it locked, I made the circuit of the house. Of course there was no one there, and I told myself that I was just like a man who looks under his bed for a burglar and would be beyond measure astonished if he found one.

My hosts were at the house when I arrived, and we spent a cheerful two hours before dinner in such desultory and eager conversation as is proper between friends who have not met for some time. Between Hugh Grainger and his wife it is always impossible to light on a subject which does not vividly interest one or other of them, and golf, politics, the needs of Russia, cooking, ghosts, the possible victory over Mount Everest, and the income tax were among the topics which we passionately discussed. With all these plates spinning, it was easy to whip up any one of them, and the subject of spooks generally was lighted upon again and again.

" Margaret is on the high road to madness," remarked Hugh on one of these occasions, " for she has begun using planchette. If you use planchette for six months, I am told, most careful doctors will conscientiously certify you as insane. She's got five months more before she goes to Bedlam.".

" Does it work ? " I asked.

" Yes, it says most interesting things," said Margaret. " It says things that never entered my head. We'll try it to-night."

" Oh, not to-night," said Hugh. " Let's have an evening off."

Margaret disregarded this.

" It's no use asking planchette questions," she went on, " because there is in your mind some sort of answer to them. If I ask whether it will be fine to-morrow, for instance, it is probably I—though indeed I don't mean to push—who makes the pencil say ' yes.' "

" And then it usually rains," remarked Hugh.

" Not always : don't interrupt. The interesting thing is to let the pencil write what it chooses. Very often it only makes loops and curves—though they may mean something—and every now and then a word comes, of the significance of which I have no idea whatever, so I clearly couldn't have suggested it. Yester-day evening, for instance, it wrote ' gardener ' over and over

again. Now what did that mean? The gardener here is a
Methodist with a chin-beard. Could it have meant him? Oh,
it's time to dress. Please don't be late, my cook is so sensitive
about soup."

We rose, and some connection of ideas about "gardener"
linked itself up in my mind.

"By the way, what's that cottage in the field by the foot-
bridge?" I asked. "Is that the gardener's cottage?"

"It used to be," said Hugh. "But the chin-beard doesn't
live there : in fact nobody lives there. It's empty. If I was owner
here, I should put the chin-beard into it, and take the rent off
his wages. Some people have no idea of economy. Why did you
ask?"

I saw Margaret was looking at me rather attentively.

"Curiosity," I said. "Idle curiosity."

"I don't believe it was," said she.

"But it was," I said. "It was idle curiosity to know whether
the house was inhabited. As I passed it, going down to the
club-house, I felt sure it was empty, but coming back I felt so
sure that there was some one there that I rapped at the door, and
indeed walked round it."

Hugh had preceded us upstairs, as she lingered a little.

"And there was no one there?" she asked. "It's odd :
I had just the same feeling as you about it."

"That explains planchette writing 'gardener' over and
over again," said I. "You had the gardener's cottage on your
mind."

"How ingenious!" said Margaret. "Hurry up and dress."

A gleam of strong moonlight between my drawn curtains
when I went up to bed that night led me to look out. My room
faced the garden and the fields which I had traversed that
afternoon, and all was vividly illuminated by the full moon. The
thatched cottage with its white walls close by the stream was
very distinct, and once more, I suppose, the reflection of the light
on the glass of one of its windows made it appear that the room
was lit within. It struck me as odd that twice that day this
illusion should have been presented to me, but now a yet odder
thing happened. Even as I looked the light was extinguished.

The morning did not at all bear out the fine promise of the
clear night, for when I woke the wind was squealing, and sheets
of rain from the south-west were dashed against my panes.
Golf was wholly out of the question, and, though the violence
of the storm abated a little in the afternoon, the rain dripped

with a steady sullenness. But I wearied of indoors, and, since the two others entirely refused to set foot outside, I went forth mackintoshed to get a breath of air. By way of an object in my tramp, I took the road to the links in preference to the muddy short-cut through the fields, with the intention of engaging a couple of caddies for Hugh and myself next morning, and lingered awhile over illustrated papers in the smoking-room. I must have read for longer than I knew, for a sudden beam of sunset light suddenly illuminated my page, and looking up, I saw that the rain had ceased, and that evening was fast coming on. So instead of taking the long detour by the road again, I set forth homewards by the path across the fields. That gleam of sunset was the last of the day, and once again, just as twenty-four hours ago, I crossed the foot-bridge in the gloaming. Till that moment, as far as I was aware, I had not thought at all about the cottage there, but now in a flash the light I had seen there last night, suddenly extinguished, recalled itself to my mind, and at the same moment I felt that invincible conviction that the cottage was tenanted. Simultaneously in these swift processes of thought I looked towards it, and saw standing by the door the figure of a man. In the dusk I could distinguish nothing of his face, if indeed it was turned to me, and only got the impression of a tallish fellow, thickly built. He opened the door, from which there came a dim light as of a lamp, entered, and shut it after him.

So then my conviction was right. Yet I had been distinctly told that the cottage was empty : who, then, was he that entered as if returning home ? Once more, this time with a certain qualm of fear, I rapped on the door, intending to put some trivial question ; and rapped again, this time more drastically, so that there could be no question that my summons was unheard. But still I got no reply, and finally I tried the handle of the door. It was locked. Then, with difficulty mastering an increasing terror, I made the circuit of the cottage, peering into each unshuttered window. All was dark within, though but two minutes ago I had seen the gleam of light escape from the opened door.

Just because some chain of conjecture was beginning to form itself in my mind, I made no allusion to this odd adventure, and after dinner Margaret, amid protests from Hugh, got out the planchette which had persisted in writing " gardener." My surmise was, of course, utterly fantastic, but I wanted to convey no suggestion of any sort to Margaret. . . . For a long time the pencil skated over her paper making loops and curves and peaks like a temperature chart, and she had begun to yawn and weary over her experiment before any coherent word emerged. And then, in the oddest way, her head nodded forward and she seemed to have fallen asleep.

Hugh looked up from his book and spoke in a whisper to me.

" She fell asleep the other night over it," he said.

Margaret's eyes were closed, and she breathed the long, quiet breaths of slumber, and then her hand began to move with a curious firmness. Right across the big sheet of paper went a level line of writing, and at the end her hand stopped with a jerk, and she woke.

She looked at the paper.

" Hallo," she said. " Ah, one of you has been playing a trick on me ! "

We assured her that this was not so, and she read what she had written.

" Gardener, gardener," it ran. " I am the gardener. I want to come in. I can't find her here."

" O Lord, that gardener again ! " said Hugh.

Looking up from the paper, I saw Margaret's eyes fixed on mine, and even before she spoke I knew what her thought was.

" Did you come home by the empty cottage ? " she asked.

" Yes : why ? "

" Still empty ? " she said in a low voice. " Or—or anything else ? "

I did not want to tell her just what I had seen—or what, at any rate, I thought I had seen. If there was going to be anything odd, anything worth observation, it was far better that our respective impressions should not fortify each other.

" I tapped again, and there was no answer," I said.

Presently there was a move to bed : Margaret initiated it, and after she had gone upstairs Hugh and I went to the front door to interrogate the weather. Once more the moon shone in a clear sky, and we strolled out along the flagged path that fronted the house. Suddenly Hugh turned quickly and pointed to the angle of the house.

" Who on earth is that ? " he said. " Look ! There ! He has gone round the corner."

I had but the glimpse of a tallish man of heavy build.

" Didn't you see him ? " asked Hugh. " I'll just go round

the house, and find him ; I don't want any one prowling round us at night. Wait here, will you, and if he comes round the other corner ask him what his business is."

Hugh had left me, in our stroll, close by the front door which was open, and there I waited until he should have made his circuit. He had hardly disappeared when I heard, quite distinctly, a rather quick but heavy footfall coming along the paved walk towards me from the opposite direction. But there was absolutely no one to be seen who made this sound of rapid walking. Closer and closer to me came the steps of the invisible one, and then with a shudder of horror I felt somebody unseen push by me as I stood on the threshold. That shudder was not merely of the spirit, for the touch of him was that of ice on my hand. I tried to seize this impalpable intruder, but he slipped from me, and the next moment I heard his steps on the parquet of the floor inside. Some door within opened and shut, and I heard no more of him. Next moment Hugh came running round the corner of the house from which the sound of steps had approached.

" But where is he ? " he asked. " He was not twenty yards in front of me—a big, tall fellow."

" I saw nobody," I said. " I heard his step along the walk, but there was nothing to be seen."

" And then ? " asked Hugh.

" Whatever it was seemed to brush by me, and go into the house," said I.

There had certainly been no sound of steps on the bare oak stairs, and we searched room after room through the ground floor of the house. The dining-room door and that of the smoking-room were locked, that into the drawing-room was open, and the only other door which could have furnished the impression of an opening and a shutting was that into the kitchen and servants' quarters. Here again our quest was fruitless ; through pantry and scullery and boot-room and servants' hall we searched, but all was empty and quiet. Finally we came to the kitchen, which too was empty. But by the fire there was set a rocking-chair, and this was oscillating to and fro as if some one, lately sitting there, had just quitted it. There it stood gently rocking, and this seemed to convey the sense of a presence, invisible now, more than even the sight of him who surely had been sitting there could have done. I remember wanting to steady it and stop it, and yet my hand refused to go forth to it.

What we had seen, and in especial what we had not seen, would have been sufficient to furnish most people with a broken night, and assuredly I was not among the strong-minded exceptions. Long I lay wide-eyed and open-eared, and when at last I dozed I was plucked from the border-land of sleep by the sound, muffled but unmistakable, of some one moving about the house. It occurred to me that the steps might be those of Hugh conducting a lonely exploration, but even while I wondered a tap came at the door of communication between our rooms, and, in answer to my response, it appeared that he had come to see whether it was I thus uneasily wandering. Even as we spoke the step passed my door, and the stairs leading to the floor above creaked to its ascent. Next moment it sounded directly above our heads in some attics in the roof.

" Those are not the servants' bedrooms," said Hugh. " No one sleeps there. Let us look once more : it must be some-body."

With lit candles we made our stealthy way upstairs, and just when we were at the top of the flight, Hugh, a step ahead of me, uttered a sharp exclamation.

" But something is passing by me ! " he said, and he clutched at the empty air. Even as he spoke, I experienced the same sensation, and the moment afterwards the stairs below us creaked again, as the unseen passed down.

All night long that sound of steps moved about the passages, as if some one was searching the house, and as I lay and listened that message which had come through the pencil of the planchette to Margaret's fingers occurred to me. " I want to come in. I cannot find her here." . . . Indeed some one had come in, and was sedulous in his search. He was the gardener, it would seem. But what gardener was this invisible seeker, and for whom did he seek ?

Even as when some bodily pain ceases it is difficult to recall with any vividness what the pain was like, so next morning, as I dressed, I found myself vainly trying to recapture the horror of the spirit which had accompanied these nocturnal adventures. I remembered that something within me had sickened as I watched the movements of the rocking-chair the night before and as I heard the steps along the paved way outside, and by that invisible pressure against me knew that some one had entered the house. But now in the sane and tranquil morning, and all day under the serene winter sun, I could not realise what it had been. The presence, like the bodily pain, had to be there for the realisation of it, and all day it was absent. Hugh felt the same ; he was even disposed to be humorous on the subject.

" Well, he's had a good look," he said, " whoever he is, and whomever he was looking for. By the way, not a word to Margaret, please. She heard nothing of these perambulations, nor of the entry of—of whatever it was. Not gardener, anyhow : who ever heard of a gardener spending his time walking about the house ? If there were steps all over the potato-patch, I might have been with you."

Margaret had arranged to drive over to have tea with some friends of hers that afternoon, and in consequence Hugh and I refreshed ourselves at the club-house after our game, and it was already dusk when for the third day in succession I passed homewards by the whitewashed cottage. But to-night I had no sense of it being subtly occupied ; it stood mournfully desolate, as is the way of untenanted houses, and no light nor semblance of such gleamed from it windows. Hugh, to whom I had told the odd impressions I had received there, gave them a reception as flippant as that which he had accorded to the memories of the night, and he was still being humorous about them when we came to the door of the house.

" A psychic disturbance, old boy," he said. " Like a cold in the head. Hallo, the door's locked."

He rang and rapped, and from inside came the noise of a turned key and withdrawn bolts.

" What's the door locked for ? " he asked his servant who opened it.

The man shifted from one foot to the other.

" The bell rang half an hour ago, sir," he said, " and when I came to answer it there was a man standing outside, and——"

" Well ? " asked Hugh.

" I didn't like the looks of him, sir," he said, " and I asked him his business. He didn't say anything, and then he must have gone pretty smartly away, for I never saw him go."

" Where did he seem to go ? " asked Hugh, glancing at me.

" I can't rightly say, sir. He didn't seem to go at all. Something seemed to brush by me."

" That'll do," said Hugh rather sharply.

Margaret had not come in from her visit, but when soon after the crunch of the motor wheels was heard Hugh reiterated his wish that nothing should be said to her about the impression which now, apparently, a third person shared with us. She came in with a flush of excitement on her face.

"Never laugh at my planchette again," she said. "I've heard the most extraordinary story from Maud Ashfield—horrible, but so frightfully interesting."

"Out with it," said Hugh.

"Well, there was a gardener here," she said. "He used to live at that little cottage by the foot-bridge, and when the family were up in London he and his wife used to be caretakers and live here."

Hugh's glance and mine met : then he turned away. I knew, as certainly as if I was in his mind, that his thoughts were identical with my own.

"He married a wife much younger than himself," continued Margaret, "and gradually he became frightfully jealous of her. And one day in a fit of passion he strangled her with his own hands. A little while after some one came to the cottage, and found him sobbing over her, trying to restore her. They went for the police, but before they came he had cut his own throat. Isn't it all horrible ? But surely it's rather curious that the planchette said ' Gardener. I am the gardener. I want to come in. I can't find her here.' You see I knew nothing about it. I shall do planchette again to-night. Oh dear me, the post goes in half an hour, and I have a whole budget to send. But respect my planchette for the future, Hughie."

We talked the situation out when she had gone, but Hugh, unwillingly convinced and yet unwilling to admit that something more than coincidence lay behind that " planchette nonsense," still insisted that Margaret should be told nothing of what we had heard and seen in the house last night, and of the strange visitor who again this evening, so we must conclude, had made his entry.

"She'll be frightened," he said, " and she'll begin imagining things. As for the planchette, as likely as not it will do nothing but scribble and make loops. What's that? Yes : come in ! "

There had come from somewhere in the room one sharp, peremptory rap. I did not think it came from the door, but Hugh, when no response replied to his words of admittance, jumped up and opened it. He took a few steps into the hall outside, and returned.

"Didn't you hear it ? " he asked.

"Certainly. No one there ? "

" Not a soul."

Hugh came back to the fireplace and rather irritably threw a cigarette which he had just lit into the fender.

" That was rather a nasty jar," he observed ; " and if you ask me whether I feel comfortable, I can tell you I never felt less comfortable in my life. I'm frightened, if you want to know, and I believe you are too."

I hadn't the smallest intention of denying this, and he went on.

" We've got to keep a hand on ourselves," he said. " There's nothing so infectious as fear, and Margaret mustn't catch it from us. But there's something more than our fear, you know. Something has got into the house and we're up against it. I never believed in such things before. Let's face it for a minute. *What* is it anyhow ? "

" If you want to know what I think it is," said I, " I believe it to be the spirit of the man who strangled his wife and then cut his throat. But I don't see how it can hurt us. We're afraid of our own fear really."

" But we're up against it," said Hugh. " And what will it do ? Good Lord, if I only knew what it would do I shouldn't mind. It's the not knowing. . . . Well, it's time to dress."

Margaret was in her highest spirits at dinner. Knowing nothing of the manifestations of that presence which had taken place in the last twenty-four hours, she thought it absorbingly interesting that her planchette should have " guessed " (so ran her phrase) about the gardener, and from that topic she flitted to an equally interesting form of patience for three which her friend had shown her, promising to initiate us into it after dinner. This she did, and, not knowing that we both above all things wanted to keep planchette at a distance, she was delighted with the success of her game. But suddenly she observed that the evening was burning rapidly away, and swept the cards together at the conclusion of a hand.

" Now just half an hour of planchette," she said.

" Oh, mayn't we play one more hand ? " asked Hugh. " It's the best game I've seen for years. Planchette will be dismally slow after this."

" Darling, if the gardener will only communicate again, it won't be slow," said she.

" But it is such drivel," said Hugh.

" How rude you are ! Read your book, then."

Margaret had already got out her machine and a sheet of paper, when Hugh rose.

" Please don't do it to-night, Margaret," he said.

" But why ? You needn't attend."

" Well, I ask you not to, anyhow," said he.

Margaret looked at him closely.

" Hughie, you've got something on your mind," she said. " Out with it. I believe you're nervous. You think there is something queer about. What is it ? "

I could see Hugh hesitating as to whether to tell her or not, and I gathered that he chose the chance of her planchette inanely scribbling.

" Go on then," he said.

Margaret hesitated : she clearly did not want to vex Hugh, but his insistence must have seemed to her most unreasonable.

" Well, just ten minutes," she said, " and I promise not to think of gardeners."

She had hardly laid her hand on the board when her head fell forward, and the machine began moving. I was sitting close to her, and as it rolled steadily along the paper the writing became visible.

" I have come in," it ran, " but still I can't find her. Are you hiding her ? I will search the room where you are."

What else was written but still concealed underneath the planchette I did not know, for at that moment a current of icy air swept round the room, and at the door, this time unmistakably, came a loud peremptory knock. Hugh sprang to his feet.

" Margaret, wake up," he said, " something is coming ! "

The door opened, and there moved in the figure of a man. He stood just within the door, his head bent forward, and he turned it from side to side, peering, it would seem, with eyes staring and infinitely sad, into every corner of the room.

" Margaret, Margaret," cried Hugh again.

But Margaret's eyes were open too ; they were fixed on this dreadful visitor.

" Be quiet, Hughie," she said below her breath, rising as she spoke. The ghost was now looking directly at her. Once the lips above the thick, rust-coloured beard moved, but no sound came forth, the mouth only moved and slavered. He raised his head, and, horror upon horror, I saw that one side of his neck was laid open in a red, glistening gash. . . .

For how long that pause continued, when we all three stood stiff and frozen in some deadly inhibition to move or speak, I have no idea : I suppose that at the utmost it was a dozen seconds. Then the spectre turned, and went out as it had come. We heard his steps pass along the parqueted floor ; there was the sound of bolts withdrawn from the front door, and with a crash that shook the house it slammed to.

" It's all over," said Margaret. " God have mercy on him ! "

Now the reader may put precisely what construction he pleases on this visitation from the dead. He need not, indeed, consider it to have been a visitation from the dead at all, but say that there had been impressed on the scene, where this murder and suicide happened, some sort of emotional record, which in certain circumstances could translate itself into images visible and invisible. Waves of ether, or what not, may conceivably retain the impress of such scenes ; they may be held, so to speak, in solution, ready to be precipitated. Or he may hold that the spirit of the dead man indeed made itself manifest, revisiting in some sort of spiritual penance and remorse the place where his crime was committed. Naturally, no materialist will entertain such an explanation for an instant, but then there is no one so obstinately unreasonable as the materialist. Beyond doubt a dreadful deed was done there, and Margaret's last utterance is not inapplicable.

A SPANISH GHOST STORY

IT is now about twenty years since I took honours in the examination qualifying me to teach in Höhere Töchterschulen. A week or two after the examination the Principal of the College called, asking me whether I would care to take a situation in Spain. He told me he had two Spanish boarders, Garcia by name, and that the mother of these boys had asked him to send her a governess for her daughters. The duties were light, and the salary good. I asked him whether he knew Mrs. Garcia?

" Personally, not at all," he answered ; " but I know that she is wealthy, and of good position."

I should have liked to know more about her than that, but the situation was too good to be refused, so I said I would go, and three weeks after I found myself in Seville.

Mrs. Garcia received me very kindly, and introduced me to my pupils—Carmen, aged thirteen, and Concepcion, aged ten. After supper, she herself showed me my rooms, which were on the first floor, close to her own. The sitting-room opened off the bedroom, not off the corridor, so that it could only be reached by going through the bedroom. It had a door opening on the staircase, but Mrs. Garcia said that door was of no use, as the staircase was unused, and the door at the foot of it locked. It was an odd arrangement altogether ; the staircase went no further than the first floor, and communicated only with two rooms—my sitting-room, and a room opposite, which Mrs. Garcia said was a lumber-room, and which was locked. This sitting-room was really a splendid room ; it had a marble floor, and was upholstered in red silk with gold fringe. I wondered that so handsome a room should have been given up to me.

I was very comfortable with the Garcias, although I disliked two members of the household—an old witch of a servant, who

634

had been Mrs. Garcia's nurse, and the father confessor. The old witch used to cross herself whenever she saw me, and mutter something which may have been a prayer for my conversion, but which sounded more like a curse. Father Avila, on the other hand, was very polite ; in fact, I had an uncomfortable feeling that if I gave him any encouragement he would be too polite. I saw him constantly, for he passed at least half of every day at the Garcias.

One night I was awakened by the sound of footsteps in my sitting-room. I thought something was the matter, and my help was wanted, so I rose, lit my candle, and opened the door between the rooms. There was nobody there. I tried the door to the staircase. It was locked and the key was inside. Certainly if Mrs. Garcia wanted me she would not have thought of going down to the courtyard, opening the door of the disused staircase, and coming to my sitting-room. She would simply have crossed the corridor from her bedroom to mine. Besides, the door was locked. I must have been mistaken. Accordingly I went back to bed.

A night or two after this I had gone to bed later than usual, and, just as I was putting out my light, I heard some one moving about in the sitting-room. A chair was pushed back from the table, and some one began to walk up and down the room. This time there could be no mistake. I distinctly heard the footsteps on the marble. Again I rose and opened the door. No one was to be seen. There was no place in the room where one could hide, and no way of getting out of the room except down the staircase or through my bedroom. The staircase door was locked, and no one could have got into my bedroom without passing me. I could not understand it. I heard the same noises now and then for the next fortnight, and could find no explanation for them. At last I resolved to speak to Mrs. Garcia.

Next morning at breakfast I told my story, and Carmen exclaimed, " It is papa ! " and began to talk quickly in Spanish. We always spoke French at meals, as Mrs. Garcia knew no German, and I knew only a few sentences of Spanish which I had picked up since I came to Seville. Most of what Carmen said was quite unintelligible to me, but I could make out that I was not the first person who had heard these noises, and that the children believed their father's ghost haunted that room.

After breakfast Mrs. Garcia came to me and said that she would like to get Father Avila to say certain prayers in the sitting-room. I said, " First tell me what it is you wish to exor-

cise." She answered, "My husband died suddenly in that
room, without having received the last rites of the church, and
I believe that his soul cannot rest." I felt that if I had to choose
between Father Avila and the ghost, I decidedly preferred the
ghost ; but I could scarcely say so to Mrs. Garcia, so I said
nothing, and Father Avila recited his prayers.

All in vain. The noises continued. I believed it was some
trick of the servants—possibly the old witch wanted to get rid
of the heretic—and was resolved to catch the offender. I was
becoming quite worn out by having my sleep so often broken,
and Carmen, too, began to be troublesome. When told to do
anything she disliked she would appeal to her mother ; and if
Mrs. Garcia took my part Carmen would say, " If you don't let
me do as I wish, I will tell. I can tell, you know I saw ; " and
thereupon Mrs. Garcia would yield.

At last I thought of a plan. A great bell hung in the courtyard to be rung in case of fire. From the window of my room
I could easily reach the bell rope. I told Mrs. Garcia that next
time I heard the noises I would ring the bell and summon the
household, and we should have the whole place searched. Mrs.
Garcia agreed. Two or three nights after, I heard the noises
again. This time the footsteps came up to my bedroom door,
and the handle of the door turned. I opened the door quickly.
No one there. Then I rushed to the window and pulled the bell-
rope with all my might. The whole household assembled. We
began by examining the staircase. No one was there, and the
door was locked, and fastened on the inside with a strong bolt.
Then the lumber-room was opened and thoroughly searched,
but we found no one. The lumber-room had no door but one
opening from the staircase. At last we gave up the search, and
went back to bed.

Next day was a festa, and we had a holiday. The German
Consul's wife invited me to accompany her to the opera. I had
brought letters of introduction to a good many Germans, and
many of them had invited me to their houses ; but Mrs. Garcia,
though she never objected in words to my making friends, always
wanted me to go somewhere with her, so that I had never been
able to accept these invitations. To-day, however, I insisted on
going to the opera, saying that I had been much agitated the
night before, and that I must have some distraction ; and Mrs.
Garcia, after many objections, consented.

There was another lady at the Consul's, a Mrs. Schröter,
who had been in Seville for many years. She seemed to take

rather a fancy to me, for she would talk to no one else, and after telling me all about her own affairs, she proceeded to ask about mine.

"And you are a governess, Fraulein Schaller? May I ask in what family?"

"In Mrs. Garcia's," answered I.

"What!" exclaimed the old lady. "Not Mrs. Garcia's? Widow of Pedro Garcia?"

"Yes," said I.

"But do you not know then, that you are in the house of a Lucrezia Borgia? Have you not heard her story?"

"I have heard no story about her," said I.

So she told me the story, and a horrible one it was. Mrs. Garcia had been the wife of Pedro Garcia, the senior partner of Garcia Brothers. They did not get on well together, and Mr. Garcia ended by becoming jealous of his own brother Carlos. One day Pedro and his wife had an unusually violent quarrel, and Pedro left the house in a rage. On his return his wife met him, all smiles and sweetness, and brought him coffee with her own hands. An hour or two later his valet, going into his sitting-room, found him sitting at the table, his head resting on his arms. Something in his master's attitude struck the man as peculiar ; he spoke, got no answer, and touched him. He was stiff and nearly cold. The valet called the servants and ran for a doctor. When the doctor came he said Mr. Garcia had been dead for some time, and asked what he had eaten last. The cook said "coffee," and pointed to the cup still on the table. "Let me see that," said the doctor, going towards the table. The old nurse jumped up, as though to hand him the cup, but managed to upset both cup and saucer, and break them.

"The matter was hushed up—people said by dint of bribery— and after a decent interval the widow married Carlos Garcia. The marriage had only lasted about a year when Carlos Garcia went mad. He accused himself of having caused his brother's death, and declared he both heard and saw the dead man continually. Six months afterwards he died. Mrs. Garcia was not well received by the Seville ladies, and was said to find her life very dull, though she consoled herself with the society of Father Avila, who had the reputation of being the worst priest in Spain.

Next day I gave Mrs. Garcia a quarter's notice. She was not well pleased and tried to persuade me to stay, but I would not. A week or two after, I went up to the music-room one evening to practise. I had to pass along a dimly-lit corridor, with recesses here and there. Suddenly a man rose from one of these recesses, and threw his arm round me, exclaiming, " My dearest, my Visitacion ! " It was Father Avila. (Mrs. Garcia's name was Visitacion.) I screamed, and tried to free myself. The moment Father Avila saw who I was he let me go, and I rushed off to my own room. I had been in a nervous state since I had heard Mrs. Garcia's story, and the fright I got made me really ill. I went to bed, and after some time fell asleep.

Some time later I awoke, to find my door open ; a light in the passage showed me Father Avila and the old nurse standing in the doorway, and Mrs. Garcia at the foot of my bed with a cup in her hand. I sat up in bed, and asked, " What is the matter ? " Mrs. Garcia started, and the contents of the cup were spilled on the bed. Instantly the light went out, and a moment after I heard the door shut. I struck a light—there was no one in the room. I lay awake trembling for a long time, but at last fell asleep again. In the morning I tried to persuade myself it was fancy, and to convince myself I examined the bed-coverings, where the cup had been spilled, to see whether there was a stain. I found them burned into holes. Having dressed as quickly as possible, I went to the house of the German Consul, telling him what I had seen, and begging his assistance. He welcomed me warmly ; and after much difficulty, and not without the use of threats of what might be revealed, induced Mrs. Garcia to hand over my things to him. I lived with the family for some time, until fortunately I got another situation in the house of a German merchant.

Mrs. Garcia I never saw again. She left Seville with her family shortly afterwards, and though I declined to have any steps taken to punish her, the story got about, and she was shunned more than before. Where she went to I do not know, but those who hated her most whispered that it was to Santa Alba, whither Father Avila had been transferred by his ecclesiastical superiors.